Clover

A NOVEL BY DORI SANDERS

. . .

Fawcett Columbine • New York

A Fawcett Columbine Book
Published by Ballantine Books

Copyright © 1990 by Dori Sanders

All rights reserved under International and Pan-American Copyright Conventions. Published in the United States by Ballantine Books, a divsion of Random House, Inc., New York, and distributed in Canada by Random House of Canada Limited, Toronto.

This edition published by arrangement with Algonquin Books of Chapel Hill.

Library of Congress Catalog Card Number: 90-93645

ISBN: 0-449-90624-8

Cover design by Jennifer Blanc

Cover photo by Erik Lee

Manufactured in the United States of America

First Ballantine Books Edition: May 1991
20 19 18 17

To my family
for their patience and humor
and
To Nancy Shulman
who saw in me something
I did not see in myself

CLOVER

I
· · · · · · ·

*T*hey dressed me in white for my daddy's funeral. White from my head to my toes. I had the black skirt I bought at the six-dollar store all laid out to wear. I'd even pulled the black grosgrain bows off my black patent leather shoes to wear in my hair. But they won't let me wear black.

I know deep down in my heart you're supposed to wear black to a funeral. I guess the reason my stepmother is not totally dressed in black is because she just plain doesn't know any better.

The sounds inside our house are hushed. A baby lets out a sharp birdlike cry. "Hush, hush, little baby," someone whispers, "don't you cry." There is the faint breathless purr of an electric fan plugged in to help out the air-conditioning, the hum of the refrigerator going on in the kitchen, a house filled with mourners giving up happy talk for the quiet noise of sorrow.

We take the silence outside to waiting shiny black cars, quietly lined behind a shiny black hearse. Drivers in worn black suits, shiny from wear, move and speak quietly, their voices barely above a whisper. It seems they are afraid they might wake the sleeping dead. It's like the winds have even been invited. The winds are still.

One of the neighbors, Miss Katie, is standing in the front yard, watching the blue light on top of a county police car flash round and round. She is shaking her head and fanning the hot air with her hand. Biting, chewing, and swallowing dry, empty air. Her lips folding close like sunflowers at sundown—opening, like morning glories at dawn.

They asked Miss Katie to stay at the house. Folks in Round Hill, South Carolina, never go to someone's funeral and not leave somebody in their home. They say the poor departed soul just might have to come back for something or another, and you wouldn't want to lock them out.

My breath is steaming up the window of the family car. It's really cold inside. Someone walks to our driver and whispers something. I see a cousin rush from a car with what Grandpa would have called a passel of chaps. They leave our front door wide open. A hummingbird flies to the open door and stands still in midair, trying to decide about entering, but quickly darts backward and away.

I press my face against the cold window. Only a few days back, my daddy, Gaten, walked out that very door, carrying a book. He headed toward the two big oak trees in the front yard and settled himself into the hammock that was stretched between them. And after awhile, like always, he was sound asleep, with the open book face down across his chest.

My daddy looked small between those big trees. But then, he was small. Everybody says I'm small for a ten-year-old. I guess I'm going to be like my daddy. Funny, it's only the middle of the week, but it seems like it's Sunday.

They say I haven't shed a single tear since my daddy died. Not even when the doctor told me he was dead. I was just a scared, dry-eyed little girl gazing into the eyes of a doctor unable to hold back his own tears. I stood there, they said, humming some sad little tune. I don't remember all of that, but I sure do remember why I was down at the county hospital.

Things sure can happen fast. Just two days before yesterday, my aunt Everleen and I walked in and out of that door, too. Hurrying and trying to get everything in tip-top shape for Gaten's wedding supper.

Gaten didn't give Everleen much time. He just drove up

with this woman, Sara Kate, just like he did the first time I met her. Then up and said flat-out, "Sara Kate and I are going to get married. She is going to be your new stepmother, Clover."

I almost burst out crying. I held it in, though. Gaten couldn't stand a crybaby. "A new stepmother," I thought, "like I had an old one." I guess Gaten had rubbed out his memory of my real mother like he would a wrong answer with a pencil eraser.

Everleen had been cooking at her house and our house all day long. My cousin Daniel and I have been running back and forth carrying stuff. I should have known something was up on account of all the new stuff we'd gotten. New curtains and dinette set for the kitchen. Everleen said, "The chair seats are covered in real patent-leather." Gaten's room was really pretty. New rug and bedspread with matching drapes.

In spite of all the hard work Everleen was doing, she had so much anger all tied up inside her it was pitiful. She was slinging pots and pans all over the place. I didn't know why she thought the newlyweds would want to eat all that stuff she was cooking in the first place. Everybody knows that people in love can't eat nothing.

Even Jim Ed tried to tell her she was overdoing it. "It didn't make any sense," her husband said, "to cook so much you had to use two kitchens."

"I don't want the woman to say I wouldn't feed her," Everleen pouted.

"I think Sara Kate is the woman's name, Everleen," Jim Ed snapped.

Well, that set Everleen off like a lit firecracker. She planted her feet wide apart, like she was getting ready to fight. Beads of sweat poured down her back. The kitchen was so hot, it was hard to breathe.

Jim Ed gave his wife a hard look. "I hope you heard what I said."

Everleen put her hands on her hips and started shaking them from side to side so fast, she looked like she was cranking up to takeoff. "I heard what you said, Jim Ed. Heard you loud and clear. What I want to know is, what you signifying?"

Everleen was so mad, she looked like she was going to have a stroke. "Let me tell you one thing. Get this through your thick skull and get it straight. You are not going to get in your head that just because some fancy woman is marrying into this family you can start talking down to me. You better pray to the Lord that you never, and I mean never, embarrass me in front of that woman. Because if you do, only the Lord will be able to help you." She waved a heavy soup spoon in his face. "Another thing, Jim Ed Hill, I am not going to burn myself to a crisp in that hot peach orchard getting my skin all rough and tore up. I'm

5

sure all Miss Uppity-class will do is sit around, and play tennis or golf. One thing is the Lord's truth, she is not going to live off what our . . ." She stopped short. "I mean what your folks worked so hard to get. Everleen Boyd will not take anything off anybody no matter what color they may be. I've been in this family for a good many years, but I sure don't have to stay."

My uncle looked at me. I guess he could see I was hurting. He put his arm around me. "Oh, baby, we ought to be ashamed, carrying on like this. We can't run Gaten's life for him. And we sure don't need to go out of our way to hurt him. Gaten told me out of his own mouth, he truly loves the woman he's going to marry. My brother deserves some happiness. You are going to have to help him, also, Clover. Getting a stepmother will be something new for you to get used to."

Jim Ed turned to his wife. "You always say you put everything in the Lord's hands. I think you better put this there, too, and leave it there, Everleen." Well, that quieted Everleen down. She never bucks too much on advice about the Lord.

Right then I couldn't even think about the stepmother bit. All I could think about was what Everleen said. Maybe she was thinking of leaving Jim Ed and getting a divorce. She called herself Boyd. I didn't think she wanted to be a Hill anymore. If she took her son Daniel and left me all alone with that strange woman, I would die. I knew in my heart, I would surely die.

I was starting to not like my daddy very much. Not very much at all. Miss Katie says, "Women around Round Hill leave their husbands at the drop of a hat these days." If Everleen leaves it will all be Gaten's fault, I thought. All because of his marriage plans.

Everleen pulled me from Jim Ed to her side. I buried my face against her sweaty arm, glad there was the sweat so she couldn't feel the tears streaming down my face. Her hot, sweaty smell, coated with Avon talcum powder, filled my nose. It was her own special smell. I felt safe.

Finally she pushed me away. "Let me dry them tears," she said, dabbing at my eyes with the corner of her apron. I should have known, I couldn't fool her.

I don't know if it was what Jim Ed said about Gaten or the Lord that turned Everleen around. Probably what he said about the Lord, but it sure turned her around. After a few minutes she was her old self again.

"All right, little honey," she said, "we better get a move on. We got us a marriage feast to cook. Now I'm going to put together the best wedding supper that's ever been cooked. Then I'm going to dress you up in the prettiest dress your daddy has ever laid eyes on." She glanced at my hair. "Lord have mercy, Allie Nell's still got your hair to fix."

Anyway, Everleen was still cooking and cleaning at the same time when the telephone rang. My daddy had been in a bad accident. Everleen snatched lemon meringue pies out of the oven and drove her pickup like crazy down to the hospital.

The sign in the waiting room said "NO SMOKING," but Uncle Jim Ed smoked anyway. He let long filter-tipped paper jobs dangle from his mouth and almost burn his lips before he remembered to take a draw.

There was an intercom system like the one at school. A voice was repeating, "Code blue—code blue. Room number 192." Nurses from everywhere hurried down the long hall.

Everleen stirred her hand around inside her pocketbook like she was stirring a pot of boiling grits. She pulled out a handful of candy without a piece of paper on it and divided it between me and Daniel. Daniel ate his. I didn't eat mine. I can't stand candy from Everleen's pocketbooks. It's the same as sucking down perfume.

It was getting later and later, and I still hadn't seen my daddy. The sun was setting. It had cast its last shadows for the day. Those long, lean shadows, they crept through the windows and clung to the clean hall floors, waiting for the darkness to swallow them up.

A state highway patrolman appeared in the doorway of

the waiting room. He inched forward slowly—it seemed as if he was afraid to enter the room. He turned his hat around and around in his hands. My uncle Jim Ed knew him. He had gone to high school with my daddy.

"I was called to the scene of the accident," he finally said.

Aunt Everleen didn't make it easy for the state trooper to tell us what had happened. Her body was shaking and drawing up like she was having spasms. Although she held Jim Ed's big white handkerchief all balled up in her fist, she did not use it. Most likely because he had blown his nose into it before he handed it to her. I guess with all that was going on, poor Jim Ed plumb forgot what he was doing.

So Everleen sat there, working her mouth back and forth to hold it back from screaming out loud. Tears flowed from her eyes too full to hold them any longer. They ran down her face and formed tiny streams around her neck, that was already dripping wet with sweat.

"Tell us what happened," she would plead. Then in the next breath, cry out, "No, no, no. I don't want to hear. I can't bear knowing." Then she'd turn right around and beg once again for him to tell her what happened.

The state trooper finally refused to listen any longer. With his hat still in his hand, he turned his back and said, "Gaten Hill's car was struck by a pickup truck when the driver ran a signal light at the intersection of North Main

Street and Highway 74. Police at the scene said alcohol is believed to have contributed to the accident which is under investigation."

He shook his head. "The car was struck on the driver's side. Gaten was driving. It looks bad," he said, "real bad." The state trooper started shaking his head again.

I thought to myself, if the wreck was all that bad, perhaps my daddy needed me. As soon as he left, I sneaked from the waiting room.

It was suppertime. I could smell the food. My daddy is always hungry for supper. I've always helped get his supper. Something seemed to tell me he needs me. I have to find him. When no one was looking I slipped down the long hall.

When a nurse popped out of a room, I hid behind a tall stack of covered trays. The nurse stopped and faced the blank wall, for a long time, studying the blank wall, looking at it as though it was some kind of picture, as though she was trying to make out a face or something. Wide fancy framed eyeglasses dangled from a chain around her neck.

I peeped from behind the trays with the little round tins covering the plates, like an Easter bonnet pulled down too far on a child's head.

While the big fat nurse with the eyeglasses studied the blank wall, I studied her shoes. White crepe-soled shoes with heels run-over so far, the shoe touched the floor. She didn't even see me when she took one of the trays from the cart.

A big set of doors swung wide open. Two doctors dressed in rumpled green started down the hall.

"This is the absolute worst part of it all," one of them said.

The other doctor loosened the mask that covered everything on his face except his eyes, "I understand there is a child. A little girl."

"At least she has one of them."

"I'll talk with the family now."

I hope they don't mean something bad has happened to Sara Kate, I thought. Gaten will be so sad. I waited until they were out of sight and hurried back to the waiting room to hear what they were going to say about Sara Kate.

A nurse led me into a small office. The doctor was speaking in a soft, soft voice, yet it was strong and heavy with sadness. Uncle Jim Ed and Everleen were carrying on like the world was coming to an end. Then I knew something was wrong. Bad wrong. A nurse offered little white pills in thimble-sized plastic cups to Aunt Everleen and Uncle Jim Ed.

Aunt Everleen buried her face in her hands and covered her ears with her fingers when the doctor tried to explain how Gaten died. For her, it was enough that he was dead.

But Uncle Jim Ed leaned forward in his chair and listened. He listened and cried. Aunt Everleen's face showed she heard the sad-faced doctor explain that my daddy's internal injuries were too extensive for them to save him.

The doctor put his hand on my shoulder. "I want to see my daddy," I said. "I need to see him." But he wouldn't take me to see Gaten. His blue eyes filled with tears. He turned away, "I'm sorry," he whispered. "We couldn't save your father."

The doctor wouldn't let me see my daddy, but he took me to Sara Kate's room to see her. The state trooper sure had been right. Sara Kate was some kind of bad bruised and cut up. Her eyes were closed. Maybe, like her lips, they were swollen shut.

The doctor's voice was soft, like our footsteps had been. Soft like snowflakes falling on the ground. "Mrs. Hill, Mrs. Hill," he repeated until she had slowly opened her eyes. Maybe she was so slow about it because she hadn't gotten used to her new name. After all, she had only had it for a few hours.

She smiled a quick weak half-smile and closed her eyes again. I guess there wasn't much for her to keep them open to see. Just a doctor in a rumpled green cotton outfit and me. I still hadn't gotten my hair fixed and, like always, I had sort of messed up my tee shirt a little scraping the bowl in which Aunt Everleen made the lemon butter creme icing for her fresh coconut lemon layer cake.

Plus, with Daniel not around, I got to lick the ice cream dasher.

Sara Kate bit her swollen lip. And even on a face that messed-up, sadness found itself a place. "Oh, little Clover," she whispered.

The doctor gave me a "say something" look.

"Hey," I said, "I'm very pleased to see you, ma'am." Then I pulled loose from the doctor's light grip on my hand and backed out of the room.

All I had heard my daddy say about her meant absolutely nothing to me. I still did not know the woman. To me she was a total stranger. How could I know her? It takes time to learn a person.

My aunt wanted to pray for me. With me. I didn't feel like praying. It seemed like all the praying I'd done hadn't helped anyway, not one single bit. While I was hiding behind those trays, I prayed for my daddy not to die. I'd prayed for my grandpa, too. Even prayed for my mama to come back to me. I just can't pray no more. It won't do me any good no way.

It's strange, but as soon as Gaten died it seems everybody sort of knew he was going to die. They could all remember some little thing he'd said, something strange about the way he was acting. They all could see some change. From the way everybody's talking, it seems Gaten visited every living soul in Round Hill, South Carolina.

All I can think is, if all those people knew something was going to happen to Gaten, wonder why they didn't do something to stop it from happening?

Some people claimed they didn't even know it was going to be Gaten. They just knew something terrible was going to happen to someone. Somebody's left eye jumped. A black cat crossed the road to the left, in front of another person's car. When that happens something bad is bound to follow.

Uncle Jim Ed doesn't seem troubled in the least that people keep coming up and saying all those kind of things. He simply said, quietly, "There is something so awesome about death, baby girl, people feel compelled to address it in some way. I suppose it's to make some peace with themselves to answer the last unknown."

With a silent owl-like swoop, the cars pulled into line and away. Car engines purring like an arrangement of music. Notes written for a sad song.

At the end of a row of rosebushes, a broken rose dangled down on one of the bushes. Broken, because I tried to break it off to pin on my dress but couldn't. You wear a white rose if your mother is dead. I don't know what color you wear when your daddy dies. I guess it probably doesn't matter.

Miss Katie is waving a big white handkerchief. They didn't tell Sara Kate that Miss Katie was left behind with the food just in case some stranger might come by, hungry and in need of a place to rest awhile. Just by chance it might be the departed soul. They only told Sara Kate it was an old custom, handed down through many generations. They did tell her, though, that the reason the hands on all clocks in the house had been stopped at 6:45 P.M. was because that was when Gaten died. People coming in only had to ask if it was morning or evening.

The only time Sara Kate said anything about the funeral arrangements was when they wanted to bring Gaten's body home and have the wake there. They said he should spend his last night on earth at home. "Oh no, oh no," Sara Kate whispered. "I don't think I can handle that." She did let them bring him by the house in the hearse the day of the funeral.

Sara Kate is sitting next to my daddy's only brother, Uncle Jim Ed. Her eyes are closed. She is twisting her new wedding band on her finger. Sara Kate is not old, but she is making the sounds with her mouth that old people make when they are beside themselves and don't know which-a-way to turn. Quiet, dry-lipped, smacking sounds. Lips slowly opening and closing, smack, smack. Just like Miss Katie.

A group of small barefoot children stand on the side of the blazing hot, hard-surfaced road. So thin, they look like stick figures. Big wide eyes pop out from faces like big white cotton balls on a blackboard. They turn and walk backwards, waving their sticklike arms until the long line of cars are out of sight. I wave back.

Sara Kate is standing alone before Gaten's casket. Her husband. My father. The funeral crowd has been held back. She has her own private time. Just a little stretch of time to be alone with Gaten. Small silent moments to say good-bye to someone already lost to her forever. All eyes are upon her. She is a white woman, a stranger to Round Hill.

Sara Kate is looking down at Gaten. Gaten's necktie is crooked. His necktie was always crooked. There was that strange connection between them that I could never understand. At least twice that I can remember, there had been a quick look from Sara Kate, and Gaten would give her a slight smile and straighten his necktie. And then smile a smile for her alone. Now Sara Kate looked at Gaten, but Gaten did not straighten his necktie.

I guess that strange and curious connection between them is gone forever.

As far as looks go, Gaten had a look for me, too. There was a certain look between us, but it sure was not the same kind of look he and Sara Kate had. For me, Gaten's look did almost everything. Most of the time he didn't have to question or punish me. His look did it all.

There was one look my daddy gave me that I don't think I'll ever forget as long as I live. It happened the day my teacher, Miss Wilson, marched me down to his office. All the years I'd gone to Gaten's school, I'd never been in any kind of trouble, much less something bad enough to be sent to the principal's office. Gaten had enough trouble at school without me adding to it.

I think my teacher hated to take me a whole lot worse than I hated to go. "Bringing Clover here, sir, was my very last resort." My daddy took off his eyeglasses. "Please don't apologize, Miss Wilson. Clover is my daughter, but she is also one of your students. I would have been disappointed in you as a teacher if you had treated her differently because of me. I'll keep Clover here with me for the rest of the day."

After Miss Wilson left I inched up to Gaten's desk. "I'm sorry, Daddy," I said. "I didn't mean to cause trouble. Honestly I didn't."

Gaten sucked in his breath. I could tell he hated for me to call him daddy at school. Calling him daddy caused a change in his feelings toward me. It showed. A two-year-old could see that. Besides, when a daddy is all you have left, you end up with double love. At least that's the way it was until Miss Sara Kate came along.

Anyway, as I was saying, Gaten looked away from me. "Get a pencil and paper, Clover, and write down everything you want to tell me that happened in your classroom this afternoon." Then my daddy looked at me. It was such a disappointed look, I could barely keep from crying.

"Maybe you'd rather tell me, Clover," he said. I studied the floor, swaying from side to side, shifting my feet one over the other. "No sir," I said. I never raised my head. No computer for me today, I can see. So I balanced my notebook on my knees and wrote. Gaten said, "Write everything you *want* to tell me that happened."

I didn't *want* to tell him nothing that really happened. How do you tell your daddy you showed off so you wouldn't have to take a test? A test you knew in your heart that you could never get a passing grade on.

When they started this thing of testing in the schools, I sure hate it that I made such a high score on that old IQ test. Made everybody think I'm so-oo smart. But I know I'm not. I've always been good in math. My grandpa taught me figures and stuff before he taught me to read. He said, "The most important thing a person needs to know is how to hold on to their money." There's no way for me not to be good in spelling. My uncle Jim Ed's wife, Aunt Everleen, has had my head buried in a dictionary since I was in the third grade. She wants me to make it to that Washington, D.C., spelling bee so bad she can taste it.

And poor old Gaten, he still thinks I'm a genius because he believes I learned to drive a tractor just by him telling me what to do. To this day he still doesn't know Grandpa taught me to drive a tractor as soon as I turned eight. He made me promise not to tell my daddy until I was older. My grandpa died that same year.

I just sort of guessed at most of the other stuff on the test. Like, I figured "ruth" would mean the opposite of "cruelty" since Grandpa said she was a good woman from the Bible. Gaten said most people knew "ruthless," but never even thought of "ruth" as a word. I didn't tell him I never did, either.

All of this was really Gaten's fault. Looks like he should have known in the first place I couldn't have learned to drive a tractor that quick, just because he told me what to do.

I was playing at the edge of our backyard when I heard a moaning sound. At first I thought it was the old stray hound having another litter of pups. And I sure didn't want to see that. Not again. Then I heard a weak cry for help and raced to the tractor shed. There was Gaten. His leg was pinned between the tractor wheel and spray machine. He had been hooking up the machine to spray peaches when the tractor probably slipped out of gear and rolled back.

Gaten's voice was getting weak. He was bleeding like a butchered hog. "Get Jim Ed," he whispered.

I started to cry. "Uncle Jim Ed went to get a load of fertilizer."

I grabbed my daddy to try and pull him out, but he made me stop. "This tractor has got to be moved," he groaned and closed his eyes.

"I can do it, Gaten," I cried. "I can, I can. Please let me."

"You can't even reach the clutch, Clover."

"I can if I stand up."

"You don't know how to change gears."

"Yes, I do," I almost said, but said instead, "I will if you tell me how to do it."

Gaten thought I was some kind of genius when I pulled that tractor off him.

Grandpa said that once I've learned something I'm like an old cooter, it's hard for me to turn it loose. I guess he thought comparing me to an old green turtle was a compliment. But what's got me worried now is, there's bound to be all new stuff in this new test. Stuff I've never heard of in my entire life. Just because I'm good at spelling and know the meaning of a whole bunch of words in the dictionary is not enough. Everything you need to know is not in there.

I tap my foot on the carpeted floor, like I'm bouncing a ball. Thump, thump. Gaten looks up. "Did you finish your report, Clover?" I shake my head, no. "Don't shake your head, Clover, say yes or no, Mr. . . ." Gaten breaks off. He never, ever made me call him mister. I giggle out loud.

There is no way I could tell Gaten why I was brought to his office. So I wrote and wrote.

I can't get away with stuff like I can when I'm waiting in Gaten's office to go home after school. I ride the school bus in the morning. Gaten has to leave before Aunt Everleen has time to fix my hair. I'm the only girl in the fifth grade who doesn't fix her own hair. Gaten says it looks too bushy when I do it.

Once I almost got away with sharpening a whole stack of pencils to a nub on his new electric pencil sharpener. Gaten didn't fuss or nothing. Just said, "I think you've sharpened enough pencils, Clover, do your homework." I do believe Gaten will be telling me to do my homework for the rest of my life. Then there was the time he told me to wear a dress on picture-taking day, and I slipped and wore my rust corduroy skirt. It was bad twisted but still pretty. When Gaten saw it, all he said was, "Straighten your skirt, Clover."

But this time it was different. My daddy was really upset with me. He didn't say much, but I could tell.

When I gave Gaten my written report, there was a trace of a smile on his face when he read it. There was real laughter in his eyes. But it was gone when he looked at me. His mouth tightened. "A bald eagle flying through an open window to attack a snake curled in a striking position behind Miss Wilson's desk?" Gaten's voice was strong. "Come now,

Clover, are you trying to tell me this happened in the classroom?"

"Shucks no, Gaten," I said. "That's what I was thinking about when Miss Wilson asked me to read my history report."

The school janitor opened Gaten's office door and jumped backwards, "Excuse, excuse me, sir," he says over and over. "I didn't aim to come in with you in here."

Gaten glanced at his watch and stood up. "It's getting late, Mr. Jackson, we'll get out of your way."

I made a grin at Gaten's back. Hot dog, Aunt Everleen will have our dinner on the stove, all warm and everything. Gaten will read while I stand on the little stool he made for me and fix his plate. If he kept on making me write everything I've ever learned in my whole life, I wouldn't have time to fix his ole plate.

The janitor was so glad Gaten called him mister. He grinned and squinted his pink eyes. Mr. Jackson is an albino. He stood tall and straight and grinned over that "mister" bit. Gaten was old enough to be his father.

People are still filing past my daddy's coffin. Sara Kate is wedged between me and Uncle Jim Ed, squeezed in between us on the crowded bench like vanilla cream between dark chocolate cookies. My daddy is dead. Stretched out in a fancy coffin right before my very eyes. And all I can think of is an Oreo cookie. An Oreo cookie.

My stepmother's body is as straight as a cornstalk. She is not crying. We sit side by side as stiff as painted leaves on a painted tree. Uncle Jim Ed puts his hand on her arm. But me and my stepmother don't touch. I can count on the fingers of one hand how many times I've laid eyes on Sara Kate. She's been my stepmother for almost four days and all I know for sure about her is, she's not a Mexican. I can spot a Mexican a mile away. Every summer if there's a big peach crop the migrant workers flood Round Hill. We have peaches, but not enough to need the Mexicans.

Chase Porter brings them in all the time. He couldn't get all those peaches picked without them. He's one of the biggest peach growers in South Carolina. Chase is at the funeral. He looks sad because he is sad. He has known my daddy all his life. Like Gaten he was born and raised in Round Hill.

I pick at a thorn in my finger until it starts to bleed. I watch a drop of blood threaten to fall. I turn my finger into a paint brush. The blood makes a round dot on my white dress. I keep adding to it until it almost becomes a flower. A daisy. The way I'm messing up my white dress, I might as well have held the baby with the stinky diaper. At first there had been just one little drop of blood that a bleeding finger could not leave alone. My dress is a mess. Sara Kate reaches for my hand. I put it behind my back.

In a way the funeral was kind of like a play. Everyone had a part. A part they played right on time, like it had been rehearsed over and over until it was down pat.

An usher leads me to my daddy's coffin. I'm supposed to cover my daddy's face with the white satin quilted blanket. He is dead. Yet he still looks some kind of fine in that fancy casket. But my arms are pasted to my sides. My knees glued together. There is no way I can pull that thing over Gaten's face. They lead me away. My feet slide across the floor like it's a sheet of ice. It's a sad, sad thing to have a ten-year-old do.

A young woman takes a picture of Gaten in the coffin. I don't think Sara Kate liked that much, either. Her face shows her feelings straight out.

The men in black suits move quickly and quietly about the casket. They close the casket. Lock the brass handles into place. It's time for the funeral to start. The Ninetieth Psalm is read. I guess my daddy is like the green grass only he was cut down before he could wither and fade. A young student sings. When a boy sings, he sings so much sadder than a girl. Everybody from the county sheriff on down is crying. Everybody but Sara Kate and me.

The women in white dresses that have stood waiting in

line take the flowers off Gaten's casket and follow as he is carried away. At the graveyard they finish their part in the play. The curtain has been dropped. It's the end.

Sara Kate places a single rose on Gaten's coffin. Gaten had been put away real fine.

A group of men in dirty coveralls and dirty shovels walked toward the grave with long smooth steps like the gliding wings of buzzards flying down to feast on the dead.

If there was a hungry stranger who stopped while we were away, he didn't eat nothing. There is still food piled up everywhere. And he didn't move or take anything either. My teddy bears are in the same place. Their eyes still have the same fixed blank stares. The snow-filled paperweight is still on Gaten's desk, right beside his new solar calculator. I shake the paperweight. A heavy snowfall twirls around, then gently settles down on a tiny village. Soon all is quiet and peaceful. The tiny snow-covered village is asleep. Not a picture is missing from the crowded piano top. Not a single piece of carnival glass moved.

Even outside everything is the same. Nothing has been changed. A soft breeze gently sways the hammock sometimes. But mostly the hammock is still. Still and empty, like it's waiting.

If there was a stranger there, one thing is for sure. He

did not disturb or take away the heavy sadness in the house. Every bit of that was left behind, right in place.

The house is soon filled with people from top to bottom. The kitchen is filled with women fixing plates. Someone brings Sara Kate a plate. She moves the food around with a fork but she doesn't eat a bite. I can understand that. I can't eat anything, either.

A mother pulls her little four-year-old boy in the middle of the room to sing. He's going to sing, just to take our minds off so much sadness, she says. He sings "America the Beautiful." He keeps his head to one side, his eyes on the floor. He sings pretty good, but how can anyone think someone would want to hear that song when their daddy is dead? But the little boy in the blue suit and red-checkered bowtie sways like he is in a swing, and sings and sings. In the end he hides his face behind his hand. He is not too shy to eat, though.

I was so sure Sara Kate was going to leave Round Hill and go back wherever she came from. I started packing my clothes to move out. I wasn't sure who I was going to live with. I only knew I was not staying in that house by myself.

I'm going to learn someday that whenever my uncle Jim Ed and his sister gather in a little cluster with Sara Kate, they're bound to be talking about me. Yes, it is me they're talking about. Sometimes Aunt Ruby Helen's voice really gets loud. She is looking cross-eyed at Sara Kate. "It will be best for my dead brother's child to be with me," she says. "I am her daddy's only sister. Actually, the only family the poor child has." Uncle Jim Ed is not about to let his sister get away with that. "Clover still has me," he says quietly. "I'm family, and she's used to us."

His sister's voice is loud again. This is the first time she's been able to even talk. She lost her voice as soon as she got off the plane. She's been crying ever since. Tears streaming down her face like rain. Her mouth was crying, but there were no crying sounds. Her brother's death took away her voice, just like death took away his life. Just sucked it up.

"You have a child, Jim Ed, a son. I have no one. Besides, Clover needs a mother." Like a child, Ruby Helen is pleading with her brother.

I guess she would make a pretty good mother. I got me a Cabbage Patch doll from her, way before anybody else in Round Hill got one. I guess Maryland is not the worst place in the world to live. If I go there I bet I'll start walking like Ruby Helen. I know she copied making short, swishing steps from Jackée on the TV program "227."

One wants me to stay, one wants me to leave. I guess they will have to do like the old wise king Grandpa told me about. Just cut me in half.

A tight-lipped Sara Kate says, "I promised Clover's father I would take care of his daughter." In her own quiet way,

Sara Kate sure said the right thing to settle that. Nobody around here messes with a dying man's wishes.

Ruby Helen looks at the corner cupboard Grandpa built with all of Grandmother's carnival glass. "My grandmother won every single piece of that glass at the county fair shooting down ducks. It is very, very valuable," she said coldly to Sara Kate.

I can see Jim Ed is embarrassed. "I'm sure Sara Kate will see that nothing is broken," he tells his sister. I'm thinking first, that was some kind of a cold thing to say to Sara Kate and second, I'd thought all along it had been *my* grandmother, Ruby Helen's mother, who did all that straight shooting.

2

. . . . . .

*I*t shouldn't have surprised me that Sara Kate and I would end up together, because she was a surprise for me from the start. She sure wasn't a purple bicycle.

"I thought I told you I was bringing a surprise home, honey. Aunt Everleen didn't get a dress ready for you," my daddy whispered. He was looking at my torn dirty dress.

I pulled on my dress, my eyes on his shiny loafers. I could tell Gaten had put a lot into making everything right for this surprise. But when he rolled up with that woman in his truck and no purple bicycle, the surprise thing was over for me.

"Everleen had a whole bunch of dresses washed," I shot back hotly, "but she just ironed this one. She claimed she was having hot flashes so bad, they were about to set her on fire. I can see her getting hot in the summertime, but she's been hot all winter.

"You may not believe this, Gaten," I went on, "but Everleen's been running as hot as an overheated radiator all winter. One day she was standing on the front porch fanning like it was the Fourth of July, and there was snow on the ground. Cross my heart and hope me die, she was."

I could see I'd hurt Gaten bad. Real, real bad. It showed in his eyes.

"I didn't know I was going to mess around and fall trying to catch that old lightning bug, Gaten," I said all sorry-like.

Now that I think about it, Everleen must have known something I didn't. She did my hair pretty and dressed me up really fine. Gaten always did have this thing about hair. He wanted my hair to look just right.

The only thing I knew was, Gaten was going to bring me a surprise and I'd been waiting all day long for it. In the back of my mind I imagined it would be a ten-speed purple bicycle. Every wish I ever made, I wanted a bicycle. Surely Gaten must have known that.

I knew it wouldn't be another doll. Ever since I cut open the high-priced one Gaten got me to see what made her cry, he hadn't bought me another one. He wasn't really that mad, though. He just looked over his glasses at me and said, "I think my little girl will become a fine surgeon one day."

He sure wouldn't have gotten me a cat or dog. Maybe

he's scared I might cut them up or something. I really don't care, though. We got more strays around now than you can shake a stick at.

The trouble was, I had to wait too long for Gaten to come. It was starting to get dark. The trees had started to show up against the evening sky like a picture under thin tracing paper. It made a pretty picture. Trees drawn in black ink on a sky framed with soft gray and pink clouds. Tiny gnats bunched together in small groups to dance their daily yo-yo dance at dusk.

When lightning bugs started darting through the sky, I jumped to catch one and landed smack dab in a pile of rotting watermelon rinds. How was I to know that's where Jim Ed threw them when we finished eating? I got me some pretty diamond rings, though.

I still wouldn't have gotten as dirty as I did if I hadn't seen the little raised furrow an old mole was making in the ground. It almost made my flesh crawl to see that dirt cracking open, like a train going through a tunnel. It kind of like drives me crazy to see dirt moving, and you can't see what's making it move. I've never, ever been able to find a mole. One day, I guess, I'll just dig my fool head clean off.

So, you see, I got some kind of dirty, waiting on Gaten all that time.

This woman, Sara Kate, is going to take some getting used to. We didn't set horses from the start. When I showed

Gaten the diamond rings I made, she shivered and eyed me coldly. "Oh, how cruel," she said, catching her breath all short and quick, like she was hurting or something. "So cruel," she whispered, when I answered, "Yes, I killed the lightning bugs." I don't know how in the world she thought I got the stuff to make my rings.

Gaten didn't say a word. He knew better than to open his mouth because he taught me how to make the rings in the first place. I guess he did it, though, to stop me from running myself to death over the dew-filled grass.

You see, on bright, sunshine-filled days, if there's been a heavy dew, the light makes diamonds everywhere. When I was little I used to race to pick up one, only to have it disappear right before my eyes. Everleen told Gaten to make me stop before I went storm crazy. Besides, she said, the sores on my legs would never heal if I kept getting dew in them.

Gaten never said a word about the dew diamonds. I just quit on my own. Just like I stopped looking for the pot of gold Grandpa said was at the end of the rainbow. I still like the lightning bug diamonds, though. To me, they look kind of real.

Sara Kate can't seem to get her mind off the fireflies, as she calls them. If she's gonna stick around us, she sure better get used to things being killed. Gaten would shoot anything that flies, except a dove. My grandpa always said, "Never kill a dove because unaware you might kill a messenger."

My daddy told me to change my dress so we could go to the fish camp for supper.

"There is no way I'm going to the fish camp to eat," I said. "For all I know they might catch them fish in the creek. Mr. Saye Willie Adams said he wouldn't eat no fish at the fish camp if he was on his dying bed and the fish would save him." I turned to Sara Kate, "And you wouldn't either if you knew what the boys in Round Hill do in the creek water."

When Gaten tried to excuse what I'd said to Sara Kate, and make me apologize for making up that awful thing, I didn't back down. I said, "All I know is what they say, and that's exactly what they say. Besides, Gaten," I added, "we have supper anyhow. I heated up the stew we had last night, and Everleen sent over a fresh pot of rice."

I knew Gaten was still plenty mad at me over this creek thing. But then I was a little mad at him, too. To this day I can't see how Gaten could think that his bringing a woman I'd never laid eyes on in my life could possibly be a surprise for me. Especially a woman that might become my stepmother. Even if I got a purple bike, I didn't want a stepmother. Even if I had to have one, I sure wouldn't pick one like Sara Kate.

Looks like anybody who knows the story about Cinderella should know that nobody in the world would want a stepmother unless they were all the way crazy.

For days on end Gaten had been walking around in a daze. He looked like he was about to die or something. Jim Ed said he'd been bitten by the love bug. In my head I think he was still mad about that creek water thing. And just maybe he knew I slipped and read that letter Sara Kate wrote him. I hate like everything I read that letter. That's the first time I'd ever read Gaten's mail in my life. But it was too late then. I couldn't unread what I'd read. Even if Gaten knew I read the thing, he surely couldn't think that I could begin to understand that letter.

My dearest Gaten,
Now that I'm faced with this dreadful thought of losing you, I'm not sure what direction my life will take. I only know that it seems necessary to convey to you how deeply I care about you. I know, as you do, that happiness cannot be built upon the pain of others. And yet, your sensitivity to this only serves to add to my reasons for loving you.

My faith is in your wisdom and my trust in your decision.

Always,
Sara Kate

I can't see why Sara Kate couldn't just say straight out what she's trying to tell my daddy. But whatever it is, I guess he must have made some sense out of it. He's mighty disturbed over something.

Everybody knew something was bad wrong with Gaten when he wouldn't eat. At Sunday's dinner Gaten didn't eat chicken or rib one. Wouldn't even eat a spoonful of Everleen's banana pudding. I could have eaten the whole thing by myself. She puts Cool Whip on top instead of that egg white stuff. They said Gaten was in L.O.V.E.

I wish I hadn't read his old letter. If I hadn't, then I wouldn't have known he'd lost her.

It was a black night outside, and Gaten was staring out the window. His eyes searched through the darkness. I wondered if he thought his Sara Kate might just come through the darkness back to him.

3
· · · · · · ·

*E*veryone at the family gathering was solid blown away when Gaten strolled up with Miss Sara Kate. Everybody, that is, except Gideon. He didn't even look up. He just kept right on eating away on a long slice of watermelon and spitting out seeds.

At least we all knew why it took Gaten so long to get back with the salt for the ice cream churn. He had been all the way to the airport in Charlotte, North Carolina.

In a way I didn't mind too much that Sara Kate was there. Maybe Gaten would get his mind settled down and his appetite back.

The relatives of our family were all gathered at our house. They've done that every year for as long as I can remember.

All the old folks pulled chairs under a shade tree. They made their way around with shaking unsteady steps, like they were picking their way barefoot through broken glass. They settled their bodies, thin from age, down among walkers and walking sticks, their voices as weak as their eyes tucked into wrinkled faces that pulled together like a gathered skirt. In the summer's heat they gathered together like sparrows warming themselves in the winter sun. Old age sure makes up its own gathering.

Deep down in my heart I knew before that day was over Sara Kate was going to be sick, sick. I could tell from the look on her face when she saw that boiling grease in that big black iron washpot. She had never seen fish cooked like that in her life. Still, whenever someone brought her a piece she ate it. Just like she ate Aunt Ruby Helen's peach walnut cake, then turned right around and ate a big hunk of store-bought Sunbeam Spanish Bar. The cake tastes all right if you can get past that awful gooey white icing that's as thick as the cake. And that's not counting the biscuits. Every time my great uncle stabs one with a fork for him, he stabs one for Sara Kate and puts it on her plate.

It seems at least the yellow jackets like the Sunbeam cake icing. I tell Sara Kate to be careful of the yellow jackets. If they sting her it might make her swell up like Uncle Jim Ed does when he gets stung. He's allergic to bees.

Poor old Sara Kate didn't even turn down the ham Gideon cooked, even after everybody tried to warn her it came from a boar. But then, the woman doesn't even know what mountain oysters are. I knew. I'd known for a long time. But I sure knew better than to tell her. You see, it's a right nasty thing to repeat.

Gaten sure needed to stay by her side. Annie Ruth, another umpteen cousin, piled macaroni and cheese on Sara Kate's plate. Annie Ruth looked plain country. Her hair was in tight separate curls all over her head. She won't comb her hair. she explained, because she is trying to save her beauty shop hairdo until Sunday. "I'm getting so worried about my mind here of late," she complained. "I get ready to use it, and Lord it's plumb left me. Sometimes I can't find it for days."

Gaten could have helped Sara Kate out on Aunt Maude's potato salad. Everyone knows she is as clean as a whistle even if she can't half see. But who wants to crunch through eggshells and spit out pieces of onion skin? But then, Gaten was eating it, too. I guess he hated to see everybody turning her potato salad down. Gaten is tenderhearted.

Sara Kate's eyes shifted from Annie Ruth's hair to yet another cousin. Her eyes were glued on the little girl's head. Her mama had her hair all corn-rowed up in the tiniest rows I'd ever seen. Rows going backwards, forwards, and all across the head. Like a cornfield planted by a drunk driving the tractor. I imagined Sara Kate was trying to count all the rows. If she wasn't, she had to be studying the haircuts. Some of the cousins, including Daniel, had razor parts cut so crazy across their heads it looked like a lightning bolt was zigzagging across.

To top all that off, our cousin California came in with even more corn-rows on her head. Her corn-rows were set in like a patchwork quilt. California is off in the head. So are her parents. They are constantly on the move all the time, moving toward and away from each other, like the checkers move about a checkerboard. Moves that form a retarded dance.

My little cousin with the corn-rows stands beside California, her eyes and head cast downward, her fat arms folded across her wide fat body.

Maybe I don't like their corn-rows because I know I can never wear them. Aunt Everleen said she'd rather be struck by a bolt of lightning than to corn-row my hair. I won't sit still long enough. Perhaps, in a way, I might be a little bit jealous.

California heads straight to a banana pudding. You better not mess around with her, though. Once Daniel was mocking the way she held her mouth open with spit drooling down. And he told her if she kept it that way they would send her back to the asylum in Columbia, South Carolina. Yes, California has been in the asylum.

Well, anyway, California got so mad she tried to ram Daniel's head into a rusty tin gallon can. I don't know what they did to her down there, but it seems like she came back worse off than she was.

Daniel knew it was wrong to mock her in the first place. Grandpa told us that long ago in Bible times the Lord sent down two bears to kill up a bunch of kids because they mocked one of his prophets.

California is taking a liking to Sara Kate. She seems drawn to her hair and keeps touching it. I know one thing, she better not let my daddy's sister from Maryland catch her combing Sara Kate's hair. Up there, Ruby Helen claims they made the people in some town change a picture of a little black girl combing a white woman's hair while they watched a polo game.

I can't name all that food on the tables. Gaten pushes Miss Eula Mae's wheelchair out of the sun into a shady spot. I go over and fan away the old nasty blow-fly buzzing around her food. When she finishes I see a dollar bill she has for me, in fingers bent over like a curved fork. Gaten is watching so I don't take it. But when he looks away that dollar is in my hands like a flash.

There was one thing I could tell right off. There was hardly a woman there who could stand Sara Kate. From a corner at the top of the stairs I can see in the dining room, but they can't see me. A cousin draws on a cigarette and slowly releases the smoke through her nose.

Ruby Helen laughs long, and hard. "I haven't seen anybody do that since old man Dan Rivers died."

"Girl, you remember some old-timey stuff."

"Remember how he used to roll his cigarettes and wet 'em with so much spit they split open?"

Their voices were drowned out by their loud laughter. I couldn't imagine Sara Kate laughing like that. All I'd heard her do that day was giggle.

Everleen comes in with a pot of soup. "I'm starting to bring in stuff," she said. "Somebody go scrape out that ice cream in the churn and put it in the freezer. Poor old Gaten will want some later. He loves homemade cream. Bless his heart, he was too shamed to eat from the dasher like he always used to. His fancy lady friend sure cramps his style."

"Seems like your brother-in-law is going to bring home a lady," someone says.

"Gaten won't marry again."

"You don't have to marry a lady to bring her home."

Everleen pulls her mouth into a tight ugly spout. "Gaten Hill does."

The cousin is dipping a homemade white potato roll into the soup. Smacking and licking her thick red lips. Everleen's jaw tightens. "Get a bowl, girl. Stop eating nasty in my soup."

They are talking about Sara Kate again.

"Can't you just die from all that beige and taupe she's wearing?"

"Girl, them some Gloria Vanderbilt's pants."

"Aw shucks now, go on, girl."

"Wonder what's wrong with her?"

"I don't know, but there is something that's caused her to be rejected by her own men."

"I say she's an epileptic," Ruby Helen puts in. The cousin puts a small slice of egg custard pie in her mouth, all at once. "How in the Lord's world did you come up with that affliction, Ruby Helen?"

"I can't stand it when someone talks with a mouth full of food."

The cousin swallowed hard. "So tell me, how do you know?"

"It's the way her eyes get that blank stare. You can be talking to her, but she's not there."

"She could be in a deep study about something."

"Well, something's wrong with her. Why else would she take up with a black dude?"

In spite of how hard they try to put down my daddy's new woman friend, trying to make her have some kind of sickness is bad. Next they will say she is retarded.

I really think it's her background that has upset them, and made them so jealous and hopping mad. You can look at the woman and see she is certainly not poor trash. Uncle

Jim Ed told me she is an only child and would never starve if she didn't hit a lick at work for the rest of her life. Not that it makes him like her any better. He hasn't made up his mind that she is the right woman for his baby brother.

He can't find fault with the way she seems to care about Gaten. Nobody can. Not over the way she looks at him. Her eyes follow his every move. She wears her feelings for him right on her face. I sure can see why she likes him. My daddy is pretty cool-looking. He is not light-skinned, but he's not dark-skinned, either. Since he cut off his mustache you can see his mouth and nose better. He's got a great mouth, especially when he smiles. And I don't care if he is a man, his nose is plain pretty. It's good Sara Kate is too old to grow anymore. Right now she and Gaten are the same height. And that's not real tall. My aunt says my daddy could stand to put on a few pounds.

I like the way they are together. They are not all over each other, hugging and kissing like some courting people. Every now and again she touches him when he is near, her hand lightly touching his, or an elbow resting on his knee.

Someone brings the cousin's little baby inside. "Well," the cousin says, dabbing spit on the tips of her fingers and wiping dried milk from around her baby's mouth, "this Sara Kate must have what Gaten likes."

"Oh, gross, Mary Kathyrn," Ruby Helen moaned. "I do hope you never let Gaten's high-class Miss Sara Kate see you do that. She'll think all black women wash their kids faces with spit."

"Sh-sh," someone whispered, "here comes Merlee Kenyon. Poor little thing. She is sure taking it hard since she and Gaten broke up. I don't know why she didn't leave when Gaten drove up with his new lady friend."

Ruby Helen eyed Merlee's tight white pants, red, red blouse and high-heeled red sandals. "Girl, you are looking bad, bad."

Miss Kenyon did look good that day, and she's got a bad shape. The prettiest shape I ever saw.

My aunt let Merlee know right off that she could not stand Sara Kate. Merlee and my aunt always were close friends.

I couldn't help thinking that it was halfway my aunt's fault that Gaten ended up with Sara Kate in the first place.

Not long after my daddy broke off with Miss Kenyon, he said he needed to get away for awhile. So he had my aunt Everleen get me all fixed up and we took off to Maryland for a long weekend.

It had been my aunt's idea to go see the King Tut exhibition. Once we got there and saw the long lines, she changed her mind. We were getting ready to leave when she spotted one of her neighbors, a doctor at Howard University Hospital, waiting in line.

While they chatted, the doctor's beeper went off. I thought that was some kind of cool. I wished my daddy had one. Gaten volunteered to hold his place in line while he made his phone call.

It turned out he was on call at the hospital and had to leave. Gaten said the position in line was too good to give up. So he stayed. My aunt and I went shopping.

At breakfast the next morning, Gaten said he couldn't believe that just by chance he had bumped into someone he hadn't seen in years. "I mean I literally bumped into her," he laughed. "When I turned to apologize, we recognized each other. We first met during my last year in college."

Ruby Helen looked at me. "So that's the reason your daddy called to say he wouldn't be home for supper. I don't think he would have missed supper if he had known I'd baked a capon and made wild rice dressing."

I sure didn't see what had been so special about the meal. Just another chicken dinner, as far as I was concerned.

"Well," she said to Gaten, "maybe I'll see more of you up here now. It's sad that it takes some woman to force a man to visit his people."

"The woman you've mentioned doesn't live in this area," Gaten said quietly. "In fact," he continued, "because of her work with the textile industry, she might temporarily move to the Carolinas. She's a textile designer."

Gaten poured syrup over his pancakes. He smiled at his sister. "Pure Vermont maple syrup. At least someone in the Hill family knows how to live."

If there is anything my aunt knows, it's food. Her husband travels in his work all the time. She stays home and eats. My aunt is as big as a house. She is still kind of pretty, though.

"Just wait until you sink your teeth into the fried cornmeal mush I'm going to cook," she promised Gaten. "Remember how Mama used to let the cooked mush set overnight in the cold on the back porch so it would slice good the next morning? We would drench those crisp golden brown fried slices with fresh butter and molasses. But you haven't tasted anything until you've had it with pure maple syrup."

Gaten laughed. "We only had it if it was cold weather. Mama never realized the refrigerator would have done the same job. She had to do it the way her mama did."

It was so good between the two of them, remembering the times when they were young. If only it had ended there. But Ruby Helen had to keep on running her mouth and jump back on the lady he had dinner with.

I had no idea what my aunt meant when she said to my daddy, "Well, there is certainly nothing wrong with a one-night stand. At least it didn't used to be, but these days," she paused and raised her eyebrows, "a decent family man sort of stays away from that kind of thing." She piled more pancakes on my plate. "If you catch my drift, big brother."

I didn't know what she meant then. I still don't know. But what I did know was, I didn't believe anyone had ever made Gaten so mad before. He put his knife and fork on his plate. In the right position, of course. Gaten eats very proper. He learned all that stuff in college. "Thanks for breakfast, Sis," he said.

If my daddy hadn't been so mad I believe he would have broken down and flat out cried.

I suppose whatever that one-night stand business was about, my aunt shouldn't have said it, or at least not in front of me. Anyway, I know that was what caused Gaten to end up cutting our visit a little short. Again, I didn't get a chance to see the White House.

"It's amazing," Miss Kenyon said, "how one single turn in your life will lead you down a road of no return. How one, single unintentional act can affect you for the rest of your life."

Miss Kenyon looked at Ruby Helen. "I don't know why you would let your brother get all tied up with a woman like her in the first place. Gaten should have sense enough to know that kind of a marriage never works out."

My aunt shrugged. "Who says he is going to marry her?"

"You know full well he will." Miss Kenyon's voice is sharp

and cutting. "And you and Jim Ed will stand by with your hands folded and let it happen."

Ruby Helen squeezed her eyes into narrow slits. "Merlee Kenyon, tell me you are not accusing me of getting my brother and that white woman together. I may look like I'm crazy, sound like I'm crazy, but listen up, honey, and listen good, I am nobody's fool."

Miss Kenyon dropped her head. "I'm sorry, Ruby Helen. So very sorry. I'm not blaming you. There is really no one to blame but myself. Me and my big mouth."

She moved to the curtained dining room windows, and stood peeking out at Gaten and Sara Kate.

A group of women dug through mounds of filled green plastic trash bags, carefully examining rolled and wadded paper napkins. Poking with sticks through chicken and rib bones. They were searching for Cousin Amphia's false teeth, of course. Every year she takes them out to eat, wraps them in a paper napkin and they get lost every time.

Amphia appears to be lost too. Wandering around worrying over her teeth. Her bright red toenails stick out of her open-toed sandals. Her toenails look as if she painted them with a spray can.

Miss Kenyon looked so lonely and sad I felt sorry for her. I knew she was crying inside. My aunt must have known it, too. She excused herself and left the room for awhile.

· · ·

When Merlee moved to Round Hill from Greenville, South Carolina, everybody said she was without a doubt the prettiest black woman they had ever seen. Merlee thought so, too. And she didn't try to hide it.

I know she was the best piano player I ever heard. I also knew she almost drove my poor daddy crazy. He couldn't keep his mind on nothing.

They were really tight for awhile. Nobody had to tell me about it. I knew it for a fact. Her car was parked at our house so much, Aunt Everleen warned her she'd better slack off some, people would start to talk.

And then some talk started. Talk got out that Miss Kenyon said she was in love with Gaten Hill, all right and enough, but she wasn't about to take on a ready-made family. She also said she sure didn't spend the best years of her life getting a master's degree in music to take care of someone else's child. Besides, little girls get on her nerves, she added.

As soon as I heard what she had said I made up my mind that I was not about to show her the killdeer's nest I'd seen. I had found a good hiding place in a tree near the edge of a field and watched the little chirping bird build the nest right on the ground. It seemed the little killdeer found the smoothest little round rocks and gravel. It rolled them into a pile with its bill, then settled down on top of the little rounded-out nest like a setting hen.

I was supposed to have started taking music lessons from Miss Kenyon every Saturday morning. I had planned to take her to see the killdeer's nest when we finished the lesson. But I didn't even start taking the old piano lessons. I didn't care what Gaten would have said. I didn't show her my bird nest, either. That was for sure.

Well, when Gaten heard what his girlfriend said about me, he stopped courting her altogether.

I kind of thought Gaten might have said something about the music lessons. But he didn't. He didn't say anything about Miss Kenyon, either.

Once when I was waiting in his office for him to finish working, I said, "Gaten, we didn't really need Miss Kenyon, did we? We can get along real good without anyone, can't we?"

Gaten leaned back in his chair and smiled at me, "Real good, Clover," he said, "real good." When my daddy smiled, he was the best-looking man in the whole world.

I don't know if it was what Merlee Kenyon said about not liking little girls, or what she said about my mama, that hurt Gaten so much. "I really don't want to wear a dead woman's shoes," she'd said, adding that even the woman's backwoods furniture made her almost throw up. She also said she could hardly keep from throwing out all the tacky little whatnots my mother left in the house.

According to Miss Katie, "A woman should never, ever

talk about a man's dead wife. They may not have gotten along worth a hoot when married. But if and when a woman dies, she suddenly becomes a saint in her husband's eyes."

Downstairs the dining room filled up with women again.

"Gaten's new lady seems to like his little Clover a lot," someone said to Miss Kenyon.

The truth is, Miss Sara Kate was singing a different tune from the first time I met her. I overheard her say to my daddy, "Clover is indeed a beautiful little girl, Gaten, you must love her dearly."

"Yes," Gaten smiled, "she is quite beautiful, and yes, I do love that little girl." He laughed. "She is also difficult sometimes, and as you well know, one can never tell what's going to come out of her mouth."

Sara Kate had laughed, a rich husky laugh that seemed strange coming from someone with a childish voice. "Tell me about it," she said.

I couldn't help but think, this woman's got the smarts to say the right thing at the right time. She may not have wanted me any more than Miss Kenyon wanted me. People don't like to take on extras. But just maybe, I figured, she had sense enough not to say it. At least not to someone who would carry it back to Gaten.

Yes, I'd decided, Sara Kate could so fool Gaten if she really wanted to. Poor old Gaten, he just might be simple-minded enough to believe that if Sara Kate would be happy with Clover, then Clover would be happy with her.

Everleen brings a platter piled high with fried chicken. "There's enough food left over to feed an army. Where's Clover? Her daddy is looking for her."

"Probably at the top of the stairs listening," laughs Ruby Helen.

I sneak out of a dormer window and, when no one is looking, slide down the chinaberry tree at the end of the porch. I need to find my daddy anyway. I got some kind of a bad stomachache and it looks like I'm not the only one.

Aunt Everleen could certainly tell something was wrong with Sara Kate. "Go find out if there is anything I can do for her, Clover," she said.

"Leave them alone," Cousin Lucille said. "When people are in love they want to be alone. Alone behind closed doors."

If anybody had looked at Sara Kate right good, they would have known by the way she looked, the way she walked, weakly leaning on Gaten. She certainly was not leaving for any hanky-panky, like they said.

Gaten and Sara Kate were in his bedroom. They were alone all right. But the door sure wasn't closed. It was wide open. Sara Kate was lying on the bed, her head propped up on a pillow. Gaten sat on the bed by her side, trying to get her not to talk. But Sara Kate talked anyway. She kept saying over and over, "I'm so sorry, Gaten, so very sorry. Why did I have to get sick?"

"It's because you've been eating like a crazy person," I said. I brought her a foaming glass of Alka-Seltzer, and put a cold damp face cloth on her forehead. My daddy hugged me, and said, "Brilliant." It wasn't anything. I've done the same thing a thousand times for Aunt Everleen when she gets one of her migraine headaches.

People are starting to leave. Sara Kate is sitting all alone at the end of a long table. What little lipstick she had on is all gone. She is as white as a sheet. She looks as sick as a dog.

A dying day brings on dying moods. A cousin up from lowlands is playing his guitar and singing the blues. "Lord, Lord," he sings, "sometimes I feel like I'm dying." He kind of looks like he's dying, with his red eyes and puffy lips that look like somebody put purple lipgloss on them.

Gideon's beagle hounds are raising some kind of fuss. Running some poor little rabbit, as hot as it is.

"Pick that thing, baby," Cousin Lucille says to the guitar player. She has put herself together as carefully as a clown. She is wearing every shade of purple I believe there is. I'm surprised her hair isn't purple. She is wearing a new wig, a frizzed one. The old one caught on fire while she was bending over a gas burner.

Lucille must have forgotten she's supposed to be a born-again Christian now and given up dancing. Because now she can't hold her dancing spirit down. Either that or it's those chiggers setting her body on fire. She's been in the blackberry thickets every day.

Somebody said, "She looks like she's having a spell the way she's twisting and carrying on."

"Leave her alone," Ruby Helen said. "She lost her husband." By that she meant, not lost like you can't find him. Everybody in Round Hill knows where he is. Right in the cemetery under an old stunted pine tree. He's dead.

So Lucille danced, all alone in the still twilight. A lonely woman whose body wins out over a guilty heart. I don't care if Lucille's getup was unlike anything you'd ever seen. It still made all the menfolk look at her. And that made the womenfolk kind of jealous. I think it's because of her walk, not her dancing. Lucille's walk is a swaying motion, her soft, curvy hips move under her skirt. I wouldn't mind having her shape when I grow up.

It's too bad Lottie Jean has gone home with the new camera she got with her S&H green stamps. I wish she could have taken Lucille's picture.

4

· · · · · · ·

Sara Kate has made Cream of Wheat for breakfast every day this week. She loaded us up with every flavor they made. I still like cinnamon apple the best.

On the back of the package there is a doodle. An easy way to draw an elephant is shown. You can do it even if you can't draw a straight line.

At the peach stand I follow the directions and draw a perfect elephant. I hide it behind my back when Everleen wants to see what I've done. If she sees it I'll be drawing elephants for the rest of my life. It will make her think I'm gifted and talented. I sure hate that they put that in people's minds about little kids. They never let you play anymore.

I like the man's picture on the Cream of Wheat box. He looks just like my grandpa. I guess my grandpa is still roaming around looking for that mansion in the sky they said he was going to go to. If he finds it I'm sure he'll get a room for me. That is, if there is any truth to that. I'm not so sure about that thing.

Everleen tells Daniel to put down the terrapin he's turning over and over in his hand. "If he bites you, he won't turn you loose until it thunders," she says, looking up at the cloudless sky. Daniel throws the terrapin down.

My uncle tells me to stack empty peach baskets. I hate to, I always hurt my hand. But I do it. Jim Ed is so worried about this peach crop I don't want to put another frown on his face. It wouldn't have any place to go, anyhow. His face is all filled up.

A late spring freeze caused the peaches to have split-seeds. That means that once the seed of a peach freezes, the peach will split wide open as soon as it starts to get ripe. When customers complain about the way the peaches look, Aunt Everleen will tell them right quick, "That's the Lord's work."

It's a real slow day at the stand. Everleen jumps to her feet when a brand new pickup truck pulls up. "I see you have Elberta peaches on your sign," the man says.

"Yes, we do," Everleen brags. "It's the finest canning peach there is. Del Monte cans Elbertas. Says so right on the can."

"Oh, I was just wanting some to eat," the customer says.

"It's the finest eating peach there is," Everleen put in quickly. She rubs one on her big fluffy shirt, and takes a big bite. "This is truly the best peach I ever tasted."

She stuffs the money he gives her into her pocket. He is a physicist down at the nuclear plant. I put his peck of peaches in his truck.

Everleen is reading the newspaper. "Just listen to this," she says. "This little girl is not even nine years old, and she's . . ." She didn't have to finish telling me. I know it's a story about some little girl doing something great. My aunt has never forgotten that Samantha Smith of Maine was invited to Russia because of a letter she wrote.

Everleen thinks if I write Mrs. Reagan I might get invited to the White House. We've been too busy with my spelling, though.

I go and get the dictionary out of the truck before she tells me to. She makes me spell five pages a day, winter or summer. "I think I'm going to have you do your C's again, Clover. You seem to have had a hard time with them." I believe I had a hard time spelling them because she had a hard time saying them. "If a C you should espy," I chant, "place the E before the I."

I watch Everleen's lips move as she whispers C-A-U-C-A-S-I-A-N. She can't whisper worth a hoot. All I have to do to spell it right is to spell after her. Finally she says, "Kak-kah-sin." "C-A-U-C-A-S-I-A-N," I spell. "My mother is a member of the Caucasian race."

She jumps up to give me a big hug, and knocks over a bushel of peaches. Peaches fly everywhere. There is a peach jigsaw puzzle on the ground. Everleen cuts me a really big piece of pineapple-coconut cake. She dances her way through the spilled peaches. "Washington, D.C., make room for Clover Lee Hill, 'cause here she comes."

To this day, I wonder if that sentence was right. I wish I could ask Gaten. Everleen doesn't know too much about stuff like that.

I open a can of Pepsi. "You'd better eat with your daddy's wife tonight, Clover," Everleen frowns. "I'm sick and tired of all the junk food your uncle piles in at this stand. If you drink another Pepsi you gonna turn into one. It's not good for you. I believe in a balanced nutritious diet."

Aunt Ruby Helen said Everleen didn't know beans about a balanced meal. Not a woman who cooked macaroni and cheese, corn pudding, fried okra, potato salad, turnip greens, candied yams, and fried chicken for an ordinary Sunday dinner.

I know what the real problem is. It's money. Jim Ed will go to a machine and pay sixty cents apiece for Pepsi. Everleen only buys them from the grocery store when they go on sale.

We've been having a lot of customers come to the stand this year. Everleen says they think they might get a glimpse of that beautiful white woman Gaten married. Jim Ed says it's because the peaches are fifty cents cheaper at our stand.

• • •

Before I leave for home Aunt Everleen combs my hair and makes me hide behind some bushes and change into clean clothes. She always keeps me a set of clean stuff, just in case I get dirty.

Everleen starts stacking peck baskets and telling me all the things I should or shouldn't say to Sara Kate. "Now, remember, Clover," she warns, "we never repeat the things we talk about here at the peach shed. This is family talk." Then she turns right around and says, "Now, remember Sara Kate is family, so be nice and tell her her cooking tastes real, real good. You know how white women are. They want you to brag on 'em all the time. To tell them you love 'em. They don't care whether it's the truth or not. So you be nice, baby girl."

Everleen knows good and well I'm not about to tell that woman I love her. I do put some nice peaches in a basket to take her, though.

"Don't you go carrying peaches to her, Clover," Daniel fusses. "Sara Kate don't hit a lick at a black snake all day long. If she wants some peaches she can bring her uppity self up here and get her own peaches. It wouldn't hurt her one bit to help Mama sometimes."

I put the peaches back. I got sense enough to know they are not Daniel's words, they're his mama's. The only thing on his mind and tongue is a dirt bike.

Here of late everybody is getting on my nerves so bad. Clover, do this. Clover, don't do that. Say this to Sara Kate, don't say that. It's no wonder my leg hurts all the time. I guess it knows my heart sure can't hold all the hurt in it. So I guess it's trying to help it out. Everleen says I've lost my hearing, completely lost it.

I might lose what little eyesight I got left in one eye for real, though. I got some peach spray in it this morning. I washed it out right good, but it still kind of burns. The warning below the poison skeleton on the bag said it could cause blindness if it got into the eyes. I would have hurried up and told Gaten if he'd been here. I know if I tell Sara Kate she'll rush me to the doctor to have it checked out. So would Everleen and Jim Ed. I've made up my mind. I'll tell one of them about it after awhile.

Sara Kate must have known we were talking about her. No sooner than I'd put the peaches back, she wheeled up and threw on her brakes. A cloud of dust blew everywhere. Everleen puffed her lips out and pushed them into a wide upsweep over her nostrils. Her mouth looked like a gorilla's mouth.

"Hi, Everleen. Hi, Clover," Sara Kate says.

I say, "Hey."

Everleen pulls her lips down. "Hey, Sara Kate."

A nasty old yellow jacket is sucking away on a piece of

candy I laid down. I know better but I still start to smash him.

"Don't kill that yellow jacket," Aunt Everleen fusses. "You know if you kill one of them their whole family will swarm in and try to sting you to death. We may not be as allergic to them as your uncle Jim Ed, but we sure don't need to invite them just because he's not here."

The truth is I did know if you kill one yellow jacket more will come. But I didn't really know why until I read in the newspaper recently that when you squash a yellow jacket they release some kind of chemical, pheromone or something, that signals a defense alarm that alerts other yellow jackets and they swarm in and sting anyone that's around.

Everleen is some kind of mad. All you have to do to tell when she is mad is look at her mouth. She is right pretty when she's not mad. She pulls a towel off her shoulder and starts dusting off peaches right fast. Sara Kate knows she's brushing her off. She turns to me. "I made your favorite supper, Clover, so don't fill up on peaches again."

Poor Sara Kate. She doesn't know it, but it's Everleen's good cooking I'm always filled up with, not peaches.

Sara Kate is trying to be friendly. "The peaches are so-oo pretty."

"Most of 'em is split wide open. And there's no size to 'em. It's a poor crop," Everleen snaps.

"They are kind of small," Sara Kate agrees. "May I take a few of them?"

"You asking me for peaches? Part of this orchard belonged to Gaten Hill. In case you've forgotten, you did marry him."

Sara Kate turned redder than a Dixie-red peach. You can tell when she's mad, too. I guess everybody's got some kind of way of letting you know they're mad without saying so. She starts toward our pickup truck. "Be sure you're home in time for supper, Clover."

"I'll ride back with you," I say. I need to tell her about my eye. Then without so much as a word, she turns back, grabs a peck basket, and marches toward the orchard. She is walking fast, her head high. She is pounding her feet on the hard baked ground harder than necessary.

Everleen rolls her eyes and grunts, "If that woman don't act like she owns this place, I'm not setting here."

When Sara Kate storms back, she just hops into the truck and speeds away. She forgot all about me. Everleen hugs me. A quick but soft hug. "Miss High-and-mighty wouldn't even let you ride home in your daddy's truck." She draws a deep breath and adds softly, "That is, it was his truck." Her eyes fill with tears.

Jim Ed drives up in his pickup. "Don't block what little air is stirring," Everleen fusses. "Park over yonder. The dust just settled down after your high-and-mighty sister-in-law drove from here like a bat out of hell. And here you come raising up another dust storm."

Everleen is having another one of her fussing spells. But her husband won't fuss back. He's scared she may get one of her bad headaches, or get mad and quit on him.

A funeral procession led by a police car with its flashing light passes along the highway. Jim Ed puts his straw hat over his heart and bows his head. Everleen starts to cry all over again. She crosses herself and mumbles something. She doesn't know why she's doing it. It's something she saw on TV and copied it.

"I can't see why you crying, Mama," says Daniel. "The cars got North Carolina tags and all the people are white, you don't even know them people, Mama."

Everleen is really crying hard. "You don't have to know people to feel sorry for them." In my heart I know she is crying for my daddy, because his brother, Jim Ed, is crying also. I'm going to cry, too.

Sara Kate had the table set real pretty. She put peach leaves around the peaches she picked. It made the peaches look like they were still on the tree.

There was a postcard from my aunt Ruby Helen beside my plate. At the end it read—"P.S. Wish you were here."

If I had gone to live with her, I would have been in Bermuda instead of eating Sara Kate's soupy grits and chicken. I sure hate that I told her I had a taste for some grits.

Sara Kate spooned the watery stuff on my plate, and some chicken swimming in tomatoes and green peppers. I drank my ice tea first. Her eyes were all over my face. Darting like the eyes of a trapped rabbit from my eyes to my mouth. The grits slid through my fork like water soup. If she cooks me grits again I will die, just plain die. "Sara Kate," I blurted out, "you sure can't cook grits." Sara Kate was hurt. I could see the red hurt under her skin. She's got the thinnest skin I've ever seen. Her eyes misted over, but she held the tears back.

I remember all the stuff Everleen said about her. Like white women being so easy to hurt and all. "You have to remember," Everleen had said, "the most of them have been sheltered and petted all their lives. The least little thing just tears them up." I take a bite of the chicken. It's got the strangest taste. But I eat it anyway. "This chicken is some kind of good, Sara Kate," I said.

Sara Kate offers to put more chicken on my plate when I finish. I shake my head, no. "Clover," she says sharply, "you know how your father felt about shaking your head for an answer. Now, would you like more chicken?"

"Uh, uh," I mutter. There was no way I could have gotten a no answer out of my mouth. It was crammed too full of grits and that tomato chicken. That was the first time Sara Kate ever laid something my daddy said on me.

Sara Kate's back had been turned to me when I'd walked into the kitchen. The radio was playing "Song Sung Blue." Her slim body swayed from side to side. A body moving not to music, but to sadness. There is a big difference, you know.

I'd tiptoed up behind her, and shouted, "boo." She jumped like I had scared the living daylights out of her. She wasn't the least bit mad, or scared for that matter. I could see she had been crying. Her green eyes were all puffed up and red. She has started crying an awful lot here of late. Just up and cries for no reason.

5

· · · · · · ·

*T*here is a lot of sadness sewed up in Sara Kate. A sadness I can't figure out. Like it's hidden on some shelf too tall for me to reach. I'm beginning to think it's not because Gaten's gone. It's because she is stuck with me. Now I'm starting to think, maybe I ought to run away. Then maybe she won't be so sad all the time. I can see she's got her own set of sorrow, a set just like mine.

Sometimes I believe she really loved my daddy. It doesn't make me love her more, though. Still, something in me wants to like her—to have her like me, too.

I guess I kind of wish I could play with her like Daniel plays with his mama. He puts his hands over her eyes and in that strange, new, high-pitched voice of his, cranks out, "Guess who?" Everleen will guess and guess till she has to finally give up. Then in that voice that changes every time he opens his mouth, Daniel will say, "It's me, Danny, your son."

If Sara Kate had done some of all the crying she's doing now at Gaten's funeral, she wouldn't have seemed so curious. There wouldn't have been so much talk about how easy she took her husband's death, either. Everleen says white folks don't cry and carry on like we do when somebody dies. They don't love as hard as we do.

We're just different, I guess. Miss Katie's still mourning over Gaten and she's not even kin. After Gaten was killed, she tried to cook but the pans fell to the floor. So she took to her rocking chair. Sometimes I would go and sit on the floor beside her. To tell you the truth, it was about the only place I could find space to sit. Anyway, she made me cry, too. I'm glad she's getting over Gaten.

People in Round Hill don't know it, but Sara Kate didn't really get over Gaten dying as fast as they think she did. Sara Kate was powerfully sad after my daddy died.

After the funeral she lit a candle and sat alone in the dark. I haven't been able to quite figure out why. People I know in Round Hill don't light candles when folks die. I didn't ask Sara Kate about the candle. I didn't even tell Everleen about it, either. I guess, in a strange sort of way, I don't want anybody thinking like, well, that Sara Kate was strange and everything. Maybe in a sly way I was trying to protect Sara Kate even if I can't stand her sometimes. Somehow, I really believe it was because I'm trying to please my dead daddy.

I'll probably find out about this candle business when I'm watching TV. I don't care what people say, you can so learn a lot of stuff from TV.

Daniel said if his grandma had watched enough TV, she would have known that the movie *57 Pick-Up* wasn't about a pickup truck, and would have never gone with him to see it. She liked to have died when they started spitting out all them nasty cuss words. And when the half-naked women started prancing about, she was more ashamed to leave than to stay. So she slid down in her seat, pulled her hat down over closed eyes and prayed and prayed that if the Lord would forgive her that time she'd never set foot in a movie place again.

Sara Kate's got to be bad lonely working in the house all day, all by herself. Sometimes she writes little notes on fancy flowered paper. I never see her mail them. I think she likes the pretty stamp too much to use.

She hurries up and mails the letters to the places that send the pictures of all them little sad-eyed dogs and cats. On the outside of the envelopes they beg, "Will You Please Help Save Them?" I do believe she sends money every time the little pictures come in the mail. It didn't take them people long to find Sara Kate in Round Hill.

Everleen says all white women give money to the animals if they have it to spare. She says it's because they feel so guilty over the way their people treated us. They think by being extra kind to animals, it'll get them into heaven. But Everleen says the Bible says "the animals are born to be destroyed." She thinks the Lord would smile down more on Sara Kate if she took some of that money and helped out the poor children right in Round Hill. Everleen knows her Bible.

I guess if I had extra money I'd feed kids before I'd feed the animals.

Sometimes Sara Kate plays the piano in a room empty now except for one new chair. It's covered in cloth that feels slick. Sara Kate bought it. She calls the cloth chintz. Everything else is pretty much like it was when Grandpa died. He made Gaten promise never to sell the mirrored umbrella and hat stand in the front hall.

I like it when Sara Kate plays. The house seems to come alive. Gaten used to play tapes of the same kind of music. Miss Kenyon used to play classical music also. Maybe that's why Gaten was in love with her too.

That kind of music is great to listen to. But it isn't hitting up on nothing for dance music.

I guess Gaten would have been happy with Sara Kate in this house. I know one thing, if Gaten could see her feeding dogs—much less stray dogs—out of the bowls we eat out of, he would just up and die again.

Sara Kate may think she is so clean, but this letting dogs eat out of dishes will never set with me. Me and Gaten didn't eat after no dogs. I bet if Jim Ed and Everleen knew about all this, they'd never eat a bite in this house.

I don't think Gaten would have liked all those little yellow notes stuck all over the refrigerator, either. Gaten couldn't stand a messed-up place.

I guess in her own way Sara Kate's not all that bad. Everleen even bragged about the way she took care of Aunt Maude. She is my great aunt and is some kind of old.

Well, after she had a stroke, she fell in her kitchen. Trying to stir up her a bite to eat, she said. It was some kind of big bite. Stewed chicken and dumplings, green onion tops and onions smothered in fried fatback drippings, green crowder peas with snaps, cornbread and grated sweet potato pudding. She made the pudding because she wanted to try out a new rum flavor she bought from a Rawleigh Product salesman.

Everleen was going to take her in, but Sara Kate offered, since Everleen was working so hard at the peach shed. That was one time Sara Kate came in real good. I couldn't help out too much with Aunt Maude, because she kept mixing me up. After her stroke her mind was affected. She lost her marbles, that's what happened. She forgot Gaten had been killed. Every day she would say, "Gaten come in yet?"

Or she'd say, "Come on, Clover, let me comb your hair. Go and change them dirty clothes. Put on a dress. I want your daddy to see he's got a little girl when he gets home from school." Then she'd tell about the time when she was teaching school. They made a fire in the big wood heater and a big snake crawled out through the grate.

Sara Kate makes mugs of coffee or tea in the microwave, does needlepoint and listens. She picks up enough of Aunt Maude's slurred speech to laugh. Sometimes when she talks about Gaten as a young boy, Sara Kate cries.

Poor Aunt Maude's mind has got to be torn up pretty bad. She's been eating Sara Kate's turnips and things cooked flat-out in water, without a speck of grease. Once she zipped her lips and wouldn't eat. And don't you know Sara Kate fixed up her plate all pretty, dotted the greens with red Jell-o cubes and Aunt Maude ate it. You got to be in mighty bad shape in the head to eat greens and Jell-o.

In no time Sara Kate had nursed her back to health. She got well enough for her daughter to come and take her to Greensboro to live.

Maybe if Sara Kate could get ahold of poor old drunk Gideon she might cure him up. They didn't do a thing for him down at that first place he went to. He is walking down the hot dusty road now, swaying from side to side. He said he's learned AA's twelve steps. It seems like he's taking twenty-three steps to make his twelve. If he keeps on he'll do a solo two-step dance.

Gideon's thin body looked like the frame of an undressed scarecrow. Leaning into the wind, his body traveled faster than his feet. Even so, that body had started to look like it housed a living creature. Gideon had spent seven days in a detox center. He'd been sober all those days and it showed. He showed off a white button he got at the AA meeting. His wife was so proud of him, she said it even tickled her bones.

I am probably kin to Gideon, but not as close kin as he makes us out to be. Good old Aunt Everleen tries to tie us up to as much kinfolk as she can. She stretches out the family line just like she stretches out sadness. She needs kinfolk to worry about, to be sad over, and make unhappiness so big she can save some over, so it'll be handy in case she needs it.

If she could see Gideon right now, she'd just pinch off a little sadness and moan, "Poor Gideon, bless his heart." Then she'd hurry up and bake him a little tin pie-pan cake. She calls it a sample cake. She never bakes a cake unless she makes a couple of samples first. She has to try out one, just in case the cake needs something. I've never seen her add anything to the cake batter. I think she just can't wait until the real cake is done. I love her sample cakes.

For a little while Gideon was sober. But then, that was

yesterday. Today he is waving a notice from Duke Power Company. They are going to shut off his lights. Today Gideon is as drunk as a blind cooter.

Sara Kate's bedroom door is closed. It's the room she and my daddy would have slept in. I stand outside for a few minutes trying to think up a way to tell her about getting poison in my eye. I clean forgot to tell her at suppertime. I'm only planning to tell her now because, now that I think about it, it's my good eye that got the poison in it.

I doubt if Sara Kate knows I don't see all that good out of one of my eyes as it is. That is, when I don't wear my eyeglasses. I hardly ever wear them. My glasses are hidden in Gaten's bottom desk drawer. I never could stand to wear the things. Like I told Gaten, "One eye will see enough of everything I need to see."

I cannot believe Gaten would have told Sara Kate about my eye. I imagine, like me, he would have thought it was something she didn't necessarily need to know.

When I finally knock on Sara Kate's door, there is no answer. I guess I did knock kind of soft. But I don't go around knocking on people's doors that much.

Gaten closed his bedroom door if he was getting dressed or something. I'm almost sure he didn't close it when he was ready to go to sleep. I kind of think he left it open so he could hear me if I was having a bad dream or something. He also had to know that ever since Grandpa died, I've been a little scared at night.

I knock again and again. In my heart I know I am knocking too softly and I know why. I really don't want her to hear me. As sure as shooting, if I tell her about my eye, she'll rush me off to the hospital. Besides, my eye had stopped burning anyway. Even so, I still splashed cold water into it until I couldn't stand it anymore.

The first thing Everleen wants to know the next day is how Sara Kate's dinner turned out. I say it was awful, that the grits were plain nasty. "That's not nice to say, Clover," she fussed. I can tell she's glad I didn't say it was all that good. I can tell you, she wants to be tops in the cooking department.

"You and Daniel, get outta the sun before you have a heat stroke, Clover," she warned us. "Anytime you have them old cicadas singing so strong this early in the day, you know it's gonna be a scorcher. They said on the evening news last night this is the hottest, driest summer we ever had in South Carolina . . .

"You know it's got to be bad here, when we make the big-time news . . . thank the Lord all them Northerners are trucking down hay, 'cause if it gets any worse . . ."

I move into the shade. Daniel and his daddy go to buy fuel oil. They're tired of listening to Everleen.

I think about Sara Kate. All alone in our quiet house. Thinking her quiet thoughts, writing quiet words. Daniel wants me to sneak out some of that writing. He thinks it might be stuff about us.

Once or twice I started into Sara Kate's room to slip the papers she'd written out. Each time something inside me stopped me. Maybe it was the hand of an angel. My grandpa used to pray for the angels to watch over me. I believe in angels.

I've known for a long time to never, ever mess with Sara Kate's drawings. Once I picked up some of the pretty little sketches on drawing paper, and forgot and left them out on the back door steps.

We looked everywhere for the sketches. We even took everything out of her big zippered artist portfolio. It's more like a briefcase for a giant. I just had a notion the sketches may have been there, but we never did find them. The white Federal Express truck came and left without them.

Well, Sara Kate was really, really angry with me that time. And she didn't mind letting me know it, either. "Clover," she fussed, "those sketches were to be sent to a company who wants me to design a line of fancy wrapping paper. I spoke with a man from the company and promised him he'd have the sketches tomorrow. There is good money in that, Clover, and right now we can use it."

Her mad spell didn't last too long. But, oh boy, let me

tell you something, when a white woman gets mad, she gets mad.

Sara Kate finally smiled and sucked in her breath when I said, "Well, Sara Kate, maybe the next day won't be too late. If you had all them pretty flowers and things in your head in the first place you ought to be able to find them again. At least we can find your head. It's not lost, that's for sure."

I still can't see how Sara Kate can stand so much sitting down all the time. If she isn't drawing or painting, she's writing. No wonder her hips are so flat.

Anyway, I've left the papers alone for good. If Sara Kate is writing something bad about us, I don't want to find out.

A little girl about my age is screaming at her mama to hurry up and buy the peaches so they can go to McDonalds. She has blue, blue eyes and hair I guess they call blonde. It sure looks white to me, though.

"Please wait, darling," says her mama sweetly, "we'll go as soon as I buy the peaches."

"I don't like peaches," the little girl screams. "I hate peaches."

I put a peck of peaches on the back seat of their car, one of them new Toyota jobs. The white-haired girl sticks her tongue out at me. I stick mine out right back at her. She makes a face as they drive away. All I can say is, if she does that to me at school, she'll get her lights punched out. She'll probably go to one of those private church schools they started setting up when the public schools started getting so many black principals.

Gideon's sister and her husband thought after they got high-paying jobs at Duke Power Company they would send their kids to one of those schools. But Everleen said the good old Baptists had no room for good old black Baptists. And to this day, there is not a single black there.

About a half a mile up the road, the signal light on an old Buick blinks for a left turn. A line of cars and eighteen-wheeled trucks brake and screech behind the Buick, slowly snaking its way to the turnoff.

"Lord, Lord," Everleen groans, "Mary Martha is gonna get herself run clean over, crawling along that busy highway. A cooter could travel faster than that."

Mary Martha has to put both feet on the ground and hold onto the door frame in order to pull her fat body out of the car. She has the body of a woman, but her face is a girl's face.

"I don't know why I'm buying peaches," she complained. "I'm so tired of working in these poor white folks' kitchens, I ain't got the strength to make a pie."

"Huh," Everleen grunts, "you and Miss Katie's the only ones still doing it that I know of."

"I know, I know. But, Everleen, what else can I do? I'm too worn out to go into one of the mills to work. James Roy's got a right good job, but we got not one, but four chaps to get ready for school. To tell you the truth, I need another little job."

Everleen tilts her head upwards and laughs about something that's making her tickled before she says it. She's really pretty when she laughs. She wears her long black hair pulled back off her dark-skinned face, and has the prettiest eyes you ever saw. "The blacker the berry, the sweeter the juice," she says about her dark skin color.

Everleen is still laughing. "I hear tell Miss Sara Kate Hill is looking for somebody to clean her house. Like she's some kind of rich white woman."

Mary Martha shakes her head. "Girl, I may be hard up, but I'd eat water and bread before I set foot in that woman's house to clean. To this day I ain't got over Gaten marrying her instead of Miss Kenyon. Seems like every time one of our fine girls have the chance for a good catch, some cracker comes along and messes it up. I'll bet the new white principal who took Gaten's place won't marry one of our black teachers."

"He won't marry a white one, either," Everleen says. They both laugh.

They wave at a passing car and moan, "Oh Lordy, Lord." It's Rooster Jones, breezing by in his brand new Pontiac.

"I'm surprised he even waved with his fine self," Mary Martha says. "Talk in town is, he's started taking up with them trashy white gals with their long dirty hair, thin lips, and slim hips. They hang around the mill every night. He'll lose the shirt off his back now."

"Girl, you are telling the Lord's truth," says Everleen, shaking her head. "If our menfolk make a plug nickel, they get the hots for them. And Lordy me, if they can shoot a basketball, those girls trail behind them like a hound dog running a coon. And when they catch them, they cling to them tighter than a green cocklebur."

"Either that, or they wise up, get their teeth fixed, and get all gussied up, then marry some old man of their own race, in his eighties with more money than they can spend. They can then live so grand, they can make their born rich sisters look pitiful, pitiful."

Everleen may be kind to Sara Kate's face, but she sure can't stand her behind her back.

They start talking about my daddy again. They must have forgotten that I was sitting right there all the time. They can't know how much it hurts me to have them talk like that about my own daddy. I thought that all the talk about Sara Kate and Gaten would all be over by now. Before Gaten died, I had to listen to all the talk he and his brother did.

People in Round Hill may not know it, but my daddy

didn't just up and marry the woman with no thought. It wasn't even an easy thing for him to do. It gnawed at his gut. And my actions sure didn't help, either. I would be so different now if I had the chance. It's too late now. My daddy is dead.

I happen to know my daddy thought long and hard before he married Sara Kate. Maybe if all these women knew what the man went through, they would stop talking so bad about him.

I am only ten years old, but certainly old enough to know that my daddy had to make a choice. There is nothing else you can do, when you have people pulling at you from every side. One thing is for sure, you can't go with everybody at the same time. So Gaten had to make a choice.

I still think of the day he brought his lady to meet me. Gaten was nervous. More so than I had ever seen him. I may not know a lot of things, but I do know a lot about my daddy's ways.

The eyes of the woman by his side clocked his every move. She was waiting for him to tell me something. Gaten tried to, but he seemed as if he could not speak. His tongue seemed to press against his teeth. He stood mute before us. I suppose he wasn't prepared for the way I treated his lady. I could tell, he really wanted me to take to her. He should have known you just can't cram that kind of thing inside a person's head and mind and make them like someone no matter what.

I cannot understand why Gaten always seemed to think I needed extra help in being raised, anyway. All my life, as far back as I can remember, I've just had one person at a time. First it was my grandpa before he died. And then I had Gaten.

When I was little I was alone with my grandpa most of the time. My uncle and aunt were in and out of the house every single day, but they didn't live with us. My daddy came home almost every weekend.

After I started going to school my daddy wanted to take me away to live with him. He was teaching school somewhere around Charleston, South Carolina. He claimed Grandpa had been too easy with me. Allowed me to pick up wrong habits. Gaten hated for me to spit and use coarse words.

Grandpa didn't teach me that kind of stuff. I learned it from my cousin Daniel. The one thing Gaten didn't really like was, I missed a lot of days at school. It was true that Grandpa did not make me go to school all that much. He said it didn't matter if I missed a few days here and there. I had the rest of my life to go to school.

To this day I believe it was my aunt Everleen who put it into Gaten's head to come and take me way down there to live with him.

I started crying when Gaten called to say he was coming for me. School or no school, I couldn't see how my daddy could begin to think of splitting up me and my grandpa. I couldn't have gone and lived away from Aunt Everleen, anyway. Who in the world would have fixed my hair? I've always been tender-headed. I've never liked people fooling with my hair.

I kind of believe my grandpa was crying also. He sucked-up real hard through his nose and wiped it with the back of his hand. I can never tell by his eyes if he is crying. He is getting kind of old and his eyes look watery all the time, anyway.

At first, Grandpa had said to my daddy, "But son, she's all I got. I just don't think I am prepared to lose her right now." In the end, though, all he said was, "I will have my baby girl ready and waiting when you come for her."

Breakfast was on the table when my daddy walked into the house. We had grits, ham and eggs, and red-eye gravy. Grandpa had spread butter and Aunt Everleen's homemade blackberry jelly on hot biscuits as soon as he took them out of the oven.

All the time we were eating breakfast, I didn't raise my head to look at my daddy. Every now and then, I did cut my eyes up to glance at him. Each time he was looking dead at me. My aunt had really fixed me up. My hair was pulled into a pony tail with a big purple bow. It matched my new purple flowered dress, with puffed sleeves and a little white pique bib in front.

I dug little ditches in my plate of hot grits and watched yellow melted butter run through like little streams of water.

When Grandpa passed my daddy the hot biscuits for the umpteenth time, he tipped the Ball mason jar with the wildflowers I'd picked, and water spilled all over the red-checkered tablecloth.

Grandpa blotted up the water with a dish towel. "You might know Clover picked these weeds, I mean flowers. The child is a spitting image of her departed mama. Even when there was snow on the ground, her mama found red berries or something to pick and put on this table. This house hasn't been the same without her."

He could never stand to talk very much about my mama. He said he loved her like she was his own daughter. I guess he now felt he was about to lose me, too. He was sad and started to cry. Real tears streamed down into the lines and wrinkles of his brown leathery face.

I sure never remembered seeing all those wrinkles in his face before. My daddy said, "Old age made them." I guess day by day old age was using its hand to carefully draw them on. "Oh Lord, oh Lord," he cried out, "help me, because I am weak. Send me your mercy to lean on."

Like lickety-split, I was by my grandpa's side. I put

my arms around his neck. "Don't worry, Grandpa," I said. "You will always have me to lean on, for as long as I live."

I hadn't said more than two words to my daddy up to then. But now I was ready to lay some kind of fussing on him. "I'm mad now," I fussed. "Really mad. You know for yourself that poor old Grandpa can't bit more take care of himself than a newborn baby. You ought to be ashamed of yourself, Gaten, to even think of taking the only help he's got in this world away." I just had to call my daddy Gaten, because for some reason the word daddy would not come out of my mouth.

I didn't know what my daddy was thinking. All I did know was, he looked at my grandpa—his own daddy—and he had to see what I saw. An old, feeble man. His eyes were even old. There was hardly any color left in them. It's strange that I'd never paid any attention to his teeth before. They looked as though they had been sawed off. Years and years of chewing had sawed them down, the same way old age had brought his voice down. A voice not half as strong as it used to be.

My daddy must have seen what I saw, because tears welled up in his eyes. Without a word, he walked into the hall, picked up my two packed suitcases, and the burlap sack that Grandpa packed for me. Only the Lord in the heavens knows what was in that sack. Anyhow, they stood waiting and ready near the front door. My daddy carried them back upstairs.

A year later, my daddy was home for good. A principal's job at the Round Hill Elementary School opened up, and my daddy got the job. The only problem for me was, it was my school. I guess that's what turned me around for good from calling my father "Daddy." I sure didn't feel right calling him Mr. Hill. So I called him Gaten. Besides, that's what everybody else in our family called him.

Things sure can happen fast in a person's life. Grandpa was dead and buried. And there was Gaten, all hurt and sad on account of a complete stranger, a woman named Sara Kate.

Uncle Jim Ed and Gaten were sitting on the front porch, talking about all they ever seem to talk about, the peach crop.

"Speak of the devil . . ." Jim Ed laughs when Chase Porter drives up. They all laugh.

"We were just talking about you, Chase, and wondering if you might have a spare spray machine belt. I had to stop short rounding a curve at full speed when I was spraying and the belt snapped." Gaten looked at his brother. "Jim Ed had left our fuel can right in the middle of a row."

Chase grinned. "I wouldn't have wanted to hear about what you said. I do have an extra belt, and come to think of it, I'm sending someone to Spartanburg tomorrow to get some parts. You can send for whatever you need if you want to."

"Well, that was perfect timing," Gaten said when Chase left.

"Speaking of timing," Uncle Jim Ed said, "I have asked you three times if we are going to spray peaches in the morning. I have yet to get a straight answer from you."

"Yep, we've got to spray all right," Gaten agreed. "I'll fix up the spray machine with water, and have it ready."

Uncle Jim Ed got up to leave. "I'll take care of the spray machine, big boy. It seems like you've got a lot on your mind today."

Gaten looked at the house. "The old home place is beginning to run down, Jim Ed. Needs painting. It's turning gray. Even the flowers seem to be struggling to hold onto the little life left in them."

Jim Ed laughed. "At least it's only the trimming that needs to be done. The old brick still looks pretty good. Remember the imitation brick siding that used to be on it? I was so glad when Papa agreed to take it off and put up real bricks." He glanced at the flowers. "You would be struggling to hold onto life, too, if you were as old as some of these flowers. Mama said she set out those crape myrtle and rose bushes right after she was married. I guess the hollyhocks and verbenas have kept reseeding over the years.

hought to myself. Jim Ed better back off. He
en some kind of mad. If he keeps on, Gaten
ow his stack. I also think, perhaps the reason
or me to get over stuff is because people keep
hat I can't, or am not, getting over it.

id not back off. "Nowadays, women like her are
set their hooks to catch any black guy that's
tle something. Especially now that so many are
make their way up in the world. As far as they
rned, all they ever need to see is the dollar sign.
aying that you have anything, but there is no deny-
you have always been an achiever. A 'first.' The
st winner ever, of a statewide oratorical contest. Also
st' black to win that honor. The 'first' black princi-
a Round Hill school. I have yet to learn if 'what-you-
call-her' even has a job."

aten is still as mad as a striking rattlesnake. He has
ys known how to keep it in. I am not quite sure how he
it. It might be in the way he keeps his voice down.

He eyes his brother. "Sara Kate Colson is a college grad-
te. Yes, she does work. She is a textile designer."

I can see Jim Ed sure didn't know what kind of work
hat was. I didn't, either, and Gaten sure was not about to
ell us. I'm not sure, but I think Jim Ed was not too pleased
to hear that, on account of his wife Everleen not having too
much schooling.

You and Miss Katie are the only ones who have them." His
face showed a trace of remembered sadness. He walked to
a small bush. His hand gently touched the leaves. That
same bush would later bloom forth with soft pink blossoms, clustered into little balls of petals that scatter and
fall like silent snowflakes.

He looked at Gaten. "We sure well remember who set
this one out." Gaten looked at me. My mother set the bush
out, just before she died. She had planted lots of things,
but it was the only one that lived. She called it a marble
bush.

Jim Ed made a play in the hopscotch game I'd drawn in
a sandy spot at the edge of our yard. "TV hasn't changed
the playing pattern of our little Clover too much," he said.
"She still plays some of the same things we did when we
were growing up." He shook his head sadly. "I can't pry
that kid of mine away from the tube."

Gaten smiled. "Clover may be a child of the eighties,
but the same person of the twenties that raised us, raised
her also."

"I've got to get a move on," Jim Ed said, stopping to take
one last look at the old brick house with shutters and dormer windows. "The house is still in great shape. I only
wish mine was half as fine." He frowned and looked directly
at Gaten. "I know it's something else that's really bothering
you, younger brother. I can tell, you are hurting, man."

When Jim Ed called Gaten "younger brother," Gaten knew he meant for him to listen because he was older. They said as soon as Gaten could talk, he told everyone not to call him baby brother.

It didn't seem to bother Gaten one bit that I was listening to every word. He must have wanted me to hear.

"I've never been able to handle hurt, Jim Ed. Especially when it involves people I love so much," he said.

I climbed out on a limb on our old chinaberry tree. "Look, Jim Ed," I laughed, swinging from my legs, "no hands, no hands."

"Get down out of that tree this minute, Clover," Gaten ordered. There was a sharpness in his voice that even shocked Jim Ed.

"Let her play," he said, "she is still only a little girl."

"That's exactly the point," Gaten snapped. "It's high time she started acting like she is a little girl. Clover has gotten out of hand here of late. I am not proud of the kind of person she is becoming."

Jim Ed studied my daddy for a long time. "It's that woman, all right," he finally said. "She has changed everything about you. You have changed the way you feel about your very own child. Up until you met her, Clover could do no wrong in your eyes. If you are not careful, that woman will wind up destroying you." My uncle was stepping on his brother's toes all right. Gaten's face showed it.

88

"I don't care, ⋯
not. To tell you t⋯
at me and stopped ⋯
to curse as good as ⋯
my presence, and he⋯
doing it.

"I am just going to ⋯
went on. "That woman ⋯
What you don't know is⋯
women don't part easily w⋯
happen to be a pretty good ⋯
odds, that woman wants you.⋯

Through closed jaws, Gaten⋯
jaws are working like a chainsa⋯
wood. "Do you care to tell me how⋯
so experienced in this kind of situa⋯
gone through a similar thing before⋯
and cruel. He did not try to hide it, ⋯

"You don't have to cut me up," Ji⋯
"If you want to get tied up with someon⋯
it's your business. All I can say is, it ⋯
load to dump on our little Clover. She h⋯
sadness in her short lifetime. Now that ⋯
just barely, getting over her grandfather's d⋯
does not need some stranger in her life to ⋯
used to."

"Whew," I t⋯
is making Ga⋯
is going to bl⋯
it's so hard f⋯
telling me t⋯

Jim Ed d⋯
starting to ⋯
worth a li⋯
starting t⋯
are conce⋯
I'm not s⋯
ing tha⋯
younge⋯
the 'fi⋯
pal at ⋯
may-⋯
G⋯
alwa⋯
doe⋯

ua⋯

t⋯
t⋯

89

When Jim Ed called Gaten "younger brother," Gaten knew he meant for him to listen because he was older. They said as soon as Gaten could talk, he told everyone not to call him baby brother.

It didn't seem to bother Gaten one bit that I was listening to every word. He must have wanted me to hear.

"I've never been able to handle hurt, Jim Ed. Especially when it involves people I love so much," he said.

I climbed out on a limb on our old chinaberry tree. "Look, Jim Ed," I laughed, swinging from my legs, "no hands, no hands."

"Get down out of that tree this minute, Clover," Gaten ordered. There was a sharpness in his voice that even shocked Jim Ed.

"Let her play," he said, "she is still only a little girl."

"That's exactly the point," Gaten snapped. "It's high time she started acting like she is a little girl. Clover has gotten out of hand here of late. I am not proud of the kind of person she is becoming."

Jim Ed studied my daddy for a long time. "It's that woman, all right," he finally said. "She has changed everything about you. You have changed the way you feel about your very own child. Up until you met her, Clover could do no wrong in your eyes. If you are not careful, that woman will wind up destroying you." My uncle was stepping on his brother's toes all right. Gaten's face showed it.

You and Miss Katie are the only ones who have them." His face showed a trace of remembered sadness. He walked to a small bush. His hand gently touched the leaves. That same bush would later bloom forth with soft pink blossoms, clustered into little balls of petals that scatter and fall like silent snowflakes.

He looked at Gaten. "We sure well remember who set this one out." Gaten looked at me. My mother set the bush out, just before she died. She had planted lots of things, but it was the only one that lived. She called it a marble bush.

Jim Ed made a play in the hopscotch game I'd drawn in a sandy spot at the edge of our yard. "TV hasn't changed the playing pattern of our little Clover too much," he said. "She still plays some of the same things we did when we were growing up." He shook his head sadly. "I can't pry that kid of mine away from the tube."

Gaten smiled. "Clover may be a child of the eighties, but the same person of the twenties that raised us, raised her also."

"I've got to get a move on," Jim Ed said, stopping to take one last look at the old brick house with shutters and dormer windows. "The house is still in great shape. I only wish mine was half as fine." He frowned and looked directly at Gaten. "I know it's something else that's really bothering you, younger brother. I can tell, you are hurting, man."

"I don't care, younger brother, if it makes you mad or not. To tell you the truth, I don't give a . . ." he glanced at me and stopped short. He and Gaten both know how to curse as good as a drunk sailor. Gaten doesn't curse in my presence, and he sure won't stand for someone else doing it.

"I am just going to come out with it, Gaten," Jim Ed went on. "That woman is about to drive you storm crazy. What you don't know is, unlike our womenfolk, those women don't part easily with something they want. You happen to be a pretty good catch. And, in spite of all the odds, that woman wants you."

Through closed jaws, Gaten is gritting his teeth. His jaws are working like a chainsaw cutting through maple wood. "Do you care to tell me how you happened to become so experienced in this kind of situation, Jim Ed? Have you gone through a similar thing before?" His voice was hard and cruel. He did not try to hide it, either.

"You don't have to cut me up," Jim Ed said quietly. "If you want to get tied up with someone like that woman, it's your business. All I can say is, it's a heavy, heavy load to dump on our little Clover. She has had so much sadness in her short lifetime. Now that she is barely, just barely, getting over her grandfather's death, she sure does not need some stranger in her life to have to get used to."

"Whew," I thought to myself. Jim Ed better back off. He is making Gaten some kind of mad. If he keeps on, Gaten is going to blow his stack. I also think, perhaps the reason it's so hard for me to get over stuff is because people keep telling me that I can't, or am not, getting over it.

Jim Ed did not back off. "Nowadays, women like her are starting to set their hooks to catch any black guy that's worth a little something. Especially now that so many are starting to make their way up in the world. As far as they are concerned, all they ever need to see is the dollar sign. I'm not saying that you have anything, but there is no denying that you have always been an achiever. A 'first.' The youngest winner ever, of a statewide oratorical contest. Also the 'first' black to win that honor. The 'first' black principal at a Round Hill school. I have yet to learn if 'what-you-may-call-her' even has a job."

Gaten is still as mad as a striking rattlesnake. He has always known how to keep it in. I am not quite sure how he does it. It might be in the way he keeps his voice down.

He eyes his brother. "Sara Kate Colson is a college graduate. Yes, she does work. She is a textile designer."

I can see Jim Ed sure didn't know what kind of work that was. I didn't, either, and Gaten sure was not about to tell us. I'm not sure, but I think Jim Ed was not too pleased to hear that, on account of his wife Everleen not having too much schooling.

Contents

Freedom and the Court

CIVIL RIGHTS AND LIBERTIES IN THE UNITED STATES

chapter *I* Introduction

Although, as David Fellman points out, the American people, both in political theory and in public law, have been committed for more than two hundred years to the "primacy of civil liberties in the constellation of human interests,"[1] these civil liberties do not exist in a vacuum or even in anarchy but in a state of society. It is inevitable that the individual's civil rights and those of the community of which he is a part come into conflict and need adjudication.[2]

It is easy to state the need for a line between individual rights and the rights of the community, but how, where, and when it is to be drawn are questions that will never be resolved to the satisfaction of the entire community. In John Stuart Mill's perceptive words in his *On Liberty and the Subjection of Women:* "But though the proposition is not likely to be contested in general terms, the practical question, where to place the limits—how to make the fitting adjustment between individual independence and social control—is a subject on which nearly everything remains to be done."[3] Liberty and order are difficult to reconcile, particularly in a democratic society such as ours. We must have *both,* but a happy balance is not easy to maintain. As a constitutional democracy, based upon a government of limited powers under a written constitution, and a majoritarianism duly checked by carefully guarded minority rights, we must be generous to the dissenter. Again citing Mill, "all mankind has no right to silence one dissenter . . . [for] all silencing of discussion is an assumption of infallibility." Even near-unanimity under our system does not give society the right

---

[1] *The Limits of Freedom* (Brunswick, N.J.: Rutgers University Press, 1959), from the Foreword (unpaginated).

[2] Although some would object, the terms "rights" and "liberties" are used interchangeably in this book. They are to be distinguished from all the other rights and freedoms individuals may enjoy under law because they are especially protected, in one manner or another, against violations *by governments.* (In Canada, the term "civil *rights*" refers exclusively to *private* law—the legal relationship between person and person in private life.) See J. A. Corry and Henry J. Abraham, *Elements of Democratic Government,* 4th ed. (New York: Oxford University Press, 1964), pp. 234–39.

[3] (New York: Holt, 1898), p. 16.

3

to deprive the individual of his constitutional rights. As Judge Jerome Frank observed, "The test of the moral quality of a civilization is its treatment of the weak and powerless."[4] "The worst citizen no less than the best," once wrote Mr. Justice Hugo L. Black, dissenting from a Supreme Court reversal of some trespassing convictions, "is entitled to equal protection of the laws of his state and of his nation"[5]—and the citizen of whom he spoke was a defiant racist. Who or what he was is irrelevant, of course; indeed, in Mr. Justice Frankfurter's often-quoted words: "It is a fair summary of history to say that safeguards of liberty have been forged in controversies involving not very nice people."[6] The basic issue was memorably phrased by Mr. Justice Robert H. Jackson in the *West Virginia Flag Salute* case,[7] in which the Supreme Court struck down, as violating the freedom of religion guarantees of the First and Fourteenth Amendments, a compulsory flag salute resolution adopted by the West Virginia State Board of Education. As Justice Jackson put it, those "who begin coercive elimination of dissent soon find themselves exterminating dissenters. Compulsory unification of opinion achieves only the unanimity of the graveyard." He elaborated in characteristically beautiful prose:

> If there is any fixed star in our constitutional constellation, it is that no official, high or petty, can prescribe what shall be orthodox in politics, nationalism, religion, or other matters of opinion or force citizens to confess by word or act their faith therein. . . . The very purpose of a Bill of Rights was to withdraw certain subjects from the vicissitudes of political controversy, to place them beyond the reach of majorities and officials and to establish them as legal principles to be applied by the courts. One's right to life, liberty, and property, to free speech, a free press, freedom of worship and assembly, and other fundamental rights may not be submitted to vote; *they depend on the outcome of no elections.*[8]

While these words raise as many questions as they state valid principles, they nevertheless point out the irreducible basis for our thinking about civil rights and liberties.

ROLE OF THE JUDICIARY

The framers of our Constitution chose a limited majority rule, but majority rule nonetheless; while tyranny by the majority is barred, so also is tyranny by a minority. And the law must be obeyed—until such time as it is validly altered by legislative, judicial, or executive action or by constitu-

4 *United States v. Murphy,* 222 F. 2d 698 (1955), at 706.
5 *Bell v. Maryland,* 378 U.S. 226 (1964), at 328.
6 *United States v. Rabinowitz,* 339 U.S. 56 (1950), at 69.
7 *West Virginia State Board of Education v. Barnette,* 319 U.S. 624 (1943).
8 *Ibid.,* at 638, 642. (Italics supplied.)

tional amendment. Notwithstanding the numerous philosophical arguments to the contrary, disobedience of the law is barred, no matter which valid governmental agency has pronounced it or what small margin has enacted it. *It must be barred.* Liberty is achieved only by a rule of law—which is as the cement of society. Government cannot long endure when any group or class of persons—no matter how just the cause may be or how necessary remedial action may seem to be—is permitted to decide which law it shall obey and which it shall flout. "Dissent and dissenters have no monopoly on freedom. They must tolerate opposition. They must accept dissent from their dissent," Mr. Justice Abe Fortas observed well.[9] Civil disobedience has often been invoked and will indubitably continue to be invoked—but those who invoke it must be willing to face the consequences. Moreover, in Professor J. A. Corry's words, civil disobedience must be *civil* not uncivil disobedience, with the basic aim persuasion, not violence.[10] No one knew this and practiced it with more conviction than the assassinated Dr. Martin Luther King, who once noted tellingly: "I believe in the beauty and majesty of the law so much that when I think a law is wrong, I am willing to go to jail and stay there."[11] And so he did, on numerous occasions.

Under our system of government some agency of course must serve as the arbiter of what is and what is not legal or constitutional. The Founding Fathers did recognize and call for the creation of an arbiter, not only between the states and the national government but also between any level of government and the individual. There was no unanimity on who might arbitrate; and the records of the debates in the Constitutional Convention now available to us demonstrate that nearly every segment of the incipient government framework received at least some consideration for the role of arbiter: the states themselves, Congress, the executive, the judiciary, and several combinations of these. But it was fairly clear that the role would fall to the judiciary and that it should include the power of *judicial review,* which authorizes the Supreme Court to hold unconstitutional, and hence unenforceable, any law, any official action based upon a law, and any other action by a public official that it deems—upon careful reflection and in line with the taught tradition of the law and judicial restraint—to be in conflict with the Constitution.[12]

Scholars continue to argue the authenticity of the power of judicial re-

[9] The phrase also appears in his definitive book on the subject, *Concerning Dissent and Civil Disobedience* (New York: New American Library, 1968), p. 126. (Fortas resigned from the U.S. Supreme Court in mid-1969.)

[10] See his 1971 CBC Massey Lectures, *The Power of the Law* (Toronto: CBC Learning Systems, 1971), p. 41. The July 1977 looting during New York City's "blackout" is an obvious example of such a totally "uncivil" response.

[11] As quoted in *The New York Times,* October 16, 1966, p. 8e.

[12] See my *The Judicial Process: An Introductory Analysis of the Courts of the United States, England, and France,* 4th ed. (New York: Oxford University Press, 1980), Ch. 7.

view. That so many doubts and challenges are raised is due preeminently to the failure of the American Founding Fathers to spell it out in the Constitution *in so many words.* Yet the records of the Philadelphia Constitutional Convention of 1787 indicate that the idea or principle of judicial review was a matter of distinct concern to the framers who, after all, had little use for unrestrained popular majoritarian government; that judicial review was indeed *known* to the colonists because the British Privy Council had established it over acts passed by colonial legislatures; that at least eight[13] of the ratifying state conventions had expressly discussed *and* accepted the judicial power to pronounce legislative acts void; and that prior to 1789 some eight instances of *state* court judicial review against state legislatures had taken place. The language of both Article Three and the famed "supremacy clause" of Article Six clearly imply the necessary but controversial weapon. Research by constitutional historians such as Charles A. Beard, Edward S. Corwin, and Alpheus T. Mason indicates that between 25 and 32 of the 40 delegates at Philadelphia generally favored the adoption of judicial review.[14] And although it remained for Mr. Chief Justice John Marshall to spell it out in 1803 in *Marbury v. Madison,*[15] the issue has been decisively settled by history—the debate over the legitimacy of judicial review is now an academic exercise.

Since the enactment of the "Judges' bill" in 1925, the Supreme Court has been complete master of its docket. The bill gave to the Court absolute discretionary power to choose those cases it would hear on a writ of *certiorari,* a discretionary writ granted only if four justices agree to do so. In theory, certain classes of cases do reach the Court as a matter of "right," i.e., those that come to it on writs of *appeal;* but even here review is not automatic since the tribunal itself must decide whether the question presented is of a *"substantial* federal nature." Its original jurisdiction docket is so small as to be dismissed for the purposes of this discussion.[16]

Since 1937 the overwhelming majority of judicial vetoes imposed upon the several states and almost *all* of those against the national government have been invoked because they infringed personal liberties, other than those of "property," safeguarded under the Constitution. This preoccupation with the "basic human freedoms"[17] is amply illustrated by the statistics

---

[13] Virginia, Rhode Island, New York, Connecticut, Massachusetts, New Jersey, North Carolina, and South Carolina.

[14] See particularly Beard's "The Supreme Court—Usurper or Grantee?," 27 *Political Science Quarterly* 1 (1912).

[15] 1 Cranch 137.

[16] See Abraham, *op. cit.,* Ch. 5, pp. 180–99, on matters of jurisdiction.

[17] See Chapter II, *infra.* As seen in these pages, they comprise the five enumerated by the First Amendment; the guarantees of procedural due process in the pursuit of criminal justice; and racial, political, ethnic, and sexual equality. (They are also known as the "cultural freedoms.") And the trend of public attitudes in the latter 1960s and evolving 1970s seemed to give fresh emphasis to the concept of privacy,

of the docket of the Supreme Court and the application of its power of judicial review.[18] More than half of all cases decided by the Court now fall into this category of "basic human freedoms." Whereas in the 1935–36 term only two of 160 written opinions had done so, in the 1979–80 term the ratio had increased to 80 out of 149.[19] A glance at the historical development of this majoritarian philosophy should help us to focus our study.

---

personified by such Supreme Court decisions as those dealing with birth control and abortions. (See especially *Griswold v. Connecticut,* 381 U.S. 479 [1965], *Roe v. Wade,* 410 U.S. 113 and *Doe v. Bolton,* 410 U.S. 179, both 1973, respectively, and their progeny.)

[18] In 1976 a total of 5,320 civil rights suits were brought in *federal* courts against *employers* alone—a 1,500 per cent increase from 1970! "I am old enough to know," commented the then 75-year old United States District Court Judge Oren R. Lewis in the fall of 1977 during a discrimination case in his Alexandria, Va., courtroom. "When I first came on the bench [in 1960] I never had a discrimination case. Now that is almost all you have." (*The Washington Post,* November 15, 1977, p. A-1.)

Another indicator: Between its enactment in 1871 and 1920, only 21 cases were brought under the former year's Civil Rights Act that authorizes suits against "every person" who "under color of law" violates the civil rights of another. In 1976 a total of 17,543 such suits were filed—a figure that has continued to increase steadily! (See A. E. Dick Howard, "I'll See You in Court: The States and the Supreme Court." Monograph, published by the National Governors' Association Center for Policy Research, Washington, D.C., 1980.)

[19] Some additional representative statistics: 1965 (39 of 120); 1966 (55 of 132); 1967 (77 of 156); 1968 (70 of 116); 1969 (51 of 105); 1970 (77 of 141); 1971 (82 of 132); 1972 (86 of 164); 1973 (85 of 156); 1974 (63 of 137); 1975 (76 of 144); 1976 (87 of 160); 1977 (84 of 142); 1978 (88 of 138); 1980–81 (71 of 123).

chapter *II* The *"Double Standard"*

The Evolution of the Double Standard

The earliest lines, drawn by the Marshall Court (1801–35), defined and strengthened the young nation, guarding the federal government against the state governments, and furthering its growth and ability to function. They were also drawn to protect the property interests of individuals. From 1836–64 Mr. Chief Justice Roger B. Taney's Court sought in a variety of ways to redress the balance in part, as it saw it, in favor of the states, while continuing to defend the ownership of land and slaves. The disastrous *Dred Scott*[1] decision bears lasting witness to that posture. The decisions of the next two rather undistinguished eras of Chief Justices Salmon P. Chase (1864–74) and Morrison R. Waite (1874–88) were predominantly concerned with confirming state authority over individuals and federal authority over interstate commerce. In general they heralded the broadly proprietarian notions of the next five decades under Chief Justices Melvin W. Fuller (1888–1910), Edward D. White (1910–21), and William Howard Taft (1921–30). The chief concern of this long era was to guard the sanctity of property. Socio-economic experimentation by the legislatures, such as minimum-wage, maximum-hour, and child-labor regulations, was regarded with almost[2] unshakable disapproval by a solid majority of the Court. Again and again the justices struck down, as unconstitutional violations of *substantive* due process of law, legislation that large majorities on both the national and state levels deemed wise and necessary. Their grounds were that, because of the *substance* of the legislation involved, such statutory experimentations deprived "persons" (i.e., property owners, chiefly businessmen) of their liberty and property without due process of law. The "deprivation" of substantive due process was then judicially regarded as proscribed by the wording and command of Amendments Five and Fourteen of the Constitution. "The Justices," as economist John R. Commons wrote in 1924, "spoke as the first authoritative faculty of political economy

---

[1] *Dred Scott v. Sandford*, 19 Howard 393 (1857).
[2] "Almost," but not quite: cf. fns. 4, 5, 6, and text on p. 9, *infra*.

in the world's history."[3] Admittedly, an occasional enactment would survive—such as maximum hours in hazardous occupations (an eight-hour Utah law for copper miners and smelters in 1896);[4] for women in most industrial establishments (an Oregon ten-hour law in 1908);[5] and even one for both men and women (another Oregon ten-hour mill and factory statute, this one in 1917).[6] But until the advent of the "Roosevelt Court" in 1937, the Supreme Court under Mr. Chief Justice Charles Evans Hughes (1930–41) continued the substantive due process veto and struck down between 1934 and 1936 a total of sixteen New Deal laws that had been enacted chiefly under the taxing and interstate commerce powers of Congress.[7] Although President Roosevelt lost his battle to "pack" the Court in February of 1937, he was able, within a matter of three months, to win the war with two favorable decisions by the Hughes Court, a victory often styled as "the switch in time that saved nine."

Here the Chief Justice and Associate Justice Owen J. Roberts joined their colleagues Louis D. Brandeis, Benjamin N. Cardozo, and Harlan F. Stone in upholding a Washington State *minimum-wage law* for women and children—the first time that such a statute was upheld by the Court.[8] (It would be another four years before the Court would have the opportunity to uphold,[9] again for the first time, a *federal child-labor law,* the Fair Labor Standards Act of 1938, which also provided for minimum wages and maximum hours for all workers in interstate commerce. It had been declared beyond the power of Congress by a lower federal court.) In the other great early spring 1937 "switch-in-time" case, the new 5:4 majority upheld the National Labor Relations Act of 1935 against the challenge that it, too, exceeded the powers of Congress.[10] When Mr. Justice Willis van Devanter retired later in 1937 after twenty-six years on the Court, and Democratic Senator Hugo LaFayette Black of Alabama replaced him, the day of resorting to declarations of unconstitutionality on grounds of alleged infringement of economic "substantive due process" had, in effect, passed beyond recall—while in the future loomed a new kind of substantive due process interest!

[3] As quoted by Arthur S. Miller in "The Court Turns Back the Clock," *The Progressive,* October 1976, p. 22.

[4] *Holden v. Hardy,* 169 U.S. 366.

[5] *Muller v. Oregon,* 208 U.S. 412. Generally credited to the first use of the "Brandeis Brief."

[6] *Bunting v. Oregon,* 243 U.S. 426.

[7] For explanatory and statistical matter through 1979, see my *The Judicial Process: An Introductory Analysis of the Courts of the United States, England and France,* 4th ed. (New York: Oxford University Press, 1980), pp. 297–310.

[8] *West Coast Hotel Co. v. Parrish,* 300 U.S. 379 (1937).

[9] *United States v. Darby Lumber Co.,* 312 U.S. 100 (1941).

[10] *National Labor Relations Board v. Jones and Laughlin Steel Corporation,* 301 U.S. 1 (1937).

Gradually the Court thus embarked upon a policy of paying close attention to any legislative and executive attempt to curb basic rights and liberties in the "non-economic" sphere. During the remaining years of the
Hughes Court and continuing through the Stone Court (1941–46), the
Vinson Court (1946–53), and particularly the Warren Court (1953–69),
the chief concern was to find a balance between the basic civil rights and
liberties of the individual and those of the community of which he is a
part. That concern continued under the Burger Court (1969–), which,
with the exception of the criminal justice sector did not reveal any clearly
demonstrable tendency to chip away at the legacy of the Warren Court (at
least not as of this writing—mid-1981).[11] This post-1937 change in judicial
attitude reflects a conviction that certain fundamental freedoms *ipso facto*
require closer judicial scrutiny lest they be irretrievably lost. A properly
lodged complaint at the bar of the Court that legislative or executive action, be it state or national, had violated the complainant's due process of
law, be it substantive or procedural—and/or the equal protection of the
law (applicable to the state level only)—would be assured at least of judicial interest and probably of close scrutiny. Whether this new concern has
not in effect created a double standard of judicial attitude, whereby governmental economic experimentation is accorded all but *carte blanche* by
the courts, but alleged violations of individual civil rights are given meticu-
lous judicial attention, is a question that we will carefully examine.[12]

Historically, the jurisprudential postures of certain justices have aided in
the evolution of a double standard.[13] True to his close adherence to a philosophy of judicial self-restraint, Mr. Justice Oliver Wendell Holmes, Jr.
spent much of his thirty-year career (1902–32) on the highest bench—
which fell in its substantive economic due process era—in dissent from
judicial vetoes of economic legislation. He did so not because he particularly liked the legislation, but because he was convinced that democracy
meant that people had the right to be foolish and unwise. In his own
words, he was willing to go so far as "to help my country go to hell if
that's what it wants." Yet he nevertheless drew the line and called a firm
halt when it came to basic "non-economic" rights. Prior to Holmes, Mr.
Justice John Marshall Harlan had been the sole consistent dissenter in the

[11] For an interesting commentary, contending that once judicially pronounced there
has never been any major policy reversal in the realm of civil rights and liberty on
the part of the Court—but with some hedging regarding future action by the Burger
Court—see an article by former Associate Justice of the Supreme Court Arthur J.
Goldberg for *The New York Times*, April 12 and 13, 1971, pp. 37c and 37m,
respectively.
[12] See especially pp. 13–21, *infra*.
[13] For contentions as to the latter-day development of a "double standard," or even
"double standards," within the original "double standard," consult the Gunther, and
Wilkinson articles cited on p. 15, footnote 38, *infra* and the Abraham and Funston
article cited on p. 21, footnote 68.

economic substantive due process era. Harlan, grandfather of President Eisenhower's appointee of the same name, served from 1877 until his death in 1911. Though a one-time Kentucky slave-holder, he, as well as Holmes, deserves the title of "great dissenter,"[14] for he believed in a full measure of judicial self-restraint regarding legislative economic-proprietarian enactments. This stance was dramatically illustrated by his solitary dissent in the 1895 case of *United States v. E. C. Knight Co.*[15] when his eight colleagues on the Court virtually wiped out the hoped-for weapons of the fledgling Sherman Antitrust Act of 1890 by ruling that "commerce succeeds to manufacture and is not a part of it."[16] On the other hand, Harlan's resolute attachment to the role of the Court as the guardian of both the letter and the spirit of the basic constitutional guarantees of civil rights and liberties is well demonstrated in his solitary dissenting opinion in *Plessy v. Ferguson.*[17] In this 1896 decision, the Court, with Mr. Justice Henry B. Brown—a native of Massachusetts, a graduate of Harvard and Yale, and a resident of Michigan—delivering the majority opinion of seven, upheld the "separate but equal" doctrine in racial segregation:

> We consider the underlying fallacy of the plaintiff's [Homer Plessy, a Louisianan, seven-eighths white, who had refused to give up his seat in a railroad car reserved for white passengers under an 1890 Louisiana statute] argument to consist in the assumption that the enforced separation of the two races stamps the colored race with a badge of inferiority. If this be so, it is not by reason of anything found in the act, but *solely because the colored race chooses to put that construction on it.*[18]

Thundered Harlan, one of only two Southerners then on the Court:

> *Our Constitution is color-blind, and neither knows nor tolerates classes among citizens.* In respect of civil rights, all citizens are equal before the law. The humblest is the peer of the most powerful. The law regards man as man and takes no account of his surroundings or of his color when his civil rights as guaranteed by the supreme law of the land are involved.[19]

---

[14] See my "John Marshall Harlan: A Justice Neglected," 41 *Virginia Law Review* 871 (November 1955). *"The"* great dissenter will presumably always be the property of Mr. Justice Douglas who, in his almost 37 (!) years on the Court (1939–75) dissented no fewer than 795 times. Holmes's dissents numbered 172, placing him 15th; Harlan penned 376, third on the list. (Dissents may be written or unwritten.)

[15] 156 U.S. 1.

[16] *Ibid.,* majority opinion by Mr. Chief Justice Fuller, at 9. (Its impact was not effectively reversed until the Court's 1937 decision in *National Labor Relations Board v. Jones and Laughlin Steel Corporation,* 301 U.S. 1.)

[17] 163 U.S. 537.

[18] *Ibid.,* at 551. (Italics supplied.) Mr. Justice David Brewer did not participate in the case.

[19] *Ibid.,* at 559. (Italics supplied.)

As we shall see below, Harlan was the first Supreme Court jurist to advocate, unsuccessfully during his time of service, the *total* applicability of the federal Bill of Rights to the several states.[20] That he and Holmes were not particularly close personally did not alter their jurisprudential kinship.

However, in this respect Harlan was even closer to Louis Dembitz Brandeis, Woodrow Wilson's close ideological ally whom the President nominated to the highest bench in 1916, five years after Harlan's death and fourteen years after Holmes's appointment to the Court. A pioneering lawyer and crusading supporter of social welfare legislation, a bitter opponent of trusts and monopolies, and the first Jew to be nominated to the Court, Brandeis won a furious and bitter four-month confirmation battle which was the longest in Court history. He was finally confirmed by a vote of 47:22, all but one[21] of the negative votes being cast by the Boston attorney's fellow Republicans![22] Mr. Justice Brandeis disappointed neither his nominator nor his "public." He and Holmes, while of widely divergent backgrounds and temperaments, not only became warm friends but were usually on the same side of the Court's decisions, particularly in the interpretation of substantive due process and the double standard. That their reasons for agreement were often quite different affected neither the basic fact of agreement nor the close relationship between them.[23] Holmes did not live to see his position vindicated; he died at 93 in 1935, three years after retiring from his beloved bench. He knew, however, that his successor, Cardozo, would follow in his footsteps, and there were ample signs that if the jurisprudential era begun by the Fuller Court had not yet run its course, it was becoming increasingly beleaguered. Brandeis did see the new era dawn. After twenty-three years on the Court, he retired in 1939 at the age of 83, secure in the knowledge that his philosophy would be followed by the post-1937 Court. F.D.R. awarded his seat to a long-time Brandeis admirer, William O. Douglas—who, during his record-setting thirty-six-and-a-

---

[20] E.g. *Hurtado v. California*, 110 U.S. 516 (1884); *Maxwell v. Dow*, 176 U.S. 581 (1900); and *Twining v. New Jersey*, 211 U.S. 78 (1908); to name just three cases. His lone success was the quasi-"incorporation" of the *economic proprietarian* concept of eminent domain in *Chicago Burlington & Quincy RR. v. Chicago*, 166 U.S. 226 (1897), an 8:1 opinion written by him (see pp. 40 ff., *infra*), obviously joined by all except Justice Brewer on the Court because the constitutional protection here conferred dealt with *property* rights as a constituent element of due process of law, although the railroad lost the case on the merits.

[21] Democrat Francis G. Newlands of Nevada.

[22] Quite a number either did not vote or were paired, however. See A. L. Todd, *Justice on Trial: The Case of Louis D. Brandeis* (New York: McGraw-Hill Book Co., 1964), for a fascinating account of the confirmation battle. Brandeis was a registered Republican, but he probably voted the Democratic ticket more frequently.

[23] See the fine analysis of the two great justices in Samuel J. Konefsky's *The Legacy of Holmes and Brandeis: A Study in the Influence of Ideas* (New York: The Macmillan Co., 1956). Also available in a later paperback edition.

half years on the Court,[24] would go well beyond his idol in the furthering of libertarian activism.

The Expression and Justification of the Double Standard

What the *post*-1937 judiciary did was to *assume* as constitutional all legislation in the proprietarian sector *unless* proved to the contrary by a complainant, but to view with a suspicious eye legislative and executive experimentation with other basic human freedoms generally regarded as the "cultural freedoms" guaranteed by the Bill of Rights—among them speech, press, worship, assembly, petition, due process of law in criminal justice, a fair trial. In short, without denying its ultimate responsibility, the Court came to accept legislative action in the economic realm, but kept and, of course, continues to keep, a very close watch over legislative activities described as "basic" or "cultural." What we have then is a judicially recognized area of "preferred freedoms." Any quest for an obvious, clear line between "property rights" and "basic human rights" is, of course, doomed to fail, because by definition and implication *both are guaranteed freedoms* under our national and state constitutions. Property, too, is a "human right," and there is a fundamental interdependence "between the personal right to liberty and the personal right in property," as Mr. Justice Stewart wrote in a 1972 opinion for the Court.[25] Committed to that philosophy, the distinguished jurist Learned Hand never failed to reject and challenge any advocacy of the "double standard." A policy urging that the courts, "when concerned with interests other than property . . . should have a wider latitude for enforcing their own predilections than when they were concerned with property itself," was to him a dereliction of the judicial function if not of the oath of office of the Constitution; "just why property itself was not a 'personal right,' " Hand observed, "nobody took the time to explain."[26] And as Paul Freund, noted scholar of constitutional law and Hand's admirer, has reminded us, it is indeed difficult to "compare the ultimate values of property with those of [for example] free inquiry and expression, or to compare the legislative compromises in the two

[24] He served until late in 1975 when debilitating illness dictated his retirement; he died in 1980.

[25] *Lynch v. Household Finance Corp.,* 405 U.S. 538 (1972), at 552. At least one student of the problem has attempted to distinguish between "personal" or "individual" and "corporate" or "institutional" property—the former being entitled to double standard inclusion, the latter not. (See Richard H. Rosswurm, "The Double Standard Under Constitution and Supreme Court: An Alternate Model," paper delivered at the 1979 Annual Meeting of the Southern Political Science Association, Gatlinburg, Tennessee, November 1–3.)

[26] "Chief Justice Stone's Conception of the Judicial Function," 46 *Columbia Law Review* 698 (1946).

realms; for laws dealing with libel or sedition or sound trucks or non-political civil service are as truly adjustments and accommodations as are laws fixing prices or making grants of monopolies."[27] However, the values of property are *not* ignored by the judiciary when, in fact, illegal legislative action takes place[28]—or when basic property rights of individuals or groups are adjudged violated beyond the legal or constitutional pale.[29]

Recently, the Court has modified the more traditional "double standard" to give "strict judicial scrutiny" to certain types of equal protection *and* due process cases, especially the former. Depending on the type of legislative statutory classification, the Court places or views the case before it in different categories or levels, accordingly affecting its treatment of the issue at hand. Thus, for the economic-proprietarian cases (which were discussed earlier in this chapter) the Court still uses the "traditional" equal protection (and due process) test of examining whether the legislature had a "reasonable" or "rational" or "relevant" basis for making its statutory classification. Yet while, ever since the 1937 "switch-in-time-that-saved nine," basic civil rights and liberties issues have led to closer case examination by the Court, the demonstration of a classification in a law which either affects so-styled "fundamental interests" (e.g., voting rights,[30] the right to interstate travel[31]) or touches a "suspect category" (e.g., race,[32] national origin or alienage,[33] and, as of 1968 but apparently no longer

[27] *The Supreme Court of the United States* (Cleveland: The World Publishing Co., 1961), p. 35.

[28] For example, in 1952 the Supreme Court by an 8:1 vote—Mr. Justice Burton dissenting—declared as a violation of substantive due process a provision of the Pure Food and Drug Act which provided for federal powers of factory inspection. The Court ruled this provision to be an unconstitutionally vague deprivation of liberty and property safeguarded by the Fifth Amendment. (*United States v. Cardiff,* 344 U.S. 174.)

[29] E.g., *Lloyd v. Tanner,* 407 U.S. 551 (1972), where the Court "balanced" the property rights of a private shopping center with the right of freedom of expression (distribution of leaflets) and found on behalf of the former by a 5:4 vote. In the words of Mr. Justice Powell's majority opinion: "Although accommodations between [speech and property values] are sometimes necessary, and the courts properly have shown a special solicitude for the [First Amendment], this Court has never held that a trespasser or an uninvited guest may exercise general rights of free speech on private property used non-discriminatorily for private purposes only." (At 567–8.)

[30] E.g., *Harper v. Virginia Board of Elections,* 383 U.S. 663 (1966).

[31] E.g., *Shapiro v. Thompson,* 394 U.S. 618 (1969)—at least when it involves, as it did here, "a basic necessity of life."

[32] E.g., *Loving v. Virginia,* 388 U.S. 1 (1967). Ironically, the first reference to it was by Mr. Justice Black in the Japanese Exclusion Case, *Korematsu v. United States,* 323 U.S. 214 (1944): "[All] legal restrictions which curtail the civil rights of a single racial group are immediately *suspect*. This is not to say that all such restrictions are unconstitutional. It is to say that courts must subject them to the *most* rigid scrutiny. Pressing public necessity may sometimes justify the existence of such restrictions [as a 6:3 Court majority here found]; racial antagonism never can." (At 216. Italics supplied.)

[33] E.g., *Graham v. Richardson,* 403 U.S. 365 (1971).

after mid-1976, illegitimacy[34]) has now received an even higher level of Court scrutiny. In some cases the category, while not "suspect," is nonetheless accorded especially close attention—sex, for example, which is second only to race in contemporary equal protection of the laws ligitation.[35] Once an issue has accordingly been placed on that special level of scrutiny, the Court in effect shifts the burden of proof of its constitutionality *to the legislature and/or the executive* and requires that *it* demonstrate a *"compelling* state interest" for its legislative classification—as it succeeded in doing, for example, in the Japanese Evacuation Case of 1944.[36] Once the "fundamental interest" or "suspect"[37] category classification is demonstrated in a case, the "strict judicial scrutiny" that thereby results leads to considerably greater judicial protection of these rights. In essence, then, we see the Court using a complicated double-standard-within-a-double-standard to accomplish this contemporary task[38]—triggering widespread accusations of judicial arrogation of legislative authority.

OF "PREFERRED FREEDOMS"

Although he did not personally use the words until four years later, the articulation of the concept of "preferred freedoms" is appropriately credited to a footnote appended to an opinion for the Court by then Associate Justice Stone in the 1938 case of *United States v. Carolene Products Company.*[39] Stone's Footnote Four probably evolved from the celebrated Cardozo opinion delivered a few months earlier in *Palko v. Connecticut.*[40] In

[34] E.g., *Levy v. Louisiana,* 391 U.S. 68 (1968); *Labine v. Vincent,* 401 U.S. 532 (1971); *Weber v. Aetna Casualty and Insurance Company,* 406 U.S. 164 (1972). For the "removal decision," see *Norton v. Mathews* and *Mathews v. Lucas,* 427 U.S. 495 (1976). But *cf. Trimble v. Gordon,* 430 U.S. 762 (1977).

[35] E.g., *Reed v. Reed,* 404 U.S. 71 (1971), *Frontiero v. Richardson,* 411 U.S. 677 (1973), and *Helgemoe v. Meloon,* 436 U.S. 950 (1978). But compare and contrast those with e.g., *Kahn v. Shevin,* 416 U.S. 351 (1974), *Schlesinger v. Ballard,* 419 U.S. 498 (1975), and *General Electric Co. v. Gilbert,* 429 U.S. 125 (1976).

[36] See fn. 32, *supra.*

[37] The "traditional indices of suspectness," viewed by Mr. Justice Stone in his Carolene footnote (see pp. 18 ff.) as "discrete and insular minorities," were characterized as follows in Mr. Justice Powell's majority opinion in *San Antonio School District v. Rodriguez,* 411 U.S. 1 (1973): "The class [is] saddled with such disabilities, or subjected to such a history of purposeful unequal treatment, or relegated to such a position of political powerlessness as to command extraordinary protection from the majoritarian political process."

[38] For two excellent recent treatments of this vexatious and complicated issue, see Gerald Gunther, "The Supreme Court: 1971 Term; In Search of Evolving Doctrine on a Changing Court: A Model for a Newer Equal Protection," 86 *Harvard Law Review* 1 (1972) and J. Harvie Wilkinson, III, "The Supreme Court, the Equal Protection Clause and the Three Faces of Constitutional Equality," 61 *Virginia Law Review* 945 (1975).

[39] In *Jones v. Opelika,* 316 U.S. 584 (1942), at 608. (See p. 17, *infra,* for further notes on the term's coinage and development.)

[40] 302 U.S. 319 (1937). (The case will be discussed more fully in Chapter III, *infra.*)

that, his last personally delivered opinion prior to his fatal illness in 1938, Mr. Justice Cardozo had established two major categories of rights: those that *are* and those that *are not* "implicit in the concept of ordered liberty." Cardozo justified this distinction, later referred to as the "Honor Roll of Superior Rights," by explaining that ". . . we reach a different plane of social and moral values when we pass to . . . freedom of thought and speech . . . [which] is the matrix, the indispensable condition, of nearly every other form of freedom."[41] Stone wrote his opinion in the *Carolene* case with Cardozo's distinction in mind. And, in a very real sense, he took it one step further: he explicitly enunciated the activist doctrine of the "double standard." *Carolene* dealt with an ordinary federal interstate commerce statute, the Filled Milk Act of 1923, which regulated adulterated ("filled") milk—and it would normally have passed into the annals of what the new Court regarded as routine exercise of valid congressional legislative power over interstate commerce. However, addressing himself to the inherent congressional regulatory power, Stone was moved to comment in the body of the opinion that

> the existence of facts supporting the legislative judgment is to be presumed, for regulatory legislation affecting ordinary commercial transactions is not to be pronounced unconstitutional unless in the light of the facts made known or generally assumed, it is of such a character as to preclude the assumption that it rests upon some rational basis within the knowledge and experience of legislators.[42]

This expression of the double standard, from one who had come to the Court from one of the largest New York corporate law offices, is a reminder that Marxian forecasts and interpretations of the attitude of justices on the highest bench are not always accurate!

Having said what he did, Stone then appended his now famous Footnote Four[43] from which we will examine the following three paragraphs:

1. There may be narrower scope for operation of the presumption of constitutionality when legislation appears on its face to be within a specific prohibition of the Constitution, such as those of the first ten amendments, which are deemed equally specific when held to be embraced within the Fourteenth.

---

[41] *Ibid.*, at 326–27.

[42] 304 U.S. 144, at 152.

[43] It is now generally accepted that most of the famed footnote was in fact authored by Stone's brilliant law clerk, Louis Lusky, and that Hughes had a hand in its first paragraph. For the footnote's popularization much credit is due to Professor Alpheus Thomas Mason, long-time McCormick Professor of Jurisprudence at Princeton University. See Lusky's book, *By What Right?* (Charlottesville: The Michie Co., 1975) for a full discussion of Footnote Four.

2. It is unnecessary to consider now whether legislation which restricts *those political processes* which can ordinarily be expected to bring about repeal of undesirable legislation, is to be subjected to more exacting judicial scrutiny under the general prohibitions of the Fourteenth Amendment than are most other types of legislation. . . .

3. Nor need we enquire whether similar considerations enter into review of statutes directed at particular religious . . . or national, . . . or racial minorities . . . ; whether prejudice against discrete and insular minorities may be a special condition, which tends seriously to curtail the operation of *those political processes* ordinarily to be relied upon to protect minorities, and which may call for a correspondingly more searching judicial inquiry. . . .

At first glance, the language in paragraph 1 may suggest to some—as it did to Mr. Justice Frankfurter[44]—that *any* legislation which on its face appears to abridge the constitutional guarantees of the Bill of Rights would have to fall *automatically*. However, as soon became evident, Stone had reference primarily to the five guarantees of the First Amendment (religion, speech, press, assembly, and petition) and secondarily to the proposition that such legislation should simply be *inspected* more critically by the judiciary than where exclusively economic rights are at issue.[45] Stone's colleagues Black, Douglas, Murphy, and Rutledge[46] embraced his position readily—although not necessarily for the same reasons—and their opinion frequently prevailed during their joint tenure on the Court between 1943 and 1949—sometimes gaining Jackson's vote, occasionally even Frankfurter's or Reed's. Thus at least five votes to carry the day were often available, and a series of memorable decisions was made in behalf of the new concept.[47] And, contrary to some reporting, justices did in fact use

[44] See, for example, his concurring opinion in *Kovacs v. Cooper,* 336 U.S. 77 (1949).

[45] For an interesting analysis of the genesis and application of the "preferred freedom" concept, see Robert B. McKay, "The Preference for Freedom," 34 *New York University Law Review* 1184 (November 1959). He is very critical of the Frankfurter position, both on factual and logical grounds.

[46] Actually it was Rutledge, not Stone, who stated the "preferred freedom" doctrine most clearly, most expressly, and most extremely, in what was the heyday of the avowed utilization of the doctrine, in the 5:4 *Union Organization* case of 1945—in which the now Chief Justice Stone dissented, together with Roberts, Reed, and Frankfurter (*Thomas v. Collins,* 323 U.S. 516, at 529–30 and 540). Rutledge referred to "the preferred place given in our scheme to the great, the indispensable democratic freedoms secured by the First Amendment." He carried his colleagues Black, Douglas, and Murphy, and Jackson concurred to make the majority of five. (Black, uncomfortable with the "preferred" concept, would later "substitute" that of "absolute," which he avowedly adapted, based upon his literalist reading of the Constitution, in 1951, in *Dennis v. United States,* 341 U.S. 494, although he did not formally employ the term "absolute" itself until a few months later in *Carlson v. Landon,* 342 U.S. 524, at 555.)

[47] E.g., *Hague v. C.I.O.,* 307 U.S. 496 (1939); *Bridges v. California,* 314 U.S. 252 (1941); *Jones v. Opelika,* 319 U.S. 103 (1943); *West Virginia State Board of Educa-*

the term "preferred position" in majority and minority opinions[48]—and they not only continued to do so but occasionally still do—notwithstanding Frankfurter's angry characterization of it as "a mischievous phrase."[49] However, when Justices Murphy and Rutledge both died in the summer of 1949, their replacements, Tom C. Clark and Sherman Minton, together with Mr. Chief Justice Fred M. Vinson (Stone had died on the bench in 1946), consigned the "preferred freedom" doctrine to relative limbo. It remained there until Earl Warren succeeded Vinson on the latter's death in 1953 and the Court renewed the emphasis on civil rights and liberties.

Paragraph 2 calls for a special judicial scrutiny of assaults on "those political processes" which in a very real sense make all other rights in our democratic society possible: equal access to the voting booth, for both nomination and election, and the ability to seek redress of political grievances, either by striving for public office or by "getting at the rascals" in office. It was this basic requirement of a representative democracy that precipitated the momentous Supreme Court decisions in the *Suffrage* cases of 1941 and 1944. In the first, *United States v. Classic*,[50] the Court overruled precedent[51] and held that the language of the Constitution equated "primaries" with "elections" in races for federal office, and that the former would henceforth be subject to congressional regulation to the same extent and in the same manner as the latter. The second case, *Smith v. Allwright*,[52] logically resulted from the first. Here, the Court, again overruling precedent,[53] outlawed, as an unconstitutional violation of the Fifteenth Amendment, the so-called "white primary," a device to bar blacks from the effective exercise of the ballot in several states of the deep South. Rejecting the contention that the Democratic Party of Texas was "a voluntary association" and thus free to discriminate in its membership, the 8:1 majority held that the Party acted as an agent of the State of Texas because of the character of its duties—such as providing election machinery and candidates. Of equal, if not greater, importance in the judicial assault on legislation restricting basic political processes is the matter of equitable represen-

---

tion v. Barnette, 319 U.S. 624 (1943); Thomas v. Collins, loc. cit.; Saia v. New York, 334 U.S. 558 (1948); Kovacs v. Cooper, loc. cit.; and Terminiello v. Chicago, 337 U.S. 1 (1949).

[48] E.g., Stone in *Jones v. Opelika*, 316 U.S. 584 (1942), at 608; Douglas in *Murdock v. Pennsylvania*, 319 U.S. 105 (1943), at 115; Rutledge in *Thomas v. Collins*, op. cit., at 530; and Reed in *Kovacs v. Cooper*, op. cit., at 88. See also *Prince v. Massachusetts*, 321 U.S. 158 (1944); *Follett v. McCormick*, 321 U.S. 573 (1944); *Marsh v. Alabama*, 326 U.S. 501 (1946), at 509; and *Saia v. New York*, op. cit., at 562.

[49] *Kovacs v. Cooper*, op. cit., at 90. For example, Black did in his dissenting opinion in *Morey v. Doud*, 354 U.S. 457 (1957), at 471.

[50] 313 U.S. 299 (1941).

[51] *Newberry v. United States*, 256 U.S. 232 (1921).

[52] 321 U.S. 649 (1944). (Mr. Justice Roberts was the sole dissenter here.)

[53] *Grovey v. Townsend*, 295 U.S. 45 (1935).

tation. In March 1962 the Supreme Court finally found sufficient votes to declare that the age-old practice of deliberate mal-, mis-, or non-apportionment of representative legislative districts in the several states was a controversy that it had the power, the right, and the duty to adjudicate. This decision in the case of *Baker v. Carr*[54]—which Mr. Chief Justice Warren[55] regarded as "the most important case we decided in my time"[56]—sharply departed from the erstwhile Court practice of regarding this kind of controversy as a "political question"[57] to be "handled" by the political rather than the judiciary branch. *Baker* broke with that precedent. Mr. Justice Frankfurter,—"the Emily Post of the Supreme Court," in Fred Rodell's nastily memorable phrase—joined by his disciple on the bench, John Marshall Harlan II, wrote an impassioned 68-page dissenting opinion reiterating his life-long judicial philosophy that the courts must stay out of what he termed the "political thicket." Warning that the Court would find itself immersed in a "mathematical quagmire," he admonished the majority of six: "There is not under our Constitution a judicial remedy for every political mischief. In a democratic society like ours, relief must come through an aroused popular conscience that sears the conscience of the people's representatives."[58] But the majority had seen one attempt after another to "sear the conscience" frustrated for generations. Indeed, in many of the transgressing states the very imbalance of representative districts rendered "an aroused public conscience" impossible. The Court, prodded by a swelling chorus of citizens who were discriminated against, notably the urban masses, had had enough, and the commands of Article One and Amendment Fourteen provided the necessary interpretative authority to bring about the "more exacting judicial scrutiny" called for in the second paragraph of Mr. Justice Stone's Footnote Four.

The decision in *Baker v. Carr*[59] that the federal courts do have jurisdiction in cases involving state legislative apportionment became a vehicle for logical substantive extensions. In 1963, in the *Georgia County Unit* case,[60] the Court, agreeing with the lower federal district court that the notorious

---

[54] 369 U.S. 186 (1962).

[55] Ironically, fifteen years earlier, as Governor of California, he had successfully opposed reapportionment. It matters what post one holds!

[56] Interview with author, Washington, D.C., May 24, 1969. Warren's view of the case's significance—whether or not one accepts his ranking—was amply vindicated, and quickly so: after but eight years following the extensions of *Baker*-opened principles *cum* yardsticks to congressional districts, the Bureau of the Census reported that the average deviation from the ideal district-size in the 93d (January 1973) Congress was but ½ of 1 per cent, as contrasted with 17 per cent in the 88th (January 1965)!

[57] E.g., *Colegrove v. Green,* 328 U.S. 549 (1946); and *South v. Peters,* 339 U.S. 276 (1950).

[58] 369 U.S. 186, dissenting opinion, at 270.

[59] The vote was 6:2. Mr. Justice Charles E. Whittaker did not participate.

[60] *Gray v. Sanders,* 372 U.S. 368.

"county unit" scheme[61] violated the equal protection of the laws clause of the Fourteenth Amendment, enunciated the principle of "one person, one vote"[62]—the equality of every voter with every other voter in the state when he casts his or her vote in a statewide election. One year later, the Court extended the principle to *Congressional* districts.[63] Then, perhaps most dramatically, in a group of six cases in June of 1964, it required that representation for *both* houses of state legislatures must be apportioned to reflect "approximate equality" (a decision not only extended subsequently to reach *local* elections of varied character,[64] but one that would ultimately result in the further extension to a Court-call for "absolute equality"![65] Wrote Mr. Chief Justice Warren for a majority of six: "Legislatures represent people, not trees or acres. Legislators are elected by voters, not farms or cities or economic interests. . . . To the extent that a citizen's right to vote is debased, he is that much less a citizen. The weight of a citizen's right to vote cannot be made to depend on where he lives."[66] Stone would have been pleased.

In paragraph 3 Stone so explicitly spells out the "double standard" as to be appropriately credited with its parenthood. It is self-evident that the

---

[61] Under it each of Georgia's counties received a minimum of two and a maximum of six electoral votes (for the eight most populous counties), with each county's vote going to the candidate receiving the largest popular vote therein—resulting in rank discrimination that saw the small counties receiving from 11 to 120 times as much representative weight as the largest.

[62] Mr. Justice Douglas spoke for the 8:1 Court here.

[63] *Wesberry v. Sanders,* 376 U.S. 1 (1964).

[64] E.g., *Avery v. Midland County,* 390 U.S. 474 (1968); and *Hadley v. Junior College Dist. of Metro. Kansas City, Mo.,* 397 U.S. 50 (1970).

[65] *Kirkpatrick v. Preisler,* 394 U.S. 526 (1969); and *Wells v. Rockefeller,* 394 U.S. 542 (1969). But the Court, 6:3, refused in 1973 to extend the principle to *elected judges* (*Wells v. Edwards,* 409 U.S. 1095) and to such special purpose governing agencies as a Board of Directors of a Water District (*Salyer Land Co. v. Tulare Lake Basin Water Storage District,* 410 U.S. 719). And, 5:3, during the same term of Court it permitted a Virginia deviation of 16.4 per cent, holding (via Mr. Justice Rehnquist) that its one-person-one-vote doctrine which it did emphatically reaffirm here, need not be applied so strictly to *state* as to *congressional* apportionment. Rehnquist reasoned that a state legislative apportionment plan could therefore include "a certain amount of arithmetical discrepancy if it was deliberately drawn to conform to the boundaries of political subdivisions." (*Mahan v. Howell,* 410 U.S. 315.) The rationale of the latter decision was subsequently confirmed in a series of cases involving 7.8 and 9.9 per cent variances in other states (*Gaffney v. Cummings,* 412 U.S. 735 and *White v. Regester,* 412 U.S. 755, both in 1973, too. On the other hand, the latter case sustained, for the first time, an attack on multi-member districts as tending "unconstitutionally to minimize the voting strength of racial groups."). But a mere 4.4 per cent deviation in congressional districting was vetoed by the Court at the same time (*White v. Weiser,* 413 U.S. 783); and an attempt by North Dakota to deviate by 20 per cent was unanimously declared unconstitutional in 1975. (*Chapman v. Meier,* 420 U.S. 1.) See also *Ball v. James,* 49 LW 4459 (1981).

[66] *Reynolds v. Sims,* 377 U.S. 533, at 562. Five other cases were decided simultaneously, all based on the same general principle, with the votes ranging from 8:1 to 6:3. (See pp. 633–713.)

special judicial protection he suggests for frequently unpopular racial, religious, and political minorities and other often helpless and small groups is preeminently designed for and directed to their political-cultural activities. Underlying his call for special scrutiny is the fact that these groups demonstrably needed or need special aid and protection to attain and maintain their full measure of constitutionally guaranteed citizenship. The current struggle of political, religious, and particularly racial minority groups bears witness to the case for the "preferred freedom" doctrine suggested by Stone on that Opinion Monday in 1938.

But is the implicit "double standard" justifiable at all? Does the Supreme Court of the United States have a moral as well as a constitutional mandate to apply such a standard, to guard against what has been called the "mistaken self-abnegation" that would allow the basic freedoms to be "eroded to the point where their restoration becomes impossible?"[67] There is considerable room for disagreement, both in legal contemplation and political philosophy,[68] some of which is outlined below.

A TRIO OF SUGGESTED JUSTIFICATIONS
FOR THE DOUBLE STANDARD

Of the numerous reasons which have been advanced in support of the double standard, three in particular have commanded potent, although not unanimous, backing:

1. *The Crucial Nature of Basic Freedoms.* As Justices Holmes, Brandeis, Cardozo, and Stone, among others, so ably demonstrated, those freedoms which can be considered basic are those upon which all other freedoms in democratic society rest. For example, when the principles of freedom of speech and press are contingent upon prior censorship, they become a mockery. When the right to worship depends upon majoritarian whims or police ordinances, it becomes meaningless. When the rights to register and vote are dependent upon the race of the applicant or the amount of his property, they become travesties of the democratic political process. To paraphrase Mr. Justice Jackson in the *West Virginia Flag Salute* case,[69] the very purpose of the Bill of Rights was to withdraw those freedoms which can be considered basic from the "vicissitudes" of political contro-

[67] Loren P. Beth, "The Case for Judicial Protection of Civil Liberties," 17 *The Journal of Politics* 112 (February 1955).

[68] See, for example, the divergent points of view presented by Richard Funston and Henry J. Abraham in 90 *Political Science Quarterly* 2 (Summer 1975), entitled respectively, "The Double Standard of Constitutional Protection in the Era of the Welfare State," and "'Human' Rights vs. 'Property' Rights: A Comment on the 'Double Standard'." See also the profoundly thoughtful analytical essay by Robert G. McCloskey, "Economic Due Process and the Supreme Court: An Exhumation and Reburial," in Philip B. Kurland, ed., *The Supreme Court Review* (Chicago: University of Chicago Press, 1962).

[69] *West Virginia State Board of Education v. Barnette,* 319 U.S. 624 (1943).

versy, from the grasps of majorities and public officials, and to hold them aloft as legal principles to be applied by the judiciary. Thus, such fundamental rights as freedom of expression and religion simply are not delegatable to the majority will; such economic-proprietarian problems as the rate of income tax assuredly are. As Justice Stone put it in a memorable dissenting opinion less than three years following his Footnote Four in *Carolene:*

> The very fact that we have constitutional guarantees of civil liberties and the specificity of their command where freedom of speech and religion are concerned require some accommodation of the powers which government normally exercises, when no question of civil liberty is involved, to the constitutional demand that these liberties be protected against the action of government itself. . . . The Constitution expresses more than the conviction of the people that democratic processes must be preserved at all costs. It also is an expression of faith and a command that freedom of mind and spirit must be preserved, which government must obey, if it is to adhere to that justice and moderation without which no free government can exist.[70]

Thus, embracing a demonstrable change in its own scale of jurisprudential values, it fell to the post-1937 Court to recognize and attempt to preserve those freedoms which are basic or crucial to the democratic process. And to achieve this, it has fallen to the Court to apply the "double standard" to them when the other branches of government have either consciously or unconsciously failed to heed or comprehend the essence of Stone's admonition—as perceived by a majority of its membership.

2. *The Explicit Language of the Bill of Rights.* An excellent case can be made for the viability of the double standard simply based upon the very language of the Bill of Rights (most of which, as we shall see,[71] has been made applicable to the several states by way of the "due process of law" clause of the Fourteenth Amendment). The economic-proprietarian safeguards of the Bill are couched in the most general of terms: the command of the Fifth and Fourteenth Amendments that no person "be deprived of life, liberty, or *property, without due process of law,"* raises more questions than it settles. Certainly the Founding Fathers did not specify what they meant by "property" except that one should not be "deprived" of it without "due process of law." As already noted, during the fifty years prior to 1937 the Court interpreted the clause so stringently that legislative efforts in the economic-proprietarian sphere were all but futile. To do so the Court had to read into the language of the "due process" clauses concepts that *may* have been implicit but were certainly not explicit. On the

---

[70] *Minersville School District v. Gobitis,* 310 U.S. 586 (1940), at 602–3, 606–7.
[71] Chapter III, *infra.*

other hand, the language governing what we commonly regard as our basic human freedoms is not only explicit, it is categorical! Madison's terminology for the First Amendment is precise:

> Congress shall make no law respecting an establishment of religion, or prohibiting the free exercise thereof; or abridging the freedom of speech, or of the press; or the right of the people peaceably to assemble, and to petition the government for redress of grievances.

Succeeding amendments in the Bill, such as those embodied in Amendments Four, Five, and Six, refer specifically to a host of other basic rights as well, be they substantive or procedural. That their interpretation has proved difficult and troublesome over the years does not, however, invalidate their explicitness, and it is their explicitness that makes a strong case for invocation of the double standard.[72]

Yet an acceptance of the double standard does not necessarily mean embracing the "literalism" of Mr. Justice Black, whose support of the doctrine was grounded on the Constitution's *verbiage.* If he found it spelled out, it became an *absolute,* which, by definition, places him in the camp of those who see a double standard, although he steadfastly refused to accept the slogan. To him it was the explicitness of the language, its categoricalness, that is decisive. Thus, his firm contention, reiterated throughout his long career on the high bench,[73] that when the First Amendment says "Congress *shall make no law . . . abridging* the freedom of speech, or of the press," it means just that: NO LAW! It most emphatically does not mean, for example, "no law except such as may be necessary to prevent the viewing of obscene movies," or "no law except what may be needed to curb seditious utterances," or "no law except one to punish libel and slander." As he put it in a famous article:

> Some people regard the prohibitions of the Constitution, even its most unequivocal commands, as mere admonitions which Congress [and by implica-

---

[72] In Mr. Justice Black's always eminently quotable exhortation: "I think that state regulations [of economic affairs] should be viewed quite differently than where it [sic] touches or involves freedom of speech, press, religion, assembly, or other *specific safeguards of the Bill of Rights.* It is the duty of this Court to be alert to see that these *constitutionally preferred rights* are not abridged." (Dissenting opinion in *Morey v. Doud,* 354 U.S. 457 [1957]), at 471. (Italics supplied.) See Archibald Cox, *The Role of the Supreme Court in American Government* (New York: Oxford University Press, 1976), p. 51, for another illustration for support of the dichotomy.

[73] Hugo L. Black, "The Bill of Rights," 35 *New York University Law Review* 866 (April 1960). See also his "follow-up" article in 37 *New York University Law Review* 569 two years later; his March 1968 Carpentier Lee Lectures; his famed TV interview with reporters Eric Sevareid and Martin Agronsky in December 1968; and his definitive book, based on the Carpentier Lee Lectures, *A Constitutional Faith* (New York: Alfred A. Knopf, 1968). He died on September 25, 1971, having served more than 34 years.

tion, the states] need not always observe . . . formulations [which] rest, at least in part, on the premise that there are no "absolute" prohibitions in the Constitution, and that all constitutional problems are questions of reasonableness, proximity, and degree. . . .

I cannot accept this approach to the Bill of Rights. It is my belief that there *are* "absolutes" in our Bill of Rights, and they were put there on purpose by men who knew what words meant, and meant their prohibitions to be "absolutes". . . . I am primarily discussing here whether liberties *admittedly* covered by the Bill of Rights can nevertheless be abridged on the ground that a superior public interest justifies the abridgement. I think the Bill of Rights made its safeguards superior.[74]

And later, discussing the First Amendment, which was to him "the heart of our Bill of Rights, our Constitution, and our nation,"[75] Black wrote: "The phrase 'Congress shall make no law' is composed of plain words, easily understood. . . . Neither as offered nor as adopted is the language of this Amendment anything less than absolute. . . ."[76] Whether or not one agrees with Black's "absolutist" thesis—and a good many observers, of course, do not[77]—it nonetheless lends strong support to the argument for the existence of a hierarchy of values and the priority within that hierarchy of those liberties specifically listed in the Bill of Rights. Even Mr. Justice Frankfurter, who rejected absolutism as well as any formula such as the double standard, declared in a significant opinion that matters like press censorship and separation of Church and State are different from economic policy matters because "history, through the Constitution, speaks so decisively as to forbid legislative experimentation" with them.[78]

3. *The Appropriate Expertise of the Judiciary.* If one accepts the first two reasons in support of the double standard, a third follows quite logically: no other agency or institution of the United States government has proved itself either so capable of performing, or so willing to undertake, the necessary role of guardian of our basic rights as the judicial branch.

[74] "The Bill of Rights," *op. cit.,* at 866–67.

[75] See especially his *A Constitutional Faith, op. cit.,* particularly Ch. III, "The First Amendment," pp. 43 ff.

[76] "The Bill of Rights," *op. cit.,* at 874. For a superb study of Black's absolutism, see James J. Magee, *Mr. Justice Black: Absolutist on the Court* (Charlottesville: University Press of Virginia, 1980).

[77] E.g., Leonard W. Levy, *Freedom of Speech and Press in Early American History: Legacy of Suppression* (New York: Harper & Row, 1963), p. xxi; Harry M. Clor, *Obscenity and Public Morality: Censorship in a Liberal Society* (Chicago: University of Chicago Press, 1969), p. 89; and Walter F. Berns, *The First Amendment and the Future of American Democracy* (New York: Basic Books, 1977), *passim.*

[78] *American Federation of Labor v. American Sash and Door Co.,* 335 U.S. 538 (1949), at 550. For a fine, perceptive, evaluative biographical essay on Felix Frankfurter, see Joseph P. Lash, *From the Diaries of Felix Frankfurter* (New York: W. W. Norton & Co., 1975).

Since the legislative and executive branches have, for reasons inherent in our political system, failed to fulfill this role, it has fallen to the judiciary. And it is a role procedurally enhanced by the Supreme Court's all but absolute prerogative of determining the kind of cases that will reach its docket—which thus enables it to concentrate on articulating the libertarian realm. As Robert H. Jackson, who came to the Supreme Court from prominent service in the executive branch, observed: "The people have seemed to feel that the Supreme Court, whatever its defects, is still the most detached, dispassionate, and trustworthy custodian that our system affords for the translation of abstract into concrete constitutional commands."[79] With these words he echoed James Madison, who, in presenting the original Bill of Rights to Congress in 1789, remarked:

> If they are incorporated into the Constitution, independent tribunals of justice will consider themselves in a peculiar manner the guardians of those rights; they will be an impenetrable bulwark against every assumption of power in the legislative or executive; they will be naturally led to resist every encroachment upon rights expressly stipulated for in the Constitution by the declaration of rights.[80]

Yet, if the Supreme Court is indeed the appropriate governmental agency to buttress and safeguard our fundamental rights, few would seriously contend that, in equal measure, its province is to rule on the validity of economic legislation and administration. Because of its insufficient expertise and its crowded docket, the Court is not prepared to make the kind of economic judgments that would veto legislative actions and intent. It is the people's representatives who are best qualified to give expression to the requirements of economic life, to the experimentation and resolution that go into public planning. "We refuse to sit as a 'superlegislature,' " as Mr. Justice Black once noted, "to weigh the wisdom of legislation . . . Whether the legislature takes for its textbook Adam Smith, Herbert Spencer, Lord Keynes, or some other is no concern of ours."[81] Or, in the words of then Associate Justice Abe Fortas: "The courts may be the principal guardians of the liberties of our people. They are not the chief administrators of its economic destiny."[82] Or, as Mr. Justice Stewart suggested in a later case, in which the Court refused to extend the "strict scrutiny" of

---

[79] *The Supreme Court in the American System of Government* (Cambridge: Harvard University Press, 1955), p. 23. Designed as the Godkin Lectures at Harvard University, the book was edited and published with the aid of Jackson's son after his father's death of a heart attack shortly before he was to deliver the lectures—a task then assumed by the son.

[80] *Annals of Congress*, 1st Cong., 1st Sess., June 8, 1789 (Washington, D.C., 1834), Vol. I, p. 457.

[81] *Ferguson v. Skrupa,* 372 U.S. 726 (1963), at 732.

[82] *Baltimore and Ohio Railroad Co. v. United States,* 386 U.S. 372 (1967), at 478.

the "new" equal protection concepts to state welfare programs, "the intractable economic, social, and even philosophical problems presented by public welfare assistance programs are not the business of this Court."[83]

Here, then, judicial self-restraint and the assumption of legislative know-how and representativeness are in philosophical accord—and it is here that the double standard thus finds perhaps its clearest justification. Few have stated this distinction as well as Mr. Justice Oliver Wendell Holmes, Jr., who was no personal friend, indeed, of legislative "fooling around" with "economic do-gooding." But he was a jurist who believed resolutely—although he was often alone and practically never carried the Court with him on that issue—that under a democratic government the people have every right to experiment legislatively with their economic fate, even if he personally were to consider their action ignorant. As he said to his colleague Stone, after more than a half-century on the Supreme Courts of Massachusetts and the United States, and at the age of ninety:

> Young man [Stone was then sixty], about seventy-five years ago I learned that I was not God. And so, when the people want to do something [in the realm of economic legislation] I can't find anything in the Constitution expressly forbidding them to do, I say, whether I like it or not, "Goddamit, let 'em do it."[84]

Holmes expressed the same judicial posture more specifically to John W. Davis, the unsuccessful Democratic nominee for the Presidency in 1924, sometime U.S. Solicitor-General, and famed corporate attorney: "Of course, I know, and every other sensible man knows, that the Sherman Law [Anti-Trust Act of 1890] is damned nonsense, but if my country wants to go to hell, I am here to help it."[85] Yet, for the First Amendment liberties, Holmes rejected this "pure democracy" approach. He was convinced that the Constitution neither provided nor intended the luxury of such risk in that sphere. Whereas property, to him, was "social" in origin, civil liberties were "human." In full concord with such post-1916 allies as Justices John H. Clarke, Brandeis, Stone, and, on occasion, Hughes,[86] he simply did not consider the average American citizen "very enlightened"—to employ Mr. Justice Jackson's phrase—on the subject of civil rights and liberties. Hence Holmes suggested that judges "should not be too rigidly bound to the tenets of judicial self-restraint in cases involving civil lib-

---

[83] Opinion for the Court in *Dandridge v. Williams,* 397 U.S. 471 (1970), at 487.

[84] As quoted by Charles P. Curtis in *Lions Under the Throne* (Boston: Houghton Mifflin Co., 1947), p. 281.

[85] As told by Francis Biddle in *Justice Holmes, Natural Law, and the Supreme Court* (New York: The Macmillan Co., 1961), p. 9.

[86] Holmes served on the Court from 1902 to 1932; Clarke, 1916–22; Brandeis, 1916–39, Stone, 1925–46 (the last five years as Chief Justice); and Hughes, 1910–16 (Associate Justice) and again 1930–41 (as Chief Justice). See Appendix A.

erties."[87] Or, as New York State Supreme Court Justice Samuel Hofstadter put the general issue: "If a judge loses his capacity for indignation in the presence of injustice, he may not be less of a judge, but he is less of a man."[88]

The above suggested trio[89] of justifications, considered separately and together, states a strong case for the existence of the judicial "double standard." In purely academic terms, the "double standard" may neither be morally nor logically convincing—and it raises very serious, indeed fundamental, questions about the nature of judicial power and that of the judicial process under the American system. Yet it stands as a practical recognition of one of that system's crucial and realistic facets of government and politics under law. Within often ill-defined limits, the case for the special protection of civil rights and liberties is strong.

[87] As asserted by Mr. Chief Justice Stone in a letter to Clinton Rossiter, April 12, 1941, and noted by Alpheus T. Mason in his *Harlan Fiske Stone: Pillar of Law* (New York: Viking Press, 1956), p. 516.

[88] Obituary, *The New York Times,* July 12, 1970, p. 65l.

[89] The three earlier editions of this book (1967, 1972, and 1977, respectively) all argued—albeit in terms of decreasing conviction—for the existence of a *fourth* justification for the application by the judiciary of the described double standard, namely the discrepancy in readily available and effective access to the judicial process, especially to the appellate levels, between economic-proprietarian and civil rights-civil liberties interests, be they on an individual or group level. If, as is patently demonstrable, that was indeed the case throughout the history of our judicial process, it is assuredly no longer. The post-World War II receptiveness by the judiciary to the docketing of allegations of denial of civil rights and liberties, which began to see its day in court under the chief justiceship of Fred M. Vinson (1946–53) and came into full bloom during that of Earl Warren (1953–69), is proof positive of the now well-established ability of once encumbered individuals and groups to be heard at the bar of the courts. This does not, of course, mean that a du Pont firm might not have more financial and personnel clout in fielding legal talent facilely than, say, a member of the Jehovah's Witnesses. But if help is needed, it is clearly available: the plethora of libertarian activist interest groups; public interest attorneys; public defenders; congressionally funded legal aid; and a generally more sympathetic and receptive judiciary have all combined to render unrealistic, indeed inaccurate, a continuing claim for the existence of that fourth factor—although it may command resuscitation.

chapter **III** *The Bill of Rights and*

Its Applicability to the States

The applicability of the Bill of Rights to the several states is an intriguing question laced with some fascinating constitutional history. Insofar as that history is any guide at all, the clear intent of Madison and his supporters in composing and in submitting the Bill of Rights to Congress in April 1789, and in seeing it approved and ratified by the necessary eleven states as the first eight amendments[1] on December 15, 1791, was that it be applicable to the *national* (federal) government. Since the states had their own bills of rights, the over-riding reason for the former's authorship and sponsorship of the federal Bill of Rights was to place demonstrably far-reaching restraints on the fledgling central government.[2] Indeed, the very first phrase of Article One of the approximately twenty-five assorted rights to be found in the 462-word Bill of Rights, is that *"Congress* shall make no law. . . ." The word "Congress" does not, however, reappear in the remainder of the eight articles of amendment, and since much of their language is more general than that of the First, the extent of their reach was bound to be litigated sooner or later.

Historical Background

The question of the applicability of the Bill of Rights to the states was raised theoretically rather quickly by elements of the propertied community. But, appropriately, it remained for Mr. Chief Justice Marshall to be the first to adjudicate the question when, in 1833, at the end of a distinguished and influential career,[3] he wrote the opinion in *Barron v. Baltimore*[4] for a unanimous Court. It has never been overruled *per se.*

---

[1] Or ten, depending upon one's point of view. At least in common parlance, Articles Nine and Ten are viewed as part of the Bill—and they were, indeed, adopted at the same time as the other eight. But their nature and language serve to set them apart.

[2] See the vivid study by Robert A. Rutland, *The Birth of the Bill of Rights, 1776–1791* (New York: Collier Books, 1962).

[3] For an excellent biography of Marshall as Chief Justice, see Albert J. Beveridge, *The Life of John Marshall,* 4 vols. (Boston: Houghton Mifflin Co., 1919).

[4] 7 Peters 243 (1833).

Mr. Chief Justice Marshall and Barron's Wharf. The basis for the litigation in *Barron v. Baltimore* was laid when the City of Baltimore, Maryland, began to pave some of its streets. In so doing its engineers found it necessary to divert several streams from their natural courses; near one, Barron's Wharf, this resulted in deposits of gravel and sand which filled up the channel and prevented the approach of vessels. John Barron's fine wharf, previously the one with the deepest water in the harbor, was thus turned into little more than a useless inlet. Not amused, Mr. Barron obtained eminent legal counsel and went to court. He alleged that Baltimore's actions had violated that clause of the Fifth Amendment of the United States Constitution which expressly proscribes the taking of private property "for public use without just compensation." Although Barron won his argument at the level of the trial court, which awarded him $4500 in damages, his joy was short-lived. Baltimore appealed the verdict to the Maryland State Court of Appeals which reversed the decision. The unhappy Barron then appealed his case to the United States Supreme Court on a writ of error.[5]

Marshall announced that "the question thus presented is, we think, of great importance, but not of much difficulty."[6] In a handful of pages he demolished Barron's fundamental contention that whatever is forbidden by the terms of the Fifth Amendment to the national government is also forbidden to the states and that the Court therefore has an obligation to construe the Fifth's "guarantee in behalf of individual liberty" as a restraint upon *both* state and national governments. The Chief Justice's response was phrased in historical and constitutional terms:

> The Constitution was ordained and established by the people of the United States for themselves, for their own government, and not for the Government of the individual States. Each State established a Constitution for itself, and, in that Constitution, provided such limitations and restrictions on the powers of its particular government as its judgment indicated. The people of the United States framed such a government for the United States as they supposed best adapted to their situation, and best calculated to promote their interests. The powers they conferred on the government were to be exercised by itself; and the limitations on power, if expressed in general terms, are naturally, and, we think, necessarily applicable to the government created by the instrument. They are limitations of power granted in the instrument itself; not of distinct governments, framed by different persons and for different purposes.

---

[5] A discontinued writ. It served to bring the entire record of a case proceeding in a lower court before the Supreme Court for its consideration for alleged "errors of law" committed below.

[6] *Barron v. Baltimore,* 7 Peters 243 (1833). It was the last constitutional law decision in which the great chief justice participated.

If these propositions be correct, the fifth amendment must be understood as restraining the power of the general government, not as applicable to the States. In their several constitutions they have imposed such restrictions on their respective governments as their own wisdom suggested, such as they deemed most proper for themselves. It is a subject on which they judge exclusively, and with which others interfere no further than they are supposed to have a common interest.

. . . These amendments [the Bill of Rights] contain no expression indicating an intention to apply them to the state governments. This court cannot so apply them.

. . . This court . . . has no jurisdiction of the cause; and [it] is dismissed.[7]

Marshall had spoken, Barron had lost, and the Court's unanimous opinion that there was "no repugnancy between the several acts of the general assembly of Maryland . . . and the Constitution of the United States,"[8] became the law of the land. Citizens like Barron were destined to have no further recourse until the ratification in 1868 of the Fourteenth Amendment, probably the most controversial and certainly the most litigated of all amendments adopted since the birth of the Republic.

The Fourteenth Amendment

The Fourteenth Amendment[9] did not in and of itself overturn the *Barron* precedent: men continue to disagree over the purpose of the framers of the Amendment and the extent of its intended application, if any, to the several states. But certain evidence does exist and merits close examination.

Some Historical Facts. The *facts* surrounding the proposal and passage of the Fourteenth Amendment in the 39th Congress (1865–67)—led by the Radical Republicans and their Committee of Fifteen[10]—are fewer than the resultant conjectures and analyses. We do know, however, that: (a) the 52 United States Senators (42 Republicans and 10 Democrats) and 191 Representatives (145 Republicans and 46 Democrats) wanted to do some-

---

[7] *Ibid.,* at 247–48, 250, 251.

[8] *Ibid.,* at 251.

[9] For a collection of fine essays, including one by Mr. Chief Justice Warren, commemorating the Amendment's Centennial in 1968, see Bernard Schwartz, ed., *The Fourteenth Amendment: Centennial Volume* (New York: New York University Press, 1970).

[10] Composed of twelve Republicans and three Democrats, it consisted of nine U.S. Representatives and six U.S. Senators, under the chairmanship of Republican Senator William Fessenden of Maine. It was essentially the congressional "policy committee," whose real leaders comprised four Radical Republicans: Representatives Thaddeus Stevens of Pennsylvania and John A. Bingham of Ohio and Senators Jacob Howard of Michigan and Lyman Trumbull of Illinois.

thing to ameliorate the lot of blacks; (b) *de minimis,* they intended to embody the provisions of the Civil Rights Act of 1866, forbidding "discrimination in civil rights or immunities . . . on account of race" in the Amendment—although *political* rights were excluded from that understanding; (c) at least to some extent, they were concerned with civil rights generally; and (d) they were interested in extending increased protection to property as well as to human rights.[11] We also know that (e) the Amendment was intended to remedy the lack of a "citizenship" clause in the original Constitution—and the initial sentence of the first of its five sections makes this clear: "All persons born or naturalized in the United States, and subject to the jurisdiction thereof, are citizens of the United States and of the State wherein they reside." This, of course, would include blacks. We further know (f) from the language of the last section, number 5, that there was some intention to provide Congress with the necessary power, if not the tools, to enforce the provisions of the Amendment: "The Congress shall have power to enforce, by *appropriate legislation,* the provisions of this article."[12] We also know (g) that, unlike the "privileges or immunities" and "due process of law" clauses, the "equal protection of the laws" clause of the Amendment had no antecedent meaning but originated in the committee that drafted it—which could hardly have foreseen its subsequent controversial history and judicial application. And finally, we know (h) that with respect to the matter of the reach of the Bill of Rights, both the heart and the greatest source of confusion and controversy of the famed Amendment is the well-known phrasing of the second, lengthy sentence of Section 1, which was chiefly composed by Republican Representative John A. Bingham of Ohio:

[11] Historians now generally agree that the word "person" instead of "citizen" was adopted by the Drafting Committee in the "due process" and "equal protection" clauses to extend protection to *corporations* as well as human beings. The Supreme Court officially adopted this point of view in 1886 in *Santa Clara County v. Southern Pacific Railroad,* 118 U.S. 394.

[12] In part thanks to this provision (italics supplied) and, by implication, to the almost identically worded Section 2 of Amendment Fifteen, Congress found authority to enact certain sections of the landmark Civil Rights Act of 1964. One of its most significant sections, that dealing with discrimination in public accommodations, was passed under the congressional power over interstate commerce, and was specifically upheld by the U.S. Supreme Court in December 1964. (See *Heart of Atlanta Motel v. United States,* 379 U.S. 241 and *Katzenbach v. McClung,* 379 U.S. 294.)

Congress also utilized the "appropriate legislation" section of the Fifteenth Amendment to enact portions of the Voting Rights Act of 1965, which met and withstood two constitutional challenges in 1966 on the strength of the section's wording and intent. (See *South Carolina v. Katzenbach,* 383 U.S. 301 and *Katzenbach v. Morgan,* 384 U.S. 641.) The 1970 amendment lowering the voting age to 18, was upheld as to *federal* elections, but struck down as to *state and local* elections in a five-opinion, 184-page decision in *Oregon v. Mitchell,* 400 U.S. 112 (1970). The Twenty-sixth Amendment resulted as a direct consequence.

No State shall make or enforce any law which shall abridge the privileges or immunities of citizens of the United States; *nor shall any State deprive any person of life, liberty, or property, without due process of law;* nor deny to any person within its jurisdiction the equal protection of the laws.[13]

There is no disagreement that the italicized portion of the Fourteenth, which was lifted verbatim from the language of the Fifth Amendment, thus was intended to provide guarantees against *state* infringement supplemental to the Fifth's mandate against federal infringement. What does cause major disagreement, however, can be illustrated by two questions: first, *did* the framers of the Amendment intend to "incorporate" or "nationalize" or "carry over" the entire Bill of Rights through the wording of its "due process of law" clause, thereby making it applicable to the several states;[14] and second, regardless of their intention, *should* the Bill of Rights be applied to the states, given the nature of the rights involved and the demands of the democratic society in which we live?

The Intention of the Framers. The Fourteenth Amendment was passed by Congress on June 16, 1866, ratified by the required three-fourths of the states—ten of these then being Southern Reconstruction governments under duress[15]—and was proclaimed in effect on July 28, 1868. The Amend-

---

[13] Italics supplied.

[14] I realize that to use the terms "incorporation," "nationalization," "application," "carrying over," and "absorption," more or less synonymously and interchangeably is heresy to a good many members of the legal and academic community, if indeed it is not regarded as simply wrong. With all due respect and deference to those who do distinguish between these terms both literally and substantively (see, for example, Mr. Justice Frankfurter's important "Memorandum" described on pages 34 and 35, *infra*), the basic issue involved clearly comes down to the answer to the following crucial question: is a certain provision in the federal Constitution, is a specific right enumerated in the federal Bill of Rights, *applicable to the states* via the "due process" clause of the Fourteenth Amendment or is it *not* applicable? If it is held to be so applicable by the judiciary, then it is "incorporated," "nationalized," "carried over," "applied," or "absorbed." To the affected litigants it does not matter what the process is called—what matters is whether or not it signifies state acquiescence with federal standards. This is not to say, of course, that I do not recognize basic historical and linguistic distinctions between the concepts of "incorporation" and "absorption," for example; and I have been fascinated and intrigued by the long-standing controversies that have engulfed them. But, given the judicio-legal developments of the past two or three decades, e.g., the 1965 decision in the *Connecticut Birth Control* case (*Griswold v. Connecticut,* 381 U.S. 479, discussed at length, on pp. 71–75, *infra*), the distinctions are blurred. What matters constitutionally, to repeat, is whether a federal provision or standard, as interpreted and declared by the Court, does or does not apply to the states.

[15] By March 1, 1867, there were 37 states in the Union including those of the old Confederacy. This meant that 28 would have to ratify the Amendment to bring it into effect. But by that time only 20 states had ratified, among them Tennessee as the sole Southern state. Consequently, the congressional Radicals passed a law which in fact put the Southern states on notice that they would not be readmitted to the Union "officially," unless they: (1) ratified the Fourteenth Amendment, and (2) extended the vote to adult males "of whatever race, color, or previous condition." This

ment had significant political overtones, for it was the key plank of the first Reconstruction platform drafted by the Radical Republicans, led by Thaddeus Stevens of Pennsylvania, Roscoe Conkling of New York, and George Boutwell of Massachusetts. Indeed, the Amendment's passage by Congress in June 1866 provided the Radical Republicans with a welcome, ready-made campaign issue for the November 1866 election campaigns. Attention directed to the Amendment was almost wholly concerned with the political implications of bestowing full citizenship upon the Negro. But there is no record of any campaign discussion or analysis of the matter of the application of the Bill of Rights to the states via its "due process of law" or any other clause. There was much talk of the Amendment giving teeth to the Thirteenth Amendment and securing the "fundamental rights and fundamental freedoms of all men."[16]

In the face of the many disagreements on the "intent" of the framers, some argue that their intent no longer matters, for the "felt necessities of the time" (Mr. Justice Holmes's celebrated phrase) and the inevitable growth of the Constitution, may *a fortiori* dictate the application of the Bill of Rights to the several states regardless of the framers' intention. However, since it is preferable to have historical data to back one's contentions, both the proponents and opponents of total or even partial incorporation continue to invoke history. A great deal of published research on historical justification is available, yet there is no conclusive answer, for the evidence is not persuasive. Originally, those opposing the incorporation interpretation enjoyed a slight edge. Briefly, they contended that had the framers of the Fourteenth Amendment intended to "incorporate" or "carry over" or "nationalize" the Bill of Rights to the states, they would have said so specifically rather than in the general language of the "due process of law" clause. The proponents, on the other hand, argued, and continue to argue, that the famous clause was adopted as "shorthand" for the Bill of Rights, and that the framers utilized it both to broaden and to strengthen fundamental guarantees of rights and liberties. It is still possible

---

resulted in action by a sufficient number of Southern states, where federal troops still attested to the Reconstruction era. President Johnson vetoed the act, but Congress passed it over his veto. The law accomplished its purpose: between April and July 1868 the legislatures of Arkansas, Florida, North Carolina, Louisiana, South Carolina, Alabama, and Georgia acquiesced and the necessary figure (28) had been attained. (Actually, in the interim New Jersey and Ohio had withdrawn their earlier ratifications—something they might no longer be able to do today, given the implications of the Supreme Court's 1939 decision in *Coleman v. Miller,* 307 U.S. 433—but Massachusetts, Nebraska, and Iowa had come aboard. Moreover, the Secretary of State *disregarded* the former two states' withdrawal votes and proclaimed the Amendment in effect, with Congress supporting his action by adopting a concurrent resolution to that effect.)

[16] The quotation is from a speech by Representative Lyman Trumbull of Pennsylvania.

to emerge with diverse conclusions, particularly in the light of the lengthy and heated congressional debates on the subject. What is certain is that since the Supreme Court first "incorporated" aspects of the Bill of Rights in 1925,[17] the process has been sporadic; but it proved to be increasingly embracing as well as continuous over the next four decades—although it may well now have run its course.

Some Protagonists. The earliest spokesman for total incorporation of the Bill of Rights was Mr. Justice John Marshall Harlan (1877–1911), but his was a lonely voice. In his 34-year career on the highest bench,[18] time and again Harlan unsuccessfully championed that interpretation.[19] He was not even partially vindicated until 1925 when Mr. Justice Edward T. Sanford delivered his dictum in *Gitlow v. New York*[20]—albeit a case could arguably be made for the contention that the concept of *eminent domain* was applied formally to the states via Amendment Fourteen in a Harlan opinion in 1897.[21] And as late as 1947 in the famous *Adamson* case,[22] Mr. Justice Frankfurter rejected the concept of incorporation as one manufactured out of whole cloth. Both the concept itself and the term "incorporation" were anathema to him. Indeed, his last publication before his death was an attack on "incorporation" and a defense of "absorption."[23] As he put it in a well-known passage:

> Of all these [43] judges [of the Supreme Court who passed on the question of incorporating the Bill of Rights via the "due process of law" clause of Amendment Fourteen] only one, *who may respectfully be called an eccen-*

[17] See text on p. 34 and fn. 21, *infra,* relative to the one earlier (1897) incorporation, i.e., of *eminent domain* guarantees.

[18] Harlan served longer than any other except Mr. Justice William O. Douglas (1939–75), Mr. Justice Stephen J. Field (1863–97), Mr. Chief Justice Marshall (1801–35), and Mr. Justice Black (1937–71).

[19] See, for example, his solo dissenting opinions in *Hurtado v. California,* 110 U.S. 516 (1884); *Maxwell v. Dow,* 176 U.S. 581 (1900); and *Twining v. New Jersey,* 211 U.S. 78 (1908). There were several others—he was a consistent advocate. See my "John Marshall Harlan: The Justice and the Man," 46 *Kentucky Law Journal* 448 (Spring 1958), especially pp. 469–70.

[20] 268 U.S. 652. Gitlow lost, but the carry-over principle was given its first public judicial notice. See pp. 61 ff., *infra.*

[21] *Chicago, Burlington & Quincy RR v. Chicago,* 166 U.S. 226. Yet in footnote four in his landmark *Palko* decision (see pp. 66 ff., *infra*) Mr. Justice Cardozo suggested that its inclusion—like that of others—was due *not* to its enumeration in the Bill of Rights, but because it is "included in the conception of 'due process of law.' " However that may be, some observers, including Mr. Justice Tom Clark, concluded that, in effect, the Harlan opinion in *Chicago, Burlington* "completely undermined" *Hurtado v. California,* 110 U.S. 516 (1884)—see pp. 57 ff., *infra*—although clearly not overruling it, and thus "laid the basis for *Gitlow v. New York.*" Yet while that was important, it was not the gravamen of the Court's intention: its overarching concern lay with the strengthening of the constitutional protection of property rights.

[22] *Adamson v. California,* 332 U.S. 46 (1947).

[23] "Memorandum on 'Incorporation' of the Bill of Rights into the Due Process Clause of the Fourteenth Amendment," 78 *Harvard Law Review* 746–83 (1965).

tric exception, ever indicated the belief that the Fourteenth Amendment was a shorthand summary of the first eight Amendments, theretofore limiting only the Federal Government, and that due process incorporated those eight Amendments as restrictions upon the powers of the States.[24]

The "eccentric exception" was, of course, Harlan—whose grandson by the same name became a Frankfurter ally on the incorporation question when he joined the Court as President Eisenhower's second appointee in 1954.[25]

Adamson v. California. It was Mr. Justice Black who became the leading proponent of incorporation—and he seized upon the aforementioned case of *Adamson v. California* to expound his views. At issue, briefly, was a provision of California law that permitted court and counsel to comment upon the failure of a defendant to explain or deny evidence against him, thus allowing the court and the jury to consider it in reaching a verdict. Admiral Dewey Adamson, under sentence of death for first degree and burglary murder and with past convictions for burglary, larceny, and robbery,[26] not only called no witnesses in his behalf but chose not to take the stand during his trial, a decision on which both the trial judge and the prosecuting attorney commented adversely. (Such comments have been statutorily proscribed on the *federal* level since 1878.) In his appeals, Adamson argued that the California law put him into an impossible situation: if he testified, the previous convictions would thus be revealed to the jury; and if he did not, comments by the judge and prosecutor would, in effect, convert his silence into a confession of guilt. (Only a few other states permitted the California procedure at the time.) In short, he claimed that the adverse comments by the two officials violated his constitutional privilege against compulsory self-incrimination under the Fifth Amendment of the federal Constitution, which he deemed incorporated and hence applicable to the states under the "due process of law" clause of the Fourteenth. He ultimately lost 5:4 at the bar of the Supreme Court. In an opinion written by Mr. Justice Stanley F. Reed, and joined by Mr. Chief Justice Vinson, and Associate Justices Robert H. Jackson and Harold H. Burton, the high tribunal held that the self-incrimination clause of the Fifth was *not* incorporated or applicable and that the State of California "may control such a situation in accordance with its own ideas of the most efficient administration of criminal justice."[27] Mr. Justice Frankfurter provided the decisive

[24] *Adamson v. California, op. cit.,* at 62. (Italics supplied.)

[25] Eisenhower's first appointee was Earl Warren to succeed the deceased Mr. Chief Justice Fred M. Vinson in 1953.

[26] Adamson had a highly prolific and interesting prison record, involving hobbies that included collecting the tops of women's stockings.

[27] *Adamson v. California,* 332 U.S. 46, at 57. (But see pp. 67–68, *infra,* for its overruling in 1964). Adamson was executed in St. Quentin's gas chamber at the end of 1949, following several additional unsuccessful appeals.

fifth vote in a long concurring opinion in which, as noted above, he took specific issue with the heart of Mr. Justice Black's dissenting opinion.

In his dissent, supported by a 33-page appendix that quoted extensively from the congressional debates involving Amendment Fourteen, Black was joined wholly by Mr. Justice Douglas and, in part, by Justices Murphy and Rutledge (who both, as we shall see later, wanted to go even beyond the Black position on incorporation—as indeed Douglas ultimately did, too). Black's opinion remains the most celebrated analysis of the intention of the framers of Section 1. Elaborately researched, it insisted that one of the chief objects to be accomplished by the first section of the Fourteenth Amendment, "separately, and as a whole,"[28] was to apply the *entire* Bill of Rights to the states. In his own words:

> My study of the historical events that culminated in the Fourteenth Amendment, and the expressions of those who opposed its submission and passage, persuades me that one of the chief objects that the provisions of the Amendment's first section, separately, and as a whole, were intended to accomplish was to make the Bill of Rights applicable to the states. With full knowledge of the *Barron* decision, the framers and backers of the Fourteenth Amendment proclaimed its purpose to be to overturn the constitutional rule that case had announced. This historical purpose had never received full consideration or expression in any opinion of this Court interpreting the Amendment. . . .[29]

Responding to Mr. Justice Frankfurter's contrary views and call for more demonstrable proof (where Frankfurter believed none existed) Black observed: "I cannot consider the Bill of Rights to be an outworn Eighteenth Century 'straight jacket.' . . ." and concluded:

> I believe [that] the original purpose of the Fourteenth Amendment [was] to extend to all the people of the nation the complete protection of the Bill of Rights. To hold that this Court can determine what, if any, provisions of the Bill of Rights will be enforced, and if so to what degree, is to frustrate the great design of a written Constitution.[30]

Mr. Justice Black, in his almost three and a half decades on the Supreme Court, never wavered from these basic convictions—convictions buttressed by the expansive support extended to them by Professor W. W. Crosskey

[28] *Ibid.*, at 71. Periodically Black made clear that, notwithstanding his emphasis on certain occasions on one or the other of the specific sentences and phrases composing Section 1 of the Fourteenth Amendment, that Amendment "*as a whole* makes the Bill of Rights applicable to the States. This would certainly include the language of the Privileges or Immunities Clause as well as the Due Process Clause." (From his 1968 concurring opinion in *Duncan v. Louisiana*, 391 U.S. 145, at 166, n. 1.)

[29] *Adamson v. California, op. cit.*, at 71–72.

[30] *Ibid.*, at 89.

of the University of Chicago in a major essay a few years after *Adamson*.[31] His staunchest historical-constitutional ally has been Professor Horace Flack. After a careful study of the debates of the 39th Congress, their newspaper coverage, and the election speeches of members of Congress in the fall of 1866, Flack concluded that Congress

> had the following objects and motives in view for submitting the First Section of the Fourteenth to the states for ratification. First, to make the National Bill of Rights applicable to the states; secondly, to give constitutional validity to the Civil Rights Act [of 1866]; and thirdly, to declare who were the citizens of the United States.[32]

Black's opinion was soon challenged in almost every detail by Professor Charles Fairman of the Harvard Law School, a leading expert on constitutional law, in an article in the *Stanford Law Review*.[33] Fairman accused Black of deliberate distortion of the verities of the debates in the 39th Congress to prove his point. In a companion article in the same issue,[34] Professor Stanley Morrison, of the Stanford University School of Law, seconded Fairman's rejection of Black's thesis. But Morrison did so with considerably less vehemence, and not so much on the basis of what was said during the congressional debates as on the strength of the judicial history of the clause following the Amendment's adoption. Noting that only the elder Harlan had consistently supported Black's incorporation interpretation, Morrison sided with Frankfurter's analysis and statistics in his concurring opinion in the *Adamson* case.[35] He refers to the refusal of such "libertarian activist" justices as Holmes, Brandeis, Stone, Hughes [sic], and Cardozo to incorporate the Bill of Rights and *seems* to score a telling point by recalling that Black himself did not dissent from, or write a separate concurring opinion to, Cardozo's famous majority opinion in the 1937 *Palko* case[36] (see pp. 56 ff., *infra*). That Cardozo opinion established a hierarchy of basic human rights which would henceforth be considered applicable to the states via Amendment Fourteen—namely, those "implicit in the concept of ordered liberty"—while at the same time establishing a *non-applicable* group.[37]

---

[31] "Charles Fairman, 'Legislative History,' and the Constitutional Limits on State Authority," 22 *University of Chicago Law Review* 1 (1954).

[32] Horace Flack, *The Adoption of the Fourteenth Amendment* (Baltimore: The Johns Hopkins University Press, 1908), p. 94.

[33] "Does the Fourteenth Amendment Incorporate the Bill of Rights? The Original Understanding," 2 *Stanford Law Review* 5 (December 1949).

[34] "Does the Fourteenth Amendment Incorporate the Bill of Rights? The Judicial Interpretation," *ibid.*, p. 140.

[35] *Adamson v. California, op. cit.*

[36] *Palko v. Connecticut,* 302 U.S. 319.

[37] Among the latter were the Fifth Amendment's safeguards against double jeopardy (at issue in *Palko*) and compulsory self-incrimination (at issue in *Adamson*).

It is only fair to note at once here in Black's defense, however, that (a) he had just joined the Court a few weeks earlier; (b) thus he might well have believed that it would be ungracious as well as foolhardy to proclaim a new jurisprudential posture; (c) the Cardozo majority opinion did, after all, announce the incorporation of the most precious of all basic human freedoms, notably First Amendment rights; and (d) as Black himself had explained in his *Adamson* dissent: "[I]f the choice must be between the selective process of the *Palko* decision applying some of the Bill of Rights to the States, or the *Twining* rule applying none of them, I would choose the *Palko* selective process."[38] He reiterated in a footnote to his dissent in *Griswold v. Connecticut* twenty-eight years after *Palko,* that he "agreed to follow" the Palko rule as a second-best method to "make [at least some of the] Bill of Rights safeguards applicable to the States."[39] Although not as dramatically critical as Fairman, Morrison does suggest that Black clearly had an ulterior motive in his interpretation of the events surrounding the framing of the Fourteenth Amendment: the establishing of a rule of law for civil rights and liberties that would be both drastic and simple and that would guarantee certainty for all future litigation, the carrying-over *in toto* of the Bill of Rights via Amendment Fourteen, through either its "due process" or its "privileges or immunities" clause.

A sixth protagonist, Professor J. B. James of Georgia Wesleyan College, in his 1956 book *The Framing of the Fourteenth Amendment,*[40] agrees with Fairman and Morrison that Black's facile and sweeping interpretation of the congressional debates of 1866 is erroneous—but only *because* it is so sweeping and facile! With some reservations, James does share Black's and Flack's conclusion that, on balance, the Amendment's framers did intend to incorporate the Bill of Rights. Although such a thought may have been entirely foreign to the collective majority who supported its passage, James, as did Flack—and Professor Jacobus ten Broek, who shares most of James's views on the entire matter[41]—presents strong evidence that the Amendment's floor managers indeed intended its incorporation.[42] This is particularly true of Representative Bingham, the author of the pertinent provisions of Section 1, whom Black called "without extravagance . . . the Madison of [that section] of the Fourteenth Amendment."[43] Contrary

---

[38] *Adamson v. California, op. cit.,* at 89. He restated this position two decades later, one of the last times he spoke on "incorporation." (*Duncan v. Louisiana,* 391 U.S. 145 [1968], at 171.)

[39] 381 U.S. 479, at 526, n. 21.

[40] (Urbana: University of Illinois Press.)

[41] See Jacobus ten Broek, *The Antislavery Origins of the Fourteenth Amendment* (Berkeley: University of California Press, 1951): "The rights sought to be protected," he asserted severally, "were men's natural rights, some of which are mentioned in the first eight amendments and some of which are not" (e.g., at 223).

[42] E.g., James *op. cit.,* pp. 85, 130 ff.

[43] *Adamson v. California, op. cit.,* at 74.

to James's and other earlier belief, we now know that, significantly, Bingham *was* fully aware of the Supreme Court's decision in *Barron v. Baltimore*[44] when he led the debates on Amendment Fourteen in House.[45] As a matter of fact, it was this ruling, he said, which made necessary "the adopting of the [Fourteenth] Amendment."[46] Certain in his belief that the Bill of Rights was designed to be *national* in scope, Bingham argued on the floor that had the 39th Congress meant the Bill of Rights to be solely applicable to the *federal* government, the wording of the Amendment's Section 1 would have so stated. James demonstrates quite convincingly that when Bingham and Republican Senator Jacob M. Howard of Michigan, the Amendment's floor manager in the upper house, spoke of the "fundamental rights of free men," they specifically meant the Bill of Rights. They wanted the proposed Amendment to overrule *Barron v. Baltimore!*

Senator Howard, in fact, clearly insisted that the national Bill of Rights *in its entirety* was incorporated into Section 1, a section that in his judgment embodied not only the "privileges and immunities" of Article Four, Paragraph 2, of the Constitution, but also all those rights guaranteed by the first eight amendments to the Constitution. Thus, in explaining the contents of the Amendment, he stated: "To these privileges and immunities [Art. Four, ¶2], whatever they may be for they are not and cannot be fully defined . . . to these should be added the personal rights guaranteed and secured by the first eight amendments to the Constitution." Enumerating these, he continued:

> [T]hese are secured to citizens solely as citizens of the United States, . . . they do not operate in the slightest degree as restraints or prohibitions upon state legislation. . . . *The great object of the first section of this amendment is, therefore, to restrain the power of the states and compel them at all times to respect these fundamental guarantees.*[47]

Nonetheless, Professor Fairman, with some support from Professor Morison, still insists that the use of the phrases "fundamental rights" or "fundamental guarantees" was specifically intended to *exclude* the Bill of

[44] 7 Peters 243 (1833).

[45] See *Congressional Globe,* 39th Cong., 1st Sess. (Washington, D.C.: Blair and Rives, 1866), pp. 1088–90.

[46] *Ibid.,* p. 1089. In 1871, during a debate on the now ratified Amendment, Bingham observed that in 1865–66 he had closely "re-examined" Marshall's decision in *Barron,* wherein the Chief Justice had stated that "had the framers of these Amendments [I–VIII] intended them to be limitations on the power of state governments, they would have imitated the framers of the Original Constitution and have expressed their intention." Bingham then significantly added, "acting upon this suggestion I did imitate the framers of the Original Constitution." *The Globe,* 42nd Cong., 1st Sess., 1871, Appendix, p. 150.

[47] *The Globe, op. cit.,* 39th Cong., p. 2765. (Italics supplied.)

Rights. Fairman does admit that Senator Howard expressly stated that the "privileges or immunities" clause of Section 1 of the Fourteenth should be construed as embracing what Howard termed "the personal rights" of the first eight amendments of the Bill of Rights. But Fairman insists that Bingham merely "talked around the point." Fairman's position received highly vocal support in 1977 with the publication of Professor Raoul Berger's fascinatingly controversial *Government by Judiciary: The Transformation of the Fourteenth Amendment.*[48] Berger concludes that his study of the "debates of the history of the period leads [him] fully to concur with Fairman," quoting approvingly Fairman's statement that the "freedom that states traditionally have exercised to develop their own systems of administering justice repels any thought that . . . Congress would . . . have attempted [to incorporate] . . . the country would not have stood for it, the legislatures would not have ratified."[49] The historians Kelly and Harbison, on the other hand, side with James's, Crosskey's, and Black's historical (and, incidentally, Black's constitutional) interpretation, and state flatly that Bingham and Howard not only agreed that the "privileges or immunities" clause "incorporated the entire federal Bill of Rights as a limitation upon the states," but that the "due process" clause was lifted from the Fifth Amendment and thus "became a guarantee against state action."[50] And independent scholarly investigations by such knowledgeable legal commentators as Louis Henkin, Frank Walker, and Michael Curtis agree that there remains no genuine doubt that the framers of Amendment Fourteen intended it as a lever for the application of the Bill of Rights to the several states of the Union—with Curtis penning a learned point-by-point rebuttal of Raoul Berger's historical arguments.[51]

A Verdict? Regardless of personal intellectual and emotional commitments on the basic question of incorporation, the various positions indicate how speculative history can be and may become. The German historian Leopold von Ranke's exhortation that it is essential to determine *"wie es eigentlich gewesen"* ("how it actually was") is noble and human, but at times futile. However, such evidence as the history of the debates provides seems to substantiate Professor James's basic point that we need not accept Mr. Justice Black's expansive evaluation of the events of the

48 (Cambridge: Harvard University Press), Ch. 8, "Incorporation of the Bill of Rights in the Fourteenth Amendment," pp. 134–156.

49 *Ibid.,* p. 156.

50 Alfred H. Kelly and Winfred A. Harbison. *The American Constitution: Its Origin and Development,* 4th ed. (New York: W. W. Norton and Co., 1970), p. 463.

51 Louis Henkin, "Selective Incorporation in the Fourteenth Amendment," 73 *Yale Law Journal* 74 (1963); Frank H. Walker, Jr., "Constitutional Law—Was It Intended that the Fourteenth Amendment Incorporates the Bill of Rights?" 42 *North Carolina Law Review* 925 (1964); and Michael Kent Curtis, "The Bill of Rights as a Limitation on State Authority: A Reply to Professor Berger," 16 *Wake Forest Law Review* 1 (1980). John Hart Ely concludes "this is an argument no one can win."

39th Congress to side with his basic conclusion: there seems little doubt that the Amendment's principal framers and managers, Representative Bingham and Senator Howard, if not every member of the majority in the two houses of Congress, did believe the Bill of Rights to be made generally applicable to the several states via Section 1. And *no* member of that Congress, before he voted on the Amendment, contradicted Bingham's and Howard's final statements to that extent.[52]

This conclusion does not, however, necessitate concurrence with the matter of the *wisdom* of such an incorporation, nor with the judicial formulae devised therefore.[53] Nor does it gainsay the fact that when Senator Howard's "privileges or immunities" clause (and his and Representative Bingham's incorporation contentions for it) had its first judicial test in the *Slaughterhouse Cases*[54] a mere five years after the adoption of the Fourteenth Amendment, it sustained a crushing and lasting defeat.

The Slaughterhouse Cases of 1873. These remarkable cases, also referred to as the "Dual Citizenship" cases, delivered the second of the one-two knockout punches to the theory of a national applicability of the Bill of Rights, the first such punch being *Barron v. Baltimore* forty years earlier. It will be recalled that in *Barron* the unanimous Court had ruled that the Bill was *not* applicable to the several states, either by expressed or by implied language. The *Slaughterhouse Cases* not only reconfirmed the *Barron* holding but went considerably further by ruling that the "privileges or immunities" ("P or I") clause of the Fourteenth Amendment did not, and was not intended to, protect the rights of *state* citizenship, but solely those of *federal* citizenship. In the words of this never-to-date overruled decision written for the narrow 5:4 majority[55] by Mr. Justice Samuel F. Miller of

---

[52] Flack, *op. cit.*, pp. 81, 87. On the entire controversy, see also Ch. 3, "The Nationalization of the Bill of Rights," of Arthur A. North, S.J., *The Supreme Court: Judicial Process and Judicial Politics* (New York: Appleton-Century-Crofts, 1966). For its specific relevance to the desegregation-segregation issues of the 1950s and 1960s, see the lengthy and learned essay, "The Original Understanding and the Segregation Decision," by Alexander M. Bickel in his *Politics and the Warren Court* (New York: Harper & Row, 1965), pp. 221–61. Bickel's conclusion is that the authors of the Fourteenth Amendment ultimately chose language which would be capable of growth. It follows that "the record of history, properly understood, left the way open to, in fact invited, a decision based on the moral and material state of the Union in 1954, not 1877" (p. 261). For an intriguing complementary—and wholly different—analysis of the intentions of Bingham (and Senator Roscoe Conkling), namely, that the due process of law clause was drafted to "take in the whole range of national economy," making *corporations* among the intended beneficiaries of the draft, see Howard Jay Graham, "The Conspiracy Theory of the Fourteenth Amendment," 47 *Yale Law Journal* 371 (1938), and Charles A. and Mary R. Beard, *The Rise of American Civilization* (New York: The Macmillan Co., 1927).

[53] See pp. 83 ff., *infra*.

[54] *The Butchers' Benevolent Association of New Orleans v. Crescent City Live-Stock Landing and Slaughter-House Co.*, 16 Wallace 36 (1873).

[55] With Miller were Associate Justices Nathan Clifford (Maine), David Davis (Illinois), William Strong (Pennsylvania), and Ward Hunt (New York).

Iowa by way of Kentucky: "It is quite clear, then, that *there is a citizenship of the United States, and a citizenship of a state, which are distinct from each other,* and which depend upon different characteristics or circumstances in the individual."[56] Thus the "citizens" protected by the "P or I" clause of Amendment Fourteen are such "citizens" only in their capacity as "citizens of the United States," *not* in their capacity or role as *"state* citizens."

The cases had arisen as a result of a statute regulating the livestock slaughtering business, which had been enacted by the Louisiana Reconstruction government in 1867. In the law, its "carpetbag"[57] legislature (unquestionably under corrupt influence) had conferred upon a single firm what, to all intents and purposes, constituted a monopoly of the New Orleans slaughterhouse business, preventing some one thousand firms and persons already established in the city from continuing in that activity. A number of the adversely affected parties filed suit in the courts of Louisiana, basing their complaint largely on alleged violation of their rights under the Fourteenth Amendment. Losing in the lower courts, they ultimately reached the State Supreme Court, which was equally unsympathetic to their claim and held that the contested Louisiana law was a valid and legal exercise of the state police power.[58] The aggrieved litigants then appealed to the United States Supreme Court.

Although four main constitutional issues were raised by the opponents of the Louisiana monopoly statute, the chief concern of the Court in its majority opinion was with the appellants' crucial contention that the law constituted a *prima facie* violation of that portion of Section 1 of Amendment Fourteen which states that "No State shall make or enforce any law which shall abridge the privileges or immunities of citizens of the United States. . . ."[59] In other words, the basic claim of the aggrieved businessmen was that the quoted clause clearly implied, indeed commanded, the protection of all civil rights and liberties *by the federal government* and that the several states could not, on pain of violating the Fourteenth Amendment, deny or abridge any rights accruing to citizens of the United States residing within their borders.

[56] *Op. cit.,* at 74. (Italics supplied.)

[57] "Carpetbagger" denotes a Northerner who went South after the Civil War to obtain office or employment by morally questionable and often corrupt methods.

[58] Accruing to the states under Article Ten of the Bill of Rights, the "police power" is generally regarded as embracing and extending to these concepts of state authority: (1) health, (2) welfare, (3) morals, (4) safety, (5) regulation of business (and labor and agricultural) activities.

[59] The other three were that the statute (1) created an "involuntary servitude" forbidden by Amendment Thirteen, (2) denied the appellants the "equal protection of the laws" under Amendment Fourteen, and (3) deprived them of their property "without due process of law," also safeguarded by Fourteen.

But the majority of five justices rejected this contention out of hand. They would have no part of this, or any related, notion of incorporating, of "carrying over," the prerogatives of the Bill of Rights so as to make them applicable to the states. Moreover, the Miller decision absolved the federal government from any obligation to protect "privileges or immunities" against state violation, a logical induction from the Court majority's basic premise that the *states* had the obligation to protect not only the rights guaranteed by their own bills of rights but the entire body of rights and liberties under the common law.

In short, the majority's decision meant that the "privileges or immunities" clause of the newly enacted Amendment really *meant nothing at all* in so far as the states were concerned. As has been well pointed out by one close student of the *Slaughterhouse Cases,* the Court's distinction between state and national citizenship made of the "P or I" clause a mere tautology since the rights of "citizens in the several states" could never have been *constitutionally* abridged by any state anyway. Thus, "the labors of the framers of the Fourteenth Amendment were nullified by a few strokes of Mr. Justice Miller's pen."[60] But *why?* The question is a natural one, given the history of the adoption of the Amendment (no matter which version) and the general acquaintance of all the justices with the activities and debates in the 39th Congress. In the opinion of most competent observers, the Court majority was simply unwilling to permit such a far-reaching alteration in the turbulent, beleaguered antebellum federal system—the relation of state and federal governments—by an "ambiguous" amendment to the Constitution.[61] Consequently, the majority of five expounded the at least plausible conception of dual citizenship, by which practically all common private rights were removed from the federal sphere of control. The majority also believed (and this idea was widely held at the time, as we have noted) that the overriding, if not the sole, purpose of Amendment Fourteen was the protection of blacks in exercising their *civil,* although not their political, rights.

But what, then, about existing "privileges or immunities" of *national* citizenship, which, by its own admission and by its creation of a "dual citizenship" the majority held to be protected against action by state governments, too? The Miller opinion avoided precise definitions and limits, but, quoting from an 1868 opinion written by himself,[62] it suggested the appropriateness of the following "rights" of the national citizen as *bona fide* "privileges or immunities":

[60] Loren P. Beth, "The Slaughterhouse Cases—Revisited," 23 *Louisiana Law Review* 487 (April 1963), at 492.

[61] See *ibid.,* at 493. This is also C. Vann Woodward's view in his *Reunion and Reaction* (New York: Doubleday Anchor, 1956).

[62] *Crandall v. Nevada,* 6 Wallace 36.

To come to the seat of government to assert any claim he may have upon that government, to transact any business he may have with it, to seek its protection, to share its offices, to engage in administering its functions . . . of free access to its seaports . . . to the subtreasuries, land offices, and courts of justice in the several states . . . to demand the care and protection of the Federal government over his life, liberty, and property when on the high seas or within the jurisdiction of a foreign government . . . the writ of habeas corpus . . . to use the navigable waters of the United States, however they may penetrate the territory of the several States. . . .[63]

Also on Miller's list, significantly re-emphasized as "rights of the citizen guaranteed by the *Federal* Constitution," were the "right[s] to peaceable assembly and petition for redress of grievances. . . ."[64] This represents, of course, a line of reasoning typical of the non-incorporation argument, then and today: that the Fourteenth Amendment extended no "rights" to citizens of the United States; that most of their rights had the same status as before, existing under *state* protection rather than national protection; that the "citizens" presumably protected by the P or I clause are "citizens" only in the sense that they are "citizens" of the United States—emphatically not in their capacity as *state* citizens.[65] As pointed out before, this kind of reasoning renders the Fourteenth Amendment useless as a legal tool, for no state could ever *constitutionally* abridge or deny the rights of "citizens in the several states." Thus, all that seemed to remain of the Amendment, given the majority's reasoning in the *Slaughterhouse Cases* a mere handful of years after its birth, was a vague, generally accepted understanding that it was intended to bring about citizenship for the Negro. In one participant's views, the Court's construction of the P or I clause had reduced it to "a vain and idle enactment."[66]

Of the three dissenting opinions by Associate Justices Noah H. Swayne— who pointedly accused the Court majority of having turned "what was

[63] *The Slaughterhouse Cases*, 16 Wallace 36 (1873), at 73–75. These rights had been originally identified as "privileges or immunities" in Mr. Justice Bushrod Washington's opinion in *Corfield v. Coryell*, 6 F. Cas. 546.

[64] *Ibid.* Depending upon one's interpretation, "the right peaceably to assemble was one of the "privileges or immunities" of United States citizenship reconfirmed three years later in *United States v. Cruikshank*, 92 U.S. 542. But in the key aspect of its holding by Mr. Chief Justice Waite, *Cruikshank* declared that Fourteen "adds nothing to the rights of one citizen as against another. It simply furnishes a federal guarantee against any encroachment by the States upon the fundamental rights which belong to every citizen as a member of society." (At 554.)

[65] James Wilson, one of Pennsylvania's delegates to the Constitutional Convention of 1787, had made a point of calling the attention of his fellow delegates to the fact that the Constitution, if ratified, would create a dual citizenship—but the significance of this was both overlooked and misunderstood.

[66] Mr. Justice Field's categorization, dissenting in the *Slaughterhouse Cases, op. cit.,* at 96.

meant for bread into a stone"[67]—Stephen J. Field, and Joseph P. Bradley, the most important was Field's, in which Mr. Chief Justice Salmon P. Chase concurred.[68] Although Field had begun his long judicial career with a general inclination in favor of individual rights, this bias ultimately resolved itself into a "special emphasis on the sanctity of economic freedom."[69] Field's *Slaughterhouse* dissent is therefore deceptive in its overall implications, for it does argue angrily for an interpretation of the Fourteenth Amendment and its P or I clause that would insist upon man's "fundamental rights, privileges, and immunities which belong to him as a free man and a free citizen."[70] To Field, the citizenship clause made state citizenship both subordinate to and derivative of national citizenship. As a result of Section 1 of Amendment Fourteen, he argued, "a citizen of a state is now only a citizen of the United States *residing* in that state."[71] But Field's cardinal argument against the majority decision was based not so much on the cause of basic human freedoms as it was on the doctrine of vested property rights—a cause he was to espouse throughout his long tenure with consistency, self-assurance, and emotion. For Field, *the* "privilege" and/or "immunity" that was at issue here was the absolute right to engage in the business of butchering. Louisiana's statutory interference with that right was to Field the crime *par excellence* of a governmental roadblock in the path of Darwinian-Spencerian economics.[72] For him, as McCloskey observed, "the property right is the transcendent value; political ambition ranks next when it is relevant; and the cause of human or civil rights is subordinate to these higher considerations."[73] Field's dissenting opinion was thus of but limited comfort to those who looked toward a

[67] *The Slaughterhouse Cases, op. cit.,* at 129.

[68] Field, whose longevity in service on the Court—almost 35 years—stood as a record until Douglas overtook him in 1975—will be remembered in the annals of constitutional law and development primarily as the "spokesman of rugged American individualism and laissez faire." (Rocco J. Tresolini, *American Constitutional Law,* 2nd ed. [New York: The Macmillan Co., 1965], p. 742.) Field had served on the California Supreme Court for six and a half years before his promotion by President Lincoln in 1863 to the U.S. Supreme Court.

[69] Robert G. McCloskey, *American Conservatism in the Age of Enterprise* (Cambridge: Harvard University Press, 1951), pp. 122–23.

[70] *The Slaughterhouse Cases, op. cit.,* at 95.

[71] *Ibid.* (Italics supplied.)

[72] Oversimplified, perhaps, this was Field's philosophy of the survival of the fittest in terms of classical nineteenth-century capitalism.

[73] McCloskey, *op. cit.,* pp. 122–23. A considerably more charitable view of Field's stance is taken by Arthur A. North, S.J., in *The Supreme Court: Judicial Process and Judicial Politics* (New York: Appleton-Century-Crofts, 1966), pp. 91–96. He flatly states that not only Harlan but Field and Brewer "accepted the theory" of incorporation (North, p. 96). North appears to have arrived at that conclusion chiefly because of Field's posture in the 1892 case of *O'Neil v. Vermont* (see footnotes 74–76 and text, pp. 45–47). But Field resigned from the Court five years later and his nephew Brewer, a fellow-dissenter—as was Harlan, of course—changed his views on the matter, with only Harlan thus remaining as an "incorporationist."

"nationalization" of basic human rights and liberties. When he spoke of the "equality of right" to labor freely, he looked toward that period of half a century when the Supreme Court would strike hard at any legislative (and administrative) action it deemed violative of the sanctity of property, and of the "freedom of contract" concept it was soon to read into the "due process of law" clause of both the Fifth and the Fourteenth Amendments.[74] Except for a handful of instances,[75] and particularly when they involved a charge against a state of "cruel and unusual" punishment,[76] Field found no such justification for protection of the basic freedoms of the Bill of Rights, however—and he was clearly disdainful of his long-time colleague John Marshall Harlan's advocacy of total incorporation. Indeed, when the Court, seven years after *Slaughterhouse,* held unconstitutional racially-based discrimination in jury impanelling by Virginia and West Virginia, Field entered a vigorous dissent, contending that the "equal protection of the laws" clause "did not prevent the outright exclusion of blacks" by states acting under their elective authority."[77]

Nonetheless, the Field dissent dramatized both the interest in the meaning of the most important of the Civil War Amendments and its possible role as a catalyst in a "nationalization" of basic rights and liberties. The *Slaughterhouse* holding of "dual citizenship" has never been overruled,[78] and the P or I clause of Amendment Fourteen has become "practically a

[74] To Field's great satisfaction, the word "person" in the latter clause was extended to corporations in 1886, via an announcement from the bench by Mr. Chief Justice Waite, in *Santa Clara County v. Southern Pacific Railroad Co.,* 118 U.S. 394—in no small measure due to the interpretative efforts of Roscoe Conkling, who had been a member of the Joint Congressional Committee that had drafted the Fourteenth Amendment.

[75] *Neal v. Delaware,* 103 U.S. 379 (1880); *Bush v. Connecticut,* 107 U.S. 110 (1882); *In re Kemmler,* 136 U.S. 436 (1890); *McElvaine v. Brush,* 142 U.S. 155 (1891); and *O'Neil v. Vermont,* 144 U.S. 323 (1892).

[76] In the last-named case he did thus note the following in his dissent:

> While, therefore, the ten Amendments, as limitations on power, and, so far as they accomplish their purpose and find their fruition in such limitations, are applicable to the Federal Government and not to the States, yet, so far as they declare or recognize the rights of persons, they are rights belonging to them as citizens of the United States under the Constitution; and the Fourteenth Amendment, as to all such rights, places a limit upon state power by ordaining that no State shall make or enforce any law which shall abridge them. If I am right in this view, then every citizen of the United States is protected from punishments which are cruel and unusual. [At 363.]

[77] See *ex parte Virginia* and *Strauder v. West Virginia,* 100 U.S. 339 and 100 U.S. 303 (1980), respectively.

[78] After the Reconstruction government was turned out of office in Louisiana, the *Slaughterhouse* statute was promptly repealed. Then the *monopoly* went to court, claiming violation of *its* due process of law under Amendment Fourteen. But, with Mr. Justice Miller again writing the opinion, the due process claim here lost 9:0. (*Butcher's Union Slaughter-House v. Crescent City Live-Stock Landing Co.,* 111 U.S. 746 [1884].)

dead letter"; it has been more or less outflanked ever since,[79] but emphatically not so the "due process of law" and the "equal protection of the laws" clauses, however—which in fact have become a "second" Bill of Rights. And, of course, Congress has begun to make use of the potentially far-reaching provisions of Section 5 of the Amendment, which gives it "power to enforce, by appropriate legislation," the Amendment's aforegone provisions.[80]

To the "due process of law" clause of the former and the incorporation problem we can now return, noting en route the criticism of *Slaughterhouse* by one of the earliest American political scientists, John W. Burgess, who pronounced the decision "entirely erroneous" from whatever view he regarded it, be that "historical, political, or juristic."[81] As he wrote in 1890 in his classic two-volume work, *Political Science and Comparative Constitutional Law*:

> I say that if history has taught us anything in political science, it is that *civil liberty is national in its origin, content and sanction* . . . if there is but a single lesson to be learned from the history of the United States, it is this: Seventy years of debate and four years of terrible war turn substantially upon this issue, in some part or other; and when the Nation triumphed in the great appeal to arms, and addressed itself to the work of readjusting the forms of law to the now undoubted condition of fact, it gave its first attention to the nationalization in constitutional law of the domain of civil liberty. *There is no doubt that those who framed the thirteenth and fourteenth amendments intended to occupy the whole ground and thought that they had done so.* The opposition charged that these amendments would nationalize the whole sphere of civil liberty; the majority accepted the view; and the legislation of Congress for their elaboration and enforcement proceeded upon that view. In the face of all these well known facts it was hardly to be doubted that . . . [the Supreme Court] *would unanimously declare the whole domain of civil liberty to be under its protection against both the general government and the commonwealths.* Great, therefore, was the surprise . . . when the decision in the *Slaughterhouse Cases* was announced. . . .[82]

Whatever one's conclusions regarding the intent of the framers of the Fourteenth Amendment, and its role as a vehicle for the applicability of the Bill of Rights to the several states, we know that there has been piece-

[79] Morrison, *op. cit.*, fn. 34, at 144.

[80] For example, sections of the Civil Rights Act of 1964. Congress has also resorted to the almost identically worded provision of Section 2 of the Fifteenth Amendment—as in the Voting Rights Acts of 1965, 1970, and 1975.

[81] *Political Science and Comparative Constitutional Law* (Boston: Ginn & Co., 1890), Vol. I, p. 226.

[82] *Ibid.*, pp. 225–26. (Italics supplied.)

meal "incorporation" or "nationalization" or "absorption" of the Bill of Rights by judicial interpretation and, as we shall see later, it came about at a steadily accelerating rate following Mr. Justice Sanford's limited initial acceptance of the concept in 1925. Thus, we now turn to the historical evolution of the incorporation issue, followed by a consideration of the various judicial "positions" on, and the wisdom of, incorporation itself.

The Evolution of "Incorporation"

PRE-1937 DEVELOPMENTS

The 1833 *Barron v. Baltimore*[83] decision firmly shut the judicial and constitutional door on any notions of incorporation until the passage of the Fourteenth Amendment appeared to open it in 1868; the *Slaughterhouse Cases*[84] relocked it in 1873; and matters seemed to be settled, *res judicata*[85]—reconfirmed in 1899, with the Court reiterating that "the first ten Amendments to the Federal Constitution contain no restrictions on the powers of the state, but were intended to operate solely on the Federal government."[86]

Mr. Justice Harlan. Only Harlan, the one-time Kentucky slaveholder,[87] continued to raise the incorporation problem with both conviction and consistency. He would never fail in appropriate cases—of which there really were not very many—to write impassioned opinions in dissent, urging his associates to accept the principle of the nationalization of the Bill of Rights.

Harlan's solitary dissenting opinions from three well-known decisions demonstrated his unshakable belief that the Fourteenth Amendment was intended to incorporate the *entire* Bill of Rights—if for no other reason than that he regarded *all* of the rights in the Bill of Rights as "fundamental" and therefore applicable to the states via the due process of law clause of Amendment Fourteen. The first of these, *Hurtado v. California* (1884),[88] turned on the question of whether California's 1879 substitution of the practice of "information"[89] for indictment by a grand jury constituted a

83 7 Peters 243.

84 16 Wallace 36.

85 *Res judicata* connotes authoritative, settled law. In other words, it represents *the* essential law involved.

86 *Brown v. New Jersey,* 175 U.S. 172, at 174. The Court, speaking through Mr. Justice Brewer, was unanimous, Harlan concurring separately without opinion.

87 See the Harlan symposium in the spring 1958 issue of the *Kentucky Law Journal.* Also, my "John Marshall Harlan: A Justice Neglected," 41 *Virginia Law Review* 871 (November 1955).

88 110 U.S. 516.

89 "Information" is a common law practice whereby the prosecuting officer merely submits his charges in the form of an affidavit of evidence, supported by sworn statements, to a trial court. It is still used widely by the states and, to a much lesser degree, by the federal government, in civil and non-capital criminal cases at the district court level.

violation of the "due process" guarantees of the Fourteenth Amendment because of the requirements of the Fifth Amendment. Joseph Hurtado was tried on the basis of "information," convicted of the murder of one José Antonio Estuardo, and sentenced to be hanged. His appeal to the United States Supreme Court accordingly alleged deficient procedural due process. But the Court, in an elaborate 7:1 decision, delievered by Mr. Justice Stanley Matthews, rejected that contention, ruling that the substitution of "information" for a grand jury indictment did not violate due process of law because it was merely a "preliminary proceeding" and thus not essential to due process; that, in any event, the Fourteenth's language simply did not contain, and did not mandate, a grand jury provision—had that been the intention, contended Matthews, it would have stated so specifically. Harlan's scholarly dissent not only disagreed with the majority's analysis, but argued at length his belief that the Bill of Rights *is* incorporated via the due process clause of Amendment Fourteen. It meant, he insisted, that "there are principles of liberty and justice lying at the foundation of our civil and political institutions which no state can violate consistently with that due process of law required by the 14th Amendment in proceedings involving life, liberty or property."[90]

The second case, *Maxwell v. Dow,*[91] came sixteen years later. Not only was the matter of the substitution of "information" for a grand jury indictment—this time by Utah—again present, but a far more important collateral issue was at stake: Charles Maxwell's trial by a Utah jury of eight instead of twelve. Convicted of the crime of armed robbery, Maxwell argued that he had been deprived of both "due process of law" and, especially, his "privileges and immunities" as a United States citizen; that the Bill of Rights' Fifth and Sixth Amendments, guaranteeing grand jury indictment and trial by jury in criminal cases, respectively, were incorporated via Amendment Fourteen. "No, not at all," said the Supreme Court, with Mr. Justice Rufus W. Peckham writing for the 8:1 majority. Peckham, heavily relying on the *Slaughterhouse* precedent, admonished his colleagues to look to the Amendment's language rather than its proponents' speeches. Not only did he see no violation of due process by the procedures employed by Utah, but neither the "due process" nor the "P or I" clause comprehended the rights listed in the federal Bill of Rights. In short, any thoughts of incorporation were to be rejected logically:

. . . [W]hen the Fourteenth Amendment prohibits abridgment by the states of those privileges and [*sic*] immunities which [the individual] enjoys as such citizen, it is not correct or reasonable to say that it covers and extends to certain rights which he does not enjoy by reason of his citizenship, but sim-

---

[90] *Hurtado v. California, op. cit.,* at 546. Hurtado died in his jail cell of a pulmonary embolism one month after the Supreme Court's decision.

[91] 176 U.S. 581 (1900).

ply because those rights exist in favor of all individuals as against Federal government powers.[92]

Harlan, the sole dissenter, was not impressed by this reasoning; scoffing at what he regarded as deliberate blindness and verbal gymnastics, he reiterated his *Hurtado* view that, indeed, the Fourteenth Amendment intended to incorporate the entire Bill of Rights. Pointing to the Court's firm 8:1 decision in favor of property rights pronounced just three years earlier,[93] he warned that "no judicial tribunal has authority to say that some of [the Bill of Rights] may be abridged by the States while others may not be abridged."[94] To him, each one of the rights was fundamental and ergo applicable to the states, for he regarded *all* federal rights possessed by citizens *prior* to the adoption of Fourteen as being among the "privileges or immunities" which were secured against encroachment by the states.

The last pertinent example of Harlan's lone stand on the issue was the 1908 case of *Twining v. New Jersey*,[95] which involved the controversial constitutional guarantee against compulsory self-incrimination. The president of the Monmouth Safe & Trust Co., Albert C. Twining, and its treasurer, David C. Cornell, had been indicted by a New Jersey grand jury for having deliberately and knowingly displayed a false paper to a bank examiner with full intent to deceive him as to the actual condition of their firm. At the trial the two defendants neither called witnesses nor took the stand in their own defense. Very much in the fashion of the trial judge in *Adamson v. California*[96] four decades later, the *Twining* trial judge, Wilbur A. Heisley, commented adversely and extensively from the bench on the defendants' failure to take the stand. His charge to the jury contained the following statements: "Because a man does not go upon the stand you are not necessarily justified in drawing an inference of guilt. But you have a right to consider the fact that he does not go upon the stand where a direct accusation is made against him." The jury returned a verdict of guilty as charged against both defendants, who ultimately appealed to the United States Supreme Court, contending first, that the exemption from self-incrimination is one of the privileges or immunities of citizens of the United States which the Fourteenth Amendment forbids the states to abridge, and second, that the alleged compulsory self-incrimination constituted a denial of due process of law. This time Mr. Justice William H. Moody spoke for another 8:1 majority that once again rejected not only the specific contentions but the larger issue of the Bill of Rights' incorpora-

[92] *Ibid.*, at 595–96.
[93] *Chicago, Burlington and Quincy Railroad v. Chicago*, 166 U.S. 226 (1897).
[94] 176 U.S. 581, *op. cit.*, at 616. Maxwell's sentence was commuted in 1903, but he was killed in a gunfight not long thereafter.
[95] 211 U.S. 78.
[96] 332 U.S. 46 (1947).

tion. However, citing *Chicago, Burlington & Quincy RR. v. Chicago,*[97] he significantly now granted the "possibility" that due process meant that "some of the personal rights safeguarded by the first eight Amendments against national action may also be safeguarded against state action."[98] Yet only, if an affirmative response is called for to the following question: "Is it a fundamental principle in liberty and justice which inheres in the very idea of free government and is the inalienable right of a citizen of such a government?"[99] Moody answered his rhetorical question by declaring it inapplicable in the instant *Twining* case because he regarded the privilege against self-incrimination as "not fundamental in due process of law, nor an essential part of it."[100] John Marshall Harlan predictably repeated his plea for incorporation, based on what he continued to regard as the commands of the Constitution. Until he died in 1911, he endeavored to convince at least a bare majority of his colleagues of the correctness of his position. But he was not to see the victory that was to come only from future judicial interpretations—one that was all but total by the late 1960s. Well might one of his biographers write that Harlan had always "maintained an unswerving faith in the role of the Supreme Court as defender of the citizen's liberties and guardian of American constitutional ideals. . . ."[101] So he had indeed, and not only in the realm of incorporation (as we shall have occasion to see later).[102]

The Gitlow Case. Despite the rising concern expressed for civil rights and liberties by Justices Holmes and Brandeis, who joined the Court in 1902 and 1916, respectively, incorporation of the Bill of Rights seemed a lost cause until June 8, 1925, when it received its first official judicial recognition, on an at least *partial* basis, in the famous case of *Gitlow v. New York.*[103]

Benjamin Gitlow, an active exponent of extreme left-wing causes and a member of the most radical wing of the Socialist Party, had run afoul of New York State's Criminal Anarchy Act of 1902—which was passed in the wake of President William McKinley's assassination in late 1901. He was

[97] 166 U.S. 226 (1897).

[98] *Twining v. New Jersey, op. cit.,* at 99.

[99] *Ibid.,* at 106.

[100] *Ibid.,* at 110.

[101] Alan F. Westin, "John Marshall Harlan and the Constitutional Rights of Negroes: The Transformation of a Southerner," 66 *Yale Law Journal* 710 (1957).

[102] See, for example, most famous of all his dissents, in *Plessy v. Ferguson,* 163 U.S. 537 (1896).

[103] 268 U.S. 652. A case can be made for the contention that a number of earlier 1920s cases had "moved" the Court to its *Gitlow* position—e.g., *Gilbert v. Minnesota,* 254 U.S. 325 (1921), but by *dictum* only; *Prudential Insurance Co. v. Cheeks,* 259 U.S. 530 (1922); *Meyer v. Nebraska,* 262 U.S. 390 (1923); and *Pierce v. Society of Sisters,* 268 U.S. 510 (1925). See Klaus H. Heberle, "From Gitlow to Near: Judicial 'Amendment' by Absent-Minded Incrementalism," 34 *The Journal of Politics,* 458–83 (1972).

tried and convicted—after forty-five minutes of jury deliberations—for having "advocated, advised, and taught the duty, necessity, and propriety of overthrowing and overturning organized government by force, violence, and unlawful means by certain writtings" (the "Left Wing Manifesto" and "The Revolutionary Age"). Appealing his conviction through the appropriate tiers of the New York State courts to the United States Supreme Court, he alleged that the New York statute violated both the Fourteenth Amendment's due process clause and the freedom of speech guarantees of the First. Gitlow lost on his basic claims, the Court ruling 6:2—Mr. Justice Stone not participating—that the statute neither violated due process in general nor free speech in particular. However, while clearing Mr. Gitlow's path to a New York jail by ruling that the latter's writings constituted not the advocacy of abstract doctrine but embodied "the language of direct incitement,"[104] the author of the Court's majority opinion, Mr. Justice Sanford, made judicial history by the first formal embrace of incorporation of provisions of the Bill of Rights, speech and press:

> For present purposes we may and do assume that freedom of speech and of the press—which are protected by the First Amendment from abridgement by Congress—*are among the fundamental personal rights and "liberties" protected by the due process clause of the Fourteenth Amendment from impairment by the States.*[105]

This renowned Sanford *dictum*[106] was fully subscribed to by all of his colleagues, including, of course, Justices Holmes and Brandeis. That the two dissented here in one of Holmes's most-celebrated opinions was not because of the incorporation announcement, but, as we shall have occasion to assess later in connection with freedom of expression in Chapter V, because they simply did not believe that Gitlow's action presented any "clear and present" danger[107] to the State of New York. Drawing the kind of line that we discussed in Chapter I, Mr. Justice Holmes pointed out that "every idea is an incitement," that "eloquence may set fire to reason. . . ." But regardless of Benjamin Gitlow's defeat—in later days he became a well-paid informant for the government in subversive activities matters[108]—the

---

104 *Gitlow v. New York, op. cit.,* at 665.

105 *Ibid.,* at 666. (Italics supplied.) Many had long treated it as such.

106 Properly known as *obiter dictum,* it is a statement of opinion by a judge that is not necessary to the conclusion on the merits of the case.

107 That famous doctrine, first enunciated in *Schenck v. United States,* 249 U.S. 47 (1919), by Holmes and Brandeis, will be fully treated in Chapter V.

108 Especially in the 1940s and 1950s (usually at $50 a day). He had served three years of a five- to ten-year sentence, being pardoned by Governor Al Smith, who opined that Gitlow had been "sufficiently punished for a political crime" (*The New York Times,* December 12, 1925, p. 1). Gitlow died in 1965, aged 73, having become a confirmed anti-Communist.

"carry-over" doctrine concerning the Fourteenth Amendment had been officially enunciated.

The Doctrine Confirmed and Expanded. That the Gitlow incorporation development was neither a fluke nor a passing pronouncement in *dictum* soon became apparent. Only two years later, the Supreme Court, again speaking through Mr. Justice Sanford, now confirmed unanimously the nationalization of *freedom of speech* in the case of *Fiske v. Kansas.*[109] Here, for the first time, it upheld a personal liberty claim under the Fourteenth Amendment, ruling specifically that a Kansas criminal syndicalism statute—very similar to the New York one in *Gitlow* (although Sanford did not discuss *Gitlow's* issues and decision at all)—did indeed violate the due process clause of the Fourteenth Amendment, as applied to Harold Fiske, because of the free speech strictures of the First Amendment. It has long been argued,[110] with considerable persuasiveness, that a more elaborate and more definitive, and hence more clearly precedent-setting case for the incorporation of speech, is the 1931 Hughes opinion in *Stromberg v. California.*[111] There, 19-year-old Yetta Stromberg, a member of the Young Communist League, had led forty 10–15-year-old children in a summer camp pledge of allegiance to a red flag, and found herself in multiple violation of a California statute prohibiting the display of such flags. The Chief Justice, speaking for a 7:2 majority (Justices Butler and McReynolds in dissent), admonished: "It has been determined that the conception of liberty under the due process clause of the Fourteenth Amendment embraces the right of free speech (citing, among others, the *Gitlow* and *Fiske* cases)."[112] In any event, incorporation of *freedom of the press* followed not long thereafter in the well-known 1931 prior-censorship case of *Near v. Minnesota.*[113]

In *Near,* this time speaking for a majority of five, Hughes declared unconstitutional, as "an infringement of the liberty of the press guaranteed by the Fourteenth Amendment," the so-called Minnesota Gag Law, which permitted prior restraint from publishing under certain circumstances. He wrote: "It is no longer open to doubt that the liberty of the press and of speech is safeguarded by the due process clause of the Fourteenth Amendment from invasion by state action. It was found impossible to conclude that this essential personal liberty of the citizen was left unprotected by the general guarantee of fundamental rights of person and property."[114]

---

[109] 274 U.S. 380 (1927). *Fiske* was sponsored by the I.W.W. Indeed, all cases involving the incorporation of the First Amendment were group sponsored.

[110] See Herberle, *op. cit.* He insists that "the question of incorporation was not settled until the decisions in *Stromberg* and *Near,*" with the Court there relying "on *Gitlow, Whitney* [*v. California,* 274 U.S. 357, (1927)] and *Fiske.*" (At 477.)

[111] 283 U.S. 359.

[112] *Ibid.,* at 368.

[113] 283 U.S. 697, at 723.

[114] *Ibid.,* at 707.

Less than a year later, the incorporation doctrine moved out of the realm of the First Amendment and, for the first time, into the area of the guarantee of a fair trial, in general, and *counsel in capital criminal cases,* in particular. The vehicle was the first of the notorious *Scottsboro Cases,*[115] *Powell v. Alabama,*[116] which was destined to become a *cause célèbre* in the records of applications of due process of law to black defendants. Writing for a majority of seven, Mr. Justice George Sutherland overturned the conviction in the Alabama courts of seven indigent, ignorant, minor Negroes, who had been falsely charged with the rape of two white girls, and convicted in a one-day trial in a mob-dominated atmosphere without the benefit of proper defense counsel. Reversing and remanding their conviction to the trial court with a stern call for a fair trial, the Court held that

> . . . the right to counsel . . . provided in the Sixth Amendment [as applied to this case] is of such a character that it cannot be denied without violating those "fundamental principles of liberty and justice which lie at the base of all our civil and political institutions." . . . [It] is obviously one of those compelling considerations which must prevail in determining *whether it is embraced within the due process clause of the Fourteenth Amendment, although it is specifically dealt with in another part of the federal Constitution.* . . . [T]he necessity of counsel was so vital and imperative that the failure of the trial court to make an effective appointment of counsel was likewise a denial of due process of law within the meaning of the Fourteenth Amendment. . . .[117]

Sutherland hinted of the applicability of the new role of law to *non-capital* criminal cases as well, but chose to state that it was not necessary to determine that question "now."[118] In any event, new ground had been broken, with Justices Pierce Butler and James C. McReynolds as the sole dissenters from the incorporation phase of the case.

The fourth aspect of the Bill of Rights to be thus nationalized was the First Amendment's guarantee of *freedom of religion* in 1934. This was determined in 1934 in the interesting and important case of *Hamilton v. Regents of the University of California.*[119] All students at the University of

---

[115] So termed because the accused were all apprehended near the Alabama town of Scottsboro.

[116] 287 U.S. 45 (1932).

[117] *Ibid.,* at 71. Sutherland also took the occasion to reaffirm the incorporation of "freedom of speech and of the press," at 67.

[118] The Court's ruling in *Betts v. Brady,* 316 U.S. 455 (1942), restricted its application to *capital* criminal cases, yet *Gideon v. Wainwright,* 372 U.S. 335 (1963), extended it to all criminal cases, save certain misdemeanors. But that holding was later interpreted as comprehending all non-traffic misdemeanors involving *any* imprisonment. (*Argersinger v. Hamlin,* 407 U.S. 25 [1972] and *Scott v. Illinois,* 440 U.S. 367 [1979]).

[119] 293 U.S. 245.

California, a public state institution, were then required to take military drill on pain of expulsion. But one among them, Albert Hamilton, holding religious convictions against the bearing of arms, refused to participate in the program and was consequently expelled. He filed suit, contending that his religious beliefs entitled him to exemption by virtue of both Amendments One and Fourteen. When his case reached the United States Supreme Court, Mr. Justice Butler, speaking for his unanimous colleagues, ruled that Hamilton's religious convictions were indeed safeguarded by the Bill of Rights, and that freedom of religion was henceforth to be regarded as incorporated via the "due process of law" clause of Amendment Fourteen.[120] However, the Court went on to rule that, despite its holding on incorporation, Hamilton was *not* entitled to an exemption from the state requirement of military training because, after all, he was not *compelled to attend* the University of California. Since he had readily chosen to attend that institution of his own free will, his due process of law was in no sense being violated by a requirement to comply with the University's, i.e., the State of California's, rules and regulations while in attendance.

In 1937, a few months earlier than the landmark incorporation case of *Palko v. Connecticut*,[121] the First Amendment's *freedom of assembly* and, by implication, its freedom "to *petition* the Government for a redress of grievances," became the fifth and sixth segments of the Bill of Rights to be "carried over." *De Jonge v. Oregon*[122] again involved a state criminal syndicalism law: Dirk De Jonge had been convicted in Oregon's Multnomah County under such a statute, which made it a criminal offense to advocate "crime, physical violence, sabotage, or any unlawful acts or methods as a means of accomplishing industrial change or political revolution." There was no record that De Jonge had advocated what the statute proscribed, nor did the indictment charge him specifically with having done so. The sole charge against him was that he had participated in an advertised political meeting of the Communist Party, of which he was an admitted member. The meeting, concededly peaceful, had been held by the Portland section of the Party to protest alleged brutality and unlawful activity by the Portland police and conditions at the county jail. Speaking for his unanimous Court, Mr. Chief Justice Hughes pointed out that "peaceable assembly for lawful discussion, however unpopular the sponsorship, cannot be made a crime," and that "the holding of meetings for peaceable political action cannot be proscribed." Further declaring that the right of peaceable assem-

[120] Some observers, including North, *op. cit.*, regard this statement of incorporation as well as a similar one made in the case by Mr. Justice Cardozo's concurring opinion (*ibid.*, at 265) as *dicta*. They prefer to point to *Cantwell v. Connecticut*, decided six years later, as the "incorporator" by rule of law rather than *dictum* of the free exercise clause (310 U.S. 296, at 303).

[121] 302 U.S. 319.

[122] 299 U.S. 353 (1937).

bly "is a right cognate to those of free speech and free press and is equally fundamental," he proceeded to hold that assembly, too, is thus one of "those fundamental principles of liberty and justice" that are made applicable to the states via the due process clause of the Fourteenth Amendment.[123]

Hence, when the *Palko* case appeared on the Court's calendar for decision, the entire First Amendment and counsel of the Sixth (at least in capital criminal cases) had been firmly incorporated. But what was needed was a more thorough discussion that would deal with the theoretical as well as the practical issues involved in "nationalizing" the Bill of . Rights. Appropriately, it fell to the eloquent Mr. Justice Benjamin N. Cardozo to perform that task. His all-too-brief six-year tenure on the Court culminated in *Palko v. Connecticut*.

THE DOCTRINE SPELLED OUT: CARDOZO AND PALKO

Frank U. Palko had been indicted by the State of Connecticut for murder in the *first* degree for the fatal shooting of two policemen. The trial jury—as juries have been known to do with predictable unpredictability—found him guilty of *second* degree murder, however, and he was accordingly sentenced to life imprisonment with a recommendation that he never be paroled. Pursuant to a statute of 1866, however, and with the permission of the trial judge in the case, the State of Connecticut then appealed the conviction on the lesser count to the highest state court, the Court of Errors. In its petition Connecticut charged that the action in the trial court constituted an "error of law to the prejudice of the state"; the Court of Errors agreed, reversing the judgment below, and ordered a new trial. Although Palko objected that the second trial would place him twice in jeopardy for the same offense—an action forbidden by the terms of the Fifth Amendment, and, as he urged, consequently forbidden also by those of the due process clause of the Fourteenth—his re-trial took place soon thereafter.

This time the trial jury returned a verdict of murder in the *first* degree, and the judge sentenced Palko to death. Having exhausted his judicial remedies at the state level, Palko then appealed to the United States Supreme Court; again he contended that "whatever is forbidden by the Fifth Amendment is forbidden by the Fourteenth also."[124] For reasons to be outlined presently, the Supreme Court, speaking through Mr. Justice Cardozo, ruled against Palko's claims on all counts; Mr. Justice Butler dissented without opinion (an intriguing but not very helpful practice).[125]

---

[123] *Ibid.,* at 364.
[124] *Ibid.,* at 322.
[125] Robert Lewis Shayon told me in November 1966 that he had discussed the *Palko* case in considerable detail with Frank Palko's court-appointed attorney, David

Frank Palko was subsequently executed by electrocution. Macabre though it may be, a cynic could comment that, given the importance of his case for the future of civil rights and liberties, he did not die in vain.

The "Honor Roll" of Superior Rights. Mr. Justice Cardozo's opinion was recognized at once as a judicial landmark for several reasons: (1) It established a yardstick by which to measure the incorporation problem, and thus govern judicial action. (2) It provided official judicial recognition for the formerly unpredictable claim that, under certain conditions, and in certain areas—based upon a hierarchy of values—the several states are beholden to the commands of the federal Bill of Rights via the Fourteenth Amendment. (3) It laid the groundwork for the support of both the theory and the practice of a judicial double standard in the interpretation of basic human rights.[126] Practically speaking, what the Cardozo opinion accomplished was to deny or reject any *general* rule of overall incorporation, while acknowledging that there are, and indeed must be, some rights in the Bill that are fundamental enough to require "incorporation" or "absorption."

Mr. Justice Cardozo's *Palko* opinion thus established the "Honor Roll of Superior Rights," to which his life-long admirer and ultimate successor on the Supreme Court, Felix Frankfurter, so irreverently referred as the "slot machine theory . . . some are in and some are out." Although he refused to regard the "due process of law" clause of the Fourteenth Amendment as "shorthand" for the Bill of Rights, Cardozo nonetheless set himself the task of distinguishing those basic rights that he and his supporters viewed as "of the very essence of a scheme of ordered liberty" from those without which "justice would not perish" and which were not therefore "implicit in the concept of ordered liberty." Explaining his rationale further, he wrote movingly of "those fundamental principles of liberty and justice which lie at the base of all our civil and political institutions," and of principles of justice "so rooted in the traditions and conscience of our people as to be ranked as fundamental."[127] (It is significant to note the recurrent use of the concept of "fundamental" rights in juxtaposition to what, as we shall see below, are termed "formal" rights on the scale of basic rights and liberties.)[128] Recognizing the difficulties of

---

Goldstein, a distinguished Bridgeport, Connecticut, lawyer. According to Goldstein, Butler's reason for dissenting—even without opinion—was based on his conviction that the State of Connecticut had in effect denied Palko's due process of law. During oral argument, Butler was "very tough" on the state's attorney, at one point shouting, "What do you want? Blood?"

[126] See the discussion in Chapter II, *supra*.

[127] 302 U.S. 319 (1937), at 325.

[128] The Court had established a dichotomy between "formal" and "fundamental" rights at the turn of the century in answering the question of how many, and which, of the rights in the Constitution were to be applicable automatically to possessions

evaluation and interpretation inherent in his dichotomy, and anticipating both the criticism and some of the problems that would follow, Cardozo resorted to the "freedom of thought and speech" as his cardinal illustration: "Of that freedom one may say that it is the matrix, the indispensable condition, of nearly every other form of freedom. With rare aberrations, a pervasive recognition of that truth can be traced in our history, political and legal. . . ."[129]

For the other group, these "formal" rights in the Bill without which "justice would not perish," Cardozo cited the right to trial by jury and the immunity from prosecution "for a capital or otherwise infamous crime" except as a result of an indictment, explaining that, indeed, they may have "value and importance," but

> even so, they are not of the essence of a scheme of ordered liberty. To abolish them is not to violate a "principle of justice so rooted in the traditions and conscience of our people as to be ranked as fundamental." . . . Few would be so narrow as to maintain that a fair and enlightened system of justice would be impossible without them. . . .[130]

Then, turning specifically to another right, the immunity from compulsory self-incrimination, he noted that "[T]his too might be lost, and justice still be done. . . . Justice . . . would not perish if the accused were subject to a duty to respond to orderly inquiry."[131] Cardozo thus insisted that in the realm of chiefly *procedural* rights, in general, and the protection against double jeopardy at issue in the *Palko* ruling, in particular, the question to be posed by the appellate tribunal must be, as Mr. Justice Harlan had phrased it decades earlier, all embracing: "Does it violate those 'fundamental principles of liberty and justice which lie at the base of all our civil and political institutions?' " "The answer," judged Cardozo, "surely must be 'no,' " for, he explained: "[Connecticut] is not attempting to wear the accused out by a multitude of cases with accumulated trials. It asks no more than this, that the case against him shall go on until there shall be a trial free from the corrosion of substantial legal error."[132] In his view, Connecticut had sought no more than parity with the defendant in the right to continue a case "until there shall be a trial free from the corrosion of substantial legal error." A defendant was given the right to appeal errors ad-

---

and territories. The "fundamental" ones only, held the Court in the series of *Insular* cases from 1901 to 1905. See especially *Hawaii v. Mankichi*, 190 U.S. 197 (1903) and *Rasmussen v. United States*, 197 U.S. 516 (1905). What is "fundamental" is of course a value judgment.

129 *Palko v. Connecticut, op. cit.*, at 327.
130 *Ibid.*, at 325.
131 *Ibid.*, at 326.
132 *Ibid.*, at 328.

verse to him. "A reciprocal privilege . . . has now been granted to the state. . . ." And he concluded on a note of assurance: "There is here no seismic innovation. The edifice of justice stands, in its symmetry, to many, greater than before."[133]

A Caveat. It is essential to recognize at once that, despite the *Palko* dichotomy between the components of the Bill of Rights that are and those that are not "implicit in the concept of ordered liberty,"[134] Mr. Justice Cardozo made it clear that the several states would still be subject to the judicial test of whether or not a duly challenged law or action constituted a violation of the "due process of law" concept of the Fourteenth Amendment *per se*. In other words, simply because only some of the rights are *ipso facto* applicable to the states via the Fourteenth Amendment, it does not mean that the states are free to violate the basic concepts of due process of law to which all persons in their jurisdictions are entitled. In such claims the judicial test then becomes the one so faithfully and ardently embraced by Mr. Justice Frankfurter during his career on the Supreme Court: does the alleged state violation constitute conduct that "shocks the conscience" or, in the less inhibited language of Mr. Justice Holmes, "does it make you vomit?" Given the divergent status of consciences, and the different physiological responses to shock, it is obvious that the answer in individual cases is difficult and often unpredictable! We shall have occasion to return to this particular problem of drawing lines when we consider the various choices or "positions" on the incorporation question offered by justices of the Supreme Court and other knowledgeable participants in the search for justice.

POST-PALKO DEVELOPMENTS

The test devised by Mr. Justice Cardozo in *Palko* presumably permitted, if it did not indeed invite, subsequent alteration of the newly created incorporation "line." That line, *as of the famous Opinion Monday in 1937*, had created the dichotomy shown in the following table.

As the limited number of "a"-marked items in the table indicates, Cardozo did not specifically cover each and every aspect of the Bill of Rights. But his language made quite clear that the underlying principles of our federal government structure demand that the states be permitted to follow their own practices and discretion in the realm of procedural due process as long as they provide a full measure of "due process of law" in each and every instance.

---

[133] *Ibid.*

[134] Louis Lusky protests that "ordered liberty is too vague to describe a national objective. . . . It is a vehicle for whatever meaning the Court gives it, and thus enables the Court to apply its own conceptions of public policy." *By What Right?* (Charlottesville: The Michie Co., 1975), pp. 105, 107.

Table 3.1

THE STATUS OF "INCORPORATION" AS OF *Palko* (1937)

AMENDMENT	"INCORPORATED"	NOT "INCORPORATED"
One	Speech.[a] Press.[a] Free Exercise of Religion.[a] Peaceable Assembly.[a] Right of Petition.	Separation of Church and State.
Two		Keep and Bear Arms.
Three		No Quartering of Soldiers.
Four		Evidence Admitted as Result of Unreasonable Search and Seizure.[a]
Five	Due Process of Law (as per Fourteenth). Eminent Domain Safeguards.[b]	Grand Jury Indictment[a] or Presentment. Double Jeopardy.[a] Compulsory Self-Incrimination.[a]
Six	Counsel in Criminal Cases[a] (later judicially abridged to read "in capital" criminal cases only—but then reinterpreted to read "all criminal cases"). Fair Trial.	Speedy and Public Trial. Impartial Jury Trial in Criminal Cases.[a] Nature and Cause of Accusation. Compulsory Process for Appearance of Witness. Confrontation of Accusers.
Seven	Fair Trial.	Jury Trial in Civil Cases.[a]
Eight	Fair Trial.	Excessive Bail and Fines. Cruel and Unusual Punishments.

[a] Specifically mentioned in the *Palko* opinion by Mr. Justice Cardozo.

[b] Alluded to in his Footnote Four. (See also footnote 20, p. 12 and footnote 21, page 34, *supra*.)

1947 and 1948: Two Additions. The Cardozo "Honor Roll" stood for almost a quarter of a century. During that period it was extended only twice: to include the concept of *"separation of Church and State"* in the already incorporated exercise of freedom of religion and to require *public* trials. The vehicle for the former was the 1947 *New Jersey Bus* case[135] (which we shall have occasion to discuss in considerable detail in Chapter VI). Pertinent here is the entire Court's acknowledgment (despite its 5:4 split on the specific merits of the case) that a *bona fide* violation of the principle of the separation of Church and State is constitutionally proscribed by *both* the terms of the First Amendment and the "due process of law" clause of the Fourteenth Amendment. The "public" trial requirement

[135] *Everson v. Board of Education of Ewing Township*, 330 U.S. 1. Mr. Justice Black preferred to think of *Murdock v. Pennsylvania*, 319 U.S. 105 (1943), as the vehicle of incorporation of separation of Church and State.

came with a 7:2 opinion by Mr. Justice Black (Justices Frankfurter and Jackson dissenting) in 1948 as a result of the secret sentencing of a Michigan citizen, William D. Oliver, by a judge serving as a one-man grand jury, a practice statutorily sanctioned in his home state's Oakland County.[136]

1961: The Cleveland Search and Seizure Case. The year 1961 heralded a new burst of judicial activity (some would say "activism"). It was the Fourth Amendment's guarantee against *unreasonable searches and seizures* that was next to be incorporated. The fruit of such seizures had long before ceased to be admissible as evidence in *federal* court.[137] But although states, too, had been judicially forbidden to engage in *unreasonable* searches and seizures as of 1949 in the 6:3 *Wolf* decision,[138] the traditions of common law—namely, that if the evidence is trustworthy, i.e., if it is "material, relevant, and competent," it is admissible regardless of how it was acquired[139]—nonetheless were held to permit their "fruit," i.e., their results, as admissible evidence in *state* court proceedings. The judicial rationale for this rather astonishing dichotomy was that the victim of such evidence could avail himself of "the remedies of private action"—namely, *sue* the procurer of the illegally obtained, but admitted, evidence for civil damages, or call for criminal proceedings against officials engaged in unlawful searches. Demonstrably, the Court thus chose to regard the *exclusionary rule as an evidentiary rule—not as a constitutional provision.*[140]

Because of her 1961 case, Ms. Dolree (Dolly) Mapp, a Cleveland woman of questionable reputation, catalyzed the carryover of the federal principle to the states. Acting on alleged information that Ms. Mapp, and possibly her daughter by an erstwhile marriage, were hiding (a) a fu-

---

[136] *In re Oliver*, 333 U.S. 257 (1948). At first blush the case seemed to turn on simple due process considerations. But in later opinions the Supreme Court specifically (e.g. *Duncan v. Louisiana*, 391 U.S. 145 [1968]) referred to *Oliver* as having incorporated "public" trials. However, a 5:4 Court ruled in a hotly criticized 1979 decision that "members of the public have no constitutional right under the Sixth and Fourteenth Amendments to attend criminal trials" *if* the defendant, the prosecutor, and the presiding judge agree to close the courtroom to press and public. (*Gannett v. De Pasquale*, 443 U.S. 368.) But see the more or less contrary 7:1 holding in 1980 (*Richmond Newspapers v. Virginia*, 48 LW 5008), confining *Gannett* to *pre*-trials.

[137] *Weeks v. United States*, 232 U.S. 383 (1914). The *judicially created* rule thus prohibits the admissibility in criminal trials of evidence seized in violation of Amendment Four.

[138] *Wolf v. Colorado*, 338 U.S. 25 (1949). Here, the Court in effect announced the "incorporation" of the Fourth Amendment's pertinent guarantees but, as explained, at once neutralized or negated it by continuing to sanction admissibility of evidence so obtained by the states—in this case the confiscation of Dr. Wolf's appointment books.

[139] The courts of England, and almost all of those of the world's other lands still maintain that particular common law approach to the acquisition of evidence.

[140] In rejecting the application of the exclusionary rule in the State of New York in 1926, Cardozo, then a judge on its Court of Appeals, had asked the celebrated question whether "the criminal is to go free because the constable had blundered?" (*People v. Defore*, 242 N.Y. 13, at 19–25.)

gitive and (b) "a large amount of policy paraphernalia" on the top floor of their two-story family dwelling, police forced their way into the house without a warrant of any kind and found, after an unedifying struggle and a widespread search, some "obscene materials." On the strength of these, Ms. Mapp was convicted of the illegal possession of obscene materials in violation of an Ohio statute. The Ohio judiciary upheld her conviction, but the Supreme Court, on appeal, reversed it in *Mapp v. Ohio*,[141] in what *The New York Times* appropriately termed "an historic step," and Harvard Law School Dean—soon to be Solicitor-General of the United States—Ervin Griswold saw as requiring "a complete change in the outlook and practices of state and local police."[142] Speaking for the 6:3 majority, Mr. Justice Tom C. Clark overruled the long-standing precedents, especially *Wolf,* and, now fully incorporating the Fourth Amendment's applicable guarantee, ruled that "all evidence obtained by searches and seizures in violation of the Constitution is, by that same authority [Amendment Four], inadmissible in a state court . . ."; and: "Since the Fourth Amendment's right of privacy has been declared enforceable against the States through the Due Process Clause of the Fourteenth, it is enforceable against them by the same sanction of exclusion as is used against the Federal Government."[143] Thus, in the words of a leading student of search and seizure problems, the *Mapp* decision "clearly catapulted the exclusionary rule into a position at the core" of the Fourteenth Amendment.[144] Yet 1974 saw a distinct dilution of its safeguards at the level of grand juries,[145] and considerable agitation for the rule's abridgment, if not its outright abolition, was manifest in Congress, segments of the judicial branch (encouraged by the Chief Justice of the United States), and the organized bar. Indeed, 1976 would see two 6:3 rulings sharply reducing the power of *lower* federal courts in *habeas corpus* proceedings to set aside *state* convictions that

---

[141] 367 U.S. 643 (1961). Actually, albeit upholding her *conviction,* the Ohio Supreme Court declared the pertinent Ohio statute unconstitutional by a majority vote of 5:2. However, since the Ohio State Constitution permits only *one* dissenting vote on the seven-man Ohio Supreme Court in cases of declarations of unconstitutionality, the law survived. (170 Ohio St. 427–28, 166 NE 2d 387, 398.) Ms. Mapp managed to run afoul of the law in subsequent years and, ironically, filed an appeal from a conviction for narcotics trafficking in New York in 1975 on the strength of the 1961 decision. (*The New York Times,* December 15, 1975, p. 35c.)

[142] June 20, 1961, p. 1, and as quoted in *ibid.,* December 15, 1975, p. 35c.

[143] *Mapp v. Ohio, op. cit.,* at 655. Federal standards of "reasonableness" were specifically confirmed as applicable to the conduct of state police officers in *Ker v. California,* 374 U.S. 23 (1963).

[144] Jacob W. Landynski, "Search and Seizure," Ch. 2 in Stuart S. Nagel, ed., *The Rights of the Accused,* Vol. I (New York: Sage Publications, Inc., 1972), p. 47.

[145] *United States v. Calandra,* 414 U.S. 338, in which the Court, by a 6:3 vote, wrote a significant exception into the rule by holding that grand juries *may* use illegally obtained evidence as a basis for questioning witnesses without violating their constitutional rights.

relied on illegally obtained evidence, and another 6:3 one refusing to apply the rule to *civil* cases.[146]

1962: The California Narcotics Addiction Proof Case. The next incorporation came scarcely a year after *Mapp*. California, a source of considerable litigation on constitutional questions, provided the vehicle that would bring about the nationalization of the Eighth Amendment's guarantees against the *infliction of "cruel and unusual punishments"* (a judicial action for which Mr. Justice Field had called seventy years earlier).[147] Because that issue itself was but fleetingly discussed and briefed, some doubt existed as to whether the Supreme Court actually intended to incorporate the provision; but the general assumption now is that Mr. Justice Stewart's language did, in effect, apply to the states those basic strictures of the last article of amendment in the Bill of Rights.[148] His allies in that interpretation were the Chief Justice and Justices Black, Douglas, and Brennan; Mr. Justice Harlan concurred, but on the narrower ground of violation of due process of law. Mr. Justice Byron R. White wrote his first dissenting opinion on the bench in the case, joined by Mr. Justice Clark. At issue was a California statute making it a crime "to be under the influence of, or be addicted to narcotics, or to make unprescribed use of them"; "status" violations were punishable by a mandatory 90-day jail sentence.

Walter Lawrence Robinson—who died a year before he won his case—had been arrested on a Los Angeles street by police, whom he told that he used narcotics; his arms bore what appeared to be hypodermic needle marks. (The case had nothing to do with the *sale* of narcotics.) He had been charged with violation of the statute and sentenced to jail. On appeal, Robinson's counsel successfully raised the "cruel and unusual punishment" issue on the grounds that the law did not require *proof* of purchase or use of the drugs. Accepting this argument for the Court majority, Mr. Justice Stewart declared the statute unconstitutional as a violation of the Eighth and Fourteenth Amendments. As he viewed it, the statute fell into the same category as one purporting to make it a criminal offense "for a person to be mentally ill, or a leper, or to be afflicted with venereal

---

[146] *Stone v. Powell* and *Wolff v. Rice,* 428 U.S. 465 and *United States v. Janis,* 428 U.S. 433, respectively. (On the other hand, in 1979 the Court reconfirmed—albeit by a mere 5:4 margin—the federal courts' *habeas corpus* authority in cases of alleged racial discrimination [*Rose v. Mitchell,* 443 U.S. 545].)

[147] See pp. 44 ff., *supra.*

[148] *Robinson v. California,* 370 U.S. 660 (1962). In the bizarre 1947 Louisiana "double electrocution" case, Mr. Justice Reed had voiced "the assumption, but without so deciding, that violation of the principles of the *Fifth* and *Eighth* Amendments, as a double jeopardy and *cruel and unusual punishment,* would be violative of the due process clause of the Fourteenth Amendment." (*Louisiana ex rel. Francis v. Resweber,* 329 U.S. 459, at 462. Italics supplied.) For an account of that grisly case see Barrett E. Prettyman, Jr., *Death and the Supreme Court* (New York: Harcourt, Brace, 1961).

disease." Carrying over the pertinent provision of Amendment Eight, he held: ". . . a state which imprisons a person thus afflicted as a criminal, even though he had never touched any narcotic drug within the state or been guilty of any irregular behavior there, inflicts a cruel and unusual punishment in violation of the Fourteenth Amendment."[149] In a significant concurring opinion, Mr. Justice Douglas regarded Robinson's conviction of being an addict as *the* specific "cruel and unusual punishment," not his confinement. Addicts, suggested Douglas, should be cured, not jailed.

1963: Clarence Earl Gideon's Right to Counsel Case. Of far greater significance, because of the large numbers of individuals affected, is the celebrated case of *Gideon v. Wainwright*.[150] It is probably the most famous "incorporation decision" since *Palko*. In effect, it nationalized the right to counsel in *all*—save certain misdemeanor—criminal cases, *be they capital or non-capital*. As indicated earlier, a good many observers had quietly assumed that Mr. Justice Sutherland's language in the *Scottsboro Case*[151] had fully intended to incorporate the right to counsel in criminal cases gener-

---

[149] *Ibid.,* at 666–67. But in 1968 the Court refused to extend the *Robinson* principle to chronic alcoholics, in a case involving one of Leroy Powell's 100 prior convictions for public intoxication. The Court held 5:4 that a Texas statute making it a crime to be "found in a state of intoxication in any public place" could not be *ipso facto* held to be "irrational" in line with the *Robinson* reasoning. For, wrote Mr. Justice Thurgood Marshall, Powell was not "convicted for being a chronic alcoholic, but for being in public while drunk on a particular occasion." (*Powell v. Texas,* 392 U.S. 514, at 532.) On the other hand, the "cruel and unusual punishment" concept became the constitutional hook on which the Court, in a nine-opinion *per curiam* decision running to 243 pages, hung the 5:4 ruling on the last day of its 1971–72 term, that capital punishment, as it was then administered under certain state laws, was unconstitutional. (*Furman v. Georgia,* 408 U.S. 238 [1972].) When Congress and thirty-five states subsequently responded by enacting new laws, designed to meet the Court's objections but to retain capital punishment, a new judicial test on the latter's constitutionality loomed as a certainty. It came on July 2, 1976 in a series of twenty-four (!) opinions in five cases covering various capital punishment laws from five states. By the decisive vote of 7:2 the high tribunal ruled that the death penalty is *not* inherently cruel or unusual, at least not in murder cases, *provided* that judges and juries have been given "adequate information and guidance" for determining whether the sentence is appropriate in a particular case. (*Gregg v. Georgia,* 428 U.S. 153.) But the Court held 5:4 in 1976 that "mandatory" capital punishment laws that require the death penalty for every defendant convicted of one or more of five categories of murder may not be imposed (*Roberts v. Louisiana,* 428 U.S. 335), and it also disallowed a similar North Carolina law (*Woodson v. North Carolina,* 428 U.S. 280). Louisiana tried to rescue the law by applying it only to anyone convicted of murdering a fireman or a policeman, but it, too, fell 5:4 (*Roberts v. Louisiana II,* 431 U.S. 633 [1977]). Georgia's attempt to render rape a capital crime was struck down by the Court 7:2, assuming it was applied to an "adult woman," as constituting an impermissible cruel and unusual punishment. Obviously the Court, although granting the constitutionality of the death penalty, has rendered its application all but impossible—lacking a specific request by the accused to be put to death (as had occurred four times at this writing, mid-1981—the number of executions since the 1972 *Furman* decision).

[150] 372 U.S. 335 (1963).

[151] *Powell v. Alabama,* 287 U.S. 45 (1932).

ally. This understanding seemed to be confirmed by Mr. Justice Cardozo's choice of words in *Palko*—"the right of one accused of crime to the benefit of counsel"[152]—but the Court held to the contrary in the case of *Betts v. Brady*[153] in 1942. There, Mr. Justice Owen J. Roberts, speaking for a 6:3 majority, had ruled that the due process clause of the Fourteenth Amendment did *not* require counsel to be furnished by a state (here Maryland) in *non-capital* criminal cases unless "special" or "exceptional" circumstances, such as "mental illness," "youth," or "lack of education," were present. It was the *Betts* ruling that was specifically overturned by a unanimous Supreme Court, some twenty-one years later, with the opinion delivered with great conviction and satisfaction by the same man who had dissented in *Betts*—Mr. Justice Black.

The *Gideon* case, about which so much has been written,[154] and for good cause, reached the highest tribunal on a writ of *certiorari* as a result of a penciled petition *in forma pauperis*,[155] composed with painstaking precision on lined prison-regulation paper by Clarence Earl Gideon. Without a lawyer and penniless, he had been committed to a Florida jail as a result of a criminal conviction for "having broken and entered a poolroom with intent to commit a misdemeanor"[156] on the strength of testimony by a man who later turned out to have been the culprit himself! Gideon's request for counsel to represent him at his trial had been refused because of Florida's then valid requirement under the *Betts* precedent, that court-appointed counsel be reserved for capital criminal cases. To Gideon's warm plea in the courtroom, "Your Honor, the United States Constitution says I am entitled to be represented by Counsel," Trial Judge Robert L. McCreary, Jr., could only say, in accordance with his Florida mandate, "I am sorry, but I cannot appoint Counsel to represent you in this case."[157] Gideon thereupon acted as his own lawyer—but not too successfully: found guilty, he was sentenced to five years' imprisonment.

No knowledgeable observer of the judicial process and the Supreme

---

[152] *Palko v. Connecticut,* 302 U.S. 319 (1937), at 324.

[153] 316 U.S. 455.

[154] The best full-length book—a superb account—is Anthony Lewis, *Gideon's Trumpet* (New York: Random House, 1964). Gideon died in 1972—his name now a household word in the annals of justice.

[155] "In the form of a pauper; as a poor man."

[156] A misdemeanor is an indictable offense, not usually serious enough to be classified as a crime—but it is so in Florida and increasingly so elsewhere. In 1972, however, all imprisonable misdemeanors, beyond mere fine cases, were accorded full *Gideon* rights (*Argersinger v. Hamlin,* 407 U.S. 25), and they were unanimously made retroactive one year thereafter (*Berry v. Cincinnati,* 414 U.S. 29). However, the Court ruled 5:4 in 1979 that *Argersinger* and *Berry* extend only to those instances in which there is a "likelihood" of actual imprisonment, as contrasted with a mere "possibility." Thus, a *fine* in a petty case would *not* trigger the *Gideon* or *Argersinger* right to assigned counsel. (*Scott v. Illinois,* 440 U.S. 367.)

[157] *Gideon v. Wainwright, op. cit.,* at 335–36.

Court was surprised that the Court overturned the *Betts* decision so decisively and unanimously[158] when Gideon managed to get his case "up"—his appeal before the Supreme Court briefed and argued by the Court-appointed, crack Washington attorney and future Associate Justice of the highest tribunal, Abe Fortas. Briefs *amicii curiae*[159] from only two states—Alabama and North Carolina—supported Florida's plea to the Court that it leave *Betts v. Brady*[160] intact; yet twenty-three states argued, in Mr. Justice Black's words "that *Betts* was an anachronism when handed down and that it should now be overruled." "We agree," concluded Black triumphantly, noting that in its *Betts* decision the Court had "departed from the sound wisdom upon which its holding in *Powell v. Alabama*[161] rested." Ruling squarely that a state's failure to appoint counsel in a non-capital case—whether requested to do so or not—deprived the indigent defendant in a criminal proceeding of due process of law under the Fourteenth Amendment, as comprehended by the right to counsel requirements of the Sixth, Black remarked that it was "an obvious truth" that "in our adversary system of criminal justice any person hailed into court who is too poor to hire a lawyer cannot be assured a fair trial unless counsel is provided for him."[162] Another long-overdue aspect of incorporation had thus been accomplished, one which, as will be determined in the next chapter, was to be significantly broadened in succeeding years.[163]

Moreover, for once Congress responded promptly and affirmatively by enacting the Criminal Justice Act (C.J.A.) of 1964, designed to provide more adequate representation of defendants in federal courts in all non-petty cases. Not only that, but within two years the legislatures and courts of twenty-three states took specific actions to implement the spirit as well as the letter of *Gideon*. As amended in 1970, the 1964 C.J.A. authorizes both the creation of federal or community public defender organizations in "high volume districts" and the necessary compensation for legal assistance at *every* step and stage of the criminal process, from the arrest to appeals, *including* post-conviction and ancillary proceedings relative to the criminal trial. No wonder the *Gideon* case stands as a landmark! And just

---

[158] Justices Douglas and Harlan wrote separate concurring opinions.
[159] A brief *amicus curiae*, i.e., "friend of the Court," enables an interested third party to enter the case, with the consent of the other litigants and/or the Court.
[160] 316 U.S. 455 (1942).
[161] 287 U.S. 45 (1932).
[162] *Gideon v. Wainwright, op. cit.*, at 355. On remand to the Florida trial court, Gideon was quickly retried and acquitted with the aid of a local attorney.
[163] See, for example, these decisions liberalizing even further the right to counsel: *Massiah v. United States*, 377 U.S. 201 (1964); *Escobedo v. Illinois*, 387 U.S. 478 (1964); the series of June 1966 cases expanding the *Escobedo* decision, headed by *Miranda v. Arizona*, 384 U.S. 436; *Orozco v. Texas*, 394 U.S. 324 (1969); *Coleman v. Alabama*, 399 U.S. 1 (1970); *Argersinger v. Hamlin*, 407 U.S. 25 (1972); and *United States v. Henry*, 447 U.S. 264 (1980).

around the corner waited another contentious sector of the Bill of Rights, the Fifth Amendment's stricture against compulsory self-incrimination.

1964: The Self-Incrimination Cases. The frequently predicted and much publicized *self-incrimination safeguards* were incorporated in a significant dual decision in the last days of the 1963–64 term. In two cases[164] the Court dramatically overruled its 1908 decision in the *Twining* case,[165] thus adopting Mr. Justice Harlan's lone dissent therein to make that case again a signal contribution to the broadening concept of criminal jurisprudence.

The first case was from Connecticut and concerned one William Malloy, who had been arrested during a gambling raid in 1959 by Hartford police. Pleading guilty to the crime of "pool-selling," he was sentenced to one year in jail and fined $500. Some sixteen months thereafter Malloy was ordered to testify in an official, court-sanctioned inquiry into alleged gambling and other criminal activities in the county. Asked a number of questions about events surrounding his own arrest and conviction, Malloy refused to answer any of them "on the grounds it may tend to incriminate me." He was held in contempt and incarcerated "until he was willing to answer the questions." His appeal via a writ of *habeas corpus* was rejected all along the judicial hierarchy in Connecticut, its highest tribunal ultimately ruling, *inter alia,* that the Fifth Amendment's privilege against self-incrimination was not available to a witness in a state proceeding and that the Fourteenth Amendment "extended no privilege to him." The Connecticut courts relied, of course, on past Supreme Court rulings to that effect. But they were now to fall. Over vigorous dissenting opinions by Justices Harlan and Clark, who firmly rejected nationalization of the Fifth, and by Justices White and Stewart, who questioned the propriety of the privilege's invocation in the instant case, a majority of five members of the Court extended the "incorporated" side of the Cardozo table. Speaking for the Chief Justice, Justices Black, Douglas, Goldberg (who had replaced the retired Frankfurter two years earlier), and himself, Mr. Justice Brennan held that the Fourteenth Amendment, which assures all citizens due process of law, guaranteed the petitioner the protection of the Fifth Amendment's privilege against compulsory self-incrimination. In language redolent with appeals for a system of "nationalized" criminal justice, Brennan pronounced the *Twining*[166] and *Adamson*[167] decisions as wrong constitutional law and announced that, *"a fortiorari,"*

---

[164] *Malloy v. Hogan,* 378 U.S. 1 (1964); and *Murphy v. Waterfront Commission of New York Harbor,* 378 U.S. 52 (1964).

[165] *Twining v. New Jersey,* 211 U.S. 78 (see p. 50, *supra*).

[166] *Ibid.*

[167] *Adamson v. California,* 332 U.S. 46 (1947). The *specifics of Adamson,* i.e., comments upon failure by the accused to take the stand, were overruled in *Griffin v. California,* 381 U.S. 957 (1965), Griffin's victorious counsel being the same attorney, Morris Lavine, who had lost in *Adamson* eighteen years earlier! In an elaborate

[t]he Fourteenth Amendment secures against state invasion the same privilege that the Fifth Amendment guarantees against federal infringement—
the right of a person to remain silent unless he chooses to speak in the un-
fettered exercise of his own free will, and to suffer no penalty . . . for
such silence.[168]

The New York companion case turned on the refusal of William Murphy to give testimony to the New York Waterfront Commission, which
was then investigating a work stoppage at certain New Jersey piers. Murphy had been promised immunity from prosecution in return for his testimony; but he refused this offer, fearing that his answers might incriminate
him under *federal* law to which the grant of immunity did not purport to
extend. Overruling its own precedents,[169] the Supreme Court, without dissent this time, categorically rejected "the established rule that one jurisdiction within our federal structure may compel a witness to give testimony
which could be used to convict him of a crime in another."[170] Although
two of the justices, in a concurring opinion by Harlan, joined by Clark,
objected to the "mixing together" of the Fifth and the Fourteenth Amendments, the Court unanimously agreed with its spokesman, Mr. Justice Arthur J. Goldberg: "We hold that the Constitutional privilege against self-
incrimination protects a state witness against incrimination under Federal
as well as state law and a Federal witness against incrimination under state
as well as Federal law."[171] While the case featured three separate opinions[172]—two of these concurring on different grounds—and the individual
justices may have accepted the Goldberg conclusion for varying reasons, it
nevertheless represented another broadening of the application of the Bill
of Rights to the states.

1965 and 1967: The Texas Confrontation of Witnesses Cases. Next in
line was the clause of the Sixth Amendment that provides: "In all criminal
prosecutions, the accused shall enjoy the right . . . to be confronted with
the witnesses against him. . . ." Did it, too, apply with equal effect to
proceedings in state courts by virtue of the due process clause of Amendment Fourteen? Yes, held a unanimous Supreme Court, although the four
opinions in the case were based on different grounds.

"follow-up" 1981 decision the Court held 8:1 that, upon a defendant's request, the
presiding judge *must* instruct the jury not to draw an adverse inference from the invocation of the Fifth Amendment by someone on trial. (*Carter v. Kentucky,* 49
LW 4225.)

[168] *Malloy v. Hogan, op. cit.,* at 8.

[169] *United States v. Murdock,* 284 U.S. 141 (1931); *Feldman v. United States,* 322
U.S. 487 (1944); *Knapp v. Schweitzer,* 357 U.S. 371 (1958).

[170] *Murphy v. Waterfront Commission of New York Harbor, op. cit.,* at 77.

[171] *Ibid.,* at 77–78. The holding was extended (7:2) in 1979 to apply to testimony
before a grand jury. (*New Jersey v. Potash,* 439 U.S. 816.)

[172] Those by Justices Goldberg, White, and Harlan.

Granville Pointer (and a cohort, Earl Dillard) had been charged with robbing Kenneth W. Phillips of $375 "by assault, or violence, or by putting in fear of life or bodily injury."[173] At the preliminary hearing before a state judge, called the "examining trial" in Texas, Phillips gave detailed testimony including an identification of Pointer who, although present throughout the hearing, had no attorney and made no effort to cross-examine Phillips. At Pointer's trial the State submitted evidence that Phillips had recently moved to California and had no intention whatever of returning to Texas. The trial judge permitted the prosecution to introduce the transcript of Phillips's testimony at the preliminary hearing, over the repeated objections of Pointer's counsel. In each instance the trial judge overruled the defense objections on the ground that Pointer had had ample opportunity to cross-examine Phillips at the preliminary hearing stage. The Texas Court of Criminal Appeals affirmed Pointer's conviction—but the Supreme Court of the United States reversed it 9:0, though it was divided on the bases for its action.

Mr. Justice Black, speaking for the Court, referred to the spate of recent decisions holding applicable to the states various guarantees in the Bill of Rights, including the Sixth Amendment's right to counsel and the Fifth's guarantee against compulsory self-incrimination. He ruled: "We hold today that the Sixth Amendment's right of an accused to confront the witnesses against him is likewise a fundamental right and is made obligatory on the States by the Fourteenth Amendment."[174] Black then observed that the inclusion in the Sixth Amendment of *the right of confrontation* "reflects the belief of the Framers . . . that confrontation was a fundamental right essential to a fair trial in a criminal prosecution."[175] And he concluded that since the right of confrontation comprehended the right to cross-examine, reversal was mandatory. Henceforth, the same standards that protect litigants against federal encroachment of this right would be applicable and enforceable against the states. A precedent of more than six decades earlier thus stood overruled.[176]

Three concurring opinions were filed, each dealing with the "incorporation doctrine." Mr. Justice Goldberg, evidently eager to go on record with *his* approach to the problem—for he had not been on the Court when the issue was joined in the *Adamson* case[177] in 1947—acknowledged that, on the record, the "incorporation doctrine" had never really commanded a

[173] *Pointer v. Texas,* 380 U.S. 400 (1965).

[174] *Ibid.,* at 403.

[175] *Ibid.,* at 404.

[176] *West v. Louisiana,* 194 U.S. 258 (1904). Unlike Clarence Earl Gideon, however, Granville Pointer, when retried below, was convicted again (Phillips now appearing as the prosecution's star witness) and was sentenced to prison from five years to life.

[177] 332 U.S. 46.

majority of the Court. However, he sternly rejected both the Frankfurter case-by-case "was it due process?" approach and the *Palko* "is it implicit in the concept of ordered liberty?" test. In effect, he embraced the applicability to the states of the *fundamental* guarantees of the Bill of Rights, and he clearly did not particularly care *how* this was done by the Court or by what name the process would be known—just so long as those guarantees were indeed made obligatory for the states via the Fourteenth Amendment.[178]

Mr. Justice Harlan, while concurring in the result of *Pointer,* nevertheless re-expressed his conviction that the majority's holding constituted "another step in the onward march on the long-since discredited 'incorporation' doctrine."[179] Exhorting the Court to return to a policy of "leaving room for differences among states," he wrote that *he* would have reversed Pointer's conviction on the basis that the procedure followed by Texas had deprived Pointer of due process of law guaranteed by the Fourteenth Amendment, "independently of the Sixth."[180] Harlan freely acknowledged that the right of confrontation is indeed "implicit in the concept of ordered liberty," which mandated its observance by Texas. But he lashed out at "incorporation" as being "incompatible with our constitutionally ordained federal system" as well as "unsound doctrine."[181] Once again he pointed to what he saw as the value of the states as "laboratories" that must not be "subordinated to federal power." Taking issue with that contention, Mr. Justice Goldberg wrote in his concurring opinion that while it was good that the states should be able to try social and economic experiments, he did not believe that this "includes the power to experiment with the fundamental liberties of citizens safeguarded by the Bill of Rights."[182]

In his brief concurring opinion, Mr. Justice Stewart took to task the Black opinion for the Court as a "questionable tour de force . . . entirely unnecessary to the decision of this case. . . ."[183] He said that *he* would have reversed Pointer's conviction on the simple ground that Pointer had been clearly deprived of liberty without due process of law in express violation of the Fourteenth Amendment—which, of course, constitutes the case-by-case approach to the applicability question. But on the same day the Court proceeded to apply the new ruling in reversing a conviction in a similar case.[184] And in 1967 it logically, and unanimously, extended the

178 *Pointer v. Texas, op. cit.,* at 414.
179 *Ibid.,* at 408.
180 *Ibid.*
181 *Ibid.,* at 409.
182 *Ibid.,* at 413.
183 *Ibid.,* at 410.
184 *Douglas v. Alabama,* 380 U.S. 415 (1965), with the same Court "line-up," although Mr. Justice Brennan wrote the opinion here.

Pointer holding to cover compulsory process to obtain and thus to confront *favorable* witnesses, too (*Pointer* having dealt with *adverse* witnesses), in another Texas controversy.[185] Again, the Court was unanimous, its decision written by Mr. Chief Justice Warren—and again Mr. Justice Harlan's concurring opinion represented an important lecture on the basic incorporation controversy.

1965: "Incorporation" Re-argued: The Connecticut Birth Control Case. As if to continue the "argument" among themselves on incorporation, which they had once again raised in the first *Texas Confrontation* case[186] in 1965, the Supreme Court justices addressed themselves to it with gusto in their controversial decision in *Griswold v. Connecticut,* now generally referred to as the *Birth Control* case.[187] Our concern here is less with the merits of the decision than with the reasoning employed by the six opinion writers on the incorporation problem (which, depending upon one's analysis, either did or did not have something to do with the holding in the case itself). It suffices to note that the Court, by a 7:2 vote, invalidated an old and generally unenforced Connecticut statute that made it a crime for any person, married or single, to *use* any drug or other article or device for the purpose of preventing conception. The Court's opinion was delivered by Mr. Justice Douglas and its judgment of reversal of the defendants'[188] convictions was agreed to by the Chief Justice and Associate Justices Clark, Harlan, Brennan, White, and Goldberg. But only Clark fully accepted Douglas's reasoning (at least he wrote no opinion); Harlan, White, and Goldberg wrote separate concurring opinions, with the Chief Justice and Brennan joining in Goldberg's. Justices Black and Stewart wrote separate dissenting opinions, each specifically also joining the other's.

Douglas noted at the outset that the Court was here confronted with a *bona fide* controversy that it could properly decide, one involving "the constitutional rights of married people with whom [the defendants, leaders of the Planned Parenthood League] had a professional relationship."[189]

[185] *Washington v. Texas,* 388 U.S. 14. Jackie Washington's Sixth and Fourteenth Amendment rights were held fatally encumbered because, under an applied Texas rule, a co-defendant was barred from appearing as a witness in his favor.

[186] *Pointer v. Texas,* 380 U.S. 400.

[187] 381 U.S. 479.

[188] They were Estelle T. Griswold, Executive Director of the Planned Parenthood League of Connecticut and Dr. C. Lee Buxton, a licensed physician, teaching at Yale University's School of Medicine, who served as medical director for the League's New Haven Center. They gave information and medical advice to married persons on means of preventing conception, were found guilty of violating the Connecticut statute at issue, and were fined $100 each. Their appeal was on Fourteenth Amendment grounds.

[189] *Griswold v. Connecticut, op. cit.,* at 481.

[190] *Ibid.,* at 484. (Italics supplied.)

He reviewed several Court decisions that, in his judgment, established "that specific guarantees in the Bill of Rights have *penumbras,* formed by emanations from those guarantees that help give them life and substance,"[190] penumbras that reached areas not specifically mentioned in the Bill. He thereupon cited five different amendments the "penumbras" of which "create zones of privacy," among them the First Amendment's protection of the right of association, the Third's prohibition of quartering of soldiers in homes, the Fourth's guarantee against unreasonable searches and seizures, the Fifth's against compulsory self-incrimination. He added, in a coup of potential trail-blazing, the *Ninth Amendment,* justifying its inclusion as a beacon to illuminate "the zone of privacy created by [the] several fundamental constitutional guarantees."[191]

Predictably, the concurring opinions raised the issue of "incorporation," and, specifically, whether—in the light of the expansive Douglas opinion—it was indeed limited to the Bill of Rights. Mr. Justice Harlan, in his solo opinion, saw the issue in terms of the requirement of basic values that are "implicit in the concept of ordered liberty"—the *Palko* and case-by-case approach to the scope of the due process clause of the Fourteenth Amendment rather than "incorporation." He was persuaded that the Connecticut statute did unconstitutionally infringe the due process clause which "stands . . . on its own bottom," and which is not dependent on "one or more provisions of the Bill of Rights . . . or any of their radiations. . . ."[192]

Mr. Justice Goldberg, whom the Chief Justice and Mr. Justice Brennan joined in his concurring opinion, made clear his conviction that the due process clause was neither limited to, nor necessarily so broad as, the Bill of Rights but rather that it "proctects those personal rights that are fundamental." In sweeping language, he emphasized the relevance of the Ninth Amendment to the Court's holding, contending that its language and history reveal that "the Framers of the Constitution believed that *there are additional fundamental rights,* protected from governmental infringement,

---

[191] *Ibid.,* at 485. Six years later, and this time squarely based on the equal protection clause as well as on considerations of "privacy," the Court, speaking through Mr. Justice Brennan—with only Mr. Chief Justice Burger in dissent—held that Massachusetts could not outlaw the distribution of contraceptives to *single* persons when these are legally available to married ones. (*Eisenstadt v. Baird,* 405 U.S. 438 [1972].) The vote declaring the 93-year-old law unconstitutional was only 4:3, however. And five years thereafter (1977), the Court struck down 7:2 New York State's broad anti-contraception advertising and distribution law on the following grounds: (1) Violation of Amendment One (the State's proscription of the advertising or display of contraceptives); (2) violation of due process of law because of the rights of privacy inherent in Amendments Fourteen and Nine (the State's limitations of sales to physicians, pharmacies, and drugstores); and, (3) again invoking the recently found prerogatives of privacy emanating from due process considerations (the State's forbidding of the dispensing of contraceptives to those aged sixteen or younger). (*Carey v. Population Services International,* 431 U.S. 678.)

[192] *Ibid.,* at 500.

which exist *alongside those fundamental rights specifically mentioned in the first eight constitutional amendments.*"[193] In other words, he viewed the Ninth Amendment—which Madison had proposed as a concession to Alexander Hamilton's and James Wilson's opposition to a Bill of Rights, opposition based on the fear that non-enumerated rights would be jeopardized—as a lever for the protection of all those "fundamental rights" not specifically protected by the first eight via the "liberty" safeguard in the due process clauses of both the Fifth and the Fourteenth Amendments. The Ninth, he reiterated several times in his opinion, "is surely relevant in showing the existence of other fundamental personal rights now protected from state as well as federal infringement."[194]

Goldberg thus rejected the Black approach to incorporation because it would *limit the rights eligible for incorporation to those specifically listed* in the Bill of Rights. For to Black, the committed literalist, it had to be spelled out verbatim in the document to be applicable.

Mr. Justice White's relatively brief concurring opinion saw a clear-cut violation of substantive due process by the Connecticut statute because of its "too sweeping" provisions which entered "a realm of family life which the state cannot enter."[195] In short, incorporation or no incorporation, the crux of the matter to White was that the due process clause, which prohibits states from depriving any person of "liberty" without due process of law, was clearly violated by the restrictions of the Connecticut law.

In dissenting, Mr. Justice Black took pains to announce his complete agreement with all of the "graphic and eloquent strictures and criticisms" leveled at what his colleague Stewart, dissenting with him, termed "this uncommonly silly law"—under which no one had ever been prosecuted—but he rejected the majority's collective reasoning. Characteristically, he noted the absence of a *specific* constitutional provision that proscribed an invasion of privacy, which he styled "a broad, abstract, and ambiguous concept,"—one he viewed merely as a "statement" of policy—and he warned

[193] *Ibid.,* at 488. (Italics supplied.)

[194] E.g., *ibid.,* at 493. Many scholars support this view; e.g., Bennett B. Patterson, the author of one of the very few works on the Ninth Amendment, *The Forgotten Ninth Amendment* (Indianapolis: Bobbs-Merrill, 1955)—although Patterson acknowledges that the Ninth may well simply be viewed as a "basic statement of the inherent natural rights of the individual" (p. 4).

[195] *Ibid.,* at 502. Since *Griswold,* a spate of Ninth Amendment litigation has been spawned. Among the claims and/or decisions: the Ninth does *not* grant a right: to smoke marijuana (*People v. Glaser,* 238 C.A.2d 819, 48 Cal. Reptr. 427 [1965]); to refuse army induction (*U.S. v. Uhl,* 436 F.2d 773, 9th Cir. [1970]); or to marry a person of the same sex (*Baker v. Nelson,* 489 U.S. 810 [1971]). The applicability of the Ninth to the long-hair syndrome remained guarded and clouded (cf. *Dawson v. School Board,* 322 F. Supp. 286 [1971] and *Davis v. Firment,* 269 F. Supp. 524), for a number of years; but a 7:2 decision in 1976 in favor of the application of state authority under duly guarded police powers seems to have settled the matter, at least for the time being. (*Kelley v. Johnson,* 425 U.S. 238.)

that the Court's reliance on the Ninth Amendment together with the due process clause would give the "federal judiciary the power to invalidate any legislative act which the judges find irrational, unreasonable or offensive."[196] To accept such an approach, he believed, was to revive the "shocking" doctrine rejected by the Court three decades earlier under which it had for so long struck down—by virtue of a power "bestowed on the Court by the Court"[197]—federal and state statutes in the *economic* realm because of alleged violations of substantive due process of law based on such notions as the sanctity of contracts. "Privacy," he declared, "is a broad, abstract, and ambiguous concept" that can be readily expanded or shrunken by later decisions.[198] Lest he be misunderstood, Black reiterated his belief that the Court does have the power, "which it should exercise," to hold laws unconstitutional where they are forbidden by the Constitution, and that he fully believed then as before, that the specifics of that document are incorporated and made applicable to the states via the due process clause of the Fourteenth Amendment. Yet, like Stewart in his dissenting opinion—who sarcastically commented that "to say that the Ninth Amendment has anything to do with this case is to turn somersaults with history"[199]—Black could find nothing in the Constitution and its amendments to forbid the passage of the Connecticut law. Quoting from his dissenting opinion in *Adamson v. California*[200] almost two decades earlier, he cautioned that

. . . to pass upon the constitutionality of statutes by looking to the particular standards enumerated in the Bill of Rights and other parts of the

[196] *Ibid.*, at 509, 511.

[197] *Ibid.*, at 520.

[198] A prophetic statement, of course: in January 1973 down came the bombshell privacy-based, six-opinion *Abortion Cases*, holding 7:2 that the right of "privacy," derived largely from the "liberty" concept of due process of law under the Fourteenth Amendment, and partly from the Ninth (*stare decisis Griswold*), rendered unconstitutional all state laws (46) that prohibited or restricted a woman's right to obtain an abortion during the first three months of pregnancy (*Roe v. Wade,* 410 U.S. 113 and *Doe v. Bolton,* 410 U.S. 179). The holding was made retroactive in a 9:0 *per cu.iam* decision in 1975 in *Louisiana State Bd. of Medical Examiners v. Rosen,* 419 U.S. 1098—and both reconfirmed and indeed extended in 1976 in a series of cases headed by *Planned Parenthood of Central Missouri v. Danforth,* 428 U.S. 52 and in 1979 in *Bellotti v. Baird,* 443 U.S. 622, although a mite equivocally. But, as Black had warned, it has also proved at least partly "shrinkable." Thus, a trio of 1977 cases held that neither the Constitution nor federal legislation *compels* states to fund non-therapeutic abortions for women in financial need. (*Beal v. Doe, Maher v. Doe,* and *Poelker v. Doe,* 432 U.S. 438, 526, and 519, respectively. See also *Colautti v. Franklin,* 439 U.S. 379 [1979].) And a six-opinion 5:4 decision in 1980 upheld the Hyde Amendment enacted by Congress, banning Medicaid financing by the federal government of abortions in all but a handful of cases (e.g., instances of promptly reported rape or incest or "where the life of the mother would be endangered if the fetus were carried to term"). (*Harris v. McRae,* 448 U.S. 297.) *Cf. H. L. v. Matheson* (1981) by backing 6:3 a Utah pre-abortion parental *notification* requirement for teenagers living at home.

[199] *Griswold, op. cit.,* at 527.

[200] 330 U.S. 46 (1947), at 90–92.

Constitution is one thing; to invalidate statutes because of application of "natural law" deemed to be above and undefined by the Constitution is another.[201]

Amplifying this position in his *A Constitutional Faith* three years later, Black observed that "even though I like my privacy as well as the next person, I am nevertheless compelled to admit that the states have a right to invade it unless prohibited by some specific constitutional provision." For he could "find in the Constitution no language which either specifically or impliedly grants to all individuals a constitutional right of privacy."[202]

Black's formula always was that the First Amendment protects freedom of *expression,* and it does that absolutely. Yet it does not protect "conduct" ("physical activities")—be that conduct a racial "sit-in"[203] or the use of contraceptive devices.[204] And he quoted with full agreement a famous statement by Judge Learned Hand on the matter of judicial invalidation of legislation offensive to the jurists' personal preferences: "For myself it would be most irksome to be ruled by a bevy of Platonic Guardians, even if I knew how to choose them, which I assuredly do not."[205] But in the footnote giving the above statement's citation, Black had to acknowledge that although he agreed with Hand's "criticism of use of the due process formula, I do not agree with all the views he expressed about construing the specific guarantees of the Bill of Rights."[206] Of course, Black could not; for, ironically, in his 1958 book, *The Bill of Rights*[207]—which contains the "platonic guardians" statement so approvingly quoted by Black—Hand, rejecting any double standard justifications as between "economic" and "civil libertarian" rights, took considerable pain to contend that the Court, on which Black then served, had gone too far, in a number of cases, in holding legislation to be in violation of *specific* guarantees of the Bill of Rights.[208]

1966: Formally Incorporating the Right to Trial by an "Impartial" Jury. The first incorporation by the Court following its thorough *reprise* analysis

---

[201] *Griswold v. Connecticut, op. cit.,* at 525.

[202] (New York: Alfred A. Knopf, 1968), p. 9. How subjective the concept of "privacy" is, and how vexatious its judicial application, may be illustrated by pointing to two lower court decisions in 1970 which, *both* citing *Griswold,* struck down a Texas sodomy statute as an unconstitutional invasion of privacy while upholding a 1796 New Jersey statute proscribing fornication! (*Buchanan v. Bachelor,* 308 F. Supp. 729 and *State v. Lutz,* 57 N.J. 314.) But late in 1977 the New Jersey Supreme Court did rule the old statute unconstitutional, 5:2, as a violation of "the right to privacy." (*State v. Saunders,* 75 N.J. 200.)

[203] See Chapter VII, *infra.*

[204] *Griswold v. Connecticut, op. cit.,* at 507–8.

[205] *Ibid.,* at 526.

[206] *Ibid.,* n. 23.

[207] (Cambridge: Harvard University Press, 1958.)

[208] *Ibid.,* pp. 35–45.

and exposition of the basic issues in *Griswold* turned out to be something that had long been assumed to have been incorporated—the right to trial by an *impartial* jury. Indeed, the requirement of a *fair trial,* a cornerstone of the judicial process, would naturally assume trial by an *impartial* jury, provided a jury trial were granted in the first place, of course. (The right to a trial by jury *per se* was not incorporated until the *Duncan* case[209]—see below—and it reached only criminal cases above the petty level.) However, although disposing of the matter in a *per curiam* opinion,[210] the Court evidently deemed it necessary and/or politic to inform the states that the Sixth Amendment's requirement for an "impartial" jury was indeed applicable to them as well as to the federal government. The case concerned a bailiff named Gladden who made the following statements to the sequestered jury trying one Lee E. A. Parker: "Oh, that wicked fellow, he is guilty. . . . If there is anything wrong, the Supreme Court will correct it."[211] The Court did—although hardly along the lines Bailiff Gladden could have expected!

1967: The Right to a Speedy Trial. With the right to a *public* trial by jury incorporated in 1948, it was only a question of time until the collateral Sixth Amendment requirement of a *speedy* trial—which had received recognition as early as 1166 in the Assize of Clarendon—would also be rendered applicable by the Court. Its vehicle became the case of a professor of zoology at Duke University, Peter H. Klopfer, who had been indicted by the State of North Carolina for criminal trespass after he took part in a sit-in at the then segregated Watts Motel and Restaurant in Chapel Hill. The controversy arose in 1964, and Professor Klopfer was indeed tried soon thereafter; however, the jury failed to agree on a verdict and a mistrial was declared by Trial Judge Raymond B. Mallard, thus heralding a new trial. A year passed without a second trial, and when Professor Klopfer officially demanded either to be tried forthwith or have his case dismissed, the judge granted, instead, State Prosecutor (District Solicitor) Thomas Cooper's motion for a *nolle prosequi* (which permits a prosecutor to place an indictment in an inactive status, without bringing the case to trial, but "retaining it for use at any future time"—a procedure then permitted by thirty states). The exasperated Professor Klopfer appealed, arguing that

---

[209] *Duncan v. Louisiana,* 391 U.S. 145 (1968). See the discussion, pp. 78–81, *infra.*
[210] An unsigned, normally very brief, opinion for the Court, its authorship unknown to the outside world, applying *res judicata* (settled law).
[211] *Parker v. Gladden,* 385 U.S. 363 (1966), at 364. In his excellent full-length study, "The Supreme Court and the Second Bill of Rights" (Madison: University of Wisconsin, 1981), Professor Richard C. Cortner disagrees with the above conclusion that *Parker* incorporated the impartial requirement of Amendment Six. Instead, he views *Parker* as a confirmation of the Sixth's confrontation and cross-examination rights. Mr. Justice Brennan for one, however, expressed agreement with my position in response to an oral *quaere* (January 15, 1969). The vote in *Parker* was 8:1, Mr. Justice Harlan dissenting (at 366).

this action denied his Sixth Amendment right to a speedy trial, which he regarded as applicable to the states. Denying his appeal, the North Carolina Supreme Court ruled in January of 1966 that a defendant's right to speedy trial—which the tribunal readily acknowledged—does not encompass "the right to compel the state to prosecute him." In Klopfer's instance this meant that he would continue to be subject to a retrial at any time, at the discretion of the state, on the basis of the "suspended" trespass indictment. He appealed to the Supreme Court of the United States.

In another milestone decision in constitutional development,[212] the Court unanimously sided with the appellant. Speaking for six justices as well as himself, Mr. Chief Justice Warren called the North Carolina practice at issue an "extraordinary criminal procedure," noting that the North Carolina Supreme Court's position "has been explicitly rejected by every other state court which has considered the question."[213] Clearly, he concluded, the procedure served to deny Professor Klopfer "the right to a speedy trial which we hold is guaranteed to him by the Sixth Amendment of the Constitution of the United States"[214]—thus incorporating the requirement. Not surprisingly on the basis of his record on the matter, Mr. Justice Harlan, while voting to reverse the North Carolina decision—noting that he "entirely agree[d] with the result reached in the Court"—wrote a separate concurring opinion in which he again voiced his rejection of what he viewed as the "rigid uniformity" in state procedures brought about by "incorporation" or "absorption," explaining that *he* would have struck down the state's procedure because it was violative of the "fundamental fairness" guaranteed by the due process of law clause of Amendment Fourteen.[215] Mr. Justice Stewart simply noted that he concurred, but did not elaborate. In 1974 Congress, led by the retiring Senator Sam J. Ervin, Jr. (D.-N.C.), enacted the Federal Speedy Trial Act, setting up a schedule to be implemented over a five-year period of time limits—ultimately (June 30, 1980) reaching a low of a hundred days—during which criminal charges must either be brought to trial or dropped. As to the precise nature of the time

---

[212] *Klopfer v. North Carolina,* 386 U.S. 213 (1967).

[213] *Ibid.,* at 219.

[214] *Ibid.,* at 222. It was on denial-of-speedy trial grounds that, in 1980, Green Beret Doctor Jeffrey R. MacDonald found his conviction of the murder of his wife and two children overturned 2:1 by the United States Court of Appeals for the Fourth Circuit. (*United States v. MacDonald,* 632 F.2d 258.)

[215] *Ibid.,* at 226–27. On remand to the trial court, the charges against Klopfer were dismissed. Had Harlan lived to witness them, he would very likely have approved the Court's actions in two 1971 cases, in which—without dissent—it declined to review two lower court holdings which, based on the facts at issue, held: (a) that an 18-months' delay from arrest to trial did not necessarily deprive a defendant of his rights to a speedy trial (*Blevins v. U.S.,* 404 U.S. 823); and (b) that neither did a governmental delay for five years of an indictment after the alleged criminal offense took place (*Quinn v. U.S.,* 404 U.S. 850).

period to be considered, the Court ruled 7:1 in 1975 that it is the period between trial and *either* arrest or indictment, whichever comes first.[216]

1968: Gary Duncan's Right to a Trial by Jury in a Criminal Case. An appeal coming up from a decision by the Supreme Court of Louisiana afforded the United States Supreme Court the long-anticipated occasion to incorporate the *right to be tried by jury in criminal cases* (above the petty level).[217] With the right to a "fair," a "public," an "impartial," and a "speedy" trial already established an incumbent upon the states, it was only a question of time until the Court would similarly deal with the fundamental right of a trial by jury *per se,* at least in criminal cases. Yet it took until 1968 and Gary Duncan's appeal of a conviction for simple battery which, under Louisiana law, was punishable by a maximum of two years' imprisonment and a $300 fine. Duncan, a 19-year-old black, convicted in Plaquemines parish[218] court of slapping a white boy on the elbow and sentenced to sixty days in jail and a $150 fine, had sought a trial by jury. But because the Louisiana Constitution granted jury trials only in cases in which capital punishment or imprisonment at hard labor might be imposed, the trial judge denied Duncan's request, and the latter appealed to the Supreme Court, contending that the Sixth and Fourteenth Amendments to the federal Constitution secured the right of jury trial in state criminal prosecutions, such as his, where a sentence as long as two years could be pronounced. The Court agreed, 7:2.

Speaking for the majority, Mr. Justice White, in a relatively brief opinion, reviewed aspects of the history of the judicially mandated application of the several provisions of the Bill of Rights to the states, and concluded simply but firmly, after reviewing the specific nature of the controversy and the history of trial by jury:

> Because we believe that trial by jury in criminal cases is fundamental to the American scheme of justice, we hold that the Fourteenth Amendment guarantees a right of jury trial in all criminal cases which—were they to be tried in a federal court—would come within the Sixth Amendment's guarantee. Since we consider the appeal before us to be such a case, we hold

216 *Dillingham v. United States,* 423 U.S. 64. (The Chief Justice dissented.) In 1977, in a speedy-trial case ruling, a federal district court declared the statute unconstitutional as an "impermissible legislative encroachment on the judiciary." (*United States v. Howard,* 440 F. Supp. 1106.) On appeal, the U.S. Court of Appeals for the Fourth Circuit affirmed on *other* grounds, finding that "the issue of constitutionality was not raised and therefore not properly before it." (*Ibid.,* 590 F.2d 564, at 568 n.4.) The United States Supreme Court denied *certiorari* in 1979. (*Ibid.,* 440 U.S. 976.) Thus, notwithstanding the trial court's holding—which may be viewed as a declaratory judgment (see my *The Judicial Process, op. cit.,* pp. 379–81)—the Act remains the law of the land (Summer 1981), as amended and strengthened in 1979.

217 *Duncan v. Louisiana,* 391 U.S. 145 (1968).

218 This oil-rich parish was long bossed by the powerful, skillful political leader Leander H. Perez—a virulent segregationist and anti-Semite.

that the Constitution was violated when appellant's demand for jury trial was refused.[219]

Justice White pointed out that so-called "petty offenses" have traditionally been tried without a jury, and said this would continue to be true under the *Duncan* ruling. He noted that, in federal cases, a "petty" offense is one carrying a maximum penalty of six months' imprisonment and a $50 fine. Beyond that, he left for future decisions the delineation of "serious" from "petty" cases because, in the Court's view, the conviction of Gary Duncan[220] was clearly a "serious" one.[221]

Three other opinions were featured in the milestone case. Mr. Justice Black, joined by Douglas, took the occasion to reiterate the convictions and beliefs concerning incorporation he had first set out so prominently in the *Adamson* case[222]—although he applauded the Court for reaching "almost" the same result via the "selective" incorporation approach (which he was thus "very happy to support" as a means to his desired end) and to dispute the stance again espoused in *Duncan* by his long-time opponent on incorporation, Mr. Justice Harlan. Black did so primarily because of Harlan's notable dissenting opinion that may well have been the latter's most eloquent in the long incorporation debate. For, joined by Stewart, Harlan not only disputed the assertion that due process of law requires the application of federal jury trial standards, but he also took pains to deliver another lecture against incorporation *per se;* against "selective" incorporation; and against the Court's reading of history which, he charged, made "no sense"—thus once again opting for a case-by-case "fundamental fairness" approach. To Harlan, the 1833 holding of *Barron v. Baltimore*[223] was still good law: he never regarded it as having been overruled by the Fourteenth Amendment,[224] warmly pleading in conclusion for a return to Mr. Justice Brandeis's "celebrated dictum" of 1932, that it is "one of the happy incidents of the federal system that a single courageous state may, if its citizens choose, serve as a laboratory. . . ."[225] Until the day he left the Court in 1971, Harlan never failed to warn against "stifling flexibility

---

[219] *Duncan v. Louisiana, op. cit.,* at 149–50.

[220] Because Louisiana refused to comply in its lower court hierarchy, Duncan was not free from the threat of further prosecution until the federal courts had effectively enjoined Plaquemines parish by late 1971! (*Perez v. Duncan,* 404 U.S. 1071, *certiorari* denied.)

[221] The Court regards as "petty" only those offenses for which a sentence of a *maximum* of six months is applicable. (See the 1970 decision in *Baldwin v. New York,* 399 U.S. 66.)

[222] See pp. 35 ff., *supra.*

[223] See pp. 29–30, *supra.*

[224] *Duncan v. Louisiana, op. cit.,* at 172.

[225] Quoting from Brandeis's opinion in *New State Ice Co. v. Liebmann,* 285 U.S. 262, at 280, 311.

in the States." He would have been pleased had he lived to see the Court's 5:4 ruling in 1976 which, seemingly narrowing the *Duncan* opinion, held that a state may indeed deny a defendant a jury in his initial trial on a criminal charge, *if* it allows that defendant, through an appeal, to get a second trial in which there *is* a jury.[226]

And in a separate concurring opinion, siding with the White holding, Mr. Justice Fortas went on record as voicing his concern lest the ruling be regarded as "automatically [to] import all the ancillary rules which have been or may hereafter be developed incidental to the right of jury trial in the federal courts." He saw "no reason whatever," for example, "to assume that [the *Duncan* decision] should require us to impose federal requirements such as unanimous verdicts or a jury of 12 upon the States."[227] When the Court had an opportunity to rule in 1970 on Florida's six-man jury in non-capital cases, it upheld the practice 7:1.[228] Mr. Justice White again wrote the opinion; Mr. Justice Marshall dissented—contending that the Sixth Amendment requires a twelve-man jury.[229] Indeed it does, ruled a bare five-man majority two years later, *but* only in *federal* cases—Mr. Justice Powell providing the key vote in his concurring opinion which, however, *upheld* 5:4 the right of Louisiana[230] to render 9:3 and that of Oregon[231] 10:2 and 11:1 verdicts in *criminal* cases. Powell insisted that the Sixth Amendment intended to require *federal* courts to employ the unanimous twelve-member jury of the English common law tradition; but he did not view the due process of law clause of the Fourteenth as requiring similarly unanimous verdicts in *state* criminal trials. Mr. Justice Blackmun, also in the majority, noted that he would have "great difficulty" in upholding a 7:5 verdict, however. Dissenting in both cases were Justices Douglas, Brennan, Stewart, and Marshall, who insisted that the federal standards apposite under Amendment Six are *ipso facto* incorporated. In 1973 down came the anticipated ruling by the Court regarding federal *civil* trials: in a 5:4 opinion, interestingly authored by one of the dissenters in the two aforementioned cases, Mr. Justice Brennan, the Court ruled that resort to less than twelve-member juries—long practiced and authorized at the level of the states—is not unconstitutional under the Seventh Amendment's guarantee of a trial by jury in civil cases if the value of the suit ex-

---

226 *Ludwig v. Massachusetts,* 427 U.S. 618.

227 *Duncan v. Louisiana, op. cit.,* at 213.

228 *Williams v. Florida,* 399 U.S. 78. The issue promised to arise again in future terms of Court.

229 In a footnote, White pointed out that the Court was not determining the *minimum* number *permissible,* "but we do not doubt that six is above that minimum." (*Ibid.,* at 91.)

230 *Johnson v. Louisiana,* 406 U.S. 356 (1972).

231 *Apodaca v. Oregon,* 406 U.S. 404 (1972).

ceeds $20, nor is it proscribed statutorily.[232] (Here a six-member federal civil jury was utilized.) Mr. Justice Powell joined his colleagues Douglas, Stewart, and Marshall in dissent. In 1978 the Court drew a line on the size of juries in *criminal* cases; however, scattering all over the legal landscape in nine (!) separate opinions, it held 6:3 that a jury of *less* than six could not stand—here striking down Georgia's use of a five-member panel, although its vote in the case had been unanimous. (*Ballew v. Georgia,* 435 U.S. 223.) Nor, said the Court 9:0 in 1979, could a 5:1 jury verdict stand—evidently thus drawing a firm line at six-member unanimous juries as the minimum constitutionally acceptable in state criminal cases. (*Burch v. Louisiana,* 441 U.S. 130.)

1969: Applying the Constitutional Prohibition Against Double Jeopardy. The *Duncan* decision had left the Fifth Amendment safeguard against being "twice put in jeopardy of life or limb" as the most fundamental among the few still not incorporated. The Court had had a number of opportunities to come to grips with the problem,[233] but it was not until the case of *Benton v. Maryland*[234] that it found an appropriate one. Granting *certiorari* in 1968, it limited itself to the following two crucial questions: (1) Is the "double jeopardy" clause of the Fifth Amendment applicable to the States? (2) If so, was the petitioner twice put in jeopardy? Its affirmative response to both questions made Court history by incorporating the contentious provision.

John Dalmer Benton had been indicted and tried in 1965 in Prince George's County for burglary, housebreaking, and larceny. He was convicted of burglary, found not guilty on the larceny charge, and the State did not press charges on the housebreaking count. He was sentenced to ten years in jail on the burglary conviction. Subsequently both his indictment and conviction were set aside by the Maryland Court of Appeals under a ruling that struck down a section of the Maryland Constitution requiring jurors to swear their belief in the existence of God as a condition of jury service.[235] Reindicted and re-tried for *both* burglary and larceny, he was now convicted on *both* charges and sentenced to fifteen years for burglary plus five years for larceny, the sentences to run concurrently. Benton's convictions were affirmed in the appropriate Maryland courts and he appealed to the highest court in the land *in forma pauperis,* arguing that the larceny conviction should be reversed on double jeopardy grounds since he had been found innocent on *that* charge in his first trial.

---

[232] *Colgrove v. Battin,* 413 U.S. 149.

[233] E.g., *Cichos v. Indiana,* 383 U.S. 966 (1966), when it granted *certiorari* only to dismiss the writ as having been "improvidentially granted," 385 U.S. 76 (1967).

[234] 392 U.S. 925 (1968), *certiorari* granted.

[235] *Schowgurow v. State,* 240 Md. 121 (1965).

He also argued that the burglary conviction could not stand on the theory that the jury was influenced by testimony on the larceny count.

Speaking for a 6:2 Court majority,[236] Mr. Justice Marshall held the double jeopardy provision to represent "a fundamental ideal in our constitutional heritage . . . that . . . should apply to the States through the Fourteenth Amendment." Adding that "[i]nsofar as it is inconsistent with this holding, *Palko v. Connecticut* is overruled," he explained:

> Our recent cases have thoroughly rejected the *Palko* notion that basic constitutional rights can be denied by the States as long as the totality of the circumstances does not disclose a denial of 'fundamental fairness.' Once it is decided that a particular Bill of Rights guarantee is 'fundamental to the American scheme of justice', *Duncan v. Louisiana*, the same constitutional standards apply against both the State and Federal Governments. *Palko's* roots had thus been cut away years ago. We today only recognize the inevitable. . . . The validity of [Benton's] larceny conviction must be judged, not by the watered-down standard enunciated in *Palko*, but under the Court's interpretations of the Fifth Amendment double jeopardy provision.[237]

Needless to relate, Mr. Justice Harlan was hardly prepared to "recognize the inevitable" so recognized by Marshall for the Court's majority! Joined by his frequent sympathizer in the incorporation cases, Stewart, he dissented sharply from the reversal of Benton's conviction because he did not think that the Court should have "reached out" to decide the merits of the case. However, if those were to be reached, he made resolutely clear that he, too, would have been prepared to reverse the larceny conviction on constitutional grounds—*but*, naturally, via the "traditional due process approach" of *Palko v. Connecticut*[238] (as he always viewed that)—rather than the majority's route of "incorporating" all of the details of the federal double-jeopardy guarantee.[239] Once more he warned against the Court's

---

[236] *Benton v. Maryland*, 395 U.S. 784 (1969). (Mr. Justice Fortas had resigned from the Court two months prior to this June 23, 1969, decision, which came on the very last day of Earl Warren's 16-year service as Chief Justice of the United States.)

[237] *Ibid.*, at 795–96. The Court apparently left undisturbed its long-standing policy of upholding separate state and federal prosecutions of the same offense, although a 6:3 ruling in 1977 seemed to open the door for its reconsideration. (*Rinaldi v. United States*, 434 U.S. 22, based on *Petite v. United States*, 361 U.S. 529 [1960].) *Res judicata* reposes in two 1959 decisions: *Bartkus v. Illinois*, 359 U.S. 121 and *Abbate v. United States*, 359 U.S. 187. For an apparent narrowing of the protection against double jeopardy in the instance of the length (or brevity) of *sentences*, see Mr. Justice Blackmun's late 1980 opinion for a 5:4 Court in *United States v. DiFrancesco*, 49 LW 4022. And in 1981 the Court 9:0 reaffirmed the constitutionality of imposing consecutive sentences for a single federal offense that violates two laws. (*Albernaz v. United States*, 49 LW 4237.) But *cf. Bullington v. Missouri*, 49 LW 4481 (1981).

[238] See pp. 56 ff., *supra*.

[239] *Benton v. Maryland*, op. cit., at 808.

"march" toward incorporation, expressing his "protest against a doctrine which so subtly, yet profoundly, is eroding many of the basics of our federal system."[240]

As the Supreme Court of the United States prepared to return to its labors in the fall of 1980—for its twelfth term under Mr. Chief Justice Warren Burger—no further provisions of the Bill of Rights had been incorporated since *Benton* did so for the double jeopardy clause in 1969. But, in effect, only a few provisions still remained "out": grand jury indictment; trial by a jury in *civil* cases; excessive bail and fines prohibitions; the right to bear arms; and the Third Amendment safeguards against involuntary quartering of troops in private homes. The close attention given during the sixteen years of the Warren Court's existence to problems of criminal justice, against the backdrop of fundamental concepts and concerns of due process of law, plus mounting legislative concern with such safeguards as bail,[241] may well leave those few that are indeed still "out" out. What is crucial is the increasing recognition and acceptance, both on and off the bench, that if there is anything at all "national" in scope and application under the United States Constitution, it is our fundamental civil rights and liberties.

Leading Positions on Incorporation

It may be useful to summarize the major judicial positions taken on the question of incorporation of the Bill of Rights by representative past and present members of the Supreme Court. Although close students of the problem can determine as many as eight or nine such positions, one may eschew fine distinctions and point to four chief ones:

The *first* position is probably, although arguably, still the current doctrine of a majority of the Court: selective incorporation, or the concept of the "Honor Roll of Superior Rights."[242] Since the *Palko* case in 1937,[243] this position has been adhered to by a majority of the members of the

---

[240] *Ibid.* Actually, the terms of the remand of the *Benton* case to the Maryland courts could not have completely displeased Harlan. For what the Supreme Court did was to send Benton's conviction back down for "re-examination," stating that it was "not obvious on the face of the record that the *burglary* conviction was affected by the double jeopardy violation." (*Ibid.,* at 809. Italics supplied.) In other words, although the provision was now incorporated, each case would still have to be examined to determine whether or not there was double jeopardy *qua* double jeopardy. And as a matter of fact, Benton's 10-year conviction for burglary in his first trial in 1965 did stand up!

[241] See the important Federal Bail Reform Act of 1966.

[242] For a scholarly view that the notion of "selective" incorporation is a misnomer and/or represents a "widespread misconception," see Jacob W. Landynski, "Due Process and the Concept of Ordered Liberty: 'A Screen of Words Expressing Will in the Service of Desire'?," 2 *Hofstra University Law Review* 1 (Winter 1974).

[243] *Palko v. Connecticut,* 302 U.S. 319.

Court—a shifting majority, but a majority nonetheless. Among those who thus labored to "incorporate" the gradually increasing string of rights from the Bill of Rights, without advocating *total* incorporation *per se,* were Chief Justices Hughes, Stone, and Warren (although it is possible to make a good, if inconclusive, case for the acceptance of not only total incorporation by the latter two but of total incorporation "plus"); Associate Justices Brandeis, Cardozo, Reed, Jackson, Burton, Clark, Stewart, White, and Stevens (but almost all with some reservations in the area of criminal procedural safeguards), and Brennan and Marshall (who may be leaning toward total incorporation or even total incorporation "plus"). This majority position—now entering its fifth decade—possesses both the virtues of flexibility and compromise and the vices of selectivity and uncertainty. These properties would be applicable even if one were to view the Court's majority position as one more adequately described as "selective incorporation *plus,*" given its recent repeatedly demonstrated willingness to broaden "due process" and "equal protection" understandings.

The *second* position on incorporation is the "fair trial" or "case-by-case" rule. This position was consistently and prominently advocated by Mr. Justice Frankfurter, and faithfully continued, with some bows toward the Cardozo reasoning in *Palko,* but not toward the *Palko* doctrine itself, by "F.F." 's jurisprudential student and companion, the younger John Marshall Harlan, and, after some initial uncertainty, by Stewart. To a lesser degree it was favored by Mr. Chief Justice Vinson and Justices Sherman Minton and Charles E. Whittaker. While it is still a bit early to essay a judgment, that also appears to be the position of Mr. Chief Justice Warren Earl Burger and Justices Harry A. Blackmun and William H. Rehnquist. Its most articulate enunciator on the "Burger Court," however, soon became Mr. Justice Lewis F. Powell, Jr., whose jurisprudence is closely akin to, and represents a blend of, that of Justices Frankfurter and Harlan. It is essentially a "case-by-case" approach which closely examines on its own merits each individual claim of violation of due process of law, determines whether or not the common law as well as statutory law principles of "a fair trial" were accorded to the petitioner, and tests his claim against the requirement of "due process of law"—as that elusive concept may be viewed by a majority of the Court. It is here that the famous Frankfurter *quaere,* whether the governmental action does in effect "shock the conscience"[244] or violate "common standards of civilized conduct," is asked. If the answer is yes, the partisans of the case-by-case approach will then

---

[244] That test was one of Mr. Justice Black's particular *bête noirs.* "I do not wish," as he once said to Edmond Cahn, "to have to pass on the laws of this country according to the degree of shock I receive! Some people get shocked more readily than others." ("Justice Black and First Amendment 'Absolutes': A Public Interview," 37 *New York University Law Review* 549 [1962], at 562.)

hold due process of law to have been violated. For the adherents to this group of justices, however, such a decision will be without any reference to incorporation of the Bill of Rights, wholly or partly. In short, the "fair trial" test adherents reject both the *selective* incorporation approach of the Cardozo test and the *total* incorporation approach of the elder John Marshall Harlan. They reject the total incorporation (and certainly total incorporation "plus") as an example of "judicial legislating," and as a clearcut violation of the principles of federalism and the commands of the Constitution. They reject selective incorporation as an unwise and unworkable resort to the vague tenets of "natural law," as the "slot machine approach," whereby, in Mr. Justice Frankfurter's words, "some are in and some are out," and as the creation of a hopeless, artificial, and unfair distinction among our basic rights and liberties. Yet to Mr. Justice Black the "due process" approach was itself plainly a "natural-law due process" formula.[245]

Pertinent illustrations of the Frankfurter "fair trial" approach are the *Adamson* case,[246] discussed earlier in this chapter, and the *Rochin* case.[247] In *Adamson,* the due process standards of Frankfurter's and his colleague Reed's majority[248] simply had not been violated and their consciences had not been shocked by California's statute that permitted official courtroom comment on the fact that the accused, Adamson, refused to take the stand in his defense. In *Rochin,* the conduct of certain Los Angeles County police officers so outraged their standards and so shocked their consciences that the accused's conviction was unanimously reversed by the Court—although two justices, Black and Douglas, concurred on separate grounds: "incorporation" of the Bill of Rights safeguards involved in *Rochin.* Also, in the 1964 self-incrimination cases, Mr. Justice Harlan's and his supporters' consciences were *not* "shocked" by Connecticut's procedures denying Malloy's self-incrimination claims,[249] but they *were* shocked by the New York Harbor Waterfront Commission's treatment of Murphy's compulsory testimony claims.[250] In *Malloy,* Harlan's case-by-case approach—one always exhortative of his consistently reiterated warning that the states should not be put into "a constitutional straitjacket"—thus enabled him to see due process accorded to the petitioner—while his five colleagues who constituted the Court majority here not only disagreed with his conclusions on the presence of due process, but, going further, incorporated the Fifth Amendment's self-incrimination issue. In *Murphy,* on the other hand, Har-

[245] E.g., *Harper v. Virginia Board of Elections,* 383 U.S. 663 (1966), at 677–79; and *Griswold v. Connecticut,* 381 U.S. 479 (1965), at 525.

[246] *Adamson v. California,* 332 U.S. 46 (1947).

[247] *Rochin v. California,* 342 U.S. 165 (1952). See Chapter IV, *infra.*

[248] They were joined by Mr. Chief Justice Vinson and Associate Justices Jackson and Burton.

[249] *Malloy v. Hogan,* 378 U.S. 1 (1964).

[250] *Murphy v. Waterfront Commission of New York Harbor,* 378 U.S. 52 (1964).

lan did see a violation of the petitioner's due process, and he thus joined his unanimous brethren to reverse Murphy's contempt conviction. In *Argersinger,*[251] which applied the *Gideon*[252] incorporation of the right to counsel to incarceratable misdemeanors as well, Mr. Justice Powell concurred in the reversal of Argersinger's conviction, but wrote an important, thoughtfully developed concurring opinion opting for the case-by-case approach. In 1978 he re-articulated his objection to "jot-for-jot" incorporation—this time in dissenting in a double jeopardy case, in which he was joined by Mr. Chief Justice Burger and Mr. Justice Rehnquist.[253] This Frankfurter-Harlan-Powell position has the virtues of extensive judicial discretion and minute individual examination and the vices of potential unpredictability and subjectivity.[254] Given the facts of all-but-total incorporation, the case-by-case approach may now, in effect, if not in theory, constitute the Court's practical position with regard to any future extension of incorporation.

The *third* judicial posture, total incorporation of the Bill of Rights, was, of course, ardently and faithfully advocated by Mr. Justice John Marshall Harlan, the elder—however he expressed it linguistically. It is a doctrine espoused after *Palko* most notably by Mr. Justice Black, with early support from Douglas, Murphy, Rutledge, and later from Goldberg (all four of whom, however, wanted to go even beyond Black's incorporation to achieve maximum application of the federal Constitution to the states and eventually did so). Simply stated, the Black formula asserts that not only do the due process of law and the privileges or immunities clauses of the Fourteenth Amendment mandate the total incorporation of the *specific* commands of the Bill of Rights,[255] but that even if history does not provide a foolproof guide, the logic of life in democratic society in our times dictates such a position as a matter of minimum fairness and necessity. Yet it should be remembered that the Black position on nationalization *in toto* extends only to those guarantees *specifically spelled out in the Constitution and its amendments.* To Black, for whom any kind of "natural law" formula was anathema, the first section of the Fourteenth Amendment absolutely incorporated the specifics of the first eight amendments, but *it was also confined to them.* Time and again he made clear that natural law may

---

251 *Argersinger v. Hamlin,* 407 U.S. 25 (1972).

252 *Gideon v. Wainwright,* 372 U.S. 335 (1963).

253 *Crist v. Bretz,* 437 U.S. 28.

254 For an articulate and warm endorsement of the Frankfurter approach to the problem, see "The Bill of Rights as a Code of Criminal Procedure," Ch. 11 in Henry J. Friendly, *Benchmarks* (Chicago: University of Chicago Press, 1967). For Harlan's reiterated support, see especially his *Duncan* dissenting opinion, *op. cit.,* 391 U.S. 145 (1968), at 171.

255 See his concurring opinion in *Duncan, op. cit.,* at 166, n. 1, for a firm reiteration of his credo just two years prior to his death.

not be employed by the judiciary either to expand or to limit legislative powers beyond the commands of the Bill of Rights—to do so he regarded as an "incongruous excrescence on our Constitution."[256] This approach possesses the undeniable virtues of both simplicity and predictability and the vices of dogmatism and questionable interpretation of the Fourteenth Amendment, in particular, and the United States Constitution, in general.

The *fourth,* and for our purposes last, position is really an extension of the third: namely, that the Bill of Rights in all its majestic guarantees may not suffice to ascertain full "due process of law," and that therefore it may be necessary to draw on a kind of total incorporation *plus* approach in order to do full justice to the allegedly aggrieved. Known as the "total incorporation plus theory," it was initially most notably expounded in the immediate post-*Palko* era by Justices Murphy and Rutledge. In their dissenting opinion in the famed *Adamson* case,[257] written by Murphy, the words and intent are clear—although they stopped well short of concise explication:

> We agree that the specific guarantees of the Bill of Rights should be carried over intact into the first section of the Fourteenth Amendment. But [we are] not prepared to say that the latter is entirely and necessarily limited by the Bill of Rights. *Occasions may arise where a proceeding falls so far short of conforming to fundamental standards of procedure as to warrant constitutional condemnation in terms of a lack of due process despite the absence of a specific provision in the Bill of Rights. . . .*[258]

Justices Black and Douglas, who had also dissented in *Adamson,* did not then address themselves to the issue raised by their two junior colleagues; they were simply content to advocate total incorporation. However, while Black would always resolutely reject the "incorporation plus" philosophy on the grounds that concepts of intrinsic justice may *neither be used to limit nor to expand* individual rights *beyond what is spelled out in the Bill of Rights,* Douglas rapidly drew closer to the Murphy-Rutledge position. In effect, not long after Murphy's and Rutledge's untimely deaths in 1949, he wholly embraced the "incorporation plus" doctrine. "The Bill of Rights Is Not Enough" was the title of one of his essays,[259] symptomatic of this intriguing position, which might be called a "super-fair-trial" rule. Mr. Justice Goldberg demonstrated his sympathy toward that constitutional posture with his important concurring opinion in the *Connecticut Birth*

---

[256] *Adamson v. California,* 332 U.S. 46 (1947), at 75. See also *Griswold v. Connecticut,* 381 U.S. 479 (1965), at 511–13; and *Harper v. Virginia Board of Elections,* 383 U.S. 663 (1966), at 675–76.

[257] *Adamson v. California, op. cit.*

[258] *Ibid.,* at 124. (Italics supplied.)

[259] 38 *New York University Law Review* 207 (April 1963).

Control case[260] in which he was significantly joined by Mr. Chief Justice Warren and also Mr. Justice Brennan. Goldberg, it will be recalled, made a point of stating that the due process clause was "neither limited to nor necessarily as broad as" the Bill of Rights, but rather that it "protects those personal rights that are fundamental."[261] Despite the theoretical loophole for a contraction of incorporation in view of the "nor as broad as" phrase of the statement just quoted, the Goldberg position, embraced also by Warren, and somewhat later by Brennan and Marshall, constitutes the acceptance of "incorporation plus"—with the possibility of a retrenchment when deemed necessary (an unlikely assumption). Moreover, it accepts the spirit and letter of the Douglas position on the Ninth Amendment announced in the *Birth Control* case, which is patently the most advanced of all positions on the basic issue[262]—one that would, of course, readily lend itself to a "selective incorporation *plus*" conceptualization for those unwilling to accept the "total incorporation *plus*" approach.

Some Guesses and a Judgment. Those very few federally ascertained rights that are still "out" of the mandatory due process of law concept of Amendment Fourteen are all likely to remain out, at least formally. Essentially, there are but five: one is the Fifth Amendment's provision for indictment by grand jury in a "capital, or otherwise infamous crime." Evidently deemed neither vital nor fundamental as a necessary prerequisite for due process in all state cases, the Court again in 1968 denied *certiorari* in a case challenging its non-applicability in certain criminal cases in Connecticut. There, one Edward R. Gyuro, convicted of breaking into a store and attempting to abscond with five fur coats, appealed his sentence of three to seven years in prison.[263] Like many other states, Connecticut utilizes "information" rather than grand jury indictment, under which the public prosecutor merely submits his charges against an accused in the form of an affidavit of evidence, supported by sworn statements, to a court of original jurisdiction for trial-docketing.

A second provision not likely to be incorporated is the Seventh Amendment right to a jury trial in *civil* cases in controversies valued at more than $20. This is obviously even less of an essential due process guarantee than grand jury indictment—and, in fact, there has been little formal demand for its application. The Court did have an opportunity to adjudicate the issue in 1968: it denied *certiorari* in a case concerning a 1964 car-train collision in Grand Praire, Texas, in which a 17-year-old University of Texas student was severely injured.[264] The student, Roger McBeth, had

260 *Griswold v. Connecticut,* 381 U.S. 479 (1965).
261 *Ibid.,* at 493.
262 *Ibid.,* at 485.
263 *Gyuro v. Connecticut,* 393 U.S. 937.
264 *McBeth v. Texas & Pacific Railway,* 390 U.S. 387 (1968).

unsuccessfully asked for a jury trial rather than the summary judgment proceeding obtained in the Texas courts by the Texas and Pacific Railway. It was hardly logical that the Supreme Court would *mandate* jury trials in civil damage suit cases, even in serious ones, and the high tribunal's refusal to hear the case had been generally predicted by observers.

Third is the matter of the Eighth Amendment exhortation against a requirement of "excessive bail . . . and fines." There is, of course, no *constitutional* guarantee of bail as such—only one against "excessive" bail, if bail is granted in the first place, and what is excessive necessarily rests upon a judicial determination[265] which also pertains to "excessive" fines.[266] However, the entire problem of bail has become a very visible issue, given the late 1960s and 1970s preoccupation with the "law and order" syndrome, and it has received considerable attention both in the legislative and the administration-of-justice arenas. Demands for bail reform were largely responsible for the Bail Reform Act of 1966 and its resultant amendments; there was also considerable clamor, partly successful, for "preventive detention" legislation. Whatever the ultimate fate of bail legislation and litigation, it does not seem likely that the Court will "incorporate" the anti-excessiveness proviso; when it does get cases relating to the problem, it is far more likely to adjudicate them on the basis of the broad and time-honored due process—fair trial requirements, as indeed it has done.[267]

Fourth is the often purposely (by opponents of gun control legislation) incompletely quoted Second Amendment proviso: "A well-regulated militia being necessary to the security of a free State, the right of the people to keep and bear arms, shall not be infringed." If any provision of the Bill of Rights seems to need no judicial protection, Amendment Two is it, so powerful have been the forces opposed to effective regulatory legislation. In the one case on record that did reach the Supreme Court, the high tribunal denied review for want of a substantial federal question, the tribunal below having held categorically that Amendment Two does not apply to the states[268]—that, indeed, "as the language of the Amendment itself indi-

---

[265] The leading decision here is *Stack v. Boyle,* 342 U.S. 1 (1951). The yardstick laid down by the Court is that fixing of bail must be based "upon standards relevant to the purpose"—i.e., the "punishment" must fit the "crime."

[266] In one of the very few Supreme Court cases on record involving fines, the high tribunal held in 1971 that it constitutes a violation of the equal protection clause of Amendment Fourteen to limit punishment to payment of a fine for those who are *able* to pay it, yet to convert a fine to imprisonment for those who are *unable* to pay it. (*Tate v. Short,* 401 U.S. 395.) But Mr. Justice Brennan's opinion emphasized that there are a number of ways to enforce judgments against those unable to pay—e.g., seven states (and England and Wales, for example) allow installment payments. (England and Wales also permit the garnishing of wages.)

[267] *Ibid.* One federal court would, however, apply the provision to the states. (*Pilkington v. Circuit Court,* 324 F.2d 45–6 [1963].)

[268] *Burton v. Sills,* 394 U.S. 812 (1969), appeal dismissed.

cates, it was not framed with individual rights in mind";[269] and that "[e]nough has been said to differentiate the second amendment from those which protect individual rights and, as such, have been carried over into the fourteenth amendment."[270]

Fifth, and last, is the seldom-perceived Third Amendment, which proscribes involuntary peacetime and illegal wartime quartering of soldiers in private homes. No record of any violations exists; no challenge under the Amendment has ever reached the Supreme Court; and the lower federal courts have seen just one, which was dismissed as being without merit.[271]

Reflecting upon these considerations involving the five "outs," perhaps it is just as well that they remain unincorporated. The "selective incorporation" concept—which, as suggested, should perhaps now be labelled as "selective incorporation *plus*"; the Court's increasingly "open-ended" omnipresent concern for "equal protection" and "due process of law," and their extension to heretofore only marginally covered groups;[272] the obvious presence of a "double standard" in favor of basic human rights;[273] and the Court's embrace of "suspect" and "almost suspect" fundamental rights categories, in which legislation must show a "compelling" state interest rather than mere legislative "rationality" in order to pass "close scrutiny" constitutional muster,[274] are now facts of constitutional law and interpretation. They all combine to render plausible the argument and plea that the federal principle might well continue to permit the states to pursue their own procedural standards in the remaining non-incorporated areas. If so, however, these standards obviously must scrupulously meet, reflect, and adhere to, the demands of due process of law. In the words of the

269 *Ibid.*, 248 A 2d 521 (1968), at 526.

270 *Ibid.*, at 528.

271 *United States v. Valenzuela*, 95 F. Supp. 363 (1951).

272 Thus note the significant 1967 decision, *In the Matter of Gault*, 387 U.S. 1, which in effect extended most of the Bill of Rights to juvenile offenders (a notable exception being the right to a trial by jury—see *McKeiver v. Pennsylvania*, 403 U.S. 528, [1971]). An intriguing extension of far-reaching implications came with the Supreme Court's contentious 5:4 decision in 1975 in *Goss v. Lopez*, holding for the first time that young people are entitled by the Constitution's due process concepts to the same sort of protection against unfair interference with their education (here summary 10-day or less suspension from public schools) that adults enjoy when the Government tries to deprive them of their rights. (419 U.S. 565.) And the same majority held shortly thereafter that school officials who unfairly discipline students cannot defend themselves against civil rights suits by claiming ignorance of the students' basic constitutional rights. (*Wood v. Strickland*, 420 U.S. 308 [1975].) On the other hand, the Court, in a 5:4 opinion, written by Mr. Justice Powell, held in 1977 that the spanking of school children by teachers or other school officials does not violate the Constitution's Eighth Amendment ban against cruel and unusual punishment, stressing the broad public acceptance of the practice. (*Ingraham v. Wright*, 430 U.S. 651.)

273 See Chapter II, *supra*, pp. 13 ff.

274 *Ibid.*

wise counsel of Mr. Justice Goldberg in his concurring opinion in *Pointer v. Texas*,[275]

> to deny to the States the power to impair a fundamental constitutional right is not to increase federal power, but, rather, to limit the power of both federal and state governments in favor of safeguarding the fundamental liberties of the individual. In my view this promotes rather than undermines the basic policy of avoiding excess concentration of power in government, federal or state, which underlies our concepts of federalism.[276]

[275] 380 U.S. 400 (1964).
[276] *Ibid.*, at 414.

chapter IV The Fascinating World of

"Due Process of Law"

The concept "due process of law" has been an integral part of much of what we have been discussing. It is both subordinate and co-ordinate to any consideration of "values and lines" in the realm of civil rights and liberties. The presence or absence of no concept is mentioned more frequently in our judicio-legal process than "due process of law"; its banner is now raised in a host of appellate cases at the level of the United States Supreme Court. Its terminology, if not its clear meaning, is found in Amendments Five and Fourteen of the Constitution, both of which issue clarion calls to national and state governments alike for the presence and maintenance of "due process of law." In the words of Amendment Five, ratified on December 15, 1791: "No person shall . . . be deprived of life, liberty, or property, *without due process of law* . . .";[1] and in the words of Amendment Fourteen, ratified on July 23, 1868: "No State shall . . . deprive any person of life, liberty, or property, *without due process of law*. . . ."[2] Towering disagreements as to the meaning of that command have plagued us and will undoubtedly continue to do so, thus complicating seriously attempts at "line drawing"—as the aforegone analysis of the question of the incorporation of the Bill of Rights has demonstrated. Yet basic guidelines do exist, and, no matter how vexatious and hazardous the task at hand may well be, they do enable us to come to grips with the central meaning of "due process of law."

Some Basic Guidelines

Although it may well be futile to attempt definitive interpretations of "due process of law," it is possible to delineate certain fundamentals. One basic requirement of the concept "due process of law" is that government may not act in an "arbitrary," "capricious," or "unreasonable" manner in

---

[1] Italics supplied.
[2] Italics supplied.

performing its task vis-à-vis the body politic. The judicial branch as the ultimate guardian of our Constitution-guaranteed civil rights and liberties has the delicate and difficult task of ascertaining the constitutional appropriateness of governmental action by weighing it against what amount to common-law notions of "arbitrariness," "capriciousness," or "unreasonableness"—although this adjectival test is vehemently and consistently rejected as a usable measure by some prominent jurists, as Mr. Justice Black as a dedicated Constitutional *literalist,* always did.[3]

Suffice it to say that opinions differ widely on the meaning of these concepts. What may be "arbitrary" to some legislators may seem reasonable to others; what may be "capricious" police behavior in the eyes of a prisoner may be fair in the eyes of the apprehending and prosecuting authorities; and what may well seem to be an "unreasonable" interpretation by an administrative agency in the view of an affected business concern or educational institution may appear reasonable to the agency's commissioners. Does the matter, then, become merely one of opinion, or are there ascertainable standards? The answer cannot be conclusive: there *are* standards, of course, but until they have been judicially tested and pronounced, they remain general standards based as much on civilized notions of fairness and decency as on any written commands, be the latter statutes, ordinances, or even constitutions, federal or state. At the *federal* level, because of the specific commands of the Constitution and the centralizing tendency of having only one final arbiter, "due process" standards are generally both more predictable and more ascertainable than at the *state* level. Fifty separate units of government, despite the mandates and exhortations of the Fourteenth Amendment and of their own bills of rights, bring normally a more fluid, less predictable, and, in the main, less "generous" interpretation of "due process of law" to the individual than is customarily true at the federal level. However, given the post-1937 stance of the United States Supreme Court, the states, too, have had to pay far more attention to the fundamental concepts of "fairness and decency," which are so vital to the presence of "due process of law."

A General Definition. Any general definition of "due process of law" must take into account the genesis of the concept. It was originally derived from English common law—probably during the reigns of Henry I (1100–

---

[3] See, among others, his scathing lecture on the subject in his *A Constitutional Faith* (New York: Alfred A. Knopf, 1968), Ch. II, "Due Process of Law," pp. 23 ff. It probably represents the fullest statement of his due process philosophy. In essence, he hinged it to Lord Coke's understanding of *per legem terrae,* "the law of the land" provision of the Magna Carta, Ch. 29, which to Black represented *already existing constitutional provisions; the Bill of Rights; plus all laws that had been passed pursuant to constitutional power at the time the alleged offense was committed.* To Coke, however, "by the due course and process of law" was almost certainly confined to *judicial proceedings*—not to substantive or contextual aspects of a statute.

1135) and Henry II (1154–89). Its more obvious antecedent is the Magna Carta of 1215, Chapter 29 (Chapter 39 in a later version), which declares: "No free man shall be taken, outlawed, banished, or in any way destroyed, nor will we proceed against or prosecute him, except by the lawfull judgment of his peers and by the law of the land." As Professor A. E. D. Howard of the University of Virginia Law School has pointed out in his commentary on the Magna Carta, as early as 1354 the words "due process" were used in an English statute interpreting the Magna Carta, and by the end of the fourteenth century "due process of law" and "law of the land" were interchangeable. The English colonists who established our courts brought the expression "due process of law" with them.[4] As it developed, "due process of law" restrained a head of government from arbitrarily depriving a member of his realm of life, liberty, or property. In due course this notion was embraced by all other departments of government as well; it has been an essential fact of governmental life on this side of the ocean from the Constitution's adoption in 1789.

Perhaps the best brief definition of due process of law was contained in the first Mr. Justice John Marshall Harlan's dissenting opinion in 1884, in *Hurtado v. California.*[5] Governments, he wrote, should be confined within the limits of those fundamental *"principles of liberty and justice,* lying at the foundation of our civil and political institutions, which no State can violate consistently with that due process of law required by the Fourteenth Amendment in proceedings involving life, liberty, or property."[6] This noble phrase, then advanced on the losing side of the judicial ledger, became firmly implanted on the majority side with its acceptance, clarification, and refinement by Mr. Justice Cardozo, more than half a century later, in *Palko v. Connecticut.*[7]

But what are those "fundamental principles of liberty and justice" constituting the irreducible minimum of due process of law? We may discover them from a variety of sources:

the body of constitutions,
bills of rights,
customs, conventions, and traditions,

[4] A. E. Dick Howard, *Magna Carta: Text and Commentary* (Charlottesville: University of Virginia Press, 1964). See also Mr. Justice Black's commentary on the subject in his *A Constitutional Faith, op. cit.,* especially pp. 30–38. But for a much more restrictive interpretation—which sees "due process" as wholly *procedural*—see Keith Jurow, "Untimely Thoughts: A Reconsideration of the Origins of the Process of Law," 19 *The American Journal of Legal History* 265 (1975). Jurow thus sides with Alexander Hamilton's interpretation of "due process of law." (See fn. 11, p. 95, *infra.*)

[5] 110 U.S. 516.

[6] *Ibid.,* at 546. (Italics supplied.)

[7] 302 U.S. 319 (1937). See Chapter III, *supra,* pp. 56 ff.

legislative enactments,
executive ordinances, decrees, and practices,
judicial interpretations and precedents;

and significantly, from what one commentator aptly termed "current views of right and wrong which collectively have come to be accepted as a part of the established law of the land."[8] The concept of due process of law and its application to our federal and state governments is based on an extensive reservoir of *constitutionally expressed and implied limitations upon governmental authority,* ultimately determined by the judicial process, and upon those basic notions of fairness and decency which govern, or ought to govern, the relationships between rulers and ruled. Although Mr. Justice Frankfurter's record is, of course, based on the subjective case-by-case approach described earlier, rather than a clearly delineated one, he viewed this flexible concept of due process of law as: ". . . compounded by history, reason, the past course of decisions, and stout confidence in the democratic faith which we profess. . . ."[9] Yet in the year he ascended the Court he had written that "[t]he due process clauses ought to go."[10]

Substantive and Procedural Due Process of Law

Any explanation of due process of law must consider its two "types" or aspects—*substantive* and *procedural*—for judicial disposition of due process litigation necessarily turns on the *kind* of violation that is alleged by a petitioner. Although neither is as readily definable nor as clearly separable from the other as is sometimes claimed, it is essential to understand at least a general distinction between the two. We may view *substantive* due process as referring to the *content or subject matter* of a law or an ordinance, whereas *procedural due process*—the more litigated of the two refers to the manner in which a law, an ordinance, an administrative practice, or a judicial task is carried out. For nearly a century procedural due process was viewed in American jurisprudence as the *only* "due process" extant,[11] substantive due process not being "discovered" by the judiciary

---

[8] Professor Jesse T. Carpenter in Edward C. Smith and Arnold J. Zurcher, eds., *Dictionary of American Politics* (New York: Barnes & Noble, 1955), p. 128.

[9] *Joint Anti-Fascist Refugee Committee v. McGrath,* 341 U.S. 123 (1951), concurring opinion.

[10] *Law and Politics: Occasional Papers of Mr. Justice Frankfurter,* ed. by Archibald MacLeish and E. F. Prichard, Jr. (New York: Harcourt, Brace, 1939), pp. 3, 6.

[11] Thus Alexander Hamilton: "The words 'due process' have a precise technical import, and are only applicable to the process and proceedings of the courts of justice; *they can never be referred to an act of the legislature." The Papers of Alexander Hamilton* (New York: Columbia University Press, 1962), p. 35. (Italics supplied.) Mr. Justice Frankfurter, deeply troubled by the increasing judicial resort to substan-

formally until the now famed *Wynehamer* case in 1856.[12] In both the substantive and procedural due process concepts the judicial test of constitutionality or legality has become more or less the same: is the governmental action "arbitrary," "capricious," "unreasonable," "invidious," "irrelevant," or "irrational" either in content or in procedure?[13] If it is, the action by government and/or its agent will then fall—and on occasion *both* substantive and procedural violations have been present.

SUBSTANTIVE DUE PROCESS

As the discussion of the post-1937 "double standard" has demonstrated,[14] the Supreme Court has largely abandoned substantive due process of law as a check on legislative economic-proprietarian regulation. This does not mean, of course, that legislatures are free to disregard the basic standards of substantive due process when legislating in the realm of the economy—indeed, the Court will permit no such obvious violation.[15] But it does mean that in line with its latter-day canons of judicial self-restraint, the Court will generally bend over backward to uphold such legislation. In the area of civil liberties, however, judicial action in the substantive due process area is relatively frequent, and while the Court is called upon to pass judgment less often in that sphere than in the procedural one, no term passes without some challenges to governmental enactments on substantive due process grounds. Many of these fall into the area of the First Amendment freedoms,[16] in particular the freedom of expression[17] and religion, and, with steadily mounting frequency since the

---

tive due process rulings at home, was instrumental, upon being asked for his advice, in having India's Constitution of 1950 adopt in its Article 21 a concept of "due process of law" that reads that no one shall be deprived of due process of law "except in accordance with *the procedure* established by law." (Italics supplied.)

[12] *Wynehamer v. People*, 13 N.Y. 358 (1856), in which a New York State prohibition law was held to violate "due process of law." Raoul Berger refers to *Wynehamer* as the *locus classicus* of substantive due process: *Government by Judiciary: The Transformation of the Fourteenth Amendment* (Cambridge: Harvard University Press, 1977), pp. 254–55.

[13] These six adjectives were listed by Mr. Justice Black in his dissenting opinion in *Harper v. Virginia Board of Elections*, 383 U.S. 663 (1966), at 673, as the governing tests for claims of violations of the Fourteenth Amendment's "equal protection of the laws" clause.

[14] See Chapter II, *supra*.

[15] E.g., *Shapiro v. Thompson*, 394 U.S. 618 (1969)—alluding to the "very means to exist," i.e., food, clothing, and shelter—and similar late 1960s and mid- and early 1970s judicial checks in the general area of welfare and poverty (when viewed as bearing upon individual constitutional rights).

[16] Space does not here permit a discussion of the following three basic substantive due-process safeguards found in the body of the Constitution (Article One): the writ of *habeas corpus, ex post facto laws*, and bills of attainder.

[17] Thus ready candidates for declarations of unconstitutionality—usually unanimously—are such patently vague enactments as "vagrancy," "loitering," and "public

1950s, Fourteenth Amendment egalitarian aspects (discussed in subsequent chapters). A pertinent illustration is sterilization legislation.

Carrie Buck Loses. Carrie Buck, an 18-year-old feeble-minded white girl, the daughter of a feeble-minded mother, and the mother of a feeble-minded, illegitimate baby, was committed in 1924 to the Virginia State Colony for Epileptics and the Feeble Minded—where her mother, Emma, had also been committed. A Virginia statute, enacted earlier in 1924, provided that the health of the patient and the welfare of society may be promoted in certain cases by the sterilization of mental defectives, under careful safeguard; that the sterilization may be effected in males by vasectomy and in females by salpingectomy, without serious pain or substantial danger to life; that the Commonwealth of Virginia "is supporting in various' institutions many defective persons who if now discharged would become a menace but if incapable of procreating might be discharged with safety and become self-supporting with benefit to themselves and to society"; and that experience has shown that heredity plays an important part in the transmission of insanity, imbecility, idiocy, feeble-mindedness, or epilepsy. The law went on to state that whenever the superintendent of certain institutions, including the State Colony at Lynchburg, where Carrie and her mother were committed, shall be of the opinion that it is for the best interests of the patient and of society, he may have the operation "performed upon any patient afflicted with hereditary forms of insanity, imbecility," etc., if he complies with the careful provisions by which the law protects the patient from possible abuse.

Bell, the Superintendent of the State Colony—prodded by the program's author, Dr. Albert S. Priddy—and acting under the statute, after many months of close observation, recommended to his Board of Directors that Carrie Buck be sterilized. The Board, again in compliance with the succinctly drawn law, ultimately so ordered. Carrie may have been feeble-minded, but she understood what was about to happen to her. Her lawyers, setting into motion the elaborate appellate procedure provided under the act, applied to the County Circuit Court for reversal of the order, but it affirmed the sterilization decree. Carrie's petitioners then appealed to the Virginia Supreme Court of Appeals, which agreed with the conclusion reached below that the application of the sterilization law in the case would be a "blessing" for feeble-minded patients like Carrie. The next legal step was an appeal to the Supreme Court of the United States, the constitu-

---

nuisance" laws. (E.g., *Papachristou v. City of Jacksonville,* 405 U.S. 156 [1972].) A "vague" statute, according to a classic 1926 definition by Mr. Justice Sutherland, is one which "either forbids or requires the doing of an act in terms so vague that men of common intelligence must necessarily guess at its meaning and differ as to its application, [and thus] violates the first essential of due process of law." (*Connally v. General Construction Co.,* 269 U.S. 385, at 391.)

tional issues raised being alleged denial of *substantive* due process and the "equal protection of the laws," both under the Fourteenth Amendment. Carrie's lawyers had no quarrel with the *procedural* aspects of the Virginia law, readily granting that they provided full due process of law; the attack was upon the *substance* of the legislation. In brief, counsel for the girl contended that not only was the sterilization order unauthorized on the existing grounds but that "in no circumstances could such an order be justified" under substantive due process of law; that it was on its face arbitrary, capricious, and unreasonable. Moreover, argued her attorneys, Virginia had violated Carrie's, and similarly afflicted candidates', equal protection of the laws because the law reached only the "small number who are in the institutions named and is not applied to the multitude outside."[18]

Over Mr. Justice Butler's dissent without a written opinion (an annoying idiosyncracy), Mr. Justice Holmes upheld Virginia's statute and action, joined by Mr. Chief Justice Taft and Associate Justices Van Devanter, McReynolds, Brandeis, Sutherland, Sanford, and Stone. Holmes reasoned that since the public welfare has more than once called, and may at almost any time call, upon the best citizens for their lives, it would be "strange if it could not call upon those who already sap the strength of the State for these lesser sacrifices often not felt to be such by those concerned, in order to prevent our being swamped with incompetence." Having established that premise the 86-year-old Holmes—a confirmed Malthusian since boyhood days—continued with an oft-quoted passage:

> It is better for all the world, if instead of waiting to execute degenerate offspring for crime, or to let them starve for their imbecility, society can prevent those who are manifestly unfit from continuing their kind. The principle that sustains compulsory vaccination is broad enough to cover cutting the Fallopian tubes. . . . Three generations of imbeciles are enough.[19]

As to the allegations of denial of the equal protection of the laws—i.e., that the Virginia statute did not reach "the multitude outside" state institutions—Holmes commented that "it is the usual last resort of constitutional arguments to point out shortcomings of this sort." The answer to *that* argument, said the dedicated exponent of judicial self-restraint, is that

> the law does all that is needed when it does all that it can, indicates a policy, applies it to all within the lines, and seeks to bring within the lines all similarly situated so far and so fast as its means allow. Of course so far as the operations enable those who otherwise must be kept confined to be returned to the world, and thus open the asylum to others, the equality aimed at it will be more nearly reached. Judgment affirmed.[20]

[18] *Buck v. Bell*, 274 U.S. 200 (1927).
[19] *Ibid.*, at 207.
[20] *Ibid.*, at 208.

Although the philosophy of *Buck v. Bell* has been subjected to heavy and trenchant criticism—partly with the hindsight of socio-medical developments since the twenties—it still serves to illustrate well some of the problems inherent in the concept of substantive due process of law. Carrie Buck was ultimately sterilized[21]—one of 8,300 Virginians between 1922 and 1972, when Virginia decided to discontinue such sterilizations. The law, which remains on the statute books, was challenged in a class action suit brought by the American Civil Liberties Union in 1981. But fifteen years after her future chance of motherhood had been surgically terminated, one man *won* his battle against sterilization on both "substantive due process" and "equal protection" grounds, in a case often regarded as a sequel to *Buck v. Bell*. His name was Arthur Skinner—and he was not precisely a pillar of the community, either.

Arthur Skinner Wins. An Oklahoman, habitually in trouble with the law, Arthur Skinner was convicted in 1926 of the crime of stealing three chickens and was sentenced to the Oklahoma State Reformatory. Three years later he was convicted of the crime of robbery with firearms and was again sentenced to the Reformatory. In 1934 he was once more convicted of robbery with firearms, and was sent to the penitentiary, where he was when, in 1935, Oklahoma enacted a new statute, known as the Habitual Criminal Sterilization Act. It was legislated in a burst of moralistic enthusiasm, with assurances not only of its wisdom but its constitutionality. The law defined a "habitual criminal" as a person who, having been convicted two or more times for crimes "amounting to felonies involving moral turpitude" either in an Oklahoma or in any other state court, is *thereafter* convicted of a *third* such felony in Oklahoma and duly sentenced to a term of imprisonment in an Oklahoma penal institution. The statute then provided that the Oklahoma attorney-general could institute "a proceeding against such a person in the Oklahoma courts for a judgment that such person be rendered sexually sterile," and continued:

> If the court or jury finds that the defendant is an "habitual criminal" and that he "may be rendered sexually sterile without detriment to his or her general health," then the court "shall render judgment to the effect that said defendant be rendered sexually sterile" by the operation of a vasectomy in case of a male and of a salpingectomy in case of a female.[22]

The Act went on to state that offenses arising out of the violation of "the prohibitory laws, revenue acts, embezzlement, or political offenses, shall

---

[21] A challenge to a Nebraska statute similar to, but not identical with, Virginia's, was dismissed by the Court well over four decades later. (*Cavitt v. Nebraska,* 396 U.S. 996 [1970].) And in the *1973 Abortion Cases* the Court reaffirmed its initial decision in *Buck* (*Roe v. Wade,* 410 U.S. 113, at 154).

[22] *Skinner v. Oklahoma,* 316 U.S. 535 (1942). Did he mean a "salpingotomy"?

not come or be considered within" its terms. In other words, one might commit a crime in these areas and *not* have them "counted" as one of the three crimes that led to the knife for those who committed felonies[23] involving "moral turpitude."

Arthur Skinner was not so fortunate. He had already committed his three felonies involving "moral turpitude." Thus he was a perfect candidate when the sterilization statute became law. For a year he seemed to have escaped, but in 1936 the attorney-general of Oklahoma began proceedings against him. Properly following every prescribed aspect of procedural due process of law under the statute, the state prosecutor steered the case through the various stages, challenged at each by Skinner's attorneys. But by a 5:4 decision, a judgment directing that the vasectomy be performed on Skinner was ultimately affirmed by the Oklahoma Supreme Court.[24] Now thoroughly frightened, Arthur Skinner appealed the statute's constitutionality to the United States Supreme Court.

Of the members of the Court that had sealed Carrie Buck's fate fifteen years earlier, all except Mr. Chief Justice Stone—who was then an Associate Justice—had either died, resigned, or retired. Stone, who had sided with the 8:1 majority in that earlier case, now joined the unanimous 1942 Court, although he disagreed with certain aspects of the expansive opinion written by Mr. Justice Douglas.[25] Be it said at once that the Supreme Court did not *reconsider* its *Buck v. Bell*[26] decision—which still stands.[27] While, in a concurring opinion, Mr. Justice Jackson pointedly warned that there are "limits to the extent to which a legislatively represented majority may conduct biological experiments at the expense of the dignity and personality and natural powers of a minority,"[28] Stone, in his own concurring opinion, made quite clear (he used the term "undoubtedly") that he still considered *Buck v. Bell* to have been properly decided.[29]

The Douglas opinion for the Court, joined by Justices Roberts, Black, Reed, Frankfurter, Murphy, and Byrnes, was actually less concerned with "due process of law" than it was with what it viewed as Skinner's denial by Oklahoma of the "equal protection of the laws." Still, the lack of substantive due process was clearly implied, since Douglas, by continuous inference if not by language, demonstrated that, in fact, the law deprived Skinner of "a basic liberty" by its "inequality," one here involving "one of

23 A felony is a crime graver in general, or more serious in nature and penal consequence, than a misdemeanor.
24 *Skinner v. Oklahoma,* 198 Okl. 235, 115 P. 2d 123.
25 *Skinner v. Oklahoma,* 316 U.S. 535.
26 274 U.S. 200 (1927).
27 See p. 99, footnote 21, *supra.*
28 *Skinner v. Oklahoma,* 316 U.S. 535, at 546.
29 *Ibid.,* at 544.

the basic civil rights of man."[30] And it was not difficult for him to find the manifold aspects of inequality that were indeed inherent in the Act. Directing his attention to the provision that *included larceny* but *excluded embezzlement* as a crime leading toward sterilization, he wrote with indignation:

> A person who enters a chicken coop and steals chickens commits a felony . . . and he may be sterilized if he is thrice convicted. If, however, he is the bailee of the property and fraudulently appropriates it, he is an embezzler. . . . Hence no matter how habitual his proclivities for embezzlement are and no matter how often his conviction, he may not be sterilized.[31]

Douglas reminded Oklahoma and the nation that when the law "lays an unequal hand" on those who have committed intrinsically the same quality of offense and sterilizes one and not the other, it has made "as invidious a discrimination as if it had selected a particular race or nationality for oppressive treatment."[32] And he concluded that while there had been "saving features" in the *Buck v. Bell* circumstances, none were present in the *Skinner* case:

> Sterilization of those who have thrice committed grand larceny with immunity for those who are embezzlers is a clear, pointed, unmistakable discrimination. Oklahoma makes no attempt to say that he who commits larceny by trespass or trick or fraud has biologically inheritable traits which he who commits embezzlement lacks. . . . The equal protection [of the laws] clause would indeed be a formula of empty words if such conspicuously artificial lines could be drawn. . . .[33]

To Stone, however, the most significant question of line-drawing involved was not one of "equal protection," but "of whether the wholesale condemnation of a class to such an invasion of personal liberty . . . satisfies the demands for due process."[34] To him and to the entire Court, it clearly did not,[35] and Arthur Skinner escaped the surgical reaches of the statute,

---

[30] *Ibid.,* at 541. "Marriage and procreation," added Douglas, "are fundamental to the very existence and survival of the race." But see p. 99, footnote 21, *supra* and Mr. Justice Marshall's dissenting opinion, *joined by his colleague Douglas,* referring to *Buck* and *Skinner,* in *San Antonio Independent School District v. Rodriguez,* 411 U.S. 1 (1973), at pp. 70 ff.

[31] *Ibid.,* at 539.

[32] *Ibid.,* at 541.

[33] *Ibid.,* at 541, 542.

[34] *Ibid.,* at 544.

[35] In 1965 the Supreme Court refused to rule whether sterilization of a California man violated the Eighth Amendment's ban on "cruel and unusual punishment." (*In re Miguel Vega Andrada,* 380 U.S. 953.) He had agreed to the vasectomy, but he

which was thus declared unconstitutional. Of course, there is a limit on the kind of laws regulating life, liberty, and property that a legislature can make.[36] Notwithstanding the high judicial regard for self-restraint vis-à-vis legislative activities, the demands of due process of law (here substantive due process) will continue to require delineation.[37]

PROCEDURAL DUE PROCESS

Despite the recent cascading of egalitarian litigation, the number of cases reaching the Supreme Court of the United States on grounds of alleged abridgment or denial of *procedural* due process of law far outweigh those concerned with alleged *substantive* infringements. This is entirely natural, for it is in the execution, administration, and interpretation of the meaning of statutes and executive ordinances that actions of the agents of the governmental process are likely to be challenged on due process grounds. "The history of liberty," once wrote Mr. Justice Frankfurter persuasively in a federal case, "has largely been the history of observance of procedural safeguards."[38] Indeed, due process of law, as already explained, was originally, and for nearly 100 years after the birth of the Republic, interpreted as a *procedural* restriction upon government. It concerned itself, more or less, not with *what* government was doing but *how*

---

later charged it was coerced and "inflicted" as punishment in a misdemeanor case in which he was charged with failure to provide for his four children by his first wife. Having later resumed payments to his ex-wife, and having married his common-law wife (by whom he had had a child out of wedlock), he subsequently sought to have the vasectomy "undone," a feat successful in only 50 per cent of such cases. On the other hand, in 1975 a Minnesota jury awarded $19,500 in damages to a couple whose eighth child was conceived six months after the husband underwent a vasectomy! (The defendants in the case, brought by Mr. and Mrs. Eugene Sherlock, were the Stillwater, Minnesota, Clinic and Dr. John Stratte, a member of the Clinic who had performed the vasectomy.) (*The New York Times,* June 11, 1975, p. 39c.)

[36] As of 1980, sterilization laws were present on the books of twenty-seven states—all of these *eugenic* in kind (and largely unenforced).

[37] A twist to the sterilization problem is illustrated by the case of one Nancy Hernandez, a 21-year-old mother of two, who faced jail in California in 1966 because she refused to submit to sterilization as a condition of probation on a misdemeanor offense. She had pleaded guilty to a minor narcotics charge, was given a suspended sentence, and freed on probation by Municipal Court Judge Frank P. Kearney provided she agreed to sterilization. At first she agreed, but then changed her mind, and her court-appointed lawyer obtained a writ of *habeas corpus.* Judge Kearney's order was subsequently overruled as "arbitrary and outside the law" by Superior Court Judge C. Douglas Smith. (See *The New York Times,* June 9, 1966, p. 51*l;* and *Time,* June 3, 1966, p. 32.)

On the other hand, a 24-year-old unwed mother agreed to be sterilized in order to reduce her sentence for killing her four-day-old son (who was her fourth child born out of wedlock). The mother, who had an I.Q. of 62 and a mental age of 12, was asked by Philadelphia Common Pleas Judge Raymond Pace Alexander if she understood the meaning of sterilization. "Yes, sir," Miss Francine Rutledge replied, "I don't want no more babies." (*The Philadelphia Evening Bulletin,* June 1, 1966.)

[38] *McNabb v. United States,* 318 U.S. 332 (1943), at 347.

it was doing it. Much is involved, of course, in the concept of procedural due process of law: it all but defies definition. It embraces a general standard of *fairness*. As a minimum, it denies to "governments the power to filch away private rights by hole-and-corner methods."[39] A host of practices falls into that category: for example, deliberately "stacked" juries; coerced confessions; lack of adequate notice; compulsory self-incrimination; denial of counsel at various stages in criminal justice; denial of counsel in criminal cases; and *unreasonable* searches and seizures. The difficulty arises, of course, in a consideration of the question of when, for instance, a confession *is* coerced, or when a search and/or seizure *is* unreasonable. The incorporation of federal standards in criminal justice cases has tended increasingly to narrow the scope of state violations of the standard of fairness, but lines must still be drawn. Among the mass of complex and contentious cases in the realms of search, seizure, counsel, notice, confession, and compulsory self-incrimination, the three to follow will illuminate both the difficulties involved and the differences of opinion on the meaning and requirements of procedural due process of law.

The Case of Antonio Richard Rochin. Rochin, habitually in difficulties with the Los Angeles police—more often than not because of drugs—lived in a modest two-story house with his mother, his common-law wife, and several brothers and sisters. For some time the County had tried to "get the goods," literally and figuratively, on Rochin. In June of 1949 the County received what its agents had reasonable ground to believe was reliable information that Rochin was selling narcotics. Hence, early on the morning of July 1, 1949, three deputy sheriffs appeared at the Rochin homestead. Finding the door open, they entered, called a soft "hello," walked to the second floor, and forced open the door of Rochin's room. The deputy sheriffs had neither search nor arrest warrants. Inside his room Rochin was sitting partly dressed on the side of the bed, on which his spouse was lying. On the night table the deputies spied two morphine capsules. When they shouted "Whose stuff is this?," Rochin quickly grabbed them and put them in his mouth. The agents of the law thereupon "jumped upon him," kicking and pummeling him, in the mistaken expectation that he would relinquish the pills. He swallowed them. The officers then administered a thorough beating to the by then prostrate Rochin, hoping that he would vomit the desired evidence. Ultimately, the deputies tied and gagged Rochin and took him to Angelus Emergency Hospital, where they ordered a resident physician to administer to the immobile yet irate Rochin an emetic through a stomach tube that had been inserted forcibly. The procedure did have the desired effect: Rochin vomited the two morphine capsules which the police agents then presented as the necessary evidence at

[39] J. A. Corry and Henry J. Abraham, *Elements of Democratic Government,* 4th ed. (New York: Oxford University Press, 1964), p. 267.

his subsequent trial. Over the defendant's objections that the police methods of obtaining evidence were not precisely in accordance with procedural due process of law, and despite the frank acknowledgment of the above-described facts by one of the participating deputies, Rochin was convicted and sentenced to a 60-day prison stint.

He immediately appealed this conviction to the proper appellate tribunal, the California District Court of Appeal. To his chagrin and surprise, that tribunal *affirmed* the trial court's holding, despite its judicial finding that the officers "were guilty of unlawfully breaking into and entering defendant's room and were guilty of unlawfully assaulting and battering defendant while in the room . . . [and] were guilty of unlawfully assaulting, battering, torturing and falsely imprisoning defendant at the alleged hospital. . . ."[40] What more is necessary to establish rank violation of procedural due process of law and a reversal of the conviction? On the *federal* level, the recovered morphine capsules would indubitably have been regarded as the fruit of an *unreasonable* search and seizure, forbidden by the Fourth Amendment and as a violation of the Fifth's guarantees against compulsory self-incrimination. But it was not until the dramatic and traumatic *Mapp* case[41] in 1961 that the United States Supreme Court ruled that all evidence obtained by searches and seizures in violation of the Fourth Amendment is inadmissible in *state* as well as federal courts in criminal trials.[42]

Since *Rochin* came almost a decade prior to *Mapp,* unless the defendant could demonstrate a violation of the due process of law clause of the Fourteenth Amendment he would have no case, for in 1952 neither the exclusionary rule of the Fourth Amendment nor the compulsory self-incrimination safeguards of the Fifth was held applicable to the states. And California, in line with standing traditions of common law then in use by roughly one-half of the states, did *not* bar the admission at the trial stage of evidence obtained illegally. It enabled the aggrieved party to *sue* the offending officers, with scant hope of success, needless to add, but such an action in no manner affected his obligation to pay fines and go to jail. This accounts for the reasoning of the District Court of Appeal. Rochin next appealed to the California Supreme Court, which denied his petition for a hearing without opinion. But two of the seven justices dissented from

---

[40] *People v. Rochin,* 101 Cal. App. 2d 140 (1950).

[41] *Mapp v. Ohio,* 367 U.S. 643. See pp. 61–63, *supra.*

[42] But note its amendatory rulings in 1976, sharply reducing the power of *lower federal courts* in *habeas corpus* proceedings to set aside *state court* convictions that relied on illegally obtained evidence. (*Stone v. Powell* and *Wolff v. Rice,* 428 U.S. 465.) Mr. Chief Justice Burger, the chief opponent of the exclusionary rule, commented in a concurring opinion that the rule's "function is simple—the exclusion of truth from the factfinding process." (At 496.)

this denial and, in doing so, expressed themselves in significant language. They contended that:

> . . . a conviction which rests upon evidence of incriminating objects obtained from the body of the accused by physical abuse is as invalid as a conviction which rests upon a verbal confession extracted from him by such abuse. . . . Had the evidence forced from the defendant's lips consisted of an oral confession that he illegally possessed a drug . . . he would have the protection of the rule of law which excludes coerced confessions from evidence. But because the evidence forced from his lips consisted of real objects the People of this state are permitted to base a conviction upon it. [We two] find no valid ground of distinction between a verbal confession extracted by physical abuse and a confession wrested from defendant's body by *physical abuse.*[43]

When the unhappy Rochin then appealed to the Supreme Court of the United States, he was granted *certiorari* and, in due course, his conviction was unanimously reversed on grounds of rank violations of the very rudiments of procedural due process of law. In what would soon be regarded as one of his most important opinions, Mr. Justice Frankfurter spoke for the Court. He not only outlined the "responsibilities" of both the state and federal courts and wrote a significant essay on the meaning of due process of law, but he restated his own case-by-case approach to the question of the applicability of the commands of the Constitution.[44]

"The vague contours of the Due Process Clause do not leave judges at large,"[45] Frankfurter explained; rather, they place upon the Supreme Court the duty of exercising a judgment "within the narrow confines of judicial power in reviewing State convictions, upon interests of society pushing in opposite directions . . . duly mindful of reconciling the needs both of continuity and of change. . . ."[46] He sternly lectured California that the proceedings by which its agents had obtained Rochin's conviction "do more than offend some fastidious squeamishness about combatting crime too energetically." Then came the sentence that represented his test, his creed, in determining the presence or absence of due process of law: *"This is conduct that shocks the conscience."*[47] And he continued to prove why it did:

[43] *People v. Rochin,* 101 Cal. App. 2d 140, at 149, 150. (Italics supplied.)

[44] See Chapter III, *supra.*

[45] Perhaps not; but there are more than a few observers who agree with Mr. Justice Douglas's frank avowal that "[d]ue process, to use the vernacular, is the wild card that can be put to use as the judges choose." (As quoted by Ray Forrester, "Are We Ready for Truth in Judging?," 63 *American Bar Association Journal* 213 [September 1977].) Douglas, of course, was a prime practitioner of that "wild card"!

[46] *Rochin v. California,* 342 U.S. 165 (1952), at 172, 173.

[47] *Ibid.,* at 172. (Italics supplied.)

Illegally breaking into the privacy of the petitioner, the struggle to open his mouth and remove what was there, the forcible extraction of his stomach's contents—this course of proceeding by agents of government to obtain evidence is bound to offend even hardened sensibilities. They are methods too close to the rack and the screw to permit of constitutional differentiation.[48]

Although Frankfurter went out of his way to assure the states that they had considerable leeway in their administration and enforcement of justice, he reminded them that it is, and must always be, axiomatic that "States in their prosecution respect certain decencies of civilized conduct." Reversing Rochin's conviction for the unanimous Court, Frankfurter terminated his opinion in words symptomatic of his judicial posture on the entire incorporation problem:

Due process of law, as a historic and generative principle, precludes defining, and thereby confining, these standards of conduct more precisely than to say that convictions cannot be brought about by methods that offend a "sense of justice."[49]

Precisely because of the vagueness of that "sense of justice" and, of course, because of their deep commitment to the underdog, Justices Black and Douglas, although naturally voting for the reversal of Rochin's conviction, wrote separate concurring opinions, contending that, while the case was rightly decided, it was decided on wrong grounds. In a judgment which has been since confirmed in the history of incorporation, the two justices held that the basic constitutional issue involved in *Rochin v. California* was not at all the one Frankfurter expressed, that is, a violation of the procedural due process guarantees of the Fourteenth Amendment. Rather, held Black and Douglas, it was that California's agents had, in fact, clearly and unmistakably violated the *specific* command of the Fifth Amendment that "No person . . . shall be compelled in any criminal case to be a witness against himself," a command which, in their view, extended to the states via the due process of law clause of the Fourteenth Amendment. To base the reversal of Rochin's conviction on a violation of procedural due process was constitutionally a Pyrrhic victory in the eyes of these two advocates of total incorporation of the Bill of Rights. The "Does it shock the conscience?" test, based on a case-by-case approach to the presence or absence of due process of law, seemed a travesty of justice to Black and Douglas. As Black put it: "I long ago concluded that the accordion-like qualities of this philosophy must inevitably imperil all the in-

48 *Ibid.*
49 *Ibid.*, at 173.

dividual liberty safeguards specifically enumerated in the Bill of Rights."[50] To him, the Frankfurter opinion was a testimonial to "what I object to most in what I consider to be an unwarranted interpretation of the Due Process Clause [for] the elaborate verbal standards offered . . . are to me merely high-sounding rhetoric[51] void of any substantive guidance as to how a judge should apply the Due Process Clause."[52]

Nonetheless, the case was decided, and Rochin owed the reversal of his conviction to considerations of procedural due process. Two related cases, decided five and fourteen years later, will illustrate both the assets and liabilities of that due process test approach.

The Case of Paul H. Breithaupt. While driving a pickup truck on a New Mexico highway, one Paul H. Breithaupt collided with a passenger car. Three occupants in the car lost their lives; Breithaupt was seriously injured but eventually recovered. When the police arrived on the scene of the collision they detected unmistakable alcoholic odors and, on investigating, not only found an almost empty pint bottle of liquor in the glove compartment of his truck but also thought they detected telling vapors on his breath. The three bodies were taken to the morgue, Breithaupt to the nearest hospital.

As he lay in the emergency room of the hospital, the smell of liquor on the unconscious man's breath was unmistakable, and one of the state patrolmen who had been at the scene of the accident requested that a sample of the patient's blood be taken. An attending physician, using a hypodermic needle, withdrew approximately 20 cubic centimeters of blood from the still unconscious man, and turned the sample over to the patrolman in charge, who submitted it for the customary laboratory analysis. The analysis proved to contain 0.17 per cent alcohol!

When Breithaupt was well enough to stand trial, the state charged him with involuntary manslaughter. The "clincher" proved to be the damaging sample analysis, which was submitted as New Mexico's chief evidence of the accused's culpability. An expert in toxicology and hematology testified that a person with 0.17 per cent[53] alcohol in his blood was decidedly under its influence. Over Breithaupt's objection on procedural due process

---

[50] *Rochin v. California,* 342 U.S. 165, at 177.

[51] "What in the world is that," he observed to his son, "but testing a law on the judges' notions of right and wrong?" (Hugo Black, Jr., *My Father: A Remembrance* [New York: Random House, 1975], p. 104.)

[52] *A Constitutional Faith, op. cit.,* pp. 29–30. Black felt similarly about the Equal Protection of the Laws clause—as he demonstrated again in one of his last opinions prior to his retirement in 1971, when, writing in dissent, he warned: "The Equal Protection Clause is no more appropriate a vehicle for the 'shock the conscience' test than is the Due Process Clause." (*Bodde v. Connecticut,* 401 U.S. 371, at 394.)

[53] In the vast majority of states, the "legally drunk" level is at a much lower percentage, usually between 0.08 and 0.15—in Virginia, for example, 0.10.

grounds, the trial judge admitted the blood test results into evidence, and Breithaupt was duly convicted. He accepted his conviction and sentence of imprisonment without appealing.

Later he had second thoughts, and sought release by petitioning the Supreme Court of New Mexico for a writ of *habeas corpus*.[54] That tribunal did hear argument on his petition, but denied the desired writ as being groundless. Breithaupt then petitioned the United States Supreme Court for a writ of *certiorari*, which the Court granted. In essence, Breithaupt contended that his conviction was a *prima facie* violation of procedural due process of law, because it was based on an involuntary blood test taken while he was unconscious. No one had asked him for his consent and he could not have responded in his "senseless condition," even if he had wanted to. Thus he pleaded violation of his liberty without the procedural due process of law guaranteed him by the Fourteenth Amendment. Relying on the Court's unanimous opinion in the *Rochin* case, he argued that the conduct of the state officers of New Mexico involved in his conviction offended that "sense of justice" of which the justices spoke in *Rochin;* that here New Mexico's conduct, just as much as California's there, represented, in Mr. Justice Frankfurter's test phrase, "conduct that shocks the conscience."

But two-thirds of the members of the Court disagreed. Seeing an important distinction between the procedures utilized by agents of government in *Rochin* and *Breithaupt,* they were quite prepared to draw a line between the two cases. Speaking for the majority of six, Mr. Justice Clark began his explanation of the distinction by holding that there is nothing "brutal" or "offensive" in the taking of a sample of blood when done, as it was in this case, under the protective eye of a physician. He acknowledged that the driver of the death-truck was unconscious when the blood was taken, but that "the absence of conscious consent, without more, does not necessarily render the taking a violation of a constitutional right; and certainly the test as administered here would not be considered offensive by even the most delicate." Furthermore, Clark went on, endeavoring to explain the labyrinth of the due process test,

> due process is not measured by the yardstick of personal reaction . . . of the most sensitive person, but by that whole community sense of "decency

[54] The "Great Writ"—the "highest remedy for anyone imprisoned"—is applicable "in all cases of a wrongful deprivation of personal liberty. Where the detention of an individual is under process for criminal or supposed criminal causes, the jurisdiction of the court and the regularity of the commitment may be inquired into." It is, to put it somewhat differently, "a writ directed to the person detaining another, and commanding him to produce the body of the person or persons detained. . . . [Its] purpose . . . is to test the legality of the detention or imprisonment, not whether he is guilty or innocent." (*Black's Law Dictionary,* 5th ed., 1979, p. 638.)

and fairness" that has been woven by common experience into the fabric of acceptable conduct. *It is on this bedrock that this Court has established the concept of due process.* The blood test procedure has become routine in our everyday life.[55]

He proceeded to point out that

as *against the right of an individual* that his person be held inviolable, even against so slight an intrusion as is involved in applying a blood test of the kind to which nearly millions of Americans submit as a matter of course nearly every day, *must be set the interests of society* in the scientific determination, one of the great causes of the mortal hazards of the road. And the more so since the test likewise may establish innocence, thus affording protection against the treachery of judgment based on one or more of the senses.[56]

Here again, we see the quest for the just line between the rights of an individual citizen and those of society at large—a line particularly difficult to draw when it comes to due process, in general, and *procedural* due process, in particular. But three justices objected vigorously to the reasoning of the majority of six. Speaking for himself and Associate Justices Black and Douglas—the latter also wrote a separate dissent—Mr. Chief Justice Warren dissented on the ground that *Rochin* was not distinguishable at all but should, in fact, be controlling. He observed that the majority's opinion suggests that an invasion of private rights—i.e., Breithaupt's body—is "brutal" or "offensive" only if the police use force to overcome a suspect's resistance. With deep conviction, the Chief Justice contended that he could not accept "an analysis that would make physical resistance by a prisoner [as in *Rochin*] a prerequisite to the existence of his constitutional rights."[57] Urging that Breithaupt's conviction be reversed, he asked rhetorically whether the taking of spinal fluid from an unconscious person would be condoned because such tests are commonly made and might be made as a scientific aid to law enforcement, and concluded that

only personal reaction to the stomach pump and the blood test can distinguish them. To base the restriction which the Due Process Clause imposes on state criminal procedures upon such reactions is to build on shifting sands. We should, in my opinion, hold that due process means at least that law enforcement officers in their efforts to obtain evidence from persons suspected of crime must stop short of bruising the body, breaking skin, puncturing tissue or extracting body fluids, whether they contemplate doing it by force or by stealth.[58]

[55] *Breithaupt v. Abram,* 352 U.S. 432 (1957), at 436. (Italics supplied.)
[56] *Ibid.,* at 439. (Italics supplied.)
[57] *Ibid.,* at 441.
[58] *Ibid.,* at 442.

In his separate dissenting opinion, joined by his colleague Black, Mr. Justice Douglas stated as the crux of the whole matter his firm belief that, under our system of government, "police cannot compel people to furnish the evidence necessary to send them to prison."[59] To Black and Douglas a case such as *Breithaupt* merely confirmed the fears and reservations they expressed in *Rochin:* that the test of whether the conscience is shocked was so uncertain and so subjective that to render justice with an equal eye and an even hand was all but impossible. Their solution, of course, was to incorporate the entire Bill of Rights via the Fourteenth Amendment and thus make the former's specific provisions applicable to the states.

Yet *Breithaupt* was confirmed by a 5:4 majority in 1966 in *Schmerber v. California*[60] even in the face of the incorporation of the self-incrimination clause that had taken place two years earlier[61]—demonstrating the vital fact of constitutional life that incorporation does not obviate the need for line-drawing but necessitates line-drawing of a different genre. This has been particularly characteristic of the problems of searches and seizures,[62] and compulsory self-incrimination. In the *Schmerber* majority opinion, written by Mr. Justice Brennan and joined by Justices Clark, Harlan, Stewart, and White, the Court held that the privilege against self-incrimination does not permit a driver to balk at giving a sample of his blood, taken by medical personnel in a medical environment, for a test to determine if he is drunk. (Schmerber's blood sample showed a blood-alcohol level of 0.18 per cent; California and most other states consider 0.15 per cent as presumptive proof of drunkenness.) The Brennan opinion relying in part on a 1910 opinion written by Mr. Justice Holmes,[63] declared that the Fifth Amendment protected an accused person from "the use of physical or moral compulsion" to extort "testimonial or communicative" evidence that could be used against him; *but* that "compulsion which makes the body of a suspect

---

[59] *Ibid.,* at 443.

[60] 384 U.S. 757 (1966).

[61] *Malloy v. Hogan,* 378 U.S. 1.

[62] See, for example, the "stop-and-frisk" and other "limited intrusion" cases: *Terry v. Ohio,* 392 U.S. 1 (1968); *Peters v. New York* and *Sibron v. New York,* 392 U.S. 40 (1968); and *Davis v. Mississippi,* 394 U.S. 721 (1969); *Adams v. Williams,* 407 U.S. 143 (1972)—which held that the police may "stop-and-frisk" a suspect on any anonymous tipster's word that the suspect is carrying a loaded pistol, and the expansive 1973 decisions of *United States v. Robinson,* 414 U.S. and *Gustafson v. Florida,* 414 U.S. 260. See also the 1980 Airport "Profile" security case of *United States v. Mendenhall,* 446 U.S. 544, and the discussion on pp. 137 ff., *infra.*

[63] Brennan paraphrased Holmes's point on obtaining evidence from the actual person of an accused, discussed in *Holt v. United States,* 218 U.S. 245, at 252–53: "The prohibition of compelling a man in a criminal court to be a witness against himself is a prohibition of the use of physical or moral compulsion *to extort communications from him,* not an exclusion of his body as evidence when it may be material." (Italics supplied.)

or accused the source of 'real or physical' evidence" that, like a blood sample, *did not involve personal communication or testimony,* did not violate the self-incrimination rule. He made it clear that arrested persons might be required by the police to submit to "fingerprinting,[64] photographing or measurements, to write[65] or speak[66] for identification, to appear in court, to stand, to assume a stance, to walk or to make a particular gesture."[67] In the majority's view the extraction of blood "performed in a reasonable manner," as here, thus did not offend that "sense of justice" of which the Court's majority spoke in *Rochin;* nor did it violate the protection now binding upon the states against unreasonable searches and seizures because (a) there was "plainly probable cause" to arrest and charge Schmerber; (b) the arresting officer "might reasonably have believed" that he was confronted with an emergency, in which the delay necessary to obtain a warrant, under the circumstances, threatened "the destruction of evidence"; and (c) the test chosen to measure Schmerber's blood-alcohol level was "reasonable." The Constitution of the United States, Brennan concluded, "does not forbid the States minor intrusions into an individual's body under stringently limited conditions [such as these at issue in *Schmerber*]." But in 1973, the Court, while affirming two California decisions, added the due process requirement that a suspect motorist *must be arrested* before a blood sample may be taken—else any subsequent conviction would fail to meet the basic strictures of the *Miranda* tests.[68]

Dissenting opinions were written by the Chief Justice and Justices Black and Fortas, with Douglas joining Black's. (Warren, Black, and Douglas had been the three *Breithaupt* dissenters.) "To reach the conclusion," wrote Black, "that compelling a person to give his blood to help the state convict him is not equivalent to compelling him to be a witness against himself strikes me as quite an extraordinary feat."[69] With obvious feeling he concluded that he deeply regretted the Court's holding and that he

[64] This includes the taking of samples from beneath the fingernails of a murder suspect. (*Cupp v. Murphy,* 412 U.S. 291 [1973].)

[65] Confirmed 6:3 (with Brennan in partial dissent) with regard to a grand jury witness who refused to furnish a specimen of his handwriting. (*United States v. Mara,* 410 U.S. 19 [1973].)

[66] Confirmed 6:3 (with Brennan again in partial dissent) with regard to a grand jury request to record a witness's voice for identification purposes. (*United States v. Dionisio,* 410 U.S. [1973].)

[67] *Schmerber v. California, op. cit.,* at 764. (Many states employ other methods of detecting inebriation, such as the drunkometer or breathing apparatus. Twenty [1981] have "implied consent laws," meaning that anyone who drives there agrees to submit to a test of some sort or lose his road privileges. Some give drivers a choice between blood, breath, and urine tests.)

[68] *California v. Hills* and *California v. Foreman,* 410 U.S. 908. *Miranda,* of course, refers to *Miranda v. Arizona,* 384 U.S. 436 (1966), discussed at length, *infra.*

[69] *Ibid.,* at 773.

would continue to believe "with the Framers that these constitutional safeguards broadly construed by independent tribunals of justice provide our best hope for keeping our people free from governmental oppression."[70]

THE DILEMMA

We know now, of course, that during the 1960s a majority of the Court gradually moved toward incorporation in a process that has come very close to totality. Thus, since *Breithaupt* in 1957, the following pertinent prohibitions and provisions of the Bill of Rights have been ruled applicable to the several states by way of the "due process of law" clause of the Fourteenth Amendment:

> 1961: unreasonable searches and seizures (Fourth Amendment);[71]
> 1962: cruel and unusual punishment (Eighth Amendment);[72]
> 1963: counsel in *all* criminal cases (Sixth Amendment),[73] (save certain non-imprisonable misdemeanors);[74]
> 1964: compulsory self-incrimination (Fifth Amendment);[75]
> 1965: confrontation by adverse witness (Sixth Amendment),[76] extended in 1967 to embrace favorable witnesses;[77]
> 1967: a speedy trial (Sixth Amendment);[78]
> 1968: trial by jury in non-petty criminal cases (Sixth Amendment);[79]
> 1969: double jeopardy (Fifth Amendment).[80]

Admittedly, the incorporation of these various constitutional safeguards of procedural due process provides significant guidelines for the application of the three adjectives, "arbitrary," "capricious," and "unreasonable." Yet differentiation in posture, analysis, and interpretation is still permitted. Thus, it is one thing to *forbid* coerced confessions, to use an obvious can-of-worms, but it is quite another to standardize the *concept* of "coerced confession." We know that a forced confession *is* forbidden *when* it has been indeed proved to have been exacted and that the Supreme Court has provided both the states and the federal government with considerable directions in interpreting the concept, of which the most important is the

---

[70] *Ibid.,* at 778.
[71] *Mapp v. Ohio,* 367 U.S. 643. (See pp. 61–63, *supra,* for necessary elaboration.)
[72] *Robinson v. California,* 370 U.S. 660.
[73] *Gideon v. Wainwright,* 372 U.S. 355.
[74] *Argersinger v. Hamlin,* 407 U.S. 25 (1972). But the holding accorded full *Gideon* rights to all likely imprisonables.
[75] *Malloy v. Hogan,* 378 U.S. 1 and *Murphy v. Waterfront Commission of New York Harbor,* 378 U.S. 52.
[76] *Pointer v. Texas,* 380 U.S. 400.
[77] *Washington v. Texas,* 388 U.S. 14.
[78] *Klopfer v. North Carolina,* 386 U.S. 213.
[79] *Duncan v. Louisiana,* 391 U.S. 145.
[80] *Benton v. Maryland,* 395 U.S. 784.

test of "voluntariness." But at what point does a confession in fact become involuntary? Because no tests, decisions, or guidelines can really gainsay the presence of procedural due process as a lodestar in both statutory and constitutional differentiation, the Court does need to test individual situations for the presence or absence of due process of law. This is a judicio-legal fact of the first magnitude unless, of course, the alleged due process violation constitutes an outright violation of an established, identifiable principle about which there is no longer any doubt. For example, the Supreme Court's decision in *Gideon v. Wainwright*[81] left no room for future doubt in its ringing mandate that, henceforth *and* retroactively,[82] there exists an absolute right to have counsel in *all* criminal cases, be they federal or state—indigents must be provided with counsel. This is now a clearcut, straightforward requirement of due process. Yet, even the *Gideon* decision has raised numerous problems; for instance, *at what point* in the judicial process must counsel be provided?[83] Both the complexity of the problem and the philosophical justifications of the inherent line-drawing need a much closer look, but first we shall attempt to summarize the current minimum requirements of procedural due process of law.

Basic Procedural Due Process Requirements. The Bill of Rights contains certain concepts inherited from common law that we have always viewed as basic to our government, be it federal or state. They are (more or less in the words of the Constitution, with the appropriate Amendment indicated in parentheses):[84]

1. the right of people to be secure in their persons, houses, papers, and effects against *unreasonable* searches and seizures (Four);
2. the issue of a search and/or arrest warrant only upon *probable cause*, supported by oath or affirmation, and *particularly* describing the place to be searched and the person or things to be seized (Four);
3. *indictment* by grand jury for capital or otherwise infamous crime (Five);
4. no *double jeopardy* (Five);
5. immunity against *compulsory* self-incrimination (Five);

---

[81] 372 U.S. 335 (1963). See Chapter III, *supra*, pp. 64 ff.

[82] *Pickelsimer v. Wainwright,* 375 U.S. 2 (1963). But see p. 65, *supra*, for a *caveat.*

[83] See, among others, the three famous cases discussed on pp. 116 ff., *infra: Massiah v. United States,* 377 U.S. 201 (1964); *Escobedo v. Illinois,* 378 U.S. 478 (1964); and *Miranda v. Arizona,* 384 U.S. 436 (1966); and such other attempts at clarification as: *United States v. Wade,* 388 U.S. 218 (1967); *Douglas v. California,* 372 U.S. 353 (1963); *Johnson v. Avery,* 393 U.S. 483 (1969); *Mempa v. Rhea,* 389 U.S. 128 (1967); *Orozco v. Texas,* 394 U.S. 324 (1969); *Coleman v. Alabama,* 399 U.S. 1 (1970); *Ross v. Moffitt,* 417 U.S. 600 (1974); *Argersinger v. Hamlin,* 407 U.S. 25 (1972); *Scott v. Illinois,* 47 LW 4520 (1980); *Estelle v. Smith* (1981).

[84] Taken verbatim, or paraphrased, from the Bill of Rights, Amendments Four through Eight. (Italics supplied.)

6. the right to a *speedy and public trial,* by an *impartial jury,* in the state and district wherein the crime was committed (Six);
7. the right to be *informed* of the nature and cause of the accusation (Six);
8. the right of the accused to be *confronted* with adverse and favorable witnesses (Six);
9. the right for compulsory process to *obtain witnesses* in the accused's favor (Six);
10. *counsel* in criminal cases (Six);
11. safeguards against *excessive bail, excessive fines,* and *cruel and unusual punishment* (Eight).

Although these safeguards, as outlined in the Constitution, are restrictions only upon the federal government, all but the third and the bail and fine aspects of the eleventh concept now also apply to the several states as a result of judicial interpretation. And even if a good many of the states do not provide all the specific safeguards inherent in those few remaining areas, they are expected to provide procedures that, in their sum total, amount to *due process of law.* In other words, the concept of a "fair trial" demands *safeguards which may not fall below a certain minimum* even if it be that vague minimum of "due process." The freedoms from arbitrary arrest, questioning, and imprisonment, from unreasonable searches and seizures, from the third degree (be it physiological or psychological), from compulsory self-incrimination, from "stacked" juries, from "quickie" trials, are as national in scope, at least in theory, as they would be if they had been derived from just one basic document rather than from fifty-one documents. In the words of Mr. Justice Black in his landmark 1940 opinion in *Chambers v. Florida:* "The requirement—of conforming to fundamental standards of procedure in criminal trials—was made operative against the States to the Fourteenth Amendment. . . ."[85] And, as Mr. Chief Justice Warren wrote at Christmas time of 1967: "The methods we employ in the enforcement of our criminal law have aptly been called the measures by which the quality of our civilization may be judged."[86]

Critical Reactions. Yet, precisely because our federal system is a multiple system of justice, particularly in the realm of criminal procedure, the United States Supreme Court has been increasingly called upon to adjudicate conflicting claims between individuals and society; and many public officials in most states have felt that, in so doing, the Court has made it

[85] 309 U.S. 227, at 241. The *Chambers* opinion contains one of *the* great Black exhortations: "Under our constitutional system courts stand against any winds that blow as havens of refuge for those who might otherwise suffer because they are helpless, weak, outnumbered, or because they are nonconforming victims of prejudice and public excitement." (*Ibid.,* at 241.)

[86] "Discriminating Against the Poor and the Fourteenth Amendment," 81 *Harvard Law Review* 435 (December 1967).

increasingly difficult for them to bring accused violators of the law to bay. The federal judiciary, in particular the Supreme Court, has been bitterly assailed—often in intemperate language. Law enforcement officers from J. Edgar Hoover to the lowliest deputy sheriff, raising their voices in protest against what they have viewed as "undue sentimentality toward lawbreakers," have charged the judiciary with making the job of the police authorities not only difficult but well-nigh impossible.

Nor have these charges and complaints been confined to the executive-administrative and legislative segments of the government; members of the judiciary itself have gone on record as viewing with alarm the tough due process standards imposed by the Warren Court, particularly in the realm of procedure in criminal cases. In the Brune Report[87] thirty-six state chief justices protested what they considered "a dangerous development in Supreme Court adjudication." The report expressed general alarm over what the majority regarded as the "erosion of the federal system," and, exhorting the Court to return to the "greatest of all judicial powers—the power of judicial self-restraint," addressed itself censoriously to most of the controversies that have embroiled the Court in the recent past. The report particularly criticized the steady evolution by Court mandate of the due process and equal protection clauses of the Fourteenth Amendment as criteria with which the states must comply in exercising their authority; it concluded that, by assuming legislative authority and acting without judicial restraint, the Court had expanded national power and contracted the power of the states. This is not the place to discuss and attempt to rebut the specific charges thus flung—it has been well done by others[88]—but there is much to be said for Paul A. Freund's contention that all the Court has really demanded of the states under the due process concepts of Amendment Fourteen is that in order to "turn square corners" in dealing with sensitive areas of human liberty, they should follow procedures that are consistent with due process of law.[89] In his study of the Brune Report, Eugene V. Rostow concluded that its findings represent "not so much a protest against the Court as against the tide of social change reflected in the Court's opinions."[90]

Most vocal of all critics has been Congress. It came within a hair's

---

[87] Named after the Chief Judge of Maryland, who headed the "Committee on Federal-State Relationships as Affected by Judicial Decisions," of the 1958 Conference of Chief Justices. The Brune Report is reprinted in full in numerous legal journals, among others, the *Harvard Law Record* of October 23, 1958.

[88] For example, E. V. Rostow's biting attack on the report in Ch. 3, "The Court and Its Critics," in his fine book, *The Sovereign Prerogative: The Supreme Court and the Quest for Law* (New Haven: Yale University Press, 1962).

[89] *The Supreme Court of the United States: Its Justices, Purposes, and Performance* (Cleveland: The World Publishing Co., 1961), p. 87.

[90] *Ibid.*, p. 111.

breadth of drastically and dramatically restricting the appellate jurisdiction of the Supreme Court in a series of 1957–58 measures, generally known as the Jenner-Butler Bill(s).[91] And the Omnibus Crime statutes of 1968 and 1970 were clearly designed to limit, if not necessarily roll back, some of the Court's most contentious holdings in the realm of criminal justice. In fact, three sections of the 1968 bill specifically endeavored to "overrule" the Court's decisions in the *Mallory* (arraignment), *Miranda* (confessions), and *Wade* (eyewitness/lineup) cases.[92]

Still, as we have seen, even some members of the Supreme Court itself have expressed serious alarm about the standards and requirements set by a majority of their fellow justices in certain instances, particularly in regard to procedural due process—e.g., the angry dissenting opinion by Mr. Justice Byron White, joined by Justices Harlan and Clark, in *Massiah v. United States*.[93] It involved questions of the Fifth Amendment's protection against compulsory self-incrimination, the Sixth Amendment's right to counsel and, by implication, the Fourth Amendment's safeguards against unreasonable search and seizure.

Winston Massiah and the Law. Massiah, a merchant seaman on the crew of the S.S. *Santa Maria* in 1958, was engaged in a narcotics traffic conspiracy, and about to transport a quantity of narcotics aboard the *Santa Maria* from South America to New York City. As a result of tips received by federal customs officers, the ship was searched on its arrival in New York. Parcels containing three and a half pounds of cocaine were found in the after-peak of the vessel, and Massiah was connected with their presence. He was arrested, promptly arraigned, and then indicted for violating the federal narcotics laws; he retained a lawyer, pleaded not guilty, and was released on bail. All of these various steps[94] fully met the requirements of due process of law. Indicted three months after Massiah as a coconspirator, and charged with the same substantive offense, was one Jesse Colson.

---

[91] For an excellent account and analysis of the fascinating background of the fate of the Jenner-Butler measures, see Walter F. Murphy, *Congress and the Court* (Chicago: University of Chicago Press, 1962); also C. Herman Pritchett, *Congress versus the Supreme Court* (Minneapolis: University of Minnesota Press, 1961).

[92] Their citations, respectively, are: *Mallory v. United States,* 354 U.S. 499 (1957); *Miranda v. Arizona,* 384 U.S. 436 (1966); and *United States v. Wade,* 388 U.S. 218 (1967). In 1972, the Court did in fact itself overrule *Wade* insofar as it applied to *pre*-grand jury indictments. (*Kirby v. Illinois,* 405 U.S. 951.) Nor does *Wade* apply to the technique of photo-identifications in the absence of the suspect. (*United States v. Ash,* 413 U.S. 300 [1973].) See also the 7:2 further widening of the eyewitness rule in 1977. (*Manson v. Brathwaite,* 432 U.S. 98.)

[93] 377 U.S. 201 (1964).

[94] For a brief description of these "steps," from apprehension to trial and beyond, see my *The Judicial Process: An Introductory Analysis of the Courts of the United States, England, and France,* 4th ed. (New York: Oxford University Press, 1980), pp. 140–45.

In November 1959, while free on bail, Massiah met Colson who was also "out" on bail. The two men went for a ride in the latter's automobile and soon parked on a New York street. There, Massiah began a lengthy discussion regarding his part in the narcotics transportation conspiracy, making innumerable incriminating statements—incriminating, that is, if they had been made in the presence of public officials. But, or so Massiah had every reason to believe, Colson was a co-conspirator—hardly a government agent!

However, his "buddy" Colson, a few days after his indictment and subsequent bailing, had decided to cooperate with government agents in their continuing investigation of the kind of activities in which the two had allegedly been engaged. Hence Colson permitted a federal agent named Finbarr Murphy to install a radio transmitter under the front seat of the Colson car. By this means, Murphy, equipped with an appropriate receiving device, could overhear from some distance away conversations carried on in Colson's vehicle. And by pre-arrangement with Colson, Murphy was parked near the spot, but out of sight, of the Colson automobile. Murphy was an eager and accurate listener to Massiah's talkathon.

At the subsequent trial, agent Murphy was permitted by the United States District Court judge to testify regarding the Massiah statements he had overheard. Massiah's defense counsel vigorously objected on two distinct and independent grounds: the alleged violation of the Fourth Amendment's proscription against the admission of evidence obtained as a result of unreasonable searches and seizures, and the alleged violation of Massiah's rights established under the Fifth *and* Sixth Amendments because of the admission in evidence of the *incriminating statements* he had made in the car *after he had been indicted* and *in the absence of his retained counsel*. The jury convicted Massiah and he was sentenced to nine years in prison. His conviction was affirmed by the U.S. Circuit Court of Appeals; he appealed to the U.S. Supreme Court, which granted *certiorari*.[95]

Addressing himself to the second argument and concentrating upon the italicized portions of the defendant's claims, Mr. Justice Stewart's majority opinion for six members of the Court did not reach the *Fourth* Amendment question at all, although it was implicit in the litigation, of course. Stewart, hardly a "bleeding heart," very simply pointed out for himself, the Chief Justice, and Associate Justices Black, Douglas, Brennan, and Goldberg that Massiah had been denied the basic protections of the Sixth and Fifth Amendments' guarantees of the right of counsel and against compulsory self-incrimination, respectively; the information that convicted him had been "deliberately elicited from him" by federal agents "*after* he had been indicted and in the absence of his counsel." Winston Massiah

---

[95] 374 U.S. 805 (1963) *Massiah v. United States.*

"did not even know that he was under interrogation by a government agent." Concluded Stewart: *"Fourth* Amendment problems aside . . . all that we hold is that a defendant's own incriminating statements, obtained by federal agents under the circumstances here disclosed, could not constitutionally be used by the prosecution as evidence against *him* at his trial."[96] And Massiah's conviction was thus reversed—which, since it had been based on what was now held to have been illegally obtained and illegally admitted evidence, meant that he went scot-free.

The majority's reasoning infuriated Mr. Justice White. His lengthy dissenting opinion for himself and Justices Clark and Harlan asked precisely the sort of questions an average observer of criminal justice might ask:

> Undoubtedly, the evidence excluded in this case would not have been available but for the conduct of Colson in cooperation with agent Murphy, but *is it this kind of conduct which should be forbidden to those charged with law enforcement?* It is one thing to establish safeguards against procedures fraught with the potentiality of coercion and to outlaw "easy but self-defeating ways in which brutality is substituted for brains as an instrument of crime detection."[97]

But in the *Massiah* case, he continued, there was no "substitution of brutality for brains, no inherent danger of police coercion justifying the prophylactic effect of another exclusionary rule." The petitioner, White went on, had not been interrogated in a police station, had not been surrounded by numerous officers, questioned in relays, or been forbidden access to others. "Law enforcement," he commented, "may have the elements of a contest about it, but it is not a game."[98]

The White dissent warned repeatedly against drawing the line in criminal justice between the rights of society and those of the accused too much in favor of the accused. It was a pungent attack on the whole approach of the Court's majority, not just in *Massiah* but in numerous other cases in this field of adjudication, in the judicial quest for a balance of interests between fairness for the criminal suspect and adequate protection for the public at large. White expressed concern lest the *Massiah* decision discourage both the ordinary citizen and the confessed criminal "from reporting what he knows to the authorities and from lending his aid to secure evidence of crime. . . . Certainly after this case the Colsons will be few and far between, and the Massiahs can breathe much easier, secure in the

---

[96] *Massiah v. United States,* 377 U.S. 201 (1964), at 207. (Italics supplied for "Fourth" only.) See *Massiah*'s extension to a prison setting in 1980. (*United States v. Henry,* 447 U.S. 264.)

[97] *Ibid.,* at 213. (Italics supplied.)

[98] *Ibid.*

knowledge that the Constitution furnishes an important measure of protection against faithless compatriots. . . ."[99] And, seconding a contention so frequently voiced by law enforcement officers, White warned that "meanwhile, of course, the public will again be the loser and law enforcement presented with another serious dilemma."[100] Less than five weeks later Mr. Justice White was to have occasion to become even more alarmed, although this time he gained the vote of Mr. Justice Stewart while retaining the support of Justices Clark and Harlan.

Danny Escobedo's Right to Counsel.[101] On the night of January 19, 1960, Manuel Valtierra, the brother-in-law of a 22-year-old Chicago laborer named Danny Escobedo, was fatally shot in the back. At 2:30 A.M. on the following morning Danny, his now-widowed sister Grace, and two of Danny's friends, Bobby Chan, 17, and Benni DiGerlando, 18, were arrested by Chicago police *without* warrants and questioned intensively at headquarters. Danny refused to make any statement whatever to his questioners. At 5:00 P.M. on that afternoon, after a full fourteen and a half hours of interrogation, he was released together with the others pursuant to an Illinois state court writ of *habeas corpus* obtained for him by attorney Warren Wolfson, who had once before represented Escobedo in a personal injury case and who had been called into the present case by Chan's mother. But on January 30, DiGerlando allegedly voluntarily confessed to his part in the crime and informed the police authorities that Danny was the one who had fired the fatal shots. Between 8:00 and 9:00 P.M. on the day of DiGerlando's assertions, Danny Escobedo was rearrested and, his hands manacled behind his back, taken to police headquarters together with the also rearrested Grace and Chan.

En route to the police station, one of the officers told Danny that DiGerlando had named him as the slayer of his brother-in-law. At his subsequent trial, Danny swore—without any contradiction from the officers involved—that "the detectives said they had us pretty well, up pretty tight, and we might as well admit to this crime," to which, Danny testified, he replied, "I am sorry but I would like to have advice from my lawyer." On arrival at the police station around 9:00 P.M. Danny had been taken to the Homicide Bureau for questioning, after having been in the "lockup" for a while. In vain he asked to see his lawyer, Wolfson. The latter, having been told of the re-arrest by Chan's mother, had immediately gone to the police station, where he arrived moments after Danny. Wolfson at once asked to see Danny, but the police told him, "Danny doesn't know you." Wolfson unsuccessfully repeated the request to see his client on some five

[99] *Ibid.,* at 212.
[100] *Ibid.*
[101] *Escobedo v. Illinois,* 378 U.S. 478 (1964).

or six separate occasions throughout the evening, but each was denied politely by the authorities, although he quoted to Homicide Bureau Chief Flynn the pertinent section of the Illinois Criminal Code which allows an attorney to see his client "except in cases of imminent escape." Wolfson and Danny did chance to catch a glimpse of one another "for a second or two" when the lawyer spotted Danny through a half-open door, waved to him, and was greeted by a similar wave by Danny—whereupon the door was quickly closed. At 1:00 A.M., realizing that he was not going to get anywhere, Wolfson signed an official complaint with Commissioner Phelan of the Chicago Police Department and left.

The interrogation of Danny Escobedo went apace, amidst his repeatedly unsuccessful pleas to see his attorney. At the trial the defendant and his interrogators disagreed on Danny's assertion that a Spanish-speaking interrogator, Officer Montejano, had offered to let his sister, Chan, and him "go home" if Danny "pinned it on DiGerlando." But the record showed that when DiGerlando and Danny were confronted with each other during the course of the night, Danny called DiGerlando a liar and said, "I didn't shoot Manuel, you did." In this manner, of course, Danny for the first time admitted to some knowledge of the crime, at least indirectly. Then, in the face of Montejano's alleged promise that a full statement would free him, Grace, and Chan, Danny further implicated himself as well as the other three accused in the murder plot. At this point, an assistant state's attorney, Theodore J. Cooper, was summoned by the interrogating officers "to take" a full statement. Mr. Cooper, an experienced lawyer, not only failed to advise Danny of his constitutional rights before, during, or after "taking" the statement, but his questions were obviously carefully framed so as to ascertain admissibility into evidence at the trial. In any event, the record stands undisputed that no one during the interrogation advised Danny of his rights and that at no time during the long evening, despite repeated requests by Danny and Wolfson, was he allowed legal counsel. Danny, Grace, and Chan were all indicted for murder, but Grace was later acquitted for lack of evidence, and the charges against Chan were dropped. DiGerlando, who charged subsequently that his confession was beaten out of him, received a life sentence. As for Danny, his defense moved, both before and during his trial, that the incriminating statement he had given to Cooper be suppressed; but the trial judge ruled the confession to have been voluntary. Danny Escobedo, thus convicted of murder and sentenced to a twenty-year term in prison—he had a record of sundry previous arrests—appealed his sentence to the Supreme Court of Illinois on several grounds of due process of law.

On February 1, 1963, that tribunal reversed Danny's conviction, holding that the defendant understood that "he would be permitted to go home if he gave the statement and would be granted an immunity from prosecution."[102] But the State petitioned for, and the court granted, a rehearing—resulting in a reversal and the sustaining of the conviction below, ruling: "[T]he officer [Montejano] denied making the promise and the trier of fact believed him. We find no reason for disturbing the trial court's finding that the confession was voluntary."[103] Danny Escobedo's counsel then appealed to the United States Supreme Court for review—his last hope—and won the first round when the Court granted a writ of *certiorari* in order to consider whether the petitioner's statement to Cooper was in fact constitutionally admissible at his trial.[104] On June 22, 1964, in the narrowest possible division, 5:4, the Court responded "no," reversed Danny's conviction and remanded it to the Illinois trial court "for proceedings not inconsistent with this opinion."[105] But the State of Illinois decided that it could not obtain a conviction without the now inadmissible statement, dropped the charges, and Danny was released from jail where he had spent almost four and a half years.

To understand the Supreme Court's majority opinion by Mr. Justice Goldberg for himself, the Chief Justice, and Associate Justices Black, Douglas, and Brennan, it is necessary to recognize not only the "toughening and tightening" of due process standards demanded of the states by the Warren Court, but also what it had done concerning both the right to counsel and the use of confessions between the day of Danny's arrest in 1960 and his appeal to the court of last resort in 1964. Regarding the right to counsel, the Supreme Court in 1961 had overruled the capital criminal conviction of Charles Clarence Hamilton on the *sole* ground, and for the first time, that the defendant had not been represented by counsel at the *arraignment,*[106] a "critical stage."[107] Two years later the *Gideon* case[108] was decided which extended the absolute right of indigents to have counsel assigned in *all* criminal cases—save those involving certain misdemeanors[109]—by making the Sixth Amendment's requirements of "the Assistance of Counsel" obligatory upon the states via the due process of law clause of the Fourteenth Amendment. (On the same day, the Court ex-

---

[102] *Ibid.,* at 483.

[103] *Ibid.,* at 484.

[104] *Escobedo v. Illinois,* 375 U.S. 902 (1964).

[105] *Escobedo v. Illinois,* 378 U.S. 478 (1964).

[106] That stage of the proceedings in criminal justice when a prisoner is called to the bar of the court of jurisdiction to be identified, to hear the formal charges against him, and to make an appropriate plea.

[107] *Hamilton v. Alabama,* 368 U.S. 52 (1961).

[108] *Gideon v. Wainwright,* 372 U.S. 335 (1963). See Chapter III, *supra,* pp. 64 ff.

[109] And these, except for non-imprisonable mere fine and traffic cases, were covered in a 1972 ruling. (*Argersinger v. Hamlin,* 407 U.S. 25.) But there must be a "likelihood" of imprisonment, as per the 1979 holding in *Scott v. Illinois,* 440 U.S. 367.

tended the right to counsel to appeals.)[110] And two weeks after *Gideon,* the Court reversed the capital conviction of one Robert Galloway White *solely* because the defendant had not been represented by counsel at an even earlier stage than arraignment, namely, the "preliminary examination."[111] The *White* decision was based on the "critical stage logic" of the *Hamilton* case.[112] Regarding the problem of "voluntary confessions" which was so crucial in the *Escobedo* ruling, the Court had for some time shown increasing concern about their use as the basis for convictions in criminal cases. Until the late 1950s, the failure to bring an accused in promptly for a preliminary examination, the number of hours of interrogation, the refusal to allow communication with counsel, and long incommunicado detention had not in and of themselves been considered enough to violate due process of law on the *state* level.[113] However, by the beginning of the 1960s, the stringent new judicial approach became readily apparent; one well-known instance of the reversal of a conviction based on a "voluntary confession" occurred in the case of Raymond L. Haynes because the State of Washington authorities had refused to permit him to telephone his wife, who would then have called an attorney.[114] Then came the decision in *Massiah.*[115]

In overturning Danny Escobedo's conviction, the five-man Supreme Court majority stated the requirements for *early* implementation of the now "nationalized" right to counsel in all criminal cases *and* a confirmed, fundamental, judicially established distrust of confessions. The basic effect of Mr. Justice Goldberg's opinion for the slender majority was to cause "the adversary system, traditionally restricted to the trial stage, [to be] hauled back slowly into the earlier stages of criminal proceedings."[116] Goldberg's specific point in *Escobedo* was quite simply and unequivocally that a person can consult with a lawyer *as soon as* a police investigation makes him a prime suspect. Anticipating the heavy professional and lay criticism that was to come as a result of the decision, and combatting the four dissenters, Goldberg concluded that the *Escobedo* decision did not

---

[110] *Douglas v. California,* 372 U.S. 535, *But* the Court in 1974 held (6:3) that does not necessarily entitle anyone to *free* legal counsel to pursue a "discretionary" *state* appeal, or a similar appeal to the U.S. Supreme Court beyond the initial "as a matter of right" appeal from a conviction. (*Ross v. Moffit,* 417 U.S. 600.)

[111] *White v. Maryland,* 373 U.S. 59 (1963). In the "preliminary examination" stage, following arrest, the apprehended is brought before a magistrate or a commissioner to determine whether he shall be released or *be held to answer* for the alleged offense.

[112] *Hamilton v. Alabama, op. cit.*

[113] E.g., *Lisenba v. California,* 314 U.S. 219 (1941); *Crooker v. California,* 357 U.S. 433 (1958); *Cicenia v. Lagay,* 357 U.S. 504 (1958).

[114] *Haynes v. Washington,* 373 U.S. 503 (1963).

[115] *Massiah v. United States,* 377 U.S. 201 (1964).

[116] *The Defender Newsletter,* November 2, 1964, p. 2.

affect the powers of the police to investigate "an unsolved crime," but *when,* as in Danny's case, *"the process shifts from investigatory to accusatory*—when its focus is on the accused *and its purpose is to elicit a confession*—our adversary system begins to operate, and, under the circumstances here, the accused must be permitted to consult with his lawyer."[117] Earlier, Goldberg had spelled out the majority's specific holding as follows:

> We hold, therefore, that where, as here, the investigation is no longer a general inquiry into an unsolved crime but has begun to focus on a particular suspect, the suspect has been taken into police custody, the police carry out a process of interrogations that lends itself to eliciting incriminating statements, the suspect has requested and been denied an opportunity to consult with his lawyer, and the police have not effectively warned him of his absolute constitutional right to remain silent, the accused has been denied "the Assistance of Counsel" in violation of the Sixth Amendment to the Constitution as "made obligatory upon the States by the Fourteenth Amendment" . . . and that no statement elicited by the police during the interrogation may be used against him at a criminal trial.[118]

The four dissenting Justices, however, were not convinced, as they made clear in three separate opinions: one by Harlan, one by Stewart—who had not only been on the other side in *Massiah,*[119] but had written its majority opinion—and one by White, who was joined by Clark and, again, by Stewart. The over-all tenor of the dissenting opinions was one of genuine concern, indeed conviction, that the decision would hamper criminal law enforcement. Harlan wrote that he regarded the new rule formulated by the majority as "most ill-conceived and that it seriously and unjustifiably fetters perfectly legitimate methods of criminal law enforcement."[120] Stewart reasoned that the decision would have an extremely "unfortunate impact" on the fair and adequate administration of criminal justice. He explained his *Massiah* stand on the basis of what he deemed the overriding fact that Massiah had already been arraigned and indicted, after which the incriminating evidence was elicited from him by trickery while he was free on bail.[121] The longest dissent was White's, who argued that the new ruling would cripple law enforcement and would render its tasks "a great deal more difficult." Bitterly, he asserted that from now on an accused's right to counsel would require "a rule wholly unworkable and impossible to administer unless police cars are equipped with public defenders and undercover agents and police informants have counsel at their side."[122] After

[117] *Escobedo v. Illinois,* 378 U.S. 478 (1964), at 492. (Italics supplied.)
[118] *Ibid.,* at 490–91.
[119] *Massiah v. United States,* 377 U.S. 201 (1964).
[120] *Escobedo v. Illinois,* 378 U.S. 478 (1964), at 493.
[121] *Ibid.*
[122] *Ibid.,* at 496.

pleading for more "reasonableness" and a more balanced approach that would eschew such a stringent and "nebulous" rule, the one-time Deputy Attorney-General of the United States concluded wistfully:

> I do not suggest for a moment that law enforcement will be destroyed by the rule announced today. The need for peace and order is too insistent for that. But it will be crippled and its task made a great deal more difficult, all in my opinion, for unsound, unstated reasons, which can find no home in any of the provisions of the Constitution.[123]

Across the country the police and prosecuting authorities alike echoed the four dissenting jurists. Yet two years later many, although not most, of the nation's top prosecutors conceded that law enforcement had not suffered from *Escobedo.*

There is no question, however, that the *Escobedo* decision, far more than *Massiah,* presented both the legal profession and the police authorities with an enormous challenge. To interrogate a suspect behind closed doors in order to secure a confession was a concept not only based on the custom and usage of centuries, but it had become a deeply entrenched police practice, strongly supported by both "traditional" and "reform" elements in the ranks of those charged with the administration of criminal justice. Fully aware of this apprehensiveness and the general unpopularity of the decision, Mr. Justice Goldberg endeavored to put matters into their proper focus by appealing for a return to the obligations and commands of law enforcement by a government in democratic society:

> We have . . . learned the . . . lesson of history that no system of criminal justice can, or should, survive if it comes to depend for its continued effectiveness on the citizens' abdication through unawareness of their constitutional rights. No system worth preserving should have to *fear* that if an accused is permitted to consult with a lawyer, he will become aware of, and exercise these rights. *If the exercise of constitutional rights will thwart the effectiveness of a system of law enforcement, then there is something very wrong with that system.*[124]

The Miranda Bombshell. By January 1966 two United States Courts of Appeals had interpreted *Escobedo* in diametrically opposite ways. Duty-bound to referee such a conflict, the Supreme Court fully sifted 170 confession appeals and accepted for review four cases involving four individuals.[125] Known by its leading case, *Miranda v. Arizona,* the package decision con-

---

[123] *Ibid.,* at 499.
[124] *Escobedo v. Illinois, op. cit.,* at 490. (Italics supplied except for "fear.")
[125] *Miranda v. Arizona, Vignera v. New York, Westover v. United States, California v. Stewart*—all 384 U.S. 436 (1966).

solidated the appeals of persons convicted on the basis of confessions made after extended questioning by officers of the law in which they were not informed of their rights to remain silent. The crimes of which they were found guilty included kidnapping, rape, robbery, and murder—all major felonies. Although *Miranda* is essentially a Fifth Amendment coerced confession case, it links naturally to the Sixth Amendment (and Fourth Amendment) problems raised by *Massiah* and, particularly, *Escobedo*.

Ernesto A. Miranda, a Phoenix, Arizona, truckdriver, had been convicted in the Arizona courts and sentenced to twenty to thirty years in prison for the kidnapping and rape of an 18-year-old girl. He was taken into custody, identified by the girl, and questioned by two police officers. Two hours later the officers—following Miranda's oral confession—also produced a handwritten one by him, on which was superimposed a typed statement that the confession was made voluntarily, without threats or promises of immunity, "and with full knowledge of my legal rights, understanding any statement I may make will be used against me." Over the objections of his defense counsel, Miranda's written confession was admitted into evidence and served as the basis for his conviction—and his appeal (plus the appeals of the similarly affected principals in the other three cases) to the highest tribunal in the land.

On June 13, 1966, in what must rank as the most bitterly criticized, most contentious, and most diversely analyzed criminal procedure decision by the Warren Court, came its 5:4 answer: the *Escobedo* rule was extended significantly to prohibit police interrogation of any *suspect in custody,* without his consent, unless a defense attorney is present at the arrest stage. In effect, the Supreme Court thus answered two years of bitter criticism over its *Escobedo* ruling with a sweeping libertarian opinion that mandated important changes in police interrogation as practiced in most of the states. While the Court did not outlaw voluntary confession, and stopped short of an *absolute* requirement that a lawyer be present before a suspect can be questioned, there is no doubt that the majority opinion intended to extend *Escobedo.* Written by the Chief Justice himself, who was joined by Justices Black, Douglas, Brennan, and Fortas, it was introduced with the dry and cautious comment, "The cases before us raise questions which go to the very root of our concepts of American criminal jurisprudence."[126] But its holding was dramatic: over the bitter dissents by Justices Clark, Harlan, Stewart, and White (Harlan, his face flushed and his voice occasionally faltering with emotion, denounced the decision orally from the bench on that Opinion Monday, terming it "dangerous experimentation" at a time of a "high crime rate that is a matter of growing concern," a "new doctrine" without substantial precedent, reflecting "a balance in

---

[126] *Miranda v. Arizona, op. cit.,* at 437.

favor of the accused"[127]), the Court, through the Chief Justice's opinion, in effect laid down the following rules which police (see also figs. 4.1, 4.2) must follow before attempting to question an *arrested* criminal suspect:

1. He must be told he has the right to stay silent.
2. He must be told anything he says may be used against him in court.
3. He must be told he has the right to have an attorney with him before any questioning begins.
4. He must be told that, if he wants an attorney but cannot afford one, an attorney will be provided for him free.[128]
5. If, after being told this, an arrested suspect says he does not want a lawyer and is willing to be questioned, he may be, provided he reached his decision "knowingly and intelligently."
6. If, after being told all his rights, a suspect agrees to be questioned, he can shut off the questions any time after they have started, whether or not he has an attorney with him.

Apprised of the Court's decision, Danny Escobedo commented, "I think it was very nice of them. Something good."[129]

In February 1967 Miranda was tried and convicted again—for the Supreme Court had only reversed his first conviction, not quashed his indictment—this time on the basis of properly admitted testimony by his common-law wife, Twila Hoffman. She told the Arizona Superior Court Trial Judge Lawrence T. Wren in open court that Miranda admitted committing the crime when she talked with him in jail—where he was serving a twenty- to twenty-five-year sentence for robbery. Their conversation occurred[130] *after* the Supreme Court had handed down its original decision. Subsequently, having been found guilty by a jury deliberating eighty-three minutes, he was thus sentenced to the same twenty- to thirty-year term in state prison. He appealed *that* case, too, but the Court refused to grant him a second hearing,[131] ditto, a third one in which three Phoenix lawyers had filed a new appeal contending that a *voluntary* confession, given to police during an interrogation,[132] was no more valid as evidence than an *involun-*

---

[127] *The New York Times,* June 14, 1966, p. 1, as reported by Fred P. Graham.

[128] A warning in the language of the Court's opinion would thus read: "The law requires that you be advised that you have the right to remain silent, that anything you say can be used against you in a court of law, that you have the right to the presence of an attorney, and that if you cannot afford an attorney one will be appointed for you prior to any questioning if you so desire." (*Miranda v. Arizona, op. cit.,* at 479.) But "no talismanic incantation" is required. (*California v. Prysock,* 49 LW 3964, 1981.)

[129] *The New York Times,* June 19, 1966, Sec. 4, p. 1e.

[130] "When I visited him in jail," testified Mrs. Hoffman, "he admitted to me that he had kidnapped the girl and roped her up, then took her into the desert and raped her." (*Time Magazine,* March 3, 1967, p. 49.)

[131] *Miranda v. Arizona,* 396 U.S. 868 (1969).

[132] *Ibid.*

tary one under such circumstances. Miranda was paroled in 1972, by now having served a total of nine years; but he again ran afoul of the law in 1974 (illegal gun possession and drug charges—subsequently dismissed because of Fourth Amendment violations); he was paroled later that year. Yet, all but magnet-like, he was returned to the Arizona State Prison for violations of his parole in early 1975—and once again released later that year. In early 1976, now 34, he was slain in a Phoenix, Arizona, skid row bar in a quarrel over a card game. When the police arrested the prime suspect they used a "Miranda Card" to read him his constitutional rights.

Reverting to the original 1966 decision,[133] despite public and private outcries that rivaled, if they did not exceed, those following such hotly opposed Warren Court decisions as the 1954 and 1955 *Public School Segregation Cases,*[134] and the 1962 and 1963 *Public Prayer and Bible Reading Cases,*[135] *Miranda v. Arizona* was now the law of the land! Indeed, the remaining three years of the Warren Court were to see a number of extensions.[136] Guidance cards such as those advocated by the Philadelphia Police Department (reproduced below) were introduced in many a jurisdiction even while the nation-wide assault on the *Miranda* decision continued. It was capped, in a very real sense, by an (aforementioned) congressional response: Title II of the Omnibus Crime Control and Safe Streets Act of 1968. That heatedly debated Title added a new section to the pertinent provision of the United States Code,[137] stating that in *federal* prosecutions a confession "shall be admitted in evidence if it is voluntarily given." Paraphrasing the five most pertinent subsections of the measure, Title II stated that judges need only consider "the totality of circumstances" in which a confession was obtained before they rule whether it was voluntary. Since that was, in effect, more or less the formula *before* Miranda, it was a foregone conclusion that the Court would find itself confronted with a test of the constitutionality of that aspect of Title II. It fell to the Burger Court to reach the specific issue of the failure of police to give the required *Miranda* warnings in the 1971 *Harris* case.[138] There, in a 5:4 decision, the Chief

---

[133] *Miranda v. Arizona,* 384 U.S. 436 (1966).

[134] *Brown v. Board of Education of Topeka, Kansas,* 347 U.S. 483 (1954); and the implementation decision, *ibid.,* 349 U.S. 294 (1955).

[135] *Engel v. Vitale,* 370 U.S. 421 (1963); and *Abington School District v. Schempp* and *Murray v. Curlett,* 374 U.S. 203 (1963).

[136] For example, to juveniles in most although not all of its aspects, *In the Matter of Gault,* 387 U.S. 1 (1967); to the questioning of prison inmates when unconnected with the incarceration offense itself, *Mathis v. United States,* 391 U.S. 1 (1967); to U.S. 324 (1969). The Burger Court would extend it to the "preliminary hearing stage," *Coleman v. Alabama,* 399 U.S. 1 (1970), and to post-arrest questioning by psychiatrists in capital punishment cases, *Estelle v. Smith,* 49 LW 4490 (1981). But it refused to extend it to the traffic court level, *David v. Strelecki,* 393 U.S. 933 (1968).

[137] Section 3501, Ch. 18 U.S.C. Note especially 3501 (b).

[138] *Harris v. New York,* 401 U.S. 222.

Justice—joined by his fellow-Nixon appointee Blackmun, and Justices Harlan, Stewart, and White (who had all been in dissent in *Miranda*)—stated that although an unwarned suspect's confession (such as Harris's) could not be admitted as *evidence,* it could henceforth be introduced in the courtroom by the prosecution in an endeavor to impeach an accused's testimony, on the central ground of the latter's *credibility, if* the accused had chosen to take the stand to testify in his behalf. In a sharp dissent, Mr. Justice Brennan, joined by his colleagues Black, Douglas, and Marshall, warned that the majority's decision in effect meant that police may now "freely interrogate an accused incommunicado," despite *Miranda.* A good many Court observers concluded that with the *Harris* decision—which, based upon what Mr. Justice White characterized as the need to "testify truthfully or suffer the consequences," was reconfirmed and perhaps even expanded in a 5:4 ruling in 1980—[139] the Court had clearly "sounded a retreat" from *Miranda.*[140] Further evidence had come with the Court's 1973 upholding of a guilty plea even though the defendant had not known that the confession he had—admittedly voluntarily—given would have been inadmissible at his trial under *Miranda.*[141] Then, in 1974, in a surprisingly lopsided 8:1 ruling—with only Mr. Justice Douglas in dissent—the Court held that the *Miranda* rules would not bar damaging evidence from a witness who, the defendant had told police questioners, would *corroborate* his alibi.[142] What defendant Tucker was entitled to, wrote Mr. Justice Rehnquist for the majority, was the barring of *his* own statements at the trial; but the testimony of his presumed friend could properly be used because it served the legitimate trial purpose of discovering the pertinent facts. Added proof that the Court no longer considered the prescribed *Miranda* warnings as a fundamental rock of criminal justice came in mid-1975: It held 6:2 that a defendant, who, once having been duly informed of his rights under the *Miranda* rules and having acknowledged understanding them, then made incriminating statements to the arresting officer in abeyance of access to his lawyer, could have these statements used against him on trial—but only to raise doubts as to his credibility after he gave *Harris*-like

---

[139] *United States v. Havens,* 446 U.S. 620. The case dealt with an Indiana lawyer who had smuggled cocaine into the country; it was seized without a warrant, and the defendant moved to exclude the evidence from the trial. His co-defendant had pleaded guilty, and lawyer Havens's seemingly false answers to the prosecution's questions on cross-examination were, the Court ruled, "reasonably suggested" by the defendant's own direct testimony.

[140] E.g., Abraham S. Goldstein, Dean of the Yale Law School, in *The New York Times,* May 3, 1971, p. 35l. But for a view that *Miranda,* though possessing significant educational value, may have been, in terms of tangible effects upon interrogation practices, "an act of judicial futility," see Otis H. Stephens, Jr., *The Supreme Court and Confessions of Guilt* (Knoxville: The University of Tennessee Press, 1973).

[141] *Schneckloth v. Bustamonte,* 413 U.S. 218.

[142] *Michigan v. Tucker,* 417 U.S. 433.

Table 4.1
RULINGS BY THE UNITED STATES SUPREME COURT (UNDER AMENDMENTS SIX AND FOURTEEN) IN FAVOR OF THE GUARANTY OF COUNSEL[a] IN CRIMINAL CASES: ARRANGED BY PROCEDURAL AND CHRONOLOGICAL STAGES

VOTE OF JUSTICES (FOR:AGAINST)	PROCEDURAL STAGE IN CRIMINAL JUSTICE SYSTEM	PROCE-DURAL ORDER[b]	CHRONOLOGICAL STAGE BY CASES (CITATION & YEAR)	CHRONO-LOGICAL ORDER
(9:0)	Arraignment	7	*Hamilton v. Alabama,* 368 U.S. 52 (1961)	1
(9:0)	Trial	9	*Gideon v. Wainwright,* 372 U.S. 335 (1963)[c]	2
(6:3)	Appeal	10	*Douglas v. California,* 372 U.S. 535 (1963)	3
(9:0)	Preliminary Hearing	6	*White v. Maryland,* 373 U.S. 59 (1963)	4
(6:3)	Post-Indictment	5	*Massiah v. United States,* 377 U.S. 201 (1964)	5
(5:4)	Pre-Indictment Confession	4	*Escobedo v. Illinois,* 378 U.S. 478 (1964)	6
(5:4)	Arrest	2	*Mi anda v. Arizona,* 384 U.S. 436 (1966)	7
(6:3)	Lineup	8	*United States v. Wade,* 388 U.S. 218 (1967)[d]	8
		8	*Gilbert v. California,* 388 U.S. 263 (1967)[d]	8
(9:0)	Probation Hearing	11	*Mempa v. Rhay,* 389 U.S. 128 (1967)	9
(6:2)	Quasi-Arrest ;	1	*O ozco v. Texas,* 394 U.S. 324 (1969)	10
(6:2)	Pre-Indictment Preliminary Hearing	3	*Coleman v. Alabama,* 399 U.S. 1 (1970)	11
(8:1)	Revocation of Probation or Parole	12	*Gagnon v. Sca pelli,* 411 U.S. 778 (1973)	12

[a] In 1975, the Court ruled (6:3) that a defendant may move to *waive* the right to counsel in favor of self-representation, if recognized as "competent" to do so. (*Faretta v. California,* 422 U.S. 806.)

[b] Number 1 represents the earliest and number 12 the latest stage in the criminal justice procedural process.

[c] Extended in 1972 (9:0) to cover *all* offenses involving possible imprisonment, whether they be classified as petty, misdemeanor, or felony, "absent a knowing and intelligent waiver." (*Argersinger v. Hamlin,* 407 U.S. 25.) Interpreted in 1979 (6:3) as extending only to those offenses in which a defendant *was in fact sentenced* to a term of imprisonment. (*Scott v. Illinois,* 440 U.S. 367 [1979].)

[d] Significantly narrowed in 1972 (5:4) so as to extend now only to post-Grand Jury indictment lineups (*Kirby v. Illinois,* 405 U.S. 951); and in 1973 (6:3) as *not* to apply to the photo-identification stage in the accused's absence (*United States v. Ash,* 413 U.S. 300).

contrary testimony on the stand.[143] And at year's end a 6:2 decision continued *Miranda's* reinterpretation: Over bitter dissents by Justices Brennan and Marshall, who predicted "ultimate overruling of *Miranda's* enforcement of the privilege against self-incrimination," the Court ruled that after a suspect exercises his right to remain silent about one crime, police may still validly question him about *another* (here after a two-hour interval).[144] Moreover, as the Court held in a less-than-crystally-clear mid-1976 multiple—although unanimous—opinion, the *Miranda* warnings need not be given to suspects called to testify before *grand juries*.[145] On the other hand, a 6:3 majority ruling in June of that year strengthened the *Miranda*-emphasized right to silence at the arrest stage by holding that a defendant's silence after being advised of his right to remain silent under questioning could not be used against him in a trial.[146] And when the Court had a seemingly golden opportunity to overrule *Miranda* in a grisly Iowa child-murder case in 1977, it demurred in an emotion-charged 5:4 decision that produced five opinions.[147] Obviously staking out a case-by-case course rather than attempting to draw a firm *Miranda*-application line, the high tribunal, three years later, distinguished its earlier Iowa decision in a not unsimilar Rhode Island case (6:3); but it now provided a definition of the meaning of "interrogation" to be used as a guide by policy in criminal cases.[148] "Interrogation," explained Mr. Justice Stewart in his opinion for the majority, should be viewed neither to be limited to direct questioning of a suspect nor be so expansive as to cover an offhand remark a police officer might make within the suspect's hearing. On the overarching question of "voluntariness" in confession cases, an issue so central to the *Miranda* rules, especially in the light of the aforementioned 1968 congressional statute supportive of voluntariness, the Court may well be on the road to the British case-by-case approach on the issue. That conclusion was strengthened by an early 1977 holding (6:3), which was supportive of pre-custodial behind-closed-door-questioning, although the suspect had admitted committing the crime, thus presumably requiring custody and the full panoply of the *Miranda* rules; but he had been permitted to leave after questioning.[149] Further proof of the all but unavoidable case-by-case approach is provided by a 1979 decision (6:3) that apparently expanded the

[143] *Oregon v. Hass*, 420 U.S. 714.

[144] *Michigan v. Mosley*, 423 U.S. 96. But *cf. Edwards v. Arizona* (1981), involving further questioning about the *same* crime, which went 9:0 the other way.

[145] *United States v. Mandujano*, 425 U.S. 564.

[146] *Doyle v. Ohio* and *Wood v. Ohio*, 426 U.S. 610.

[147] *Brewer v. Williams*, 430 U.S. 387 (known as the *Christian Burial Speech* case. On remand for a new trial, Williams was again found guilty of first-degree murder (carrying a mandatory life sentence in Iowa).

[148] *Rhode Island v. Innis*, 446 U.S. 291 (1980).

[149] *Oregon v. Mathiason*, 429 U.S. 492.

right to questioning in the absence of an attorney,[150] while one in 1980 reversed (8:1) the armed conviction robbery of a Louisiana man because there was no evidence that he had "knowingly and intelligently" waived his rights before making the inculpatory statement.[151]

That, of course, brings us back to the basic dilemma of values and lines. The presence of lines and limits, and the need to draw them wisely and well, is at least as pressing and arguably more widely perceived in the realm of criminal justice than in any of the other areas under discussion in the civil libertarian spectrum.

Due Process of Law in Perspective

No one challenges the basic contention that both the individual and society are entitled to a full measure "due process of law." In the opinion of a good many observers, however, the balance has of late shifted to the side of the potential or actual lawbreaker. Thus, the Supreme Court and the lower federal judiciary have come under fire because of their tightening of due process concepts in its decisions, particularly in the field of criminal justice. Has the judiciary, in particular, has the Supreme Court, gone too far—or not far enough? There is no answer that will please everyone but it is possible to consider some fundamental points.

"THE CRIMINAL GETS THE BREAKS"

This caption in an article in *The New York Times Magazine,* written by Dean Daniel Gutman of the New York Law School[152] after *Escobedo,* but almost two years prior to *Miranda,* has lost neither its pertinency nor timeliness with the passage of the years. Then, as Mr. Chief Justice Burger has endeavored to drive home at every opportunity both on and off the bench,[153] Dean Gutman, with unassailable statistics demonstrating a continued upward trend in crime—a trend that has not only persisted but has exacerbated into the 1980s—warned that "we do not solve the problem of dealing with those who make crime their business by providing procedural methods of escape for the guilty, to the detriment of the law-abiding who

---

[150] *North Carolina v. Butler,* 441 U.S. 369.

[151] *Tague v. Louisiana,* 444 U.S. 469. For a perceptive, lucidly written summary article on aspects of the Fifth Amendment, see David M. O'Brien, "The Fifth Amendment: For Hunters, Old Women, Hermits, and the Burger Court," 54 *Notre Dame Lawyer* 26 (October 1978). See *Edwards v. Arizona* and *Estelle v. Smith, supra.*

[152] November 29, 1964, p. 36 ff. (The New York Law School is not to be confused with the New York University School of Law.)

[153] E.g., his annual "State of the Judiciary Messages" and his opinions in such opposite cases as *Bivens v. Six Unknown Named Agents,* 403 U.S. 388 (1971) and *Stone v. Powell,* 428 U.S. 465 (1976). In his 1981 Message he pointed out that in 1980 Washington, D.C., with a population of 650,000, had more criminal homicides than Sweden and Denmark with an aggregate population of more than 13,000,000!

FIGURE 4.1

PHILADELPHIA POLICE DEPARTMENT

Standard Police Interrogation Card

WARNINGS TO BE GIVEN ACCUSED

We have a duty to explain to you and to warn you that you have the following legal rights:

A. You have a right to remain silent and do not have to say anything at all.

B. Anything you say can and will be used against you in Court.

C. You have a right to talk to a lawyer of your own choice before we ask you any questions, and also to have a lawyer here with you while we ask questions.

D. If you cannot afford to hire a lawyer, and you want one, we will see that you have a lawyer provided to you, before we ask you any questions.

E. If you are willing to give us a statement, you have a right to stop any time you wish.

75-Misc.-3
(10-9-67)

are victimized by the lawless." After reciting a number of the more controversial Supreme Court decisions "in favor of criminals"—among them the *Massiah* and *Escobedo* rulings—the author called for a series of steps to be taken "within the framework of the Constitution and the Bill of Rights" to remedy the situation. Among them were (a) legislation to permit wiretapping, pursuant to court order, for evidence of major crimes; (b) "recodification" of procedural requirements for search and seizure, "which are distinctive for ancient strictures no longer valid"; (c) extension of the right to detain and interrogate, with due safeguards against coercion or other violation of constitutional rights; (d) classification of the "extent and application" of the concept of right to counsel; and (e) "relaxation of the rule excluding all evidence improperly obtained, so as to vest discretion as to admission in the trial judge." Such a list prompts recognition of the paradox that the administration of justice poses to thoughtful and committed Americans like Dean Gutman, the members of the Supreme Court, and their respective supporters and detractors in the lay as well as the professional public. The basic issues are likely to continue to remain unre-

FIGURE 4.2

PHILADELPHIA POLICE DEPARTMENT

Reverse Side of Standard Police Interrogation Card

QUESTIONS TO BE ANSWERED BY ACCUSED

1. Do you understand that you have a right to keep quiet, and do not have to say anything at all?

2. Do you understand that anything you say can and will be used against you?

3. Do you want to remain silent?

4. Do you understand that you have a right to talk with a lawyer before we ask you any questions?

5. Do you understand that if you cannot afford to hire a lawyer, and you want one, we will not ask you any questions until a lawyer is appointed for you?

6. Do you want either to talk with a lawyer at this time, or to have a lawyer with you while we ask you questions?

7. Are you willing to answer questions of your own free will, without force or fear, and without any threats or promises having been made to you?

solved—notwithstanding the recurrent, variegated, earnest efforts of such qualified professional and lay, public and private groups as the American Bar Association; the President's National Commission on the Causes and Prevention of Violence; the Council of States; nation-wide organizations of chiefs of police and district attorneys; Ralph Nader; Common Cause; local crime-fighting citizen's groups; educators or, for that matter, the perpetual, if uneven, and not infrequently incomprehensibly self-defeating activity by Congress in the popular "law-and-order" realm.

Has the Court Been Too Lenient? It is entirely natural to ask whether the courts have not in fact tipped the balance of justice in favor of the criminal to the detriment of the public? Given a post-1938 rise in crime at a rate eight to ten times faster than the growth of America's population— and still climbing in 1980–81—it is understandable that professionals and laymen alike should be fond of quoting Mr. Justice Cardozo's well-known observation that "[J]ustice is due the accused, but it is also due the accuser," coupled with the memorable Cardozo *quaere* whether the "criminal is to go free because the constable has blundered."[154] In the words of

[154] *People v. Defore*, 242 N.Y. 13 (1926).

Mr. Justice Stanley Reed, the "purpose of due process is not to protect an accused against a proper conviction, but against an *unfair* conviction."[155] Or, as Mr. Justice Robert H. Jackson pointed out in a case involving the question of due process in connection with the composition of a "blue ribbon"[156] jury: "Society also has a right to a fair trial. The defendant's right is a neutral jury. He has no constitutional right to friends on a jury."[157]

Yet in insisting upon strict standards of decency and fairness in governmental law-making, law-enforcing, and prosecuting, the courts simply perform the historic function of protecting the rights of the individual against the alleged unlawful acts of government. Mr. Justice Brennan once put the matter well in speaking for the 7:1 Supreme Court in a reversal of the conviction of union leader Clinton E. Jencks, a suspected perjurer of Communist persuasion, who had not been permitted to attempt to impeach testimony given to the F.B.I. on the basis of which he had been found guilty and convicted in the trial court below: ". . . the interest of the United States in a criminal prosecution . . . [and any of the several states] *is not that it shall win a case, but that justice shall be done.*"[158] There is no doubt that this philosophy is "hard to take" in specific instances—but can there really be any compromise with it under our form of government? The answer must be a firm "No!"

True, indeed, that men and women like Rochin, Jencks, Mapp, Mallory,[159] Massiah, Escobedo, Robinson, Malloy, Murphy, and Miranda are

---

[155] *Adamson v. California,* 330 U.S. 46 (1947), at 130. (Italics supplied.)

[156] A special jury which in some jurisdictions—e.g., Manhattan—may be selected by the jury commissioner from those qualified as trial jurors on the basis of special or superior qualifications. With the enactment of the Federal Jury Selection Act of 1968 it is no longer *legal* on the *federal* level (but it has never been held to be *unconstitutional*).

[157] *Fay v. New York,* 332 U.S. 261 (1947), at 288–89, upholding New York's "blue ribbon" jury.

[158] *Jencks v. New York,* 353 U.S. 657 (1957), at 668, quoting from Mr. Justice Sutherland's opinion in *Berger v. United States,* 295 U.S. 78 (1935), at 88. (Italics supplied.)

[159] Of the famed "Mallory Rule," under which the Court ruled in 1957 (*Mallory v. United States,* 354 U.S. 449) that officers must take an arrested person "without unnecessary delay" before the nearest available commissioner (he had been held overnight and interrogated by the police for seven hours ere this was done)—thus reversing Mallory's conviction and death sentence in a rape case. Mallory later went on to assault another woman and to burglarize a house and rape the housewife. Convicted on the latter two counts, he was ultimately sentenced to twenty-two years in the Pennsylvania State Penitentiary. After having served eleven and one-half years, he was released late in 1971. Soon thereafter, in July 1972, he was caught in the acts of robbing a couple and raping the woman and was shot fatally by Philadelphia Fairmount Park police when he tried to flee and pulled a gun on two officers. The *Mallory* "without unnecessary delay" rule became a focal point of congressional attacks on the Court and the subject of one of the "repealer" provisions—in Title II of the Omnibus Crime Control and Safe Streets Act of 1968 (discussed, pp. 114 ff. and 131 ff. *supra*). A confession is now admissible if a judge rules that it was indeed voluntary and that the delay before its presentation to a magistrate was not "unrea-

neither paragons of citizenship nor likely to "stay out of trouble," despite their "victories" at the bar of the Supreme Court. Indeed, almost all of them did run afoul of the law again. That, however, is not the main issue; what *is* the issue is the need to provide justice in accordance with the commands of our constitutional principles, in this case due process of law—which, on the other hand, knows and should know limits, too.

But to devote some thought to certain of the specific attacks upon Supreme Court rulings, *just which* of the more recent controversial issues would we have the Court or—failing its acquiescence to a hearing—the legislative branches alter, if not negate? The famed *Gideon* decision that guaranteed counsel in state criminal proceedings for indigent defendants in non-capital as well as capital criminal cases?[160] Or its subsequent extension to the preliminary hearing stage?[161] Or its further extension to the interrogation stage following arrest?[162] Can any member of a democratic society *honestly* argue the point that counsel in a criminal case is a luxury, that he who cannot afford it is not entitled to it? Or that, as in Danny Escobedo's situation, a request to consult with one's attorney prior to a police interrogation is somehow loading the dice against the government?

Or to consider an allied area of due process, are we really prepared to oppose or even reverse the Court's 1964 decision that the Fifth Amendment's tradition-heavy guarantee against compulsory self-incrimination is applicable to the states as well as the federal government?[163] Admittedly, there are matters of degree involved here—as there are in all of these areas—but there can hardly be any compromise with the elementary command that a suspect need not "sing" unless he so desires or unless he is given full statutory immunity.[164] The initial fears, and subsequent charges,

---

sonably longer than necessary." (The outer limit seems to be six hours.) *Mallory* remains judicially untested specifically, but the Burger Court appears to have more or less accepted it.

[160] *Gideon v. Wainwright*, 372 U.S. 335 (1963).

[161] *White v. Maryland*, 373 U.S. 59 (1963).

[162] *Miranda v. Arizona*, 384 U.S. 436 (1966).

[163] *Malloy v. Hogan*, 378 U.S. 1 (1964).

[164] See *Ullmann v. United States*, 350 U.S. 422 (1956), *Murphy v. Waterfront Commission of New York Harbor*, 378 U.S. 52 (1964), and *New Jersey v. Portash*, 440 U.S. 450 (1979). The sufficiency of the protection provided by the "immunity bath" section of the 1970 federal omnibus crime statute, and almost identical state legislation, came under simultaneous constitutional attack in 1971 in both a state (*Zicarelli v. New Jersey State Commissioner of Investigation*, 406 U.S. 472) and a federal case (*Kastigar v. United States*, 406 U.S. 441). Both pieces of legislation—which provided a more limited type of immunity, known as *"use"* immunity rather than the normal complete or *"transactional"* immunity—were upheld in 5:2 opinions, written by Mr. Justice Powell, with Justices Douglas and Marshall in dissent (Brennan and Rehnquist not participating). The essential difference between "use" and "transactional" immunity is that the latter covers *any and all aspects* of a matter for which a respondent is given immunity in return for waiving his rights against self-incrimination. Whereas "use" immunity, while barring "investigatory leads" against

that the *Miranda* decision would seriously interfere with the normal tendency to confess has not been borne out by resulting statistical evidence.[165]

Of course, it is revolting to find obvious, confessed murderers go scot-free (indeed, the phrase "getting away with murder" applies here literally) as, for example, one Arthur Culombe did in a grisly, multiple-murder case in Connecticut.[166] But the partially demented Culombe's confession had been *coerced* by Connecticut authorities in the most devious and patently illegal manner, involving the accused's family. True, one may well ask why the State was not justified in utilizing *any* methods that would bring such a criminal to justice. The answer is simple: because of our civilized standards of decency, fair play, and due process, our Constitution simply and resolutely proscribes such methods. In the words of Mr. Justice Clark in the 1961 *Mapp* case: "Nothing can destroy a government more quickly

---

an "immunized" respondent, does *not* prevent the prosecution from using evidence against him *if* such evidence is derived and developed from a source wholly independent of the "immunized" respondent's testimony. Not an easy line to draw! (*Zicarelli v. New Jersey,* 401 U.S. 933.)

[165] Following the uproar caused by this and the other *Miranda* rules, the findings of a major statistical study were disclosed by Evelle E. Younger, then District Attorney of Los Angeles County (which has the largest case load in the country) and later Attorney-General of California. The survey, which covered 4,000 felony cases, and the results of which frankly "amazed" Mr. Younger, showed that confessions were needed for successful prosecution in fewer than 10 per cent of the 4,000 cases, and that 50 per cent of the suspects were confessing *despite* the warning by the police. "The most significant things about our findings," commented Younger (a former F.B.I. agent), "are that suspects will talk regardless of the warning and furthermore it isn't so all-fired important whether they talk or not." (*The New York Times,* August 21, 1966, Sec. 1, p. 52). The Younger study confirmed similar findings by Brooklyn Supreme Court Justice Nathan R. Sobel and by Detroit Chief of Detectives Vincent W. Piersante. (See Sidney Zion, "So They Don't Talk," *The New York Times, op. cit.,* Sec. 4, p. 13.) An 18-month study of the effects of *Miranda* in Pittsburgh, Pa., reconfirmed the above: while confessions had dropped slightly since the June 1966 decision, the number of suspects who pleaded guilty had increased slightly as well. (*The New York Times,* December 31, 1967, Sec. 1, p. 25.) An 11-week Yale University study in 1967 yielded similar results. (*Ibid.*) So did a May 1968 Washington, D.C. study. (*Ibid.,* May 14, 1968, p. 60.) And so did a separate project observing custodial police interrogation in the District of Columbia. (66 *Michigan Law Review* 1347–1422, May 1968.) By 1970, after four years of close concern with the problem, Fred P. Graham concluded in a lengthy report that "despite evidence that crime has been steadily outstripping" the capacity of big-city law enforcement officers to control it, they "are becoming less disturbed by the Supreme Court's rein on their conduct towards suspects." (*The New York Times,* April 6, 1970, p. 1*l.*) See also the 1967 report of the International City Managers Association, *Public Management* (July), pp. 183–90, which confirms the above. The Yale and Washington, D.C. studies cited above, as well as similar compliance studies in Green Bay, Kenosha, Racine, and Madison, Wisconsin, showed that while implementation of *Miranda* was slow, grudging, and sometimes ineffective, overt flouting of the Court's norms by the police was a rarity. For the Wisconsin results, see Neal Milner, "Comparative Analysis of Patterns of Compliance with Supreme Court Decisions: *Miranda* and the Police in Four Communities," 5 *Law and Society Review* (August 1970), pp. 119–34.

[166] *Culombe v. Connecticut,* 367 U.S. 568 (1961).

than its failure to observe its own laws, or worse, its disregard of the charter of its own existence."[167] Which does not gainsay the frustrations of public officials such as Warren Earl Burger who, just prior to his accession to the Chief Justiceship of the Supreme Court of the United States wrote:

> The seeming anxiety of judges to protect every accused person from every consequence of his voluntary utterances is giving rise to myriad rules, subrules, variations and exceptions which even the most alert and most sophisticated lawyers and judges are taxed to follow. . . . We are approaching the predicament of the centipede on the flypaper—each time one leg is placed to give support for relief of a leg already "stuck," another becomes captive and soon all are immobilized. . . . We are well on our way to forbidding any utterance of an accused to be used against him unless it is made in open court. Guilt or innocence becomes irrelevant in the criminal trial as we flounder in a morass of artificial rules—poorly conceived and often impossible of application.[168]

The Fourth Amendment Can-of-Worms. We have neither time nor space to survey each of the various contentious and difficult areas in which the lines of private and public rights converge. But one last illustration: the complex matter of permissible search and seizure—which may well be *the* most complex to analyze as well as to adjudicate. Under the Fourth Amendment, *unreasonable*[169] searches and seizures are forbidden; out of this grew the so-called exclusionary rule applied to the federal government as of 1914[170] and, as we noted in the *Mapp* case,[171] to the states as of 1961. The exclusionary rule now forbids the use of *any* illegally obtained evidence to convict an accused in *court,* although the as yet (spring 1981) largely untested Organized Crime Control Act of 1970 contains a provision of questionable constitutionality which sets a five-year statute of limitations on challenges by defendants of evidence from leads picked up by officers during *illegal* searches.[172] The basic exclusionary rule also means that an otherwise illegal search is not rendered legal simply by what it turns up;

[167] *Mapp v. Ohio,* 367 U.S. 643, at 659.

[168] As quoted in Alpheus T. Mason and William M. Beaney, *American Constitutional Law,* 5th ed. (Englewood Cliffs, N.J.: Prentice-Hall, Inc., 1972), p. xv.

[169] An eternally controversial adjective! For a recent 5:4 split on the subject, see *United States v. Edwards,* 415 U.S. 800 (1974).

[170] *Weeks v. United States,* 232 U.S. 383. See Yale Kamisar's extensive supportive discussion of the rule, "Is the Exclusionary Rule an 'Illogical' or 'Unnatural' Interpretation of the Fourth Amendment?," 62 *Judicature* (August 1978), pp. 67–84. For a contrary view, see Judge Malcolm Richard Wilkey, "The Exclusionary Rule: Why Suppress Valid Evidence?," *ibid.* (November 1978), pp. 215–32. The rule has spawned an enormous amount of passionate as well as dispassionate commentary in books, journals, the press, other media, and the *Congressional Record.*

[171] *Weeks v. United States, op. cit.* See also pp. 102–12, *supra.*

[172] It *was* upheld as to the questioning of grand jury witnesses. (*United States v. Calandra,* 414 U.S. 338 [1975].)

ergo, "fishing expeditions" on the part of police in search of evidence are thus out. Before asking for an arrest warrant,[173] the police officer must convince the warrant-issuing magistrate of his "personal knowledge" of "probable cause." To obtain a search warrant, the place to be searched and the object(s) to be seized must be described "particularly." When, surprisingly, the Supreme Court ruled (5:3) in 1978 that police can get warrants to make *un*announced searches of places owned or occupied by persons believed to be innocent of criminal activities,[174] Congress responded two years later by enacting the Privacy Protection Act of 1980, severely limiting such searches. In any event, warrants are not issuable for "general" searches. Nor does a warrant to search a particular place *automatically* authorize the police to search anyone who happens to be there—as, for example, in a public bar.[175]

But there are, because there must be, situations in which the search of a person or the *immediate* surroundings is lawful *if* it is "incidental" to a legal arrest—i.e., one authorized by an arrest warrant or on the basis of probable cause—but such an "incidental" search, to be considered "reasonable," must *really* be "confined to the immediate vicinity of the arrest . . . to the area within the arrestee's reach at the time of his arrest, the area from which he might gain possession of a weapon or destructible evidence."[176] *Mere* "suspicion," without more, is never enough to meet the constitutional commands, yet the concept of *"reasonable* suspicion" has been judicially justified in, for example, upholding "profile"-triggered airport searches of drug traffic[177] and hijacking suspects. And, of course, there are instances, other than the narrowly drawn "incidental" search rule, in which it *is* possible to search without a search warrant, *provided there is probable cause.*[178] Some examples would be: to discover weapons and/or

---

[173] It may be either a daytime or nighttime warrant. (*Gooding v. United States,* 416 U.S. 430 [1974].)

[174] *Zurcher v. Stanford Daily,* 463 U.S. 547. "The critical element in a reasonable search," wrote Mr. Justice White in this highly controversial case, "is not that the owner of the property is suspected of crime, but that there is reasonable cause to believe that the specific things to be searched for and seized are located on the property." (At 556.) Because the case involved the press, sundry First Amendment issues were also raised and disposed of.

[175] *Ybarra v. Illinois,* 444 U.S. 85 (1979). But otherwise admissible evidence is not suppressible simply on the ground that it was unlawfully seized from a third party not before the court in a trial. (*United States v. Payner,* 447 U.S. 727 [1980].)

[176] *Chimel v. California,* 395 U.S. 752 (1969), at 763, which "toughened" the standards of *United States v. Rabinowitz,* 399 U.S. 56 (1950).

[177] *United States v. Mendenhall,* 446 U.S. 554 (1980). But *cf. Reid v. Georgia,* 48 LW 3847 (1980).

[178] "Probable cause" is, of course, enormously difficult to define—and to disprove. The Court's most frequently quoted definition is taken from Mr. Justice Douglas's opinion in *Henry v. United States,* 361 U.S. 98 (1959): "Probable cause exists if the facts and circumstances known to the officer warrant a prudent man in believing that the offense has been committed." (At 102.)

prevent the destruction of evidence,[179] the common-law right of an arresting police agent to search when he has reasonable grounds to believe that a crime is being committed or that an individual on the scene is "armed and dangerous,"[180] and, again always assuming the presence of "probable cause" in the case of *moving* vehicles.[181] No such justifiable "probable cause" exists, however, the Supreme Court held (7:1) in 1979, in standard so-called police "spot checks" of automobile drivers' credentials on the public highways, *unless* the officer has some "articulable and reasonable suspicion that the motorist is unlicensed or [the auto] unregistered or [there is some other] violation of law.[182] Nonetheless, the Court made clear unanimously in 1981, police may indeed stop vehicles when "the totality of circumstances" suggests its occupants may be involved in a crime (here the transportation of illegal aliens in Arizona).[183] Moreover, as it had ruled (6:3) in 1973, *if* there is "probable cause" to take a person into custody, "the fact of lawful arrest establishes the authority to search" the person "reasonably" (and not just in instances of suspected *serious* crimes;[184] nor does it have to be justified, like the *Terry* "stop-and-frisk" case,[185] which did *not* initiate an incident that led to an arrest but turned on the grounds of protecting the police officer from harm). And the Court added (6:2) in 1976 that the Constitution does *not* require law enforcement officials to obtain warrants before they make arrests in *public places*—even when there is adequate time to obtain a warrant—provided there is probable cause that a felony has been committed.[186] But, as the Court held in 1980, a warrant *is* needed for routine felony arrests in *private* homes, absent "exigent circumstances."[187] Frustrating as it may be, the constitutional rules must be observed—by the protagonists on both sides.

---

[179] *Agnello v. United States,* 268 U.S. 20 (1925).

[180] See the several late 1960s and early 1970s "stop-and-frisk" cases cited in footnote 62, on p. 110, *supra.* See also *Pennsylvania v. Mimms,* 434 U.S. 106 (1977).

[181] *Carroll v. United States,* 267 U.S. 132 (1925). *Cf. New York v. Belton* (1981).

[182] *Delaware v. Prouse,* 440 U.S. 648. The decision still allows the police to set up roadblocks for license and registration checks, however—prompting the dissenting Mr. Justice Rehnquist to observe that motorists, "like sheep, are much less likely to be 'frightened' or 'annoyed' when stopped en masse"; that, therefore, police can now stop *"all* motorists," but not *"less* than all motorists." (At 664.)

[183] *United States v. Cortez,* 49 LW 4099. See also *Robbins v. California* (1981).

[184] *United States v. Robinson* and *Gustafson v. Florida,* 414 U.S. 218 and 414 U.S. 260, respectively, and a contraband search warrant provided police power for "temporary detention." (*Michigan v. Summers,* 49 LW 4776, 1981.)

[185] *Terry v. Ohio,* 392 U.S. 1 (1968), an 8:1 decision, written by Mr. Chief Justice Warren, Mr. Justice Douglas dissenting.

[186] *United States v. Watson,* 423 U.S. 411. See *Donovan v. Dewey* (1981).

[187] *Payton v. New York,* 445 U.S. 573. For an excellent analysis—as of 1966—of the entire search-and-seizure syndrome see J. W. Landynski, *Search and Seizure and the Supreme Court* (Baltimore: The Johns Hopkins Press, 1966). See also that author's work cited in footnote 144, p. 62, *supra.* For a more recent study see J. D. Hirschel, *Fourth Amendment Rights* (Lexington: D.C. Heath Co., 1979).

The Case Study of Wiretapping. To illustrate further, wiretapping, one of the most vexatious of the due process problems, is *not* unconstitutional—or at least the Supreme Court has never so held it. The famous 5:4 *Olmstead* case of 1928 set the tone,[188] Mr. Chief Justice Taft holding it *not* to be a Fourth Amendment violation because the telephonic messages at issue did not involve a physical intrusion on the defendant's premises, nor was any "material thing" seized. Mr. Justice Holmes's vigorous dissent that it is "dirty business,"[189] and Mr. Justice Brandeis's prophetic warning about the "progress" of science, also rendered in a separate dissenting opinion—one of *the* great dissents in the Court's annals[190]—failed to command a majority. The response to *Olmstead* was the Federal Communications Act of 1934 which (like some state statutes) expressly forbade it; yet the F.B.I. successfully qualified it with the interpretation that mere "interception" is not a violation of the Act's famous Section 605 *unless there* is also *"divulgence"*—an interpretation that served as the agency's rationale for much of its wiretapping, despite the language of Section 605. Hence we had something that was proscribed yet went on constantly!

But does not wiretapping make the citizen prey to the very kind of "fishing expedition" which is theoretically forbidden under the Fourth Amendment? The modern scientific "advances" in the realm of detection, so perceptively predicted by Brandeis, are rapidly reducing privacy to a shibboleth. Thus, as was vividly demonstrated to a subcommittee of the United States Senate's Committee on the Judiciary,[191] we now have available such eavesdropping devices as tiny radio transmitters that can be concealed in a martini olive, with the toothpick serving as the antenna; in a woman's purse or her brassiere—even in the cavity of a tooth of an intimate associate! Then there is the laser, a device which can transmit a concentrated beam of light to a room several blocks away so as to reflect back a television picture of everything happening in the room, including the sound! Perhaps it was specters such as these that caused Mr. Justice Nathan R. Sobel of the New York State Supreme Court (Brooklyn Division) to declare unconstitutional on March 1, 1965, the New York State law that had authorized court-approved electronic eavesdropping on a suspect's private premises. In his 32-page opinion, Justice Sobel held the law invalid because the eavesdropping orders it authorized could not, in his judgment,

[188] *Olmstead v. United States,* 277 U.S. 438. (Italics supplied.)

[189] "We have to choose," he observed, "and for my part I think it a less evil that some criminals should escape than that the government would play an ignoble part." (*Ibid.,* at 470–471.)

[190] Among its memorable language: "The makers of our Constitution . . . conferred, as against the government, the right to be let alone—the most comprehensive of rights and the right most valued by civilized men. . . . Men born to freedom are naturally alert to repel invasions of their liberty by evilminded rulers. The greatest dangers to liberty lurk in insidious encroachment by men of zeal, well-meaning but without understanding." (At 478.)

[191] See *Life,* May 20, 1966, pp. 38–47.

meet the standards required for the issuance of search warrants under the Fourth Amendment.[192] Just a year later, the Federal Communications Commission issued an order prohibiting private citizens from using radio devices to eavesdrop. Theoretically, the F.C.C. order made illegal such equipment as the tiny radio transmitters described above (unless everyone present knew the equipment was being used). Yet it did *not* affect the use of a miniature tape recorder directly connected to a small camouflaged microphone, since no radio transmission is involved—although the same kind of eavesdropping may take place. Nor did the ban affect law enforcement agencies, such as the F.B.I., the Internal Revenue Service, or state and local police and similar authorities. However, in July 1967 the then Attorney-General, Ramsey Clark, in a dramatic order going far beyond any previously issued governmental limitations in the wiretapping and eavesdropping field, issued sweeping new regulations forbidding all wiretapping and virtually all eavesdropping except in national security cases. The new rules generated considerable controversy and opposition among federal agents and prosecutors.[193]

Indeed, by that time a number of legal experts had become convinced that the Supreme Court's *Griswold* ruling in June 1965[194] which, as noted in Chapter III, invalidated Connecticut's birth control statute by enunciating a new "right of privacy," had laid the basis for an eventual judicial outlawing of wiretapping and other forms of electronic eavesdropping. It was argued that the new right of privacy could be held to override the technical distinction of a physical intrusion that the Court made both in the *Olmstead* case[195] and in subsequent decisions involving other electronic eavesdropping,[196] and thus render all such intrusions unconstitutional.[197] On the other hand it might well be asked, could not and should not the

---

[192] *People v. Grossman,* 257 N.Y.S. 2d 266. He was reversed a year later by the Appellate Division, but he was more or less vindicated in 1967 when the United States Supreme Court declared the New York law unconstitutional in *Berger v. New York,* 388 U.S. 41.

[193] Thus F.B.I. Director J. Edgar Hoover referred to Clark as the "worst Attorney-General" he had served under in fifty years in Washington, "even worse than Bobby Kennedy." (*Time,* November 30, 1970, p. 11.)

[194] *Griswold v. Connecticut,* 381 U.S. 479. See pp. 71 ff., *supra.*

[195] *Olmstead v. United States,* 277 U.S. 438 (1928). The vote in that case, as noted earlier above, was 5:4; the majority opinion was written by Mr. Chief Justice Taft and joined by Associate Justices Van Devanter, McReynolds, Sutherland, and Sanford. The dissenters, in addition to Holmes and Brandeis, were Justices Butler and Stone—all of whom wrote dissenting opinions.

[196] E.g., *Goldman v. United States,* 316 U.S. 129 (1942) and *On Lee v. United States,* 343 U.S. 747 (1952). (*Lee* was reconfirmed, 5:4, in 1971, in *United States v. White,* 401 U.S. 745.)

[197] Such a ruling would presumably reach the so-called distinction between "wiretapping" and "bugging," a distinction that sees the latter as not proscribed. It was embraced by sundry law-enforcement officials, apparently including the then ex-U.S.-Attorney-General Robert F. Kennedy. (See David Lawrence, "Rightfully Bugging," the *New York Herald Tribune* [International Edition], July 9, 1966, p. 8.)

kind of search and seizure represented by wiretapping be authorized under our Constitution? Although wiretapping and electronic eavesdropping are clearcut invasions of the basic rights of privacy, perhaps they *are* necessary in cases of subversive activities, seditious conduct, espionage, kidnapping, and certain other major crimes. Perhaps a good case *can* be made for eavesdropping in the fields just mentioned when the act is duly requested *and judicially authorized before the fact,* notwithstanding the reprehensible nature of the incursions of privacy involved. However, it would be much harder to make a viable case for such intrusions on privacy in crimes like fraud, racketeering, prostitution, and gambling, or for the "investigation" of public and private employees in anything but highly secret positions.[198] In the final analysis, our response must turn first on the constitutionality of any such proposed action and second on its wisdom. And even assuming the former, any thoughts on the wisdom of such action must confront the basic issues raised by Mr. Justice Brandeis in his memorable dissent in the *Olmstead* case, when he wrote:

> The makers of our Constitution undertook to secure conditions favorable to the pursuit of happiness. They recognized the significance of man's spiritual nature, of his feelings and of his intellect. They knew that only a part of the pain, pleasure and satisfactions of life are to be found in material things. They sought to protect Americans in their beliefs, their thoughts, their emotions and their sensations. They conferred, as against the Government, *the right to be let alone—the most comprehensive of rights and the right most valued by civilized men.* To protect that right, every unjustifiable intrusion by the Government upon the privacy of the individual, whatever the means employed, must be deemed a violation of the Fourth Amendment. . . .[199]

The Court—the recipient of so many governmentally, especially legislatively, "passed bucks"—in its 1967 catalytic *Katz* case[200] seemed to take a long stride toward a possible solution of at least the eavesdropping ("bugging") aspect of the problem, and by implication, of the entire privacy/intrusion dilemma. In that decision, with a solo dissent by Mr. Justice Black—who consistently rejected the contention that the specific safeguards of the Fourth Amendment, as spelled out therein, apply to eavesdropping because the Amendment speaks only of "persons, houses, papers, and effects"—the Court *eased curbs* on "bugging" *while adding safeguards* against it! Mr. Justice Stewart's majority opinion, noting that

---

[198] An interesting case for such a balancing approach to the use of wiretapping and electronic eavesdropping was made by Alan Westin in his *Privacy and Freedom* (New York: Atheneum, 1967), *passim.*

[199] *Olmstead v. United States, op. cit.,* at 478. (Italics supplied.)

[200] *Katz v. United States,* 389 U.S. 347. The vote was 7:1, Mr. Justice Marshall not participating.

the Fourth Amendment should not "be translated into a general constitutional right of privacy,"[201] made clear that the Constitution does not forbid electronic "bugging" by law enforcement officers *if* they first obtain warrants authorizing the eavesdropping—warrants being a basic requirement of the Fourth Amendment, of course. *But,* at the same time, with *Katz* the Court extended the reach of that Amendment by holding that the search warrant procedure must be followed by the police officers even when they plan to eavesdrop on persons in semi-public places, such as a phone booth. Moreover, and significantly, the Court threw out its old "physical trespass" test by ruling that the trespass *per se* was not the crucial point, that the Fourth Amendment "protects people not places."[202] In effect, *Katz* thus overruled both the "material things seized" rationale of the *Olmstead* holding[203] and the "physical intrusion" distinction of the *Goldman* case[204] (which had come midway between the *Olmstead* and *Katz* decisions). The latter also lessened the effect of the Court's 5:4 decision in *Berger v. New York* a few months earlier in 1967,[205] when it had narrowly invalidated the aforementioned New York statute authorizing electronic eavesdropping because, as Mr. Justice Tom Clark—an ex-Attorney-General of the United States—wrote for the majority, the "statute is too broad in its sweep, resulting in a trespassory intrusion into a constitutionally protected area" and did not provide for "adequate judicial supervision or protective procedures."[206] What *Katz* did, then, was to enable the enactment of both wiretapping and eavesdropping ("bugging") statutes, *provided* the carefully delineated Fourth Amendment safeguards against unreasonable searches and seizures would be scrupulously observed by *all* branches of the government, both statutorily and procedurally.[207]

Against the backdrop of the rising controversy of the "law and order" issue, Congress took the *Katz* cue, and enacted Title III of the Omnibus Crime Control and Safe Streets Act of 1968, headed "Wiretapping and Electronic Surveillance." It permits *court-approved* interceptions by both federal and state law enforcement officials in the investigation of a large

---

[201] *Ibid.*, at 350.

[202] *Ibid.*, at 351. See the Court's 7:2 majority emphasis of that crucial point in its 1977 striking down of a conviction obtained in a federal case involving a 200-pound footlocker filled with marijuana. (*United States v. Chadwick,* 433 U.S. 1.) But the Court also pointed out three years later that the *legality* of a search is challengeable only if an accused can demonstrate "an expectation of privacy in the premises searched." *United States v. Salvucci,* 448 U.S. 83 (1980).

[203] *Katz v. United States, op. cit.,* at 351.

[204] *Goldman v. United States,* 316 U.S. 129 (1942).

[205] 388 U.S. 41.

[206] *Ibid.*, at 44, 60.

[207] See the informative analysis of privacy by David M. O'Brien, "Reasonable Expectations of Privacy: Principles and Policies of Fourth Amendment—Protected Privacy," 13 *New England Law Review* 663–738 (1978), and the same author's *Privacy, Law, and Public Policy* (New York: Frederick A. Praeger, 1979).

number of listed crimes[208]—there were 302 such court-authorized, although not necessarily applied, orders in 1969; 816 in 1971; 864 in 1973; 871 in 1974; and 626 in 1977 (549 of these state and 77 federal). Almost three-quarters involved gambling offenses, which consistently lead the "tap" field, followed by those for drug-related crimes (that now cover *circa* one-fifth of the total) throughout the United States.[209] The sharp drop as of 1976 reflects a cutback in gambling investigations (in part because of mounting costs). Replete with procedural safeguards—with an eye toward *Katz*—the law has a contentious "exemption" section in the case of "an emergency situation exist[ing] with respect to conspiratorial activities threatening the national security interest or to conspiratorial activities characteristic of organized crime."[210] Under its terms, and if the action at issue is so classified by either the United States Attorney-General or the principal prosecuting attorney of any state or its subdivisions, interception may proceed *without* court order, provided an application for an order is obtained and entered "within forty-eight hours after the interception has occurred or begins to occur."[211] Here, then, is the loophole—which may, or may not be justifiable and constitutional, and will assuredly be judicially tested.[212]

A different, and perhaps even more significant test, however, had come in 1971 when, breaking new ground in a surprisingly bold decision, United States District Judge Warren J. Ferguson ruled in Los Angeles that the federal government's "no-warrant-needed" national security wiretap policy, allegedly inherent in a perhaps even more contentious section of the 1968 statute than the one discussed above, which states that the law's provisions "do not restrict the constitutional powers of the President,"[213] was unconstitutional as applied to *domestic* cases (rather than foreign ones). As he put the issue:

> National security cannot be invoked to abridge basic rights. . . . To guarantee political freedom, our forefathers agreed to take certain risks which

[208] E.g., for the *state* level: murder, kidnapping, gambling, robbery, bribery, extortion, or dealing in narcotics, marijuana, or other dangerous drugs, etc. (Section 2516–[2]). Some of these also apply in the federal sector.

[209] Based on annual reports by the United States Attorney-General.

[210] Section 2518(7).

[211] Section 2518(7)(b).

[212] By mid-1981 lower federal courts had reached conflicting results; but no Supreme Court test had occurred. *United States v. Chavez*, 416 U.S. 562 (1974), in the eyes of at least some observers, seemed to approve the procedure tangentially in a 5:4 holding.

[213] Section 2511(3). Among other things, it states: "Nothing contained in this chapter . . . shall limit the constitutional power of the President to take such measures as he deems necessary to protect the nation against actual or potential attack or other hostile acts of a foreign power. . . ."

are inherent in a free democracy. It is unthinkable that we should now be required to sacrifice those freedoms in order to defend them.[214]

Shortly thereafter, Judge Ferguson's ruling was echoed in an even more strongly worded decision against the government's interpretation of its asserted authority under the 1968 Wiretapping Act by United States District Judge Damon J. Keith in a Detroit case.[215] The government appealed; lost 2:1 at the bar of the United States Court of Appeals for the Sixth Circuit in April, which held, *inter alia,* that there was not "one written phrase" in the Constitution or statutes to support the Administration's view that federal agents might legally wiretap radical domestic groups without court order;[216] and took a further appeal to the Supreme Court.[217] In one of those decisions that render the study of the judicial process so fascinatingly unpredictable, down came the Burger Court's response in its next term: in an 8:0 opinion—Mr. Justice Rehnquist abstaining—written by Mr. Justice Powell who, as a private citizen not so long theretofore had *supported* publicly the Government's claim of constitutional authority for wiretapping of radical domestic groups *sans* warrant, the unanimous Justices declared the practice of doing so *without prior judicial approval* to be an unconstitutional invasion of Fourth Amendment guarantees, as well as being unauthorized under the 1968 statute![218] "The price of lawful public dissent," in Powell's words, "must not be a dread of subjection to an unchecked surveillance power. Nor must the fear of unauthorized official eavesdropping deter citizen dissent and discussion of government action in private conversation."[219]

The Court left open the statute's application to *foreign* groups suspected of subversive activity—a facet it refused 3:5 pointedly to explore when it had an opportunity to do so in 1974.[220] Four years thereafter, however, Congress—allowing for but narrow exceptions—enacted legislation requiring federal court approval before the government can conduct electronic surveillance in *foreign* intelligence cases. Concurrently, Congress further

[214] *United States v. Smith,* 321 F. Supp. 424.

[215] *Plamondon v. Mitchell,* decided January 25, 1971. (See following footnote.)

[216] *United States v. United States District Court for the Eastern District of Michigan,* 444 F. 2d 651 (1971).

[217] A collateral issue had reached the Court in 1969, when it held that any criminal defendant had the right to see directly all transcriptions unexpurgated by a judge of his conversations picked up by an "illegal" police listening device. The purpose of the decision was to let defendants rest assured that no illegally obtained evidence was used against them—the government being forced either to turn the transcripts of the "illegal" tap over to defendants or to drop the case against them. (*Alderman v. United States,* 394 U.S. 165.)

[218] *United States v. United States District Court for the Eastern District of Michigan,* 407 U.S. 297 (1972).

[219] *Ibid.,* at 314.

[220] *Ivanov v. United States,* 419 U.S. 881 (1974).

narrowed the government's authority to obtain judicial warrants for *domestic* national security wiretaps and bugging. Chairman Birch Bayh (D.-Ind.) of the Senate Intelligence Committee hailed the measure as "a landmark in the development of effective legal safeguards for constitutional rights."[221] On a related matter involving the 1968 wiretapping law, it had administered another defeat to the Government's attempts to use tapping more facilely: in two devastating, unanimous decisions in mid-1974, the Court threw out the convictions of two accused criminals[222] because of "shortcuts" under the 1968 statute taken by Attorney-General John N. Mitchell some years earlier. While the Justices acknowledged that the law had indeed vastly expanded federal investigative authority to tap, that authority hinged expressly on the personal approval in advance by the Attorney-General or by an especially designated assistant. But dozens of authorizations, including those involved in the two cases before the Court, had simply been initialled "JNM" by a minor Mitchell aide, Sol Lindenbaum, or sometimes even just by the latter's secretary! That irregularity, held the normally decidedly "pro" law-and-order Mr. Justice White, was no mere technicality: Congress had clearly and carefully required that "the mature judgment of a particular, responsible official" would be involved in any decision to tap. As a result of the Court's ruling, nearly two years of determined, hard work by federal investigators was wiped out, and at least sixty cases involving no fewer than 626 accused gamblers, narcotic dealers, and other racketeers were imperiled.[223] Such, however, is the price of constitutional guarantees: shortcuts à la Mitchell's can simply not be condoned nor, it is to be hoped, will they be as long as we are governed by our Constitution's letter and spirit.

Law, Order, and Justice Reconsidered. Notwithstanding the great, and entirely understandable, public outcry to do something about the now so shockingly predictable annual, upwards of 10 per cent, rise[224] in crime, there are no shortcuts in democratic society to regulation, prosecution, and conviction. But it would be sophistry to gainsay the genuine concern, both lay and professional, over the contemporary broadening of judicial "supervision" in the realm of criminal justice and the resultant stringent new rules of procedure that have evolved. Given the epidemically increasing rate of crime—of which less than 20 per cent is officially reported[225]—are there

[221] *The Washington Post*, October 26, 1978, p. A2. (The new legislation was in 18 USCS §2511.) See the Foreign Intelligence Surveillance Act of 1978.

[222] *United States v. Giordano*, 416 U.S. 505 and *United States v. Chavez*, 416 U.S. 562.

[223] See the account in *Time*, May 27, 1974, p. 57.

[224] *Annual Reports* of the Federal Bureau of Investigation, 1970 ff. Its report for 1979 showed a 9.1 per cent overall increase, but an 11.0 per cent one in violent crime—the sharpest rise in four years.

[225] See *The New York Times*, April 15, 1974, p. 1. See also the works by Wilson and Silberman, fn. 226, *infra*, and the F.B.I.'s annual *Uniform Crime Report*.

alternatives to "easy" or "shortcut" apprehensions, prosecutions, and convictions that either cricumvent, dilute, or disregard basic constitutional guarantees? Among them may well be such fundamental ones as deterrents and, arguably most significantly, the certainty of punishment—hardly a hallmark under our criminal justice system! And since according to the most authentic and reliable recent statistics,[226] between 65 and 92 per cent of those booked on criminal charges were recidivists ("repeaters"), it seems entirely reasonable to ask whether our courts have not been "too soft" on them and, instead, thus might well be more severe in the type and length of sentences meted out to recidivists. The public has the right to be protected from habitual criminality; and perhaps longer, less readily commutable, and less easily parolable sentences[227] may well be in order,[228] especially since only one out of fifty *reported*—and but one out of every

[226] See James Q. Wilson's estimate of 87 per cent in his fine *Thinking About Crime* (New York: Basic Books, 1975); among others, the President's Crime Commission's conclusion that 85 per cent of those arrested for crimes more serious than a traffic offense have been arrested before, and that the average man who has been arrested once will be arrested seven more times. (*The New York Times Magazine*, May 11, 1969, p. 136.) According to Mr. Chief Justice Burger, 65 per cent of the 200,000 persons serving prison sentences in 1970 would be reconvicted. (*The Philadelphia Evening Bulletin*, February 23, 1970.) According to ex-Attorney-General Ramsey Clark, 87 per cent of the major crimes committed in the United States are committed by youths who were previously convicted of an earlier offense. (Speech at Temple University, April 1970.) The F.B.I.'s *Uniform Crime Report* of 1967 reported that of 17,000 randomly selected prisoners released in 1963, a total of 92 per cent had been rearrested by 1967 (p. 28). According to the same source, almost 90 per cent of those who were arrested for major crimes during 1967 had been arrested previously; 70 per cent had been convicted; and 50 per cent had served jail sentences of over ninety days (p. 23). Although hardly without a considerable number of critics on grounds of reliability or accuracy, the F.B.I.'s annual *Uniform Crime Reports* are an important source of a host of pertinent statistics. "The public notion and the police idea of revolving door crime is thus borne out," reported Marvin E. Wolfgang, head of the Center for Studies in Criminology and Criminal Law at the University of Pennsylvania in releasing a 1969 pilot study of 9,978 boys born in 1945. Six per cent of those boys committed 5,305 crimes, nearly nine apiece. (Release to the press, September 28, 1969.) Of 14,214 adults arrested for major crimes in 1971, 69 per cent had been arrested before and averaged 5.8 arrests each. (The *Philadelphia Inquirer*, April 1, 1972, p. 7.) For a recent, widely acclaimed study of crime in America and its attempted control, see Charles E. Silberman, *Criminal Violence, Criminal Justice* (New York: Random House, 1978; Vintage Books, 1980). The author's "Appendix: Notes on Crime Statistics" (pp. 606–17) represents an unique approach to and analysis of their gathering and utilization.

[227] For a useful compendium on diverse criminal sentencing, see the special issue of 60 *Judicature* 5 (December 1976), "Criminal Sentencing: A Game of *Chance.*" And see 63 *Judicature* 4 (October 1979) for some fascinating, thought-provoking comparative data on the utilization of fines in lieu of imprisonment in sentencing in England and Wales.

[228] I am aware of the general opposition to that suggestion by most sociologists and psychologists. But there is also considerable support from experts on criminology and urbanology as, prominently, James Q. Wilson (see p. 147, footnote 226, *supra*). Thus, in arguing for longer jail terms as a practical deterrent to the growing crime menace, Wilson is scornful of utopian-minded "intellectuals" who, in his view, refuse to acknowledge that "wicked people exist" and are loathe to be critical of "humankind."

To the Editor:

I, along with a vast number of my fellow citizens, am in contempt of court. The reason? Typical articles in today's *Times*, to wit:

* Page 1: A story about the capture of Nathan Giles, convicted murderer who was out on parole when he allegedly committed the particularly horrible murder of a nurse.

* Page B1: Davreaux Wiggins, convicted of pushing a stewardess in front of a subway train, then kicking her in the face when she tried to escape. He told police this was his fourth recent such incident. Judge George Roberts gave him half the sentence that could have been imposed. Beware of subway platforms four years hence when Mr. Wiggins may be back at work.

* Page B3: Because of the technicality that a convicted rapist committed his crime in Queens rather than Brooklyn, the New York State Court of Appeals, in its infinite wisdom, ruled that he must be retried. Three members of the court expressed doubt that the defendant would be tried again. And, if he will be retried, imagine the anguish that his victim must suffer for the second time.

I once was under the impression that one of the functions of the courts was to see that justice was done so that the public would be protected. Until there is more evidence of this I will remain in contempt of court.

Max Kohn
Philadelphia, Dec. 1, 1978

[The writer is a consultant to the Citizens Crime Commission of Philadelphia.]
SOURCE: *The New York Times,* December 8, 1978, p. A28.

five such crimes *is* reported—crimes results in conviction![229] It does seem that trial judges and parole officers have often been guilty of the kind of leniency in criminal cases involving "repeaters" that may be appropriate only for an initial offense; that—and this is more troubling—the criminal is not infrequently regarded as the victim of society rather than society as the victim of the criminal; that, in the view of many on-lookers, "there is more concern with the criminal than with the victim." But there is another aspect to that suggestion.

Because "bigger and better" prison sentences will not solve the problem of crime, a plea for toughness in sentencing must join one for more effec-

[229] 58 *Judicature* 10 (May 1975), p. 466. See also, 63 *Judicature* 4 (October 1979).

tive efforts in prison rehabilitation; for more modern institutional facilities; and for more appropriately trained professional personnel. Revelations in 1969 and 1970 of conditions in prisons, styled "universities of crime" by President Nixon, gave shocking proof of the state of America's prisons—of which six that were still in use in 1971 were built in the eighteenth century, and four prior to George Washington's inauguration.[230] In the last two decades, at least eight presidential commissions, dozens of legislative reports, and more than 800 books and articles have pleaded for prison reform. Although we have witnessed some *bona fide* groping for such reform,[231] the future still looked bleak in the early 1980s. Coordination and improvement of federal, state, and local systems is vital. Of course, there is a limit to the type of rehabilitation that a prison can provide—but much more can be done than is done at present—although some leading experts, James Q. Wilson for one, contend that hardened criminals are not rehabilitable,[232] and Charles E. Silberman, while somewhat less pessimistic, perhaps, on overall solutions to crime prevention and control, concludes that "[n]o approach to rehabilitation seems to work."[233] The public, however, must be willing to foot the bill for such measures; insistence on more protection has been accompanied, all-too-often and contradictorily, by opposition to paying for it.

Whether or not these suggestions might help us come to grips with important aspects of the problem and assuage the very real and justifiable[234] fears of the lay and professional public, or whether such statutes as the Organized Crime Control Act of 1970, with its drastic provisions, has some answers—when it comes to the fundamental standards of due process of law under our Constitution, there can be no compromises, no shortcuts. "The interest of . . . [the government]," to quote again Mr. Justice Brennan, ". . . is not that it shall win a case, but that justice shall be done."[235] There should be no reason whatsoever why, in our democratic society,

[230] *The New York Times,* January 7, 1971, Sec. 1, p. 1. See also "U.S. Prisons: Schools for Crime," *Time,* January 18, 1971, p. 48.

[231] E.g., the imaginative new federal prison complex in Butner, North Carolina, which opened in mid-1976, designed and organized to try a new tack in penology. Another is the ultra-modern federal minimum security prison at Eglin Air Force Base in Florida (where Maryland's deposed Governor Marvin Mandel began to serve his three-year sentence in 1980).

[232] "I have not heard an intellectually respectable defense of criminal rehabilitation." (Quoted by *Time,* June 30, 1975, p. 22.) See also his book cited in fn. 226, *supra* and Mr. Chief Justice Burger's imaginative May 1981 proposals.

[233] Silberman, *op. cit.,* p. 247.

[234] Thus, from 1961 to 1979 the rate of robberies increased 256 per cent, forcible rape 174 per cent, aggravated assault 176 per cent, and murder 107 per cent. And the rate for these violent crimes as well as property crimes like burglary is still rising sharply, averaging 10 per cent per category. (See F.B.I. *Uniform Crime Report,* released September 29, 1980.)

[235] *Jencks v. United States,* 353 U.S. 657 (1957), at 668.

well-trained, professional agents of the law cannot apprehend and convict alleged criminals without, in the process, becoming criminals themselves. As Arnold S. Trebach put it so well in his *The Rationing of Justice,* the argument against greater protection for the rights of the accused "reduces itself to an argument *for* violation of the law in order to enforce it. It is a crime to violate the rights of *any* person," whether he be a criminal or a saint. Under our system, in the words of Mr. Chief Justice Warren to *New York Times* correspondent Anthony Lewis, the prosecutor "is not paid to convict people. He is there to protect the rights of the people in our community and to see that when there is a violation of the law, it is vindicated by trial and prosecution under fair judicial standards."[236] A poignant Warren trademark thus was to interrupt a learned counsel's argument citing precedent and book, with the simple, almost naive-sounding *quaere:* "Yes, but was it fair?" Deeply concerned with social justice, that remarkable, if hardly non-controversial, public servant once mused: "You sit there, and you see the whole gamut of human nature. Even if the case being argued involves only a little fellow and $50, it involves justice. That's what is important."[237]

As he did so frequently, Mr. Justice Brandeis went to the heart of the matter in his dissent in the *Olmstead* case in 1928:

> "Decency, security, and liberty alike demand that government officials shall be subjected to the same rules of conduct that are commands to the citizen. In a government of laws, existence of the government will be imperilled if it fails to observe the law scrupulously. Our government is the potent, the omnipresent teacher. For good or for ill, it teaches the whole people by example. Crime is contagious. If the government becomes a lawbreaker, it breeds contempt for law; it invites every man to become a law unto himself; it invites anarchy. To declare that in the administration of the criminal law the end justifies the means—to declare that the government may commit crimes in order to secure the conviction of a private criminal—would bring terrible retribution. Against that pernicious doctrine this court should resolutely set its face."[238]

In the main the Supreme Court has for some time now[239] been setting its

---

[236] A Talk with Warren on Crime, the Court, the Country," *The New York Times Magazine,* October 19, 1969, p. 126.

[237] From *Time's* obituary essay, July 22, 1974, p. 66.

[238] *Olmstead v. United States,* 277 U.S. 438 (1928), at 485. Mr. Chief Justice Warren would echo these haunting thoughts well in his opinion for the Court in *Spano v. New York,* 360 U.S. 315 three decades later: "The police must obey the law while enforcing the law; . . . in the end life and liberty can be as much endangered from illegal methods used to convict these thought to be criminals as from the actual criminals themselves." (At 320.)

[239] For an intelligent critique of aspects of that dénouement, see Henry J. Friendly, *Benchmarks* (Chicago: University of Chicago Press, 1967), especially Ch. 11, "The

face "against that pernicious doctrine," and it has done so regardless of criticism. Still, it is obliged to ever be alive to the admonition by one of its most thoughtful and literate members, Mr. Justice Robert H. Jackson, that it must not en route "convert the constitutional Bill of Rights into a suicide pact."[240]

Bill of Rights as a Code of Criminal Procedure." See also the aforementioned somber, enlightening, critical Wilson and Silberman works, fns. 226, 232, and 233, *supra,* and *Time's* issues of June 30, 1975 and March 23, 1981, devoted to "The Crime Wave."

[240] Dissenting opinion, *Terminiello v. Chicago,* 337 U.S. 1 (1949), at 37. See text and fn. 110 on p. 176, *infra,* for a fuller discussion of that statement. For an echo see Mr. Chief Justice Burger's 1981 majority opinion in *Haig v. Agee,* 49 LW 4869.

chapter *V* The Precious Freedom of Expression

If we Americans have, and practice, "ambivalence"[1] as our primary ideology, the realm of the precious freedom of expression is assuredly a case in point. The commonplace expression "It's a free country, isn't it—so I can darn well say what I please!" is in fact sincere, for its underlying philosophy is ingrained in the body politic's notion of what democratic America means. But its paradox is that throughout history we so often permit, wink at, even encourage, its violation in practice. Thus we have been quite willing to curb the "dangerous," the "seditious," the "subversive," the "prurient," the "obscene," the "libelous," and a host of other presumably undesirable modes and manners of expression that—at a particular time and place—seemed to justify repression. Yet, unless one accepts the absolutist approach advocated so consistently by Mr. Justice Black and his supporters (an approach that nonetheless still necessitates an answer to the basic question of just what "expression" *is*), the need to draw some line is primary, for, as Black observed in a famous 1941 dissenting opinion: "Freedom to speak and write about public questions is as important to the life of our government as is the heart of the human body. In fact, this privilege is the heart of our government! If that heart be weakened, the result is debilitation; if it be stilled, the result is death."[2] Mr. Justice Brandeis, whose last two years of service on the bench of the highest court coincided with Black's first two, tried to provide a memorable guideline when, in a concurring opinion joined by his colleague Holmes, he defended the "chance-taking" aspects of freedom of expression in ringing terms:

> [Those who won our independence] believed that freedom to think as you will and to speak as you think are means indispensable to the discovery and

---

[1] This was cogently suggested by Professor Robert G. McCloskey of Harvard University in "The American Ideology," an essay in Marian D. Irish, ed., *Continuing Crisis in American Politics* (Englewood Cliffs, N.J.: Prentice-Hall, 1963).

[2] *Milk Wagon Drivers Union v. Meadowmoor Dairies,* 312 U.S. 287, at 301–2.

spread of political truth; that without free speech and assembly, discussion would be futile; that with them, discussion affords ordinarily adequate protection against the dissemination of noxious doctrine; that the greatest menace to freedom is an inert people; that public discussion is a political duty; and that this should be a fundamental principle of the American government.[3]

To draw the line for freedom of expression is an enormously difficult task; yet, as they have done elsewhere, our courts have valiantly endeavored to find and draw that line.

Some Basic Concepts

Since we cannot here attempt to cover all, or even most, aspects of "freedom of expression," we shall concentrate on those that illustrate the fundamental problem and are of enduring interest.

A Basic Definition. In its overall context, freedom of expression connotes the broad *freedom to communicate*—a concept that far transcends mere speech. It embraces the prerogative of the free citizen to express himself—verbally, visually, or on paper—without *previous* restraint, and, if the expression meets the test of truth, the prerogative necessarily extends to the post-utterance period. It is vital to recognize at the outset that the freedom of expression extends not only to speech and press but also to areas of *conduct* laced or tinged with expression such as those of press, assembly, petition, association, lawful picketing, and other demonstrative protests. To point to its diversity and range, freedom of expression now apparently extends also to independent *spending* by and for a candidate for federal elective office, but *not* in the form of unlimited *contributions;*[4] to purely "commercial speech,"[5] including even the right of professionals to advertise their fees (on a "limited, factual basis");[6] to banks and business corporations making contributions or expenditures for the purpose of influencing votes on referenda proposals (even those not materially affecting their assets or property), of expressing their views on public issues, and of promoting their products (even by advertising or inserting them in customer utility bills);[7] to realtors posting "for sale" or "sold" signs in front

---

[3] *Whitney v. California,* 274 U.S. 357 (1927), at 375.

[4] See the complex 6:2 decision by the Court in 1976, in which it tested the Federal Election Campaign Act of 1974. (*Buckley v. Valeo,* 424 U.S. 1.) See also the related 5:4 one in *California Medical Association v. Federal Election Commission,* 49 LW 4842 (1981).

[5] *Virginia State Board of Pharmacy v. Virginia Citizens Consumer Council,* 425 U.S. 748 (1976).

[6] *Bates v. Arizona State Bar,* 433 U.S. 350 (1977).

[7] *First National Bank v. Bellotti,* 435 U.S. 765 (1978); and *Consolidated Edison v. Public Service Commission* and *Central Hudson Gas Co. v. Public Service Commission,* 100 S. Ct. 2326 and 2343 (1980), respectively.

of a home in a racially tense community;[8] and to persons marching in Nazi uniforms replete with the hated swastika symbol in a community peopled largely by survivors of Nazi concentration camps.[9] Astonishingly, freedom of expression even extends to the time-honored practice of dismissal of public employees because of their political beliefs, unless, as Mr. Justice Stevens explained ultimately, "party affiliation is an appropriate requirement for the effective performance of the public office involved."[10] The Court's rulings here voided a "patronage" practice as old as the nation itself!

Yet, since—*pace* Mr. Justice Black—none of these freedoms can be absolute, any basic definition must consider the inevitability of limits—limits that recognize the rights of the minority in a majoritarian system, without, however, subscribing to a philosophy of the "tyranny of the minority." Thus, the Court has repeatedly pointed out that the First Amendment does *not* "afford the same kind of freedom" to communicate *conduct* as to that which it extends to "pure speech."[11] There is no doubt that picketing, for example, is a vital prerogative of the freedom of expression; however, mass picketing; picketing that applies physical force to those who might wish to exercise their equal rights of freedom of expression by disregarding the picket line; or certain kinds of picketing violative of a picketee's property rights or picketing utterly unrelated to a picketee's "operations"; or picketing in derogation of secondary boycott statutes, is *not*.[12] Screaming "fire" in a crowded theater—to use the famed Holmesian illustration—upon discovery of a blaze is not only "freedom of speech" but a dutiful exercise of citizenship; but if there is *no* fire, the call is not freedom of expression but license. *Actual, overt* incitement of the overthrow of the government of the United States by force and violence, accompanied by the language of direct and imminent incitement, is not freedom of expression

---

[8] *Linmark Associates v. Willingboro,* 431 U.S. 85 (1977).

[9] *Smith v. Collin,* 436 U.S. 953 (1978), the controversial Skokie, Illinois, case that caused problems of consistency for some of the most devoted exponents of freedom of expression.

[10] *Elrod v. Burns,* 427 U.S. 346 (1976) and *Branti v. Finkel,* 445 U.S. 507 (1980). The former decision had confined its application to "below public policy-making levels," but the latter one expunged any such distinction.

[11] E.g., see Mr. Justice Goldberg's opinion for the Court in *Cox v. Louisiana,* 379 U.S. 536 (1965), at 555.

[12] Compare and contrast *Thornhill v. Alabama,* 310 U.S. 88 (1940) with *Giboney v. Empire Storage and Ice Co.,* 336 U.S. 490 (1949); *Amalgamated Food Employees Union v. Logan Valley, Inc.,* 391 U.S. 309 (1968) with *Lloyd Corp. Ltd. v. Tanner,* 407 U.S. 551 (1972) and *Hudgens v. N.L.R.B.,* 424 U.S. 507 (1976); and *Pruneyard Shopping Center v. Robins,* 447 U.S. 74 (1980), *Carey v. Brown,* 447 U.S. 455 (1980), and *National Labor Relations Board v. Retail Store Employees Union,* 447 U.S. 607 (1980) with the last three aforementioned cases. There is patent need for more judicial clarifying of the problems created in picketing.

but a violation of Court-upheld legislative proscriptions; yet the *theoretical* advocacy of such overthrow, on the other hand, has been a judicially recognized protected freedom since 1957.[13] If a written work has "literary, artistic, political or scientific value," it is not proscribable as being "pornographic";[14] but this safeguard may be vitiated by its publisher's "pandering."[15] Publicly addressing someone as "damned Fascist" and "Goddamned racketeer" can hardly be considered as freedom of speech—in fact, those terms have been judicially held to be "fighting words" that are proscribable *if* (and it is a big "if") the proscribing statute is carefully and narrowly drawn[16]—but calling a duly convicted thief "thief" or "crook" presumably can be considered freedom of speech—at least until the epithet's target has paid his debt to society. Nor is there a constitutionally protected right to libel or slander, but what constitutes libel or slander, and what the exercise of First Amendment rights, has proved to be a veritable public-law snake pit! Broadly speaking, at least of this writing (mid-1981), the law seems to be that a *public* official or even a public "figure" is not entitled to damages unless he or she can prove "actual malice," i.e., proof that the defamatory statement was made "with knowledge that it was

---

[13] See *Yates v. United States,* 354 U.S. 298 (1957), particularly Mr. Justice Harlan's opinion for the 6:1 Court.

[14] *Jenkins v. Georgia,* 418 U.S. 153 (1974).

[15] *A Book Named "John Cleland's Woman of Pleasure" v. Massachusetts,* 383 U.S. 413 (1966).

[16] *Chaplinsky v. New Hampshire,* 315 U.S. 568 (1942)—opinion for the unanimous Court by Mr. Justice Frank Murphy, then its leading civil libertarian. The New Hampshire statute had enacted the common-law "fighting words" doctrine: "No person shall address any offensive, derisive or annoying word [directly] to any other person who is lawfully in any street or other public place, nor call him by any offensive or derisive name." The state court had interpreted it to ban "words likely to cause an average addressee to fight," and "face to face words" likely to produce an immediate violent breach of the peace by the addressee. Although the "fighting words" test has continued to be relied upon, it has presented major problems when applied to the "profane," the "obscene," and the "libelous," as noted *infra* pp. 155–60. By and large the Court's posture has been *one of focusing on* the specific "circumstances" in which the contested speech is uttered and, increasingly, on proof that the "fighting words" were intentionally, directly, and specifically addressed to an *identifiable individual rather than to a group.* See, for example, its 5:2 distinction of *Chaplinsky* in the 1972 Georgia "bad language" case of *Gooding v. Wilson,* 405 U.S. 418, which disallowed a Georgia statute as "on its face" unconstitutionally vague and overbroad. On the other hand, the same Court *declined* (8:1) to review a lower-court decision that there is no "constitutional privilege to shout four-letter words on a public street" in a case in which a policeman arrested a man for disorderly conduct on the grounds that he had used obscene language. (*Von Schleichter v. United States,* 409 U.S. 1063). For proof that the Court continues to find the Chaplinsky test extremely vexatious in application, see Mr. Justice Powell's diverse, pained opinions in the 1972 "foul language trilogy" cases of *Rosenfeld v. New Jersey, Lewis v. New Orleans,* and *Brown v. Oklahoma,* reported as 408 U.S. 901, 913, and 914, respectively—all propounding definitional "overbreadth" and/or "vagueness" problems in the free-speech realm.

false or with reckless disregard of whether it was false or not"—which, rather than simple truth or falsehood, thus becomes the test.[17] Furthermore, only those false statements made with a "high degree of awareness of their probative falsity," may be the subject of either civil or criminal sanction[18]—which, however, does not mean that in *no* circumstances will a public official be judicially found to have been libeled.[19] Although the test is naturally less stringent in the instance of *private* or *quasi-private* persons,[20] who may win cases by proving carelesness, irresponsibility, or a similar "lapse"—the line remains ambiguous.[21] Thus, while in 1971 the Court applied its free press doctrine to *news* "about private individuals involved in matters of public or general interest"[22] rendering collection of damages extremely difficult—it distinguished that decision three years later when it held 5:4 that an ordinary citizen "elevated to sudden prominence by news events" can sue any newspaper or radio or television station that circulated a false and defamatory account of his role in those events; that a publisher or broadcaster of *defamatory falsehoods* about a *private* individual's involvement in a public issue may *not* assert the 1964 *"New York Times* Rule" as protection against liability for actual damages, at least there "the substance of the defamatory statement makes substantial

---

[17] *The New York Times v. Sullivan,* 376 U.S. 254 (1964). This important test, since referred to as *"The New York Times* Rule" was initially expanded in *Ocala Star Banner v. Damron,* 401 U.S. 295 (1971), but then narrowed in *Time, Inc. v. Firestone,* 424 U.S. 448, a narrowing that was patently continued in two 8:1 holdings in 1979, in which the Court made clear that it would no longer be very generous in protective-characterizations of "public"; that, to qualify for the "public" label, there would have to be proof that an individual made a deliberate, affirmative injection-effort for the public limelight or be a policy-maker. In other words, it would now no longer neither be so difficult to recover for an alleged libel nor so easy to hide under the "public" characterization. (*Hutchinson v. Proxmire,* 443 U.S. 111 and *Wolston v. Reader's Digest Association,* 443 U.S. 157.) See also the implications of the interesting verdicts against Novelist Gwen Davis and her publisher, Doubleday, one year later. (*Mitchell v. Bindrin* and *Doubleday v. Bindrin,* 444 U.S. 984; *certiorari* denied.) An early 1981 Court refusal to review appeared designed to continue the narrowing of "public" characterization. *London Times—Mirror v. Arctic Co.,* 49 LW 3481.

[18] *Garrison v. Louisiana,* 379 U.S. 64 (1964).

[19] E.g., *Ginzburg v. Goldwater,* 396 U.S. 1049 (1970); *Indianapolis Newspapers, Inc. v. Fields,* 400 U.S. 930 (1970); and *Cape Public. Co. v. Adams,* 434 U.S. 943 (1977).

[20] See *Curtis Publishing Co. v. Butts,* 338 U.S. 130 (1967), *Matus v. Triangle Publications,* 408 U.S. 930 (1972), and *Patrick v. Field Research Corp.,* 414 U.S. 933 (1973). See also the cases noted in fn. 17, *supra.*

[21] E.g., compare *Associated Press v. Walker,* 388 U.S. 130 (1967) with the three cases listed in footnote 19, *supra,* and *Greenbelt Coop. Pub. Assn. v. Bresler,* 298 U.S. 6 (1970). And compare them with *Time, Inc. v. Firestone, op. cit.,* in fn. 17, *supra,* and the three 1979 and 1980 cases also cited there.

[22] *Rosenbloom v. Metromedia,* 403 U.S. 29 (1971) at 44: "Voluntarily or not we are all public men to some degree," in Mr. Justice Brennan's words, at 48. See also *Edwards v. New York Times Co., certiorari* denied, 434 U.S. 1002 (1977).

danger to reputation apparent."[23] Nonetheless, by 1974 the Court had drawn a *seemingly* sharp distinction between an ordinary citizen libeled by a news account and "public officials and public figures [who] have voluntarily exposed themselves to incurring risk or injury from defamatory falsehoods."[24] The new doctrine raised doubts about such famed past (1967) decisions as *Time, Inc. v. Hill*[25] in which "newsworthiness" had narrowly triumphed over "privacy." However, in 1975 an 8:1 majority, striking down a Georgia law that made it a misdemeanor to print or broadcast the name of a rape victim, and barring the right of the victim or her parents to invoke "invasion of privacy" as a basis for a suit, held that the media cannot be subjected to either civil or criminal liability for disseminating *accurately* data that are available from public law enforcement records.[26] Moreover, the Court ruled (5:3) in 1976 that "reputation" is neither "liberty" nor "property" for purposes of an alleged civil rights violation.[27] Justices Black and Douglas, of course, never had difficulty in the realm of libel: they considered an "unconditional right to say what one pleases about public affairs to be the *minimum* guarantee" under Amendments One and Fourteen.[28] They would have been aghast had they been on the Court in 1979 when it ruled 6:3 that, given the "malice aforethought" test-requirement of *The New York Times* case, a public official had a right to request reporters to testify on their "state of mind" in connection with their levelling of charges against him or her.[29]

As a further illustration of the elusiveness of drawing the line for freedom of expression: petitioning and demonstrating against the draft are both *bona fide* manifestations of freedom of expression, but the burning

[23] *Gertz v. Robert Welch, Inc.*, 418 U.S. 323, at 348. (But see text for fn. 24, *infra*.)

[24] *Gertz*, fn. at 345. That it was but a "seemingly" sharp one was demonstrated by its 5:3 narrowing of the "public *figure*" concept in 1976 when it upheld a $100,000 libel award won by a prominent Palm Beach (Fla.) socialite, Mary Alice Firestone, whose notorious divorce proceedings had been publicized by *Time Magazine*. (*Time, Inc. v. Firestone*, 424 U.S. 448.) The gravamen of Mr. Justice Rehnquist's opinion was that Mrs. Firestone was not a "public figure," since she had not assumed "any role of especial prominence in the affairs of society other than perhaps Palm Beach society," and because she had not thrust herself to the forefront of any particular public controversy in order to influence the resolutions of the issues involved in it. (*Ibid.*, at 453). Room for doubt about that analysis of the facts persists, however!

[25] 385 U.S. 374. It involved *Life's* review of the play, "The Desperate Hours"; Richard M. Nixon represented Hill (the loser), Harold Medina, *Time, Inc.* (the winner).

[26] *Cox Broadcasting Corp. v. Cohn*, 420 U.S. 469.

[27] *Paul v. Davis*, 424 U.S. 693.

[28] See *The New York Times v. Sullivan*, *op. cit.*, at 296, Mr. Justice Black's concurring opinion, for a comparative analysis of the right to denounce. (Italics supplied.)

[29] *Herbert v. Lando*, 441 U.S. 153. The majority opinion in this contentious decision was written by Mr. Justice White, the dissenters being Justices Brennan, Stewart, and Marshall.

of draft cards is not. "We cannot accept the view," wrote Mr. Chief Justice Warren in the leading case for his 7:1 Court, with only Mr. Justice Douglas in dissent, "that an apparently limitless variety of conduct can be labelled 'speech.' "[30] Mr. Justice Black, who drew the line at "conduct" rather than "expression," was in the majority here. And he strongly dissented from the Court's 7:2 holding, just a year later, that the wearing of black armbands by high school students constituted constitutionally protected "symbolic" free speech.[31] Only Mr. Justice Harlan sided with him in what they viewed as a matter of proscribable *conduct*. Again Black, this time joined in dissent by Justices Fortas and White and Mr. Chief Justice Warren, saw as proscribable conduct rather than symbolic free speech the action of Sidney Street, a Brooklyn bus driver, who, while loudly cursing an American flag, burned it in outrage in 1966 after he had learned that James Meredith, the civil rights activist, had been shot and wounded in an ambush.[32] To compound the difficulties *and* unpredictabilities of this realm, the majority opinion was written by Mr. Justice Harlan who had dissented in the black armband case![33] On the other hand, the Court found no difficulty at all in unanimously declaring unconstitutional a part of a federal law that barred theatrical performers from wearing a United States military uniform *if* their role was intended to discredit the armed forces;[34] the law had permitted performances that were laudatory! Appropriately, that classic symbolic freedom of expression opinion was written by Mr. Justice Black. But it was by a mere one-vote margin (5:4) that the Court ruled in 1971 that the display on a jacket of the epithetical phrase "Fuck the draft" in a corridor of the Los Angeles courthouse is constitutionally protected speech and may not be made a criminal offense[35]—with the Court

[30] *United States v. O'Brien* and *O'Brien v. United States*, 391 U.S. 367 (1968), at 376.

[31] *Tinker v. Des Moines Independent Community School District*, 393 U.S. 503 (1969). The *Tinker* decision was confirmed in 1972 when the Court refused to review a lower tribunal's decision permitting a public school teacher of English to wear a black armband on Vietnam Moratorium Day—despite his subsequent suspension for continued political activity and educational disruption. (*Board of Education v. James*, 409 U.S. 1042.)

[32] *Street v. New York*, 394 U.S. 576 (1969). "We don't need no damn flag," Street had shouted. "I burned it! If they let this happen to Meredith, we don't need an American flag." So called "Do-Not-Dishonor-the-Flag" statutes—e.g., *Smith v. Goguen*, 415 U.S. 566 (1974)—came before the Court increasingly in the mid-1970s, most of them falling to challenges of "vagueness."

[33] He was joined by Justices Douglas, Brennan, Stewart, and Marshall.

[34] *Schacht v. United States*, 398 U.S. 58 (1970).

[35] *Cohen v. California*, 403 U.S. 15. Relatedly, see *Papish v. Board of Curators of University of Missouri*, 410 U.S. 667 (1973), that 6:3 overturned a student's expulsion for circulating "offensive ideas" in print in a campus publication that used the "M_____ F_____" expletive with obvious relish in connection with the trial and acquittal of the member of an organization called "Up Against the Wall, Motherfucker." (A headline story was entitled "M_____ F_____ acquitted," and it printed

for the first time spelling out that Anglo-Saxon term (Mr. Justice Harlan, of all people!, writing for the Court). Yet his colleague Black was one of three dissenters who saw "mainly conduct," very little "expression." As he frequently did, Black here evidently drew the proverbial line based on his belief that, in words he employed elsewhere, "a law which primarily regulates conduct but which might also indirectly affect speech can be upheld if the effect on speech is minor in relation to the need for control of the conduct."[36]

Throughout our history, law-making and judicial authorities have had to wrestle with these and similar questions—including such, perhaps less than earthshaking, ones as to the right of public school boards and other public agencies to prescribe the length of the hair sported by those under their aegis.[37] Limitations, today almost entirely of a statutory nature, are thus present on both the national and state levels of government—a phenomenon almost unknown prior to World War I. Thus, there is scant doubt that Congress has the authority to guard against sedition and subversion[38]; it has asserted it rather widely, especially in periods of national emergency and throughout the Cold War, enacting three controversial pieces of legislation in less than fifteen years: the Smith Act of 1940, the Internal Security Act of 1950 (passed over President Truman's veto), and the Communist Control Act of 1954. The problem implicit in this legislation is, of course, where to draw the line between the individual's cherished right to espouse and express unpopular causes and the right of the community to protect itself against the overthrow of government. As the courts have ultimately been called upon to demonstrate time and again—as, for instance, in granting to members of the armed forces a lower degree of protection against the "chilling effect" which broad and vague regulations would normally be viewed as imposing upon the exercise of free expression[39]—democratic society has the right and duty to maintain concurrently *both* freedom of expression and national security.

To re-allude briefly to another area, one in which the states have pre-

---

a political cartoon depicting police raping the Statue of Liberty and the Goddess of Justice.)

[36] Dissenting opinion, *Barenblatt v. United States,* 360 U.S. 109 (1959), at 141.

[37] Although the Court has been on both sides of the issue in its decisions, and may well have to come down with a definitive one ultimately, by and large it has sided with duly constituted authorities, assuming reasonable rules are at stake. See, e.g., *Olff v. East Side Union High School District,* 404 U.S. 1042 (1972); *Jackson v. New York City Transit Authority,* 419 U.S. 831 (1974); and *Kelley v. Johnson,* 425 U.S. 238 (1976).

[38] *Sedition* consists of publications, utterances, or other activities, short of treason, which are deemed to encourage resistance to lawful authority. *Subversion* comprehends participation in or advocacy of any organized activity to overthrow an existing government by force.

[39] *Parker v. Levy,* 417 U.S. 733 (1974) and *Greer v. Spock,* 424 U.S. 828 (1976).

dominated, what of the matter of prohibiting the sale and dissemination of "obscene" literature? Statutes abound, yet many of these quickly run afoul of First and Fourteenth Amendment safeguards of freedom of expression. To what extent then, may the community protect itself against "obscenity"? Do particular publications possess the "redeeming social value" which presumably underlies the exercise of responsible freedom? Is demonstrable obscenity a "civil right"? The anticipated negative chorus to those rhetorical questions must be discounted at least in part because of (a) hypocrisy and (b) the enormously difficult definition of the "obscene." Hence, here again the judicial branch has had to endeavor to draw lines—which it has done more than once by reading the allegedly "obscene" book, and, especially, by screen-viewing the allegedly "obscene" film.[40] Some justices, as was ever true of Black and Douglas, have no problem here: Not only do they not "go" to "those movies"—in Black's case, at least, cordially loathing them—but they do not have to: for any prior censorship of the visual (or the written) is a *prima facie* violation of freedom of expression.

The following capsule illustrations will indicate the at once fascinating and frustrating line-drawing problem involved in freedom of expression—one the Supreme Court, in particular, has been repeatedly called upon to solve amid the inevitable jeers and cheers.

Drawing Lines: Some Brief Examples

1. *Press Freedom and Fair Trial and Prior Restraint.* "The basis of our government being the opinion of the people, the first object shall be to keep that right; and were it left for me to decide whether we should have a government without newspapers, or newspapers without government, I should not hesitate a moment to choose the latter." So wrote Thomas Jefferson in 1787.[41] But even the embrace of that noble statement does not gainsay the need to face the reality of difficult and timely line-drawing. Thus, where *does* one draw the line between the seminal right of a free press to comment and criticize and the fundamental duty of the judiciary to ensure a fair trial? Freedom and responsibility are sides of the same coin.

Thus, the 1946 ruling in *Pennekamp v. Florida*[42] is a relatively early

[40] E.g., the "Miracle" decision (concerning Roberto Rossellini's controversial movie) of *Burstyn v. Wilson,* 343 U.S. 495 (1952); that of the film "Lady Chatterley's Lover," *Kingsley Corporation v. Regents of the University of New York,* 360 U.S. 684 (1959); and *Jenkins v. Georgia,* 418 U.S. 153 (1974), endeavoring to regulate the sexually suggestive "Carnal Knowledge."

[41] Letter to Edward Carrington in Paul Leicester Ford, ed., *Thomas Jefferson's Works,* Vol. IV (New York: G. P. Putnam's Sons, 1894), p. 359.

[42] 328 U.S. 331 (1946). Five years earlier, in what was long regarded at the leading case on the subject, the Court ruled through Mr. Justice Black's 5:4 opinion that highly intemperate published attacks upon the judiciary in pending cases by West Coast union leader Harry Bridges and editors of the *Times-Mirror,* did not present

contemporary illustration of the ever-alive issue of the people's alleged "right to know" *versus* the judicial duty to administer justice fairly: The publisher and the associate editor of the *Miami Herald* were fined for contempt because they had printed a cartoon and written an editorial designed to demonstrate that a Miami trial judge had, by certain rulings, favored criminals and gambling establishments. Their conviction was justified by Florida on the grounds that their actions had reflected upon and impugned the integrity of the trial court, had tended to create public distrust for it, and had obstructed the fair and impartial justice of pending cases. In a unanimous decision, written by Justice Reed, the Supreme Court reversed the lower court, holding that the newspaper's and its personnel's freedom of speech and press had been violated. Reed admitted that some of the *Herald*'s comments were directed at pending cases and, moreover, were not even truthful. But justifying his drawing a generous line here, he argued that

> in the borderline instances where it is difficult to say upon which side of the line the offense falls, we think the specific freedom of public comment should weigh heavily against a possible tendency to influence pending cases. Freedom of discussion should be given the widest range compatible with the essential requirement of the fair and orderly administration of justice.[43]

Not long thereafter, the Court, although splitting 6:3, reaffirmed the aforegone cases in *Craig v. Harney*[44] which involved an intemperate and inaccurate attack on a lay judge who had directed a verdict in a civil suit. Reversing the resultant contempt citations by the judge against a Corpus Christi, Texas, publisher, editorial writer, and news reporter, the Court, although admitting that the "news articles were by any standard an unfair report of what had transpired," held through Mr. Justice Douglas:

> The vehemence of the language used is not alone the measure of the power to punish for contempt. The fires which it kindles must constitute an imminent, not merely a likely, threat to the administration of justice. The danger must not be remote or even probable; it must immediately imperil.[45]

And the Court sustained this general approach to the problem in the most recent case on the issue when it held, 5:2, in *Wood v. Georgia*[46] that an

---

a "clear and present danger" to the course of an orderly administration of justice. (*Bridges v. California* and *Times-Mirror Co. v. Superior Court of California*, 314 U.S. 252 [1941]. What tied the two cases together was that both appellants challenged their contempt citations by the Superior Court of Los Angeles County on free-speech-and-press grounds.

[43] *Pennekamp v. Florida, op. cit.,* at 347.
[44] 331 U.S. 367 (1947).
[45] *Ibid.,* at 376.
[46] 370 U.S. 375 (1962).

elected sheriff in Bibb County, Georgia, could not be cited for contempt of court because, in "An Open Letter to the Bibb County Grand Jury," he expressed his "personal ideas" when he criticized a judge of the Superior Court who had instructed the grand jury in racially charged, intemperate tones. Over dissents by Justices Harlan and Clark, Mr. Chief Justice Warren's opinion for the Court concluded that the majority's examination of Sheriff Wood's actions "did not present a danger to the administration of justice that should vitiate his freedom to express his opinions in the manner chosen."[47]

Another facet of the vexatious issue is personified by the resolution of *Irvin v. Dowd*[48] in which a unanimous Supreme Court struck down a state conviction *solely* on the ground of prejudicial pre-trial publicity—a case that emphasizes the collateral question of the impact of broad press freedom on the individual on trial rather than its impact upon the tribunal itself. Nothing happened to the offending newspapers or their "roving reporters" in Gibson County, Indiana, nor to the Evansville radio and television stations that blanketed the county with the news of petitioner Irvin's alleged crime of six murders in the vicinity of Vandenburgh County. But the accused's detention and death sentence were vacated and remanded in an opinion by Mr. Justice Clark, replete with criticism of an irresponsible press. Mr. Justice Frankfurter, concurring, administered a lecture to the news media, reminding them warmly that freedom implies responsibility:

> . . . this is, unfortunately, not an isolated case that happens in Evansville, Indiana, nor an atypical miscarriage of justice due to anticipatory trial by newspaper instead of trial in court before a jury. . . . But, again and again, such disregard of fundamental fairness is so flagrant that the Court is compelled, as it was only a week ago, to reverse a conviction in which prejudicial newspaper intrusion has poisoned the outcome. . . . This Court has not yet decided that the fair administration of criminal justice must be subordinated to another safeguard of our constitutional system—freedom of the press, properly conceived. The Court has not yet decided that, while convictions must be reversed and miscarriages of justice result because the minds of jurors or potential jurors were poisoned, the poisoner is constitutionally protected in plying his trade.[49]

[47] *Ibid.,* at 395. On the other hand, as Mr. Justice Goldberg made clear in *Cox v. Louisiana,* 379 U.S. 559 (1965)—*op. cit.,* p. 154, fn. 11—a state has the right to enact a statue forbidding picketing or parades in or near a court house "with intent of interfering with [the] administration of justice or [of] influencing any judge, juror, witness, or court officer." (At 560, 567.)

[48] 366 U.S. 717 (1961). During *voir dire* 370 of 430 admitted believing Irvin guilty.

[49] *Ibid.,* at 729, 730. We should note here that—perhaps as a precursor of the *Estes decision* (see pp. 164–65, *infra*)—the Court, in *Rideau v. Louisiana,* 373 U.S. 723 (1963), voided on due process grounds the murder conviction of a defendant whose confession to a sheriff had been televised and thrice beamed at potential jurors throughout the area. Three seated jurors admitted viewing it!

In other words, the Court's resolution here was—as it has often been the case—to effect a "compromise" under which both the press and the accused "win"—and society loses.

It is difficult enough to find the line when responsibility obtains, but how much more so when the press ignores its responsibility? Must we really continue to believe that there is an unlimited right to conduct *ex parte* public trials in the press, on the radio, and on television? The British have long since answered that fundamental question in the negative. There, any publication of information about a defendant in a criminal case *before* the trial starts leads to punishment for contempt of court. Nothing that might conceivably affect the attitude of a potential juror may be revealed unless and until it is formally disclosed in court. Large fines have been meted out to newspapers that have violated the so-called Judges Rules, some of which have been enacted into formal statutes. To cite some examples: a small weekly newspaper in Eastbourne (on England's south coast) was fined the equivalent of $500 for saying that a defendant wore a dark suit and glasses, had been married on New Year's Day, and was being held on a serious charge.[50] A Scottish newspaper, *The Daily Record* of Edinburgh, was fined $21,000, for using on its front page a picture of a soccer star charged with "indecent exposure." In addition, Chief Assistant Editor Robert Johnson— who was in charge when the issue went to press—was fined $1,400 and the only reason no individual was sent to jail for contempt was that the editor responsible had been at home sick that night. "How is a judge or jury to know," asked the presiding judge in the case, "that the witness is identifying the man seen on the occasion of the crime and not the man whose photograph has been blazoned on the front page of a newspaper?"[51] In general, it is British doctrine that from the moment the police announce that an individual will be charged to the final disposition of the case—including appeals—nothing may be published about a defendant that might in any way influence the proceedings against him. Usually the only exception made is for information that comes out in the courtroom.[52]

Two significant United States Supreme Court rulings in 1965 and 1966 well pinpoint the omnipresent fact that, under our system, fundamental fairness cries out for a "balance" between freedom of the press and the right of the public to be informed, on the one hand, and the press's re-

[50] *The New York Times,* March 22, 1974, p. 4.
[51] As reported by the Associated Press in the *New York Herald Tribune,* February 12, 1960, p. 6. See also "British Verdict on Trial-by-Press," by Anthony Lewis, in *The New York Times Magazine,* June 20, 1965, p. 31, and the excellent comparative column by Richard Eder, "Curbs on Press Shield British Suspect," in *The New York Times,* March 22, 1974, p. 4.
[52] An average "allowable" report is this account from *The Daily Telegraph* (August 8, 1970, p. 9): "A man was . . . charged with the attempted murder of . . . two women. He will appear at Exmouth magistrates' court today."

sponsibilities and the right of the accused. The first ruling involved the conviction for swindling of Texas financier and "wheeler-dealer" Billie Sol Estes, who had been tried and convicted (among several other earlier convictions) in a Tyler, Texas, courtroom in 1962. During the pre-trial hearing, extensive and obtrusive television coverage took place: "The courtroom," reported *The New York Times,* "was turned into a snake-pit by the multiplicity of cameras, wires, microphones and technicians milling about the chamber."[53] Estes's appeal to the United States Supreme Court alleged denial of his constitutional rights of "due process of law." In a six-opinion, 5:4 decision, the Court laid down a rule that televising of "notorious" criminal trials is indeed prohibited by the "due process of law" clause of Amendment Fourteen, and it reversed Estes's conviction.[54] But it was a far from clear decision in so far as the basic problem of freedom of the press and fair trial goes. Four justices,[55] through Mr. Justice Clark, said that "the time honored principles of a fair trial" are violated when television is allowed in any criminal trial. A fifth, Mr. Justice Harlan—supplying the winning vote—agreed, but only because the Estes trial was one of "great notoriety," and he made clear that he would reserve judgment on more routine cases. Four dissenting justices[56] objected on constitutional grounds to the blanket ban at this stage of television's development, holding that there was insufficient proof that Estes's rights had here been violated.[57]

The second case involved the Court's striking down of the 1954 second-degree-murder conviction of a Cleveland, Ohio, osteopath, Dr. Samuel H. Sheppard, for the bludgeon-murder of his pregnant wife.[58] Dr. Sheppard had been in jail until 1964 when a federal district judge in Dayton granted a writ of *habeas corpus* and released him from the Ohio penitentiary, ruling that prejudicial publicity had denied him a fair trial. Two years later the Supreme Court affirmed that action by a vote of 8:1, giving Ohio authorities a choice of retrying him or of dismissing the case against him. (Ohio decided to retry him on the murder charge; the jury acquitted him

[53] June 9, 1965, p. 31c.
[54] *Estes v. Texas,* 381 U.S. 532 (1965).
[55] Clark, Warren, Douglas, and Goldberg.
[56] Stewart, Black, Brennan, and White.
[57] Fifteen years later, *Estes v. Texas* still provided the law. But the use of television in courtrooms had become much more frequent; by mid-1981 thirty states permitted at least some form of TV coverage; and the Supreme Court almost eagerly confronted the issue in what gave promise of becoming a seminal decision: *Chandler v. Florida,* 49 LW 4141 (1981). Its 8:0 ruling—Mr. Justice Stevens not participating—held that, notwithstanding objections by the defendant, states may permit the news media to televise, i.e., to photograph and broadcast, criminal trials; that controlled televising (in Florida one camera and one cameraman) did not necessarily jeopardize the constitutional guarantees to a fair trial. While *Chandler* dealt only with a *state* trial, the extension of its gravamen to the federal sphere was a distinct possibility.
[58] *Sheppard v. Maxwell,* 384 U.S. 333 (1966).

in November 1966 after a trial that was a model of courtroom decorum!)
Mr. Justice Clark's majority opinion pointed to the circus atmosphere that
attended Dr. Sheppard's sensationalized trial. For example, the trial judge,
Edward Blythin, positioned the press inside the lawyer's rail so close to the
bench that it was in effect impossible for defense attorneys to consult with
either their client or the judge without being overheard. When the jurors
viewed the scene of the murder at Dr. Sheppard's home, a representative
of the press was included in the group, while other reporters hovered over-
head in a press helicopter. Radio and television commentators, among
them Bob Considine, Dorothy Kilgallen, and Walter Winchell, kept up a
drum-fire of accounts of alleged multiple illicit liaisons by the defendant.
Television broadcasts spewed forth from the room adjacent to the jury
deliberation chamber. Jurors were photographed and interviewed by the
news media as were witnesses. In setting aside Dr. Sheppard's conviction,
Clark restated the Court's concern that had led it to void Billie Sol Estes's
conviction just a year earlier, namely, that the presence of a large, ill-
controlled news media contingent can deny a defendant that "judicial
serenity and calm" which the "due process of law" guarantees of the Constitution manadate for a fair trial—even in the absence of proof that the
jury was in fact prejudiced by the publicity. And Clark added significantly
that although the various officials involved could probably stifle most
sources of prejudicial trial publicity, he would not rule out the possibility
that *a judge could take direct action* against a newspaper, for example, if
it persisted in violating defendants' rights.[59] The lone dissenting vote was
cast by Mr. Justice Black—but without a written opinion, the record merely
noting "Mr. Justice Black dissents."[60]

The dilemma remains; but in *Estes* and *Sheppard* the Court probably
gave a signal in the direction of considerably more concern for fairness to
those on trial.[61] Such a trend was also indicated by the actions taken by
bar associations and jurists in a number of states, among them New Jersey,
New York, and Pennsylvania, and, perhaps most significantly, by a widely
circulated 226-page report by the American Bar Association's Advisory
Committee on Fair Trial and a Free Press. Known as the Reardon Report
for its chairman, Massachusetts Supreme Judicial Court Justice Paul C.
Reardon, it set out detailed rules aimed at drastically curtailing the flow of
information about arrested persons that is made available to the press in

[59] *Ibid.,* at 357–62.
[60] *Ibid.,* at 363.
[61] In October 1966 the Texas Court of Criminal Appeals reversed the murder conviction of Jack Ruby, who had been sentenced to death in 1964 for the slaying of
Lee Harvey Oswald, presumed assassin of President Kennedy. The Court cited the
rampant publicity (as well as inadmissible evidence) and, for Ruby's new trial,
ordered a change of venue from Dallas County where the shooting took place. But
Ruby's fatal illness intervened.

most communities. Sharply tightening the canons of legal ethics, it also recommended that judges be given the power to punish newsmen for contempt.[62] The resultant uproar from the media was at least in part instrumental in the adoption of a new set of rules by The Judicial Conference of the United States, recommended by a special committee headed by Judge Irving Kaufman of the United States Court of Appeals for the Second Circuit. In part patterned upon the Reardon Report, the Judicial Conference rules attempt to discourage publicity that might influence a jury and result in an unfair trial but, unlike the Reardon-ABA code, do not attempt to define any standards for the news media or police working beyond the confines of the courtroom.[63] In particular, the "Kaufman Rules" do not include the three most controversial Reardon provisions: (1) exclusion, under some circumstances, of newsmen from preliminary hearings and other hearings held out of the presence of the jury; (2) extension to policemen of the curbs covering lawyers; and (3) recommendation that judges bring contempt-of-court citations against newsmen who publish material "wilfully designed" to influence a trial's outcome. Predictably, it was the Kaufman Committee's recommendations, not Reardon's, that seem to have become part of the rules, more or less, in every federal and many a state court in the nation. But, despite a helpful 1969 "Code of Professional Responsibility" for lawyers issued by the American Bar Association,[64] and some encouraging signs that judges are indeed committed to the Kaufman rules—with some prepared to go even beyond them toward those suggested by the Reardon Report[65]—the basic dilemma[66] of drawing lines between the right to a fair trial and that of freedom of the press remains. It was back before the highest court in 1976 involving a sensational Nebraska multiple-murder case, in which Hugh Stuart, the trial judge, had imposed a very broad "gag order" sharply restricting pre-trial coverage.[67] The Supreme Court's answer came quickly, 9:0, and to the delight of the media—although the five different opinions delivered in the case[68] evinced considerable line-drawing difficulties: in general, judges may *not* impose such

---

[62] For its text see *The New York Times,* February 20, 1968, pp. 1, 35c.

[63] For their text see *The New York Times,* September 20, 1968, p. 32c.

[64] See *The Philadelphia Evening Bulletin,* September 10, 1969, p. 26.

[65] Thus in 1973 the Supreme Court declined to review—Mr. Justice Douglas dissenting—the contempt of court convictions of two Louisiana reporters who had defied an order by a federal trial judge not to write articles about an open hearing in his court. The United States Court of Appeals for the Fifth Circuit had found the secrecy order unconstitutional, but ruled that the reporters were subject to contempt proceedings anyway. (*Dickinson v. United States,* 414 U.S. 979.)

[66] See the Alfred Friendly and Ronald L. Goldfarb proposals in their *Crime and Publicity: The Impact of News on the Administration of Justice* (New York: The Twentieth Century Fund, 1967).

[67] *Nebraska Press Association v. Stuart,* 427 U.S. 539.

[68] By Mr. Chief Justice Burger and Justices Brennan, White, Powell, and Stevens.

orders on the press that forbid publication of information about criminal cases—even if, in the judge's opinion, such an order would help to assure the defendant a fair trial by preventing prejudicial publicity.

The ABA entered the *Stuart* decision's spirit by adopting a new set of guidelines in late 1978, prohibiting a judge to seal off any portion of a trial or pre-trial proceedings and from limiting comments to the press by attorneys—unless it could be shown that publicity would "create a clear and present danger" to a criminal suspect's ability to obtain an impartial jury, and unless other less restrictive alternatives, such as changing the location of the trial, would be impossible.[69] If these developments seemed to have a settling effect, it was a short-lived one, for down came the Supreme Court with its contentious, momentous 5:4 decision in the 1979 case of *Gannett Co. v. DePasquale*.[70] Two defendants in a New York State prosecution for second-degree murder, robbery, and grand larceny, arguing that their Sixth Amendment right to a fair trial had already been seriously threatened by a redolent building up of pre-trial publicity, moved at a *pre-trial* hearing that the press and the public were to be excluded from the hearing during which the trial judge, Daniel DePasquale, was to hear arguments and rule on a defense motion to suppress certain physical evidence and alleged involuntary confessions. The New York District Attorney did not oppose the motion; a reporter present said nothing—and the trial judge, granting the defense motion, held a closed hearing. When, on the following day, the reporter objected and requested access to any and all pertinent records of the hearing, the judge declined, contending that, at least at this stage of the proceedings, the defendants' Sixth Amendment rights to a fair trial outweighed any First Amendment rights of the press or the public to disclose the contents of the suppression hearing. The Gannett newspaper organization sought a writ of prohibition and mandamus against Judge DePasquale and the Appellate Division of the New York Supreme Court vacated the closure order as an impermissible *prior restraint* in violation of Amendments One and Fourteen and an invasion of the public's interest "in open judicial proceedings." On further appeal, however, the highest New York tribunal, its Court of Appeals, upheld Judge DePasquale—who, ironically, in the meantime had made the suppression hearing transcripts available—and the United States Supreme Court promptly granted *certiorari*.

Regrettably, the Court's multi-divided, five-opinion (four on the majority side) ruling, while upholding the suppression order, did little to clarify the gravamen of the basic controversy of the First versus the Sixth Amendment. Some among the five prevailing Justices (Stewart, who au-

[69] Published August 25, 1978.
[70] 443 U.S. 368.

thored the controlling plurality opinion, Burger, Powell, Rehnquist, and Stevens) seemed to confine their holding of suppressibility to the *pre*-trial stage, e.g., the Chief Justices; others, e.g., Rehnquist, to both pre-trial *and* trial; others, personified by the controlling plurality opinion by Stewart, seemed to leave the matter to another day by simply asserting that "members of the public have no constitutional right under the Sixth and Fourteenth Amendment to attend criminal trials."[71] All five on the prevailing side in effect thus agreed that these guarantees, hallmarked by the Sixth Amendment, mandated only the right to a *public trial* to the defendant—a right dating from 11th century England; that, however, it provides no such guarantee to the press or the public. Writing for his dissenting colleagues Brennan, White, and Marshall, Mr. Justice Blackmun, however, saw a clearcut right of press access in the Sixth Amendment—except in "highly unusual circumstances . . . not present here"[72]—both at the pre-trial *and* the trial stage of a criminal case, all events observed being publishable and reportable consistent with the First Amendment.

Given the multi-faceted, quasi-confusing opinions in the DePasquale case, that "another day" was not long in coming—especially since some 200 state and local judges had attempted to bar the press from their courts in the interim: At the very end of its 1979–80 term, the Court returned to the fray with its eagerly awaited decision in *Richmond Newspapers v. Virginia.*[73] With native Virginian Mr. Justice Powell abstaining, the high tribunal now ruled firmly 7:1—Mr. Justice Rehnquist in solitary dissent—that "absent an overriding interest to the contrary," the *trial* of a criminal case must be open to the public. Six of the Justices agreed—in what was a constitutional "first"—that there is a First Amendment guarantee of *access* to open trials; a seventh preferred to see it as a Sixth Amendment right. The controlling opinion—among seven rendered—written in twenty-four pages of ringing tones of support for press access by the press's latter-day villain, Mr. Chief Justice Burger, emphasized that the public and the press have a constitutional right to witness criminal trials—a right that is "implicit in the guarantees of the First Amendment for freedom of speech, of the press and of assembly" and in the Ninth Amendment's grant to "the people" of "certain rights" not specifically enumerated elsewhere.[74] Acknowledging that a trial may be closed in "rare circumstances" (that were unspecified), the Chief Justice held that, to have justice carried out, the process must also "satisfy the appearance of justice . . . that can best be provided by allowing people [and, of course, the press] to observe it."[75] It was clearly a watershed decision—a signal victory for freedom of communication.

[71] *Ibid.,* at 379.
[72] *Ibid.,* at 448.
[73] 48 LW 5008 (1980).
[74] *Ibid.,* at 5012.
[75] *Ibid.,* at 5013.

The Pentagon Papers Case. Central to the embattled "free press *versus* fair trial" syndrome is, of course, the fundamental issue of *access by and to the media*—access without prior restraint, again involving that ubiquitous line between societal and individual rights. What had appeared at first glance to be a golden opportunity in 1971 for the Supreme Court to find and draw a significant portion of such a line, while concurrently enunciating a ringing defense of freedom of the press on First Amendment grounds, had in fact turned out little more than a qualified one, at best, on both counts. At issue was the now famous *Pentagon Papers,* the publication—initially by *The New York Times* and then by several other leading newspapers—of a massive 7,000-page series of secret governmental documents dealing with the origins of the United States's involvement in Vietnam. These classified documents, compiled some years earlier by order of Secretary of Defense Robert S. McNamara, had been written by a team of distinguished experts; they had fallen into the hands of *The Times* through the instance of one of their authors, Daniel Ellsberg. Their publication became an immediate *cause célèbre.*

A series of legal maneuvers commenced instantly, with the United States Government, through Attorney-General John N. Mitchell, asking for an injunction against *The Times* (and subsequently *The Washington Post*) to suppress any further publication of the "Pentagon Papers" on the grounds of national security. It represented the first time in the history of the Republic that such *prior* restraint had been requested by the federal government.[76] Without going into the details of the legal maneuvers—all of which are carefully set forth in what became an instant all-time "best seller," *The Pentagon Papers*[77]—some federal courts granted, and some denied, injunctions in whole or in part. Inexorably, but with uncommon speed, what promised to be a major case at constitutional law wound its way to the Supreme Court of the United States, which proceeded to delay its sched-

---

[76] The only time to date (mid-1981) in which the federal government ever succeeded in obtaining a prior restraint order came in the 1979 "Hydrogen Bomb Article" case, *United States v. Progressive, Inc.* (467 F. Supp. 990). There U.S. District Judge Robert W. Warren, painfully and with the utmost reluctance, became the first federal jurist in our history to issue an injunction imposing prior restraint on the press in a national security case. However, in July 1980, the federal government decided to drop the litigation as a result of an agreement with *The Progressive,* under which 38 of 72 impounded documents would be released in their entirety, along with parts of most of the others. Judge Warren readily agreed to dismiss the case. *Snepp v. United States,* 444 U.S. 507 (1980) was another controversial press decision: There the Court ruled (6:3) that an agreement requiring employees of the Central Intelligence Agency not to publish "any information" about the agency without specific prior approval is a judicially enforceable contract that applies to both classified and non-classified information—and Frank W. Snepp, a former C.I.A. officer who published his account of the fall of Saigon, *Decent Interval,* without such permission, was compelled to turn over to the C.I.A. the entire earnings of the book ($142,090 by August 1980).

[77] *The New York Times,* based on investigative reporting by Neil Sheehan (New York: Bantam Books, Inc., 1971).

uled summer adjournment in order to hear oral argument in *The Times* and *The Washington Post* cases on June 27. The eagerly awaited decision was handed down three days later.[78]

The case had been expected to produce a landmark ruling on the circumstances under which prior restraint could be imposed upon the press, but because no opinion by a single justice commanded the support of a majority, only the unsigned *per curiam* opinion, read for his Court by Mr. Justice Burger, will serve as a precedent. There was a judicial outpouring of *nine* opinions! Six of these[79] rejected the government's contention that the further publication of the "Papers" be enjoined on the grounds of national security because, as the justices held variously, to do so would impose an *unconstitutional prior restraint* upon the freedom of the press guaranteed by the First Amendment. The three dissenters,[80] on the other hand, held that courts should not refuse to enforce the executive branch's conclusion that material be kept confidential on matters affecting foreign relations—so long as a Cabinet-level officer personally so decided.

In effect, however, with the exception of Justices Black and Douglas, who restated their long-held absolutist belief that the First Amendment forbids *any* judicial restraint on speech and press, the difference of opinion among the justices turned on whether the government had *proved* that publication of the "Pentagon Papers" would constitute "immediate and irreparable harm to the nation." Only Mr. Chief Justice Burger and Justices Harlan and Blackmun believed that the government had made such a case; Justices Brennan, Stewart, White, and Marshall did not, although on varying grounds and in varying degrees. In brief, then, the highest tribunal of the land held (6:3) that the government had failed to meet the heavy burden it must in any attempt to block news articles *prior* to publication: namely, the presumption *against* the constitutionality of such an interference with basic First Amendment rights. Yet, fascinating though the dénouement was, the Court's ruling was on narrow grounds—there was no "seismic innovation" here.

On a tangential question, however, the Court did rule (5:4) in 1972 that there was *no* First Amendment right to refuse to provide grand juries in *criminal* cases with the names of confidential sources and related information obtained by journalists in their line of duty[81]—a principle that was even extended to appropriate *civil* cases in 1977.[82] It was reconfirmed below in the much publicized 1978–79 litigation involving the refusal of *The*

---

[78] *The New York Times v. United States*, 403 U.S. 713 (1971) and *United States v. The Washington Post*, 403 U.S. 713 (1971).
[79] By Justices Black, Douglas, Brennan, Stewart, White, and Marshall.
[80] The Chief Justice and Justices Harlan and Blackmun.
[81] *Branzburg v. Hayes*, 408 U.S. 665.
[82] *Tribune Publ. Co. v. Caldero*, 434 U.S. 930.

New York Times's ace reporter, Myron A. Farber, to turn over defense-requested notes in the sensational alleged multiple-murder case of Dr. Mario E. Jascalevich. And to date (Spring 1981) the Court has committedly adhered to its precedent.[83] The Court also held 5:4 that congressional immunity did not prevent a grand jury from asking Senator Mike Gravel (D.-Alaska) or his aides certain questions about his version of the "Pentagon Papers"—including where he had obtained them.[84]

A further press-freedom-limiting decision by the same 5:4 majority,[85] came in June 1973 when the Court sustained a Pennsylvania ordinance prohibiting newspapers from carrying sex-designated employment advertisements.[86] On the other hand, friends of freedom of the press rejoiced in June 1974 when, speaking through Mr. Chief Justice Burger, it unanimously struck down a Florida law requiring newspapers to print *replies*—as distinct from *retractions* from defamation—from political candidates attacked in their columns. "A responsible press is an undoubtedly desirable goal," wrote Burger, "but press responsibility is not mandated by the Constitution, and, like many other virtues, it cannot be legislated."[87] The aforegone *Tornillo* decision was not a surprise, of course: for while the Court's 1939 holding in *Red Lion Broadcasting Co. v. F.C.C.*[88] appeared to recognize a *limited* right of access to the broadcast media under the Commission's "fairness" doctrine, the Court concluded in its 1973 *C.B.S. v. Democratic National Committee* ruling that neither First Amendment principles nor the congressional mandate that the F.C.C. act in the "public interest" required an F.C.C. ruling that broadcasters accept paid editorial advertisements.[89] Nor does that Amendment bar the F.C.C. from prohibiting radio broadcasting of "offensive words," to wit, what the Court in its 5:4 ruling characterized as the "seven dirty words," used by comedian

[83] Farber went to jail for forty days for contempt of court. The controversy ended when a jury acquitted Dr. Jascalevich. Farber's contention that New Jersey's press "shield law" vitiated any obligation to turn over his notes was rejected by the state's Supreme Court. *In re Farber*, 78 N.J. 259, certiorari denied, *New York Times Co. v. New Jersey*, 439 U.S. 997 (1978). Yet two years later, in 1980, that same tribunal upheld, by a 6:1 vote, *Shrewsbury Daily Register* reporter Robin Goldstein's refusal to do likewise under the now amended law, which requires the utilization of "less intrusive" sources. (*In the Matter of the Application of Robin Goldstein re: Subpoena*, 82 N.J. 446.)

[84] *Gravel v. United States*, 408 U.S. 697 (1972).

[85] Mr. Chief Justice Burger and Associate Justices White, Blackmun, Powell, and Rehnquist. Dissenters were Justices Brennan, Stewart, Marshall, and Stevens.

[86] *Pittsburgh Press Co. v. Pittsburgh Commission on Human Relations*, 413 U.S. 376—obviously because of the Court's "close scrutiny" test (Ch. II, *supra*) applied to gender. See also a similarly intriguing line-drawing decision affecting competing interests, here race and religion, in *Norwood v. Harrison*, 413 U.S. 455 (1973). But *cf. Linmark Associates v. Willingboro*, fn. 8, *supra*, involving expression and race.

[87] *Miami Herald Publishing Co. v. Tornillo*, 418 U.S. 241, at 256.

[88] 395 U.S. 367. Strengthened in *C.B.S. v. F.C.C.*, 49 LW 4891 (1981).

[89] 412 U.S. 94. But it *must* sell time in federal campaign races. (See fn. 88, *supra*.)

George Carlin in a 12-minute monologue over station WBAI-FM New York.[90] And the above-outlined *Pittsburgh Press* case[91] was distinguished in 1975 when the Court held (7:2) that Virginia had violated the First Amendment when it tried to punish a newspaper editor for publishing an advertisement telling of New York abortion services because abortions were illegal in Virginia.[92]

2. *Free Speech and Freedom from Noise.* In a different although related form of the dilemma, during the 1948 presidential elections, two interesting cases involving sound trucks caused the Court to draw two different lines between "freedom and order"—lines that are illustrative of the inherent complexities.

In the first case, *Saia v. New York,*[93] the petitioner was a minister of the Jehovah's Witnesses. Wishing to broadcast his gospel in Lockport, New York, Samuel Saia had run afoul of a city ordinance forbidding the use of sound-amplification devices except for "public dissemination of items of news and matters of public concern provided that the same be done under permission obtained from the Chief of Police." Refused a new permit on the grounds that complaints had been made about his prior sound-amplified speeches on religious (and not exactly very popular) subjects, Saia nevertheless decided to proceed to lecture, by means of loudspeakers, in a small city recreational park. He was convicted, fined, and sentenced to jail. Speaking for a closely divided Court (5:4), Mr. Justice Douglas held the ordinance "unconstitutional on its face, for it establishes a *previous restraint* on the right of free speech."[94] The right to be heard, concluded Douglas, was here placed impermissibly at the "uncontrolled discretion of the Chief of Police." However, to the four dissenting justices—Frankfurter, Reed, Jackson, and Burton—this was not a free speech issue at all since no one, they contended, had stopped Saia from using his voice; rather, it was a question of the protection of society's unwilling listeners by a non-arbitrary, noncapricious, non-discriminatory ordinance. But they lost.

They *won,* however, only eight months later in *Kovacs v. Cooper,*[95] with a ruling concerning the validity of a Trenton, New Jersey, ordinance. This time Henry Wallace's Progressive Party was involved. The case went 5:4 *contra,* Mr. Chief Justice Vinson switching sides and thus providing the

---

[90] *F.C.C. v. Pacifica Foundation,* 438 U.S. 726 (1978). The words, characterized by the majority as "patently, offensively, referring to excretory and sexual organs and activities," were "shit, piss, fuck, cunt, cocksucker, motherfucker, and tits." (At 751–55.)

[91] See fn. 86, *supra.*

[92] *Bigelow v. Virginia,* 421 U.S. 809. Justices Rehnquist and White dissented.

[93] 334 U.S. 558 (1948).

[94] *Saia v. New York, op. cit.,* at 559–60. (Italics supplied.) Douglas was joined by Mr. Chief Justice Vinson and Associate Justices Black, Murphy, and Rutledge.

[95] 336 U.S. 77 (1949).

key vote for the upholding of Trenton's law, which prohibited the use on the city's "public streets, alleys or thoroughfares" of any "device known as a sound truck, loud speaker or sound amplifier . . . [that] emits therefrom loud and raucous noises. . . ." Speaking for the new majority, Mr. Justice Reed, while emphasizing the "preferred position of free speech in a society that cherishes liberty for all," distinguished *Kovacs v. Cooper* from the *Saia* case on the grounds that the Trenton ordinance was carefully drawn and that the kind of discretionary power that the Court had found fatal to the Lockport ordinance was not present in Trenton's. The four dissenters (who, with the Chief Justice, had made up the majority in the *Saia* case) saw a rank violation of Charles Kovacs's right to freedom of expression under Amendments One and Fourteen.[96]

3. *Freedom of Street Corner Exhortation.* Two famous decisions, illustrating the importance of specific facts in particular court cases, were announced by the Supreme Court on the same day in 1951. The first, which favored free-speech claimant Carl Jacob Kunz, an ordained Baptist minister of rather unsavory reputation and long a thorn in the side of New York City police authorities because of his penchant for inflammatory addresses against Jews and Catholics in areas abounding with these two groups (minorities in most areas of the country, but certainly not in New York City). Preaching under the auspices of what he called the "Outdoor Gospel Work," of which he was the self-appointed director, Kunz had in 1946 asked for and received a permit under a New York City ordinance that made it unlawful to hold public worship meetings on the streets without first obtaining a permit from the City Commissioner of Police. Aware of what Kunz had done with his 1946 permit—that was revoked after a hearing—the Commissioner several times refused a new one to Kunz, each time pointing to the fact that the 1946 revocation was based on clear evidence that Kunz had publicly ridiculed and denounced other religious beliefs in his meetings. In 1948 Kunz, having decided to hold one of his meetings *without* a permit, was arrested for speaking at Columbus Circle, and fined $10 for violating the New York City ordinance in question. In an 8:1 opinion for the Court, Mr. Chief Justice Vinson addressed himself exclusively to the matter of prior suppression of free speech, concluding

---

[96] The issue has a habit of recurring. Thus in 1966 U.S. District Court Judge Alfred L. Luongo ruled that the city of Chester, Pennsylvania, was entitled to establish certain controls over operation of a sound truck, but could not charge a $25 fee for its operation. His decision came in a suit brought by the NAACP. (*The Philadelphia Evening Bulletin,* April 28, 1966.) And in 1970 the Maryland Supreme Court struck down a Baltimore ordinance banning the use of loudspeakers without a permit. The law allowed the mayor and police commissioner to issue permits for "events of public interest"; it exempted newspapers, which were allowed to broadcast important news and sports items throughout the city. In effect, this accorded authorities the right to decide who would be permitted to exercise free speech! (For an account see 270 *Civil Liberties* 7 [July 1970].)

that "it is sufficient to say that New York cannot vest restraining control over the right to speak on religious subjects in an administrative official where there are no appropriate standards to guide his action."[97] There was a solitary, but lengthy and vigorous, dissenting opinion by Mr. Justice Jackson. He pointed to the kind of "preachings" Kunz made, which, on his arrest in 1948, included the following observations:

> The Catholic Church makes merchandise out of souls . . . [Catholicism] is a religion of the devil . . . [the Pope] is the anti-Christ. . . . The Jews . . . are Christ-killers. . . . All the garbage [the Jews] that didn't believe in Christ should have been burnt in the incinerators. It's a shame they all weren't.[98]

To Jackson, the Chief American Prosecutor at the Nürnberg War Crimes Trials, this public speech was too "intrinsically incendiary and divisive," given the delicate and emotional nature of the two subjects of "race and religion," to permit the type of constitutional protection claimed by Kunz and confirmed by Jackson's eight fellow judges. "The consecrated hatreds of sect," concluded the lone dissenter, "account for more than a few of the world's bloody disorders. These are the explosives which the Court says Kunz may play with in the public streets, and the community must not only tolerate but aid him. I find no such doctrine in the Constitution."[99]

Yet, on the same day of Court, just a few pages along in the same *United States Reports*,[100] the majority seemed to adopt the very ideas that Jackson alone expressed in the *Kunz* case! Involved here was the free speech claim of one Irving Feiner, an adolescent sidewalk orator, who, using derogatory language about public officials and certain interest groups, had harangued a crowd of some 75 to 80 white and black persons in a predominantly black residential area of Syracuse, New York. He was publicizing a "Young Progressives" meeting to be held that evening in a local hotel rather than in the public school auditorium originally scheduled, because the permit granted for the latter had been revoked as a result of local pressure-group activities. In the course of his speech Feiner referred to President Truman as a "bum"; to Mayor Costello of Syracuse as a "champagne-sipping bum" who "does not speak for the Negro people"; to Mayor O'Dwyer of New York City as a "bum"; to the American Legion as "a Nazi Gestapo"; and, in what the record described as "an excited manner," yelled: "The Negroes don't have equal rights; they should rise up in arms and fight for them."[101]

[97] *Kunz v. New York,* 340 U.S. 290 (1951), at 295.
[98] *Ibid.,* at 296.
[99] *Ibid.,* at 314.
[100] The official volumes reporting all Supreme Court decisions.
[101] *Feiner v. New York,* 340 U.S. 315 (1951), at 330.

Feiner's statements "stirred up a little excitement," and one of the by-standers called out that if the police did not get that "sonafabitch" off the stand, he would do so himself. (The police later admitted that there was "not yet a disturbance," but that there did occur "angry muttering and pushing.") At this point one of the two police officers detailed to the area stepped forward and arrested Feiner to "prevent [the events] from result-ing in a fight," since Feiner—who had been holding forth for over thirty minutes—had disregarded two earlier requests by the policeman to stop speaking. The New York State trial judge concluded that the police officers were justified in taking the action "to prevent a breach of the peace," and the intermediate appellate tribunal concurred. New York State's highest court, the Court of Appeals, then affirmed the findings below, stating that Feiner, "with intent to provoke a breach of the peace and with knowledge of the consequences, so inflamed and agitated a mixed audience of sympa-thizers and opponents that, in the judgment of the police officers present, a *clear danger* of disorder and violence was threatened."[102] Speaking for himself and five of his colleagues—Associate Justices Reed, Frankfurter, Jackson, Burton, and Clark—Mr. Chief Justice Vinson agreed with the find-ings of "three New York courts" that Feiner's free speech claims were spurious: that, while his right to hold his meeting and utter the derogatory remarks was uncontested and uncontestable, the police officers were justi-fied in making the arrest because they

> were motivated solely by a proper concern for the preservation of order and protection of the general welfare, and that there was no evidence which could lend color to a claim that the acts of the police were a cover for suppression of [Feiner's] views and opinions. Petitioner was thus neither arrested nor convicted for the making or the content of his speech. Rather, *it was the reaction which it actually engendered.*[103]

It was precisely from this last sentence that Justices Black, Douglas, and Minton dissented strongly in two separate opinions, Minton joining Doug-las's, and Black writing his own. In brief, the dissenters rejected the ma-jority's two key points, namely, that danger of a riot existed and that Feiner had perpetrated a breach of the peace. They denied that the facts demonstrated "any imminent threat of riot or uncontrollable disorder,"[104] and declared that the record merely showed "an unsympathetic audience and the threat of one man to haul the speaker from the stage. *It is against that kind of threat that speakers need police protection,*" concluded Mr. Justice Douglas,[105] pointing to what he and the other dissenting jurists

102 *Ibid.,* at 319, n. 2. (Italics supplied.)
103 *Ibid.,* at 319–20. (Italics supplied.)
104 *Ibid.,* Black, dissenting opinion, at 325.
105 *Ibid.,* dissenting opinion, at 331.

viewed as the duty of the police: to, as Black put it, protect Feiner's "constitutional right to talk" rather than to arrest him.

And there, of course, lies the dilemma: at what point should speech be prohibitable? When it stirs to anger? When it creates opposition? When it creates disorder? But who is to say that the latter cannot be artificially stimulated, even created? Could not, as Black, Douglas, and Minton tried to plead in *Feiner,* a strong point be made that the police have an obligation to protect the *maker* of the speech *against* a hostile audience? To raise these fundamental questions is to recognize the difficulty of any all-embracing response! Does it depend not only upon the *content* of a speech but *how* it is *delivered?* And with what identifiable purpose and direction?[106] What of such emotion-charged issues as those that informed the wrenching 1978 Skokie, Illinois, Nazi Party activities?[107] What of the nature of the mass protests and demonstrations in the context of the contemporary youth and race "evangelism"? "Incitement," too, is a double-edged sword. After all, as Mr. Justice Holmes put it so perceptively in his memorable dissenting opinion in the *Gitlow* case,[108] "[E]very idea is an incitement. . . . The only difference between the expression of an opinion and an incitement in the narrower sense is the speaker's enthusiasm for the result. Eloquence may set fire to reason."[109] Whatever the elusive answer, democratic society demands that it be a generous one. If that means taking chances, so be it—but, as Mr. Justice Jackson put it so eloquently in his already alluded-to dissent in the *Terminiello* case, we are assuredly not obliged to be so doctrinaire and so devoid of practical wisdom as to "convert the constitutional Bill of Rights into a suicide pact."[110]

4. *Free Expression and Association and Subversive Activity: The National Security Syndrome.* The fact and concept of subversive activity and

[106] See *Chaplinsky v. New Hampshire,* fn. 16, *supra,* and its subsequent interpretation.

[107] See *Village of Skokie v. National Socialist Party,* 69 Ill. 2d 605; 373 N.E. 2d 21 (1978). See also *Smith v. Collin,* fn. 9, *supra,* on the same case.

[108] *Gitlow v. New York,* 268 U.S. 652 (1925).

[109] *Ibid.,* at 673.

[110] *Terminiello v. Chicago,* 337 U.S. 1 (1949), at 37, an interesting and troublesome case, demonstrating that very problem. In *Terminiello,* the Court, dividing 5:4, reversed the breach-of-peace conviction of a professional rabble rouser (a suspended Catholic priest) who had *really* caused a riot. But the year was 1949—with Justices Murphy and Rutledge still on the bench (they both died later that year). And Douglas's majority opinion was based on a dubious procedural analysis: that the oral charge of the jury by the trial judge was ambiguous and imprecise in its explanation of the municipal ordinance defining "disorderly conduct" under which Terminiello had been tried and convicted. In fact, Douglas had initially voted to *sustain* the conviction—but then changed his mind and was assigned the writing of the opinion for the Court by Black (the senior justice on that side of the issue, Mr. Chief Justice Vinson being in dissent). Reed provided the decisive fifth vote, persuaded by Douglas's reasoning. (The other three dissenters were Frankfurter, Jackson, and Burton, with Jackson there penning his celebrated warning.)

how to meet it have concerned the nation sporadically since its birth. From the hated Alien and Sedition Acts of 1798 through the trying eras of the Civil War, World War I, the "red scare" of the 1920s, post-World War II, McCarthyism, and the Cold War, the legislative and administrative remedies, adopted to deal with the problem of national security have often been dominant concerns. And the resultant statutes, executive orders, and legislative investigations have almost all, sooner or later, found themselves in judicial hot water, agitated by the friction between freedom of expression and association and national security and how to draw viable and allowable lines. Answers given by the judicial branch in this area—if answers they be—have understandably been perhaps more cautious and more circumspect, than for any other aspect of the freedom at issue. Nonetheless, as the McCarthy-tinged 1950s turned into the 1960s, the courts became increasingly generous toward the individual's constitutional claims as against those of majoritarian society. Hence, for example, while necessarily recognizing the right and duty of the legislative branch to keep itself informed in order to legislate more wisely, both to "oversee" the executive branch and to inform the public, the Supreme Court has also recognized that there are, and must be, limits on the range and extent of the power to investigate. Among these are the witness's right to decline to respond by invoking the Fifth Amendment's privilege against compulsory self-incrimination, though in many areas he may be compelled to testify in return for immunity from prosecution,[111] to refuse to reply if the question is beyond the investigating committee's mandate;[112] and to have "explicit and clear" knowledge of the subject to which the interrogation is deemed pertinent.[113] Yet as other decisions of the Court have shown, great difficulties here are the matters of "pertinency"[114] and just what constitutes "exposure for the sake of exposure."[115]

Similarly troublesome has been the matter of "loyalty and security." The Court has been called upon repeatedly to draw lines between the rights of the individual under the Bill of Rights, which he assuredly does not surrender simply because he works for the government, and the rights

[111] E.g., *Ullmann v. United States,* 350 U.S. 422 (1955) and *Murphy v. Waterfront Commission of New Jersey Harbor,* 378 U.S. 52 (1964).

[112] E.g., *United States v. Rumely,* 345 U.S. 41 (1953).

[113] E.g., *Watkins v. United States,* 354 U.S. 178 (1957).

[114] E.g., *Barenblatt v. United States,* 360 U.S. 109 (1959).

[115] E.g., *Braden v. United States,* 365 U.S. 431 (1961). *Cf. DeGregory v. Attorney-General of New Hampshire,* 383 U.S. 825 (1966). Most notoriously prominent in these investigations was "HUAC" (the House Committee on Un-American Activities). Restyled the Internal Securities Committee—its constitutionality upheld in 1968 in *Stamler v. Willis,* 393 U.S. 212—it was abolished in 1975 and its functions transferred to the House Committee on the Judiciary. The Senate's counterpart, the Judiciary Committee's Internal Security Subcommittee, was disbanded in 1977; but a Subcommittee on Security and Terrorism was constituted early in 1981.

of the state, which has a basic obligation to protect its citizenry from subversion by disloyal elements. Grave problems have surrounded the nature and meaning of the terms "loyalty" and "security," as well as the compatibility of appropriate security legislation and ordinances with the prerogatives of free citizens. Avoiding the constitutional issues whenever possible, the Court handed down several significant guidelines, chiefly by statutory interpretation. Thus, federal employee loyalty-security regulations, which initially seemed to have a rather free rein, found themselves increasingly confined in coverage and held to ever more strict requirements of procedural due process as of the mid-1950s.[116] At least one key aspect of the issue was more or less settled when a special three-judge federal court ruled in 1969 that the statute on which the then 25-year-old *loyalty oath* requirement for federal employees was based was "unconstitutionally vague" not only as a violation of the Fifth Amendment's due process of law clause but also, in the ruling of the 2:1 majority opinion by Judges J. Skelly Wright and Harold Leventhal of the United States Court of Appeals for the District of Columbia, as a violation of the strictures against "odious test oaths" inherent in Article Six of the Constitution.[117] When the U.S. Department of Justice decided not to appeal the decision to the Supreme Court, the Civil Service Commission quietly informed all federal departments and agencies that prospective employees would henceforth no longer have to sign the controversial affidavit stating that the applicant was neither a Communist nor a Fascist nor sought to overthrow the United States Government by force and violence.[118]

The Warren Court did squarely face the constitutional issue in a related matter—namely, the government's policy of barring employment to otherwise qualified individuals *merely* because of their beliefs and/or associations. While never having wavered from basic erstwhile, and entirely logical, holdings that there is no *ipso facto* constitutional *right* to work for the *government*,[119] the Court nonetheless made clear in a series of cases in the late 1960s that the First Amendment is not vitiated simply because someone happens to be, or aspires to be, a governmental employee. Thus, in

---

[116] *Peters v. Hobby*, 349 U.S. 341 (1955); *Cole v. Young*, 351 U.S. 356 (1956); *Service v. Dulles*, 354 U.S. 363 (1957); *Vitarelli v. Seaton*, 359 U.S. (1959); *Greene v. McElroy*, 361 U.S. 374 (1959).

[117] *Stewart v. Washington*, 301 F. Supp. 610. Judge John Lewis Smith, the third member of the tribunal, agreed that the oath was invalid, but he did not agree that the wording of the law itself was unconstitutional.

[118] *The New York Times*, January 7, 1970, p. 1. And in late 1976 it ordered elimination of *all* political loyalty questions on federal job application forms. (*Ibid.*, September 9, 1976, p. 1.) Four years later, the Carter Administration forbade government officials from inquiring into the sexual habits of employees or individuals seeking most federal jobs—an order that represented a major boost for the rights of homosexuals. (*The Washington Post*, May 14, 1980, p. C2.)

[119] *United Public Workers v. Mitchell*, 330 U.S. 75 (1947).

1967, in the *Robel* case, speaking through Mr. Chief Justice Warren, it declared unconstitutional (6:2)—as a violation of First Amendment rights of freedom of association—a provision of the Subversive Activities Control (McCarran) Act of 1950 that made it a crime for members of the Communist Party to work in defense plants—regardless of the "quality and degree" of that membership.[120] And the Court extended the aforegone ruling to the maritime industry early in 1968, holding unanimously that Herbert Schneider, a Seattle marine engineer and former Communist Party member who had applied for clearance in 1964, could not be barred from employment simply because of his beliefs or associations.[121] The government, wrote Mr. Justice Douglas for the Court, has every right to enact legislation to safeguard American shipping from subversive activity, but Congress had not, under the applicable statute—the Magnuson Act of 1950—given the executive branch the power "to ferret out the ideological strays."[122]

A host of state "loyalty" statutes and allied requirements have fallen on grounds of both substantive and procedural due process, often in concord with freedom of expression guarantees. Thus, while some practices have been upheld as valid exercises of the state police power—particularly *affirmative* rather than *disclaimer* loyalty oaths[123]—others have fallen, more often than not because of the "vice of vagueness": the sweeping implications of such terms as "subversive organizations," "subversive persons," or "sympathetic association with."[124] In fact, state loyalty oaths began to fall like veritable flies as of 1966, and by 1969 the vast majority of the disclaimer-type state oaths as well as "mixed" disclaimer-affirmative types[125] were a thing of the past.[126] And attacks, albeit unsuccessful,[127] were also launched even against the simple "positive" type.

---

[120] *United States v. Robel,* 389 U.S. 258. (See discussion, *infra.*)

[121] *Schneider v. Smith,* 390 U.S. 17. In that case, however, the Court applied statutory construction to the Magnuson Act 1950 rather than hold it unconstitutional.

[122] *Ibid.,* at 26. Congress threatened to overturn the two decisions, but never did.

[123] *Garner v. Board of Public Works of Los Angeles,* 341 U.S. 716 (1951); *Gerende v. Board of Supervisors,* 341 U.S. 56 (1951); *Adler v. Board of Education of New York,* 342 U.S. 485 (1952), but overruled by *Keyishian,* see fn. 125, *infra; Knight v. Board of Regents of New York,* 390 U.S. 36 (1968); *Hosack v. Smiley,* 390 U.S. 744 (1968); *Lisker v. Kelly,* 410 U.S. 928 (1971).

[124] *Wieman v. Updegraff,* 344 U.S. 183 (1952); *Shelton v. Tucker,* 364 U.S. 479 (1960); *Baggett v. Bullitt,* 377 U.S. 360 (1964).

[125] *Elfbrandt v. Russell,* 384 U.S. 11 (1966); *Keyishian v. Board of Regents of New York,* 385 U.S. 589 (1967), overruling *Adler,* fn. 123, *supra; Whitehill v. Elkins,* 389 U.S. 54 (1967).

[126] E.g., *Rafferty v. McKay,* 400 U.S. 954 (1970), in which the Court affirmed a lower-court holding that struck down California's loyalty oath for teachers by relying on *Baggett v. Bullitt, op. cit.* The oath at issue was the "mixed" type, reading: "I solemnly swear (or affirm) that I will support the Constitution of the United States of America, the Constitution of the State of California, and the laws of the United States and the State of California, and will . . . promote respect for the flag and . . . respect for law and order and . . . allegiance to the government of the United

Here, again, the advocates of maximum security and those who believe that democratic society must take risks for the sake of freedom are at loggerheads. It is far easier to criticize than to solve. And it has been understandably rare for the Court to be unanimous in any such cases unless the restrictions involved were clearly and patently unconstitutional.[128]

In the three major federal statutes that have been enacted since 1940 to combat subversion and increase national security, heavy judicial involvement was inevitable, given the nature of the controversy and the delicacy and difficulty of producing legislation that would achieve the desired goal without impinging upon fundamental individual liberties. The triumvirate of laws, in the order of their enactment, are the Smith Act of 1940, the Subversive Activities Control (McCarran) Act of 1950, and the Communist Control Act of 1954. We need not here be concerned with this last, hastily enacted, largely floor-legislated statute since it has been more or less ignored by the Department of Justice as a basis for possible prosecution. Although it did figure tangentially in three cases in 1956, 1961, and 1970,[129] it had not been frontally adjudicated by the Court as of mid-1981, and it is not likely to be.

The first major test of anti-Communist legislation involved the Smith Act: the 1951 case of *Dennis v. United States*.[130] Here, in a 6:2 decision, featuring five separate opinions (the opinion for the Court by Mr. Chief Justice Vinson, two separate concurring opinions by Justices Frankfurter and Jackson, and two separate dissenting opinions by Justices Black and Douglas), the Supreme Court upheld the Smith Act's constitutionality. It did so against the contentions by Eugene Dennis and his ten co-leaders of the American Communist Party that the statute infringed on First Amendment guarantees of freedom of expression, in addition to violating substantive due process guarantees under the Fifth Amendment because of vagueness. The eleven top leaders had been indicted and tried in United

---

States." Had the oath stopped with "California" and before "and will" it would undoubtedly have been upheld as a simple affirmative oath (like those enumerated in fn. 123, *supra*). However, narrowly dividing 4:3, the Court in 1972 upheld a two-part Massachusetts loyalty oath which, in addition to the standard "uphold and defend" clause, requires public employees to pledge that they will "oppose" the overthrow of the federal and state governments by force, violence, "or by any illegal or unconstitutional methods." (*Cole v. Richardson*, 405 U.S. 676.)

[127] E.g., *Fields v. Askew*, 414 U.S. 1148 (1974).

[128] E.g., *Wieman v. Updegraff, op. cit.*, in which the Court unanimously struck down an Oklahoma loyalty oath law that made even *innocent* membership in a proscribed organization an offense.

[129] *Pennsylvania v. Nelson*, 350 U.S. 497, *Communist Party v. Catherwood*, 367 U.S. 389 and *Mitchell v. Donavan*, 398 U.S. 427, respectively. In the 1961 case it ruled 9:0 (via Harlan) that the Communist Party could not be banned from state unemployment systems; and in the 1970 case it pointedly declined to rule on the Act's constitutionality.

[130] 341 U.S. 494.

States District Court Judge Harold Medina's tribunal, and after a sensational nine-months' trial were found guilty of a conspiracy[131] to teach and advocate the overthrow of the United States Government by force and violence, and a conspiracy to organize the American Communist Party to teach and advocate the same offenses proscribed and rendered criminal by the terms of the Smith Act. Their appeal to the United States Court of Appeals for the Second Circuit had been unanimously rebuffed. In upholding the challenged segments of the Act, the Chief Justice, speaking for himself and Associate Justices Reed, Burton, and Minton,[132] focused on what the majority regarded as the conspiratorial nature of the defendants' activities. Calling upon the "clear and present danger" formula—a judicial doctrine utilized in freedom of expression cases, to be discussed below— Vinson ruled that these activities transgressed the permissible line between the exercise of individual rights of peaceful advocacy of change and the right of society to ascertain national security as viewed by the Smith Act. But in invoking the concept that the activities of the eleven did indeed constitute a clear and present danger which Congress had a right and duty to prevent, he added an important qualification originally expressed by Chief Judge Learned Hand in the case of the Court of Appeals below: "In each case [courts] must ask whether the gravity of the 'evil,' discounted by its improbability, justifies such invasion of free speech as is necessary to avoid the danger."[133] "We adopt this statement of the rule," the Chief Justice went on, because it is "as succinct and inclusive as any other we might devise at this time. It takes into consideration those factors which we deem relevant, and relates their significance. More we cannot expect from words."[134] Explaining the community's justification for its national security policy, he continued:

> The formation by [the convicted Communist Party leaders] of such a highly organized conspiracy, with rigidly disciplined members subject to call when the leaders, these petitioners, felt that the time had come for action, coupled with the inflammable nature of world conditions, similar uprisings in other countries, and the touch-and-go nature of our relations with countries with whom the petitioners were in the very least ideologically attuned, convince us that their convictions were justified on this score.[135]

"And this analysis," wrote the Chief Justice determinedly, "disposes of the contention that a conspiracy to advocate, as distinguished from the ad-

[131] A conspiracy is commonly regarded as any combination of two or more persons to commit an unlawful act or accomplish some unlawful purpose by illegal means.

[132] Mr. Justice Clark, who, as President Truman's Attorney-General, had brought the indictments in the case, did not participate.

[133] *Dennis v. United States,* 183 F. 2d 201 (1950), at 212.

[134] *Dennis v. United States,* 341 U.S. 494 (1951), at 510.

[135] *Ibid.,* at 510–11.

vocacy itself, cannot be constitutionally restrained, because it comprises only the preparation. *It is the existence of the conspiracy which creates the danger.*"[136] Earlier, he had anticipated one objection by commenting that "clear and present danger" cannot mean that before the "Government may act, it must wait until the *putsch* is about to be executed, the plans have been laid and the signal is awaited."[137] And he rejected success or probability of success as a criterion.

Mr. Justice Frankfurter's concurring opinion was characteristic of his jurisprudential philosophy: to him, the decisive consideration was the Court's obligation to exercise judicial self-restraint by recognizing that the legislative assumption in passing the Smith Act was a reasonable one, consummated by reasonable representatives of the body politic. He was troubled by the law, however, and warned that "it is a sobering fact that in sustaining the conviction . . . we can hardly escape restriction on the interchange of ideas"; that without "open minds there can be no open society."[138] Yet he emphatically held to his creed that even "free-speech cases are not an exception to the principle that we are not legislators, that direct policy-making is not our province."[139] Only if the legislative determination on how competing interests might best be reconciled is clearly "outside the pale of fair judgment," would the Court be justified in exercising its veto. The obvious difficulty, of course, remains: how and when to judge what is "outside." On the other hand, Mr. Justice Jackson, in his concurring opinion, pursued a different tack; waving aside the intricate free-speech problem line *per se*—he rejected application of the clear and present danger doctrine "to a case like this"—he concentrated almost exclusively on what he chose to see as *the* crux of the case—a conviction of and for *conspiracy*—"as that is the case before us." Eleven times in two paragraphs of his opinion he used the noun "conspiracy," commenting that the "Constitution does not make conspiracy a civil right."[140]

Justices Black and Douglas dissented vehemently. In separate opinions they *denied* the existence of a danger either clear or present enough to justify what they regarded as a rank invasion of the prerogatives of freedom of expression (although Douglas, unlike Black, granted that "freedom to speak is not absolute"); charged that the Court's majority had, in effect, introduced a formula far less "tough" for the government to cope with than the "clear and present danger" concept Mr. Chief Justice Vinson ostensibly employed; and fervently argued for "full and free discussion even of ideas we hate." Mr. Justice Douglas belittled the alleged internal

[136] *Ibid.*, at 511. (Italics supplied.)
[137] *Ibid.*, at 509.
[138] *Ibid.*, at 556.
[139] *Ibid.*, at 539.
[140] *Ibid.*, at 572.

strength and threat of the Communist movement, pointing out that in America "they are miserable merchants of unwanted ideas: their wares remain unsold."[141] Mr. Justice Black closed his opinion with the observation that

> Public opinion being what it now is, few will protest the conviction of these Communist petitioners. There is hope, however, that in calmer times, when present pressures, passions and fears subside, this or some later Court will restore the First Amendment liberties to the high preferred place where they belong in a free society.[142]

Whatever the substantive merits of the Black position, this statement proved to be correct both as an analysis and as a prophecy. By June 1957, the federal authorities had obtained 145 indictments and 89 convictions under the Smith Act. But then, a six-man majority of the Supreme Court[143] with only Mr. Justice Clark in dissent—drastically and dramatically limited the application of the Act by handing down a series of significant amendatory interpretations in the difficult case of *Yates v. United States*.[144] Writing an intricate opinion for the Court, Mr. Justice Harlan narrowed the meaning of the term "to organize"—one that Congress, clearly in retaliation, again broadened in 1962—and endeavored to establish an important legal distinction under the Smith Act between the *statement of a philosophical belief and the advocacy of an illegal action*. The Court took pains to make clear that the Smith Act still stood and there was no attempt to overrule the *Dennis* case, but it was obvious that the federal government would now no longer be statutorily able to punish members of the American Communist Party, such as Oleta O'Connor Yates and her co-defendant "second-string Communists," *for expressing a mere belief in the "abstract idea"* of the violent overthrow of the government. It would now have to prove that individuals on trial for alleged violations of the Smith Act had *actually intended,* now or in the future, to overthrow the government by force and violence, or to persuade others to do so. Moreover, the government would still have to demonstrate that the language employed by the advocates of actual overthrow was in fact "calculated to incite to action . . . to *do* something, now or in the future, rather than merely *believe* in something."[145] This, of course, it should be observed, was no longer the Vinson Court of 1951; the Chief Justice had died in 1953 and was re-

---

[141] *Ibid.,* at 589.

[142] *Ibid.,* at 581.

[143] Justices Brennan and Whittaker did not participate in the case.

[144] 354 U.S. 298 (1957).

[145] *Ibid.,* at 325. The Court did distinguish the cases of the fourteen petitioners in *Yates,* however, ordering the acquittal of five, and remanding the case of the remaining nine for a new trial—based on the newly created *Yates* line.

placed by Earl Warren; Robert Jackson, who died a year later, was replaced by John Marshall Harlan; and although they took no part in the consideration or decision of *Yates,* William Brennan and Charles Whittaker had supplanted the resigned Sherman Minton and the retired Stanley Reed. Remaining were Tom Clark, who had not participated in *Dennis* and now dissented in *Yates;* Felix Frankfurter and Harold Burton, who made up part of the *Yates* majority; and the *Dennis* dissenters, Hugo Black and William Douglas—who concurred in the decision in part, but also dissented in part because of their insistence that Amendment One renders any such legislation unconstitutional on its face.

The public reaction to *Yates* was adverse; the line created by the Court between "theoretical" and "actual" advocacy did not assuage the uneasy feelings of both the opponents and proponents that it would prove to be a vexatious distinction, indeed. Hence it came as less than a total surprise that four years later the Court, in *Scales v. United States,*[146] in the first test involving the so-called "membership clause"[147] of the Smith Act, upheld that clause in the face of stringent constitutional challenges on the grounds of First and Fifth Amendment infringements. Mr. Justice Harlan, speaking for the 5:4 majority, ruled that a person who was a "knowing, active" member of a subversive group, and who personally had a "specific intent to bring about violent overthrow of the government," could be convicted under the statute—and Junius Irving Scales, whose membership in the Party the Harlan opinion categorized as "indisputably active," went to jail.[148] Yet in a companion case decided on the very same day, also testing the validity of a conviction under the "membership clause," Harlan, adhering to his *Yates* dichotomy between a philosophical belief and advocating an illegal action, *switched* sides, together with his four *Scales* supporters, to bring about a 9:0 vote *against* the culpability of one John Francis Noto.[149] Noto, held Harlan for the Court, including the Chief Justice, and Justices Black, Douglas, and Brennan—who had all dissented from the *Scales* decision[150]—did not meet the "knowing, active" membership test necessary for

[146] *Scales v. United States,* 367 U.S. 203 (1961).

[147] The Act, among other things, made a felony the acquisition or holding of knowing membership in any organization which advocates the overthrow of the Government of the United States by force or violence. (18 U.S.C. #2385, 18 U.S.C.A. #2385.)

[148] After having served fifteen months of his six-year sentence, he was pardoned by President Kennedy on Christmas Day 1962. Ironically, he had broken with the Communist Party four years before he went to jail!

[149] *Noto v. United States,* 367 U.S. 290 (1961).

[150] These four now *concurred;* they would have preferred to dismiss the indictment, not merely to reverse the conviction. Speaking for the four, Black wrote: "I cannot join in an opinion which implies that the existence of liberty is dependent upon the efficiency of the Government's informers" (at 302). He viewed the majority opinion as a clarion call to the government to maintain a permanent staff of informers who are prepared to give up-to-date information with respect to the Communist Party's present policies.

conviction. Again we see the difficult and delicate balancing problem in freedom of expression.

As if to demonstrate that fact of governmental and societal life, on the very day of the two decisions in *Scales* and *Noto,* a 5:4 verdict upheld the registration requirements of the second national security statute, the Mc-Carran or Subversive Activities Control Act of 1950,[151] the Court's line-up being the same as in *Scales.* Under that statute, the Subversive Activities Control Board (S.A.C.B.) could, after a due hearing, order any Communist "action" or "front" group to register—and it had so ordered the American Communist Party. But for more than a decade the Party had refused to register, and it challenged the order as a violation of freedom of expression and association and (in view of the Smith Act's criminal sanction) as compulsory self-incrimination under the Fifth. In one of the longest opinions in the Court's history, Mr. Justice Frankfurter, speaking also for his colleagues Clark, Harlan, Whittaker, and Stewart, upheld the forced disclosure of Communist Party members' names. With characteristic caution, and deference to the legislative branch, the Frankfurter opinion failed to consider the basic issue of compulsory self-incrimination under Amendment Five (or any of several other constitutional questions raised by the defense). Rather, he based his ruling strictly upon a judgment that the "registration requirement of #7 [of the McCarran Act], on its face and as here applied, does not violate the First Amendment."[152] Dissenting, Warren, Black, Douglas, and Brennan, in three separate opinions, not only flayed the Court majority for ducking the crucial self-incrimination issue, but they also exhorted it to recognize, in Mr. Justice Douglas's words, that "our Constitution protects all minorities, no matter how despised they are."[153]

Yet the Court's hand was forced on the compulsory self-incrimination issue just two years later when the United States Court of Appeals for the District of Columbia *did* squarely meet that aspect of the registration issue by *reversing* the Communist Party's conviction in a federal trial court for its failure to register under the McCarran Act's commands. The reversal[154] was on narrow grounds and did not necessarily settle the self-incrimination matter,[155] but it did uphold the Communist Party's constitutional argument that since the Smith Act treats it as a criminal conspiracy, compelled registration would *ipso facto* be self-incriminating. Since "mere association with

---

[151] *Communist Party v. Subversive Activities Control Board,* 367 U.S. 1 (1961).

[152] *Ibid.,* at 105.

[153] *Ibid.,* at 190.

[154] *Communist Party v. United States,* 331 F. 2d 807 (1963).

[155] "We hold only that the availability of someone to sign the forms was an element of the offense; that the officers, who should otherwise have signed, were unavailable by reason of their valid claim of the privilege against self-incrimination; that the government had the burden of showing that a volunteer was available; and that its failure to discharge this burden requires reversal of this conviction." (*Ibid.,* at 815.)

the party incriminates," ruled the unanimous intermediate appellate tribunal in its opinion by Chief Judge Bazelon, statutory registration would indeed force self-incrimination in the face of Fifth Amendment guarantees to the contrary. When the United States Government appealed that holding to the Supreme Court, the latter eschewed the opportunity to expound on the problem and, by refusing without comment to review the decision, maintained the Government's defeat.[156]

Two weeks later, however, the Court did come to constitutional terms with another section of the McCarran Act, which it had also purposely ignored in the 1961 decision: the denial of passports to members of the American Communist Party, and its "fronts." In a 6:3 decision, written for the Court by its most junior member in point of service, Mr. Justice Goldberg, the majority ruled the provision "unconstitutional on its face" as a deprivation of liberty guaranteed by the "due process of law" concept of the Fifth Amendment because it "too broadly and indiscriminately restricts the right to travel."[157] The three dissenters, Justices Clark, Harlan, and White contended with feeling that that right was not absolute, and that its denial on national security grounds was entirely reasonable under the circumstances at issue. Subsequently the Court granted *certiorari* in two cases again challenging the McCarran Act requirement that *individual members* of the Communist Party, rather than the Party itself, register with the government.[158]

It took until 1965, but when the Court's decision was announced, it was unanimous. Speaking through Mr. Justice Brennan, it held *unenforceable* the Justice Department orders requiring two alleged subversives, William Albertson and Roscoe Quincy Proctor, to register under the McCarran Act, ruling that such registration would expose them to prosecution under other federal laws "in an area permeated with criminal statutes."[159] The opinion stopped short of declaring the "individual membership registration" provision of the Act *unconstitutional,* because a Party member could waive his self-incrimination privilege and register. But the obvious effect of the Court's holding was to make the registration requirement governmentally unenforceable and thus unusable. In an area of freedom of ex-

[156] *United States v. Communist Party,* 377 U.S. 968 (1964).

[157] *Aptheker v. Secretary of State,* 378 U.S. 500 (1964), at 514. The Act's controversial Title II, its detention provision, was repealed by the Senate by unanimous vote in 1969, the House followed suit (356:49) in 1971. But *cf. Haig v. Agee* (1981).

[158] *Albertson v. Subversive Activities Control Board,* 381 U.S. 910; and *Proctor v. Subversive Activities Control Board,* 381 U.S. 910 (1965). Earlier, the Court had vacated two orders requiring Communist "fronts" to register, ruling that the record in the cases was "too stale" for a serious constitutional adjudication. *American Committee for Protection of Foreign Born v. Subversive Activities Control Board,* 380 U.S. 503; and *Veterans of the Abraham Lincoln Brigade v. Subversive Activities Control Board,* 380 U.S. 513 (1963).

[159] *Albertson v. Subversive Activities Control Board,* 382 U.S. 70 (1965).

pression in which unanimity is so demonstrably hard to attain, the Court thus stood as one with Brennan's holding that "the requirement to accomplish registration by completing and filling [the required form] is inconsistent with the protection of the self-incrimination clause [of the Fifth Amendment to the Constitution of the United States]."[160]

In 1968, faced with a now practically toothless Subversive Activities Control Board, Congress enacted a compromise measure designed to keep the S.A.C.B. in business, notwithstanding the several damaging Supreme Court and lower-court rulings affecting its functions. It provided that the S.A.C.B. could hold hearings to determine whether individuals were Communists and whether organizations were either Communist "front" or Communist "action" groups. If it so determined, the S.A.C.B. could then *itself* register them. The dubious constitutional provisions of the 1968 statute were tailor-made for a judicial test, and Simon Boorda, a Utah teacher, ordered by the S.A.C.B. to register, and then registered as "Communist" by the Board itself upon his refusal to do so, brought suit in 1969. The United States Court of Appeals for the District of Columbia declared the registration procedures authorized under the 1968 law unconstitutional as a rank violation of the First Amendment's guarantee of freedom of association.[161] The Justice Department appealed, but the Supreme Court denied review, thus upholding the lower tribunal's decision.[162] President Nixon revitalized the S.A.C.B. by executive order in 1971, indeed expanding its scope. Although Congress approved that move in 1972, it slashed the S.A.C.B.'s budget by 50 per cent later, and the President's budget message for 1973 omitted all funds for it. It died a quiet death on June 30, 1973.

Foreshadowing its increasing strictness vis-à-vis legislative experimentations in the internal security realm, the Court had entered virgin territory in 1965 in the battleground between freedom of expression and national security by declaring unconstitutional for the very first time a *congressional* statute on grounds of First Amendment freedom of speech. While federal statutes had heretofore fallen on other grounds, frequently because of due process violation, for one, and many a state law had been struck down on the freedom of expression issue by its incorporation via Amendment Fourteen, this was a novel development. Unanimously, the Court now threw out a 1962 federal law that had required persons to whom "Communist political propaganda" from abroad was addressed to make a special request to the Post Office to deliver it. Under the statute—which did not cover sealed letters—the Customs Bureau gave the Post Office Department a list of countries from which printed Communist propaganda emanated. At the eleven entry points postal officials examined the material and, if

160 *Ibid.*, at 76.
161 *Boorda v. Subversive Activities Control Board,* 421 F. 2d 1142 (1969).
162 *Subversive Activities Control Board v. Boorda,* 397 U.S. 1042 (1970).

they decided that it was "Communist political propaganda," intercepted it. The Department then notified the persons to whom it was addressed that they could receive it only if they returned an attached reply card within twenty days; if they did not respond, the mail was destroyed! Mr. Justice Douglas's opinion:

> We conclude that the act as construed and applied is unconstitutional because it requires an official act [returning the reply card] as a limitation on the unfettered exercise of the addressee's First Amendment rights. . . . The addressee carries an affirmative obligation which we do not think the Government may impose on him. . . . The regime of this *act is at war with the "uninhibited, robust, and wide-open" debate and discussion that are contemplated by the First Amendment.*[163]

Perhaps more than any of the other examples of "line-drawing," that of the riddle of national security in the days of the Cold War may serve to demonstrate that there are no easy answers to the problem of the balance between freedom of expression and the security requirements of the land. It is a demonstrable fact of life that dedicated democrats may well find themselves on opposite sides of the question.[164] A less vital but intriguing, titillating, and vexatious question concerns the line between freedom of expression and "obscenity."

5. *What Is Obscene and When Is It?* The temptation to wallow a bit here is strong, but space demands confinement to some fundamental considerations. The obvious difficulty is again the problem of definition—Mr. Chief Justice Warren regarded it, in retrospect, as the Court's "most difficult" area of adjudication.[165] What is "obscenity" to some is mere "realism" to others; what is "lascivious" in the eyes of one reader is merely "colorful" in those of another; what is "lewd" to one parent may well be "instructive" to another. One Southern city, the censorship board thus once ruled "obscene" a movie which showed black and white children playing together in a school yard.[166] In cosmopolitan Chicago, the Police Board of Censorship, held "obscene" Walt Disney's film on a vanishing prairie,

---

[163] *Lamont v. Postmaster-General* and *Fixa v. Heilberg,* 381 U.S. 301 (1965). (Italics supplied.)

[164] Carl Friedrich, a close student of the problem and convinced that it defies satisfactory solution by the judiciary—let alone the legislature—suggested that a *constitutional* amendment be passed specifically to deal with the security issue. (See his "Rights, Liberties, Freedoms: A Reappraisal," 57 *American Political Science Review* 853 [December 1963].)

[165] Interview, Sacramento, California, June 26, 1969, as quoted in *The New York Times,* June 27, 1969, p. 1*l*. It did not take the Court's then newest and youngest member, Mr. Justice John Paul Stevens, long to observe in 1977 that its "thinking on obscenity is intolerably vague and makes evenhanded enforcement virtually impossible." (*The Daily Progress,* March 2, 1977, p. A-8.)

[166] *The New York Times,* June 27, 1969, p. 1*l*.

that showed a mother buffalo giving birth in a snow storm.[167] New York's Board of Regents—that state's official censor of movies—was never troubled by the charming little movie, *The Moon Is Blue,* in which its actors used such commoplace terms as "pregnant" and "virginity"; but Maryland and the United States Navy deemed it "lewd" and "lascivious," and accordingly banned the showing of the film—lest it have dire effects on the viewers. On the other hand, New York banned the distribution of *Lady Chatterley's Lover,* charging that "the whole theme of this motion picture is immoral [under the applicable New York statute], for that theme is the presentation of adultery as a desirable, acceptable and proper pattern of behavior."[168] In unanimously reversing the New York action, the Supreme Court issued a number of opinions,[169] but they turned, more or less specifically, on the vagueness of the concept "immorality" and the problem of censorship generally. In this concurring opinion, Mr. Justice Frankfurter stated the crux of the matter—differences of opinion as to the meaning of terms and differences of taste:

> As one whose taste in art and literature hardly qualifies him for the *avant-garde*, I am more than surprised, after viewing the picture, that the New York authorities should have banned "Lady Chatterley's Lover." To assume that this motion picture would have offended Victorian moral sensibilities is to rely on the stuffiest of Victorian conventions. Whatever one's personal preferences may be about such matters, the refusal to license the exhibition of this picture . . . can only mean that [the portion of the New York statute in question] forbids the public showing of any film that deals with adultery except by way of sermonizing condemnation or depicts any physical manifestation of an illicit amorous relation.[170]

In general, the trend has been to throw out, on constitutional or statutory grounds, most state visual *prior* censorship laws, or, if not the laws themselves, the *procedures* involved. And in 1975 *live theatrical productions*—here the musical *Hair*—were judicially recognized for the first time as enjoying the same kind of constitutional safeguards against prior restraints as do the press, books, and the movies.[171] At the end of 1975 only a handful of states had such state-wide laws, and the *procedures* used by several had been declared unconstitutional.[172] A good many cities still do have

[167] *Ibid.*

[168] *Kingsley International Pictures v. Regents,* 4 N.Y. 2d 349 (1957).

[169] *Kingsley International Pictures v. Regents,* 360 U.S. 684 (1959). Opinions were by Justices Stewart, Black, Frankfurter, Douglas, Clark, and Harlan—the latter five all concurring in the result, but on varying grounds.

[170] *Ibid.,* at 691–92.

[171] *Southeastern Promotions, Ltd., v. Conrad,* 419 U.S. 892.

[172] E.g., *Freedman v. Maryland,* 380 U.S. 51 (1965), where the law had provided *no* judicial participation in barring of a film, nor a time limit for the required administrative hearing. The Ohio obscenity statute fell unanimously in 1973 because it

censorship ordinances, but where the requirement is for licensing *in advance* of exhibition, only three were still enforced in 1980, Chicago's having been declared unconstitutional in 1968.[173] These statistics do not, however, cover state criminal statutes against the showing of obscene films *not subject to prior censorship;* these are still widespread and, of course, raise a different, no less difficult, issue. Moreover, when it comes to *general* anti-obscenity laws, the federal government as well as all states except New Mexico had such laws on their books in late 1980.[174] Thus, while there is now fairly general consensus about the illegality of *prior* censorship, whatever the medium of expression, there still exists broadly general agreement that obscenity, at least in public, is at best of no redeeming social value and at worst actively corruptive of morals and must be both interdictable *and* punishable. The increase in printed smut throughout the country that seems to have accompanied judicial reversals of state obscenity convictions has thus given rise to fairly widespread outcries and demands for curbs—both genuine and hypocritical—from citizens and citizen groups. If only we could agree on just what is obscene! How can ideas and morality be protected concurrently? In 1968 President Johnson, in response to statutory authority, appointed a blue-ribbon eighteen-member Federal Commission on Obscenity and Pornography. Its report, two years later, *inter alia* recommending the elimination of all restrictions on *adults* wishing to obtain sexually explicit books, pictures, and films, not only caused a storm of righteous controversy, but was officially denounced and formally rejected by the pure United States Senate by a roll call vote of 60:5[175]—an action warmly endorsed by President Nixon, who agreed with the Reverend Dr. Billy Graham that the report was "one of the worst, most diabolical reports ever made by a Presidential Commission."[176]

---

failed to provide a prior adversary hearing for an "obscenity" determination. (*Huffman v. United States District Court for Northern District of Ohio,* 414 U.S. 1021.) And a Louisiana law, under which *Last Tango in Paris, The Stewardesses,* and several magazines had been banned as "lewd, lascivious, filthy or sexually indecent," was declared unconstitutional in 1974 on both substantive ("vague") *and* procedural (no "probable cause" had to be shown) grounds. (*Louisiana v. Gulf State Theatres,* 417 U.S. 911.)

[173] *Teitel Film Corp. v. Cusack,* 390 U.S. 139. Here the prescribed administrative process stretched from fifty to fifty-seven days, and it lacked a provision for judicial review.

[174] In 1971 the Supreme Court, by 7:2 and 6:3 votes respectively, upheld the constitutionality of the federal statute that prohibits the knowing use of the mails for delivery of obscene matter and the right of customs agents to seize obscene "photographs, books, and advertisments coming into the country from abroad." (*United States v. Reidel* and *United States v. Thirty-Seven Photographs,* 402 U.S. 363.)

[175] The five courageous libertines who bucked the Puritan tide were Clifford Case (R.–N.J.), Jacob K. Javits (R.–N.Y.), George S. McGovern (D.–S.D.), Walter F. Mondale (D.–Minn.), and Stephen M. Young (D.–Ohio). Evidently neither political party had a corner on purity!

[176] *The New York Times,* October 14, 1970, p. 30.

Other democracies throughout the world have also wrestled with this problem, admittedly under different national and cultural traditions, and their solution has been far from easy. For example, the *Chambre de Droit Public* of Switzerland's highest tribunal, the *Tribunal Fédéral Suisse,* had to deal with "indecency" charges against one Werner Kunz, a Zürich producer of three "naturalist" films, who found himself censored because he had shown "nudism" on the beaches and on snow-covered mountains. Now, did this showing of nudity constitute "naturalist beauty" or "indecent character"? The seven jurists rendered a split decision on each count: Yes, 5:2, it was indecent to exhibit nudity publicly in the white snow; but no, 4:3, it was not indecent to show it publicly on the beach.[177]

On the other hand, small and homogeneous Denmark—and the two preceding adjectives, particularly the second, are crucial to the *modus operandus*—decided to pioneer in 1967, when its *folketing* (the unicameral legislature) abolished all sanctions against the "production," import, export, and distribution of *written* pornography. The Danish Commission on Criminal Law, which had initially recommended both laws, had done so because it had been fully convinced by psychologists and sociologists that there was no *provable* nexus between pornography and corruption of sexual mores. The results were such that exactly two years later Denmark became the first state formally to abolish *every* legal sanction against pornography for *adults*. Its 1969 statute does continue to provide prison terms of up to six months for purveying pornography to children (defined as being under age sixteen) and the police do act against the "related" realms of brothels and narcotics.[178]

Turning back to the large and heterogeneous United States of America— and those two appropriate adjectives assuredly make a major difference in any attempted resolution of the problem, as all public and private sectors that have been brave enough to resolve it have repeatedly found out—most attempts to censor *written publications* have turned on the use of certain famous or infamous Anglo-Saxon four-letter words. Generally, books and allied media have enjoyed at least as much judicial protection against unbridled censorship as have movies. Obviously, obscenity, or more precisely, "hard-core pornography"—as it has been increasingly classified by the Court—may be forbidden, but the problems of classifications, sanctions, and punishment are indeed vexatious. Mr. Justice Stewart, for one, who backs censorship *solely* if the material represents "hard-core pornography," threw up his judicial hands when specifically asked its meaning in 1964,

---

[177] *Chambre de Droit Public,* P110/CG, Séance du 7 décembre 1960, at 7–8. See Francis William O'Brien's perceptive account, "Movie Censorship: A Swiss Comparison," 1966 *Duke Law Journal* 3 (Summer), pp. 634–68.

[178] See the account by Bernard Weintraub in *The New York Times,* January 26, 1976, p. 5.

responding "[all I can say is that] I know it when I see it."[179] And he has stuck to this position ever since. Mr. Justice Harlan tried to be more precise when he explained that, to him, "hard core" signifies "that prurient material that is patently offensive or whose indecency is self-demonstrating"[180]—which is not crystal clear either, as definitions go!

One person's smut may well be another one's Chaucer! Or, as Harlan put it once, "One man's vulgarity is another man's lyric."[181] But, logically, as the Supreme Court held 8½:½ (Mr. Justice Harlan concurred in part and dissented in part) in *Smith v. California*,[182] the proprietor of a bookstore cannot constitutionally be punished for offering an "obscene" book, here *Sweeter than Life,* for sale—an act banned by the terms of a Los Angeles city ordinance—if he was *unaware* that the book was in fact obscene. And Eleazar Smith was thus absolved of the charges against him. Yet, it may be asked, if the book had already been adjudged "obscene" in another jurisdiction, could Mr. Smith really plead ignorance, or lack of *scienter,*[183] regarding continued sales of the volume? At least one student of the field observed that he certainly could not,[184] and fourteen years later the Supreme Court seemed to agree.[185] Actually, the Court ruled on the *scienter* matter in the *Smith* case only tangentially: the controlling point there was that the burden of proof of criminal violation was held to rest upon the state. To shift that burden to the individual constitutes an impermissible requirement, which the Court underscored again in 1971 when it declared two *federal* "mail block" laws unconstitutional because they had placed the burden of proof on the individual rather than on the government—the latter not being required to obtain a prompt judicial determination whether, in fact, the material was obscene.[186] The highest tribunal has gone further to condemn on constitutional grounds the kind of "informal censorship" by the "Rhode Island Commission To Encourage Morality in Youth," a unit statutorily created and empowered to educate the public "concerning any book, picture, pamphlet, ballad, printed paper or other things containing obscene, indecent or impure language, or manifestly tending to the cor-

[179] *Jacobellis v. Ohio,* 378 U.S. 184, concurring opinion, at 197.

[180] *A Book Named "John Cleland's Woman of Pleasure" v. Massachusetts,* 383 U.S. 413 (1966), dissenting opinion.

[181] *Cohen v. California,* 403 U.S. 15 (1971), at 25, majority opinion.

[182] 361 U.S. 147 (1959).

[183] *Scienter* means having such knowledge as charges a man with the consequences of his actions.

[184] Paul G. Kauper, *Civil Liberties and the Constitution* (Ann Arbor: University of Michigan Press, 1962), p. 71.

[185] In 1973 it thus dismissed 5:4 a challenge to a New York statute that created a presumption that the seller of obscene materials knows the character of its contents. (*Kirkpatrick v. New York,* 414 U.S. 948.) The four dissenters argued that the word "obscene" was impermissibly vague.

[186] *Blount v. Rizzi* and *United States v. The Book Bin,* 400 U.S. 410.

ruption of the youth . . . and to investigate and recommend the prosecution of all violations of [the statute involved]."[187] Such action, held Mr. Justice Brennan for the 8:1 Court, constituted "in fact a scheme of state censorship effectuated by extra-legal sanctions; they acted as an agency not to advise but to suppress."[188]

That the Court's search for a viable standard has been extremely difficult[189] is illustrated by some additional examples. In a well-known 1957 case, *Butler v. Michigan,* it held unconstitutional a Michigan law that forbade "any person" to sell or give away anything "containing obscene, immoral, lewd or lascivious language . . . tending to incite minors to violent or depraved or immoral acts, *manifestly tending to the corruption of the morals of youth.*"[190] Speaking for the unanimous Court, Mr. Justice Frankfurter set aside the conviction of Alfred E. Butler who had sold such a book (*The Devil Rides Outside*) to another adult, here a policeman. (The book is a story of a young American's visit to a Benedictine monastery in France to study Gregorian chants. As a result of his observations of the monks he aspires to resemble them, particularly in the virtue of chastity, although he is obsessed by sex and indulges in several sordid amours.) The Court's ruling was on the ground that the state could not, under its police power, quarantine "the general reading public against books not too rugged for grown men and women in order to shield juvenile innocence. . . . Surely, *this is to burn the house to roast the pig.*"[191] Frankfurter, hardly a foe of reasonably drafted, tightly drawn[192] police-power legislation, continued:

> We have before us legislation not reasonably restricted to the evil with which it is said to deal. The incidence of this [law] is to reduce the adult population of Michigan to reading only what is fit for children. It thereby arbitrarily curtails one of those liberties of the individual, now enshrined

[187] *Bantam Books, Inc. v. Sullivan,* 372 U.S. 58 (1963), at 59–60.

[188] *Ibid.,* at 72. The lone dissenter was Harlan.

[189] In the 11-year period between the 1957 *Roth* and *Alberts* decisions and that of *Ginsberg v. New York* in 1968 (see below for discussion and citation), the Court undertook a full-scale review of obscenity law in thirteen major cases. In those thirteen cases, members of the Court turned out fifty-five separate opinions. "The subject of obscenity . . . that intractable problem," as Mr. Justice Harlan observed laconically in 1968, "has produced a variety of views among the members of the Court unmatched in other courses of constitutional adjudication." (*Interstate Circuit v. Dallas,* 390 U.S. 676, at 704–5.) It is no wonder, then, that Mr. Chief Justice Warren would regard *it* as the most vexatious of all lines to draw in the eternal contest between individual and societal rights. His successor found the going equally rough— the Burger Court dividing 5:4 in a bloc of eleven cases decided on a single 1973 opinion day, for example! Does smut perhaps lie "in the groin of the beholder"?

[190] 352 U.S. 380 (1957). (Italics supplied.)

[191] *Ibid.,* at 383. (Italics supplied.)

[192] E.g., see his opinion for the Court in *Kingsley Books, Inc. v. Brown,* 354 U.S. 436 (1957).

in the due process clause of the Fourteenth Amendment, that history has attested as the indispensable conditions for the maintenance and progress of a free society.[193]

A few weeks later, a divided Court attempted to provide a viable yardstick, which has since proved to be but partly successful. In the combined *Roth* and *Alberts* cases,[194] featuring five opinions, the justices who joined in the majority's holding[195] did their best to "balance" the rights involved by establishing the "prurient interest" test[196]—and thereby at last abandoned the 19th-century standard, based upon an English case, *Regina v. Hicklin:*[197] its test was "whether the *tendency* of the matter charged as obscenity is to *deprave and corrupt* those whose *minds are open* to such immoral influences and into whose hands a publication of this sort may fall." Here, speaking through Mr. Justice Brennan—frequently called upon to write opinions in this sphere—the Court upheld both a federal statute forbidding the transportation through the mails of "obscene, lewd, lascivious, indecent, filthy or vile" materials *and* a state statute forbidding the sale or advertisement of "obscene or indecent matter" on the strength of the new "prurient interest" concept. This test, as elucidated by Brennan, was to determine "[w]*hether to the average person, applying contemporary community standards, the dominant theme of the material, taken as a whole, appeals to prurient interests,"*[198] and whether, in addition, the material "goes substantially beyond the customary limits of candor." That Brennan cited "impure sexual thoughts" as one example of "prurient interests" ought to demonstrate the intriguingly difficult nature of the test. On the other hand, he made clear that by "obscenity" the Court had in mind only material that was *"utterly without redeeming social importance"*[199] (a concept *cum* test of which Mr. Justice Black would write later that is "as uncertain, if not more uncertain, than is the unknown substance of the Milky Way").[200]

---

[193] *Butler v. Michigan, op. cit.,* fn. 190, *supra,* at 383–84. (Italics supplied.)

[194] *Roth v. United States* and *Alberts v. California,* 354 U.S. 476 (1957).

[195] Justices Brennan, Frankfurter, Burton, Clark, and Whittaker. The Chief Justice concurred separately; Justice Harlan concurred in *Alberts* but dissented in *Roth;* Justices Black and Douglas dissented in both.

[196] "Prurient," according to *Webster's,* signifies "itching; longing; of persons, having lascivious longings; of desire, curiosity, or propensity, lewd." (5th ed., Springfield, Mass.: 1943, p. 801.)

[197] L.R.3Q.B.360 (1868). (Italics supplied.)

[198] *Roth v. United States* and *Alberts v. California,* 354 U.S. 476 (1957), at 489. (Italics supplied.)

[199] On this point see his fine article, based on the 1965 Meiklejohn Lecture at Harvard University, "The Supreme Court and the Meiklejohn Interpretation of the First Amendment," 79 *Harvard Law Review* 1–20 (November 1965). (Italics supplied.)

[200] Dissenting in *Ginzburg v. United States,* 383 U.S. 463 (1966), at 480. Seven years later the Court would abandon that test—but substitute a new one which would

What Brennan himself regarded as the "difficult, recurring and unpleasant task" of setting a national moral criterion for a heterogeneous people such as the citizenry of the United States, was accentuated by the wistful dissenting opinion of Mr. Justice Douglas, joined by his colleague Black. He questioned "prurience" as a viable standard, commenting that "the arousing of sexual thoughts and desires happens every day in normal life in dozens of ways."[201] He cited a questionnaire sent to female college and normal school graduates in the late 1920s which asked "what things were most stimulating sexually?" Of 409 replies, 218 responded "man."[202] After a lengthy lecture on the First Amendment guarantees of free expression, Douglas concluded that he, for one, "would give the broad sweep of the First Amendment full support. I have the same confidence in the ability of our people to reject noxious literature as I have in their capacity to sort out the true from the false in theology, economics, politics, or any other field."[203]

Yet the Court seemed to have created a line with its "prurient interest" test, which it further refined, perhaps liberalized, in 1962 in *Manuel Enterprises, Inc. v. Day*.[204] There, Mr. Justice Harlan, writing for the 6:1 Court majority—which was badly split, however, on just what was being decided—held that not only must the matter challenged be "so offensive as to affront current community standards of decency," but that the indecency must be "self-demonstrating." In other words, Harlan joined "patently offensive" to "prurient interest" in an attempt to find a more precise line.[205] Another explanation and refinement came in a multiple 1964 decision, in which it was Mr. Justice Brennan who, speaking for a majority of six, made clear that the *Roth-Alberts* test reference to "contemporary community standards" was intended to establish a *national* standard rather than a "particular local community standard"[206]—an interpretation that would hold for almost a decade.[207]

Thus the Court by 1964 had established a basic constitutional require-

---

have been equally unacceptable to the now deceased champion of absolutist freedom of expression. (*Miller v. California*, 413 U.S. 15 and *Paris Adult Theater v. Slaton*, 413 U.S. 49, discussed on pp. 199–201, *infra*.)

[201] *Roth v. United States* and *Alberts v. California, op. cit.,* fn. 194, *supra*, at 509.

[202] Douglas quoted from Leo M. Alpert, "Judicial Censorship of Obscene Literature," 52 *Harvard Law Review* 40 (1938), at 73. Ninety-five girls said "books," 40 "drama," 29 "dancing," 18 "pictures," 9 "music."

[203] *Roth v. United States* and *Alberts v. California, op. cit.,* fn. 194, *supra*, at 514.

[204] 370 U.S. 478.

[205] *Ibid.,* at 482.

[206] *Jacobellis v. Ohio*, 378 U.S. 184, at 193. For an interesting study, which comprises a major appeal for reliance on the good sense of the *local* community, see Harry M. Clor, *Obscenity and Public Morality: Censorship in a Liberal Society* (Chicago: University of Chicago Press, 1968).

[207] It fell in favor of *"local"* in *Miller* and *Paris Adult Theatre* in 1973. (See fn. 200, *supra*, and the discussion of the two cases, *infra*, pp. 199–204.)

ment that material attacked on grounds of "obscenity," or any other similar concepts, *must be judged not by its isolated parts, but by the dominant theme of the material as a whole.* The Court had made clear that freedom of expression carries with it the inherent privilege of "unconventional," "controversial," even "immoral" advocacy, *provided* the manner in which this is done is not "obscene" under the established guidelines. Moreover, the Court would obviously not permit loosely drawn administrative and/or legislative procedures, nor would it assume automatic *scienter* of possession of obscene matter on the part of vendors.

However, in March of 1966 along came the rather surprising *Ginzburg* decision.[208] There, in a welter of fourteen opinions by seven justices in three cases decided together,[209] the Court, narrowly dividing 5:4 in the lead case (*Ginzburg*), demonstrated that, notwithstanding its recent "liberalizing" decisions in the obscenity field, it was also by no means necessarily averse to "toughening" its *Roth-Alberts* test. Ralph Ginzburg, publisher of the magazine *Eros* and other erotic literature[210] stood convicted on twenty-eight counts of violating the federal obscenity statute at issue in the *Roth* case, not because the material in itself was obscene, but *because of the manner in which it was "exploited," i.e., advertised*—advertisement permeated "with the leer of the sensualist."[211] As Mr. Justice Brennan, the Court's "obscenity expert," put the matter for himself, the Chief Justice, and Associate Justices Clark, White, and Fortas (with Justices Black, Douglas, Stewart, and Harlan dissenting in four separate opinions):

> Where an exploitation of interests in *titillation by pornography* is shown with respect to material lending itself to such exploitation through pervasive treatment or description of sexual matters, such evidence may support the determination that the material is obscene even though in *other contexts* the material would escape such condemnation.[212]

In other words, in "close cases," evidence of pandering may be "probative with respect to the nature of the material."[213] But to Mr. Justice Black,

---

[208] *Ginzburg v. United States*, 383 U.S. 463.

[209] *Ibid.* (decided 5:4); *Mishkin v. New York*, 383 U.S. 502 (6:3); and *A Book Named "John Cleland's Woman of Pleasure" v. Massachusetts*, 383 U.S. 413 (6:3).

[210] *Eros*, a hard-cover magazine of expensive format; *Liaison*, a bi-weekly newsletter; and *The Housewife's Handbook on Selective Promiscuity*, a short book. (He also published the controversial magazine *Fact*, which figured in the *Ginzburg v. Goldwater* libel case. See p. 156, *supra*.)

[211] *Ginzburg v. United States*, *op. cit.*, fn. 208, *supra*, at 468. After unsuccessfully seeking mailing privileges from the postmasters of Intercourse, Pa. and Blue Ball, Pa., Ginzberg finally obtained them from Middlesex, New Jersey.

[212] *Ibid.*, at 475. (Italics supplied.) Ginzburg's five-year sentence was eventually reduced to three. He did not begin to serve it until February 1972, and was paroled and released that October.

[213] *Ibid.*, at 474. (Reconfirmed in 1977 in *Splawn v. California*, 431 U.S. 595.)

the majority's stance fatally misinterpreted the First Amendment, for, as he put it: "I believe that the Federal Government is without power whatever under the Constitution to put any type of burden on speech and expression of ideas of any kind (as distinguished from conduct). . . . I would reverse this case and announce that neither Congress nor the states shall pass laws which in any manner abridge freedom of speech and press—whatever the subjects discussed."[214]

The quest for a viable line continued apace after *Ginzburg,* and while no new rule emerged readily, there were definite signs that one would—sooner or later—and that it would attempt to distinguish between minors and adults, between private and public exposure, and between the "captive" and the "escapable." It began to take shape with three decisions—known as the Redrup group[215] that were rendered *per curiam* in 1967. As usual, the justices remained divided on the meaning of "obscenity," and sidestepped a great many issues. However, in this group of three cases involving ten "girlie" magazines and two paperbacks which had all been ruled "obscene" by state courts in Arkansas, Kentucky, and New York, the Warren Court, in joining the three cases and reversing the convictions in each, pronounced three identifiable "rules of thumb" (although still ducking such ticklish issues as just what is a "girlie magazine"). Rule 1 noted that in none of the three cases did the state law in question reflect a "specific and limited state concern for juveniles." Rule 2 explained that in none of the cases was there any effort of "pandering" à la *Ginzburg.* And Rule 3 pointed out that none of the materials in question was "forced" on an unwilling public.[216] These rules or guidelines now began to be present in whole or in part, expressly or impliedly, in most of the important subsequent cases. Thus, in 1968, the Court in a very real sense seemed to "codify" its majoritarian conviction—with Black and Douglas always, and

---

[214] *Ginzburg, op. cit.,* fn. 208, *supra,* at 476. (Parentheses in original.)

[215] *Redrup v. New York, Gent v. Arkansas,* and *Austin v. Kentucky,* 386 U.S. 767. Shortly after these decisions, the Court upheld a conviction based on a public display of allegedly obscene sculpture in its owner's backyard since it was "positioned" in a manner so obtrusive as to be unavoidable. (*Fort v. City of Miami,* 389 U.S. 918, [1967].)

[216] What of an outdoor movie screening of conceivably obscene movies visible from twelve to fifteen homes and passing motorists? Unless the obscenity statute involved explicitly gives fair and due notice concerning "context" or "location," its application, ruled an unanimous Court in 1972, is "impermissibly vague" under Due Process considerations. (*Rabe v. Washington,* 405 U.S. 313.) It affirmed this stance in 1975 when it struck down 6:3 as an unconstitutional interference with free speech a Jacksonville, Florida, ordinance making drive-in theatres criminally liable for showing films including nudity that are visible outside the theatre grounds. Speaking for the majority, Mr. Justice Powell held that "the privacy interest of persons on the public streets cannot justify this censorship of otherwise protected speech on the basis of its contents." (*Erznoznik v. Jacksonville,* 419 U.S. 822.) But zoning either concentrating or dispersing "adult" movies is constitutional. (*Young v. American Mini Theatres,* 427 U.S. 50 [1976].) See also *Schad v. Mount Ephraim* (1981).

Stewart often, in dissent—that it would *not* strike down carefully drawn statutes aimed at the protection of juveniles. In the leading case of *Ginsberg v. New York* (no relation to *Ginzburg v. United States*) the Court ruled 6:3 that New York could indeed make it a crime knowingly to sell "to minors under 17 years of age material defined to be obscene to them whether or not it would be obscene to adults." Hence Sam Ginsberg, who in 1965 had sold two "girlie magazines" to a 16-year-old boy in Ginsberg's Bellmore, Long Island, "Sam's Stationary and Luncheonette," found himself in trouble with New York State's law on the subject, and appealed his resultant conviction on First Amendment grounds. Speaking for the Court majority, Mr. Justice Brennan made clear that New York's "prohibition does not bar parents who so desire from purchasing the magazines for their children," and, of course, they were free to buy them for themselves—for they were *not obscene for adults*. Dissenting Justices Black, Douglas, and Fortas mocked this distinction, with Douglas angrily writing: "As I read the First Amendment, it was designed to keep the state and the hands of all state officials off the printing presses of America and off the distribution systems for all printed literature."[217] Yet the double standard of obscene-for-child-not-obscene-for-adult had been firmly embraced—and it has stood to date (mid-1981).

An additional principle was established, firmly and unanimously (although there were three separate opinions) in 1969 in the case of *Stanley v. Georgia*.[218] Federal and state agents had entered the Atlanta home of Robert Eli Stanley in 1967 to search for proof of suspected bookmaking. They failed to unearth any evidence of gambling, but they did find three reels of film that, as they later testified in court, depicted "successive orgies of seduction, sodomy, and sexual intercourse." Stanley was jury-convicted under a Georgia law that forbids *possession* of obscene material and was sentenced to a year in prison. Delivering the opinion for the Court, its then junior member, Mr. Justice Thurgood Marshall, agreed with Stanley's contention that his First and Fourteenth Amendment rights had been violated, for the mere *private* possession of obscene matter cannot constitutionally be made a crime. The Court took pains to note that its holding in no way infringes upon the right of states or the federal government to make possession of other items, such as narcotics, firearms, or stolen goods a crime. But, in Marshall's words:

> Whatever may be the justifications for other statutes regulating obscenity, we do not think they reach into the privacy of one's own home. If the First Amendment means anything, it means that a State has no business telling a

[217] 390 U.S. 629, at 655. In a concurring opinion, Mr. Justice Harlan criticized the Court for avoiding a definition *cum* explanation of "girlie magazines."
[218] 394 U.S. 557.

man, sitting alone in his own house, what books he may read or what films he may watch. Our whole constitutional heritage rebels at the thought of giving government the power to control men's minds.[219]

Hence it was entirely within that spirit that the Court, a year later, would uphold the right of individuals privately to show "stag" movies—even of women masturbating.[220] On the other hand, as the Court ruled ingeniously 6:3 in 1972, states, acting under their authority derived from the Twenty-First (!) Amendment, may—without doing violence to the First—shut down state liquor-licensed bars that, in the words of Mr. Justice Rehnquist's majority opinion, feature nude dancers and other "bacchanalian revelries."[221] And in 1976 it upheld a Virginia law that provided criminal penalties for committing adult, consensual, homosexual acts.[222]

But while these several landmark decisions settled, or at least seemed to settle, some of the major problems involved on the obscenity front, they did not—for they really could not—settle the basic problem of just what "obscene" means.[223] *Roth-Alberts, Ginzburg, Redrup, Ginsberg,* and *Stanley* had indeed provided some guidelines, but the very nature of the subject, and the public's understandable schizophrenic approach toward it, rendered additional litigation a certainty. And it was not long until the Court handed down a new—or perhaps another or additional—set of guidelines, intended to bring a degree of order into the vexatious subject.

Those new guidelines were announced in two 1973 cases.[224] Decided by the narrowest of margins (5:4), they were hardly conducive to future stability; yet they represented a significant development. Mr. Chief Justice Burger, speaking for himself and the three other Nixon appointees—Associate Justices Blackmun, Powell, and Rehnquist—plus Justice White, triumphantly noted that it was for "the first time" in sixteen years (referring to *Roth-Alberts*) that "a majority of this court has agreed on concrete guidelines to isolate 'hard core' pornography from expression protected by

[219] *Ibid.,* at 565.

[220] *California v. Pincus,* 400 U.S. 922 (1970).

[221] *California v. La Rue,* 409 U.S. 109. As Rehnquist delicately described the night club's activities: "Customers were found engaging in oral copulation with women entertainers; customers engaged in public masturbation; and customers placed rolled currency either directly into the vagina of a female entertainer, or on the bar in order that she might pick it up herself." (At 111.) See also *New York v. Bellanca* (1981).

[222] *Doe v. Commonwealth Attorney for the City of Richmond,* 425 U.S. 901 (1976). (See p. 203, *infra.*)

[223] For an excellent analysis and definition of the concept and application of "hard-core pornography," see William B. Lockhart and Robert C. McClure, "Obscenity Censorship: The Core Constitutional Issue—what is Obscene?" 7 *Utah Law Review* 289 (1961). Their suggestion is that obscenity, in the constitutional sense, be limited to material *treated* like hard-core pornography by the *primary* audience to which it is addressed.

[224] *Miller v. California,* 413 U.S. 15 and *Paris Adult Theatre v. Slaton,* 413 U.S. 49.

the First Amendment."[225] Designed to enable states and municipalities to ban books, magazines, plays, and motion pictures that are offensive to *local* standards, rather than the heretofore presumed prevalent single *national* standard,[226] the five-man majority identified and promulgated the following trifold requirements as henceforth applicable guidelines for the obscenity-law-of-the-land: In order to substantiate a charge of proscribable pornography, (1) "the *average* person applying contemporary [*local,* or, as later expanded, *state*] community standards," must convincingly demonstrate that the allegedly obscene work in question, *taken as a whole* (not by its isolated parts) appeals to prurient interests; (2) that the material depicts or describes, *"in a patently offensive way,* sexual conduct *specifically defined* by applicable state law"; and (3) that, taken as a whole, the work *"lacks serious literary, artistic, political, or scientific value"* (which quickly became known as "The LAPS Value Test").[227] In bitter, often sarcastic dissent, Justices Douglas, Brennan, Stewart, and Marshall predicted "raids on libraries"; contended that the new guidelines impinged seriously on free speech and free press; and warned that the necessary vagueness of any definition based on "local community" was redolent with censorship postures. Brennan, the author of *Roth, Jacobellis, Ginzburg, Mishkin,* and *Memoirs,* clearly abandoning his "compromise" or "balancing" position in those decisions, now concluded with deep feeling that "the time has come to make a significant departure from that approach," and offered the following formula as *the* viable, sensible approach to the obscenity problem:

> [W]hile I cannot say that the interests of the State—apart from the question of juveniles and unconsenting adults—are trivial or nonexistent, I am compelled to conclude that these interests cannot justify the substantial damage to constitutional rights and to this Nation's judicial machinery that inevitably results from state efforts to bar the distribution even of unprotected materials to consenting adults. . . . I would hold, therefore, that at least *in the absence of distribution to juveniles or obtrusive exposure to unconsenting adults,* the First and Fourteenth Amendments prohibit the state and Federal governments from attempting wholly to suppress sexually oriented materials on the basis of their allegedly "obscene" content.[228]

But he spoke for the minority. The Burger majority had indeed fashioned new interpretative guidelines that embraced two major changes in the heretofore applicable obscenity law: (1) the substitution of *local* or, at most, *state* for *national* standards; and (2) the adoption of the LAPS value test for the erstwhile one of "utterly without redeeming social value."

[225] *Miller v. California, op. cit.,* at 29.
[226] *Jacobellis v. Ohio,* 378 U.S. 184 (1964).
[227] *Miller v. California, op. cit.,* at 24. (Italics supplied.)
[228] *Paris Adult Theatre v. Slaton, op. cit.,* fn. 224, *supra,* at 112–13.

Those observers who were skeptical as to the clarity and finality of the now pronounced—though not retroactive[229]—*Miller* and *Paris Adult Theatre* guideline triad did not have to wait long for confirmation of their analysis. Thus notwithstanding its "old" (1971) guidelines vote (4:4), which upheld Maryland's highest court's 4:3 ruling that the controversial Swedish film *I Am Curious Yellow* was obscene,[230] the "new" guidelines court ruled unanimously in 1974 that *Carnal Knowledge* was *not* obscene and could thus not be banned by Georgia.[231] Speaking through Mr. Justice Rehnquist, it emphasized that only material showing "patently offensive hard core sexual conduct" may be banned under the now applicable rules.[232] On the other hand, on the very same opinion day, an advertisement for an illustrated version of the report of the Presidential Commission on Obscenity and Pornography was held to be hard-core pornography, with Rehnquist now speaking for a 5:4 majority![233] To muddy the waters a mite further, the Court ruled 5:4 three years later that individuals are subject to the federal Comstock Act of 1873 ban on sending obscenity through the mail even if the state of their activity (here Iowa) has more permissive standards *and* despite the fact that the material's dissemination was wholly in-state.[234] And, of course, it was not at all astonishing that the Court would run into a host of difficulty as to jury determinations of lines and limits governing the concepts of "average person" and "community standards."[235]

In the visual media, such as movies, the problem is, of course, considerably less complicated than in the realm of the printed word. For one thing, the movie-maker is usually acutely conscious of what he perceives as the public consensus and the reaction of the public's pocketbook. Moreover, the American movie industry has tried to bestow its own formal or pre-release seal of approval.[236] Self-policing is not, of course, a guarantee of good taste, but it does lodge responsibility and judgment where it ought to lie: with the industry itself.[237] (The same may be said for the press.) The

[229] *Marks v. United States,* 430 U.S. 188 (1977).

[230] *Grove Press, Inc. v. Maryland State Board of Censors,* 401 U.S. 480.

[231] *Jenkins v. Georgia,* 418 U.S. 153. (The four *Miller* and *Paris Adult Theatre* dissenters concurred only in the judgment, in effect saying "we told you so," while reiterating their previous objections to the majority's doctrine.)

[232] *Ibid.,* at 160 (quoting *Miller,* at 27).

[233] *Hamling v. United States,* 418 U.S. 87 (1974). Similarly, see the White-written 5:4 decision in *Ward v. Illinois* in 1977 (431 U.S. 767.)

[234] *Smith v. United States,* 434 U.S. 830 (1977).

[235] *Pinkus v. United States,* 436 U.S. 293 (1977).

[236] *The Man with the Golden Arm,* produced in 1955, dealing with the narcotics problem (producer Otto Preminger, United Artists Release) was the *first* movie released without that "ok."

[237] Perhaps partly copying the practices extant in, for example, the Scandinavian countries and in the United Kingdom, the movie industry published a much-heralded, simple Motion Picture Code of Self-Regulation late in 1968 which—amended early

adult public, of course, should be free to patronize or to refuse to patronize the visual as well as the written media without governmental interference, or injunction by administrative or legislative fiat, or the censorial tactics of a powerful or vocal pressure group. If a movie is offensive to the sensibilities of a minority or majority group, that group is entirely free to advise and campaign against its patronization. But it is emphatically not free to prevent those who desire to patronize it from so doing. Freedom of expression is a two-edged sword. So is democracy.

Given the sizable number of federal and state statutes on the books, the obscenity question remains both current and vexatious in the absence of some such unlikely action as that taken by the Danes or that recommended by the abortive Presidential Commission on Obscenity and Pornography. This means, in effect, that we may expect continued, close, independent, case-by-case judicial scrutiny of findings of "obscenity," but with the aid of the new *Miller* and *Paris Adult Theatre* rules and guidelines, which were fashioned out of the experience of such earlier endeavors to determine lines and limits as those of *Roth-Alberts, Ginzburg, Redrup, Ginsberg,* and *Stanley.* Censors will continue to find it difficult, indeed, to obtain judicial confirmation or support. On the other hand, it must not be assumed that the government has been, or is being, denied the authority to ban the sale and/or "pandering" of "hard-core pornography"—genuine smut—which, by self-demonstration, is patently offensive to current local or state community standards of decency, and thereby clearly appeals to prurient interests, particularly if advertised in "titillating" or "pandering" fashion. Presumably that type of filth and its method of dissemination would be classified as "hard-core pornography." Sex, which Mr. Justice Brennan—in his majority opinion in the key *Roth* and *Alberts* cases[238]—dubbed "a great and mysterious motive force in human life," has indeed "indisputably been a subject of absorbing interest to mankind through the ages; it is one of the vital problems of human interest and public concern."[239] And, as he went on to point out, "sex and obscenity are not synonymous. On the other hand, obscene material is material which deals with sex in a manner appealing to prurient interests."[240] Moreover, to reiterate, since *Ginzburg,* something need *not* have a "prurient appeal" to the public at large to be declared obscene. It can now be so judged even if it panders merely to a "clearly de-

---

in 1970—did provide the public with the following (and for harried parents rather helpful) rating symbols:

G = All ages admitted.

PG = All ages admitted. Parental guidance suggested.

R = Restricted. Children under seventeen require accompanying parent or adult guardian.

X = No one under seventeen admitted.

[238] *Roth v. United States* and *Alberts v. California,* 354 U.S. 476 (1957).

[239] *Ibid.,* at 487.

[240] *Ibid.*

fined deviant sexual group," such as homosexuals or masochists.[241] A book is not obscene because of "isolated parts"; the work must be viewed "as a whole," based on its "LAPS" (literary, artistic, political, or scientific) value.[242] But this anti-censorship rule may be vitiated by evidence of a publisher's pandering.[243] Thus the post-*Roth-Alberts* history, without settling the entire matter, has brought us closer to the possibility of drawing some lines, however serpentine they may well be. The lines inevitably deal with sex, a subject that, in Mr. Justice Black's dissenting words in the *Ginzburg* case, is "pleasantly interwoven in all human activities and involves the very substance of life itself."[244] As the 1970s turned into the 1980s, four aspects of the obscenity puzzle seemed to be *res judicata*—notwithstanding the *Miller* and *Paris Adult Theatre* "retrenchment," namely, that: (1) just about everything goes in the privacy of one's home—although the Court raised serious questions about that verity in 1976, when by simply affirming 6:3 a 2:1 Three-Judge U.S. District Court decision below, it upheld a Virginia law that provides felony penitentiary sentences of one to three years[245] for committing consensual, adult homosexual acts *in private!*,[246] (2) *public* hard-core pornography is not constitutionally protected,[247] (3) there now exists a judicially sanctioned "double

[241] *Mishkin v. New York,* 383 U.S. 502 (1966).

[242] *Miller v. California,* 413 U.S. 15 (1973), at 24.

[243] *A Book Named "John Cleland's Woman of Pleasure" v. Massachusetts,* 383 U.S. 413 (1966).

[244] *Ginzburg v. United States, op. cit.,* at 481. For an anthology dealing with diverse viewpoints on sexuality and the law, see Note, School of Law, Duke University, "Sex Offenses," 25 *Law and Contemporary Problems* 214 (1960).

[245] Va. Code §18.1–212 (Cum. Supp. 1974): "Crimes against nature.—If any person shall carnally know in any manner any brute animal, or carnally know any male or female person by the anus or by or with the mouth, or voluntarily submit to such carnal knowledge, he or she shall be guilty of a felony and shall be confined in the penitentiary not less than one year nor more than three years."

[246] *Doe v. Commonwealth Attorney for the City of Richmond,* 425 U.S. 901 (1976), reconfirmed in *Enslin v. Bean,* 436 U.S. 912 (1978). The Court came under heavy criticism for deciding so privately crucial a matter without hearing oral argument and without issuing a formal opinion. Cf. the case of the dismissal of a homosexual high school teacher in Washington State, *Gaylord v. Tacoma School District,* 434 U.S. 879 (1977). But see the supportive freedom-of-speech-and-assembly decision in the "campus recognition" of "Gay Lib" at the University of Missouri, *Ratchford v. Gay Lib,* 434 U.S. 1060 (1978) and *Onofre v. New York,* 49 LW 3854 (1981).

[247] Space does not permit a discussion of the fascinating clash between the competing constitutional values of freedom of expression and *privacy* that faced the Burger Court early in 1970. At issue was a 1967 federal anti-pandering law (enacted post-*Ginzburg*) which empowers any citizen to cut off the flow of mailed ads that he personally considers "erotically arousing or sexually provocative." The recipient simply notifies the Post Office which then orders his name removed from the mailing lists. Unanimously, the Supreme Court upheld the law, Mr. Chief Justice Burger affirming every citizen's right "to be let alone." He added: "A mailer's right to communicate must stop at the mailbox of an unreceptive addressee." (*Rowan v. United States Post Office Department,* 397 U.S. 728.) See also *U.S. Postal Service v. Council of Greenburgh Civic Assns.,* 49 LW 4813 (1981).

standard" vis-à-vis obscenity legislation directed at minors and adults; and (4) while there is no judicially recognized *national* community standard, *local* (or *state*) standards *are* relevant[248] in obscenity litigation[249]—absent *federal* precedence.[250]

Judicial Line Formulae

The difficulty of any attempt to establish viable standards in the realm of freedom of expression is apparent. Yet, as the five key example areas should have indicated, attempts at judicial tests, doctrines, or formulae have been of lasting concern to the Court. Much depends on the definition of terms which determine a particular judicial decision. But—in addition to the self-evident one of "balancing" competing interests—we can isolate at least two, perhaps three, major judicial "tests," all of them post-World War I phenomena.

The "Clear and Present Danger" Test

Certainly the best-known is the "clear and present danger" test. Credit for its authorship has generally been given to Mr. Justice Holmes, actively supported by Mr. Justice Brandeis, although there are some observers who would grant United States Court of Appeals' Judge Learned Hand an important assist in the birth of the doctrine, if not with its central idea. It was first used in 1919 in the *Schenck* case.

Schenck v. United States.[251] In 1917 Charles T. Schenck, general secretary of the Socialist Party, and some of his associates, sent out some 15,000 leaflets to potential and actual draftees under the Conscription Act, urging the young men—in impassioned language—to resist the draft. The leaflets' text intimated that conscription was despotism in its worst form and a "monstrous wrong against humanity, in the interest of Wall Street's chosen few." It urged not to "submit to intimidation . . . from cunning politi-

---

[248] A flurry of activity by various communities, led by Cleveland, Ohio, commenced in 1977, to "determine" such obscenity standards and lines (often by way of questionnaires distributed by trash collectors!). Note, for example, the accounts in *The New York Times*, June 11, 1977, and June 26, 1977, p. 8E. The head of the Cleveland branch of the American Civil Liberties Union, doubting that the poll, if incorporated in a projected anti-smut law, would survive a serious court challenge, commented: "In our opinion it will probably wind up where it started—with the garbage men." (As quoted, June 26, *ibid.*)

[249] For a view warmly praising the Burger Court for adding "clarity to the constitutional law of obscenity by drawing lines which are in most respects clearer than those of earlier cases," see Lane V. Sunderland, *Obscenity: The Court, the Congress and the President's Commission* (Washington, D.C.: American Enterprise Institute for Public Policy Research, 1974), pp. 114–15.

[250] See *Smith v. United States, supra,* p. 243, where the federal standard was ruled to govern (5:4).

[251] *Schenck v. United States,* 249 U.S. 47 (1919).

cians and a mercenary capitalist press" and referred to the Constitution as an "infamous conspiracy."

Under the Espionage Act of 1917, which had specifically proscribed the kind of activities in which Schenck and his colleagues had engaged, the federal government indicted them on three counts: (1) conspiracy to cause insubordination in the armed forces of the United States, and to obstruct the recruiting and enlisting services; (2) conspiracy to use the mails for the transmission of matter declared to be non-mailable under the Espionage Act; and (3) the unlawful use of the mails for the transmission of the matter under (2). Schenck and his co-defendants were convicted in a federal trial court over their objections that the pertinent provisions of the Espionage Act constituted a violation of the freedom of speech and press guaranteed by the First Amendment. Unanimously rejecting the petitioners' contentions, the Supreme Court, speaking through Mr. Justice Holmes enunciated its new "clear and present danger" doctrine. As the then 78-year-old jurist explained in a memorable passage:

> We admit that in many places and in *ordinary times* the defendants in saying all that was said in the circular would have been within their constitutional rights. *But the character of every act depends upon the circumstances in which it is done.* . . . The most stringent protection of free speech would not protect a man in *falsely* shouting fire in a theatre and causing a panic. It does not even protect a man from an injunction against uttering words that have all the effects of force. . . . *The question in every case is whether the words used are used in such circumstances and are of such a nature as to create a clear and present danger that they will bring about the substantive evils that Congress has a right to prevent.* When a nation is at war many things that might be said in time of peace are such a hindrance to its effort that their utterance will not be endured so long as men fight and that no Court could regard them as being protected by any constitutional right.[252]

The doctrine was designed to draw a sensible and usable line between the rights of the individual and those of society at the point where the former's actions or activities tended to create a danger to organized society so "clear and present" that government, the servant of the people—here the representative legislative branch by way of a wartime emergency statute—had a right to attempt to prevent the individual's actions or activities in *advance*. Schenck and his associates deemed such a statute to be an unconstitutional invasion of their First Amendment rights. But the Court—here handing down its *first* ruling on a claim that an act of *Congress* violated freedom of expression *per se*—resorted to its new doctrine and concurred with the government that the exigencies of wartime provided sufficient justification for

[252] *Ibid.,* at 52. (Italics supplied.)

its passage; that, indeed, any government worthy of the name would protect itself against the danger "clear and present" of interference with the
so basic element of conscription for military service. It would be difficult
to quarrel with that contention. And just one Opinion Day after *Schenck,*
Holmes again was the author of two unanimous opinions for the Court upholding the Act of 1917 anew, in which he again invoked the "clear and
present danger" test, but without elaborating. One of the cases involved a
pro-German newspaperman,[253] the other the famous Socialist leader Eugene V. Debs.[254] Not entirely happy with the nomenclature, Brandeis—as
would Jackson in the *Dennis* case in 1951[255]—preferred to categorize the
doctrine as a "rule of reason"[256]—which, of course, it has to be. As he saw
the test, correctly applied it would preserve the right of free speech both
from "suppression by tyrannous, well-meaning majorities, and from abuse
by irresponsible, fanatical minorities."

Abrams v. United States.[257] As if to demonstrate almost immediately the
difficulties inherent in the "clear and present danger" formula, its two leading champions found themselves in the minority in the celebrated *Abrams*
case barely six months after the *Schenck* decision. This time the Sedition
Act of 1918, which went considerably beyond its predecessor, the Espionage Act of 1917, was at issue. It made punishable what two subsequent
observers have justly called "speech that in World War II would have
been deemed mere political comment."[258] It thus rendered punitive any
"disloyal, profane, scurrilous, or abusive language about the form of government, the Constitution, soldiers and sailors, flag or uniform of the
armed forces," and it also made unlawful any "word or act [favoring] the
cause of the German Empire . . . or [opposing] the cause of the United
States." Under the statute, Jacob Abrams, a 29-year-old self-styled "anar-
chist-Socialist," and five young associates (all aliens) were apprehended
for distributing certain English- and Yiddish-language leaflets from roof-
tops on New York City's Lower East Side late in August 1918. These

[253] *Frohwerk v. United States,* 249 U.S. 204 (1919). Frohwerk had inserted several
articles in a Missouri German-language newspaper, challenging the purposes of the
War as well as the merits and constitutionality of the draft.
[254] *Debs v. United States,* 249 U.S. 211 (1919). Debs was charged with an attempt
to cause insubordination in the Army and to obstruct recruiting.
[255] See Jackson's concurring opinion, discussed at p. 182, *supra.*
[256] See his dissenting opinion in *Schaefer v. United States,* 251 U.S. 466 (1920):
"If the words were of such a nature and were used under such circumstances that
men, judging in calmness, could not reasonably say that they created a clear and
present danger that they would bring about the evil that Congress sought and had a
right to prevent, then it is the duty of the trial judge to withdraw the case from the
consideration of the jury; if he fails to do so, it is the duty of the appellate court
to correct the error." (At 483.)
[257] 250 U.S. 616 (1919).
[258] Alpheus T. Mason and William M. Beaney, *American Constitutional Law,*
4th ed. (Englewood Cliffs, N.J.: Prentice-Hall, 1968), p. 495.

leaflets urged the "workers of the world" to resist the Allied and American military intervention against the Bolsheviki in Russia's Murmansk and Vladivostok areas during the summer of 1918. They bitterly denounced President Woodrow Wilson for his decision to intervene and exhorted "the workers of the world" to a general strike in order to prevent future shipment of munitions and other war materials to the anti-Soviet forces. The English-language leaflet closed with the following observation: "P.S. It is absurd to call us pro-German. We hate and despise German militarism more than do your hypocritical tyrants. We have more reasons for denouncing German militarism than has the coward in the White House."[259]

Four of the five defendants were found guilty in the United States District Court for the Southern District of New York. The judge[260] sentenced three of them, including Abrams, to the maximum of 20-years' imprisonment in a federal penitentiary and a $4,000 fine each; the lone girl received fifteen years and a $500 fine; and one defendant got three years. (Four years later President Harding commuted their sentences on condition that they would all embark at once for the Soviet Union—which they did.) When their appeal reached the Supreme Court, Mr. Justice John H. Clarke, in a 7:2 opinion, agreed that the defendants had intended to "urge, incite, and advocate" curtailment of production deemed necessary to the conduct of the war effort, a crime under the Sedition Act and its predecessor statute. Clarke granted that the "primary purpose and intent" of the petitioners "was quite obviously to aid the cause of the Russian Revolution"— which was not forbidden *per se* under either of the statutes involved. But, he ruled,

> the plan of action which they adopted necessarily involved, before it could be realized, defeat of the war program of the United States, for the obvious effect of this appeal, if it should become effective, as they hoped it might, would be to persuade persons . . . not to aid government loans and not to work in ammunition factories.[261]

The question that arises at once, of course, is whether the advocacy of a general strike constituted the kind of direct threat to the war effort that the laws under which they were indicted and sentenced envisaged. A plausible case could certainly be made, as indeed it was made by Zechariah Chafee, that "interference with the war was at the most an incidental consequence of the strikes [they clamored for], entirely subordinate to the longed-for

---

[259] As quoted by Zechariah Chafee, Jr., in his classic *Freedom of Speech in the United States* (Cambridge: Harvard University Press, 1954), p. 110. See his Ch. III for a fascinating account of the *Abrams* case.

[260] Visiting Trial Judge Henry DeLamar Clayton of Alabama (author of the Clayton Anti-Trust Act of 1914).

[261] *Abrams v. United States,* 250 U.S. 616 (1919), at 621.

consequences of all this agitation, withdrawal from Russia . . ." and should certainly *not* be made the main basis for punishments restricting open discussion.[262]

And while the majority of seven saw a "clear and present" danger, the doctrine's authors *dissented* in an opinion written by Mr. Justice Holmes. With Brandeis concurring, Holmes penned the best that he (or anyone else, one may add) could say on the matter, to which the following impassioned excerpt testifies:

> . . . when men have realized that time has upset many fighting faiths, they may come to believe even more than they believe the very foundations of their own conduct that the ultimate good desired is better reached by *free trade in ideas*—that the best of truth is the power of the thought to get itself accepted in the competition of the market, and that *truth is the only ground* upon which their wishes can be safely carried out. That at any rate is the theory of our Constitution. *It is an experiment, as all life is an experiment.* Every year if not every day we have to wager our salvation upon some prophecy based upon imperfect knowledge. While that experiment is part of our system I think that we should be *eternally vigilant against attempts to check the expression of opinions that we loathe and believe to be fraught with death,*

—and here, of course, he draws the line—*"unless they so imminently threaten immediate interference with the lawful and pressing purposes of the law that an immediate check is required to save the country."*[263] Holmes and Brandeis saw no such interference in what Holmes called the "surreptitious publishing of a silly leaflet" by an unknown man. Assuredly, noted Holmes, this did in no sense constitute "a present danger of immediate evil," and he warned his fellow countrymen and their legislators that "[o]nly the emergency that makes it immediately dangerous to leave the correction of evil counsels to time warrants making any exception to the sweeping command, 'Congress shall make no law abridging freedom of speech.' "[264] Holmes was not speaking of *acts,* but of *"expressions of opinions and exhortations,* which were all that were uttered here." He con-

---

[262] *Freedom of Speech in the United States, op. cit.,* p. 134.

[263] *Abrams v. United States, op. cit.,* at 630. (Italics supplied.) Mr. Justice Frankfurter wrote of those deeply moving (and provocative) words: "It is not reckless prophecy to assume that his famous dissenting opinion in the *Abrams* case will live so long as English prose retains its power to move." (*Justice Holmes and the Supreme Court* [Cambridge: Harvard University Press, 1938], pp. 54–55.) And Max Lerner commented that Holmes's language "has economy, grace, finality, and is the greatest utterance on intellectual freedom" by an American, ranking in the English language with Milton and Mill." (*The Mind and Faith of Justice Holmes* [Boston: Little, Brown & Co., 1943], p. 50.)

[264] *Abrams v. United States, op. cit.,* at 630–31.

cluded that beyond doubt they "were deprived of their rights under the Constitution of the United States."[265]

The "Bad Tendency Test"

If the *Abrams* majority did not theoretically modify the "clear and present danger" doctrine, it assuredly sidetracked it practically. The *official* modification came six years later in the *Gitlow* case.

Gitlow v. New York.[266] The facts and circumstances surrounding this famous decision have been amply outlined and discussed earlier.[267] However, we must examine here the Supreme Court majority's holding, over the dissenting opinion by Mr. Justice Holmes, in which once again Mr. Justice Brandeis concurred, that "certain writings" of Benjamin Gitlow constituted a *"bad tendency"* to "corrupt public morals, incite to crime, and disturb the public peace." The majority thus affirmed Gitlow's conviction under New York State's Criminal Anarchy Act of 1902, which prohibited the "advocacy, advising, or teaching the duty, necessity or propriety of overthrowing or overturning organized government [New York's] by force or violence" and the publication or distribution of such matters. Despite the fact that there was no evidence of any effect from the publication of Gitlow's "Left Wing Manifesto," Mr. Justice Sanford, speaking for the Court, contended that the "State cannot reasonably be required to measure the danger from every such utterance in the nice balance of a jeweler's scale"[268] and ruled that because a

> single revolutionary spark may kindle a fire that, smoldering for a time, may burst into a sweeping and destructive conflagration . . . [the State] may, in the exercise of its judgment, suppress the threatened danger in its incipiency.[269]

Obviously, this was no longer the "clear and present danger" test. When the State is empowered to suppress a mere *threat* in its very *incipiency,* the line is being drawn on the basis of a "bad tendency" rather than on that of a "clear and present" danger. There was hardly anything very "clear" or "present" in Gitlow's activities, confined as they were to the written exhortations of a rather pathetic individual. As Professor Chafee, America's leading expert on freedom of expression during the second quarter of the twentieth century, commented: "Any agitator who read these thirty-four pages to a mob would not stir them to violence, except possibly against

---

[265] *Ibid.,* at 631. (Italics supplied.)
[266] *Gitlow v. New York,* 268 U.S. 652 (1925).
[267] See Ch. III, *supra,* on "incorporation," especially pp. 51–53.
[268] *Ibid.,* at 669.
[269] *Ibid.*

himself. This Manifesto would disperse them faster than the Riot Act."[270]

In asking itself whether Gitlow's activities had created or constituted *a "bad tendency" to bring about a danger* (a phrase from the *Schaefer*[271] decision five years earlier), the majority shifted the balance between the individual and the state toward the latter. Thundered Holmes:

> If what I think the correct test is applied it is manifest that there was no present danger of an attempt to overthrow the government by force. . . . It is said that this manifesto was more than a theory, that it was an incitement. *Every idea is an incitement.* It offers itself for belief and if believed it is acted on unless some other belief outweighs it or some failure of energy stifles the movement at its birth. The only difference between the expression of an opinion and an incitement in the narrower sense is the speaker's enthusiasm for the result. *Eloquence may set fire to reason.*[272]

Holmes pointed out, as he had in similar circumstances in his *Abrams* dissent, that the charges against the defendant alleged *publication,* and nothing more. And, calling a democratic spade a democratic spade, he commented:

> If in the long run the beliefs expressed in proletarian dictatorship are destined to be accepted by the dominant forces of the community, the only meaning of free speech is that they should be given their chance and have their way.[273]

He was naturally confident, as was Mr. Justice Douglas in his dissenting opinion in the *Dennis* case[274] a quarter of a century *later,* that "the American people want none of Communism [whose] doctrine is exposed in all its ugliness . . . its wares unsold."[275] In a very real sense the issue for both Holmes and Douglas came down to a matter of faith in the ability of the American people to choose their destiny, in the absence of demonstrable, overt, illegal *actions* or conduct.

---

[270] *Freedom of Speech in the United States, op. cit.,* p. 319.

[271] *Schaefer v. United States,* 251 U.S. 466 (1920).

[272] *Gitlow v. New York, op. cit.,* at 673. (Italics supplied.)

[273] *Ibid.* In 1968 the Court would refuse to *review,* with Mr. Justice Douglas in a long dissenting opinion from that refusal, the conviction under the same statute of Marxist William Epton. (*Epton v. New York,* 390 U.S. 29, appeal dismissed.) In 1971, it also refused to review another New York case, which in 1969 had been construed below like *Gitlow* and *Epton* (*Samuels v. Mackell,* 401 U.S. 66); ditto a similar California case (*Younger v. Harris,* 401 U.S. 37 [1971]). But it had declared Ohio's criminal syndicalism law unconstitutional in 1969 in the significant *Brandenburg* case, discussed in connection with *Whitney,* pp. 211–13, *infra.* (*Brandenburg v. Ohio,* 395 U.S. 444.)

[274] *Dennis v. United States,* 341 U.S. 494 (1951).

[275] *Ibid.,* at 588–89.

EXPANDING "CLEAR AND PRESENT DANGER"

Holmes and Brandeis recognized that some amplification of their "clear and present danger" test was needed to prevent its demotion to the "bad tendency" level. Their opportunity came some two years following the *Gitlow* decision in *Whitney v. California*.[276]

Whitney v. California. Miss Charlotte Anita Whitney, a niece of one of the pillars of *laissez faire* American capitalism, Mr. Justice Stephen J. Field, was one of the band of disenchanted adventurers who, in 1919, helped to organize the Communist Labor Party of California. Motivated largely by her passionate espousal of the cause of the poor, she readily permitted herself to be elected as a member of the C.L.P.C. during its 1919 convention held in Oakland. The Party's constitution was quite clear on its affiliation with both the Communist Labor Party of America and the Communist International of Moscow. Miss Whitney's activities brought her into conflict with California's Criminal Syndicalism Act of 1919. She soon found herself indicted on five counts, and subsequently convicted of one: that on November 28, 1919, she "did then and there unlawfully, willfully, wrongfully, deliberately and feloniously organize and assist in organizing, and was, is, and knowingly became a member of an organization, society, group and assemblage of persons organized and assembled to advocate, teach, aid and abet criminal syndicalism."[277]

On appeal, Miss Whitney protested, as she had during her trial, that at no time did she wish her Party to engage in any acts of violence or terror, but the intermediate appellate tribunal affirmed her conviction and the State Supreme Court refused to review her case, which then went on to the United States Supreme Court. At issue was the association between due process of law and First Amendment guarantees, against the basic charge of a criminal conspiracy—an activity that falls outside the protection of free speech. Again Miss Whitney lost. Mr. Justice Sanford, here writing the opinion for a unanimous Court that *included* Justices Holmes and Brandeis, agreed that the State of California had an inherent right to guard statutorily against the alleged conspiracy—and neither Holmes nor Brandeis disputed the Court's finding that there was sufficient evidence to point to the existence of such a conspiracy to violate the Criminal Syndicalism Act. However, in a highly significant concurring opinion, joined by Holmes, Brandeis rejected the majority's interpretation of a section of the law that not only made it a crime to advocate or teach or practice criminal syndicalism, or conspire to do so, but also to be in "association with those who proposed to teach it." Here Brandeis and Holmes saw a lurking and

---

[276] 274 U.S. 357 (1927).
[277] *Ibid.*, at 358.

grave threat to the concept of "clear and present danger" as they had conceived of it; thus, with the *Gitlow* "bad tendency" doctrine in mind, the two jurists endeavored not only to resurrect their original "clear and present danger" concept but to strengthen it. In a ringing admonition—which reportedly so moved the then Governor of California, C. C. Young, that he later pardoned Miss Whitney—Brandeis's concurrence—which, in effect, reads like a dissent[278]—attempted to clarify, expand, and liberalize the doctrine by joining to its basic test the requirement of *"imminence":*

> Fear of serious injury cannot alone justify suppression of free speech and assembly . . . there must be reasonable ground to fear that serious evil will result if free speech is practiced. There must be reasonable ground to believe *that the danger apprehended is imminent.* There must be reasonable ground to believe that the evil to be prevented is a serious one. . . . In order to support a finding of clear and present danger *it must be shown either that immediate serious violence was to be expected or was advocated, or that the past conduct furnished reason to believe that such advocacy was then contemplated.*
>
> Those who won our independence by revolution were not cowards. They did not fear political change. They did not exalt order at the cost of liberty. To courageous, self-reliant men, with confidence in the power of free and fearless reasoning applied through the processes of popular government, *no danger flowing from speech can be deemed clear and present, unless the incidence of the evil apprehended is so imminent that it may befall before there is opportunity for full discussion.* If there be time to expose through discussion the falsehood and fallacies, to avert the evil by the processes of education, *the remedy to be applied is more speech, not enforced silence.*[279]

In his and Holmes's opinion, "such . . . is the command of the Constitution."[280]

Specific vindication of the Brandeis-Holmes view in their *Whitney* concurrence did not really come until they were long dead. A United States District Court declared the California Criminal Syndicalism Law unconstitutional in 1968 in the *Younger v. Harris* case, although the Supreme Court set the verdict aside on technical grounds two years later.[281] But the Court did dispose of Ohio's similar statute in the key 1969 *Brandenburg*

---

[278] And so it was! *But* it had been written originally for *Ruthenberg v. Michigan,* 273 U.S. 782 (1927), a case mooted by Ruthenberg's death and dismissed that March. Brandeis subsequently seized upon the opportunity of *Whitney* to incorporate the central points of that dissent into what is his concurring opinion for *Whitney.* (See Klaus H. Heberle, "From Gitlow to Near . . . ," 34 *Journal of Politics* 468 [1972].)

[279] *Ibid.,* at 377. (Italics supplied.)

[280] *Ibid.*

[281] *Younger v. Harris,* 281 F. Supp. 507 and *Younger v. Harris,* 401 U.S. 37 (1971), respectively.

decision,[282] in which it *specifically* overruled its 1927 *Whitney* holding. Clarence Brandenburg, a Ku Klux Klan leader, was convicted, fined, and sentenced to jail under the law at issue,[283] and challenged the latter on First and Fourteenth Amendment grounds. Pointing to a spate of intervening decisions,[284] the Court's unsigned (*per curiam*) opinion re-emphasized the

> principle that the constitutional guarantees of free speech and free press do not permit a State to forbid or proscribe advocacy of the use of force or of law violation *except* where such advocacy is directed to inciting or producing *imminent* lawless action and is likely to incite or produce such action.[285]

Mere advocacy is thus no longer punishable on pain of violating Amendments One and Fourteen; but *direct incitement to imminent action* is.[286]

Thus, we again see the basic dilemma inherent in the two approaches to freedom of expression in democratic society. No matter what the language employed, no matter what the rationalization by individuals in specific situations, it comes down to a reading of the Constitution in its historical-evolutionary setting, against what Holmes called "the felt necessities of the time." And underlying the entire problem is, inevitably and necessarily, the faith one has in a free people's willingness and ability to experiment, to take chances, to govern itself in democratic society.

"Preferred Freedoms" and Beyond. We noted in Chapter II that the Supreme Court in the late 1930s and much of the 1940s—in line with the Brandeis-Holmes philosophy expressed in *Whitney* and other cases—

---

[282] *Brandenburg v. Ohio,* 395 U.S. 444 (1969).

[283] Brandenburg had invited a television cameraman to a cross-burning ceremony, where he was filmed vowing "revengeance" against the nation's leaders and making slurring and vile remarks about "niggers" and "kikes," e.g., that "the nigger should be returned to Africa, the Jew returned to Israel." During the "organizational meeting," some in the group of about twelve hooded Klansmen were seen brandishing firearms.

[284] E.g., *Dennis v. United States,* 341 U.S. 494 (1951); *Yates v. United States,* 354 U.S. 298 (1957); *Noto v. United States,* 367 U.S. 290 (1961); and *Bond v. Floyd,* 385 U.S. 116 (1966).

[285] *Brandenburg v. Ohio, op. cit.,* at 444. (Italics supplied.) Supported by Mr. Justice Black in separate concurring opinions, Mr. Justice Douglas restated the two libertarians' firm faith, namely, that there is "no place in the regime of the First Amendment for any 'clear and present danger' test, whether strict and tight as some would make it, or free-wheeling as the court in *Dennis* rephrased it." (At 454.) Judge Learned Hand's opinion in *Masses Publ. Co. v. Patten,* 244 Fed. 535 (1917), considered but rejected Holmes's future test as "too slippery, too dangerous to free expression." Instead he urged the adoption of a "strict," "hard," "objective" test, focusing on the speakers words: if the language used was solely that of a direct incitement to illegal action, speech could be proscribed; otherwise it was protected. However, Hand evidently abandoned this approach a few years later and embraced the "clear and present danger" test.

[286] For a pertinent later illustration, see *Hess v. Indiana,* 414 U.S. 105 (1973).

adopted the view that there should be "more exacting judicial scrutiny" of First Amendment freedoms. The Court thus identified a constitutionally protected area of "preferred freedom," based upon the famous footnote by Mr. Justice Stone in *United States v. Carolene Products Co.*,[287] where the future Chief Justice had called for a special niche for "legislation which restricts the political processes."[288] A concept enthusiastically embraced by Justices Black, Douglas, Murphy, and Rutledge when they served together with Stone from Rutledge's appointment in 1943 to the deaths of Stone, Rutledge, and Murphy, it was to be joined to the "clear and present danger plus imminence" doctrine.

But when Harlan Stone died in 1946, Fred Vinson replaced him as Chief Justice, foreshadowing trouble for the new "line" established by the civil libertarians. And when Murphy and Rutledge both died in the summer of 1949, their replacements, Justices Clark and Minton, together with the new Chief Justice and the "holdovers"—Justices Reed, Frankfurter, Jackson, and Burton—constituted a majority that almost at once departed from the philosophy of "preferred freedom." Indeed, in the landmark *Dennis*[289] internal security case even the "clear and present danger" doctrine underwent a rather dramatic transformation into what some observers viewed as a "grave and probable" test patterned upon Judge Learned Hand's lower court opinion,[290] on which Mr. Chief Justice Vinson leaned very heavily in his *Dennis* majority opinion.[291] Others felt that in fact the Court had adopted as its new freedom of expression doctrine a "possible and remote danger" test![292] Unquestionably, "bad tendency" had taken over from "clear and present danger." However, soon after Earl Warren became Chief Justice on Vinson's death in 1953, the Court returned to the "clear and present danger" test, even restoring its "imminence" appendage. Indeed, some even felt that the new Court adopted a "super-preferred" standard vis-à-vis claims of racial discrimination and due process standards of criminal justice. It did retain the "bad tendency" test in the national security field for a while longer but, by the *late* 1950s, in cases such as *Yates v. United States*,[293] the Court, after some wavering and broken-field strategy, returned to the "clear and present danger" plus imminence test for the national security field also. With the advent of the "Burger Court" in 1969, Warren Earl Burger having replaced Earl Warren in the center chair, a change of direction could not be ruled out. However, as of

[287] 304 U.S. 144 (1938).
[288] *Ibid.*, at 152.
[289] 341 U.S. 494 (1951).
[290] *Dennis v. United States,* 183 F. 2d 201 (1950), at 212.
[291] *Op. cit.,* fn. 289, *supra,* at 510 ff.
[292] Alfred H. Kelly and Winifred A. Harbison, *The American Constitution: Its Origins and Development,* 2nd ed. (New York: W. W. Norton & Co., 1955), p. 893.
[293] 354 U.S. 298 (1957). See the discussion of the case, pp. 183 ff., *supra.*

mid-1981 there had been no return to the Vinson approach. Indeed, despite some narrowing in the realms of "obscenity" and aspects of freedom of the press,[294] freedom of expression was given generous interpretations by the Burger Court, notwithstanding the departures from the Court of its great champions, Justices Black and Douglas, in 1971 and 1975, respectively. Thus, a 1978 opinion by the Chief Justice strongly reaffirmed a tough "clear and present" standard upon any legislative attempts to bridle freedom of speech.[295] The Burger Court in fact emphasized an additional type of "preferred freedom," the so-called "suspect" categories of race, alienage and national origin, and—although not quite so clearly—sex, which were accorded special judicial protection alongside other fundamental rights regarded as entitled to "close scrutiny" by the courts. If any retrenchment was in evidence, it was in the field of criminal justice, but even there the Court's record was not one-sided.[296] On the other hand, as 1981 entered the annals, it was obvious that none of the Nixon-Ford appointees to the high bench[297] would be committed to the *absolutist* reading of freedom of expression brought to the Court by Black and Douglas for almost four decades.

Some Concluding Thoughts

No other branch of our government is as qualified to draw lines between the rights of individuals and those of society as the Supreme Court of the United States. The legislative and executive branches yield all too easily to the politically expedient and the popular. Admittedly, the "clear and present danger" approach to freedom of expression, however amended and augmented, is far from perfect. But the sole alternative to it would be an almost total absence of immunity in the face of legislative actions. Freedom of expression cannot be absolute; but it can be protected to the widest degree humanly feasible under the Constitution. And there are giants of liberal democracy who bridle at *any* restraint on free expression. Thus we had Mr. Justice Black in his absolutist approach to the problem[298] and, al-

---

[294] See pp. 199 ff. and pp. 170 ff., *supra*, respectively.

[295] *Landmark Communications, Inc. v. Virginia*, 435 U.S. 829 (1978). He quoted a passage from Mr. Justice Brandeis's concurrence in *Whitney v. California* (*op. cit.*, pp. 211 ff.) that began: "A legislative declaration does not preclude enquiry into the question whether, at the time and under the circumstances, the conditions existed which are essential to validity under the Federal Constitution. (At 843–44.)

[296] See Chapter IV, *supra*.

[297] In addition to the 1969 Burger for Warren switch, the following replacements had taken effect by mid-1981: Blackmun for Fortas (1970); Powell and Rehnquist for Black and Harlan (1971); Stevens for Douglas (1975).

[298] E.g., his "The Bill of Rights," 35 *New York University Law Review* 865–81 (April 1960); and his *A Constitutional Faith* (New York: Alfred A. Knopf, 1968), especially Ch. II, "The First Amendment," pp. 43 ff. (See also, generally, Chapter II, *supra*.)

most as absolute, the late educator-philosopher Alexander Meiklejohn, who held that while the First Amendment "does not forbid the abridging of *speech* . . . it does forbid the abridging of *freedom of speech.*"[299]

For Alexander Meiklejohn who, like Hugo Black, rejected the "clear and present danger" approach in favor of a more liberal standard there is thus *never,* under the *First* Amendment, any right or reason to curb or abridge *freedom* of speech—at least not *public* speech (see below); dangers, even in wartime, are irrelevant; and the time of danger is precisely the time to show people that one means what one says and has the right to say it:

> If, then, on any occasion in the United States it is allowable to say that the Constitution is a good document it is equally allowable, in that situation, to say that the Constitution is a bad document. If a public building may be used in which to say, in time of war, that the war is justified, then the same building may be used in which to say that it is not justified. If it be publicly argued that conscription for armed service is moral and necessary, it may likewise be publicly argued that it is immoral and unnecessary. If it may be said that American political institutions are superior to those of England or Russia or Germany, it may, with equal freedom, be said that those of England or Russia or Germany are superior to ours. . . . When a question of policy is "before the house," free men choose it not with their eyes shut, but with their eyes open. To be afraid of ideas, any idea, is to be unfit for self-government.[300]

This stirring language should serve as a beacon to us all; but the fact remains that there *are* limits to the precious freedom and that we do need some such doctrine as "clear and present danger." Meiklejohn, however, proposed a different solution: he created a dichotomy of *public speech* and *private speech,* "public" speech pertaining to any matter that concerns politics—i.e., public policy and public officials. This type of speech, Meiklejohn held, is given *absolute* protection, in the interests of a self-governing free and democratic society, by the First Amendment and the "privileges or immunities" clause of the Fourteenth, and cannot be abridged at all. *"Private"* speech, he contended, pertains to speech that concerns only private individuals in their personal, private concerns, and can therefore be regulated or restricted—but *only* in accordance with the "due process of law" safeguards under the Fifth and Fourteenth Amendments. Noble as the Meiklejohn dichotomy may be,[301] it is burdened with what is clearly an

[299] *Free Speech and Its Relation to Self-Government* (New York: Harper & Brothers, 1948), p. 19. (Italics supplied.)

[300] *Ibid.,* p. 27.

[301] For a similar dichotomy see George Anastaplo, *The Constitutionalist: Notes on the First Amendment* (Dallas: Southern Methodist University Press, 1970). He accepts "the First" as *absolute* in the "political" ("public business") area, *but* denies

unresolvable dilemma of its own: how to draw the line pragmatically between "public" and "private" speech. Much speech is private but has definite public ramifications—a viable line seems impossible to attain. Yet shortly before he died in 1965 Meiklejohn voiced the belief that the Supreme Court had, in effect, adopted his "public speech" approach because of its developing stance on litigation concerning libel, slander, and defamation of character, highlighted by the 1964 decision in *New York Times Co. v. Sullivan*.[302] There the Court held that a *public* official cannot recover libel damages for criticism of his official performance *unless he proves that the statement was made with deliberate malice*.[303] "It is an occasion for dancing in the streets," exclaimed Meiklejohn, according to Mr. Justice Brennan—who, however, preferred to leave to his readers "to say how nearly Dr. Meiklejohn's hope has been realized."[304]

Yet a staunch supporter of the Holmes-Brandeis "clear and present danger plus imminence" doctrine, Zechariah Chafee, Jr., the aforementioned towering advocate of free expression, had publicly disagreed with his revered teacher and friend Meiklejohn in 1949. Reviewing Meiklejohn's *Free Speech and Its Relation to Self-Government*,[305] Chafee charged that Meiklejohn, in his repeated challenge to Holmes and the "clear and present danger" doctrine, simply showed no realization of the long uphill fight that Holmes had to wage in order to secure free speech. After all, as Chafee explained appropriately in his review, it *was* Holmes who

> worked out a formula which would invalidate a great deal of suppression, and won for [free speech] the solid authority of a unanimous Court. Afterwards, again and again, when the test was misapplied by the majority, Holmes restated his position in ringing words which, with the help of Brandeis and [later, after he had become Chief Justice] Hughes, eventually inspired the whole Court.[306]

---

it in the "private" sector, specifically "artistic expression" and "problems of obscenity." He confines his reading to the *First* Amendment, not reaching the states via the Fourteenth, Meiklejohn, of course, does not exempt the states. The two also differ somewhat on the meaning of "public."

[302] 376 U.S. 254.

[303] See discussion on pp. 155 ff., *supra*. Note that the Court has wavered on the degree of extending the "public" concept to "persons" and/or "figures" as well as "officials."

[304] See William J. Brennan, Jr., "The Supreme Court and the Meiklejohn Interpretation of the First Amendment," 79 *Harvard Law Review* (November 1965). Actually, the first to report Meiklejohn's "dancing in the streets" statement was Harry Kalven, Jr., in "A New Look at the Central Meaning of the First Amendment," *The Supreme Court Review* (1964).

[305] 62 *Harvard Law Review* 891 (1949). See also Meiklejohn's "charges which I would bring against the 'clear and present danger' theory," in another important work of his on the freedom of speech problem, *Political Freedom: The Constitutional Powers of the People* (New York: Harper and Bros., 1948 and 1960); and the Oxford University Press edition (New York: 1965), pp. 75–76.

[306] *Op. cit.*, p. 901.

Of course, to support the "clear and present danger" doctrine, or that of "clear and present danger plus imminence," is not to ignore *its* inherent dilemmas—as the preceding discussion demonstrates. The very adjectives "clear" and "present" raise problems of great magnitude. Still, both in its basic philosophy and its application, the doctrine's overriding tenets are realistic in approach and reflect an attitude which is both liberal *and* conservative in the classic connotations of those two misunderstood terms. It is simply not possible to get away from the concept of "balancing"—a contentious term in some quarters[307]—liberty and authority, freedom and responsibility.[308] But when "balancing" is called for, and in the absence of a danger clear, present, and imminent, we must presume the scale to be weighted on the side of the individual.

The philosophical test[309] to be applied is clear: will the forbidding of freedom of expression further or hamper the realization of liberal democratic ideals? The sole manner in which to moderate, remedy, or remove rankling discontent is to get at its causes by education, remedial laws, or other community action. Repression of expression will only serve to sharpen the sense of injustice and provide added arguments and rationalizations for

[307] See, for example, the intriguing law review debate between Professors Laurent Frantz and Wallace Mendelson over the validity of "balancing" as a technique in free speech cases: Frantz, "The First Amendment in the Balance," 71 *Yale Law Journal* 1424 (1962); Mendelson, "On the Meaning of the First Amendment: Absolutes in the Balance," 50 *California Law Review* 821 (1962); Frantz, "Is the First Amendment Law? A Reply to Professor Mendelson," 51 *California Law Review* 729 (1963); and Mendelson, "The First Amendment and the Judicial Process: A Reply to Mr. Frantz," 17 *Vanderbilt Law Review* 479 (1964). Speaking broadly, Professor Frantz was anti-, Professor Mendelson pro-"balancing"—but the reader is cautioned against over-simplification. See also the challenging article by Dean Alfange, Jr., "The Balancing of Interests in Free Speech Cases: In Defense of an Abused Doctrine," 2 *Law in Transition Quarterly* 1 (1965). See also Mr. Justice Black's scathing denunciation of "balancing" in his *A Constitutional Faith, op. cit.,* and my pp. 22–24, *supra.* To him, of course, the "clear and present danger" doctrine—be it with or without the "imminence" requirement—was just another form of "balancing" and hence unacceptable under his reading of the absolutist commands of the First (and Fourteenth) Amendment. "[I]t has no place in [their] interpretation," as he admonished again shortly prior to the end of his long and distinguished career on the Court, in his concurring opinion in *Brandenburg v. Ohio,* 395 U.S. 444 (1968), at 449–50.

[308] In his interesting position essay on the overall question, *Freedom of Speech: The Supreme Court and Judicial Review* (Englewood Cliffs, N.J.: Prentice-Hall, 1966), Professor Martin Shapiro contends that although balancing "may still occasionally be useful in particular instances, it cannot be maintained as a general formula for a Court bent on fulfilling its First Amendment responsibilities" (p. 105). Issuing a clarion call for judicial activism, he sees the "preferred freedom" position as the only viable formula, one that he insists must "again become the dominant First Amendment doctrine of the Supreme Court" (p. 172). Again and again calling for judicial activism, judicial policy-making, in the freedom of speech sphere, he argues that American democracy "not only permits but invites and requires a strong measure of judicial activism here."

[309] See J. A. Corry and Henry J. Abraham, *Elements of Democratic Government,* 4th ed. (New York: Oxford University Press, 1964), pp. 262 ff.

desperate, perhaps reckless measures. Surely the loyalty of the mass of men to liberal democracy has been immensely strengthened by the right to free expression and the consequent feeling of a genuine stake in society, a society that allows the expression of our deepest and most rankling grievances. Hence repressive laws will fail to maintain "loyalty." While they may give a false sense of temporary security, since we would be excused from arguing the case for our ideals and for the carefully developed procedures for pursuing them, we must also recognize that freedom of utterance, even though it be rebellious, constitutes a safety valve that gives timely warning of dangerous pressures in our society. Committed to the principles of Western liberal democracy, we have a lasting obligation to leave open the political channels by which a governing majority can be replaced when it is no longer able to command popular support. However, to plead for a generous approach to freedom of expression is not to say that it is absolute. It is not; it cannot be. In the final analysis we must confidently look to the Court to draw a line based on constitutional common sense. No other agency of government is equally well qualified to do so.

chapter *VI* Religion

If line-drawing in the realm of due process is difficult because of the ambiguity of the concept, and if it is elusive in determining the freedom of expression, it is pre-eminently delicate and emotional in the matter of religion. Religion, like love, is so personal and irrational that no one has either the capacity or justification to sit in judgment.[1] Any attempt by society to find and draw a line here is bound to be frustrating. Our own society is certainly no exception—although it is to America's credit that in probably no other area of civil rights and liberties have our agencies and agents of government maintained such a consistently good record. Even more than the freedom of the press has the freedom of religion been safeguarded from governmental interference. This is not to say, of course, that we have a perfect record; our early history is replete with both public and private discrimination against religious creeds, particularly Catholics, Quakers, and Jews. However, as we grew and developed as a nation, discrimination *by government* declined perceptibly and fairly rapidly. *Private* religious discrimination—which does still exist, and presumably always will to some degree—is no longer, if it ever was, sanctioned by government, and when it occurs it is pre-eminently of a "social" rather than a "religious" nature. The problems arise when attempts are made to commingle matters of religious belief with matters of state and to conduct policy in line with spiritual commitments.

The election of the first Roman Catholic president of the United States in 1960; the rise to public prominence and power of a host of members of religious minority groups; and the steadily increasing official proscription of public or quasi-public discrimination because of race, sex, religion, color, and national origin—brought to a dramatic climax in the Civil Rights

---

[1] Still, I am tempted to profess a modicum of "expertise": a product of secular secondary schools, I spent one year at a Roman Catholic university; was graduated from an Episcopal college; married a Christian Scientist; our children went to Quaker schools (and to the same college as their father); and I was a long-time member of the Board of Trustees of an old Reform Jewish Congregation.

Act of 1964—all augur well for a continuing increase in understanding and a continuing decline of the barriers built of religious discrimination. Nevertheless, problems of religious freedom still do arise and lines must be drawn. Our concern here lies predominantly in the *public* sector, and in how and where lines are drawn between the prerogatives of the free exercise of religion, and all the concept entails, and the right of society to guard against activity that would infringe upon the rights of other members of that society. The distinction is compounded by the unique collateral problem of the constitutional command against the "establishment" of religion; *it* has proved to be a hornet's nest, indeed!

Some Basic Considerations

Basic to our understanding of the problem are three constitutional facts.

1. *The Proscription of Religious Tests in Article Six of the Constitution.* It is often forgotten that there exists in the body of our Constitution an important provision dealing directly with a crucial religious right, the forbidding of religious tests as qualifications for public office. The third section of Article Six, following the famed supremacy clause[2]—which constitutes all of Section 2—reflects the concern for religious liberty of four Virginians to whom, although they were not all participants in the Constitutional Convention, is due chief credit for our constitutional theory of freedom of religion: Thomas Jefferson,[3] James Madison, George Mason—who refused to sign the final draft of the Constitution because of the absence of a Bill of Rights—and, perhaps with an occasional aberration, Patrick Henry.[4] The Journal of the Convention for August 30, 1787, bears the following entry: "It was moved and seconded to add . . .—'but no religious test shall *ever* be required as a qualification to *any* office or public trust under the authority of the United States.'; which passed unanimously in the affirmative."[5] Only North Carolina voted against the adoption of this

---

[2] "This Constitution, and the Laws of the United States which shall be made in Pursuance thereof; and all Treaties made, or which shall be made, under the Authority of the United States, shall be the supreme Law of the Land; *and the Judges in every State shall be bound thereby, any Thing in the Constitution of Laws of any State to the Contrary notwithstanding.*" (Italics supplied.)

[3] Symptomatic of Jefferson's strong feelings about religious freedom is the following excerpt from a letter he wrote to Mrs. M. Harrison Smith on August 6, 1816: "I never told my own religion, nor scrutinized that of another. I never attempted to make a convert, nor wished to change another's creed. I have never judged the religion of others, and by this test, my dear Madame, I have been satisfied yours must be an excellent one to have produced a life of such exemplary viture and correctness. For it is in our lives and not from our words that our religion must be read."

[4] Anson Phelps Stokes and Leo Pfeffer, *Church and State in the United States,* rev. one-vol. ed. (New York: Harper & Row, 1964), pp. 65 ff.

[5] Jonathan Elliot, *The Debates in the Several State Conventions,* 2nd ed. (Philadelphia: Lippincott & Co., 1854), Vol. I, pp. 277. (Italics supplied.)

clause.[6] Later, referring to the clause's significance, Mr. Justice Joseph Story commented: "The Catholic and the Protestant, the Calvinist and the Armenian [sic], the infidel and the Jew, may sit down to the Communion-table of the National Council, without any inquisition into their faith or mode of worship."[7]

Although this ban against religious test oaths settled matters at once in so far as public office under the federal government was concerned, it did become an issue in state and municipal public employment, and remained so for a good many years. Most states removed their mandated disqualifications against Jews and members of other theistic religions, but others, such as Arkansas, Maryland, Pennsylvania, and Tennessee, retained constitutional provisions compelling all would-be public office-holders to take an oath or make an affirmation of their belief in God. Inevitably, however, judicial nationalization of civil rights and liberties via the "due process of law" clause of the Fourteenth Amendment ultimately reached the area of religion.[8] And in 1961 the Supreme Court addressed itself specifically to the religious oath clause in *Torcaso v. Watkins*.[9]

In that case Roy Torcaso, an aspirant for the minor state office of notary public in Maryland, refused to abide by his state's requirement, imbedded in a clause of its Constitution, that all office-holders declare their belief in the existence of God as a part of their oath of office. On Torcaso's refusal to take the oath his application was denied, and he appealed to the Maryland courts for a reversal of that ruling, alleging violation of the religious liberty guaranteed to him by the United States Constitution. When the state courts sided with Maryland, Torcaso took his case to the United States Supreme Court, which not only agreed with Torcaso's contentions, but declared the oath requirement unconstitutional as a violation of the "free exercise of religion" clause of the First Amendment of the federal Constitution. Unanimously, the Court, without any inquiry into what belief, if any, Roy Torcaso held—he was an atheist—declared that the state test oath constituted a clear invasion of "freedom of belief and religion." Moreover, wrote Mr. Justice Black for the Court, in placing Maryland on the side of "one particular sort of believer," namely, theists—those who believe in the existence of God—the constitutional requirement imposed a burden on the free exercise of the faiths on *non-believers* in violation of the free exercise clause.[10] To emphasize this point, Black appended what

[6] With the substitution of a semicolon for the dash before "but" and of a period for the semicolon after "States," it became the last phrase of Article Six, Section 3.

[7] As quoted in Phelps and Pfeffer, *op. cit.*, p. 91.

[8] See Chapter III, *supra* and, *inter alia, Hamilton v. Board of Regents of California,* 293 U.S. 245 (1934); *Cantwell v. Connecticut,* 310 U.S. 296 (1940); and *Everson v. Board of Education of Ewing Township,* 330 U.S. 1 (1947).

[9] 367 U.S. 488.

[10] *Ibid.,* at 495.

has become a well-known footnote in constitutional law: "Among religions in this country which do not teach what would generally be considered a belief in the existence of God are Buddhism, Taoism, Ethical Culture, Secular Humanism and others."[11] In other words, the Court made categorically clear that not only were religious test oaths barred, but that theistic belief could not be a requirement for religious belief.[12] Put somewhat differently, the Court affirmed what has been, or should have been, apparent all along: that the Constitution of the United States, in guaranteeing freedom of religion, by implication also guarantees freedom of *irreligion*. Four years later, the Maryland Court of Appeals specifically extended that guarantee to invalidate a requirement that all Maryland jurors declare a belief in God.[13]

2. *The "Nationalization" of the Religion Clauses.* As we already know from Chapter III, the wording of the First Amendment, of which the religion phrases constitute the opening statements, confined the inherent prohibitions against governmental action to the *federal* government. This made particular sense in the case of religion, for at the time of the adoption of the Constitution of the United States many of the original thirteen *states* had specific religious establishments or other restrictive provisos. In fact, in the earliest days of the fledgling nation only Virginia, led by Jefferson, Madison, and Mason, and Rhode Island conceded full, unqualified freedom, and New York *almost* did.[14] Two states, Delaware and Maryland, demanded Christianity, Delaware also insisting on assent to the doctrine of the Trinity; four, Delaware, North Carolina, Pennsylvania, and South Carolina, called for assent to the divine inspiration of the Bible, with Pennsylvania and South Carolina further requiring a belief in heaven and hell, and South Carolina—the only one among the thirteen—still speaking of religious "toleration"; three, Maryland, New York, and South Carolina excluded all ministers, even Protestants, from any civil office; five, Connecticut, Maryland, Massachusetts, New Hampshire, and South Carolina insisted on "Protestantism," or "Christian Protestantism"; and six, Connecticut, Georgia, New Hampshire, New Jersey, North Carolina, and South Carolina, specifically adhered to religious establishments (Protestant).[15] Hence it is not surprising that the First Amendment was widely regarded as a protection of state establishments *against* congressional action. By 1833, however, following the capitulation of the Congregationalists in Massachusetts, the fundamental concepts of freedom of religion had, to all

[11] *Ibid.,* n. 11.

[12] In this connection see the problem of the draft and conscientious objectors, discussed on pp. 226 ff., *infra*.

[13] *Schowgurow v. State,* 240 Md. 121 (1965).

[14] In addition to barring ministers from public office, New York required naturalized citizens to abjure allegiance in all foreign ecclesiastical as well as civil matters.

[15] See Stokes and Pfeffer, *op. cit.,* Ch. 3, for a full account.

intents and purposes, become a recognized fact and facet of public law, with only minor aberrations, throughout the young United States of America.

It was thus but a matter of time for religious freedom and its attendant safeguards for the separation between Church and State to become binding under our Constitution *de jure* as well as *de facto*. As the "incorporation," "absorption," or "nationalization" of the Bill of Rights guarantees achieved judicial recognition, beginning with the Sanford opinion in *Gitlow v. New York*[16] in 1925, it was but a question of time until the Court would address itself to religion. And so it did, first to the free exercise of religion in 1934 and 1940,[17] then to the separation of Church and State in 1947.[18]

3. *The Two Aspects of the Religion Clause.* One of the difficulties in the interpretation of the religion clause is that its language speaks of both the "establishment" *and* the "free exercise" of religion. Certainly the two clauses are interrelated, but they are also separable.[19] The author of the First Amendment, usually regarded as Madison, even separated the two by a comma: "Congress shall make no law respecting an establishment of religion, or prohibiting the free exercise thereof. . . ." When the Supreme Court first undertook to "nationalize" the religion clauses in the *Hamilton* case[20] in 1934, Mr. Justice Butler's opinion confined itself to Albert Hamilton's claim of free exercise; the matter of "establishment" or separation of Church and State was not properly at issue. Nor did it play a meaningful role in the next great freedom of religion case to be decided by the Supreme Court six years later, *Cantwell v. Connecticut*,[21] which elaborated upon the *Hamilton*[22] rationale. It was not until the *New Jersey Bus* case,[23] seven years after *Cantwell*, that the Court, speaking through Mr. Justice Black, held that the First Amendment's prohibition against legislation respecting an establishment of religion is also applicable to the

[16] 268 U.S. 252. See Chapter III, *supra*.

[17] *Hamilton v. Regents of University of California*, 293 U.S. 245 (1934); and *Cantwell v. Connecticut*, 310 U.S. 296 (1940).

[18] *Everson v. Board of Education*, 330 U.S. 1.

[19] This is not to say that commentators and students have not at times been puzzled both as to the choice determined by the judiciary in specific cases and as to the viability of a distinction in others. Illustrative of the problem is the challenge brought in 1974 by four Roman Catholic students and priests against the University of Delaware's ban against religious services on its property. The University argued—ultimately unsuccessfully—that the establishment clause compelled it to ban such services; the students and priests argued that the free exercise clause entitled them to hold such services. The Delaware courts upheld the latter's claim and the U.S. Supreme Court declined to review the case, thereby leaving the state's judgment in force. (*University of Delaware v. Keegan*, 424 U.S. 934.)

[20] *Hamilton v. Regents of California*, op. cit.

[21] 310 U.S. 296 (1940).

[22] *Ibid.*

[23] *Everson v. Board of Education of Ewing Township*, 330 U.S. 1 (1947).

several states by virtue of the language and obligations of the Fourteenth Amendment. Thus, by 1947, *both* aspects of the religion guarantee had been judicially interpreted to apply to *both* the federal government and the several states of the Union. Far more complicated, however, was the determination of the meaning, range, and extent of the two famous clauses.

ATTEMPTING TO DEFINE "RELIGION"

To state the problem is to see its complications. Yet in a government under law, whatever an individual's personal idea of religion might be, formal definitions have to be ventured. Each individual does, of course, possess the basic right, now one universally guaranteed and protected under our Constitution, to believe what he or she chooses, to worship whom and how he or she pleases, always provided that it does not impermissibly interfere with the right of others. Hence, we have those who believe in nothing; those who believe but doubt; those who believe without questioning; those who worship the Judeo-Christian God in innumerably different ways; those who adhere to Mohammed's creed; those who worship themselves; those who worship a cow or other animals; those who worship several gods—to mention just a few of the remarkable variety of expressions of belief that obtain.

Webster's New Collegiate Dictionary provides the following choices under the heading "religion":

> 1(a): the service or worship of God or the supernatural; (b): commitment or devotion to religious faith or observance; 2: a personal faith or institutionalized system of religious attitudes, beliefs, and practices; 3 (*archaic*): scrupulous conformity; 4: a cause, principle, or system of beliefs held to with ardor and faith.[24]

At best such a definition can offer a broad guideline of a non-binding nature. The same is more or less true of the kind of psychological guideline furnished by such thoughtful commentators as Professor Gordon W. Allport, who wrote that religion encompasses a value that every democrat "must hold: the right of each individual to work out his own philosophy of life, to find his personal niche in creation as best he can."[25] He further elaborated:

> A man's religion is the audacious bid he makes to bind himself to creation and to the Creator. It is his ultimate attempt to enlarge and to complete his own personality by finding the supreme context in which he rightly belongs.[26]

[24] 8th ed. (Springfield, Mass.: G. & C. Merriam Co., 1975), p. 724, col. 1.
[25] Gordon W. Allport, *The Individual and his Religion* (New York: The Macmillan Co., 1962), p. vii.
[26] *Ibid.*, p. 142.

One may agree with Allport's approach to a definition or interpretation—or Alfred North Whitehead's that it is "what each individual does with his own solitariness"[27]—but the authoritative definition *cum* constitutional interpretation had to come from the Supreme Court, acting either upon a congressional definition or within the confines of its common-law responsibilities.

The Supreme Court Defines Religion. The classic Court definition was authored by Mr. Justice Stephen J. Field in an 1890 case in which the Court unanimously upheld[28] a lower court judgment that one Samuel Davis, a Mormon residing in the then Territory of Idaho, should be disqualified as a voter for falsifying his voter's oath "abjuring bigamy or polygamy as a condition to vote" since, as a Mormon, he believed in polygamy. Polygamy, then as now a criminal offense, constituted a disqualification under territorial voting and other statutes. Field wrote for the Court:

> [T]he term "religion" has reference to one's view of his relations to his Creator, and to the obligations they impose of reverence for his being and character, and of obedience to his will. It is often confounded with the cultus or form of worship of a particular sect, but is distinguishable from the latter. . . . With man's relations to his Maker and the obligations he may think they impose, and the manner in which an expression shall be made by him of his belief on those subjects, no interference can be permitted, provided always the laws of society, designed to secure its peace and prosperity, and the morals of its people are not interfered with.[29]

Thus, although giving religion the widest feasible interpretation in terms of individual commitment, Field found that Davis had violated the reservation of the last qualifying clause.

The "C.O." Problem. This Supreme Court definition of religion was most often tested in cases dealing with military exemptions and conscientious objectors. Exemption from the draft and/or combat service for those who oppose war on religious grounds is deeply rooted in American tradition and history—although it was not really formalized until post-Civil War days. Much litigation has attended this problem, frequently involving the Jehovah's Witnesses, who contend that every believing Witness is a "minister" and as such ought to be exempt from military service. Both the Society of Friends (the Quakers) and the Mennonites have made pacifism a dogma. And, of course, there has been a continuous stream of individual

---

[27] "Religion in the Making," in F. C. S. Northrop and Mason W. Gross, eds., *Alfred North Whitehead: An Anthology* (New York: The Macmillan Co., 1953), p. 472.

[28] *Davis v. Beason,* 133 U.S. 333 (1890).

[29] *Ibid.,* at 342.

conscientious objectors, coming chiefly from small Protestant sects but from other faiths as well—a stream that in the 1960s became a formidable river with our lengthy Southeast Asia involvement.[30] Congress has been generous in recognizing *bona fide* conscientious objectors and in exempting these from military service,[31] although it is not at all clear that there exists a *constitutional* rather than a *moral obligation* to exempt conscientious objectors. It is quite possible to argue either—or both—sides of the issue. The two major draft statutes of this century, those of 1917 and 1940, both included exemption provisions. The former exempted from combat only members affiliated with some "well-recognized religious sect or organizations," such as "peace churches" or a "pacifist religious sect" like the Quakers. In 1940, however, Congress discarded *all* sectarian restrictions so that conscientious objectors no longer had to belong to a church or other religious organization, provided their opposition to war was based upon "religious training and belief." Subsequent amendments to the 1940 statute, enacted in 1948 and 1951, expanded the prerogatives; but 1967 saw a distinct retrenchment.[32]

The problem in granting these exemptions has been, and is, the distinction between *bona fide* and not so *bona fide* claims. It is axiomatic in democratic society that men of abiding religious conviction who, either as individuals or as members of pacifist sects, hold creeds and beliefs that proscribe participation in war or related strife should neither be compelled to participate nor be jailed for refusing to do so. Yet, what of those whose objections are not of a clearly identifiable, *bona fide* religious nature, but are probably pre-eminently moral and/or sociological, philosophical, or even political? Where does personal "policy-making" begin? Can it ever be given preference over duly enacted public policy, one that recognizes C.O. status in law, but chooses to establish definite, limiting, guidelines? And, to compound the inherent complexities, what of those whose conscientious objection is limited to a *particular* war, e.g., that in Viet Nam?[33]

[30] In June 1970 alone, for example, 14,440 "C.O." claims were officially filed. (*The New York Times,* July 25, 1970, p. 6*l.*)

[31] A C.O., who first claimed conscientious objector status *after* he received an induction notice when, he asserted, his C.O. views "matured," appealed unsuccessfully for Supreme Court review of his problem in 1967. (*Gearey v. United States,* 389 U.S. 959, *certiorari* denied.)

[32] For an excellent treatment of the subject, although now dated, see Mulford Q. Sibley and Philip E. Jacobs, *Conscription of Conscience: The American State and the Conscientious Objector, 1940–1947* (Ithaca, N.Y.: Cornell University Press, 1952).

[33] This issue faced the Court repeatedly as of the late 1960s, often coupled with a challenge to the *legality* of the undeclared Indo-China involvement. On several occasions, the Court denied review on the "legality" question involving individuals, e.g., twice in 1967, Mr. Justice Douglas dissenting from the denial in *both* cases, Mr. Justice Stewart in the second (*Mitchell v. United States,* 386 U.S. 972 and *Mora v. McNamara,* 389 U.S. 934); and, late in 1970, with the two dissenters joined by

In 1965 the Supreme Court handed down a momentous decision in three cases involving the most recent provisions in the draft law exempting religious objectors from combat training and service. At issue was the restriction established by Congress in 1951 of exemption to "persons who by reason of religious training and belief are conscientiously opposed to any participation in war." The definition spelled out "religious training and belief" as follows:

> Religious training and belief in this connection means an individual belief in a relation to a Supreme Being involving duties superior to those arising from any human relation, but does not include essentially political, sociological or philosophical views, or a merely personal moral code.[34]

Three men were involved in these 1965 *Draft Act* cases,[35] Daniel A. Seeger, Arno S. Jakobson, and Forest B. Peter. Seeger and Jakobson had been convicted by the United States District Court in New York, and Peter by the United States District Court in San Francisco, of refusing to submit to induction. Both New York convictions were reversed by the United States Court of Appeals for the Second Circuit, but the Appeals Court for the Ninth Circuit upheld the Peter conviction. Seeger had told the Selective Service authorities that he was conscientiously opposed to participation in war in any form because of his "religious" belief, but that he preferred to leave open the question of his belief in a Supreme Being rather than answer "yes" or "no." Jakobson asserted that he believed in a Su-

---

Harlan, it refused to entertain a lawsuit by the Commonwealth of Massachusetts which, based on a law it had passed, challenged the President's power to carry on the Viet Nam war without a formal declaration of war (*Massachusetts v. Laird*, 400 U.S. 886). One year and one-and-one-half years later, with only Douglas and Brennan dissenting in both cases, it refused again (*Orlando v. Laird*, 404 U.S. [1971] and *Da Costa v. Laird*, 405 U.S. 979 [1972]). A different effort, basing the appeal on the question of congressional power to appropriate funds for an undeclared war, also failed in 1972, Douglas and Brennan dissenting. (*Sarnoff v. Schultz*, 409 U.S. 929.) And so did a similar one in 1973. (*Attlee v. Richardson*, 411 U.S. 94.) On the matter of conscientious objection to a *particular* war—or, as it may also be styled, *selective* conscientious objection—the Court had a test case before it in 1970, but (a) the issue came up tangentially in connection with the more pressing one of "non-religious conscientious objection" and (b) a majority of 5:3 held that the case had been improperly appealed to it from the District Court below (*United States v. Sisson*, 399 U.S. 267, an 83-page decision). To make clear that it was not engaging in an artful evasion—something of which it is eminently capable, and often for excellent reasons—the Court granted two appeals by selective conscientious objectors, of which it disposed in March 1971 (*Gillette v. United States* and *Negre v. Larson*, 401 U.S. 437). See pp. 233 ff., *infra*.

[34] 50 App. U.S.C.A., §456 (j) (1951).

[35] *United States v. Seeger*, 380 U.S. 163 (1965). For a complete case study of *Seeger* (from start to conclusion), see Clyde E. Jacobs and John F. Gallagher, *The Selective Service Act: A Case Study of the Governmental Process* (New York: Dodd, Mead & Co., 1967), pp. 138–89.

preme Being who was "Creator of Man," in the sense of being "ultimately responsible for the existence of" man, and who was the "Supreme Reality" of which "the existence of man is the result." Peter said the source of his conviction was "our democratic American culture, with its values derived from the Western religious and philosophical tradition." As to his belief in a Supreme Being, Peter added that he supposed "you could call that a belief in the Supreme Being or God. These just do not happen to be the words I use."[36]

In affirming the reversals by the Second Circuit Court of Appeals and in reversing the decision of that of the Ninth Circuit, the United States Supreme Court, while sidestepping constitutional questions, clearly broadened construction of the statutory provision quoted above. The test of belief "in a relation to a Supreme Being," the Court held, is whether a sincere and meaningful belief which occupies in the life of its possessor, a place *parallel* to that filled by the God of those admittedly qualifying for the exemption comes within the statutory definition.[37] Applying this liberalizing test, the Court ruled that the beliefs expressed by the three men involved in the cases before it consequently entitled them to the exemption. Thus they created a new definition of the concept of religion under the Constitution, at least for pertinent statutory purposes. However, the Court, in a unanimous opinion written by its foremost religious layman, Mr. Justice Clark, added:

> We also pause to take note of what is not involved in this litigation. No party claims to be an atheist or attacks the statute on this ground. The question is not, therefore, one between theistic and atheistic beliefs. We do not deal with or intimate any decision on the situation in this case.[38]

Indeed, the Clark opinion and a concurring one by Mr. Justice Douglas read like a short course in theology, as *The New York Times* commented on the morning after.[39] The majority opinion quoted Paul Tillich, the Bishop of Woolwich, John A. T. Robinson, and the schema of the most recent Ecumenical Council at the Vatican to prove, as Clark put it, the "broad spectrum of religious beliefs found among us." These quotations, the opinion went on,

> demonstrate very clearly the diverse manners in which beliefs, equally paramount in the lives of their possessors may be articulated. They further reveal the difficulties inherent in placing too narrow a construction on the provisions [of the particular sections of the Draft Act here at issue] and

[36] *United States v. Seeger, op. cit.,* at 165.
[37] *Ibid.,* at 176.
[38] *Ibid.,* at 173.
[39] March 9, 1965, p. 43*l.*

thereby lend conclusive support to the [broad] construction which we today find that Congress intended.[40]

Other than from Congress and the executive branch, there was astonishingly little criticism of this dramatic decision that recognized "a sincere and meaningful belief" as occupying a place "parallel to a belief in God." This abstemiousness differed markedly from the reaction which had greeted (if that is the word!) the Court's memorable decision in the *New York Prayer* case[41] and the *Bible Reading* cases[42] a few years before. What the 1965 *Draft Act* cases proved conclusively is that there is less certainty in, and less emphasis on, a strictly construed traditional definition of religion. Instead, and without getting into the matter of distinctions between theistic and atheistic creeds and dogmas, a unanimous Supreme Court adopted broadened concepts of religious liberty and conscience by declaring that a conscientious objector need not believe in the orthodox concept of a Supreme Being. A "religious motivation," however vague or existential, was apparently still required, nonetheless.

On the other hand, neither the Administration nor Congress was happy with the *Seeger* decision, especially not the House of Representatives, where the powerful, hawkish L. Mendel Rivers (D.–S.C.), then the chairman of the House Armed Services Committee, was livid with rage, and threatened immediate revenge. At first, he attempted to push through Congress a revised version of the 1951 C.O. provisions, which would have mandated the presence of a belief in an "organized" (and presumably "recognized") religion before an individual could qualify as "a *bona fide* C.O." When his move failed, he proposed a new version of the 1951 language, which became law in 1967. Rivers was aided by his Senate counterpart, Chairman John Stennis (D.–Miss.) as well as a general wave of resentment against eligible draftees because of the spate of draft-card burnings. The 1967 provision—coded as Section 6(j)—reads: *"Religious training and belief does not include essentially political, sociological or philosophical views, or a merely personal moral code."* A quick comparison with the 1951 language of the provision (cf. p. 274, *supra*) will show that the term "Supreme Being" was deleted from the 1967 draft law amendment, and with it the Supreme Court's generous interpretation of the term in the *Seeger* case. Or at least so Representative Rivers and his supporters thought. But it was a short-lived triumph. The warnings voiced by a sizable number of Mr. Rivers's colleagues, that Congress was about to create a troublesome constitutional *cul de sac*,[43] proved to be prophetic. In 1969

[40] *United States v. Seeger, op. cit.,* at 183.

[41] *Engel v. Vitale,* 370 U.S. 421 (1962).

[42] *Abington School District v. Schempp* and *Murray v. Curlett,* 374 U.S. 203 (1963).

[43] Fred P. Graham, "Again the Tough Issue of the C.O.," *The New York Times,* April 6. 1969, Sec. 4, p. 10.

and 1970 three different United States District Courts ruled the new provision unconstitutional, on a veritable smorgasbord of grounds, as violative of the establishment clause of the First Amendment and of its free-exercise clause; of the due-process-of-law clause of the Fifth Amendment; even of the equal-protection-of-the-laws clause of the Fourteenth Amendment, which is not applicable to the federal government.[44] The lead case came from Judge Charles E. Wyzanski's tribunal in Boston: *United States v. Sisson*,[45] alluded to earlier, concerned the refusal of one John H. Sisson, a "selective" Viet Nam war objector, to be inducted into the armed forces. The colorful trial judge ruled that Sisson could not "constitutionally be subjected to military orders which may require him to kill in the Vietnam conflict." A jury had found him duly guilty of refusing to submit to induction, but Judge Wyzanski sustained two of Sisson's contentions: (1) a "broad," primarily "free exercise" claim "that no statute can require combat service of a conscientous objector whose principles are either religious *or akin thereto*"; and (2) a "narrower" assertion concerning separation of Church and State, that "the 1967 draft act [section 6 (j)] invalidly discriminates in favor of certain types of religious objectors to the prejudice of *Sisson*."[46] Heavily relying on the Clark opinion in *Seeger*, Wyzanski concluded:

> In short, in the draft act Congress unconstitutionally discriminated against atheists, agnostics, and men, like Sisson, who, whether they be religious or not, are motivated in their objection to the draft by profound moral beliefs which constitute central convictions of their beings.[47]

The Supreme Court, for technical and procedural reasons, would not then deal with the key *Sisson* issue on its merits, but it did docket two cases on the "selective" conscientious objection problem,[48] *and* it did come to grips with at least some of the aspects of the basic "religious" problem in its 1970 decision in the case of *Welsh v. United States*.[49]

Elliott A. Welsh, II, a 28-year-old Los Angeles commodities broker, had applied for draft exemption on C.O. grounds in 1964. In filling out the special form he took pains to cross out the words "religious training"—partly to demonstrate that he was opposed to war on broader historical, philosophical, and sociological grounds. His application was denied all along the line for want of proof of a "religious basis" for his beliefs; he refused induction; and he was sentenced to a three-year prison term. By a

---

[44] *United States v. Sisson*, 297 F. Supp. 902 (D. Mass. 1969); *Koster v. Sharp*, 303 F. Supp. 836 (E.D. Pa. 1969); and *United States v. McFadden*, 309 F. Supp. 502 N.D. Cal. 1970).

[45] See pp. 227–28, footnote 33, *supra*, for *United States v. Sisson*.

[46] *Ibid.*, at 906. (Italics supplied.)

[47] *Ibid.*, at 911.

[48] See pp. 233–35, *infra*.

[49] 398 U.S. 333.

vote of 5:3, with Mr. Justice Black—a captain in the Army in World War
I—writing for four of the five justices on the majority side, the Court re-
versed his conviction. Mr. Justice White—a lieutenant commander in the
Navy in World War II—dissented sharply, joined by Mr. Chief Justice
Burger, and Mr. Justice Stewart—another naval officer in World War II.
The Black opinion, which was joined by Justices Douglas—a private in the
Army in World War I—Brennan—an Army colonel in World War II—and
Marshall, was based on a broad and generous construction of the *Seeger*
rationale of five years earlier. Welsh's conviction, wrote Black, was inconsistent with the *Seeger* holding. He admitted that the draft law bars exemption based on "essentially political, sociological or philosophical views, or
a merely personal moral code"—but he suggested that such views can
readily be held so firmly as to be "religious" within the meaning of the
law. According to Black's interpretation, then, the draft law actually
exempts "all those whose consciences, spurred by deeply held moral, ethical or religious beliefs, *would give them no rest or peace* if they allowed
themselves to become a part of an instrument of war."[50] In view of the
explicit religious terminology in the crucial section 6(j) of the statute, one
might be pardoned for blinking a bit—and the three dissenters did more
than blink. "Saving #6(j) by extending it to include *Welsh* cannot be done
in the name of a presumed congressional will but only by the Court's taking upon itself the power to make draft-exemption policy,"[51] wrote Mr.
Justice White.

To the majority, however, the key element had become Welsh's docu-
mented assertion that he believed "the taking of life—anyone's life—to be
morally wrong." Because he held this belief "with the strength of more
traditional religious convictions," he was, in the considered judgment of
the four members joining in the Court's majority opinion, entitled to
exemption under the statute. Mr. Justice Harlan—an Air Force colonel
during World War II—wrote his own concurrence, agreeing that Welsh
was entitled to exemption, but for a dramatically different reason. In retrospect unhappy with the *Seeger* construction—although he had concurred in
that decision, too—Harlan was even more unhappy with its expanded construction here. He now wanted to reach the constitutional question and,
addressing it, urged that to deny Welsh an exemption *would show favorit-
ism to religion* as opposed to non-religion, and thus violate the First
Amendment's ban against governmental "establishment of religion."[52]
This, of course, raises again the fascinating *quaere* of whether Congress

---

[50] *Ibid.,* at 344. (Italics supplied.) In 1973, with Justice Douglas and Stewart dissenting, the Court declined to consider applying the decision retroactively. (*Avery v.
United States,* 414 U.S. 922.)

[51] *Ibid.,* at 369.

[52] *Ibid.,* at 357.

could be *compelled* to grant C.O. exemptions under the "free exercise" (conscience?) clause of the First Amendment in the face of the Harlan assumption—one held by many others—that to do so would constitute a violation of its "establishment" clause. White, in his dissent, while acknowledging that Congress could not be *compelled* to grant exemption on religious grounds, contended that it certainly could legislate to recognize free exercise values—thus rejecting the Harlan posture on establishment. Given *that* dilemma, the Black solution may well be the most viable suggestion for a usable line, after all. Yet to apply that line equitably throughout the land presented a dilemma—as the Selective Service Director, Dr. Curtis Tarr, made clear, while valiantly attempting to issue guidelines to his 4,101 local draft boards.[53] There was much sympathy with his, and Congress's, unhappiness with the Welsh decision; but there was also much agreement with James Reston's poignant observation that, while recognizing the existence of what amounts to a "privileged sanctuary of conscience," there is

> something reassuring philosophically about the Supreme Court's support of ethical as distinguished from religious opposition to the war, something even exciting and ennobling about the American system that struggles with life's great imponderables.[54]

Those who were unhappy with *Welsh* would soon find themselves somewhat, if not totally, mollified, and those who were happy with *Welsh* would soon be somewhat, if not totally, disappointed in the face of the Court's momentous early 1971 decision in two cases that clearly raised the issue of "selective" conscientious objection. In other words, did the congressional, and judicially interpreted, provision for conscientious objection permit objection to only *some* wars, to "unjust" rather than "just" wars, to the Viet Nam rather than some other past, present, or future wars? The Court responded "No!" without equivocation, in a joint 8:1 decision in *Gillette v. United States* and *Negre v. Larsen*.[55] Speaking for all members of the Court except the dissenting Mr. Justice Douglas, Mr. Justice Marshall held that Congress acted constitutionally when it ruled out "selective" conscientious objection by authorizing exemptions only for those men who were "conscientiously opposed to participation in war in *any*

[53] The primary criterion for a C.O. henceforth, he told the boards, would be whether his beliefs were "sincere and deeply held," and not whether they were "comprehensible" to board members. A man must hold his "beliefs with the strength of traditional religious conviction," he wrote and he must "demonstrate that his ethical or moral convictions were gained through training, study, contemplation or other activity, comparable in rigor and dedication to the processes by which traditional religious convictions are formulated." (*The New York Times,* July 6, 1970, p. 1*l*.)

[54] *Ibid.,* June 21, 1970, p. 16e.

[55] 401 U.S. 437 (1971).

form," that the statutory provisions at issue did not unconstitutionally favor religious denominations that teach total pacifism and did not infringe upon the freedom of religion of those who believe that only "unjust" wars must be opposed. Declaring that the "affirmative purposes underlying §6(j) are neutral and secular"; that the rule against conscientious objection was "essentially neutral" in its treatment of various religious faiths— that there were ample "neutral, secular reasons to justify the line that Congress has drawn"—and that any "incidental burdens" felt by particular draftees were justified by "the Government's interest in procuring the manpower necessary for military purposes."[56] Marshall thus rejected both the free exercise of religion and the separation of state and church claims lodged by the appellants. Douglas, on the other hand, saw a violation of both, especially of the former, and observed wistfully: "I had assumed that the welfare of a single human soul was the ultimate test of the vitality of the First Amendment."[57]

The government had readily conceded that Guy Porter Gillette and Louis A. Negre were sincere in their conscientious objection to the Viet Nam war, but it insisted that they did not qualify for the C.O. exemption created by Congress because *they said that they did not oppose all wars.* Gillette, a rock musician, had told his draft board in Yonkers, New York, that his belief in the religion of humanism prevented him from serving in the military during the Viet Nam war, which he considered unjust. The board denied him C.O. status because he frankly conceded that he would fight in defense of the United States or in a peace-keeping effort by the United Nations; he was convicted and given a two-year jail sentence for refusing to report for induction. Negre, a Bakersfield, California, gardener, a devout French-born Roman Catholic, who had studied the writings of St. Thomas Aquinas and other Catholic theologians who taught that "unjust" but not "just" wars should be opposed, had been drafted and had not reported for duty. However, when he was subsequently compelled to do so, he applied for a C.O. discharge; he was turned down, although the Army granted that his objections to the Viet Nam conflict were indeed sincere. The lower courts concurred and Negre found himself transferred to Viet Nam, where he began his quest for release.

Here, then—unlike the widespread protests that accompanied the successful draft-evasion-conviction-appeal by Cassius Clay, *alias* World Heavyweight Boxing Champion Muhammed Ali[58]—no one deemed questionable or "phony" the allegations or motivations of the two men involved, for they were obviously sincere in their opposition to the Viet Nam conflict

---

56 *Ibid.*, at 462.
57 *Ibid.*, at 469.
58 *Clay v. United States*, 403 U.S. 698 (1971). That opinion, rendered *per curiam* (probably authored by Mr. Justice Stewart) relied heavily on a procedural aberration by the Department of Justice in its prosecution.

per se. But could they claim C.O. status under Section 6(j) of the Military Selective Service Act of 1967? In its firmly negative response, the eight-man majority dwelt at length on the government's assertions that its military capacity might be paralyzed if selective conscientious objection were recognized as a constitutional right. Mr. Justice Marshall pointed out that, among other touchy tasks connected with any such recognition, draft boards would be saddled with that of divining which draftees were sincere and which were having convenient attacks of selective conscience, inviting the very "real danger of erratic or even discriminatory decision-making in administrative practice."[59] Moreover, he opined, the nature of an unpopular war might change so that those who once considered it unjust would—or should—change their minds. It would be difficult to fault the logic of these basic contentions. Policy making by individual draftees would create a chaotic situation: the Court-defined C.O. line, which Congress reluctantly accepted but soon made the law of the land, seems to be the most generous and most liberal obtainable in the light of our democratic society's constitutional fundamentals.[60]

The Free Exercise of Religion

"Free exercise" brackets freedom of religious belief *and* freedom of religious action; it is linked closely with those other bastions of the First Amendment, freedom of speech, of the press, of assembly, and of petition. Indeed, any reading of the religion clause guarantee of the First Amendment that does not consider its dependence upon the other four guarantees spelled out in that provision of the Bill of Rights, and now carried over to the states via the Fourteenth Amendment, does a disservice to constitutional analysis and interpretation. The interrelationship is as real as it is significant.

A BASIC DILEMMA

The very language of the "free exercise" segment of the religion phrase poses a dilemma. It clearly militates against any governmental action "pro-

---

[59] *Op. cit.,* at 462–3.

[60] That line *has* other limits, of course. Thus, in an 8:1 opinion, written by Mr. Justice Brennan in 1976, the Court rejected free exercise and due process appeals by an "alternate service" C.O. that he was entitled to "G.I. Bill" educational benefits, despite congressional statutory exclusion therefrom. (*Johnson v. Robison,* 415 U.S. 361, with Douglas in lone dissent.) Nor, again 8:1, Douglas once more the only dissenter, can an employer withhold a lower rate from the income taxes due from C.O.s who object to supporting the defense budget. (*United States v. American Friends Service Committee,* 419 U.S. 7 [1974].) For a generally sympathetic analysis of selective conscientious objection, see Martin S. Sheffer, "The Free Exercise of Religion and Selective Conscientious Objection: A Judicial Response to a Moral Problem," 9 *Capital University Law Review* 6–29 (1979). For an even more supportive one, see Walter S. Griggs, Jr., "The Selective Conscientious Objector: A Vietnam Legacy," 21 *Journal of Church and State* 1 (Winter 1979).

hibiting the free exercise thereof." Unquestionably, the phrase is designed to mean what it says: Congress—and by interpretation the states—may not interfere with the sacred rights of freedom of religious "belief" and "exercise." But, as Mr. Justice Roberts pointed out in his opinion for a unanimous Court in the 1940 *Cantwell* case, while "freedom of exercise" embraces both the freedom to *believe* and the freedom to *act,* "the first is absolute but, in the nature of things, the second cannot be. *Conduct* remains subject to [governmental] regulation for the protection of society. The freedom to act must have appropriate definition to preserve the enforcement of that protection."[61]

In every case, Roberts continued, "the power to regulate must be so exercised as not, in attaining a permissible end, unduly to infringe the protected freedom."[62] This, of course, raises as many *practical* questions as it settles. But the general line is at least perceivable in *Cantwell,* and it remains a landmark chiefly for three reasons: it embraces the dual aspects of "belief" and "action"; it reaffirms the absorption or incorporation of the freedom of religion guarantees into the Fourteenth Amendment; and it emphasizes the close link of the free exercise of religion with the other freedoms spelled out in the First Amendment.

The Jehovah's Witnesses. The *Cantwell* case was the first freedom of religion case involving the Jehovah's Witnesses to be decided by the United States Supreme Court. Actually, the initial litigation concerning that fundamentalist sect had come two years earlier, but it was decided in reference to the freedom of speech and press rather than those of the freedom of religion.[63] The Jehovah's Witnesses have won over 90 per cent of the host of significant First and Fourteenth Amendment cases which have come before the Court since the mid-1930s—their success due in considerable measure to the talents of their long-time chief legal counsel, Hayden C. Covington.[64] A dedicated sect of approximately 1,250,000 members throughout the world who believe that Armageddon is imminent, their creed is based on what they regard as utter obedience to the Bible. They accept the Biblical prophecy that Satan will be defeated in the cataclysm of Armageddon, followed by eternal life for the righteous. Their movement began in 1872, largely as the result of the efforts of Charles Taze Russell, a Pittsburgh merchant, who had become disenchanted with his Congrega-

---

[61] *Cantwell v. Connecticut,* 310 U.S. 296 (1940), at 303. (Italics supplied.)

[62] *Ibid.,* at 304.

[63] *Lovell v. Griffin,* 303 U.S. 444 (1938). The next Jehovah's Witnesses case, also decided under the freedom of speech and press guarantees, was *Schneider v. Irvington, New Jersey,* 308 U.S. 137 (1939)—one year prior to *Cantwell,* which was thus the third Supreme Court case involving the Witnesses.

[64] He was also Cassius Clay's—Muhammad Ali's—attorney in his aforementioned, eventually successful battle to attain ministerial exemption as a Muslim. When apprised of his 8:0 *per curiam* victory in the Supreme Court, Ali told reporters that he "thanked Allah." (*The Philadelphia Evening Bulletin,* June 28, 1971, p. 1.)

tionalist Church. Russell began to preach the Adventist doctrine that the imminent second coming of Christ will trigger Armageddon, which he finally pegged at 1914. With a rapidly increasing following, Russell incorporated in 1884 the Watch Tower Bible and Tract Society, now generally known as the Jehovah's Witnesses ("Ye are my Witnesses, saith Jehovah," Isaiah 43:10). They deem Abel the first Witness, Christ the Chief Witness, and themselves direct descendants, from whose ranks Jehovah will select 144,000 members who will reign in heaven after Armageddon.

An impressively organized hierarchy with totalitarian overtones, the Witnesses—who shun all political activity, even voting—are fiercely evangelistic, and publicly so. Although inevitably polite, they persistently solicit and proselytize, push their two journals, *Awake!* and the *Watchtower*, and, if given permission, play their gramophone or tape recordings. To the Witnesses, the chief villains on earth are the leaders of organized religion in general, and the Roman Catholic Church in particular: the Witnesses' notorious gramophone record "Enemies" characterizes the Roman Catholic Church as "a great racket." It is no wonder then, that they often find themselves in considerable litigation involving such matters as leaflet distribution, local and state censorship ordinances, parade permits, flag salutes, license taxes, conscientious objection to the draft (indeed, they insist that, as "ministers," they are *all* entitled to military deferments so that they may go about their primary task of proclaiming the impending Kingdom), public meetings, and blood transfusion requirements.[65] The United States Reports for the past five decades list some fifty cases involving the Witnesses in one or more of the above problems. *Cantwell v. Connecticut*[66] was *not* one of the very few they lost.

Cantwell v. Connecticut. Newton Cantwell and his two teen-aged sons, Jesse and Russell, approached three pedestrians on Cassius Street in New Haven, an area whose inhabitants were 90 per cent Roman Catholic, and asked their permission to play them a record on their portable phonograph. Obtaining that permission, the Cantwells put on "Enemies." One portion of the record stated in particular that the Roman Catholic Church was an instrument of Satan that had for fifteen hundred years brought untold sorrow and sufferings upon mankind by means of deception and fraud. The three listeners were, according to their own testimony, "rather tempted

---

[65] See, *inter alia, Minersville, School District v. Gobitis*, 310 U.S. 596 (1940); *Cox v. New Hampshire*, 312 U.S. 569 (1941); *Martin v. Struthers*, 319 U.S. 141 (1943); *Jones v. Opelika*, 316 U.S. 584 (1942); *Prince v. Massachusetts*, 321 U.S. 158 (1944); *Marsh v. Alabama*, 326 U.S. 501 (1946); *Niemotko v. Maryland*, 340 U.S. 268 (1951); *Jehovah's Witnesses in the State of Washington v. King County Hospital*, 390 U.S. 598 (1968); *Wooley v. Maynard*, 430 U.S. 705 (1977); *Palmer v. Board*, 444 U.S. 1026 (1980); and many others. The listing here is designed merely to be representative, not exhaustive.

[66] 310 U.S. 296 (1940).

to strike the Cantwells," but confined themselves to an exhortation to "shut the damn thing off and get moving"—which the Cantwells did forthwith. No violence of any kind occurred, nor was it alleged. Nonetheless, the Cantwells were arrested, indicted, charged with, and convicted of two separate violations of Connecticut law.

One count of a five-count indictment charged them with soliciting funds and subscriptions for the Witnesses' cause without obtaining in advance— as required by a 1917 statute—a "certificate of approval" from the Secretary of the Connecticut Public Welfare Council, who was specifically empowered to determine, again in advance, whether the cause was either a "religious" one or one of a *"bona fide* object of charity." The second charge against the Cantwells was a breach of the peace, based on their stopping pedestrians on New Haven's public streets and asking them for permission to play the described phonograph record. The Cantwells appealed their convictions to the United States Supreme Court on both substantive and procedural grounds, alleging infringement of freedom of religion rights under both the First and Fourteenth Amendments on the first (substantive) count and violations of the Fourteenth Amendment alone on the second (procedural) ground. Agreeing, the Court reversed the convictions unanimously as constituting unconstitutional violations of the free exericse of religion, Mr. Justice Roberts authoring the opinion. It provided the Court with the opportunity to comment upon and endeavor to explain the difficulties of drawing the line between freedom of religious belief and proscribable action in the realm of the free exercise of religion.

Roberts emphasized that there can be no doubt that a state has the right to guard against breaches of the peace and thus punish those who would incite, or be guilty of, such breaches—even as a result of religious motivations or considerations. Yet just because an individual, in his religious fervor, resorts to exaggeration and even vilification, thereby arousing public anger and ill will, does not *per se* render him liable to punishment unless there is a demonstrably clear and present danger to public peace. In the instance of the Cantwells there was no such danger or menace: no assault took place; there was no intentional discourtesy, no threatening bearing, no personal abuse—their arrest was patently unconstitutional. The Connecticut statute, which gave such broad prior censorship powers to an official of Connecticut's government, was held to constitute on its face an impermissible infraction of free exercise of religion guaranteed by the First Amendment, as absorbed by the Fourteenth. The Court ruled that for religious groups such as the Jehovah's Witnesses, Connecticut's requirement, as applied here, represented a "censorship of religion as a means of determining its right to survive"—a clear violation of the basic guarantee. Roberts took pains to acknowledge that nothing he had said for the Court was "intended even remotely to imply that, under the cloak of religion, persons may, with impunity, commit frauds upon the public." Endeavoring to establish a viable line, he observed that, certainly, penal laws are properly available to punish such proscribed conduct, and emphasized that even the exercise of religion may be at some slight inconvenience in order that the State may protect it citizens from injury:

> Without doubt a State may protect its citizens from fraudulent solicitation by requiring a stranger in the community, before permitting him to solicit funds for any purpose, to establish his identity and his authority for the cause which he purports to represent. The State is likewise free to regulate the time and manner of solicitation generally, in the interest of public safety, peace, comfort or convenience. But to condition the solicitation of aid for the perpetuation of religious views or systems upon a license, the grant of which rests in the exercise of a determination by state authority as to what is a religious cause, is to lay a forbidden burden upon the exercise of liberty protected by the Constitution.[67]

The Cantwells had thus won an important victory not only for themselves, but for the cause of religious liberty.

The Flag Salute Cases. But two weeks later, the next case to involve the Jehovah's Witnesses did not augur well in its decision for a continuing generous interpretation of the religious liberty clause. As a condition of attending the public schools of Minersville, Pennsylvania (population 10,000), *all* children were required to salute the national flag as part of a daily school exercise. Twelve-year-old Lillian Gobitis and her brother William, aged ten, children of Walter Gobitis, a member of the Jehovah's Witnesses, were expelled from the public schools for refusing to comply. To them, any compliance with such a requirement would have been tantamount to paying homage to a graven image—a mortal sin under the precepts of the Witnesses.[68] For a while Walter Gobitis bore the burden of sending them to private schools that did not mandate the flag salute. Unable to sustain that expense, however, and seeing three more of his children expelled from public school, Gobitis sued to enjoin the public authorities from continuing to

---

[67] *Ibid.,* at 306.

[68] The daily ceremony, in which all teachers as well as students participated, was a familiar one, with the following pledge recited in unison; "I pledge allegiance to my flag, and to the Republic for which it stands; one nation indivisible, with liberty and justice for all." While the words were spoken, teachers and pupils extended their right hands chest high in salute to the flag. In a letter to Superintendent of Schools Charles E. Rondabush, Lillian explained her three reasons for not saluting the flag: "1. The Lord clearly says in Exodus 20:3, 5 that you should have no gods besides Him and that we should serve Him. 2. The Constitution of [the] United States is based upon religious freedom. According to the dictates of my conscience, based on the Bible, I must give full allegiance to Jehovah God. 3. Jehovah my God and the Bible is my creed. I try my best to obey the Creator." William wrote a similar letter. (*Minersville School District v. Gobitis,* 310 U.S. 586 [1940], at 592.)

exact participation of Lillian and William in the daily flag salute ceremony as a condition of their public school attendance. To his surprise and gratification, the United States District Court in Philadelphia granted his plea on the grounds that the expulsions violated the First, and through it the Fourteenth, Amendment's guarantees of religious liberty! Now it was the Minersville School District's turn to appeal, and it did so, first to the Circuit Court of Appeals, which sustained the District Court, and then to the Supreme Court which granted *certiorari.* The nation awaited its decision with considerable interest; both the Committee on the Bill of Rights of the American Bar Association and the American Civil Liberties Union had sought, and been granted, permission to enter the case in behalf of the Witnesses as *amici curiae.*

But to the astonishment of many—including some of those who consider themselves experts on the Court and its personnel—the Court *reversed* the judgment below and upheld the Minersville flag salute requirements by a resounding 8:1 vote.[69] Delivering the Court's opinion, Mr. Justice Frankfurter contended that religious liberty does not exempt citizens from obedience to general laws applicable to all and not designed to restrict religious beliefs as such. Explaining that "we live by symbols," Frankfurter—Vienna-born, who came to the United States at the age of twelve—exhorted the country that the "flag is the symbol of our national unity, transcending all internal differences, however large, within the framework of the Constitution."[70] He rejected the plea that the Gobitis children should be excused from "conduct required of all other children in the promotion of national cohesion," adding that "we are dealing with an interest inferior to none in the hierarchy of legal values. National unity is the basis of national security. . . ."[71] Frankfurter acknowledged that many might well doubt the effectiveness of the compulsory flag salute in the promotion of national unity and loyalty, but he insisted—characteristically for one so committed to the doctrine of judicial self-restraint—that, lest the Supreme Court become "the school board of the country,"[72] this was a decision to be made by the elected school officials against the backdrop of the basic "legislative judgment." He continued: "But to the legislature no less than to the courts is committed the guardianship of deeply-cherished liberties."[73] Joining the Frankfurter opinion were Mr. Chief Justice Hughes, Associate Justices McReynolds, Roberts, Reed, and—amazingly—Associate Justices Black, Douglas, and Murphy, whom prognosticators confidently expected to side with the sole dissenter, Mr. Justice Stone.

[69] *Minersville School District v. Gobitis,* 310 U.S. 586 (1940). The requirement was administrative, not legislative.

[70] *Ibid.,* at 596.

[71] *Ibid.,* at 595.

[72] *Ibid.,* at 598.

[73] *Ibid.,* at 600. There are many, however, who rest more comfortably in the knowledge that the courts do have the final word on the subject.

Conceding that the personal liberty guarantees under the Constitution are by no means "always absolutes," and that "Government has a right to survive," Stone's dissent nonetheless bitterly assailed the majority's opinion as doing violence to "the very essence of liberty . . . the right of the individual to hold such opinions as he will and to give them reasonably free expression, and his freedom, and that of the state as well, to teach and persuade others by the communication of ideas."[74] He contended that the very essence of the liberty, which the freedom of the human mind and spirit, and the freedom of reasonable opportunity to express them guarantee, is

> the freedom of the individual from compulsion as to what he shall think and what he shall say, at least where the compulsion is to bear false witness to his religion. If these guarantees are to have any meaning they must . . . be deemed to withhold from the state any authority to compel belief or the expression of it where that expression violates religious convictions, whatever may be the legislative view of the desirability of such compulsion.[75]

His noble spirit simply could not see how any inconveniences that might attend what he called "some sensible adustment of school discipline" would present a problem "so momentous or pressing as to outweigh the freedom from compulsory violation of religious faith which has been thought worthy of constitutional protection."[76] He did not have to wait long, however, to witness his reasoning become the majority opinion of the Court and thereby the law of the land!

To attain that constitutional turnabout, some crucial developments took place—all significant elements in the judicial process. One was the retirement of Mr. Chief Justice Hughes in 1941 and his replacement by Attorney-General Robert H. Jackson—although as an Associate Justice, President Roosevelt having seen fit to elevate Mr. Justice Stone to the Chief Justiceship. A closely related denouement was the resignation of Mr. Justice Byrnes late in 1942[77] and his replacement by the one-time dean of the University of Iowa School of Law, Wiley B. Rutledge. On paper, at least, the two new appointees could be expected to be more sympathetic to the Stone point of view than to that of Frankfurter. The third important development was a dramatic announcement by Justices Black, Douglas, and Murphy, who joined in a separate memorandum in a 1942 case[78] that upheld (5:4) the validity of a license tax on bookselling levied upon Jehovah's Witnesses, as well as other activities considered "commercial" by the

[74] *Ibid.*, at 604.
[75] *Ibid.*
[76] *Ibid.*, at 607.
[77] He had replaced Mr. Justice McReynolds who had retired in 1941.
[78] *Jones v. Opelika,* 316 U.S. 584 (1942).

city of Opelika, Alabama. (In 1943, just one year later, that ruling was reversed on rehearing[79] in conjunction with another decision favoring the Witnesses.[80]) Apparently authored by Black, the six-sentence, one-paragraph memorandum—which followed two dissenting opinions[81] on the merits of the case—simply observed, *inter alia,* that "since we joined in the opinion in the *Gobitis* case, we think this is an appropriate occasion to state that *we now believe that it was also wrongly decided.*"[82] The test of these developments came but a few months later in 1943, when the Court overruled the *Gobitis* precedent in a new flag salute case, *West Virginia State Board of Education v. Barnette.*[83]

Following the Court's decision in *Gobitis*[84] three years earlier, the State of West Virginia legislature had amended its statutes to require all of its schools to conduct courses of instruction in history, civics, and both the federal and West Virginia Constitution "for the purpose of teaching, fostering and perpetuating the ideals, principles and spirit of Americanism, and increasing the knowledge of the organization and machinery of government."[85] In 1942, the Board of Education adopted a resolution based largely on *Gobitis,* which ordered the salute to the flag to become "a regular part of the program of activities in the public schools"; that all teachers and pupils "shall be required to participate in the salute honoring the Nation represented by the Flag; provided, however [sic], that refusal to salute the Flag be regarded as an Act of insubordination, and shall be dealt with accordingly."[86] The "accordingly" meant expulsion—with readmission denied by the statute until compliance. Meanwhile, the expelled child was considered "unlawfully absent," was subject to delinquency proceedings, and his parents or guardians were liable to prosecution and punishment by fine and/or imprisonment. Members of the Jehovah's Witnesses like the Gobitis family, Walter Barnette and his relatives, Paul Stull and Mrs. Lucy Barnette McClure, refused to comply and saw their seven

---

[79] *Jones v. Opelika,* 319 U.S. 103 (1943).

[80] *Murdock v. Commonwealth of Pennsylvania,* 319 U.S. 105.

[81] One was written by Mr. Chief Justice Stone, in which Justices Black, Douglas, and Murphy joined; the other was by Murphy, in which Stone, Black, and Douglas concurred.

[82] 316 U.S. 584, at 623. (Italics supplied.) Black elaborated some twenty-five years later in his great *A Constitutional Faith:* "Reluctance to make the federal Constitution a rigid bar against state regulation of *conduct* thought inimical to the public welfare was the controlling influence that caused me to consent to the *Gobitis* decision. Long reflection convinced me that although the principle was sound, its application in the particular case was wrong, and I clearly stated this change of view in a concurring opinion in *Barnette* which Justice Douglas joined. Life itself is change and one who fails to recognize this must indeed be narrow-minded . . ." (New York: Alfred A. Knopf, 1968), p. xv. (Italics supplied.)

[83] 319 U.S. 624 (1943).

[84] 310 U.S. 586 (1940).

[85] *West Virginia State Board of Education v. Barnette, op. cit.,* at 625.

[86] *Ibid.,* at 626.

children expelled from school for "insubordination." The crucial difference between their and the Gobitis's fortunes was that the Barnette families won!

They won because the two new Associate Justices, Jackson and Rutledge, added to the three "mind-changers," Black,[87] Douglas, and Murphy,
and the one steady holdover from the *Gobitis* decision, the now Chief Justice Stone, constituted a new six-man majority! Three *Gobitis* holdovers,
Associate Justices Frankfurter, Reed, and Roberts, continued to cling to
their then majority reasoning in that case. The Barnettes had won a victory
for a liberal construction of the line between the individual's freedom of
conscience and the state's claims for conformance to majority policy in
regard to symbols. It was a significant victory—one that is not likely to be
overturned. And, appropriately enough, it came on Flag Day, June 14,
1943.

It would have been fitting had Mr. Chief Justice Stone assigned the majority opinion to himself, being the only member on that side of the decision who had consistently supported it. Yet he chose Mr. Justice Jackson,[88]
who held that the guarantees of freedom of speech and conscience imply
the freedom *not* to speak and *not* to make any other symbolic expression,
even the saluting of the national flag. Jackson acknowledged that public
officials did naturally have the right to foster national unity and might well
employ a symbolic public ceremony to achieve this, but that they might
not render participation in such ceremonies compulsory. To the dissenters'
contention that, if laws such as those of Pennsylvania and West Virginia
were unwise, the manner to alter or abolish them was not through court
action but through the electoral process—what Mr. Justice Frankfurter, the
author of the dissenting opinion, was later on several occasions[89] to call
the "searing of the legislators' conscience"—Jackson responded that it de-
pended necessarily upon the type of claim involved. In situations like
Barnette, judicial action was not only necessary but essential, because,
"[o]ne's right to life, liberty, and property, to free speech, a free press,
freedom of worship and assembly, and other fundamental rights may not
be submitted to vote; they depend on the outcome of no elections."[90]

The closing paragraphs of the Jackson opinion for the Court contain
language both seminal and magnificent. Stressing the futility of compelling

[87] Black wrote in his concurring opinion: "Words under coercion are proof of
loyalty to nothing but self-interest. Love of country must spring from willing hearts
and free minds." *Ibid.,* at 644. (See p. 242, footnote 82, *supra.*)

[88] See Glendon Schubert, *Dispassionate Justice: A Synthesis of the Opinions of
Robert H. Jackson* (Indianapolis: The Bobbs-Merrill Co., 1969), pp. 1–34.

[89] Particularly on the "political question" in redistricting and reapportionment cases
such as *Colegrove v. Green,* 328 U.S. 549 (1946); note, especially, his last signed
opinion (appropriately in dissent—running to more than sixty pages) in *Baker v.
Carr,* 369 U.S. 186 (1962).

[90] *West Virginia State Board of Education v. Barnette, op. cit.,* at 641.

conformity and coherence in such sacred First Amendment guarantees as the freedom of belief, conscience, and expression, the great stylist warned that "[T]hose who begin coercive elimination of dissent soon find themselves exterminating dissenters. Compulsory unification of opinion achieves only the unanimity of the graveyard." And he concluded memorably: "If there is any fixed star in our constitutional constellation, it is that no official, high or petty, can prescribe what shall be orthodox in politics, nationalism, religion, or other matters of opinion or force citizens to confess by word or act their faith therein."[91]

Predictably, and justly, the dissenting opinion was written by the author of the *Gobitis* majority opinion, Mr. Justice Frankfurter—and it was one of his most important and longest, representing, as it did, his passionate dedication to the creed of judicial self-restraint, the *raison d'être* of his judicial career. Probably quoted only slightly less than the Jackson passages outlined above are the opening passages of Frankfurter's exhortation:

> One who belongs to the most vilified and persecuted minority in history is not likely to be insensible to the freedoms guaranteed by our Constitution. Were my purely personal attitude relevant I should wholeheartedly associate myself with the general libertarian views in the Court's opinion, representing as they do the thought and action of a lifetime. But as judges we are neither Jew nor Gentile, neither Catholic nor agnostic. We owe equal attachment to the Constitution and are equally bound by our judicial obligations whether we derive our citizenship from the earliest or the latest immigrants to these shores. As a member of this Court I am not justified in writing my private notions of policy into the Constitution, no matter how deeply I may cherish them or how mischievous I may deem their disregard. . . . Most unwillingly, therefore, I must differ from my brethren with regard to legislation like this. I cannot bring my mind to believe that the "liberty" secured by the Due Process Clause gives this Court authority to deny to the State of West Virginia the attainment of that which we all recognize as a legitimate legislative end, namely, the promotion of good citizenship, by employment of the means here chosen.[92]

Frankfurter did not prevail, yet some schoolboards have continued to read his dissent as a majority opinion. Thus in 1966, almost a generation later, the New Jersey Supreme Court had to rule unanimously, quoting *Barnette,* that children cannot be suspended from school if they refuse to salute the flag on the grounds of conscientious scruples![93] And in 1973 Mrs. Susan

---

[91] *Ibid.,* at 642.

[92] *Ibid.,* at 646, 647. Associate Justices Roberts and Reed were the other two dissenters in the case. Philip Elman, a law clerk of Frankfurter's, argued vainly against the dissent, but his Justice put his foot down: "This is my opinion, not yours." (As recounted to Israel Shenker, *The New York Times,* October 22, 1977, p. 34.)

[93] *Holden v. Board of Education, Elizabeth,* 46 N.J. 281 (1966). In 1964 Governor Richard J. Hughes had vetoed a compulsory flag salute bill for all school children, enacted by the New Jersey legislature, and other states have attempted similarly unconstitutional evasion and downright violation of *Barnette.*

Russo had to fight all the way to the Supreme Court for reversal of her dismissal as a public school arts teacher, which had come as a result of her refusal to recite the pledge of allegiance to the flag with pupils in her homeroom.[94]

A Catalogue of Line Decisions. So manifold have been the Supreme Court's decisions concerning the free exercise of religion that it is impossible to detail them in the limited space available. But the tables below will at least serve to indicate a pattern—a pattern of demonstrable liberality on the part of the highest tribunal, a liberality based, in large measure, on the kind of basic convictions about individual freedom of conscience so well expressed by Mr. Justice Jackson in his *Barnette* opinion. Table 6.1 illustrates those instances in which the Court held *against* constitutional claims of freedom of religion and thus *in favor* of society's constitutional prerogative to promulgate and enforce the official statutes, ordinances, or practices involved. Table 6.2, in turn, demonstrates those instances in which the highest tribunal held in favor of the individual's contentions *versus* those of the state. Neither table is intended to be, nor could it be, exhaustive; rather, each will simply indicate the kind of values that America has embraced through the instrumentalities of the legislative and judicial processes.

THE DILEMMA COMPOUNDED

Before considering the far more intricate concept of the "establishment" of religion, its close relationship with the "free exercise" aspect may be demonstrated—following the above tabular analysis—by pointing to at least one complex example,[95] namely, the Court's handling of the 1961 *Blue*

[94] The Court based its decision on freedom of speech, however. (*Central School District # 1 v. Russo,* 411 U.S. 932.)

[95] Space does not permit an examination of the tragic problem of drawing lines between the rights of parents and the right of the state, in *loco parentis,* when the parents' faith precludes submittal to medical treatment. It is clearly established in statutory law that parents have the right to determine treatment—of whatever type or kind. Since Christian Science practice, for example, *is* legal in every state of the Union, such parents have the right to determine the nature of the medical care, if any, their children who are minors are to receive. What then if a Christian Science child dies as a result of the parents' deliberate decision not to submit the child to orthodox medical treatment? For a pertinent illustration, see the case of *Commonwealth of Pennsylvania v. Cornelius, Philadelphia County* (*Pennsylvania*) Quarter Sessions, April Term, #105 (1956), which was *nolle prossed* at the request of the then district attorney, Victor H. Blanc. Numerous other examples could be readily cited, of course, involving particularly Jehovah's Witnesses and Seventh Day Adventists who have frequently refused—with varying degrees of success—to submit to such standard medical practices and/or legal requirements as blood transfusions or compulsory smallpox vaccinations. For a case involving the latter, see *Jacobson v. Massachusetts,* 197 U.S. 11 (1905). For one dealing with a Christian Scientist's successful refusal to take tranquilizers, see *Winter v. Miller,* 404 U.S. 985 (1971), *certiorari* denied. See also the fascinating case of *Karen Ann Quinlan,* in which the New Jersey Supreme Court ultimately ruled unanimously that the mechanical respirator that had kept her alive artificially for a year, could be disconnected if her father so decided, subject to medical and hospital concur-

Table 6.1
"Free Exercise" Cases Decided Against the Individual

DATE	CASE	VOTE	CONSTITUTIONAL ISSUES RAISED	DECISION AND COMMENTARY
1878	*Reynolds v. United States*, 98 U.S. 145.	9:0	Validity of Congressional statute proscribing practice or advocacy of polygamy against claim of freedom of religious practice.	The first of the *Mormon* cases, holding religious beliefs not to justify polygamy.
1890	*Davis v. Beason*, 133 U.S. 333.	9:0	Validity of Idaho Territorial statute requiring an "Oath abjuring bigamy or polygamy as a condition to vote."	Bigamy and polygamy regarded as crimes, not religious exercise.
1890	*The Late Corp. of the Church of Jesus Christ of Latter-Day Saints v. United States*, 136 U.S. 1.	9:0	Validity of 1877 Congressional statute annulling charter of the Mormon Church and declaring all its property forfeited save for a small portion used exclusively for worship.	Law came as a result of the continued defiance of the Mormon Church regarding the practice of polygamy. Court saw no constitutional infirmities.
1929	*United States v. Schwimmer*, 279 U.S. 644.	6:3	Denial of naturalization application to 50-year-old Hungarian Quaker woman for refusing to pledge to "take up arms" on behalf of U.S.	First of the naturalization cases. Holmes, Brandeis, and Sanford dissented from the Butler opinion upholding denial. (*Overruled in 1946.*)
1931	*United States v. Macintosh*, 283 U.S. 605.	5:4	Denial of naturalization application to Canadian Baptist minister, a professor of theology and chaplain at Yale, for refusal to agree to defend U.S. by arms unless he were convinced of "moral justification."	Second of the naturalization denial cases. Hughes, Holmes, Brandeis, and Stone dissented from the Sutherland opinion. (*Overruled in 1946.*)
1934	*Hamilton v. Regents of the University of California*, 293 U.S. 245.	9:0	Refusal of Hamilton (and others) on grounds of conscience to take state-required courses in military science and tactics at state university.	Concurring opinion by Cardozo, joined by Brandeis and Stone, warned against carrying compulsion too far, but joined in Court's decision in favor of California.
1940	*Minersville v. Gobitis*, 310 U.S. 586.	8:1	Validity of compulsory flag salute contested by Jehovah's Witnesses.	Discussed in detail in text above, pp. 239 ff. (*Overruled in 1943.*)

Year	Case	Vote	Validity	Outcome
1941	*Cox v. New Hampshire*, 312 U.S. 569.	9:0	Validity of N.H. statute requiring a permit to hold a procession or parade on a public street, but considering only time, manner, and place of the parade.	Jehovah's Witnesses failed to apply for a permit; engaged in a parade. Court upheld the "exercise of local control over the use of streets for parades and processions."
1942	*Chaplinsky v. New Hampshire*, 315 U.S. 568.	9:0	Validity of narrowly drawn N.H. law proscribing the "address [of] any offensive, derisive or annoying word to any other person who is lawfully in any street or other public place or call[ing] him by any offensive or derisive names."	Law upheld unanimously. A Jehovah's Witness called city marshal "God-damned racketeer" and "damned Fascist." Murphy wrote opinion. (See discussion in Ch. V, "The Precious Freedom of Expression," *supra*, pp. 154–56.)
1942	*Jones v. Opelika* [I], 316 U.S. 584.	5:4	Validity of Opelika ordinance imposing license taxes on bookselling—here by Jehovah's Witnesses.	Stone, Black, Douglas, and Murphy dissented from upholding of law. (*Overruled in 1943*.)
1944	*Prince v. Massachusetts*, 321 U.S. 158.	8:1	Validity of Mass. statute forbidding boys of under 12 and girls of under 18 to sell newspapers or periodicals on streets or in other public places. Jehovah's Witness Prince allowed her under-age children and ward to help sell and distribute J. W. literature.	Freedom of religious exercise here must give way to state's interest and right to protect the health and welfare of children under the state's *parens patriae* position. Murphy dissented.
1945	*In re Summers*, 325 U.S. 561.	5:4	Validity of Illinois's denial of admission to the bar of an otherwise qualified applicant who was a conscientious objector to war and who would therefore not serve in the state militia if called upon to do so under the state's constitutional provisions.	State's regulatory power upheld. Black, Douglas, Murphy and Rutledge dissented, contending unsuccessfully that a state has no right to "bar from a semi-public position, a well-qualified man of good character solely because" of his religious conviction.
1949	*State v. Bunn*, 336 U.S. 942.	No vote	Validity of North Carolina prohibition of handling of poisonous snakes in a "religious ceremony."	One of several such state laws upheld as valid exercise of police power via denial of writ of *certiorari*—most recently again in 1976. (*State ex rel. Swann v. Pack*, 424 U.S. 954.)

Table 6.1 (continued)

DATE	CASE	VOTE	CONSTITUTIONAL ISSUES RAISED	DECISION AND COMMENTARY
1951	*Breard v. City of Alexandria,* 341 U.S. 622.	7:2	Validity of ordinance banning the practice of summoning occupants of a residence to the door *without prior consent* for the purpose of soliciting orders for the sale of goods.	Upheld. Distinguished from other solicitation cases because of the presence of the commercial element here. Similarly, *Heffron v. Krishna Consciousness,* 49 LW 4762 (1981) by involving state fair soliciting.
1961	The Four Sunday Law cases: a. *McGowan v. Maryland,* 366 U.S. 420. b. *Two Guys from Harrison-Allentown, Inc. v. McGinley,* 366 U.S. 582. c. *Braunfeld v. Brown,* 366 U.S. 599. d. *Gallagher v. Crown Kosher Market,* 366 U.S. 617.	8:1 8:1 7:2 6:3	Validity of a series of so-called state Blue Laws, variously forbidding sales on Sundays. Challenges were brought on several grounds, including "due process of law" and "equal protection" of the laws, and the individual facts and circumstances of the cases varied. However, in all cases both the religious liberty *and* the establishment of religious claims were raised, particularly the former, in the attacks on the statutes' constitutionality.	Laws upheld. Discussed in detail in text below, pp. 253 ff.
1967	*Garber v. Kansas,* 389 U.S. 51.	6:3	Alleged constitutional right of the Amish to refuse to send their children to *any* state-accredited schools.	*Per curiam* opinion upheld Kansas's requirement, because Amish may have own schools and own teachers—simple *accreditation* being the sole state requirement. Warren, Douglas, and Fortas dissented.
1971	*Gillette v. United States and Negre v. Larsen,* 401 U.S. 437.	8:1	Does the "free exercise" concept extend C.O. status to those whose opposition to war is confined to only "certain" or "just" wars rather than "unjust" wars, but not to *all* wars?	Rejection of "selective" conscientious objection claim is discussed in detail in text above, pp. 233-35.
1974	*Johnson v. Robinson,* 415 U.S. 361 (1974).	8:1	Does the performance of "alternate" instead of regular military service entitle a "C.O." to educational benefits under the "G.I. Bill of Rights"?	With but Douglas dissenting, the Court, through Brennan, ruled that the statutorily authorized withholding of educational benefits to those who do not perform regular military service "involves only an incidental burden upon appellee's free exercise of religion—if indeed any burden exists at all."

Table 6.2
"Free Exercise" Cases Decided in Favor of the Individual

DATE	CASE	VOTE	CONSTITUTIONAL ISSUES RAISED	DECISION AND COMMENTARY
1892	Church of Holy Trinity v. United States, 143 U.S. 226.	9:0	Can a Congressional statute prohibiting the importation of foreigners "under contract or agreement to perform labor in the United States" forbid, without violating "free exercise" of religion, a New York Church from contracting with an English clergyman to migrate to the U.S. and act as its rector and pastor?	Marshaling much evidence that "we are a religious people," the Court held that such a restrictive intent as claimed could not be validly imputed to the statute by the Government. Has overtones of Church-State "separationist" problem in addition to "free exercise."
1940	Cantwell v. Connecticut, 310 U.S. 296.	9:0	(a) Validity of Conn. statute requiring certificate from State Secretary of Welfare before soliciting funds, to let him determine whether the "cause is a religious one." (b) Cantwell's conviction for breach of the peace.	Both aspects discussed in body of text above. First case under the "freedom of religion guarantees" clause decided by Court to be applicable to states as well as government. Jehovah's Witness Cantwell won on both counts (a) and (b).
1943	Jones v. Opelika [II], 319 U.S. 103.	5:4	Court's reconsideration of the Jones v. Opelika decision (see Table 6.1) of 1942, questioning validity of Opelika's ordinance imposing license tax on book-selling here by Jehovah's Witnesses.	Switch in favor of "J.W.s" was made possible largely by the new stance of Black, Douglas, and Murphy, the constancy of Stone, plus the replacement of the resigned Byrnes by Rutledge.
1943	Murdock v. Commonwealth of Pennsylvania, 319 U.S. 105. (See also Follett v. McCormick, 321 U.S. 573 [1944]).	5:4	Validity of statute requiring payment of a tax ranging from $1.50 to $20.00 a day for three weeks for the privilege of canvassing or soliciting orders for articles, as here applied to Jehovah's Witnesses.	Douglas opinion, joined by Stone, Black, Murphy, and Rutledge, held statute inapplicable to Witnesses, for "a person cannot be compelled to purchase, through a license fee or a license tax, a privilege freely granted in the Constitution."
1943	Martin v. Struthers, 319 U.S. 141.	5:4	Validity of Struthers, Ohio, ordinance forbidding knocking on door or ringing of doorbell of a residence in order to deliver a handbill to occupant without his invitation.	Ordinance declared an unconstitutional abridgment of freedom of religion as applied to Jehovah's Witnesses who distribute their literature in this way.

Table 6.2 (continued)

DATE	CASE	VOTE	CONSTITUTIONAL ISSUES RAISED	DECISION AND COMMENTARY
1943	*Douglas v. City of Jeanette,* 319 U.S. 157.	9:0	Can public evangelism and proselytizing be stopped by police on Sundays, acting on numerous citizens' complaints?	Douglas's opinion held "no"—that Jehovah's Witnesses had right to do so; that since these activities have the same claim to protection as the more orthodox and conventional exercises of religion. Angry Jackson concurrence exhorted community rights.
1943	*West Virginia State Board of Education v. Barnette,* 319 U.S. 624.	6:3	Validity of W. Va. compulsory flag salute—upheld in *Minersville* case (see above)—again contested on free exercise grounds.	Famed overruling of the *Minersville* decision. (Discussed in detail in body of text above pp. 242 ff.)
1943	*Taylor v. Mississippi,* 319 U.S. 583.	6:3	Validity of Mississippi statute making it unlawful to urge people, on religious grounds, not to salute the flag.	If the Constitution bans enforcement of a regulation to salute the flag, it also prohibits the imposing of punishment for advising and urging, on religious grounds, that citizens refrain from saluting the flag.
1943	*Jamison v. Texas,* 318 U.S. 413.	8:0	Validity of Dallas ordinance prohibiting distribution of handbills in city streets.	A state may not prohibit distribution of handbills in city streets in the pursuit of a clearly religious activity merely because the handbills invite purchase of books or promote raising of funds for religious purposes.
1944	*United States v. Ballard,* 322 U.S. 78.	5:4	May secular authority—in connection with alleged mail fraud—determine the truth of religious claims and beliefs, here the "I Am" movement?	No matter how "preposterous" or "incredible" they may be, religious beliefs are not subject to findings of "truth" by fact-finding bodies.
1946	*Girouard v. United States,* 328 U.S. 61. (See also *Cohnstaedt v. Immigration and Naturalization Service,* 339 U.S. 901	5:3	Re-examination of the *Schwimmer* and *Macintosh* question (see Table 6.1, *supra*) regarding denial of naturalization to conscientious objectors.	Court overruled its 1929 and 1931 decisions, adopting the then dissenting opinions of Justices Holmes and Hughes that religiously motivated refusal to bear arms does not manifest a lack of attachment to the U.S. Constitution.

Year	Case	Vote		
1946	*Marsh v. Alabama*, 326 U.S. 501. (See also companion case of *Tucker v. Texas*, 326 U.S. 517 [1946].)	5:3	Validity of Alabama statute making it a crime to enter or remain on private premises—here the privately owned ship-building wharf of Chickasaw—after having been duly warned by the owner not to do so.	Distribution of religious literature by Jehovah's Witnesses cannot be banned even on the privately owned streets of a company town. First and Fourteenth Amendments guarantees apply here.
1951	*Niemotko v. Maryland*, 340 U.S. 268.	9:0	Validity of city of Havre de Grace ordinance allowing use of public parks for public meetings, including religious groups, by custom requiring an advance permit to be issued by City Council.	Denial of permit by City Council to Jehovah's Witnesses, evidently based on "unsatisfactory responses" to questions concerning their views of flag salutes, military service, Roman Catholicism, etc., held to be prior censorship, violative of First and Fourteenth Amendments.
1953	*Fowler v. Rhode Island*, 345 U.S. 67.	9:0	Application of Pawtucket public park meetings ordinance that, by interpretation, did not forbid church service in public parks to Catholics and Protestants, but did ban the Jehovah's Witnesses.	By treating the religious services of the Witnesses differently from those of other faiths, Pawtucket had unconstitutionally abridged the religious freedom commands of the First and Fourteenth Amendments.
1961	*Torcaso v. Watkins*, 367 U.S. 488.	9:0	Validity of Maryland Constitution's provision of test oath of belief in the existence of God as prerequisite to holding public office.	Held a fatal invasion of freedom of belief and religion, violative of both the free exercise and establishment concepts. (See discussion *supra* in body of text, pp. 222–23.)
1963	*Sherbert v. Verner*, 374 U.S. 398.	7:2	Legality of South Carolina State's ruling that Seventh Day Adventist Sherbert's refusal to work on Saturdays (her Sabbath Day), a refusal for which she was discharged by her employers, did not constitute "good cause" under the law, and therefore did not entitle her to unemployment compensation benefit payments.	Despite its 1961 precedents in the *Blue Law Cases* (see Table 6.1 *supra* and discussion *infra*, pp. 253 ff.), the Court held that the denial of benefits to Sherbert constituted infringement of her constitutional rights under the First Amendment because her disqualification imposed a burden on the free exercise clause by forcing her to choose between adhering to her religious precepts and forfeiting benefits for abandoning these precepts and accepting employment. (See text, *infra*, pp. 255 ff.)

Table 6.2 (continued)

DATE	CASE	VOTE	CONSTITUTIONAL ISSUES RAISED	DECISION AND COMMENTARY
1965	*United States v. Seeger, et al.,* 380 U.S. 163.	9:0	Validity of claim by Seeger and two others, alleging their exemptability under Draft Act provision governing conscientious objection "by reason of religious training and belief."	Delicate question of meaning of "an individual's belief in a relation to a Supreme Being" interpreted broadly and liberally by unanimous Court. (See discussion *supra* in text, pp. 228 ff.)
1970	*Welsh v. United States,* 398 U.S. 333.	5:3	Does the Seeger decision and the Draft Act permit draft exemption as C.O. for purely moral and ethical reasons of conscience?	Broadening the "parallelism" of *Seeger* to extend to "strong beliefs about our domestic and foreign policy." (See text, *supra,* pp. 231–233.)
1971	*Winter v. Miller, et al.,* 404 U.S. 985.	9:0	May a Christian Scientist, involuntarily interred in a mental institution, be compelled to take tranquilizers in violation of her religion?	Court denied *certiorari* without comment. Court of Appeals below was divided, but upheld Ms. Miller's free exercise claim.
1972	*Wisconsin v. Yoder,* 406 U.S. 205.	6:1	May the Amish, given their well-established belief that education beyond the 8th grade teaches worldly values at odds with their religious creed, be thus compelled to attend school nonetheless?	In what was the first Supreme Court holding that ruled a religious group immune from compulsory attendance requirements, Mr. Chief Justice Burger found a violation of the Amish's free exercise of religion but made clear that this holding would *not* apply to "faddish new sects or communes."
1977	*Wooley v. Maynard,* 430 U.S. 705.	7:2	May N.H. require passenger automobiles to bear license plates with the motto, "Live Free or Die," if contrary to J.W.'s religious creed?	Free exercise of religion (joined to freedom of expression), ruled the Chief Justice, includes "both the right to speak freely and the right to refrain from speaking at all." The N.H. law here compelled the J.W.s to be a "mobile billboard," objectionable to their beliefs. Rehnquist and Blackmun dissent.
1979	*International Assn. of Machinists v. Anderson,* 440 U.S. 960.	7:2	Given the non-discrimination provisions of the Civil Rights Act of 1964, may a Seventh Day Adventist, on free exercise grounds, refuse to pay union dues?	With but Justices Brennan and White wishing to review the case, the Court upheld lower court's holding that, absent the union's ability to demonstrate "undue hardship," religious freedom had preference over payment of union dues.

Laws Cases[96] as seen against its decision, just two years later, in *Sherbert v. Verner,*[97] a case involving South Carolina unemployment compensation claims.

The Sunday Law Cases and Sherbert v. Verner. The underlying principle of the manifold "Sunday" or "Blue Laws"—which in 1980 still existed in one-half of the states in various forms and contain manifold inconsistencies and incongruities—is the right of a state, under its police power, to enact legislation providing for the Sunday closing of certain business enterprises, while permitting others to remain open. Undoubtedly there must be some logic to such intriguing provisions as those that—under the very same state laws—ban the sale of hosiery in hosiery shops on Sundays yet do not forbid it in drugstores; or those that permit the sale of "antiques," but not "reproductions"; or those that require candy stores to be closed but permit roadside candy counters to be open; or those that allow clam-digging but forbid oyster-dredging![98] Such logic, if any, is difficult to detect and certainly subject to some question. It was just such questioning and reasoning that brought a spate of Sunday law litigation to the bar of the Supreme Court two decades ago. In addressing itself to the basic constitutional question, the Court combined four cases coming to it, some of them reaching the Court with diametrically opposed judgments from lower federal tribunals! Two of them[99] involved owners of highway discount department stores that were open for business seven days a week; the other two concerned smaller stores, owned and operated by Orthodox Jews who, given their religious convictions, closed their establishments on Saturdays but wanted them open on Sundays.[100] The four cases came from three different "Blue Law states," Maryland, Massachusetts, and Pennsylvania, and in all of them the constitutionality of the several statutes involved was under attack on the grounds that they infringed upon religious liberty in

---

rence. (*In the Matter of Karen Ann Quinlan*, decided March 31, 1976.) The United States Supreme Court denied review. (*Garger v. New Jersey*, 429 U.S. 922 [1976].) Similar actions followed elsewhere in the United States. Miss Quinlan was still alive in August 1981 (!); but other cases, e.g., those of Celia Cain and Rodney Poindexter, resulted in instantaneous death. (Duval County, Florida, December 4, 1976, and Los Angeles, California, October 8, 1980, respectively.) See my "Religion, Medicine, and the State," 22 *Journal of Church and State* 3 (1980).

[96] *McGowan v. Maryland*, 366 U.S. 420; *Two Guys from Harrison-Allentown, Inc. v. McGinley*, 366 U.S. 582; *Gallagher v. Crown Kosher Super Market of Massachusetts*, 366 U.S. 617; and *Braunfeld v. Brown*, 366 U.S. 599.

[97] 374 U.S. 398 (1963).

[98] For an illuminating analysis of this crazy-quilt pattern of exemptions and exceptions, see Richard Cohen, *Sunday in the Sixties* (New York: Public Affairs Committee, 1962).

[99] *McGowan v. Maryland* and *Two Guys from Harrison-Allentown, Inc. v. McGinley, op. cit.*

[100] *Gallagher v. Crown Kosher Super Market of Massachusetts* and *Braunfeld v. Brown, op. cit.*

violation of the First Amendment; that they contravened the First's constitutional proscription against the establishment of religion; and that they constituted an unreasonable, arbitrary, and capricious classification, thus denying to the merchant involved the equal protection of the laws guaranteed under the Fourteenth Amendment.

Depending upon how one wishes to count or number opinions that are listed as "concurring and dissenting in part," at least eight and perhaps a dozen separate opinions were handed down in these four cases by an obviously uncomfortable and unhappy Court. It suffices to point to the fact that the prevailing majority opinion—where one could be said to exist at all—in each one of the four cases was written by Mr. Chief Justice Warren, whereas Mr. Justice Douglas dissented in each. The other justices ranged across an opinion spectrum that varied from 8:1 to 6:3. It is clear that the Court did not believe that a demonstrable case for the laws' unconstitutionality had been made; nor did it wish to strike down legislation that, to such a large degree, was based upon either legislative discretion or popular demand, legislation that not only varied widely in character and substance but that also was enforced only sporadically for the simple reason that so many consumers evidently did not wish it enforced—legislation that, moreover, was in some cases at least based upon popular referenda.[101] Hence, although avowedly recognizing the "religious origin" of Sunday laws, the Chief Justice, in his four opinions, hit hard upon the general theme that, in effect, their religious purposes were no longer present; that the present-day purpose of a legislature in enacting such laws was to set aside a day not for religious observance but for "rest, relaxation, and family togetherness," with the motivation thus being "secular rather than religious"; that—with an eye toward the Orthodox Jewish merchants—although the freedom to hold religious beliefs and opinions is absolute, what was involved in the cases at issue was not freedom to hold religious beliefs or opinions *but freedom to act;* and that such freedom, even when motivated by *bona fide* religious convictions, is not wholly free from legislative restrictions, duly enacted under the state police power. The Chief Justice indicated strongly that, although the Court would have wished that the states had passed so-called "Sabbatarian" laws designating Sunday as a day of rest while providing an exemption, or the choice of another day (as some states have done), it obviously could not compel the states to adopt such legislation in their sovereign discretion. Wisdom could not be the issue; constitutionality was—and it was deemed to have been met in view of what the Court regarded as the overridingly secular nature of the various laws. To Mr. Justice Douglas and his supporters in dissent, however, there was a patent violation of both the free exercise and the establishment

---

[101] See the discussion by Murray S. Stedman, Jr., in his *Religion and Politics in America* (New York: Harcourt, Brace & World, 1964), especially pp. 71–4.

clauses. Rejecting the majority's finding of predominating "temporal considerations," Douglas contended with feeling that when the laws are applied to Orthodox Jews or to "Sabbatarians," their absence of justice is accentuated. As he put it:

> If the Sunday laws are constitutional, Kosher markets are on a five-day week. Thus those laws put an economic penalty on those who observe Saturday rather than Sunday as the Sabbath. For the economic pressures on these minorities, created by the fact that our communities are predominantly Sunday-minded, there is no recourse. When, however, the State uses its coercive powers—here the criminal law—to compel minorities to observe a second Sabbath, not their own, the State undertakes to aid and "prefer one religion over another—" contrary to the command of the Constitution.[102]

Whatever the realities of the Sunday Closing Laws, and their degree of enforcement, there can be little doubt that, as Mr. Justice Stewart wrote in dissent in the pertinent Pennsylvania case,[103] the Orthodox Jew is forced into "a cruel choice . . . between his religious faith and his economic survival . . . a choice which . . . no State can constitutionally demand. . . . [T]his is not something that can be swept under the rug and forgotten in the interest of enforced Sunday togetherness."[104] To Justices Stewart, Brennan, and Douglas this was a gross violation of the constitutional right to the free exercise of religion. In a sense, Pennsylvania responded by enacting a "Sabbatarian" law in 1967: it permits *bona fide* other-than-Sunday observers to remain open on Sunday, assuming they keep another Sabbath.

If the majority's reasoning in the *Sunday Closing Law Cases* raised professional and lay eyebrows, they were *really* raised by the Court's opinion and decision in *Sherbert v. Verner*[105] two years later. As indicated in Table 6.2 above, this free exercise of religion case was brought by Mrs. Adell H. Sherbert, a member of the Seventh Day Adventist Church. For thirty-five years a loyal employee of the Spartan Mills, a textile mill in Spartanburg, South Carolina, she was on a five-day week when she formally joined the Church in 1957, thus enabling her to have her Sabbath on Saturdays in accordance with the Church's precepts. Yet in 1959 the firm changed the work week to six days for all three shifts that operated in the mill. When she refused to work on Saturdays she was fired. Finding herself unable to obtain similar work because she would not labor on Saturdays, she filed a claim for unemployment compensation under the South Carolina Unemployment Compensation Act. But the State Employment Security Commission ruled that Mrs. Sherbert's restriction upon her availability for Satur-

[102] *McGowan v. Maryland,* 366 U.S. 420 (1961), dissenting opinion, at 577.
[103] *Braunfeld v. Brown,* 366 U.S. 599 (1961), dissenting opinion, at 616.
[104] *Ibid.,* at 616.
[105] 374 U.S. 398 (1963).

day work disqualified her for benefits under the Act, which denies benefits to any insured workers who fail, "without good cause, to accept suitable work when offered by the employment office or the employer." The South Carolina Supreme Court sustained the Commission's finding 4:1 for, in its judgment, no restriction was placed upon Mrs. Sherbert's freedom of religion since she remained free to observe her religious beliefs in accordance with the dictates of her conscience.

In language that could have been applied in the *Sunday Closing Law Cases* to obtain results *opposite* from those reached here, the majority of seven, speaking through Mr. Justice Brennan—who had been unhappy about at least two of the *Sunday Closing Law Cases*[106]—now *reversed* the South Carolina authorities! It did so on the grounds that the denial of benefits to Mrs. Sherbert constituted a clear infringement of, and burden upon, her constitutional rights of free exercise of religion under the First Amendment:

> *The ruling forces her to choose between following the precepts of her religion and forfeiting benefits, on the one hand, and abandoning one of the precepts of her religion in order to accept work, on the other hand.* Government imposition of such a choice puts the same kind of burden upon the free exercise of religion as would a fine imposed against appellant for her Saturday worship.[107]

Mr. Justice Stewart wrote a separate concurring opinion, and Mr. Justice Harlan dissented in an opinion joined by his colleague White.

The disappointed owners of the Braunfeld and Crown stores had much cause to wonder why the Brennan language—particularly the portions italicized here—did not also fit *their* cases. Yet although Justices Stewart, Harlan, and White did indeed believe that the *Sherbert* decision had the effect of overruling the *Braunfeld* and *Crown* judgments, Brennan's majority opinion *distinguished* the former on the ground that the same practical difficulties and considerations arising from the granting of exemptions in Sunday Closing Laws did not apply and were not present in the South Carolina unemployment insurance problem. It is quite obvious that what the Court did here was to try to draw a line: to balance considerations of public policy against infringement on religious liberty. In the 1961 *Sunday Closing Law Cases* the Court was *not* willing to make exemptions in laws of general application on grounds of claims of religious liberty *versus* economic hardship—in the 1963 *Sherbert* case it was. And this distinction was emphatically not due to changes in personnel since Justices White and Goldberg, the successors to retired Justices Whittaker and Frankfurter, did

---

[106] *Braunfeld v. Brown*, 366 U.S. 599 and *Gallagher v. Crown Kosher Market of Massachusetts*, 366 U.S. 617 (1961).

[107] *Sherbert v. Verner, op. cit.*, at 404. (Italics supplied.)

not numerically or substantively affect the different results in the latter decision. Although the facts in the settings of the two cases differed, the difference was surely one of rationalization rather than of substance. The conclusion is inevitable that the distinction made in the *Sherbert* case is neither very logical nor very convincing.[108] The distinction advanced by Brennan that in the applicable *Blue Law Cases* there was a "less direct burden upon religious practices" is highly questionable—or as Mr. Justice Stewart put it in his concurring opinion, in which he strongly criticized the Brennan rationale, "[W]ith all respect, I think the Court is mistaken, simply as a matter of fact."[109] If anything, the secular purpose of the South Carolina statute was clearer than that of Pennsylvania's and Massachusetts's. The line the Court endeavored to establish here is simply not viable as a basic rule of law.[110] The Court's 1970 denial of *certiorari* in the case of a California Seventh Day Adventist construction worker, who unsuccessfully attempted to invoke *Sherbert* below, may represent some second thoughts—although the facts were rather different and his case did not involve similar hardship.[111] A 1981 case, however, relied on *Sherbert* (8:1).

In a sense, the Court was given "a hand" by virtue of a provision of the Title VII of the Civil Rights Act of 1964, as amended, that—since the mid-1970s—requires employers "to make reasonable accommodations to the religious needs of employees [where] such accommodation can be made without undue hardship on the conduct of the employer's business." In the face of that provision's obvious judgmental flexibility, a 7:2 majority thus found in 1977 that Larry S. Hardison, a clerk at a large TWA maintenance base, who had joined the Worldwide Church of God—a sect that proscribed work on Saturday—had not been deprived of his free exercise of religion since TWA had made every good faith effort to accommodate him. Hardison did not have enough seniority to select a non-Sabbath shift as a matter of right under the union agreement, and the union steward, at TWA's urging, had tried, but failed, to find someone who would exchange

---

[108] See the interesting analysis of this general problem in Paul G. Kauper, *Religion and the Constitution* (Baton Rouge: Louisiana State University Press, 1964), Chapter 2, "Religious Liberty: Some Basic Considerations."

[109] *Sherbert v. Verner, op. cit.,* at 477.

[110] For an interesting, perceptive analysis of the *Sherbert* decision, see Warren L. Johns, "The Rights to Rest," 66 *Liberty* 1 (January–February 1971), pp. 7 ff. See also his *Dateline Sunday, U.S.A.* (Mountain View, Calif.: Pacific Press Publishing Association, 1967).

[111] *Stimpel v. California State Personnel Board,* 400 U.S. 952 (1970). A somewhat related subject matter was addressed by the Court in 1972 to the same result when it declined to review a lower-court decision that required a member of the Seventh Day Adventist Church to join a union, despite his religious belief in freedom of choice, since he was employed in a plant with a duly adopted union shop contract. (*Hammond v. United Papermakers,* 409 U.S. 1028.) The 1981 case was *Thomas v. Review Board,* 49 LW 4341.

shifts.[112] Assuredly, other cases will reach the Court, but the provision's elasticity will afford considerable leeway.

Yet if the results in *Sherbert* and some of its offspring signify a more generous interpretation of the "free exercise" phrase, it may be welcomed in the light of the fundamental question of whether more harm is done to the democratic process by permitting an eccentricity of personal code or behavior, so long as no valid law is broken, than by trampling upon the non-conformist in the interest of the power of majoritarianism.[113] Because lines must be drawn along the way, and the drawing usually seems to fall to the Court, it is not surprising then, that it would be guided on occasion, as it evidently was there, by certain judgments based on considerations of realistic subjectivity that inevitably characterize the political process. After all, the Supreme Court of the United States is a body at once legal, governmental, and political. With this thought we now turn to the Pandora's Box of "establishment."

"Establishment": The Separation of Church and State

If the clause "Congress shall make no law respecting an establishment of religion" is commanding in tone and clear in syntax, it is utterly unclear in its intention. What does it mean? What does it forbid? References to history only intensify the riddle. And because the "establishment" and "free exercise" clauses are closely related, the complexities of establishment simply cannot be understood if they are treated or considered in isolation from the central problem of religious liberty itself.

A GLANCE INTO HISTORY

Among America's revolutionary and post-revolutionary leaders, the persons who were initially responsible for the concept of non-establishment and its incorporation into the Bill of Rights were Thomas Jefferson, James

[112] *Trans World Airlines, Inc. v. Hardison,* 432 U.S. 63. The dissenters were Justices Marshall and Brennan, who joined in an opinion by the former that was described by Mr. Justice White's majority opinion as including "hyperbole and rhetoric." (Intriguingly, the provision at issue had been declared unconstitutional in 1977 (at 83) by United States District Court Judge Manuel Real as a violation of the First Amendment's guarantee of separation of Church and State. (*Yott v. North American Rockwell Corporation,* 428 F. Supp. 763.) But the United States Court of Appeals for the Ninth Circuit reversed Judge Real in 1979. (*Ibid.,* 602 F. 2d 904.)

[113] But, needless to say, there are limits: thus, in 1973 the Supreme Court dismissed the appeal of defendants in a marijuana case who contended that the use of the drug was part of their religious beliefs, protected by the free exercise clause. (*Gaskin v. Tennessee,* 414 U.S. 886). Dr. Timothy Leary, the stormy petrel of the 1960s and 1970s, had unsuccessfully endeavored to peddle a similar argument earlier. (*Leary v. United States,* 383 F. 2d 851 [1967].) See my "The Status of the First Amendment's Religion Clauses: Some Reflections on Lines and Limits," *Church and State* (Spring 1980).

Madison, George Mason, Patrick Henry (on a somewhat different plane), and the Reverends Samuel Davies and John Leland.[114] Virginians all, they led and fought the good fight in the struggle that took place during Virginia's last days as a colony and early days as a state, a struggle similar to that which took place almost a century and a half earlier in Rhode Island and neighboring areas under Roger Williams. Williams, who has been appropriately called "the most advanced and effective advocate of religious freedom in colonial times,"[115] and his supporters fought less on the specific matter of "establishment" than on the general one of 'freedom." Hence it is the Virginians who must receive chief credit for the notion and coinage of American theories of the separation of Church and State. Their influence was decisive and their debates and writings on establishment are indeed still valuable sources of reference even though they can be differently interpreted. A matter on which there is agreement, however, is that they strived, above all, for separation of Church and State in the sense that there should not be an Established Church—as the Episcopal (Anglican) Church was in Virginia at the time—and that there should never be "the preferred position of a favored Church." To achieve those minimum aims, Jefferson, Madison, Mason, and their allies struggled for more than a decade until they succeeded in bringing about the "disestablishment" of the Episcopal Church as the State Church in Virginia. This they accomplished, with the enactment, after a nine-year battle, of Jefferson's great Bill for Establishing Religious Freedom in 1786. The effect of this legislation—hereafter commonly referred to as the Disestablishment Bill—was far-reaching: Virginia's victory over establishment decisively influenced not only the ultimate course of action of her sister states but also that of the federal government. No wonder that Jefferson requested notation of his role in the epic struggle for religious freedom on his tombstone at Monticello, along with the other achievements he considered of greater significance than his eight-year Presidency.[116]

Moreover, Madison's widely circulated and highly influential "Memorial and Remonstrance" of 1785, against the proposal of Virginia's House of Delegates to provide, through assessments, for teachers of the Christian religion, is as classic a statement as may be found in support of the separation of Church and State. Supported by Jefferson, the eloquent and lengthy 15-point document argued persuasively that the State as the secular au-

---

[114] Of course, others, who labored long before the Virginians (such as Roger Williams and the Reverend John Clarke), have carved their niche in the history of religious liberty, but at a different moment in history, under different circumstances, and with different impact.

[115] Stokes and Pfeffer, *op. cit.,* p. 65.

[116] "And not a word more," were his instructions for the epitaph he composed: "Here was buried Thomas Jefferson. . . ." First he listed his authorship of the Declaration of Independence, next that of the "Statute of Virginia for Religious Freedom," next "Father of the University of Virginia."

thority must have jurisdiction over *temporal* matters; that such authority does not extend over *spiritual* matters, which lie in the domain of private belief and the churches (note: "churches," not "Church"). He warned persuasively that once they look to government for the achievement of their various purposes, the churches invite the sacrifice of their spiritual independence; and that when government enters upon the religious scene, it, in turn, enters into competition with the churches in seeking favors—thereby incurring the risk of ecclesiastical domination, with the attendant dangers of coercion of belief and persecution of dissenters.

Thus, to Jefferson and Madison, "children of the Enlightenment [who] represented the secular and humanistic view that supported religious liberty and the separation of church and state,"[117] the principle of separation was absolutely indispensable to the basic freedoms of belief, conscience, and dissent. They were in no sense hostile to religion—far from it—they simply regarded it as an entirely private matter. Overridingly determined to keep religion out of the domain of public affairs, they were as much concerned with freedom *from* religion as with freedom *of* religion—a concern still reflected in Virginia's Constitution today (the 1971 revision retaining it in full).[118]

Difficulties of Historical Application to Contemporary Problems. Following the obvious intent of Jefferson and Madison, it is clear that there can be neither an *official* Church nor even an especially *favored* Church in the United States or in any of its constituent subdivisions. What is far less clear, however, is the matter of state *aid* to religious activities and that of state *cooperation.* If government treats *all* religions with an equal eye and an even hand, may it not, wholly in conformity with the Jefferson-Madison injunction, aid in furthering the spiritual development of Americans, whom the Supreme Court has repeatedly styled "a religious people"?[119] Is the government, in the words of an experienced student of philosophy and politics, "furthering a legitimate purpose when it acts to encourage, support, or aid the institutions of religious life," or is it "precisely the point of the 'no establishment' clause that it precludes government action to this end"?[120] How authoritative and decisive can the intent of men who wrote and lived almost two centuries ago be regarded when applied to the current scene? The principle of "separation" *is* demonstrably present in both

[117] Paul G. Kauper, *op. cit.,* p, 48.

[118] The tough prohibitory language of its Bill of Rights bars "any appropriation of public funds, or personal property, or any real estate to any church, or sectarian society, association, or institution of *any kind whatever,* which is *entirely or partly directly or indirectly,* controlled by any church or sectarian society." (Italics supplied.) (Article I, Section 16.)

[119] E.g., Mr. Justice Douglas's majority opinion in *Zorach v. Clauson,* 343 U.S. 306 (1952), at 313.

[120] Joseph Tussman, *The Supreme Court on Church and State* (New York: Oxford University Press, 1962), p. xv.

the spirit and the letter of the Constitution. Once again, then, we are faced with the line-drawing problem; once again we must look to the Court, even if its role has evolved as much by default as by affirmation.

A Solution That Is No Solution. Striving for a solution, the Court seized upon Jefferson's concept of the "wall of separation between Church and State," which he expressed in a letter to the Danbury Baptist Association in 1785. The idea that the clause against establishment of religion by law was intended to erect "a wall of separation between Church and State" was initially expounded in the *First Mormon Polygamy* case[121] in 1879 by Mr. Chief Justice Waite, who wrote for a unanimous Court. The "wall of separation" clause reappeared in a far more significant, highly contentious, opinion by Mr. Justice Black for a 5:4 Court in the *New Jersey Bus* case[122] in 1947, when the narrow majority found that "wall" had *not* been breached by granting state subventions of $354.74 for bus fares to parents of twenty-one children in Ewing Township's four non-public, if non-profit (which here meant Roman Catholic) parochial schools as well as to public school children. As we shall have occasion to note again, Black reaffirmed the "wall" principle but ruled that it had *not* been breached here; his colleague Frankfurter, however, was not so sure and saw the "wall" "not as a fine line easily overstepped"; Mr. Justice Jackson quipped that that "wall" may become as winding as Jefferson's celebrated "serpentine wall" of single bricks on the grounds of his beloved University of Virginia at Charlottesville; and Mr. Justice Reed objected to drawing a rule of law from what he viewed as "a figure of speech." Fifteen years later, Reed's point was echoed by Robert M. Hutchins: "The wall has done what walls usually do: it has obscured the view. It has lent simplistic air to the discussion of a very complicated matter. Hence it has caused confusion wherever it has been invoked. . . . The wall has been offered as a reason. It is not a reason: it is a figure of speech."[123] And, to compound the basic problem for generations yet unborn, one of the five "wall"-upholders in that *New Jersey Bus* case, Mr. Justice Douglas, seized upon the opportunity of the *New York Bible* case[124] to announce from the bench

---

[121] *Reynolds v. United States,* 98 U.S. 145 (1879), at 164. Actually, that case rested essentially on the "free exercise" question.

[122] *Everson v. Board of Education of Ewing Township,* 330 U.S. 1 (1947). The case was brought as a taxpayer's suit by Arch R. Everson, executive vice-president of the New Jersey Taxpayers' Association, an economy-in-government group. The litigation was in fact sponsored and paid for by the Junior Order of United American Mechanics, a Protestant fraternal organization active in New Jersey. (Letter to me from Professor Daryl R. Fair of Trenton State College, December 13, 1974. Professor Fair has authored a fascinating background study of the statute and the several court cases involved. *"Everson v. Board of Education:* A Case Study of the Judicial Process," delivered as an address to the 1975 Meeting of the New Jersey Political Science Association, held at Rider College, Trenton, N.J., April 12, 1975.)

[123] *Christian Century,* December 4, 1963, p. 1512.

[124] *Engel v. Vitale,* 370 U.S. 421 (1962), at 443.

that he *now* (1962) believed the *Bus* case to have been wrongly decided by him and his four colleagues who then (1947) constituted the majority![125]

Obviously, then, that famous "wall of separation" seems to be made of different stuff and be of rather different height depending on its viewers, be they Supreme Court justices, other jurists, or subjective or objective commentators, lay or professional. As Harold Hammett put it intriguingly in his "The Homogenized Wall," for the wall to function properly, "one must not be able to climb over, dig under, break through or sneak around to the other side."[126] Accordingly, he suggested not one wall between Church and State but two: with Church on one side, State on the other, and joint functions permitted by the First Amendment in the middle. Mr. Justice Black had firmly insisted that in the instance of the New Jersey bus subsidies to children attending the Township's non-profit parochial schools, the "wall" stood high and unbreached:

> The "establishment of religion" clause of the First Amendment means at least this: Neither a state nor the Federal Government can set up a church. Neither can pass laws which aid one religion, aid all religions, or prefer one religion over another. Neither can force or influence a person to go or remain away from church against his will or force him to profess a belief or disbelief in any religion. No person can be punished for entertaining or professing religious beliefs or disbeliefs, for church attendance or nonattendance. No tax in any amount, large or small, can be levied to support any religious activities or institutions, whatever they may be called, or whatever form they may adopt to teach or practice religion. Neither a state nor the Federal Government can, openly or secretly, participate in the affairs of any religious organizations or groups and vice versa. In the words of Jefferson, the clause against establishment of religion by law was intended to erect a "wall of separation between Church and State."[127]

In the light of the above manifesto, Black's concluding passage in his opinion must have come as a bit of a surprise to some of his readers as well as some of his colleagues: "The First Amendment has erected a wall between church and state. The wall must be kept high and impregnable. *We could not approve the slightest breach. New Jersey has not breached it here.*"[128] Had it not? In a lengthy, troubled dissent (in which his colleagues Frank-

---

[125] Writing in 1967, Professor William A. Carroll, in a lengthy article, called the *Everson* definition "untenable . . . a sham" and urged its discard for the sake of "ordered coherence." (See "The Constitution, the Supreme Court, and Religion," 51 *American Political Science Review* 663 [September 1967].)

[126] 53 *American Bar Association Journal* 929 (October 1967).

[127] *Everson v. Board of Education of Ewing Township, op. cit.,* at 15–16.

[128] *Ibid.,* at 16. (Italics supplied.) The Court thus *affirmed* the judgment of the tribunal whence the case had come, the New Jersey Court of Errors and Appeals, which in turn had reversed a lower New Jersey court.

furter, Jackson, and Burton joined), and to which he appended Madison's "Memorial and Remonstrance Against Religious Assessment," Mr. Justice Rutledge found, on the contrary, that the "wall" *had* been breached, flagrantly and inexcusably. According to Mr. Justice Murphy's notes, Rutledge had already stated bluntly in the Justices' Conference on the case: "First it has been books, now buses, next churches and teachers. Every religious institution in [the] country will be reaching into [the] hopper for help if you sustain this. We ought to stop this thing at [the] threshold of [the] public school."[129] Now, writing his dissenting opinion, and rejecting the majority's so-called "child benefit" and/or "public purpose" theory—namely, that New Jersey's subsidy was meant for, and went to, the *child* rather than to the Church—Rutledge warned the majority that separation must be strictly construed. It is only by rigidly observing the prohibition against establishment, he contended, that

> the state can maintain its neutrality and avoid partisanship in the dissensions inevitable when sect opposes sect over demands for public moneys to further religious education, teaching or training in any form or degree, *directly or indirectly*.[130]

And in response to the many who have argued long and persistently that such aid would be no more than simple equity to atone for the fact that people whose children go to non-public schools must pay public taxes and often tuition too, Rutledge observed:

> Like St. Paul's freedom, religious liberty with a great price must be bought. And for those who exercise it most fully, by insisting upon religious education for their children mixed with secular, *by the terms of our Constitution the price is greater than for others*.[131]

In another well-known dissent, Mr. Justice Jackson argued—quite plausibly—that the Black opinion was inconsistent with the Black decision, and that he (Jackson) was reminded of "Julia who, according to Byron's reports, whispering 'I will ne'er consent,' consented."[132] And, referring to the Rutledge warnings, Jackson noted that "Catholic education is the rock on which the whole structure [of the Church] rests."[133] The divergent views of such devotees to the Constitution and the basic freedoms of man-

[129] Murphy Papers (located at the Michigan Historical Collections, University of Michigan, Ann Arbor), Docket Notes and Conference Notes, No. 52, Box 138. See also J. Woodford Howard, Jr.'s illuminating biography of Murphy, *Mr. Justice Murphy: A Political Biography* (Princeton: Princeton University Press, 1968), p. 448.

[130] *Everson v. Board of Education of Ewing Township, op. cit.*, at 59. (Italics supplied.)

[131] *Ibid.* (Italics supplied.)

[132] *Ibid.*, at 19.

[133] *Ibid.*, at 24.

kind as Justices Black and Douglas and Rutledge and Jackson are proof positive that the doctrine of the "wall" is no solution *per se*.[134] It fails because the necessary line depends overridingly on public policy considerations—and on the interests of contending groups[135]—even if one believes, with Senator Sam J. Ervin (D.-N.C.), "in a wall between Church and State so high that no one can climb over it."[136]

SOME PRINCIPAL THEORIES OF SEPARATION

Since the "wall" approach is hardly definitive, let us analyze those principal theories of separation that have made themselves felt in the interpretation of the First Amendment. Again, in considering them we ought to keep in mind that a strict segregation between the "establishment" and "exercise" clauses of the First Amendment is not only an oversimplification, but that it is misleading and a disservice to the discussion of the basic problem. A close reading of the major Supreme Court opinions specifically governing the issue of "establishment" or separation of Church and State,[137] rather than the specific issue of "free exercise"—assuming that dichotomy can ever be thus clearly delimited—presents three more or less identifiable Court theories[138]—depending upon one's count. (One can find more).

1. *The Strict Separation or "No Aid" Theory.* Presumably incorporating the "wall" approach to the problem, this theory holds that there must be a strict separation of Church and State, and that government may not constitutionally provide support of religion or religious interests. The theory was demonstrably applied in the "released time" case of *McCollum v. Board of Education*,[139] where the Supreme Court ruled 8:1—the majority opinion written by Mr. Justice Black, the dissenting one by Mr. Justice Reed—that the "no aid" concept had been violated. At issue was Mrs. Vashti Cromwell McCollum's challenge[140] of the constitutional validity of

[134] For some interesting data concerning the justices' maneuverings and misgivings on *Everson*, see J. Woodford Howard, Jr., "On the Fluidity of Judicial Choice," 52 *American Political Science Review* 43 (March 1968).

[135] Withal, *Everson* continues to be reaffirmed; e.g., in late 1971 the Court refused to disturb a New Jersey law providing for free school transport for many private and parochial school students. (*West Morris Regional Board of Education v. Sills*, 404 U.S. 986.)

[136] As quoted in *Time Magazine*, March 8, 1971, p. 30.

[137] These major opinions are indicated in Tables 6.3 and 6.4, *infra*. Probably the most significant ones for our present purposes are the *Everson, Zorach, Allen, Walz, McCollum, Earley, Lemon, Tilton, Nyquist, Engel, Schempp, Roemer, Wolman,* and *Regan* cases. (See tables for citations.)

[138] These are discussed in detail in Kauper, *op. cit.*, Chapter 3. See also Richard E. Morgan, *The Supreme Court and Religion* (New York: The Free Press, 1972), Chapter 3 ff., and J. C. Choper, "The Religion Clauses," 41 *University of Pittsburgh Law Review* 4 (Summer 1980). The latter two present other theories.

[139] *Illinois ex rel. McCollum v. Board of Education*, 333 U.S. 203 (1948).

[140] See her interesting book on the case, *One Woman's Fight* (Boston: Beacon Press, 1961).

a practice by the Board of Education of Champaign, Illinois, which enabled the interfaith Champaign Council on Religious Education to offer classes in religious instruction to public school children, on public school premises. The religious classes were attended from thirty to forty-five minutes on Wednesdays by those public school students whose parents submitted written authorizations. Teachers were provided by the Council at no charge to the Board, but they were subject to the approval of Champaign's Superintendent of Schools. The classes were conducted in the regular school classrooms during school hours; those students who did not wish to stay for the religious sessions were required to go elsewhere in the building to pursue "meaningful secular studies." Evidently, these were not very meaningful in the case of those few students—such as young James Terry McCollum, whose family were professed agnostics—who did not stay for the Protestant, Catholic, or Jewish classes. Attendance at both the religious and lay classes was enforced strictly by secular teachers.

Strongly reiterating the "wall" principle that he had pronounced as the author of the majority opinion in the *Everson Bus* case,[141] Mr. Justice Black here found clear violations of the First and Fourteenth Amendments. He rejected the Board of Education's argument that, if the Court were to hold that a state cannot consistently, under these two Amendments, utilize its public school system to aid any or all religious faiths or sects in the dissemination of their doctrines and ideals, then the Court would "manifest a governmental hostility to religion or religious teachings." Black pointed to *Everson,* repeating its—his—language: ". . . the First Amendment has erected a wall between Church and State which must be kept high and impregnable." Because there was much lingering doubt as to just what had really happened to that "wall" in *Everson,* Black evidently felt constrained to spell out his conclusions on the violation of separation of Church and State again, and he closed his opinion with this admonition:

> Here [in *McCollum*] not only are the State's tax-supported public school buildings used for the dissemination of religious doctrines. The State also affords sectarian groups an invaluable aid in that it helps to provide pupils for their religious classes *through use of the State's compulsory public school machinery.* This is not separation of Church and State.[142]

On the other hand, Mr. Justice Reed, in solitary dissent, believed that the principle of *Everson* could accommodate the facts in *McCollum.* Sounding the frequently voiced argument that "devotion to the great principle of religious liberty should not lead us into a rigid interpretation of the constitu-

[141] *Op. cit.,* 330 U.S. 1 (1947).
[142] *Illinois ex rel. McCollum v. Board of Education,* 333 U.S. 203 (1948), at 212. The supplied italics point to Black's key objection (as he would have cause to point out five years later in the *Zorach* decision, discussed *infra,* pp. 275–79).

tional guarantee that conflicts with accepted habits of our people," he observed sadly that here was "an instance where, for me, the history of past practices is determinative of the meaning of a constitutional clause not a decorous introduction to the study of its text."[143] Justices Reed and Black had been on the same side in the *Everson* case although it will be recalled that Reed, perhaps sensing the expansiveness and uncertainty of the "wall" doctrine, and reflecting the fear of those who well recognized that it could "give" in either direction, had there objected to "drawing a rule of law from a figure of speech."

In the light of his position in the separation cases that were yet to follow,[144] and which would be consistent with his *McCollum* reasoning, Black's position in the *New Jersey Bus* case can best be explained in terms of a distinction he was willing to make under the strict separation theory between "incidental" aid to religion and "direct" aid. The situation in the *Bus* case was for him an entirely viable example of *incidental* aid—which, to him, constituted *"no aid."* He reasoned that since the purpose of the New Jersey ordinance was to provide nothing more than the *general public purpose* one of safe transportation of school children who were attending school under compulsory education laws, the fact that they happened to attend Roman Catholic parochial schools was not constitutionally fatal. For Black and his (then) supporters, the purpose of that aid was "secular" and "incidental" to the requirements of the compulsory school attendance statute, *hence appropriately directed to secular objectives.* In other words, the financial assistance given to the parochial school students was not the kind of "aid" forbidden under the "wall" doctrine of the *Everson* decision itself.

Some fifteen years after the *Everson* and *McCollum* cases, Black returned to the fray to author what quickly became one of the most contentious and most misunderstood opinions of our time in the *New York Prayer* case.[145] Here, writing for an 8:1 majority, Black endeavored to make clear that the principle of the separation of Church and State could not permit the recitation in the public schools of a rather innocuous, 22-word, non-denominational daily prayer that had been drafted by the New York State Board of Regents, a state agency composed of state officials. The prayer read as follows: "Almighty God, we acknowledge our dependence upon Thee, and we beg thy blessings upon us, our parents, our teachers, and our country." It was recommended, although not required, for *viva voce* reading by teachers and students in the classrooms of the New York State public schools at the beginning of each school day. Numerous school boards adopted the recommendation, among them that of

[143] *Ibid.*, dissenting opinion, at 256.
[144] See discussion and Tables 6.3 and 6.4, *infra.*
[145] *Engel v. Vitale,* 370 U.S. 421 (1962).

New Hyde Park, Long Island, which did so in 1958. Five parents[146] of ten children attending the school involved brought suit on the ground that the use of the official prayer in the public schools violated both separation of Church and State and freedom of religion. In his neither very lengthy nor very complex opinion for the Court, Mr. Justice Black agreed with the contentions of the parents and held the practice unconstitutional as a violation of the First and Fourteenth Amendments' ban on establishment of religion. "We think," he wrote,

> that by using its public school system to encourage recitation of the Regents' prayer, the State of New York has adopted a practice wholly inconsistent with the Establishment Clause. *There can, of course, be no doubt that New York's program of daily classroom invocation of God's blessing as prescribed in the Regents' prayer is a religious activity. It is a solemn avowal of divine faith and supplication for the blessings of the Almighty.*[147]

Anticipating the public outcry that was to follow the decision—and it proved to be quite an outcry, one that has hardly subsided, giving rise to a host of proposed constitutional amendments designed to overturn the decision—he tried hard to put into words that the public might accept, and perhaps even appreciate, the manifold problems of personal commitments and drawing lines in case of majority-minority religion that continue to bedevil these controversies. Thus, he explained,

> [T]he constitutional prohibition against laws respecting an establishment of religion must at least mean that in this country it is no part of the business of government to compose official prayers for any group of the American people to recite as part of a religious program carried on by government.[148]

And over the objections of the one dissenter, Mr. Justice Stewart, who contended that the Court "has misspelled a great constitutional principle" by ruling that "an 'official religion' is established by letting those who want to say a prayer say it,"[149] Black concluded on a frank, terse, and hardly illogical note:

> It is neither sacrilegious nor antireligious to say that each separate government in this country should stay out of the business of writing or sanctioning official prayers and *leave that purely religious function to the people themselves and to those the people look to for religious guidance.*[150]

[146] One Unitarian, one non-believer, one a member of the Ethical Culture Society, and two Jews.

[147] *Engel v. Vitale, op. cit.,* at 424. (Italics supplied.)

[148] *Ibid.,* at 425.

[149] *Ibid.,* dissenting opinion, at 445. (Bills, designed to strip the federal courts of jurisdiction over state-authorized voluntary prayers in public schools, passed the Senate 61:30 and 51:40 in 1979 but died in the House.)

[150] *Ibid.,* at 435. (Italics supplied.)

In an important footnote (#21), unfortunately largely ignored by the news media, Black tried to make clear—as he also did in two additional remarks he made orally from the bench on that Opinion Monday in June 1962— that, contrary to his colleague Douglas's concurring opinion, he in no sense of the term intended his opinion for the Court to extend to ceremonial functions and observations with religious mottos or religious characteristics.

The *New York Prayer* decision seemed a confirmation of the Court's adherence to an even stricter interpretation of the separation of Church and State concept than heretofore pronounced. Additional confirmation came just one year later with the extension of the *New York Prayer* case in two momentous decisions that fall under the second principal theory of separation of Church and State. Then, in 1970, the Court let stand a ruling by the Oregon Supreme Court that a 50-foot lighted cross, which had been erected on a hill owned by the City of Eugene, had to be removed because its presence on public land violated the principle of separation of Church and State.[151] And in 1972, it affirmed a lower-court decision prohibiting the service academies from *requiring* attendance at chapel religious services.[152]

2. *The Governmental Neutrality Theory*. Under this theory, the establishment clause is viewed as requiring government to be resolutely "neutral" regarding religious matters. So neutral, in fact, that, in the interesting interpretation and application of the theory advanced by Professor Philip B. Kurland of the University of Chicago Law School, government cannot do anything which *either aids or hampers religion*[153]—that there must be, in other words, *a secular legislative purpose and primary effect that neither advances nor inhibits religion.* Professor Kurland reads the freedom and separation segments of the religion phrases as "a single precept that government cannot utilize religion as a standard for action or inaction because these clauses prohibit classification in terms of religion *either to confer a benefit or to impose a burden.*[154] This, of course, leaves us with the delicate and intriguing question as to the meaning not only of "benefit" and "burden" but of "neutral"—and, in the final analysis, of *religion* itself. It also leaves us with the suspicion that the suggested doctrine might well be rather hard on individual religious dissenters, which is something Kurland seems to acknowledge but does not quite concede.[155]

---

[151] *Eugene Sand and Gravel, Inc. v. Lowe,* 397 U.S. 591. (But the City promised to try to take steps to circumvent the Court "legally"!)

[152] *Laird v. Anderson,* 409 U.S. 1071. *Cf. Citizens Concerned v. Denver* (1980).

[153] He has expressed this thesis frequently and in various media. See, for example, his essay "The School Prayer Cases," in Dallin H. Oaks, ed., *The Wall Between Church and State* (Chicago: University of Chicago Press, 1963), p. 160.

[154] *Ibid.*, n. 83. (Italics supplied.)

[155] See his *Religion and the Law* (Chicago: Aldine Publishing Co., 1962), especially pp. 40 ff.

The Supreme Court resorted to the neutrality theory most obviously—and indeed avowedly—in the *Bible Reading* cases of 1963, *Abington School District v. Schempp* and *Murray v. Curlett,*[156] which were "follow-up" cases to the *New York Prayer* case. Briefly, the *Schempp* portion of the two cases—which were decided together in a 144-page, five-opinion compendium—challenged the validity of a Pennsylvania law requiring the reading without comment of ten verses from the King James version of the Holy Bible[157] on the opening of public school each day, although provision was made for a child to be excused from the exercises on the written request of a parent or guardian. The Schempps were faithful Unitarians; Mrs. Madalyn E. Murray and her son, William J. Murray, III, on the other hand,[158] were avowed atheists, contesting rulings of the Baltimore School Board that required reading of a Bible chapter "and-or the Lord's Prayer" at daily opening exercises in the public schools of that state. William had apparently been subjected to taunts and even physical assault in school because of his consistent opposition to these morning exercises.[159] (An inter-

[156] 374 U.S. 203. A later (1968) prominent example of resort to the neutrality doctrine is the Court's unanimous declaration of unconstitutionality of Arkansas's "monkey law," which prohibited the teaching in its public schools and universities of the theory of evolution. (*Epperson v. Arkansas,* 393 U.S. 97.) But note its new 1982 law.

[157] Bible reading has always engendered emotional reaction. One of the most tragic on record came in 1842 after Francis Kenrick, the Roman Catholic Bishop of Philadelphia, asked that either the Catholic (Douay) as well as the Protestant (King James) Bible be read in the public schools or that Catholic public school children be excused from Bible reading. Rumors began to sweep the city that "Catholics were trying to drive the Bible from the schools." In May and July 1844 the worst riots in the city's history erupted over the Bible issue, leaving a dozen persons dead and two Catholic churches, a seminary, and fifty houses in Kensington in ruins. (*The Philadelphia Sunday Bulletin,* April 21, 1968.) A direct result was the development of a strong, separate Catholic school system.

[158] In 1970, now Mrs. M. M. O'Hair, William's mother, unsuccessfully sought Supreme Court review of her contention that the reading of the Bible from outer space (by astronauts!) violated the establishment clause. (*O'Hair v. Paine,* 397 U.S. 531, appeal dismissed.) Another attempt by the tenacious Mrs. O'Hair failed in 1971. (*Ibid.,* 401 U.S. 955.) But she did win her claim to tax-exempt status of an Atheist Library she set up in 1972—the I.R.S. agreeing to her demands rather than do battle in a lawsuit she was about to bring. (*The New York Times,* June 12, 1972, p. 19c.) In 1976 she announced her "resignation" as leader of "the American atheist community." (*Ibid.,* March 26, 1976, p. 28.) But, denounced as a "demon-directed damsel," she returned to the fray in 1978, filing suits to have the motto "In God We Trust" removed from the coin on which the image of suffragette Susan B. Anthony—alleged by Mrs. O'Hair to be an atheist—appears, and indeed to have that motto expunged from all United States currency. She and her supporters also established a "Dial-an-Atheist" telephone message service in English and Spanish in New York and Chicago, designed to counter the "Dial-a-Prayer" inspirational message service long available in cities across the country. And in 1981 she filed suit to stop the United States Court of Appeals for the Fifth Circuit from using its standard opening prayer, "Oyez, oyez, God save our nation and this honorable court."

[159] Two decades later, Bill Murray found God, quit his job, and set about making friends, embraced as a prodigal son. Surrounded by fundamentalist ministers and right-wing congressmen, he publicly broke with, and indeed scathingly condemned, his mother in a dramatic, well-advertised appearance before a large "In God We

esting, although not uncommon, by-product of the two cases involved was that the two different lower courts, through which the cases passed to the United States Supreme Court, had reached opposite conclusions on the same constitutional issues.)

The Chief Justice assigned the writing of the decision to Mr. Justice Clark, a devout Presbyterian active in his church, who delivered an opinion redolent with diplomacy and acknowledgment of the significant place religion is presumed to hold in American society. He clearly endeavored to avoid the hostile, however uninformed, outcries that followed the Black opinion in the *Engel* decision. In the 8:1 ruling—from which only Mr. Justice Stewart dissented but, unlike his *Engel* dissent, now rather heavily on *procedural* grounds—Clark chose to rest both the decision and the burden of the opinion on a different plane, that of *governmental neutrality*. How well he succeeded is perhaps tellingly illustrated by the fact that dozens of newspapers selected as the decisive segment of opinion the following explanation and exhortation by Clark:

> The place of religion in our society is an exalted one, achieved through a long tradition of reliance on the home, the church and the inviolable citadel of the individual heart and mind. We have come to recognize through bitter experience that *it is not within the power of government to invade that citadel, whether its purpose or effect be to aid or oppose, to advance or retard. In the relationship between man and religion, the state is firmly committed to a position of neutrality.*[160]

Not only was the opinion written by a devout Protestant, but among the five lengthy, separate concurring opinions was one delivered by the Court's Roman Catholic, Mr. Justice Brennan (whose comments embraced 77 pages), and one by its Jewish member, Mr. Justice Goldberg. All five authors took great care to acknowledge the hallowed place of religion, yet all five firmly, and indeed repeatedly, referred to governmental neutrality as the *sine qua non* of the problem. Thus, the Court's emphasis was clearly on the theory of neutrality, a requirement based—as Mr. Justice Clark put it—on the possibility that "powerful sects or groups might bring about a fusion of governmental and religious functions or a concert or dependency of one upon the other."[161] The language, although evidently not the full intent, of the application of the principle of neutrality thus becomes that

---

Trust" sign at the United States Capitol. (*The Washington Post,* May 21, 1980, p. C-1.)

[160] E.g. (from the conclusion of the opinion), "Quotation of the Day," in *The New York Times,* June 18, 1963, p. 39*l.* (Italics supplied.) The citation is from 374 U.S. 203, *op. cit.,* at 226.

[161] *Abington School District v. Schempp* and *Murray v. Curlett,* 374 U.S. 203 (1963), at 222.

advanced by Professor Kurland, which asks whether the "purpose or primary effect" of an enactment is "either the enhancement or inhibition of religion":

> [T]o withstand the strictures of the Establishment Clause there must be a *secular legislative purpose and a primary effect that neither advances nor inhibits religion.* . . . [And] the fact [advanced by Pennsylvania and Maryland] that individual students may absent themselves upon parental request . . . furnishes no defense to a claim of constitutionality under the Establishment Clause.[162]

The religious practices authorized by Pennsylvania and Maryland, and challenged by the Schempps and Murrays, thus failed to meet the demands of the "neutrality" test, a test under which *both* religion clauses of the First Amendment place the government in a "neutral position" vis-à-vis religion. As for the allegation that a logical concomitant of that "neutrality" policy would be, in effect, to render government hostile to religion, Mr. Justice Clark explained that the Court—and through it the country's constitutional framework—

> cannot accept that the concept of neutrality, which does not permit a State to *require* a religious exercise even with the consent of the majority of those affected, collides with the majority's right to free exercise of religion. While the Free Exercise Clause clearly prohibits the use of state action to deny the right of free exercise to *anyone,* it has never meant that a majority could use the machinery of the State to practice its beliefs.[163]

What Clark says here is surely a basic premise of our government under law: that majorities, even near-unanimous ones, cannot violate the Constitution! Thus, when Florida attempted to continue required prayers and Bible-reading in its public schools, a practice approved by its state supreme court, the United States Supreme Court, without even hearing argument, promptly reversed the tribunal by an 8:1 vote one year later.[164] When in 1965 the principal of P.S. 184 in Queens, New York, ruled that not even a "voluntary" recitation of a nursery school prayer in public schools could be said, the Supreme Court upheld him by refusing to review an appeal from his ruling.[165] The Court even let stand a 1968 lower-court ruling that a verse recited by *public* kindergarten children in De Kalb, Illinois, represented a violation of the separation principle, notwithstanding the deletion

---

[162] *Ibid.,* at 222, 224. (Italics supplied.)

[163] *Ibid.,* at 225–26. (Italics supplied.)

[164] *Chamberlin v. Dade County Board of Instruction,* 377 U.S. 402 (1964).

[165] *Stein v. Oshinsky,* 382 U.S. 957. The prayer, said before eating cookies and drinking milk: "God is great, God is good, and we thank him for our food, Amen."

of the word "God,"[166] Mr. Justice Stewart dissenting. In 1971 the Court, 7:2, agreed with the New Jersey courts that to use the prayers in the *Congressional Record* as "voluntary devotional exercises" in the public schools constituted an impermissible "subterfuge."[167] And late in 1975 it declined an opportunity to consider whether public school children have a right to "pray aloud voluntarily" while in school, as the mother of a Massachusetts girl had sought unsuccessfully in the courts below.[168] Undaunted—and in concert with the actions by numerous other states, e.g., New Jersey and New Hampshire—Massachusetts enacted a law in 1980 that permitted ritual prayer, with provisions for abstention, in its public schools, only to see it struck down as "an unconstitutional sponsorship of religion," the 12-page opinion citing the United States Supreme Court precedents.[169]

That the volatile, emotion-charged issue of public school prayer does not subside is manifested not only by the continuing efforts of states to come up with legislation that will pass judicial muster, and by the demonstrable fact that a plethora of communities still defies or ignores the now established law of the land, but also by repeated efforts in and by Congress to "overrule" the highest court in the land. Thus, both constitutional amendments and statutes have been introduced en masse with predictable regularity. Although none had passed both houses of Congress as of mid-1981, the United States Senate, trying a new approach, in 1979 had voted 49:37 and 51:40 to *deny appellate jurisdiction* to the Supreme Court of the United States in *Engel*-type and *Schempp*-type cases—obviously realizing that the Court would not reverse itself on the merits. The House failed to concur on both occasions; yet the 1980 presidential election campaign rang with clarion calls to "put God back into the lives of our school children." The controversy is indeed alive!

The concept of governmental neutrality can be interpreted in various ways, depending upon the interpreter and his philosophy. Thus, to Wilbur Katz, it means that in order to be truly neutral, the government is in some instances *obliged* to give aid to religion in order to avoid restricting the

---

[166] The prayer: "We thank you for the flowers so sweet; We thank you for the food we eat; We thank you for the birds that sing; We thank you for everything." A principle, alas, is a principle. (*De Kalb v. De Spain,* 390 U.S. 906 [1968].)

[167] *Board of Education of Netcong, N.J. v. State Board of Education,* 401 U.S. 1013.

[168] *Warren v. Killory,* 423 U.S. 929 (1975). An attempt by an Albany, New York, student group, Students for Voluntary Prayer, to hold prayer meetings in a public school came to naught on separation grounds in a late 1980 unanimous 23-page opinion by the United States Court of Appeals for the Second Circuit. (*Brandon v. Board of Education of Guilderland Central School District,* 487 F. Supp. 1219.)

[169] Massachusetts Supreme Judicial Court, March 13 and 27, 1980, opinions by Justices Herbert P. Wilkins and Benjamin Kaplan. (*Kent v. Commissioner of Education,* 402 N.E. 2d 1340, 1980 Mass. Adv. Sh. 803, 1980.)

complete enjoyment of religious liberty.[170] To some, anything but total neutrality is anathema,[171] to others, a neutrality that prevents a "just measure of governmental aid" is a violation of "the old American principles" of freedom of religion,[172] and to still others, it signifies that since government and religion both have roles to play in public life and the public order, and since they share some overlapping concerns and functions, neutrality can only mean that government policy must place religion neither at a *special advantage* nor a *special disadvantage*.[173] Professor Carroll suggests that the "neutrality" definition and test assume a *complementary* interpretation of the religion clauses to the end that religion be defined "neutrally" so as to include "both belief and non-belief in God in regard to both the free exercise and the establishment clauses."[174]

How, then, does the "no aid" theory expounded in the *Everson Bus* case[175] differ from the "neutrality" theory expounded in the *Public School Prayer Cases?*[176] Although the response depends upon interpretation, one *can* with some assurance say that the "no aid" test inquires whether government is acting *in aid of religion* (in *Everson* the Court found that New Jersey's subsidy aided the *child* rather than the *Church*), whereas the "neutrality" test inquires whether government is placing religion at a patent advantage or disadvantage (which the Court answered in the former in the *Public School Prayer Cases*).[177] There remains the third theory, which frankly recognizes governmental "accommodation"—to which an interesting "bridge" might be Richard E. Morgan's controversial proposition that "there is no anomaly in banning even modest prayers in the common public schools, while financially aiding specialized independent parochial schools where sectarian prayer is routine."[178]

3. *The Governmental Accommodation Theory.* In his very lengthy concurring opinion in the *Public School Prayer (Pennsylvania/Maryland)*[179]

---

[170] *Religion and American Constitutions* (Evanston: Northwestern University Press, 1964), *passim*.

[171] E.g., Professor Leo Pfeffer, a distinguished student of the field.

[172] Father John Courtney Murray, S.J., "Law and Prepossessions?" 14 *Law and Contemporary Problems* 23 (1949).

[173] Professor Paul G. Kauper, *op. cit.*, Chapter 3, *passim*.

[174] Carroll, *op. cit.*, p. 664 ff., see especially pp. 664–66 and 673–74.

[175] *Everson v. Board of Education of Ewing Township*, 330 U.S. 1 (1947).

[176] *Engel v. Vitale*, 370 U.S. 421 (1962); and *Abington School District v. Schempp* and *Murray v. Curlett*, 374 U.S. 203 (1963).

[177] An interesting aspect of the problem of the Bible in the public schools was presented in New Jersey in 1953, in *Tudor v. Board of Education of Rutherford*, 14 N.J. 31, where the New Jersey Supreme Court held unconstitutional the state law sanctioning free distribution of Gideon Bibles (the King James version) at a group of public schools.

[178] Morgan, *op. cit.*, p. 207. See also Choper, *op. cit.*, fn. 138 for a different approach.

[179] 374 U.S. 203 (1963), commencing at 230.

decisions, Mr. Justice Brennan, while acknowledging that the accommodation theory had no place in the particular cases at issue, was moved to explain that only a concept such as that of "accommodation" could effectively reconcile the natural clash between the free exercise and separation clauses; that *some* accommodation between government and religion and between Church and State could and should be accepted. Readily granting that Pennsylvania and Maryland had gone beyond "accommodation" with their Bible-reading and public prayer legislation, thereby violating the basic concept of governmental neutrality required by the Constitution, he catalogued activities that could *not,* in his opinion, be held to be constitutional violations,[180] activities that, although religious in origin, have ceased to have religious meaning—such as: the motto "In God We Trust" on currency and the belief expressed in the Pledge of Allegiance that the nation was founded "under God";[181] provisions for churches and chaplains in the armed forces and in penal institutions; draft exemptions for ministers and divinity students; the recital of invocational prayers in legislative assemblies; the appointment of legislative chaplains; inclusion of prayers in public school commencement programs;[182] teaching *about* religion in the public schools, i.e., the *study* of the Bible and other religious literature; *uniform* tax exemptions incidentally available to religious institutions;[183] other pub-

---

[180] *Ibid.,* at 296–303.

[181] Indeed, in 1964 the Court refused to review—and thereby let stand—a ruling by the Appellate Division of the New York Supreme Court that upheld the use of the words "under God" in the Pledge of Allegiance (*Lewis v. Allen,* 379 U.S. 923).

[182] *Wood v. Mt. Lebanon Township School District,* 342 F. Supp. 1293 (W.D. Penn., 1972), affirmed 412 U.S. 967 (1974).

[183] In 1966 the Supreme Court seemed to reaffirm that sensitive issue by declining to review a unanimous decision by the Maryland Court of Appeals that the time-honored state tax exemptions for church buildings were *not* an unconstitutional "establishment of religion." (*Cree v. Goldstein,* 385 U.S. 816, and *Murray v. Goldstein, ibid.*) And in 1970, in the *Walz* case, with Mr. Justice Douglas in lone dissent, the Court specifically upheld the tax exemption of property used exclusively for religious purposes. Mr. Chief Justice Burger, contending that "there is room for play in the joints productive of a benevolent neutrality which will permit religious exercise to exist without sponsorship and without interference"—provided there results no "excessive entanglement" with religion—held for his 7:1 Court that there was no relation between tax exemption and establishment, and explained: "The grant of a tax exemption is not sponsorship since the government does not transfer part of its revenue to churches but simply abstains from demanding that the church support the state." (*Walz v. Tax Commission of the City of New York,* 397 U.S. 664, at 669–70.) To Douglas—and many another observer—however, "a tax exemption is a subsidy" pure and simple (at 704) and assuredly a far cry from the "wall of separation." It was the *Walz* case, and the Burger opinion therein, that in effect spelled out in detail the now widely accepted "three-pronged" test of constitutionality under any "accommodation" scheme, namely, (1) there must be a *primary secular* legislative purpose; (2) its effect must neither inhibit nor advance religion; and (3) its result must not foster an *"excessive* entanglement" of government and religion. (At 674, 675.)

The question of whether tax exemption could also be granted to church-owned

lic welfare benefits which government makes available to educational, charitable, and eleemosynary groups that *incidentally* aid individual worshippers; excuse of children from required school attendance on their respective religious holidays; the temporary use of public buildings by religious organizations when their own facilities have become unavailable because of disaster or emergency.

As if to indicate the difficulty of drawing such lines, Mr. Justice Douglas in *his* concurring opinion in the *Pennsylvania/Maryland* decisions essentially reiterated his strong stand in the *New York Prayer* case, where he had said that the "First Amendment . . . prevented secular sanctions to *any* religious ceremony, dogma, or rite."[184] But lest he be misunderstood, he emphasized his now firm conviction that the concept of the "wall" brooked no infraction or circumvention, whatever the circumstances, whatever the rationale:

> the First Amendment does not say that some forms of establishment are allowed; it says that "no law respecting an establishment of religion" shall be made. What may not be done directly may not be done indirectly lest the Establishment Clause become a mockery.[185]

This stand, of course, rejects *any* theory of "accommodation." Ironically, Mr. Justice Douglas had not only provided the necessary fifth vote that upheld New Jersey's public funds subsidy to students attending Catholic parochial schools, a position he then publicly repudiated in *Engel v. Vitale*[186] and would again attack in the *New York Text Book* case in 1968;[187] but it was he who had written (a decade prior to the *Public School Prayer Cases*) the majority opinion in *Zorach v. Clauson,* the *New York Released Time* case,[188] which well illustrates the accommodation theory that he now in effect rejected.

Zorach v. Clauson presented a situation ostensibly different from the one that faced the Court in the *Champaign, Illinois, Released Time* case[189] four years earlier in 1948. It will be recalled that the Court's 8:1 decision in that Illinois case struck down as a clearcut violation of the separation of Church and State the Champaign School Board's practice of permitting the use of its public school facilities for weekly "released time" religious

---

property that is used for business purposes was answered in the negative by the Court in 1972 (6:1). (*Diffenderfer v. Central Baptist Church of Miami,* 401 U.S. 412.)

[184] *Engel v. Vitale,* 370 U.S. 421 (1962), at 442 n. 7.

[185] *Abington School District v. Schempp, op. cit.,* at 230, concurring opinion. He took pains publicly to reiterate that posture in 1964 in the *Chamberlin* case, cited p. 271, footnote 164, *supra.*

[186] 370 U.S. 421 (1962).

[187] *Board of Education v. Allen,* 392 U.S. 236.

[188] 343 U.S. 307 (1952).

[189] *McCollum v. Board of Education,* 333 U.S. 203 (1948).

classes. The New York released-time arrangement differed on its face principally in that those public school students whose parents requested their attendance at religious instruction classes were in fact *released* from classes at school to journey outside to the site of the religious classes. Those who did not participate in the released time program were required to remain in the public school buildings for instructional or study hall purposes. Theoretically, the public school teachers took neither public notice nor attendance of the student releases, but under the regulations promulgated by the Board of Education, the religious teachers did have to take attendance and file it with the individual's home-room teacher or the principal, who was required to keep a card attendance record.

The Supreme Court's six-man majority,[190] per the Douglas opinion, found critical differences between *McCollum* and *Zorach*. Douglas, while acknowledging that the public school teachers "cooperated" with the program to the extent of enabling voluntary attendance of the religious classes, held that the New York program, unlike that struck down in Illinois, involved neither religious instruction in the public school classrooms nor the expenditure of public funds *per se*. He insisted that the Court was indeed following the *McCollum* case, but he added that this did not mean that the Court had to read into the Bill of Rights a "philosophy of hostility to religion." Musing that the constitutional standard of the separation of Church and State, like many problems in Constitutional Law, "is one of degree," he declared that Church and State need not be hostile to one another. Although granting that "[g]overnment may not finance religious groups nor undertake religious instruction or blend secular and sectarian education nor use secular institutions to force one or some religion on any person,"[191] he added in language that ultimately came to haunt him in light of his concurring opinions in the *Public Prayer* cases of 1962 and 1963: "But we find no constitutional requirement which makes it necessary for government to be hostile to religion and to throw its weight against efforts to widen the effective scope of religious influence."[192] The First Amendment, he had said earlier in his opinion, "does not say that in every and all respects there shall be separation of Church and State";[193] and he elaborated later in a phrase much quoted by those opposed to later decisions by the Court in general and Douglas opinions in particular that "we are a religious people whose institutions presuppose a Supreme Being."[194]

But three dissenters, Justices Black, Frankfurter, and Jackson, not only

---

[190] Douglas, with Mr. Chief Justice Vinson and Justices Reed, Burton, Minton, and Clark.
[191] *Zorach v. Clauson,* 343 U.S. 306 (1952), at 314.
[192] *Ibid.*
[193] *Ibid.,* at 312.
[194] *Ibid.,* at 313.

regarded the majority's findings as going far beyond any constitutionally permissible "accommodation," but they also saw no difference "even worthy of mention" (in the words of Mr. Justice Black, the author of the *McCollum* opinion) between the Illinois and New York programs, except for the use of public school buildings. Black especially objected to what he regarded as the compulsory process aspects of the New York practice: "New York," he wrote angrily, "is manipulating its compulsory education laws to help religious sects get pupils. *This is not separation but combination of Church and State.*"[195] As for the different use of the school buildings, Black noted: "As we attempted to make categorically clear, the *McCollum* decision would have been the same if the religious classes had *not* been held in the school buildings."[196] He concluded his opinion with an impassioned warning:

> State help to religion injects political and party prejudices into a holy field. It too often substitutes force for prayer, hate for love, and persecution for persuasion. Government should not be allowed, under cover of the soft euphemism of "co-operation," to steal into the sacred area of religious choice.[197]

To Mr. Justice Frankfurter, "the pith of the case" was that under New York's program, formalized religious instruction is instituted for other school activity which those who do not participate in the released time program are *compelled* to attend. He suggested that this coercion might well be met, and met constitutionally, if the public schools were to close their doors completely for an hour or two, leaving the pupils to go where they will, "to God or Mammon." This practice, known as "dismissed time," was then in vogue in three states, and had been readily upheld by the courts. Caustically, Mr. Justice Jackson, the third dissenter, commented that "my evangelistic brethren confuse an objection to compulsion with an objection to religion."[198] In his view the New York program operated to make religious sects beneficiaries of the power to compel children to attend secular schools, holding that the public school thereby "serves as a temporary jail for a pupil who will not go to Church."[199] He cautioned that "the day this country ceases to be free for irreligion it will cease to be free for religion— except for the sect that can win political power."[200] He ended his dissent on a note of combined alarm and sarcasm:

[195] *Ibid.,* at 318. (Italics supplied.)
[196] *Ibid.,* at 316. (Italics supplied.)
sioned warning:
[197] *Ibid.,* at 320.
[198] *Ibid.,* at 324.
[199] *Ibid.*
[200] *Ibid.,* at 325.

. . . the *McCollum* case has passed like a storm in a teacup. The wall which the Court was professing to erect between Church and State has become even more warped and twisted than I expected. Today's judgment will be more interesting to students of psychology and of the judicial processes than to students of constitutional law.[201]

The *Zorach* decision, however, has not only *not* been overruled[202]—none of the above have, no matter which theory they might reflect—but the "accommodation" approach received further impetus when the Court in 1968 upheld New York's controversial 1965 law that *requires* public school systems to *lend* textbooks to students in private and parochial schools.[203]

In that *New York Textbook* case the Court ruled 6:3—in a case that appeared to open ever wider the door of accommodation—that the law directing school districts to lend $15 worth of textbooks each year to each pupil in grades 7 through 12 in non-public schools, and which then cost the state *circa* $25,000,000 annually, was an entirely permissible "student benefit" rather than an impermissible "school benefit" program, and hence not violative of the First Amendment's strictures against establishment. In the majority opinion, Mr. Justice White—joined by Mr. Chief Justice Warren and Justices Brennan, Harlan, Stewart, and Marshall—thus clearly adopted the "child benefit" rationale of the *Everson* decision of two decades earlier.[204] He agreed that it would be unconstitutional for the state to purchase the books and *give* them *gratis* to parochial school students, but he noted that the law forbids that and merely requires the state to *lend* them. Underlying the legislature's action and the rationale of the earlier "child benefit" cases, contended White,

> has been a recognition that private education has played and is playing a significant and valuable role in raising national levels of knowledge, competence, and experience.[205]

But three opinions by three dissenters, Justices Black, Douglas, and Fortas, saw matters quite differently. Douglas pointed out that, in fact, the "statutory system provides that the parochial school will ask for the books that *it wants*"[206] with the local public school board then simply (or not so simply) having to decide whether to veto the selection made by the parochial school. And, he asked, with rather difficult-to-refute logic: "Can there be the slightest doubt that the head of the parochial school will ask

---

[201] *Ibid.*
[202] Presented with a golden opportunity to reconsider it in 1976, the Court pointedly refused to do so. (*Smith v. Smith,* 429 U.S. 806, *certiorari* denied.)
[203] *The New York Textbook* case (*Board of Education v. Allen,* 392 U.S. 236).
[204] *Everson v. Board of Education of Ewing Township, N.J.,* 330 U.S. 1 (1947).
[205] *Board of Education v. Allen,* 392 U.S. 236 (1968), at 247.
[206] *Ibid.,* at 256. (Italics supplied.)

for the book or books that best promote its sectarian creed?"[207] Black, passionately contending that his *Everson* line had not only been over-stepped but utterly misinterpreted—for he saw all the difference in the world between *bus* aid and *book* aid, the first being "incidental" or "ancil-lary" to the educational process, while the latter being crucial to and an integral part of that process—warned (with a wary eye toward the Federal Aid to Education Act of 1965, discussed below, and its impending judicial tests):

> It requires no prophet to foresee that on the argument used to support this law others could be upheld providing for state or federal government funds to buy property on which to erect religious school buildings or to erect the buildings themselves, to pay the salaries of the religious school teachers, and finally to have the sectarian religious group cease to rely on voluntary contributions of members of their sects while waiting for the Government to pick up all the bills for the religious schools.[208]

Fortas, in what would be one of his last decisions prior to his resignation from the bench in 1969, categorically stated that *Allen* was simply and patently *not* within the principles of *Everson,* for:

> Apart from the differences between textbooks and bus rides, the present statute does not call for extending to children attending sectarian schools the same service of facility extended to children in public schools. *This statute calls for furnishing special, separate, and particular books, specially, separately, and particularly chosen by religious sects or their representa-tives for use in their sectarian schools.* This *is the infirmity.*[209]

But there were six votes on the majority side—cast by justices who evi-dently believed the New York Textbook Law to fit into the now widely ac-cepted "child benefit" syndrome, who were willing, in White's words, to stipulate "evidence that parochial schools are performing, in addition to their sectarian function, the task of secular education."[210]

While the thrust of the times, the evolving nature of governmental aid to education, seemed then clearly to be on the side of the majority's rea-soning in *Allen,* and while the latter's principle of the constitutionality of textbook *loans* was reaffirmed in 1973, 1975, and 1977 (in cases that, however, disallowed other state-devised attempts to "accommodate"),[211]

[207] *Ibid.*
[208] *Ibid.,* at 253.
[209] *Ibid.,* at 271 (Italics supplied.)
[210] *Ibid.,* at 248.
[211] *Committee for Public Education and Religious Liberty v. Nyquist,* 413 U.S. 476; *Meek v. Pittenger,* 421 U.S. 349; and *Wolman v. Walter,* 433 U.S. 229, respectively.

there are obvious limits: thus, as the Court ruled unanimously in 1973—
in a not necessarily overly convincing Burger opinion that professed to distinguish *Allen*—such free textbook aid may *not* constitutionally be extended to private academies (here under the terms of a 1940 Mississippi
law) that have racially discriminatory admission policies.[212] Nor, 6:3, does
Allen by any means sanction state-forays that would provide *funds* for the
purchase of textbooks to *parents* of non-public school students.[213]

That there are constitutional limits to "accommodation," even when the
1968 *Allen* textbook case decision appeared to have made these academic,
had been made crystal clear by two 8:0 and 8:1 decisions handed down in
1971 that dealt with attempted aid going well beyond textbook loans or
bus subventions. With only Mr. Justice White dissenting in the second, the
Supreme Court, speaking through Mr. Chief Justice Burger—hardly a doctrinaire opponent of "accommodation"—declared unconstitutional as *"excessive entanglement* between Government and religion"—and therefore
violative of the separation of Church and State mandated by the First
Amendment—programs enacted by Pennsylvania in 1968 and Rhode Island in 1969 that provided *public funds* for *direct* aid for instruction in
"non-religious subjects" to Roman Catholic and other church-related primary and secondary schools. The aid involved in the Pennsylvania statute
included the partial payment of salaries of parochial school teachers by
professing to "purchase secular services" for their teaching of such "secular" subjects as mathematics, physical education, physical science, and
modern foreign languages (Latin, Hebrew, and Classical Greek were expressly excluded) and also for the purchase of textbooks and instructional
materials. Lower federal courts had subsequently declared the Rhode Island law, which provided for a 15 per cent supplement to private school
teachers of secular subjects using the same instructional materials as those
in the public schools, unconstitutional as violative of the establishment
clause; but Pennsylvania's statute had been upheld.

In agreeing with the Rhode Island and disagreeing with the Pennsylvania decisions below, the Supreme Court gave renewed firm notice that
while it did not retreat from its earlier "accommodation" holdings—such
as its bus and textbook decisions—there were definite limits to "accommodation" lest it violate the separation of Church and State, that "excessive
entanglement" would and could not be tolerated. Explaining that the Court
was thus obligated to draw lines with reference to the three main evils
against which the establishment clause was intended to afford protection,

---

[212] *Norwood v. Harrison,* 413 U.S. 455. "The leeway for indirect aid to sectarian
schools has no place in defining the permissible scope of state aid to private racially
discriminatory schools." (At 464.) The *Norwood* case was reaffirmed in 1974 in
Evangeline Parrish School Board v. United States, 416 U.S. 970.
[213] *Marburger and Griggs v. Public Funds for Public Schools,* 417 U.S. 961 (1974).

"sponsorship, financial support, and active involvement of the sovereign in religious activity," the Chief Justice ruled:

> In order to determine whether the government entanglement with religion is excessive, we must examine the character and purposes of the institutions which are benefited, the nature of aid that the state provides, and the resulting relationships between the government and the religious authority. . . . Here we find that both statutes foster an impermissible degree of entanglement.[214]

And in concluding, he reiterated the basic dimensions of the new line:

> The merit and benefits of these schools . . . are not the issue before us in these cases. The sole question is whether state aid to these schools can be squared with the dictates of the Religious Clauses. *Under our system the choice has been made that government is to be entirely excluded from the area of religious instruction and churches excluded from the affairs of government.*[215]

Along the way, the Chief Justice had restated the governing three-pronged "cumulative criteria" as follows: "First, the statute must have a secular legislative purpose; second, its principal or primary effect must be one that neither advances nor inhibits religion; finally, the statute must not foster an excessive entanglement with religion."[216] But Mr. Justice White disagreed; he theorized that aid to a "separable secular function" of a church-related school was *not* unconstitutional, contending that it does not matter if religious interests "may substantially benefit" from the aid.[217]

As if to underscore future problems for the "excessive entanglement" doctrine, on the very same opinion day, the Chief Justice, speaking for himself and Justices Harlan, Stewart, White, and Blackmun, *upheld* 5:4 the Federal Higher Educational Facilities Act of 1963 under which $240 million in federal funds were paid for the construction of academic buildings on the campuses of private colleges—*including* religious colleges.[218]

[214] *Lemon v. Kurtzman,* 403 U.S. 602 (1971), at 615.

[215] *Ibid.,* at 625. (Italics supplied.) Yet in a rather grotesque postscript, the Court—through the Chief Justice—held 5:3 two years later that Pennsylvania could and indeed should release the $24 million in special aid for those private sectarian schools which it had authorized and appropriated for the school year *preceding* the 1971 holding of unconstitutionality! (*Lemon v. Kurtzman,* 411 U.S. 192, [1973].)

[216] 403 U.S. 602, at 612–13. See the editorial, "Bureaucratic Governmental Regulation of Churches and Church Institutions," 21 *Journal of Church and State* 2 (Spring 1979).

[217] Dissenting opinion in *Earley v. Dicenso,* 403 U.S. 602 (1971), at 664.

[218] *Tilton v. Richardson,* 403 U.S. 672 (1971). The Court did strike down unanimously a provision of the law which enabled the colleges to use the buildings for *any* purpose twenty years after receiving the funds. The right of states to help pri-

Over a sarcastic dissenting opinion by Mr. Justice Douglas—which was also signed by Justices Black and Marshall—charging that evidently "small violations of the First Amendment over the years are unconstitutional while a huge violation occurring only once is *de minimus*,"[219] the Chief Justice distinguished the federal higher education case from the two state secondary and primary school cases under three headings: that pre-college church schools are more involved in religious indoctrination than colleges; that there are fewer entanglements between Church and State in the "one-time, single purpose construction grant than in continuing salary-supplement programs"; and that what he viewed as the evil of bitter political battles, which he regarded as fatally damaging and divisive at the state programs' level, "is not likely to erupt" over aid to colleges. (Five years later he would join Mr. Justice Blackmun's opinion, utilizing the same general distinctions between college and below-college levels, in the Court's 5:4 decision upholding Maryland's aid-to-higher educational facilities program.[220]) The only Roman Catholic on the Court, Mr. Justice Brennan, echoing Jefferson's and Madison's warnings, dissented separately, deploring what he saw as the secularizing impact of public assistance on church schools. By accepting government funds, he reasoned, not only do the religious activities of a sectarian institution become compromised—for there must inevitably be "policing" by the secular authorities—but there is really no way to separate out the religious and secular functions. Brennan restated his deeply held conviction that "the establishment clause forbids the federal government to provide funds to sectarian universities in which the propagation and advancement of a particular religion is a function or purpose of the institution."[221]

Obviously, neither the "excessive entanglement" line, nor the allegedly governing "three-pronged cumulative criteria" thus settled the establishment clause controversies—but they did serve notice to policy makers across the land that the First Amendment contained certain basic strictures against the commingling of Church and State—especially on pedagogical levels *below* college. Hence when Ohio passed a law for direct tuition grants of $90 annually to all parents of children in private and parochial schools, the Court barred it 8:1, with once again only Mr. Justice White in

---

vate colleges and universities borrow money to build *non-sectarian* facilities, even those that are owned and operated by a religious sect, was upheld 6:3 in 1973. (*Hunt v. McNair*, 412 U.S. 734.) See also *Roemer v. Maryland Public Works Board*, 426 U.S. 736 (1976), *infra*, pp. 284–85.

[219] *Ibid.*, at 692.

[220] See pp. 284–85, 296, and 301–302, *infra*. For an interesting discussion of the dichotomy between aid to higher and pre-college institutions, see Edward N. Leavy and Eric Alan Raps, "The Judicial Double Standard for State Aid to Church-Affiliated Educational Institutions," 21 *Journal of Church and State* 2 (Spring 1979).

[221] 403 U.S. 602, *op. cit.*, at 689.

dissent.[222] And down in three 1973 cases went sundry formidable, ambitious non-public school aid attempts by New York and—again—Pennsylvania, the votes ranging from 8:1 to 6:3.[223] Included among them were such attempts as direct grants for maintenance and repair, for full and/or partial reimbursement of tuition, for testing and record keeping, and for tax relief. Such an endeavor, wrote Mr. Justice Powell for the Court, "advances religion in that it subsidizes directly the religious activities of sectarian elementary and secondary schools"; and he specifically viewed the programs as constituting a crass violation of the injunctions against any programmatic *effect* of advancing religion.[224]

The controlling Powell opinion in the above three mid-1973 decisions demonstrated clearly that, at least as of that period of history, the applicable test on separation between Church and State was the already repeatedly alluded-to "purpose-effect-entanglement" trilogy yardstick. In the five cases at issue in the New York and Pennsylvania litigation, the first ("purpose") passed muster; the third ("entanglement") was but briefly discussed; the second ("effect") became decisive. When, undismayed, undaunted, and stubborn Pennsylvania tried once more in 1975, with a host of provisions for state aid to private and parochial schools for such services as counseling, testing, remedial classes in speech and hearing therapy, and for instructional equipment like charts, maps, records, films, tape recorders and projectors, as well as an additional textbook loan program, all, except—predictably—the last, which survived 6:3, fell 3:6. With Mr. Justice Stewart speaking for the majority, joined wholly or partly by his colleagues Douglas, Brennan, Powell, Marshall, and Blackmun—the Chief Justice, and Justices White and Rehnquist dissenting, more or less—and again zeroing in on the *effect* of the multiple legislation plus what it regarded as patent "political [and] administrative entanglement," the Court, in a stern, broadly sweeping opinion, saw grave potential for conflict between Church and State. Provision of such services, wrote Stewart, raises "the danger that religious doctrine will become intertwined with secular instruction"[225] and creates a "serious potential for divisive conflict over the issue of aid to religion"[226] as legislation providing financial support comes up in the legislature year after year. The program, which cost $12 million for non-public schools in 1972–73, "inescapably" results in the direct and substantial ad-

[222] *Essex v. Wolman,* 409 U.S. 808 (1972).
[223] *Levitt v. Committee for Public Education and Religious Liberty,* 413 U.S. 427; *Committee for Public Education and Religious Liberty v. Nyquist,* 413 U.S. 756; and *Sloan v. Lemon,* 413 U.S. 825.
[224] *Committee for Public Education . . . v. Nyquist, op. cit.,* at 774. For reconfirmation of Nyquist's tax relief negation, see also the Court's summary disposition in *Byrne v. Public Funds for Public Schools,* 442 U.S. 907 (1979).
[225] *Meek v. Pittenger,* 421 U.S. 349, at 370.
[226] *Ibid.,* at 372.

vancement of religious activity, Stewart held for the majority, "and thus constitutes an impermissible establishment of religion."[227]

In fine, what the Court held in that 1975 landmark decision of *Meek v. Pittenger* was—speaking somewhat oversimplifiedly but accurately—that tax-raised funds may plainly not be used to finance the operations of church schools. Few, if any, Court watchers seriously believed, however, that the determined and numerous supporters of aid to non-public schools would cease and desist. Indeed, the Court's docket for the following term contained a number of possible candidates for renewed Church-State legal strife. And one of them—to the astonishment (and dismay) of a number of close students of the Court—may have done more than "open a small crack in the 'wall' of separation," as *The New York Times* put it.[228] In a 5:4 decision in the *Roemer* case, featuring a welter of opinions, but *no* majority agreement (the five-man victorious side splitting two ways in their reasoning),[229] the Supreme Court upheld Maryland's program of *non-categorical* financial aid to church-related *colleges,* thereby, for the first time in history, approving a system of state *general purpose* subsidies benefitting church-related educational institutions. Over the troubled, fervent, often biting dissents by Justices Brennan, Stewart, Marshall, and Stevens (Mr. Justice Douglas's recent replacement), who viewed the subsidies as demonstrably involving "the disease of entanglement," the five Justices comprising the high tribunal's marginal majority—Mr. Chief Justice Burger and his colleagues Blackmun, Powell, White, and Rehnquist—saw no constitutional violation for a variety of reasons. The decision seemed to be controlled by a less than totally persuasive rationale—which had also governed in the 5:4 holding four years earlier in *Tilton v. Richardson,*[230] which upheld limited *federal* aid to higher educational facilities for construction purposes. The "character" of the colleges, the ability of these colleges "to separate their secular and religious functions," and the lower "impressionability" of college students[231]—as contrasted with students on the secondary and primary levels—were held to lessen the dangers of indoctrination and thus sufficed to meet the trifold requirements of non-religious purpose, non-religious effect, and avoidance of excessive entanglement. The controlling plurality opinion by Mr. Justice Blackmun did admit "entanglement," but since he and his supporters did not deem it "excessive," it was not viewed as constitutionally fatal to the program.[232]

---

[227] *Ibid.,* at 366. With respect to the described expenditure, see p. 281, footnote 215, *supra*.

[228] Sec. 4, p. 7E, June 27, 1976.

[229] *Roemer v. Maryland Public Works Board,* 426 U.S. 736 (1976).

[230] 403 U.S. 672 (1971). See discussion, *supra,* pp. 281–83.

[231] For a different point of view, see Howard L. Reiter, "Do Professors Persuade Students?," *News for Teachers of Political Science* (Winter 1980), pp. 5–7.

[232] And for Justices White and Rehnquist only the first two requirements were

Needless to relate, however, the *Roemer* holding and reasoning encouraged pro-parochial aid forces on all levels of the pedagogical and political ladder. Thus, a scant year later, in the 1977 *Wolman* case, when the Justices split five ways in ruling on a welter of six "aid" issues and their votes ranged from 8:1 to 3:6—new authority to aid parochial education was established by another Blackmun opinion, which was joined in all of its aspects only by Mr. Justice Stewart. Among the Wolman rulings were: therapeutic, remedial, and guidance counseling services, if provided on "neutral" sites off school premises (7:2); diagnostic services "on ground" (8:1); standardized tests and test-scoring services (6:3);—but *not* the loan to either parents or children of classroom paraphernalia like wall charts, maps, globes, science kits, and slide projectors (3:6); nor subsidized field trips (4:5).[233] The Justices' five opinions were hardly models of clarity! Indeed, they constituted a mishmash of interpretations, which naturally invited further litigation. That December, perhaps in an effort to send a message that its broadening *Wolman* decision earlier in 1977 had decidedly not pulled out all the proverbial First Amendment stops, the Court ruled unconstitutional (6:3) a New York law that had provided for *direct financial reimbursement* to parochial schools for record-keeping and testing services,[234] the Chief Justice and Justices White and Rehnquist predictably dissenting.

Although 1978 and 1979 passed without any significant new development on the Church-State litigation front, the Court returned to the fray with a major decision in 1980, spawned by the 1977 *Wolman v. Walter* confusion.[235] The new case, *Committee for Public Education and Religious Liberty v. Regan*,[236] arose as a result of New York's revised 1974 version of its 1970 law that the Justices had struck down 3:6 in the 1973 *Nyquist* decision.[237] Now, however, in an opinion by Mr. Justice White—the Court's most ardent and consistent champion of widespread accommodation—the Court distinguished the latter decision (5:4) by pointing to the fact that the 1974 statutory revision mandated that the state-required tests and supporting procedures, for which *all* schools were to be reimbursed, were *prepared by officials of the state* rather than by the school teachers themselves, as had been the case under the 1970 law. White's opinion, joined by his close allies on the issue, Mr. Chief Justice Burger and Mr. Justice Rehn-

---

constitutionally mandated. The Court, without opinion, affirmed similar college assistance programs in North Carolina and Tennessee in 1977—although Justices Brennan, Marshall, and Stevens wanted to hear oral arguments. (*Americans United for Separation of Church and State v. Blanton*, 434 U.S. 803.)

[233] *Wolman v. Walter*, 433 U.S. 229 (1977).

[234] *New York v. Cathedral Academy*, 434 U.S. 125 (1977).

[235] 433 U.S. 229, *op. cit.*

[236] 444 U.S. 646.

[237] *Committee for Public Education and Religious Liberty v. Nyquist*, 413 U.S. 476.

quist, and "swing" Justices Stewart and Powell, contained numerous *caveats* and frankly acknowledged a course that "sacrifices clarity and predictability for flexibility."[238] Not surprisingly, the four dissenters, Justices Blackmun, Brennan, Marshall, and Stevens perceived, and warned against, a demonstrable primary effect of advancing religion and an entanglement patently violative of the First Amendment's strictures.

Notwithstanding the broadening of the open door implications of its *Regan* ruling,[239] the Court continues to recognize limits, such as it had done in the same term with its proscription of New Jersey's attempt to provide *special income tax deductions* for parents who send their offspring to non-public schools.[240] Its 6:3 *per curiam* opinion again endeavored to make clear that neither tax credits nor tax deductions nor exemptions nor rebates, nor any form of *direct* financial aid to parents or teachers, will now pass muster with six (Brennan, Stewart, Marshall, Blackmun, Powell, and Stevens) of the current (mid-1981) nine members of the Court, at least not in the absence of some permissible type of federal statutory sanction. Mr. Chief Justice Burger and Justices White and Rehnquist, on the other hand, appear to be firmly on record as finding constitutional support for almost any type of "accommodation," provided they can detect *some* kind of secular purpose. In the instance of the Chief Justice, this posture obtains only so long as he does not perceive an entanglement that is "excessive." But Justices White and Rehnquist, especially the former, do not seem to be concerned at all about either the "primary effect" of the state involvement or the attendant "entanglement." If they see a viable *secular* purpose, they will vote to uphold the measure or action. For them, the Court's three-pronged test on the establishment front has been reduced to the single one of the presence of a secular purpose as perceived by them.

A tabular recapitulation of the more significant Supreme Court decisions on separation of Church and State is given in Table 6.3 and Table 6.4, plus the subsequent textual discussion. They are designed to demonstrate that of all the questions posed by the delicate and emotion-charged issue of establishment, the leading one has been on the type, degree, and conditions under which governmental aid may be constitutionally extended to non-public schools. To all intents and purposes, this means predominantly Roman Catholic schools. Regardless of which of the three theories of separation one may regard as most appropriate, there are no easy answers—either on procedural or substantive grounds. The facts of life (1980), on the other hand, are plain: the parents of some 4,800,000 parochial children,[241] 83 per cent of them Roman Catholic, are members of the body

---

[238] *Regan, op. cit.,* at 653.
[239] *Ibid.*
[240] *Byrne v. Public Funds for Public Schools,* 442 U.S. 907 (1979).
[241] *Standard Educational Almanac* (Marquis Academic Media, 1979–80).

Table 6.3
"Separation of Church and State" Cases* in Which the Court Found No Constitutional Violation

DATE	CASE	VOTE	CONSTITUTIONAL ISSUES RAISED	DECISION AND COMMENTARY
1872	*Watson v. Jones,* 13 Wallace 679.	5:2	Can decisions by appropriate ecclesiastical tribunals as to which of two Louisville Presbyterian church factions had the legal right to possess and operate a local church be held binding on the civil authorities as well as the churches?	The U.S. Supreme Court recognized here that the freedom and independence of churches would be in grave danger if *it* or any other organ of civil government undertook to define religious heresy or orthodoxy or to decide which of two factions was the "true faith." (Reconfirmed, more than a century later, in a 7:2 decision: *Serbian Orthodox Diocese v. Milivojovich,* 429 U.S. 873 [1976] and, but somewhat more equivocally, in the 5:4-decided case of *Jones v. Wolf,* 443 U.S. 595 [1979].)
1899	*Bradfield v. Roberts,* 175 U.S. 291.	9:0	May Congress appropriate funds ($30,000) for a District of Columbia hospital, operated by a sisterhood of the Roman Catholic Church but chartered by Congress?	Peckham held for unanimous Court that the 1st Amendment was *not* violated, since the hospital, as a corporation chartered by Congress, is a "purely secular agency" and does not become a religious one merely because its members are Catholic nuns.
1908	*Quick Bear v. Leupp,* 210 U.S. 50.	9:0	Could U.S. Government legally disburse treaty and other funds of which it was trustee for Indians (their real owners) to private religious schools, at the designation of the Indians, to defray their tuition costs?	Arrangement held constitutional on grounds that the U.S. Government is necessarily "undenominational" and cannot make any law respecting an establishment of religion. It merely held the funds in a fiduciary capacity for the Indians.
1930	*Cochran v. Louisiana State Board of Education,* 281 U.S. 370.	8:0	Validity of a Louisiana statute providing for purchase of *secular* textbooks for use by public *and* non-public, including parochial, school children.	Initial application of the "*child benefit*" approach. Here, Court held that benefits went to the "children of the state," not to the "private schools *per se.*" Decision based chiefly on due process.

* Some "mixed" cases, such as *The Sunday Closing Cases,* in which the "free exercise" issues predominated, are found in Table 6.1.

Table 6.3 (continued)

DATE	CASE	VOTE	CONSTITUTIONAL ISSUES RAISED	DECISION AND COMMENTARY
1947	Everson v. Board of Education of Ewing Township, N.J., 330 U.S. 1.	5:4	Validity of New Jersey statute authorizing bus fare reimbursement to parents of private (non-profit) and here parochial, as well as public, school students.	Statute upheld. The famed "wall" decision. (See body of chapter, pp. 261–64, for discussion and analysis.) "Public purpose" "child benefit" doctrine applied.
1952	Zorach v. Clauson, 343 U.S. 306.	6:3	Validity of New York's "released time" program in New York City's public schools.	Upheld because of its special circumstances. (See body of chapter, pp. 275–78 for discussion and analysis.)
1968	Board of Education v. Allen, 392 U.S. 236.	6:3	Constitutionality of 1965 New York State statute requiring local school districts to lend books gratis to seventh- to twelfth-grade children in private and parochial schools.	Sustained on basis of broad application of the "child benefit" theory. Stinging dissents by Justices Black, Douglas, Fortas. (See discussion in text, supra, pp. 278–80.)
1970	Waltz v. Tax Commission of the City of New York, 397 U.S. 664.	7:1	Constitutionality of tax exemption of property used exclusively for religious purposes.	Sustained on the basis of "benevolent neutrality," i.e., on grounds that no particular religion is singled out for favorable treatment, and partly on the historical grounds that church tax exemptions have been accepted without challenge in all states for most of the nation's history.
1971	Tilton v. Richardson, 403 U.S. 672.	5:4	Constitutionality of $240 million Federal Higher Education Facilities Act of 1963 which funds construction of academic buildings on private sectarian as well as secular colleges.	Narrowly sustained—except for its twenty-year "quit-claim" provision, which fell 9:0—on grounds that the admitted "entanglement" of Church and State was "not enough" to invalidate (unlike that in the Lemon and Earley decisions made on the same day). Saved as a "one-time, single purpose construction," rather than a "continuing" grant. Justices Black, Douglas, Brennan, and Marshall dissenting in two separate opinions.

Year	Case	Vote		
1973	*Hunt v. McNair*, 413 U.S. 734.	6:3	Validity of a South Carolina state bond issue designed to aid all types of institutions of higher learning in construction, financing, and refinancing of projects of non-religious purpose buildings.	Upheld on the strength of *Tilton* precedent in the absence of any showing that the recipient Baptist College involved was "any more of an instrument of religious indoctrination" than the institutions involved in *Tilton*.
1975	*Meek v. Pittenger*, 421 U.S. 349.	6:3	Constitutionality of that portion only of a Pennsylvania statute that authorized loan of secular textbooks to private and parochial as well as public schools.	Sustained pre-eminently on the basis of the *Cochran* and *Allen* precedents, *supra*, pp. 287 and 278–80, 288, resp.
1976	*Roemer v. Maryland Public Works Board*, 426 U.S. 736.	5:4	Validity of Maryland law providing general purpose funds for non-sectarian purposes to church-affiliated colleges and universities— even if religion and theology are mandatory courses there.	Upheld by seriously divided majority on grounds that the aid neither violates the three-pronged test of "purpose," "effect," and "entanglement," nor is "pervasively sectarian." Dissenters, however, saw grants as "the disease of entanglement" between government and religion that the Constitution expressly forbids. (Reconfirmed in 1977 in North Carolina and Tennessee cases.)
1977	*Wolman v. Walter*, 433 U.S. 229.	5:4	Constitutionality of a compendium of Ohio law providing a host of services to non-public primary and secondary schools, upheld by votes ranging from 8:1 to 6:3.	Included were certain diagnostic, therapeutic, testing services, "off-ground" or "neutral," as well as book loans. (See body of text, pp. 284–85, for details. Some parts of law were struck down: see Table 6.4.)
1980	*Committee for Public Education and Religious Liberty v. Regan*, 444 U.S. 646.	5:4	Validity of New York statute designed to overcome the constitutional defects found by the *Court* in *Nyquist*. (See text, supra, pp. 285–86, and Table 6.4.)	Seriously divided Court reluctantly sanctions reimbursement for certain expenses incurred by non-public schools in connection with state record-keeping and testing requirements (the latter prepared by the state rather than the teachers). Strong dissents by Brennan, Marshall, Blackmun, and Stevens.

Table 6.4

"SEPARATION OF CHURCH AND STATE" CASES* IN WHICH THE COURT DID FIND CONSTITUTIONAL VIOLATION

DATE	CASE	VOTE	CONSTITUTIONAL ISSUES RAISED	DECISION AND COMMENTARY
1815	*Terrett v. Tyler*, 9 Cranch 43.	5:0	Validity of Virginia recession statute that negated the charter of the Virginia Episcopal Church as a corporation and directed that its parish lands be sold and its proceeds used for the poor of the parish.	Not *truly* a "separation" issue, for the case was decided under principles of general corporate law. Nonetheless, this case established the principle that a state cannot deny to members of a religious corporation the right to retain a corporate charter and continue to act as a corporation.
1925	*Pierce v. Society of Sisters of the Holy Names of Jesus and Mary*, 268 U.S. 510.	9:0	Constitutionality of Oregon's Compulsory Education Act of 1922 requiring every child from eight to sixteen to attend *public* school. (The "Sisters" conducted a group of *private* schools, according to the tenets of the Roman Catholic Church.)	The Act held to interfere "unreasonably" with the liberty of parents and guardians to direct the upbringing and education of children under their control. (Also not purely a "separation" case issue—it was decided on due process grounds—but related to it.) Similarly, see *Meyer v. Nebraska*, 262 U.S. 390 (1923) and the free exercise case of *Wisconsin v. Yoder*, 406 U.S. 205 (1972).
1948	*Illinois ex rel. McCollum v. Board of Education*, 333 U.S. 203.	8:1	Validity of Champaign, Illinois, arrangements permitting "released time" programs on public school property under attendance sanctions.	Struck down as violative of separation concepts inherent in Amendments One and Fourteen. (See body of chapter, pp. 264–66, for discussion and analysis.)
1952	*Kedroff v. Saint Nicholas Cathedral*, 344 U.S. 94.	8:1	Authority of New York State to deprive the Moscow hierarchy of the Russian Orthodox Church of control over all its Church property in New York by forceful statutory transfer to the local "Russian Church in America."	A state is no more allowed than the federal government to enact a law impairing the separation of Church and State. Government has no capacity to intervene in religious controversies or determine which is "the true faith."

* Some "mixed" cases, such as *Torcaso v. Watkins*, involving *both* separation and free exercise issues, are found in Table 6.2.

Year	Case	Vote	Issue	Holding
1962	*Engel v. Vitale*, 370 U.S. 421.	8:1	Constitutionality of New York State composed 22-word non-denominational prayer administered in public schools.	"The New York laws officially prescribing the Regents' prayer are inconsistent with both the purposes of the Establishment Clause and with the Establishment Clause itself." (See text, pp. 266–68, *supra*, for full discussion.)
1963	*Abington School District v. Schempp* and *Murray v. Curlett*, 374 U.S. 203.	8:1	Validity of Pennsylvania's statutory requirement of reading of 10 versus from Holy Bible in public schools and Maryland's practice of daily Bible reading and Lord's Prayer recitation in public schools.	All three procedures held to violate the establishment clause, following *Engel*. (See text, *supra*, pp. 269–73, for discussion and analysis.)
1968	*Epperson v. Arkansas*, 393 U.S. 97.	9:0	Constitutionality of Arkansas "Monkey Law," a statute which made it unlawful to teach the theory that mankind is ascended or descended from a lower order of animals.	Law violates establishment of religion clause by embodying the idea of a particular segment of religious beliefs and proscribing all others.
1969	*Presbyterian Church v. Mary Elizabeth Blue Hull Memorial Church*, 393 U.S. 440.	9:0	May civil courts award church property to dissident congregations on the grounds that the parent church has lost the faith?	"First Amendment values are plainly jeopardized when church litigation is made to turn on the resolution by civil courts of controversies over religious doctrine and practice." (Cf. first entry on p. 287, *supra*.)
1971	*Lemon v. Kurtzman* and *Earley v. Dicenso*, 403 U.S. 602.	8:0 / 8:1	Constitutionality of direct aid to Pennsylvania and Rhode Island parochial schools, involving state "purchase" of secular "services" from sectarian schools, including the use of public funds to pay salaries of parochial school teachers.	Both statutes struck down as involving "excessive entanglement between government and religion." Chief Justice Burger also pointed to "divisive political potential" of the laws, an "evil" the First Amendment was designed to avoid. White, in the solo dissent, saw no "excessive entanglement," finding "separable" secular functions.
1972	*Essex v. Wolman*, 409 U.S. 808.	8:1	Constitutionality of an Ohio plan for direct tuition rebates of $90 annually per child attending a private or parochial school.	Struck down as "excessive entanglement," as a violation of the establishment clause, because "the effect of the scheme is to aid religious enterprises."

Table 6.4 (continued)

DATE	CASE	VOTE	CONSTITUTIONAL ISSUES RAISED	DECISION AND COMMENTARY
1973	Levitt v. Commission for Public Education and Religious Liberty, 413 U.S. 476; Commission for Public Education and Religious Liberty v. Nyquist, 413 U.S. 756; and Sloan v. Lemon, 413 U.S. 825.	8:1 6:3 6:3	Validity of several New York and Pennsylvania programs of diversely attempted financial aid to private, chiefly parochial, schools, including tuition reimbursement, repairs, and maintenance, testing, remedial classes, instructional equipment, and counseling.	All statutes involved fell as "eroding . . . the limitations of the establishment clause now firmly implanted." Powell's opinions stressed that the programs all advanced religion in that they directly subsidized "the religious activities" of sectarian schools.
1974	Marburger and Griggs v. Public Funds for Public Schools, 417 U.S. 961.	6:3	Constitutionality of two New Jersey programs providing money to parents of parochial school students, and also providing supplies and auxiliary services to those schools at public expense.	Court, per curiam, affirmed declaration of unconstitutionality below on basis of absence of bona fide child benefit theory applicability and on the basis of its own 1973 Nyquist rulings.
1975	Meek v. Pittenger, 421 U.S. 349.	6:3	Constitutionality of another Pennsylvania attempt to provide sundry auxiliary services to private and parochial as well as public schools, including counseling, testing, remedial classes, and equipment. (Textbook loan provision was upheld.)	Same majority as Nyquist, Sloan, and Marburger held such provisions raised "the danger that religious doctrine will be intertwined with the secular institutions" and created "a serious potential for divisive conflict over the issue of aid to religion." Dissents by Burger, White, and Rehnquist.
1977	Wolman v. Walter, 433 U.S. 229.	6:3	Validity of certain services by Ohio to nonpublic primary and secondary schools. Some upheld (see Table 6.3); some struck down, 6:3 and 5:4.	While upholding four such services (see p. 285 and Table 6.3) Court struck down financial aid for field trips (5:4) and for certain class paraphernalia (6:3).
1977	New York v. Cathedral Academy, 434 U.S. 125.	6:3	Constitutionality of direct reimbursement to parochial schools for record-keeping and testing services.	Over dissents by Burger, White, and Rehnquist, six members held law to be unconstitutional by providing either direct aid to religion or produce: "excessive state involvement in religious affairs." (But cf. its 1980 Regan holding, text, supra, pp. 285–86 and Table 6.3.)

Year	Case	Vote	Question	Ruling
1979	*National Labor Relations Board v. Bishop of Chicago*, 440 U.S. 490.	5:4	May a sectarian institution, such as a Roman Catholic school, be required to bargain collectively with a union?	Ducking the constitutional issue(s), the narrow majority ruled that there was no clearcut affirmative Congressional intention ascertainable in the National Labor Relations Board that would extend its coverage to teachers in Church-operated schools.
1979	*Byrne v. Public Funds for Public Schools*, 442 U.S. 907.	6:3	Constitutionality of New Jersey statute providing a special income tax deduction for parents who send children to non-public schools.	In a one-sentence order, the Court here affirmed two lower federal courts that had held that the tax deduction had the "primary effect of advancing religion."
1980	*Stone v. Graham*, 49 LW 3369.	5:4	Constitutionality of a Kentucky law requiring posting of a copy of the Ten Commandments in every public school classroom in the state.	Although paid for with private rather than tax funds, the practice fell as not being a "permissible state objective under the establishment clause."
1981	*Hall v. Bradshaw*, 49 LW 3637.	9:0	Constitutionality of a North Carolina practice of publishing a "motorist's prayer" on its official highway map.	Denying review, the Court, without dissent, upheld a decision below that saw a patent violation of the Constitution's bar against state establishment of religion.
1981	*St. Martin's Lutheran Church v. South Dakota*, 49 LW 4575.	9:0	Are religious schools that are "integrated into a church's structure," and have no separate identity, obliged to pay unemployment taxes for their employees?	Ducking the constitutional issue, the Court ruled that Congress had not intended to reach such schools, in contrast to those that are church-related but not directly church-run.

politic and wield political power. When all is said and done, the issue ultimately falls into the *policy field,* heavily surcharged with considerations of public welfare in a pluralistic society with a democratic base. The sole remaining question then becomes that of the *constitutionality* of such programs as government, be it state or federal, does choose to adopt. *Is* the program a violation of the pertinent aspects of the First and/or Fourteenth Amendments?

Obviously, the judiciary, and the Supreme Court of the United States in particular, has not provided a clearcut response to the constitutional question. At times it has upheld certain policies; at others it has struck them down. It must never be forgotten, however, that an additional consideration at the bar of judicial decision-making is the Court's strong predisposition to exercise judicial self-restraint vis-à-vis legislative enactments. The Court's avowed purpose, given at least some doubt about a measure's legitimacy, is to *save,* not to destroy. It is a recognition of this basic maxim of judicial self-restraint that will facilitate an understanding of decisions that, at least on paper, would seem to be diametrically opposite. Thus, we have witnessed three levels of approach which the Court has utilized:

Level 1. The Court *strikes down* a measure or practice as a clearly and demonstrably unconstitutional infringement of the no establishment clause —*because,* in whole or in part, it is simply and patently unconstitutional (and usually, although not always, so regarded by a large majority of the justices). Some pertinent examples are:

the *Illinois Released Time* case,[242] in which the released time programs were held on public school property (8:1);

the *Oregon Compulsory Education Law* case,[243] in which that State *required* attendance at public schools (9:0);

the *New York Prayer* case,[244] in which the New York State composed and administered public school prayer was declared unconstitutional (8:1);

the *Pennsylvania and Maryland Bible Reading* cases,[245] in which statutes and practices requiring public school reading of Bibles and the Lord's Prayer met a like fate (8:1 and 8:1);

the *Arkansas "Monkey Law"* case,[246] in which the proscription of the teaching of evolution fell (9:0);

[242] *Illinois ex rel. McCollum v. Board of Education,* 333 U.S. 203 (1948).
[243] *Pierce v. Society of Sisters of the Holy Names,* 268 U.S. 510 (1925).
[244] *Engel v. Vitale,* 279 U.S. 421 (1962).
[245] *Abington School District v. Schempp* and *Murray v. Curlett,* 374 U.S. 203 (1963).
[246] *Epperson v. Arkansas,* 393 U.S. 97 (1968).

the *Pennsylvania and Rhode Island "purchase of secular services and direct salary supplemental laws,"*[247] and the *Ohio* direct tuition reimbursement grants statute,[248] which fell on grounds of "excessive entanglement" of Church and State (8:0, 8:1, and 8:1); the five *New York and Pennsylvania* laws,[249] providing numerous forms of financial aid to non-public schools, and the renewed 1975 *Pennsylvania* statutory endeavors[250] to attain the same end, all of which fell in 1973 as having a primary *effect* of aiding religion (8:1, 6:3, 6:3). The Court also struck down *Ohio's* renewed efforts to provide certain class paraphernalia (6:3 and 5:4);[251] *New York's* move *directly to reimburse* parochial schools for record-keeping and testing services (6:3);[252] and *New Jersey's* attempt to legislate income tax deductions for parents of parochial school students (6:3).[253]

Although fully aware of the relative unpopularity of some of its decisions, especially in the third and fourth illustrations (which evoked an emotional, popular reaction that was often uninformed and sometimes absurd, given the clear limits of the decisions involved), the Court did not hesitate to do what it clearly considered its duty under the commands of the Constitution. And it did so with but twenty-eight dissenting votes cast of the 152 cast above all together, one of the former coming on procedural rather than substantive grounds.

Level 2. The Court perhaps somewhat uncomfortably at times, and often severely divided, *upholds* a measure or practice because it believes that it can stand under the principle of "auxiliary" or "general public policy" rather than as "primary" or "specific" governmental aid to a nonpublic school—often rationalized under the controversial "child benefit" theory. Appropriate illustrations are:

the *Louisiana Textbooks to All* case,[254] which enabled use of textbooks purchased with public funds by pupils of public *and* non-public schools (8:0); although this case was actually decided on "due process" grounds rather than on the religious issue *per se*, it was confirmed and expanded (6:3) by the 1968 *New York Textbook* loan case,[255] which did deal with the establishment issue directly; it was the only provision that escaped

[247] *Lemon v. Kurtzman* and *Earley v. Dicenso,* 403 U.S. 602 (1971).
[248] *Essex v. Wolman,* 409 U.S. 808 (1972).
[249] *Levitt v. Committee for Public Education and Religious Liberty,* 413 U.S. 472, *Committee for Public Education and Religious Liberty v. Nyquist,* 413 U.S. 756, and *Sloan v. Lemon,* 413 U.S. 825 (1973).
[250] *Meek v. Pittenger,* 421 U.S. 349.
[251] *Wolman v. Walter,* 433 U.S. 229 (1977).
[252] *New York v. Cathedral Academy,* 434 U.S. 125 (1977).
[253] *Byrne v. Public Funds for Public Schools,* 442 U.S. 907 (1979).
[254] *Cochran v. Louisiana State Board of Education,* 281 U.S. 370 (1930).
[255] *Board of Education v. Allen,* 392 U.S. 236.

(6:3) unconstitutionality in the 1975 Pennsylvania *Meek v. Pittenger* hold-ing,[256] and it was upheld (6:3) in the 1977 Ohio *Wolman v. Walter* litiga-tion;[257]

the *New Jersey Bus* case,[258] the famous "wall" decision, upholding public subventions for transportation of parochial as well as public school stu-dents (5:4);

the *New York Released Time* case,[259] where religious classes were held *outside* public school buildings during the school day for those wishing to attend, with the others continuing secular education (6:3);

the tax exemption of wholly church-owned property in the *New York Tax Exemption* case (7:1);[260]

the *Federal Education Facilities Act* case, narrowly (5:4) upholding con-struction grants to both sectarian and non-sectarian colleges;[261]

the 1973 *South Carolina Aid to Education* case,[262] which sanctioned (6:3) a scheme providing state bond aid to *all* educational institutions of higher learning;

the 1976 *Maryland Aid to Church-Affiliated Colleges and Universities* case,[263] which upheld (5:4) a program of general grants for non-sectarian use even in institutions where religion is mandatory;

the 1977 *Ohio Multiple Primary and Secondary Aid to All* case,[264] uphold-ing such heretofore unapproved state services to nonpublic schools as cer-tain testing, diagnostic, and therapeutic services (6:3, 8:1, and 7:2, respec-tively); and the *New York 1980 Aid to Parochial and Other Nonpublic Schools Aid* case,[265] sanctioning (5:4) reimbursement for certain state required administration and testing services, provided these were prepared by the state rather than by the teachers.

Here, although much more sharply split, with 34 of 124 votes cast in dis-sent (more than one-third, compared with *circa* one-sixth in the Level 1 group), the Court believed itself justified in accommodating public policy that raised questions about, but was not regarded as violative of, separation of Church and State.

Level 3. The Court, on the basis of the principle of judicial self-

256 *Meek v. Pittenger,* 421 U.S. 349.
257 *Wolman v. Walter,* 433 U.S. 229.
258 *Everson v. Board of Education of Ewing Township,* 330 U.S. 1 (1947).
259 *Zorach v. Clauson,* 343 U.S. 306 (1952).
260 *Walz v. Tax Commissioners of New York City,* 397 U.S. 664 (1970).
261 *Tilton v. Richardson,* 403 U.S. 672 (1971).
262 *Hunt v. McNair,* 413 U.S. 734.
263 *Roemer v. Maryland Public Works Board,* 426 U.S. 736.
264 *Wolman v. Walter,* 433 U.S. 229.
265 *Committee for Public Education and Religious Liberty v. Regan.* 444 U.S. 646.

restraint or because it adjudges the matter *res judicata*, either refuses to accept a case for review or simply affirms the decision below. This judicial practice may well have the effect of sanctioning practices in one state that are unconstitutional in another, since in each separate instance they were so held by the state courts concerned; but considerations of federalism are far from absent in the judicial process! Some random instances are:

Despite its decision confirming Louisiana's, New York's, Ohio's, and Pennsylvania's free loan of textbooks for parochial schools laws,[266] the Court denied *certiorari* in an Oregon case,[267] thereby upholding a 6:1 decision by Oregon's Supreme Court that school districts must *stop* providing free textbooks to parochial schools; it even reconfirmed that decision one year later; New Mexico's and South Dakota's highest courts ruled likewise; it affirmed (6:3) a New Jersey decision declaring unconstitutional two state programs that provided cash funds to parents of non-public school students for the *purchase* of textbooks, and further provided supplies and auxiliary services to such schools at public expense,[268] and the Court declined to review a Missouri Supreme Court decision invalidating a Missouri law that authorized textbook *loans* to children in church-related as well as those in public and nonsectarian private schools.[269]

Despite its decision in the *New Jersey Bus* case of 1948[270] the Court has refused to review, or has simply summarily affirmed,[271] innumerable state court decisions declaring *unconstitutional*, as violative of the respective state constitutions, free transportation provisions for parochial as well as public school children in, among other states, Alaska, Iowa, Missouri, New Mexico, Oklahoma, Washington, and Wisconsin. In fact, all of these came after the *New Jersey Bus* case—although by mid-1981 twenty-five of the states provided some type of transportation aid to parochial schools, several of which had found state judicial approval (e.g., Connecticut)—and subsequent Supreme Court sanction by virtue of refusal to review (e.g., Pennsylvania).[272]

Despite other state precedents *to the contrary,* the Court refused to review,[273] and thereby upheld, a Vermont Supreme Court decision holding unconstitutional the use of public funds for tuition payable to children attending either public or private schools of their own choice in the instance of towns that had no high schools of their own. Again, despite other

---

[266] See pp. 295–96, footnotes 254–257, *supra.*
[267] *Dickman v. School District, Oregon City,* 371 U.S. 823 (1962).
[268] *Marburger and Griggs v. Public Funds for Public Schools,* 417 U.S. 961 (1974).
[269] *Reynolds v. Paster,* 419 U.S. 1111 (1975).
[270] *Everson v. Board of Education of Ewing Township,* 330 U.S. 1.
[271] *Luetkemeyer v. Kaufmann,* 419 U.S. 888 (1974).
[272] See *Rhoades v. Washington,* 389 U.S. 11 (1967); and *Worrell v. Matters,* 389 U.S. 846 (1967).
[273] *Anderson v. Swart,* 366 U.S. 925 (1961).

state practices to the contrary, the Court refused to review,[274] and thus upheld, a 4:3 Court of Appeals of Maryland decision that declared unconstitutional as a violation of the *First* Amendment the subvention of matching state grants for construction purposes to two Maryland Roman Catholic colleges (Notre Dame and St. Joseph) and one Methodist college (Western Maryland), while upholding similar grants to Hood College. It had regarded Hood's character "essentially secular," but deemed the other three as clearly projecting a religious "image" (only to reverse itself 5:4 a decade later!).[275] And it summarily affirmed (6:3) a lower federal court decision invalidating a California law that authorized state income tax reductions for parents of parochial school students.[276] (On the other hand, as noted above,[277] the Court had also affirmed a decision by Maryland that *upheld* state tax *exemptions* for church buildings.)

Obviously, the issue is far from settled. Notwithstanding *constitutional* proscriptions in thirty-six states, fully thirty-eight (!) provided some sort of aid to church-related schools early in 1981—often in the face of these constitutional prohibitions. Thus, twenty-four states provided pupil transportation; ten, textbooks; eight, health services; five, "general auxiliary" services; and three still "purchased services" from non-public schools and paid salary supplements to teachers in these schools—notwithstanding Supreme Court holdings to the contrary in similar cases.

In terms of experience these three "levels" are readily explainable and just as readily serve to re-emphasize the difficulty, if not perhaps the utter impossibility, of creating and drawing a viable, predictable line between the permissible and the impermissible in the realm of the establishment clause in general and in that of the subsection of public and private education in particular. Still, some outlines of the lines that can be drawn are perceptible in general terms—if not in specific Court judgments. They can be identified, although their application cannot be predicted safely.

Some Overall Policy Positions. A number of these outlines have clearly emerged and may be stated broadly as follows:

First, because it is intended to serve pupils of all religious faiths, a public school in democratic society is *ipso facto* a secular institution. This, of course, does not mean that the public school either is, should be, or is in-

---

[274] *Board of Public Works of Maryland v. Horace Mann League of U.S.*, 385 U.S. 97 (1966); and *Horace Mann League of United States v. Board of Public Works of Maryland*, 385 U.S. 97 (1966).

[275] The issue had been revived in 1974–75 when Maryland, having reinstituted a somewhat revamped program, won a victory in a Three-Judge District Court ruling, which was appealed to the U.S. Supreme Court; the latter sustained the lower tribunal in 1976. (*Roemer v. Maryland Public Works Board*, 426 U.S. 736.) See pp. 284–85, *supra*.

[276] *Franchise Tax Board v. United Americans*, 419 U.S. 890 (1974).

[277] See p. 274, footnote 183, *supra*.

tended to be anti- or irreligious—and the judiciary as well as the legislature have made this amply clear.

Second, freedom of conscience in all its religious aspects and concepts must be, and is, protected.

Third, while it is axiomatic that it is incumbent upon the federal government to protect freedom of religion, and to ascertain the separation of Church and State in the several states of the Union, responsibility for public school curriculum and administration lodges with the State. Just as applicable provisions of the Civil Rights Act of 1964 and the Federal Aid to Elementary and Secondary Education Act of 1965, both as amended, have had far-reaching impact in altering that tradition, so indeed have they indubitably had at the level of higher education.

Fourth, notwithstanding the contemporary changes just described, public education in the several states is controlled preeminently by duly appointed and/or elected public state officials.

Fifth, although attendance of public schools is inevitably one of the hallmarks of the body politic in the several states, no state may *compel* school-age students to attend *public* as distinct from private or parochial schools, and no state has tried to do so since Oregon's defeat at the hands of a unanimous Supreme Court in the *Pierce* case[278] in 1925.

Sixth, on the other hand, a state constitutional provision (e.g., Missouri's) that *forbids* the expenditure of public funds to church-related schools does *not* violate the religious freedom (free exercise) of parents who choose to send their children to sectarian schools.[279] This posture was firmly reiterated by Mr. Chief Justice Burger for the Court in 1973: "Even assuming that the equal protection clauses might require state aid to be granted to private nonsectarian schools in some circumstances—health care or textbooks, for example—a State could rationally conclude as a matter of legislative policy that constitutional neutrality as to certain schools might best be achieved by withholding all state assistance."[280]

Seventh, either by constitutional provision or by statute most states have endeavored to prevent the "direct" disbursement or subvention of any funds from the public state treasury to any parochial or otherwise denominational school—although at least some states have acted to "purchase services," pay salaries, and rebate taxes, sometimes called "parochaid," devices that were declared unconstitutional severally by the Supreme Court in 1971, 1973, 1974, 1975, 1977, and 1979.[281] Most states have permitted, or even encouraged, the providing of one or more, or even all, of the fol-

[278] *Pierce v. Society of Sisters of the Holy Names,* 268 U.S. 510.
[279] *Brusca v. State Board of Education of Missouri,* 405 U.S. 1050 (1972).
[280] *Norwood v. Harrison,* 413 U.S. 455 (1973), at 462. (Italics supplied.)
[281] See discussion on preceding pages and Table 6.4.

lowing "auxiliary" services to be extended to accredited non-public schools: tax exemptions; free lunches; free medical care; free protective services; free school nurse services; free textbook loans; free bus transportation; certain diagnostic, testing, therapeutic, and record-keeping services; and other similar governmental aid, usually termed "indirect," "general," or "auxiliary." It should be noted again here, however, that many of these practices have either been specifically forbidden in some states and/or held to be unconstitutional by their state courts, while the precise *opposite* has been held in others.[282]

Eighth, even prior to the *Illinois Released Time* case[283] the type of denominational or sectarian teaching there at issue was specifically forbidden by most states. Yet a number always did, and still do, permit the kind of "released time" practiced in New York and upheld in the *New York Released Time* case.[284]

Ninth, state-mandated religious observances in the public schools, such as prayers, Bible-reading, and recitation of the Lord's Prayer, practiced widely in various states[285] and banned in a good many others[286] even *prior to* the New York, Pennsylvania, and Maryland 1962 and 1963 Supreme Court decisions,[287] are no longer legal. And as it has already demonstrated repeatedly,[288] the Supreme Court will make short shrift of any subterfuges—provided a case is appealed to it (which of course does not necessarily occur in all, or even most, instances). The collateral question of the observance in the public schools of Christmas and other religious holidays has not squarely reached the Supreme Court. At the state court level, this matter—which raises such emotion-charged, difficult social issues—has seen one adverse[289] and one partly favorable and partly adverse ruling by courts

---

[282] The continuing controversy is demonstrated by the successful veto by Delaware Governor Charles L. Terry, Jr., early in 1966 of a bill that would have provided free bus transportation for parochial and other private school students. At approximately the same time Governor W. W. Scranton of Pennsylvania *signed* a similar measure. Both chief executives acted—or at least professed to act—in accordance with constitutional mandates governing such aid. Similarly diverse postures continue.

[283] *Illinois ex rel. McCollum v. Board of Education,* 333 U.S. 203 (1948).

[284] *Zorach v. Clauson,* 343 U.S. 306 (1952).

[285] E.g., Alabama, Arizona, Indiana, Idaho, Maine, New Jersey.

[286] E.g., Alaska, Illinois, Nevada, Wyoming, Washington.

[287] *Engel v. Vitale,* 370 U.S. 421 (1962); and *Abington School District v. Schempp* and *Murray v. Curlett,* 374 U.S. 203 (1963).

[288] See p. 272, footnotes 167–169, *supra.*

[289] Florida: *Chamberlin v. Dade County Board of Public Instruction,* 143 So. 2d 21 (Fla., 1962). Yet baccalaureate services were upheld, albeit on a procedural judicial point, in the same-named case, but recorded as 160 S. 2d 97 (1964). The Supreme Court dismissed an appeal on the issue for want of a properly presented federal question. (*Ibid.,* 377 U.S. 402, [1964].) And in late 1980 the Court affirmed summarily, with two dissents, a South Dakota ruling allowing the use of religious materials in public school observances of holidays, such as Christmas. (*Florey v. Sioux City School District,* 49 LW 3345.)

and at least one adverse ruling by an attorney-general.[290] But a 5:4 ruling by the Supreme Court in 1980 struck down a Kentucky law that required the posting of a copy of the Ten Commandments in every public classroom in the state.[291] Schools with a substantial Jewish enrollment have increasingly tried to deal with the problem either by diminishing, or even eliminating, the more theological aspects of Christmas, or by commemorating the Jewish holiday of Hanukkah, which usually falls at the same time of year.

Tenth, a reasonably predictive, albeit narrow, Court majority has continued to take a relatively "hard" line on the "secular purpose/effect/entanglement" triad, resulting in a fairly close reading of the First Amendment's injunctions for separation. But such decisions as those in the *Roemer* (1976), *Wolman* (1977), and *Regan* (1980) cases[292] render inevitable the conclusion that an erosion of Church-State separation has taken place. That there are limits is demonstrated by the Court's 6:3 interdictive rulings in the *Cathedral Academy* (1977) and *Byrne* (1979) cases.[293] Yet there is little doubt that in a host of areas, broadly describable as financial support for "auxiliary" governmental aid and services to parochial schools, a more permissive judicial attitude toward separation of Church and State appears to have become *res judicata.*

SEPARATION AND THE PROBLEM OF FEDERAL AID
TO NON-PUBLIC SCHOOLS

The above ten guidelines to policy on the separation of Church and State vis-à-vis aid to non-public schools and/or recognition of sectarian practices therein are firmly established. But a new complexion may well have been triggered with the enactment of the 1965 Federal Aid to Elementary and Secondary Education Act, which contains controversial provisions of potentially crucial importance to the meaning of the First Amendment.

The 1965 Federal Aid to Elementary and Secondary Education Act. The concept of federal aid to education is not, of course, new. What is new is the revolutionary departure from precedent embraced in the 1965 bill. Breaking historic ground, it provided subventions of *federal money for elementary and secondary instruction for children in both public and paro-*

---

[290] *Baer v. Kolmorgen,* 14 Misc. 2d 1015 (N.Y., 1960) was the court decision; the attorney-general's opinion, the first of its kind, was issued by Minnesota at the request of the Rochester (Minnesota) School District, 256 *Civil Liberties* 7 (July 7, 1968).

[291] *Stone v. Graham,* 49 LW 3369. The unsigned majority opinion observed that the "pre-eminent purpose [was] plainly religious" because the document is "undeniably a sacred text" for Jews and Christians.

[292] *Roemer v. Maryland Public Works Board,* 429 U.S. 736; *Wolman v. Walter,* 433 U.S. 229; and *Committee for Public Education and Religious Liberty v. Regan,* 444 U.S. 646, all discussed in the text, *supra,* pp. 284 ff.

[293] *New York v. Cathedral Academy,* 434 U.S. 125 and *Byrne v. Public Funds for Public Schools,* 442 U.S. 907, also discussed in the text, pp. 285 and 286 respectively.

chial as well as all other schools. Sundry measures in the field of education, in which private schools and colleges participated, had been passed prior to 1965, but none of these had tackled the ticklish problem of instructional federal aid to non-public schools below the college level. Among the former were: the "G.I. Bill," the National School Lunch Act, the Special Milk Program, subsidized college housing, the Higher Education Facilities Act, the National Defense Education Act, the College Housing Loan Program, the National Science Foundation Program, and Atomic Energy Commission Fellowships. But because of the lasting opposition of educators, lawyers, and churchmen, instructional aid was never included—and as a result no general federal aid to education measure was put forward effectively until the presidency of Lyndon B. Johnson, who submitted his bill in 1964 and saw it become law in 1965.

To the surprise of many, notwithstanding full recognition of the remarkable Johnson domestic political *savoir faire,* the bill went through both houses of Congress without a big Church-State fight, without a Conservative-Liberal battle, without a racial row. Indeed, it passed without a single major change after it had been first introduced for the administration by Representative Carl D. Perkins (D.–Ky.). It passed because the President managed to convince most of those either involved or interested that the entire scheme would collapse if anyone were to tinker with his bill. Although it may well have pleased no one entirely, all the traditional protagonists supported the measure, or at least did not oppose it: the National Education Association, the National Catholic Welfare Conference, the American Federation of Teachers, the American Jewish Congress, Americans for Democratic Action, Baptists, Methodists, and a coterie of other religious, educational, labor, and civil rights organizations. Heretofore, every past effort to see a general federal aid to education bill pass Congress had faltered for three overriding reasons: (1) the opposition of the hard core of anti-big-government, conservative members of Congress; (2) that of the diehard Southerners whose districts were in need of the kind of financial aid only the federal treasury could provide, but who steadfastly opposed the legislation because of the perennial "Powell Amendment"[294] that barred segregated use of funds; and (3) the controversy engendered by the delicate religious issue, with almost all Roman Catholics opposed to any bill that by-passed their parochial schools, and most Protestants and Jews opposed to any bill that did *not* by-pass aid to parochial schools.

President Johnson licked all three problems. The first was eliminated by the drastic reduction of conservative senators and congressmen as a result of the landslide Johnson-over-Goldwater victory in the 1964 election. The race issue was by-passed by Title VI of the Civil Rights Act of 1964,

[294] Named after then Representative Adam Clayton Powell (D.–N.Y.).

which banned the use of federal funds for segregated activities. The religious issue was the most difficult, of course; yet the superb and experienced parliamentarian and tactician was equal to the task—one his Roman Catholic predecessor in office had been unwilling even to consider: for President Kennedy believed the inclusion of direct federal financial assistance to elementary and secondary schools to be unconstitutional, or at least he chose to give that impression publicly in the Administration's 1961 Ribicoff Brief.[295] And Senator Robert F. Kennedy publicly agreed with his murdered brother's posture during his tragedy-truncated presidential campaign in 1968.

Determined to get a general aid-to-education measure through the 89th Congress, and given a two-thirds Democratic majority, President Johnson, however, was not to be stopped by the religious issue. He met it in several ingenious ways. First, he drafted his program as one in line with the Supreme Court's "child benefit" approach. Second, the control of funds was to be in the hands of public authorities. Third, all aid was to be "categorical" rather than "general." Fourth, he more or less restricted the bill to the poor and needy; its primary benefits were assigned to counties and school districts with ten or more children of families with a yearly income of less than $2,000. Next, the United States Office of Education was initially authorized to allocate $100 million for grants to the states for the purchase of textbooks and library materials to go to Church-controlled and other private non-profit as well as public schools. The language of this particular provision was closely tailored to the principle of textbook *grants*-to-students Louisiana statute[296] that had survived subsequent constitutional onslaughts with the terms of the aid changed now to emphasize *loans* rather than grants.[297] To the irrefutable argument that some states expressly *forbid* that type of book grant or even loan, the administration's response was that *it,* rather than the states, would be the "owner" of the books and could, of course, loan them to the children concerned. The last aspect of the Johnson strategy in defeating or isolating the religious issue as a factor of opposition to the over-all program, was an on-the-record promise by the President to a number of balky, key Northern urban and suburban

[295] See its reproduction in *The New York Times*, March 29, 1961, p. 22l. A.o., he said: "[T]he Constitution clearly prohibits aid to the . . . parochial schools. I don't think there is any doubt of that. . . . The Supreme Court made its decision in the *Everson* case by determining that the aid was to the child, not to the school. Aid to the school—there isn't any room for debate on the subject. It is prohibited by the Constitution, and the Supreme Court has made that very clear. And therefore there would be no possibility of our recommending it." Mr. Justice Douglas quoted this as "the correct constitutional position" in his dissent in *Tilton v. Richardson* in 1971. (403 U.S. 672.)

[296] Upheld in *Cochran v. Louisiana,* 281 U.S. 370 (1930).

[297] *Board of Education v. Allen,* 392 U.S. 236 (1968), *Meek v. Pittenger,* 421 U.S. 349 (1975), and *Wolman v. Walter,* 433 U.S. 229 (1977).

members of Congress to go "all out" to alleviate the overcrowded class-rooms and half-day sessions so prevalent there. In typically forceful language he assured these critical legislators in March 1965 that he would "use every rostrum and every forum and every searchlight that I can to tell the people of this country and their elected representatives that we can no longer afford over-crowded classrooms and half-day sessions."[298] On the morning following this clinching declaration, the House Committee on Education and Labor reported the bill out favorably. The House ultimately passed it by a vote of 263:153, and the Senate, where the bill had been entrusted to Senator Wayne Morse (D.–Ore.), followed suit early in April by a vote of 73:18. For the first time, both houses of Congress had thus approved a broad ($1.3 billion)[299] federal program to aid elementary and secondary education, regardless of the school's secular or non-secular character. The President triumphantly signed the bill into law on April 11, 1965.

The Constitutional Attack on the 1965 Act. Exactly two days later the first steps were taken to mount the anticipated constitutional attack on the revolutionary measure. The National Governing Council of the American Jewish Congress, which has a record of close alliance with liberal Protestant denominations on the Church-State issue, announced that it would seek a court test of the three most controversial and most innovative provisions of the Act. Urging that the "grave issues that have been raised during the long debate on the [statute] must be resolved promptly—before the church-state separation guarantee in the Bill of Rights is eroded to the point of extinction,"[300] the A.J.C. moved to ask for constitutional tests of the following:

1. The dual enrollment or "shared time" arrangements authorized under the bill—to the extent that these result in the "commingling" of public and parochial school faculties, facilities, and/or administration. (Under "shared time" programs the time of parochial school children is divided between public and parochial schools; i.e., for "religiously neutral" subjects—such as languages and physics—the child goes to the former, for the social sciences to the latter.)
2. Those provisions under which public school teachers and public school

[298] *The Philadelphia Evening Bulletin*, April 9, 1965, p. 1.

[299] Predictably, this relatively modest-sounding figure had risen to $2.4 billion for the three-year budget period 1970–73 and to over $4.1 billion for 1981. This figure does not include other types of federal grants for state and local education—the *total* approaching $20 billion by the early 1980s. Not surprisingly, House votes to renew now passed with overwhelming margins (380:26 in 1974)—a far cry from the initial vote a decade earlier. The legislation's principle, if not all of its components, is no longer controversial.

[300] As quoted in the *Christian Science Monitor*, April 13, 1965, p. 4. The A.J.C., as noted on p. 302, *supra*, had not opposed passage of the statute, but was eager for a rapid constitutional test.

equipment may be sent into parochial schools under the bill's program of "supplementary educational centers." (Under Titles I and III, $100 million was initially allocated for remedial instruction, teaching machines, and laboratory equipment, teachers, and other services to public *and* non-profit private schools.)

3. The aforementioned provisions in Title II of the Act under which textbooks purchased with an initial $100 million of federal funds were made available to Catholic, Protestant, and Jewish parochial schools—the vast majority to the first—as well as to public schools.

But in order to be able to mount the desired Court test, it would first be necessary to obtain the kind of *federal* taxpayer standing to sue that had been consistently denied by the Supreme Court as a result of a famous 1923 decision.[301] Matters looked hardly promising for a Court reversal of that posture, especially given the delicate subject at issue—but the would-be litigants received aid from a powerful quarter: Senator Sam J. Ervin, Jr. (D.–N.C.), the Senate's leading constitutional authority and, conveniently, an implacable foe of aid to parochial schools. The Senator would *himself* argue the case for Supreme Court reversal of the "standing to sue" issue here. And he did so successfully! On June 10, 1968, the Court ruled 8:1 in a suit requesting an injunction against the 1965 statute in *Flast v. Cohen*[302] that the 1923 decision was *not* a barrier to suits, contending that the government was infringing on *specific Bill of Rights guarantees,* here the First Amendment's religion clauses.[303]

Although that momentous decision did not address itself to the substantive merits of the separation of Church and State problem *per se,* it opened the door to a direct challenge of the huge federal expenditures under the 1965 law. By February 1971 fully fifty-two cases were "in the mill"—al-

[301] There, in the case of *Frothingham v. Mellon,* 262 U.S. 447, the Supreme Court had held unanimously that a *federal* taxpayer lacked "standing" to sue and had not presented a *bona fide* "case or controversy" under the Constitution for federal court review of a challenge to appropriations under the federal Maternity Act of 1921. This holding did not then, nor has it since, applied to *state* "taxpayer suits" acting under *state* laws, but it was *res judicata* for federal cases. For a detailed examination of "standing" and "case or controversy," see my *The Judicial Process: An Introductory Analysis of the Court of the United States, England and France,* 4th ed. (New York: Oxford University Press, 1980), Chapter IX.

[302] 392 U.S. 83.

[303] The opinion by Chief Justice Warren, which "distinguished" rather than overruled the 1923 case (*Frothingham v. Mellon, op. cit.*), with only Mr. Justice Harlan in dissent, went further, however, to open the door to any taxpayer's allegation that "congressional action under the taxing and spending clause is in derogation of those constitutional provisions which operate to restrict the exercise of the taxing and spending power" (*Flast v. Cohen, op. cit.,* at 106). It did this by setting two conditions, a "two-part nexus" test: (1) the taxpayer must establish a link between his status and the statute attacked by alleging that an Act of Congress is unconstitutional under the taxing and spending power; (2) the taxpayer must allege that the challenged enactment exceeds a specific limit placed on the exercise of the taxing and spending power.

though, perhaps surprisingly, only one had reached the Supreme Court's decisional stage on the merits by the end of 1980: it upheld 8:1 the Act's Title I provision for the sending of public school teachers into parochial (and other private) as well as public schools during normal school hours, a practice forbidden in Missouri whence the case was appealed.[304] Mr. Justice Blackmun, speaking for the Court, pointed to the law's rationale, which was based on programs for special federal aid for *all* children classified as "disadvantaged," be they in public or non-public schools. Over Mr. Justice Douglas's solitary dissent, Blackmun told Missouri that a state was not required to engage in Title I programs of the kind at issue, if state law prohibits same—but that a comparable program must be provided. Missouri's failure to do so triggered the statutorily mandated federal one.

As the country entered the last fifth of the 20th century, federal aid to education on *all levels* of schooling and to *all* schools, public or private, was an established fact. It is highly unlikely that the Court would be willing to strike down provisions that form the very heart of a law such as the 1965 one at issue, that was passed, and consistently extended and renewed, by an almost two-thirds majority of the people's representatives in Congress. After all, had the latter not evidently been converted to the proposition that a price, even perhaps a questionably constitutional one, had to be paid to get the much-needed and much-sought aid to our schools as a matter of public policy? It must never be forgotten that in the long run the Court reflects even as it reveals the nature of American society; that although it is often an effective educator and teacher in the short run, there are limits to which it can go in the face of determined, overwhelming *long-run* opposition by the body politic—a body politic wedded to those pluralistic concepts of which diverse schools form such an important part. What the Supreme Court of the United States says and holds indeed "reflects not only the competing interests and values at stake, but also its own role in accommodating constitutional interpretation to the demands of a pluralistic society."[305]

To reiterate, this is not to say that there are not limits. The Court, as we have seen time and time again, does ultimately determine lines—however uncertain their future may well be. Moreover, as it has demonstrated throughout its history, no amount of popular reaction and vilification will stop the Court from speaking as it perceives the command of the basic law of the land; when, convinced of its rightful duty under our Constitution, it knows it must say "no" to government and the society which it serves—and thus says so. It is a role crucial to the survival of our constitutional system, one it must continue to exercise with resolve.

[304] *Wheeler v. Barrera*, 414 U.S. 908 (1974).
[305] Kauper, *op. cit.*, p. 79.

chapter *VII* Race: *The American Dilemma, and Gender*

In theory *race,* the dominant subject of this chapter, should not present the sort of difficult line-drawing that has pervaded considerations of the topics already discussed. Surely, in the last quarter of the 20th century race could hardly, in enlightened democratic society, determine the outcome of an individual's quest for equality before the law and equality of opportunity—nor should gender or ethnic origin or creed or religion, or any other immutable characteristics not relevant to egalitarian and libertarian imperatives. Yet theory does not necessarily govern practice, and although—beyond question—we have seen enormous strides taken toward the egalitarian goals of black Americans, both under law and in the mores of society, racial discrimination is still a fact of life. That great progress has been made since World War II, especially since the late 1950s, both in the private *and* the governmental sphere is obvious. Yet ingrained sentiments and prejudices of large segments of the people in the North as well as in the South, die hard—if indeed they die at all. And government, under the Constitution the great line-drawer in the absence of voluntary action, has had to be cautious lest it move too far in advance of those sentiments and prejudices. For full enforcement of the civil rights of all, there must be mutual trust and respect—and although government can accomplish much to promote such trust and respect, it cannot be a finite substitute for the slower processes of education. Still, as the race problem has shown well, indeed, leadership by responsible public officials is not only desirable but crucial at all stages. When the race controversy attained a degree of no longer ignorable public concern at the highest governmental level in the late 1940s, it was the judicial branch of the government, with the Supreme Court at its apex, which led the other branches in tackling the problem. While it probably did not lead eagerly or joyously, a people's rightful claims could no longer be ignored merely because the political, in particular the legislative, branches refused to become involved beyond the most cursory of levels, and in fact, consistently passed the problems on to the Court. It is an intriguing question how much strife might have been spared

307

and how much understanding might have been engendered, had the elective branches of the government provided the decisive leadership with which they are charged and, as subsequent events proved, of which they are capable when pressed.

By the end of 1980 there were some 26 million blacks in the United States—roughly 11.7 per cent of a total population of about 225 million. Segregation barriers had tumbled or were tumbling everywhere; the federal government and now also state governments—whether voluntarily or as a result of enforceable orders from the judiciary—had made crystal clear that race would no longer be permitted as a valid factor of adverse classification in any public or quasi-public sphere—and even the demonstrably private sector of society found itself under intense and mounting pressure to fall into line with the spirit of the times. The tough Civil Rights Act of 1964 and the equally tough Voting Rights Act of 1965, with their numerous subsequent amendatory extensions and expansions, were being vigorously enforced; desegregation of public educational facilities, on all levels, but particularly in the deep South,[1] had advanced from the tokenism of two decades earlier to an all but complete stage—with exceptions still extant, however, largely because of housing patterns and ethnic clusters that do not readily lend themselves to rapid alterations (of which much more later in these pages); the increase in college and university enrollment of blacks had become so dramatic during the 1970s—some 300 per cent in five years—that by late 1980 the U.S. Bureau of the Census could report that blacks were entering higher education in numbers *exceeding* their representation in the total population (although their dropout rate was significantly higher than that of whites).[2] Jim Crow[3] legislation was legally dead everywhere; public accommodations were open to all; registered black voters numbered close to 10 million—almost four times as many as in 1960; and over 5,000 blacks held elective public office—an increase from but 72 in 1965 and 480 in 1967, including almost 2,500 black officials in the South (where the most dramatic gains took place). Nationally, there were over 400 black judges[4] almost 15 per cent of whom were appointed to the *federal* bench by President Carter.

[1] Generally speaking, five Southern states are usually classified as the deep South: South Carolina, Georgia, Louisiana, Alabama, and Mississippi. The six other members of the Confederacy are commonly simply called Southern: Virginia, North Carolina, Florida, Arkansas, Tennessee, and Texas. Six are normally classified as Border states: Delaware, Kentucky, Maryland, West Virginia, Oklahoma, and Missouri (although the Bureau of the Census no longer includes Missouri).

[2] See the Bureau's *Annual Report* for the years of the 1970s and for 1980.

[3] A slang term applied to the black, derived from the title of a minstrel song, popularized about 1835 by F. D. Rice: "Wheel About and Turn About and Jump, Jim Crow."

[4] See statistics provided regularly by the U.S. Bureau of the Census, the U.S. Bureau of Labor Statistics, *Statistical Abstract of the United States,* the Joint Center of Political Studies, *The Christian Science Monitor, The Washington Post,* and *The New York Times.*

High-ranking black officials were in evidence at all levels of government—including some 200 mayors. Thus, among others, the Northern cities of Los Angeles, California; Detroit and Grand Rapids, Michigan; Gary, Indiana; Cleveland and Dayton, Ohio; and Newark and East Orange, New Jersey—all had elected black mayors, 45 of these in cities with white majorities. The year 1969 saw the election of black mayors in the Southern cities of Chapel Hill, North Carolina, and Fayette, Mississippi; and that of 1973 not only brought the same to Raleigh, North Carolina, but witnessed the first election of a black mayor for a Southern metropolitan center, Atlanta, Georgia, in the person of 33-year-old attorney Maynard Jackson. Birmingham, a symbol of Southern intransigence on race, elected a black mayor in 1980. Massachusetts was a state with only 3 per cent of its population black when it sent Republican Edward W. Brooke to the U.S. Senate in 1966 to replace retiring New England Brahmin Leverett Saltonstall. Brooke, the first black Senator since Reconstruction—who had easily defeated a distinguished Massachusetts Yankee of unquestioned civil-libertarian persuasion, Endicott Peabody—was re-elected by a margin of better than 2:1 in 1972.[5]

In 1967 President Johnson had appointed Thurgood Marshall to the Supreme Court—the first black ever to receive this honor. In that same year, Robert H. Lawrence became the first black astronaut; in 1976 Alabama Democrats had elected the first black ever to serve as a member of the state's regular delegation to the Democratic National Committee; and neighboring Mississippi, which now led all Southern states in the number of elected black officials, saw the installation of a black as the state's Roman Catholic Auxiliary Bishop. There were 481 black delegates at the 1980 Democratic Convention, a good many of them from the deep South. In the fall of 1980, seventeen blacks were elected to the 97th Congress (1981–83), more than double the number (only seven then) that had served there at the height of the Reconstruction from 1873 to 1877. (The 97th Congress also held a record twenty-one women and five Hispanics.) In the realm of national law enforcement, in 1963 there were 1,600 whites for every black in the F.B.I.; by 1980 the ratio had dropped to 35:1, and two of the 59 special agents in charge were black. Indeed, the catalogue of accomplishments was proud and impressive. Moreover, between the Civil War and the Korean War the rate of Negro illiteracy had dropped from 90 to less than 5 per cent. There was now a rising black middle class (family incomes of upward of $15,000–20,000 annually, with more than 500,000 black families earning more than $25,000 and 32,000 more than $50,000 in 1977.) Despite the economic turndown during the mid and late 1970s, the rise in family incomes was at a rate greater than that of

[5] His record tainted by some questionable financial transactions, Senator Brooke was defeated in his quest for a third term in 1978 by Democrat Paul E. Tsongas—a man with an even more liberal record.

whites, while—for the first time in many years—blacks generally were moving into the poverty class at a lesser rate than whites. The number of nonwhite professional workers had more than quintupled between the *Brown* decision[6] and mid-1981; life expectancy for blacks had commenced to increase markedly, accompanied by a striking reduction in black mortality rates under one year of age; black migration to the suburbs increased 39 per cent during the 1970s; and blacks had begun to feel sufficiently confident about the evident improvement in the South's racial climate so as to commence to move *into* the South in greater numbers than *out* of it as of 1974—a phenomenon that has continued at an accelerated pace.[7]

Yet while there was indubitably demonstrable and truly commendable progress on every level of public and private life, the picture was not universally bright. Although the median black family income in 1975 had maintained its recent annual increase of close to 8 per cent to reach almost $8,000, that figure was still only 65 per cent as much as that earned by white families, and inflation hit blacks harder. At the same time, the number of black families with only a mother· at home (there were *circa* 2.1 million such families in July 1975) had jumped to a total of 35 per cent of all black families as opposed to 9 per cent of all white families—and the majority of these fatherless families are poor, their children especially vulnerable to delinquency, crime, and premarital pregnancy. There were dramatic income gains at all age levels during the 1960s and 1970s, with one-third of the black families' earnings reaching the $10,000 threshold. But the jobless rate for blacks in 1979 stood at 13.7 per cent versus 7.6 per cent for whites. Upward of 40 per cent of all food stamp purchases were being made by black families. More than three times as many black women were separated or divorced than were white women. The high school dropout rate for blacks, after improving somewhat between 1960 and 1970, had begun to augment again—and was still almost twice as high as that for whites.[8] Unquestionably, enormous, readily recognizable progress had been made on almost all fronts of the racial dilemma—yet much remained to be accomplished.

[6] *Brown v. Board of Education of Topeka,* 374 U.S. 483 (1954).

[7] See *The New York Times,* June 23, 1974, Sec. 4, p. 15; the 1975 report of the U.S. Bureau of the Census; "Geographical Mobility: March 1975 to March 1977," a release by the U.S. Bureau of the Census; Bernard E. Anderson, "The Black Middle Class," *The Pennsylvania Gazette,* March 1979, p. 37; Robert Reinhold, "Progress of Blacks Traced," *New York Times* News Service; *The* [Charlottesville, Va.] *Daily Progress,* July 1, 1979, p. B9; *The Daily Progress,* June 2, 1980, p. A12; and U.S. Department of Commerce, Bureau of the Census, P-23 *Current Population Reports* 80, "The Social and Economic Status of the Black Population in the United States: An Historical View, 1790–1978" (1980) and *The New York Times,* July 3, 1981.

[8] For sources of statistics see those cited on p. 308, footnote 4, *supra,* and p. 310, footnote 7, *ibid.;* plus "Decade of Progress," *Time Magazine,* April 16, 1973, p. 16; the Annual Economic Surveys of the National Urban League; Paul Delaney, "Economic Survey Cites Black Loss," *The New York Times,* July 29, 1975, p. 27c.

Moreover, the demonstrable psychological toll inflicted on America's blacks over almost three centuries was clearly in evidence; impatience, however understandable, threatened to play havoc with the newly established lines of equality of opportunity. Racial prejudice was not only still a factor but, because of the assertive and highly visible civil rights clamor, was engulfing areas it had not hitherto reached, especially in Northern urban and suburban areas. The frightful August 1965 riots in the Watts section of Los Angeles lasted six days and resulted in 34 deaths, 1,032 injuries, the arrest of 3,952 persons, and $40 million in property damage (more than 600 buildings were damaged, 200 totally destroyed). Those around Detroit's Twelfth Street in 1967 constituted the bloodiest uprising in the country in half a century, and the costliest ever in terms of property damage: the five days of rioting, looting, burning, and killing resulted in 43 deaths, 347 injuries, 3,800 arrests, 5,000 made homeless, 1,300 buildings reduced to ashes, and $500 million in damages. Watts and Detroit—and the disorders that in subsequent years engulfed such Northern centers as Newark, Buffalo, Kansas City, Cleveland, Chicago, St. Louis, San Francisco, and many others, reaching into Miami (16 deaths) and Chattanooga again in 1980—served as shocking and costly reminders that the mere removal of legal barriers to equality was not enough. The principle of equality now not only included demands for economic and even social equality, but also included demands for compensatory, preferential "affirmative action." Yet fear and lack of communication were still rampant, and frustration, engendered by rising expectations, could readily lead to anger and thence to blind unreasoned violence. The President's National Commission on the Causes and Prevention of Violence thus reported late in 1969 that extensive violence had occurred in 239 hostile outbreaks by blacks, which resulted in more than 8,000 casualties and 191 deaths.[9] Prejudice and poverty still stood in the way. And the bitter school-busing controversies that crested in the 1970s—of which more below—would demonstrate that resort to violence is not confined to either one race or one section of the land!

Thus, whereas the gulf of opportunity and achievement was clearly narrowing, it remained wide for a good many blacks, especially at the lower socio-economic levels. And the desire to bridge it not only fully but rapidly, coupled with a demonstrable measure of success, gave rise to insistent and greater demands, not infrequently backed by what became known as "action in the streets" rather than in the courts or in legislative halls. This action, in turn, prompted considerable feeling on the part of the white community that what had hitherto been regarded as legitimate grievances based on legitimate demands had now become unreasonable and unjusti-

[9] Chapter 5, "American Society and the Radical Black Militant," in *Law and Order Reconsidered: A Staff Report* (New York: Bantam Books, Inc., 1970), pp. 85–117.

fiable demands for "special" or "privileged" treatment—increasingly characterized as "preferential treatment" or "reverse discrimination." Public authorities thus found themselves faced with the problem of drawing lines particularly between *public* and *private* action and the attendant legal and governmental responsibilities, a difficult and uncomfortable task. Just how, where, and by whom could or should such a line be established? How to find accommodations between the twin basic rights of liberty and equality—*both* being constitutionally mandated? Is it purely—is it properly—a judicial function? A summary glance into the history of racial discrimination in the United States may serve as a prolegomenon to some answers, if we can speak of answers at all.

A Glance at History

Although the Declaration of Independence had stipulated, as a self-evident truth, that "all men are created equal," it soon became obvious that, in the words of George Orwell, "some men are created more equal than others." The second section of the first article of the Constitution clearly recognized the existence of slavery in the United States by directing the inclusion of "three-fifths of all other persons," i.e., the *slaves,* in the enumeration which was to form the basis for representative apportionment and taxation. True, Section 9 of Article One did make it possible to stop the "migration or importation" of slaves after 1808, provided Congress chose to do so then, and the Thirteenth Amendment was designed to settle the matter by outlawing slavery in 1865. But it was not really until the ratification of the Fourteenth Amendment in 1868, five years after Lincoln's Emancipation Proclamation, that the white-supremacy concept inherent in Article One was removed from the Constitution. In the language of the Amendment's second section: "Representatives shall be apportioned among the several States according to their respective numbers, *counting the whole number of persons in each State,* excluding Indians not taxed. . . ."[10]

Yet despite these enactments, despite the mandates of Amendment Fourteen (quoted below), and despite the language of the Fifteenth Amendment of 1870 that on its face seemed to assure to blacks the privilege of the ballot, neither the myth of white supremacy nor the fact of color prejudice was wiped out. Section 1 of the Fourteenth Amendment, now so significant but then so ineffective, would have to wait more than eight decades for its triumphs on behalf of the black:

> *All persons born or naturalized in the United States, and subject to the jurisdiction thereof, are citizens of the United States and of the State*

[10] Opening sentence. (Italics supplied.)

wherein they reside. No state shall make or enforce any law which shall abridge the privileges or immunities of citizens of the United States; *nor shall any State deprive* any person of life, liberty, or property, without due process of law; *nor deny to any person within its jurisdiction the equal protection of the laws.*[11]

The Emancipation Proclamation and these three Civil War amendments intended, above all, to ameliorate the lot of blacks by attacking the constitutional silence on federal protection of civil rights, a protection that had, until then, been left wholly to the several states. They proved to be ineffective. True, Reconstruction seemed to offer genuine hope: twenty-two Southern blacks went to Congress and two became United States Senators from Mississippi. True also that in the decade following the passage of the Thirteenth Amendment, Congress enacted five major civil rights statutes, spelling out the rights of the new black freedom and providing penalties for their denial.[12] But the South proved itself equal to the challenge of restoring the *status quo ante* via a host of ingenious and disingenuous devices. By 1910 every former Confederate state, for example, had succeeded in disfranchising blacks either by state statute—e.g., the "white primary" and the "grandfather clause"[13]—by state constitutional amendment, or with the direct or indirect aid of such United States Supreme Court decisions as those in *United States v. Harris*,[14] the *Slaughterhouse Cases*[15] and the *Civil Rights Cases*.[16] The Court's position, as noted earlier,[17] was that the Fourteenth Amendment did not place under federal protection "the entire domain of civil rights heretofore belonging exclusively to the states," and that the protection offered by the Fourteenth and Fifteenth Amendments was *against state action only,* not against private action. And in 1896 the Court upheld the convenient discriminatory concept of "separate but equal" in the case of *Plessy v. Ferguson*.[18] To all intents and purposes the black was at the mercy of the states—there was no Warren Court to redress grievances. Indeed, until World War II the federal government assumed at most a highly limited role in the protection of civil rights on the state level.

In 1900 almost 90 per cent of America's blacks lived in the South and the Border (a figure that had declined to 70 per cent in 1950, to 60 in

[11] Entire section quoted. (Italics supplied.)
[12] Among them were the "Anti-K.K.K." Act of 1871 and the Public Accommodation Act of 1875.
[13] See pp. 354 ff., *infra.*
[14] 106 U.S. 629 (1882).
[15] 16 Wallace 36 (1873).
[16] 109 U.S. 3 (1883).
[17] See Chapter III, *supra.*
[18] 163 U.S. 537.

1960, and to 51 in 1978[19]); the core of racial discrimination was naturally found there, on both the public and the private level. Thus, *public* authorities at the state and local levels, usually under the guise of the Court-upheld "separate but equal" concept, enacted measures (sometimes taking the form of a constitutional provision) *permitting* or even *requiring* segregation of buses, streetcars, taxicabs, railroads, waiting rooms, comfort stations, drinking fountains, state and local schools, state colleges and universities, hospitals, jails, cemeteries, sport facilities, beaches, bath houses, swimming pools, parks, golf courses, courthouse cafeterias, libraries, dwellings, theaters, hotels, restaurants, and other similar facilities—be these public, quasi-public, or private in nature; and interracial marriages were widely proscribed.[20] *Private* individuals and groups, on their own initiative, and not infrequently encouraged by state authorities, acted to deny blacks, and often other non-Caucasians as well, access to social clubs, fraternities and sororities, private schools, colleges, and universities, churches, cemeteries, funeral parlors, hospitals, hotels, dwellings, restaurants, movies, bowling alleys, swimming pools, bath houses, sporting events, comfort stations, drinking fountains, barber and beauty shops, employment agencies, and employment itself. There was nothing particularly secretive about either public or private discrimination; it was simply an accepted way of life—accepted by many blacks as well as by almost all whites.

Yet the onset of World War II—which witnessed many blacks fighting side-by-side with whites and which saw increasing migration of blacks northwards—prompted the federal government to take notice of the problem. Although his administration recommended no civil rights legislation *per se* to Congress—which, needless to say, did not act on its own—President Franklin D. Roosevelt did take two far-reaching executive actions. In 1939, at the prompting of Attorney-General Frank Murphy (who would soon be promoted to the Supreme Court), he created a Civil Liberties Unit[21] in the Criminal Division of the Department of Justice. Then, since Congress would not have passed such legislation, he established by executive order[22] the first Committee on Fair Employment Practices (to be known as the F.E.P.C.). The President created it largely at the behest of black leaders, other civil rights advocates, and, significantly, his spouse, Eleanor Roosevelt—whose entire life was dedicated to the eradication of

[19] *United States Department of Commerce News,* October 23, 1970, p. 5 and U.S. Bureau of the Census, 1979. (See also p. 310, footnote 7, *supra.*) The decline appeared to have been arrested at the end of the 1970s; and a reversal began to take place. (See text and fn. 7, p. 310, *supra.*)

[20] It was not until 1967 that this particular prohibition was unanimously declared unconstitutional as a violation of both equal protection and due process guaranties under Amendment Fourteen in *Loving v. Virginia,* 388 U.S. 1. See also its 1964 precurser, *McLaughlin v. Florida,* 379 U.S. 184, also decided 9:0.

[21] Subsequently to be called the Civil Rights Section.

[22] Exec. Order 8802, *Federal Register,* Vol. VI (1941), p. 3109.

injustice. Although its enforcement powers were severely circumscribed, and its domain was exclusively in the federal sphere, the F.E.P.C. did make some progress toward the elimination of discriminatory employment practices in those companies and labor unions that had government contracts or were engaged in activities connected with World War II. Yet Congress abolished the Committee in 1946.

The end of the war brought increasing pressure on the federal government to combat the various manifestations of racial discrimination. But the political power of entrenched Southern forces, both in Congress and out, often combined with Northern conservative elements, was able to prevent, or at least to delay, any meaningful legislative aid. The House of Representatives, by definition theoretically "closer to the people" and more sensitive to the currents and tides of change, did pass in 1946 and 1950 such potentially remedial measures as bills establishing a permanent F.E.P.C.; but both were rejected by the more tradition-bound Senate, in which Southern influence was still decisive in such matters. Again, the House passed legislation designed to outlaw the poll tax in 1945, 1947, and 1949, yet in no instance would the Senate accept it. (It would take another thirteen years before Congress legislated against the poll tax in *federal* elections by way of the Twenty-fourth Amendment, which was ratified in 1964.) No action at all was taken on the host of anti-lynching proposals introduced at every session of Congress.

Winds of Change: President Truman. Because Congress was unwilling or unable to make progress on the race problem, President Harry S. Truman—a son of Missouri, with Confederate ancestors—determined to take matters into his own hands. In a sense, the catalyst for his first move was Congress's deliberate failure to include a widely backed anti-discrimination provision in the important Selective Service Act of 1948. Angry, the President issued a no-nonsense executive order[23] that specifically banned "separate but equal" recruiting, training, and service in the armed forces. While this did not affect the National Guard and Reserve units under state aegis, it was an important step in an area of public activity in which discrimination based on race was particularly heinous: military service for one's native land. President Truman was convinced that he had to move on his own, insofar as that was legal and possible, because of the fate that the report of his President's Committee on Civil Rights had suffered at the hands of Congress: in 1946 he had appointed a fifteen-member blue-ribbon committee,[24] and charged it specifically with the careful investigation of the need for legislative and other procedures designed to further and protect civil rights and liberties. One year later, the Committee reported that al-

[23] Exec. Order 9981, *Federal Register,* Vol. XIII (1948), p. 4313.
[24] Exec. Order 9808, *Federal Register,* Vol. XI (1946), p. 14153. The Committee was headed by Charles E. Wilson ("Electric Charlie"), president of General Electric.

though civil rights were indeed better and more generally protected than ever before, there were still alarmingly widespread violations. In its broadly distributed report, *To Secure These Rights,* the Committee made numerous recommendations designed to ensure that every violation of a civil right by any individual be treated as a criminal offense. Were these recommendations to be followed, the enforcement of civil rights would become a new and vigorous government activity on a much extended scale. Specifically, the Committee's proposals included federal laws to forbid lynching; to outlaw discrimination in voting requirements; to create a permanent Fair Employment Practices Commission and a permanent Commission on Civil Rights; and to expand into a Civil Rights Division the small, undermanned Civil Rights Section in the Department of Justice that Attorney-General Murphy had established eight years earlier.

Like all proposals for the extension of government activities, these quickly became a political issue. Still, President Truman committed himself to the implementation of the report as far as federal action was feasible —in the face of considerable risks to his party position and his campaign for re-election in 1948. Indeed, that campaign witnessed the "Dixiecrat" revolt in the Democratic Party, resulting in the bolting from the Democratic party of four Southern states[25] and their formation of the Dixiecrat party under Strom Thurmond of South Carolina. Nonetheless, the President made *To Secure These Rights* an issue throughout his campaign. He won re-election, but he did not obtain—as already noted—congressional acquiescence. In fact, Congress took no action during the remaining four years of the Truman Administration, a hiatus that extended through the first four and a half years of the Eisenhower Presidency. But Truman attempted to salvage what he could by executive order. Shortly before his 1948 order banning segregation in the armed forces, he had issued an executive order[26] establishing a Fair Employment Board to oversee announced policy that henceforth all federal jobs were to be distributed without any regard to "race, color, religion, or national origin." Three years later the President created the Committee on Government Contract Compliance, requiring any business holding a contract with the federal government not only to pledge but to provide *bona fide* fair employment policies and practices.[27] The tenor of these several executive moves gradually began to pervade much of the executive establishment.

President Eisenhower continued his predecessor's civil rights policies. Resorting to the technique of the executive order,[28] the new Chief Executive created the President's Committee on Government Contracts, headed by Vice-President Nixon. The Committee was empowered to receive com-

---

[25] Alabama, Louisiana, Mississippi, and South Carolina.
[26] Exec. Order 9980, *Federal Register,* Vol. XIII (1948), p. 4311.
[27] Exec. Order 10308, *Federal Register,* Vol. XVI (1951), p. 12303.
[28] Exec. Order 10479, *Federal Register,* Vol. XVIII (1953), p. 4899.

plaints alleging discrimination by government contractors, and to cancel contracts if necessary. Various cabinet departments and agencies continued the policy of earlier administrations against sundry types of obvious internal discrimination.

The Watershed. These activities were of course not lost on the several states. A good many Northern states turned to F.E.P.C. and similar devices to combat discrimination. The air was filled with the beginnings of change. Yet the South was determined not to budge, and in Congress it had a seemingly eternal ally. President Eisenhower did not recommend any new civil rights legislation until his Administration's Civil Rights Bill of 1956. It failed to be enacted, but Congress did pass a modified version, the Civil Rights Act of 1957, the first major piece of civil rights legislation since Reconstruction. It is fair to say, however, that it would never have become law had not the Supreme Court, swung into the fray with its monumentally significant ruling in the *Public School Segregation Cases*[29] on May 17, 1954.

That decision was one of the most far-reaching in our history in terms of its social impact.[30] It catalyzed the issue of racial discrimination; it focused responsibility for remedial action on government officials everywhere; and, especially, it pointed an accusing finger at that branch of government presumably responsible for social action: the legislature. The controversy triggered by the 1954 *Public School Segregation Cases* may have subsided, but it will not die. Conscious of its position as a national moral goad as well as a teacher in a continuing national constitutional seminar, the Court had led. Recognizing the necessarily limited options open to the executive branch, and the immobility of the legislative on the issue, the Supreme Court had decided unanimously that it had to create a line. As Mr. Justice Jackson remarked laconically during oral argument in *Brown*, "I suppose that realistically the reason this case is here was [*sic*] that action could not be obtained from Congress."[31] After two and a half years of painful deliberation, it chose to attack the concept of "separate but equal" in the field of public school education on the grounds that separate facilities are "inherently unequal," and that the very concept of "separate but equal" in matters of race violates the "equal protection of the laws" clause of the Fourteenth Amendment and (on the federal level) the "due process of law" clause of the Fifth.[32]

---

[29] *Brown v. Board of Education of Topeka,* 347 U.S. 483 (1954); and *Bolling v. Sharpe,* 347 U.S. 497 (1954).

[30] Mr. Chief Justice Warren ranked it in second place behind *Baker v. Carr,* 369 U.S. 186 (1962)—see pp. 19–20, *supra*—in terms of the significance of cases his Court decided during the sixteen-year tenure from 1953 to 1969.

[31] Oral argument in the Virginia and South Carolina segments of the suit, p. 244.

[32] *Brown v. Board, op. cit.*—which involved four different states: Kansas, Virginia, Delaware, and South Carolina, and *Bolling v. Sharpe, op. cit.*—which concerned the District of Columbia only.

"Separate but Equal": Rise and Demise

We know that the intent of the three Civil War amendments was to abolish the institution of slavery, to bestow the full benefit of American citizenship upon blacks, and to enable them to exercise the franchise. And for a brief period of roughly two decades, give or take a few years depending upon the individual state involved, blacks were indeed in a position to exercise their newly confirmed civil rights relatively effectively—backed, to be sure, by federal Reconstruction forces. But, as we also know—and as C. Vann Woodward, among others, has told us so well[33]—the dominant white elements in the old Confederacy were not about to grant blacks anything like genuine, lasting freedom and equality; indeed, they utilized every conceivable covert and overt device to bar the one-time slaves from attaining even the semblance of first-class citizenship. As the evangelism and fervor of Northern abolitionists began to subside, especially after the Hayes Compromise of 1877 had resulted in the withdrawal of the troops from the South, Southern leadership all but restored the *status quo ante*—with the overwhelming support of the Southern constituency. By 1900, the Southern black had been pushed back into second-class citizenship. Jim Crow, with certain refinements, again reigned supreme.

THE RISE OF "SEPARATE BUT EQUAL"

Black leaders endeavored to battle this trend. Unable to expect any aid in their efforts from either the executive or legislative branches, they turned to the state judiciary. But it, too, quickly proved itself generally in sympathy with the point of view of the region's population and its leadership. The black's only hope thus hinged on the United States Supreme Court. And *it* proved for a long time to be a vain hope.[34]

An Ill Omen: Slaughterhouse. When the famous *Slaughterhouse Cases*[35] were handed down by the Court in 1873, things began to look bad for the black cause. Ironically, blacks were *not* involved in that litigation, and the Court's language even seemed to give distinct comfort to them. There were ringing phrases regarding the purposes of the Civil War amendments: the achievement of "freedom for the slave race," the "security and firm establishment of that freedom," and the protection of the "newly-made freeman and citizen from the oppressions of those who had formerly exercised unlimited dominion over him."[36] But, as noted in the earlier discussion[37]

[33] See his *The Strange Career of Jim Crow*, rev. ed. (New York: Oxford University Press, 1966).
[34] For an engaging account of the story of the Supreme Court of the United States and black petitioners, written by the son of a black slave and his white wife, see Loren Miller's *The Petitioners* (New York: Pantheon Books, 1966).
[35] 16 Wallace 36.
[36] *Ibid.*, at 71.
[37] See Chapter III, *supra*, pp. 41–47.

of these cases, the Court's *real* point was that there must be a careful distinction between the "privileges or immunities" of *United States* citizens and *state* (here Louisiana) citizens; that the only privileges attaching to national citizenship are those that "owe their existence to the Federal Government, its National character, its Constitution, or its laws";[38] that, in effect, a citizen of a state derived his "privileges or immunities" from *state* citizenship, a thing quite "distinct" from federal citizenship rights, which "depend upon different characteristics or circumstances in the individual."[39] In other words, if blacks had hoped to rely on the "privileges or immunities" clause of that Amendment as a source of salvation in their struggle for equal rights, the Supreme Court's narrow construction of the clause—one never really altered to this day (1981)—rendered it of little value as a restraint upon state regulation. But what of the "due process of law" and "equal protection of the laws" clauses of the Fourteenth?

Another Hope Shattered: The Civil Rights Cases. Things seemed to look up when Congress, in an effort to aid blacks, passed the Civil Rights Act of 1875, which made it a *federal* crime for any owner or operator of, *inter alia,* a hotel, public conveyance, or theater, to "deny the full enjoyments of the accommodations thereof" because of race or color. Various blacks were nonetheless denied access and brought suit in a series of five cases,[40] ultimately consolidated by the Supreme Court as *The Civil Rights Cases of 1883.*[41] The Court, in an 8:1 decision written by Mr. Justice Joseph P. Bradley, with only Mr. Justice John Marshall Harlan in dissent, declared the Act of 1875 unconstitutional. The Court did so on the grounds that the Fourteenth Amendment applied to *state* action only and did not give Congress authority to forbid discrimination by *private* individuals (a point it had already made a few months earlier in *United States v. Harris,*[42] in which it declared unconstitutional a section of the Ku Klux Klan Act of 1871 as being inapplicable to the acts of *private* persons); that if the state did not assist the discrimination of an individual against another individual, the matter is purely between the two as private persons. Thus not only had the Supreme Court sharply limited the "privileges or immunities" that had, hopefully, come with national citizenship, it now read the phrase "no state shall" in the Fourteenth and Fifteenth Amendments to mean solely and literally the actions of state government *officials*. The decisive Court majority refused to accept the contention that it was in fact state action when individuals and corporations *licensed by a state* to "serve all without

[38] *The Slaughterhouse Cases, op. cit.,* at 79.

[39] *Ibid.,* majority opinion by Mr. Justice Miller, at 74.

[40] One each from California, Kansas, Missouri, New Jersey, and Tennessee.

[41] 109 U.S. 3. Their story is well known and well told. See, for example, Alan F. Westin, "The Case of the Prejudiced Doorkeeper," in John A. Garraty, ed., *Quarrels That Have Shaped the Constitution* (New York: Harper & Row, 1964), pp. 128–44.

[42] 106 U.S. 629 (1882).

discrimination" used race as a criterion. As for alleged violation of the Thirteenth Amendment, it regarded restrictive public accommodations as having nothing to do with slavery or involuntary servitude. Indeed, Bradley commented in an oft-quoted dictum that blacks should cease endeavoring to obtain "special treatment"; that there had to be a time when blacks stopped being "the special favorite of the law," and adopted "the rank of a mere citizen" (a refrain that became highly audible again in the face of the "affirmative action" programs of the 1960s and beyond).[43] Harlan, however, not only flayed Bradley for these comments, but firmly voted to uphold the Civil Rights Act of 1875. He insisted that it was well settled that "railroad corporations, keepers of inns, and managers of places of public amusement are *agents or instrumentalities of the State*"[44] and that the Act regardless could and should have been upheld under the congressional power over interstate commerce—foreshadowing the Civil Rights Act of 1964 and its quick, unanimous upholding by the Supreme Court.[45]

Gradually taking their cue from the *Slaughterhouse, Harris,* and *Civil Rights* decisions, most of the states of the old Confederacy not only closed their eyes to the steadily spreading segregation practices that either had sprung up or were revived within their borders, but in the four-year period between 1887 and 1891 alone eight of them enacted legislation *requiring* railroads, for example, to maintain *separate* facilities for whites and blacks.

Enter Plessy v. Ferguson. There had been earlier legal skirmishes at the state level; indeed, the "separate but equal" concept had been heavily attacked, albeit unsuccessfully, by Charles Sumner when Massachusetts Chief Justice Lemuel Shaw adopted it almost half a century earlier in 1849 in *Roberts v. the City of Boston*[46] by ruling in favor of Boston's "police power" to segregate schools. But the issue was first joined at the highest federal level in the case of *Plessy v. Ferguson,*[47] which was destined to remain law for fifty-eight years. Before the Court was the constitutionality of Louisiana's Jim Crow Car Act of 1890, euphemistically entitled "An Act To Promote the Comfort of Passengers." It required that railroads "provide equal but separate accommodations for the white and colored races" and that "no person be permitted to occupy seats in coaches other than the ones assigned to his race." Here then it was: "EQUAL but SEPARATE." With

---

[43] *The Civil Rights Cases, op. cit.,* at 25. For an analysis of the "affirmative action"/"reverse-discrimination" syndrome, see pp. 396 ff., *infra.*

[44] *Ibid.,* at 58. (Italics supplied.)

[45] See pp. 384–51, *infra.*

[46] Cush. (59 Mass.) 198 at 206. Sumner here unsuccessfully represented Sarah C. Roberts, a black child, who brought suit against the City of Boston under an 1854 statute that provided for recovery of damages from "the city or town" that supported instruction from which any child was unlawfully excluded. Sumner's argument—to the effect that segregated schools can never be equal—prophetically antedated the NAACP brief in *Brown v. Board of Education* (see pp. 328 ff., *infra*).

[47] 163 U.S. 537 (1896).

the exception of an 1892 decision in which the State of Louisiana Supreme Court had held the new law to be inapplicable to an *interstate* passenger—a decision the state did not appeal—all prior tests of the 1890 Act at the state level had ended in victory for the new doctrine. Now at last the Supreme Court would hear and adjudicate the problem of "separate but equal," a problem which had been brought to it through the efforts of a group of eighteen blacks who had formed a "Citizens' Committee To Test the Constitutionality of the Separate Car Law." As their attorney they selected Albion Winegar Tourgee of Mayville, then residing in New York, a leading carpetbagger during Reconstruction who, an Ohioan by birth, had served in the Union Army and then had moved to Greensboro, North Carolina, to practice law. There he became a leader of the Radical Republican Party, took an active part in the creation of the State's Radical Constitution, and served as a judge of the Superior Court of his adopted state for six years. Tourgee had been chosen by the Citizens' Committee even prior to the 1892 Louisiana "victory," which he obtained. That case had not met the needs and aims of the Jim Crow Act's challengers. Homer Adolph Plessy's case did.[48]

Plessy was seven-eighths white; his one-eighth "African blood" was not apparent. The Citizens' Committee had seen to it that the East Louisiana Railroad knew of his background. Selected by the Committee to test the statute, Plessy boarded in New Orleans, having purchased a ticket to Covington, Louisiana, and took a seat in the "Whites Only" coach; when the conductor requested that he move to the "Colored Only" section, Plessy refused, whereupon he was promptly arrested by Detective Christopher C. Cain, and charged with violating the "Jim Crow Car Act of 1890." Tourgee's defense contended that the Louisiana statute under which Plessy had been arrested and charged was null and void as a violation of both the Thirteenth and Fourteenth Amendments. The argument turned on the latter's proscription of the denial of the "equal protection of the laws." Partly because of the fundamental requirement inherent in the judicial process that all remedies "below" must be exhausted before the Supreme Court will consider an otherwise properly qualified case, and partly because of its own work load, the high tribunal did not hand down its decision until four years later. These intervening years saw a further attrition of black post-Civil War gains—and unless the Court were to strike down the "separate but equal" doctrine, Jim Crow would be perpetuated.

The opinion of the Court—with Mr. Justice David J. Brewer not participating—upheld the statute 7:1. Once again, the lone dissenter was John Marshall Harlan, whose grandson and namesake was destined to help pre-

---

[48] For a lively and illuminating description of the case and its setting, plus an engaging sketch of the principals, see C. Vann Woodward's "The Case of the Louisiana Traveler," in Garraty, *op. cit.,* pp. 145–58.

side over Jim Crow's judicial demise in the Court six decades later.[49] The majority opinion in *Plessy* was written by Mr. Justice Henry B. Brown, one of seven Northerners then on the Court.[50] Brown's opinion frankly acknowledged Louisiana's action to have been "state action," thus falling under Fourteenth Amendment consideration; *but,* he held, the action was *not discriminatory* since the whites were separated just as much from the blacks as the blacks were separated from the whites! As for the charge that the basis for the separation was race, Brown ruled that was not in and of itself a violation of the Constitution's equal protection clause, for a state had every right under that document to "classify" as long as that classification[51] was not capricious, arbitrary, or unreasonable. "Separate but equal" did not run afoul of these considerations, said Brown, since the claim that the concept intended to "stamp the colored race with a badge of inferiority" (a phrase that would be quoted and construed quite differently by Mr. Chief Justice Earl Warren fifty-eight years later) was "not by reason of anything found in the act, but *solely because the colored race chooses to put that construction upon it."* And Brown could not forbear to add: "If one race be inferior to another socially, the Constitution of the United States cannot put them upon the same plane."[52] He admitted that the Fourteenth Amendment was "undoubtedly designed to enforce the absolute equality of the two races before the law," but that "it could not have been intended in the nature of things . . . [to] abolish distinction based upon color or to enforce social, as distinct from political equality."[53]

In eloquent anger, Mr. Justice Harlan rejected what he viewed as the majority's social Darwinism. To him, as to many others who would follow, the line drawn here by his colleagues reflected "a compound of bad logic, bad history, bad sociology, and bad constitutional law."[54] Moreover, it flew in the face of recent precedent.[55] "The thin disguise of 'equal' accommoda-

[49] He joined the Supreme Court approximately one year after the 1954 *Public School Segregation Cases, op. cit.,* and was on the bench when the Court handed down its implementation decision in the second *Public Segregation Cases (Brown v. Board of Education of Topeka, et al.,* 349 U.S. 294 [1955]).

[50] The Southerners were Harlan and Mr. Justice Edward D. White of Louisiana.

[51] For a discussion of "classification" see Jewell Cass Phillips, Henry J. Abraham, and Cortez A. M. Ewing, *Essentials of American National Government,* 3rd ed. (New York: American Book Co., 1971), Ch. VI, pp. 110 ff.

[52] *Plessy v. Ferguson,* 163 U.S. 537 (1896), at 551.

[53] *Ibid.,* at 544.

[54] Robert J. Harris, *The Quest for Equality: The Constitution, Congress, and the Supreme Court* (Baton Rouge: Louisiana State University Press, 1960), p. 101.

[55] *Strauder v. West Virginia,* 100 U.S. 303 (1880), in which the Court had struck down on Fourteenth Amendment "equal protection" grounds a state law that limited jury duty to *white male* citizens—although it proved to be a Pyrrhic victory. See also *ex parte Virginia,* 100 U.S. 339 (1880), where the Supreme Court upheld the conviction of a county court judge for having excluded blacks from jury lists compiled by him, solely because of their race. He had acted in violation of a federal law specifically forbidding such discrimination.

tions for passengers in railroad coaches will not mislead anyone, nor atone for the wrong this day done,"[56] Harlan warned the majority. He attacked the decision as one redolent with sociological speculation: "The arbitrary separation of citizens on the basis of race, while they are on a public highway, is a badge of servitude wholly inconsistent with the civil freedom and the equality of the law established by the Constitution. It cannot be justified upon any legal grounds."[57] And in memorable language he went on to note that

> in view of the Constitution, in the eye of the law, there is in this country no superior, dominant, ruling class of citizens. There is no caste here. *Our constitution is color-blind, and neither knows nor tolerates classes among citizens. . . .*[58] The law regards man as man, and takes no account of his surroundings or of his color when his civil rights as guaranteed by the supreme law of the land are involved.[59]

But this was a *dissenting* opinion. The separate but equal concept had not only been adopted; now it had been judicially sanctioned. It proved to be most detrimental to the blacks' cause in education, public accommodations, the franchise, the administration of justice, housing, employment, and, needless to add, social relationships. White supremacy seemed to have triumphed; assuredly this was true in most of the states below the Mason-Dixon line. For that matter, when Brown spoke in *Plessy,* not only the Southern and Border states, but a total of thirty states of the Union, including most of those in the West, as well as Indiana, Kansas, and New York, had "separate but equal" public school statutes.

CHIPPING AT THE DOCTRINE

Yet, however slowly and imperceptibly, the legal chisels were being readied, the chipping away at the "separate but equal" line probably began with the case of *Missouri ex rel. Gaines v. Canada*[60] in 1938; actually, the *first* court-enforced admission of a black to a heretofore segregated higher institution of learning had come two years earlier, when the Maryland

[56] 163 U.S. 537, at 562.

[57] *Ibid.*

[58] Almost 180 years later, with *Plessy* overruled twenty years earlier in *Brown v. Board,* Mr. Chief Justice Hale of the Supreme Court of Washington, speaking in dissent in the "reverse discrimination" case of *De Funis v. Odegaard,* 507 P. 2d 1169 (1973), at 1189, asked whether the Constitution may be color conscious in order to be color blind—an ironic dénouement. (See pp. 396 ff., *infra.*) He believed not, but events since seem to have demonstrated the contrary.

[59] *Ibid.,* at 559. (Italics supplied.) According to his colleague Brewer, Harlan "went to sleep with one hand upon the Constitution and the other on the Bible, and thus secured the untroubled sleep of the just and the righteous." Quoted in G. Edward White, *The American Judicial Tradition* (New York: Oxford University Press, 1976), p. 129.

[60] 305 U.S. 337.

Court of Appeals—that state's highest tribunal—ordered Donald Murray admitted to the University of Maryland Law School.[61] But it was *Gaines* which initially gave notice to the nation that the winds of change had begun to blow. That change had its practical roots in certain attitudes, both legal and social, which were growing partly as a result of what might be called a heightened egalitarian national conscience and partly because of the imminence of war. In any event, it manifested itself chiefly in the gradual but unquestionably progressive shift in rulings of the United States Supreme Court from acceptance of the separate but equal doctrine to a close examination of the alleged "equality" to, ultimately, the firm rejection of the constitutionality of the doctrine. It took almost two decades to proceed from stage one to stage three. Although the Supreme Court clearly led— and it did so despite vilification and abuse—it did have an important ally, however tenuous, in what might be called the national conscience.

The Gaines Case. Lloyd Gaines was a black citizen of Missouri who sought, but was denied, admission to the School of Law of the state-owned University of Missouri after his graduation from Lincoln University, an all-black Missouri institution. There was no claim of lack of qualifications— S. W. Canada, the University's registrar, simply pointed to a Missouri statute under which the two races were to be educated "separately but equally." Mr. Canada told Gaines that he could, of course, avail himself of another feature of Missouri law applying specifically to black law school applicants, whereby state funds were made available to qualified blacks for their legal education in schools of *adjacent states* that offered unsegregated facilities—e.g., Kansas, Nebraska, Iowa, Illinois. But, encouraged in his stand by the increasingly active and influential National Association for the Advancement of Colored People (NAACP), Gaines declined. What he wanted, he said, was what was his due as a full-fledged citizen and taxpayer of his home state of Missouri: the right to attend the state law school and to practice law in Missouri. Mr. Canada again refused. The NAACP then financed Gaines's appeal through the lower courts and ultimately to the Supreme Court of the United States. Mr. Chief Justice Charles Evans Hughes wrote the opinion, speaking also for Justices Brandeis, Stone, Cardozo, Roberts, Black, and Reed; only Justices McReynolds and Butler— the two surviving members of the so-called Arch-Conservative Quads[62]— dissented, pleading for a continuation of a practice that, they agreed, was in the "best interests" of Missouri's people.[63]

[61] *Pearson v. Murray,* 169 Md. 478 (1936). He was admitted and ultimately graduated.
[62] The other two were Justices Van Devanter and Sutherland, replaced by Black and Reed, in 1937 and 1938, respectively. Yet it is entirely plausible that—based on their records in the civil rights and liberties realm—the two departed justices would have joined the majority opinion.
[63] *Missouri ex rel. Gaines v. Canada,* 305 U.S. 337 (1938), dissenting opinion, at 353.

The Chief Justice praised the state of Missouri for the financial arrangements outlined, but held that since there was no law school for blacks in the entire state—Lincoln University had none—the equal protection guarantee of the Fourteenth Amendment was in fact denied Lloyd Gaines. Hughes, continuing to give comfort to the partisans of the "separate but equal" doctrine, explicitly stated that Missouri could have fulfilled its obligation to provide legal instruction to its black citizens "by furnishing equal facilities in separate schools, a method the validity of which has been sustained by our decisions."[64] In other words, he ruled that while the Constitution did not guarantee Gaines's admission to the School of Law of the University of Missouri, it did guarantee a legal education in Missouri substantially equal to that afforded by the state to members of the white race. That Gaines happened to be the only black wishing such an education was beside the point. The state subsequently decided to set up a separate law school for blacks at Lincoln University, but Lloyd Gaines, perhaps overcome by notoriety and pressure, disappeared shortly before the Court's decision was handed down. While it remained for someone else then to test the "separate but equal" doctrine *per se,* the *Gaines* case had laid the foundations based on the "equal protection of the laws" clause of Amendment Fourteen. It was this clause that would bring ultimate victory to the blacks' strivings; it was this clause that cast the black into the role of the Supreme Court's "unwilling ward," its "constant petitioner."[65]

Post-Gaines. Almost ten years of pre-war, war, and post-war preoccupation elapsed before the Court dealt with the doctrine again. Inconclusively but nonetheless pointedly, in 1948 it ordered the state of Oklahoma to provide a duly qualified, NAACP-backed black woman applicant with an equal legal education in a state institution.[66] The results were less than satisfactory in terms of the ultimate goal, but there was no longer any question that, at the very least, *equal* facilities would have to be state provided.

Two years later, however, the Court handed down a set of decisions which made painfully clear to the South that while "separate but equal" might still not be unconstitutional, it was patently on its last legs. The two 1950 cases were announced on the same Opinion Monday, and both were decided unanimously in opinions written by Mr. Chief Justice Vinson. Although neither outlawed the "separate but equal" doctrine *per se,* the conditions posited by the Court for its continued constitutionality were in fact unattainable. Both cases had once again been stimulated and backed by the NAACP's capable, increasingly active, legal team. One, *Sweatt*

---

[64] *Ibid.,* majority opinion, at 344.

[65] Terms used repeatedly, and appropriately, by Judge Loren Miller in his *The Petitioners, op. cit.*

[66] *Sipuel v. Oklahoma,* 322 U.S. 631 (1948) and *Fisher v. Hurst,* 333 U.S. 147 (1948), both decided *per curiam.* Miss Sipuel had become Mrs. Fisher in the intervening period.

v. Painter,[67] concerned the University of Texas's statutorily sanctioned denial of Herman Sweatt's request for admission to its law school solely because he was black. Sweatt, a Houston mail carrier aspiring to be a lawyer, had refused to attend the separate law school for blacks established by Texas as a result of the *Gaines* case. He argued that because it was inferior, it would deprive him of the equal protection of the laws. The second case, *McLaurin v. Oklahoma State Regents,*[68] dealt with an ingenious requirement by the Oklahoma legislature, which enabled qualified blacks, such as Professor G. W. McLaurin, to do graduate study (here toward a doctorate in education) at the state-owned University of Oklahoma *if* the University's authorities admitted them as candidates on a "segregated basis"—defined as "classroom instruction given in separate classrooms, or at separate times."

Sweatt's argument that the Texas State University for Negroes was simply "inferior" and hence *unequal* found willing listeners. The Chief Justice's brief but lucid opinion pointed not only to the obvious physical differences between the two schools—which alone would have made them sufficiently unequal—but, far more significantly, to those "qualities which are incapable of objective measurement but which makes for greatness in a law school."[69] Among these qualities he noted "reputation of the faculty, experience of the administration, position and influence of the alumni, standing in the community, tradition and prestige."[70] Tongue in cheek, Vinson commented that it was indeed difficult to believe that one who had a free choice between the two law schools involved would "consider the question close."[71] And he went on to identify some of the intensely practical considerations that rendered the new law school for blacks so decidedly inferior:

> The law school to which Texas is willing to admit [Sweatt] excludes from its student body members of the racial groups which number 85 per cent of the population of the State and include most of the lawyers, witnesses, jurors, judges, and other officials with whom [Sweatt] will inevitably be dealing when he becomes a member of the Texas Bar. With such a substantial and significant segment of society excluded, we cannot conclude that the education offered [Sweatt] is substantially equal to that which he would receive if admitted to the University of Texas Law School.[72]

While the Court thus held that there was simply no way to make the two schools equal and yet separate, it still had stopped short of declaring the

[67] 339 U.S. 629 (1950).
[68] 339 U.S. 637 (1950).
[69] *Sweatt v. Painter, op. cit.,* at 634.
[70] *Ibid.*
[71] *Ibid.*
[72] *Ibid.,* at 634. Sweatt was duly admitted, but flunked out.

doctrine null and void. Yet its willingness to look at socio-political, philo-sophical, and psychological "intangibles" of the "separate but equal" doc-trine inexorably pointed the way to the 1954–55 *Public School Segregation Cases*.

The circumstances surrounding McLaurin's case were just as unpropitious for the future of the "separate but equal" concept. After McLaurin had been ordered admitted to the University of Oklahoma's School of Educa-tion to work for his doctorate in education, and since he was the only black so admitted at the time, the University administration endeavored to comply with the state-mandated provisions for "segregated admission" by resorting to the following degrading devices: rather than arranging for separate classes for him, the University required him to sit apart at a desig-nated desk in what was variously described as a "hallway" or an "ante-room adjoining the classroom," where he and the instructor could see and hear each other, but from which vantage point he would presumably not contaminate the superior race of his fellow students. In the library he was assigned a special desk on the mezzanine floor, but told that he could not use the desks in the regular reading room. In the school cafeteria he was directed to eat at a specifically designated table and to do so at a different time than his white fellow-students. And, as the Chief Justice described it in his opinion:

> For some time, the section of the classroom in which [McLaurin] sat was surrounded by a rail on which there was a sign stating, "Reserved for Col-ored," but these have been removed. He is now [at the time of the litiga-tion] assigned to a seat in the classroom in a row specified for colored students.[73]

This hocus-pocus, declared the unanimous tribunal, was neither "equal" nor constitutional—and McLaurin was promptly admitted to full student citizenship and the equal protection of the laws.

After the 1950 triumphs of Messrs. Sweatt and McLaurin, the barriers prevalent in higher education in the Border states and the South began to give way, however gradually. But it would take the death of the "separate but equal" doctrine and the employment of federal troops in Tuscaloosa, Alabama, and Oxford, Mississippi, thirteen years later, before *every* state in the heretofore segregated area would admit at least one black to at least one of its graduate or professional institutions of higher learning.

Although the effective catalyst would be the *Public School Segregation Cases* of 1954 and 1955, collateral developments[74] also assisted in chip-ping away at the "separate but equal" doctrine. Transportation was one of

[73] *McLaurin v. Oklahoma State Regents, op. cit.,* at 640.
[74] See pp. 323 ff., *supra*.

these. As early as 1946, a Virginia segregation statute, as applied to interstate buses, was declared unconstitutional by the Supreme Court.[75] Four
years later, compulsory segregation on interstate trains was outlawed—
first by another Supreme Court decision,[76] then by the Interstate Commerce Commission, which particularly referred to sleeping and dining cars.
Ultimately, the I.C.C. ordered the cessation of all racial segregation on interstate buses and trains and their public waiting rooms in stations and ter-
minals. To the advocates of segregation, if there was to be an effective last
stand at all, it would have to come in *intra*-state matters—of which, they
hoped, public schools would be one of the most important. Then, on what
would be known to arch-segregationists as "Black Monday," May 17,
1954, came *Brown v. Board of Education of Topeka, et al.*[77] Powerful
rear-guard actions continued to be fought, but the "separate but equal"
doctrine was lost as a legal force. When the colorful Mississippi politician
and rabid segregationist James K. Vardaman cautioned at the turn of the
century that "[t]his education is ruining our Negroes. They're demanding
equality,"[78] he did not realize how prophetic his words would prove to be
some five or six decades later.

THE DEATH OF THE "SEPARATE BUT EQUAL" DOCTRINE

The *Public School Segregation Cases* of 1954, and their implementation
decision one year later, transferred, in the words of one commentator, "the
legal sanction and moral authority of the nation's basic law from the segregationist forces to the civil rights advocates."[79] It marked the end of an era
and the beginning of a new one. In the words of Alpheus T. Mason: "On
May 17, 1954, the Court initiated the greatest social revolution of this
generation."[80] Most of the considerable political, economic, and social
progress blacks have been able to achieve since 1954 stems demonstrably
from *Brown v. Board* and its offspring—and much of the contemporary
criticism of the authority of the Supreme Court is traceable to that decision
and its results. It richly deserves explanation and analysis.

Some Groundwork. Following the *Sweatt* and *McLaurin* decisions, the
NAACP's now highly encouraged lawyers, headed by Thurgood Marshall,
bided their time in the hope that the South might show some disposition to

---

[75] *Morgan v. Virginia,* 328 U.S. 373 (1946).

[76] *Henderson v. United States,* 333 U.S. 816 (1950).

[77] 347 U.S. 483.

[78] As quoted in Walter Lord, *The Past That Would Not Die* (New York: Harper
& Row, 1965), p. 43.

[79] Alan F. Westin, in Redford, Truman, Hacker, Westin, and Wood, *Politics and
Government in the United States* (New York: Harcourt, Brace & World, 1968),
p. 588.

[80] *The Supreme Court: Palladium of Freedom* (Ann Arbor: University of Michigan Press, 1962), p. 170.

comply with the spirit of those two decisions and embark upon some "gradualist" program of desegregation. It is idle to speculate whether more courageous leadership by Southerners and non-Southerners, in and out of government, might have brought about the desired change. The fact is that no such leadership of any consequence was forthcoming. The evolving Southern strategy now seemed to follow the candid public statement of Governor James F. Byrnes of South Carolina that, indeed, the South had failed to properly facilitate the education of its blacks and that "to remedy a hundred years of neglect" a crash building program of fine new schools for blacks had to be started instantly. Byrnes readily admitted that the South would have to act, and act at once, to preserve the "separate but equal" concept, lest the Supreme Court, as he—once (1941–42) a member of that tribunal himself—put it, "take matters out of the state's hands." When all overt and covert entreaties for a gradualist approach were rejected, particularly by Virginia and South Carolina, Marshall and his battery of attorneys determined that the time had come to wage an all-out battle in the courts against "separate but equal." They had no difficulty in finding appropriate vehicles for the desired litigation, and five separate desegregation suits were instituted in carefully selected parts of the country. Four were begun in the states of Delaware, Kansas (Topeka), South Carolina (Clarendon County), and Virginia (Prince Edward County), and one at the federal level in the District of Columbia. Each suit, painstakingly presented by NAACP attorneys, charged not only that the several local black schools involved were *inferior* to their white counterparts, but that the "separate but equal" rule itself violated the "equal protection of the laws" clause of Amendment Fourteen.

To no one's great astonishment the suits lost everywhere, save in Delaware where a limited victory was achieved. However, the Supreme Court granted *certiorari* during 1952, hearing extensive oral arguments from both sides that December. According to one source, the vote to grant review came by the requisite bare minimum of four.[81] Thurgood Marshall's forces, augmented by other friendly lawyers, and buttressed by a brief *amicus curiae* brought by President Truman's Attorney-General Edward T. McGranahan, were supported in their argument in what was to become a famous appendix to their brief. In it, thirty American social scientists of national and international reputation[82] not only supported the NAACP's fundamental charge of segregation as constituting discrimination but—even more significantly from the standpoint of the Court's ultimate opinion—contended at length that segregation as such was harmful to the psyche of

[81] Fred Rodell, "It Is the Earl Warren Court," *The New York Times Magazine*, March 13, 1966, p. 93.

[82] Among them Kenneth Clark, Floyd Allport, Robert M. MacIver, Robert Redfield, and Alfred McC. Lee.

both black and white children, causing irreparable damage to their development as members of a healthy heterogeneous community. Arguing—without fee—on behalf of the segregation status quo, as represented by the five cases, was one of America's foremost constitutional law experts, trial attorney John W. Davis, who had not only held numerous high-ranking jobs in government but had been the unsuccessful Democratic nominee for President in 1924. It would be the now 80-year-old Davis's last appearance before the Court.

Conscious of the significance of the issue at bar, the Supreme Court bided its time. In June 1953, it not only rescheduled the cases for *re-argument* but submitted a set of fundamental questions to opposing counsel with directions for appropriate responses, questions that dealt chiefly with the meaning and intent of the Fourteenth Amendment vis-à-vis segregation and certain practical aspects of desegregation. However hypothetically they were phrased, the nature of the Court's questions caused the hopes of the NAACP and its supporters to soar. But the battle was not yet won, and Marshall, especially in view of what seemed to be the controversial historical aspect of the Court's basic *quaere*,[83] once again turned to the academic community. In September 1953 he enlisted the expertise of some 130 distinguished, chiefly academic, specialists in constitutional history, law, and interpretation. The impressive array of scholars met, chiefly in New York City, and aided Marshall and his immediate lieutenants in the preparation of the new brief.[84] It was filed on November 15, 1953, and argued orally on December 8, 1953, before a new Chief Justice, Earl Warren, Vinson having died just prior to the re-argument. The brief's chief historical contention was that the framers of Amendment Fourteen had *intended* to ban segregation "as a last vestige of slavery"—a contention elaborately disputed by a good many historians.[85] Davis's response was geared to judicial self-restraint as much as to contrary history; neither the Supreme Court nor any other judicial body had the power, he argued, to

[83] The 39th Congress—the framers of the Fourteenth Amendment—denied almost to a man that its equal protection of the laws clause required the desegregation of public institutions; they applied the same reasoning to racial discrimination in the exercise of the suffrage. The latter was reached, of course, by the Fifteenth Amendment two years later.

[84] Among them C. Vann Woodward, John Hope Franklin, Alfred H. Kelly, Robert E. Cushman, Robert K. Carr, Milton R. Konvitz, John P. Frank, Walter Gellhorn, Horace Bond, Howard J. Graham. For an excellent description of their work see Alfred H. Kelly, "The School Segregation Cases," in Garraty, *op. cit.,* pp. 243–68.

[85] One of these is Raoul Berger, most of whose mammoth and controversial *Government by Judiciary: The Transformation of the Fourteenth Amendment* (Cambridge: Harvard University Press, 1977) is intended to demonstrate that the Amendment's framers and supporters specifically rejected its application to segregated schools and to the franchise. (E.g., Chapter 15, "The Rule of Law"; and Chapter 20, "Conclusion.")

declare unconstitutional or *ultra vires* on sociological or psychological bases a school system, a way of life, duly enacted by the people's representatives, that "has stood for three-quarters of a century." If there was change in the offing, it would have to come either by evolution or by the legislative process. The now Republican Administration's Attorney-General, Herbert Brownell, although not quite so assertive in his support of desegregation as McGranahan had been, filed a brief *amicus curiae* in favor of desegregation. It did not accept the historical rationale of the main brief but called for a one-year transition period to permit the South to adjust its social and educational problems. Listening intently to these various arguments in the jammed Supreme Court chamber, the full bench of justices peppered counsel with searching questions.

May 17, 1954. Five months after oral argument, and four years after the *Sweatt* and *McLaurin* decisions, the Supreme Court of the United States gave its decision.[86] It did not resort to the historical issue in which it had expressed so much interest; obviously, and quite wisely, it did not believe it to be either convincingly resolvable or necessary to the unanimous conclusion it would reach through its new Chief Justice, who, as he would recall two decades later, assigned himself to write the opinion, "for it seemed to me that something so important ought to issue over the name of the Chief Justice of the United States."[87] Evidently Warren had labored hard and long to get a unanimous opinion;[88] there are reliable indications that two justices were inclined to dissent—albeit on differing grounds—for at least some time during the Court's deliberations;[89] that, indeed, the initial,

[86] *Brown v. Board of Education of Topeka, et al.,* 347 U.S. 483 and *Bolling v. Sharpe,* 347 U.S. 497. The "Brown" in the case was the Rev. Oliver Brown, a welder on the Rock Island Railroad, who filed suit on behalf of his daughter, Linda.

[87] Lecture, University of Virginia Legal Forum, April 18, 1973.

[88] At a celebration of his ten years on the Court, Warren noted that when the decisions were announced, "the Clerk of our Court for weeks was beset by scores of requests for copies of the 'dissenting opinion.' When told that there was no dissenting opinion, many of them demanded to know by whose order the dissenting opinion had been abolished. Others, believing that there must be a dissenting opinion, threatened to have him investigated for suppressing it." (As quoted in Jacobus ten Broek, *Equal Under Law,* new enl. ed. [New York: Collier, 1965], p. 7.)

[89] See Rodell, *op. cit.* Evidently, they were Reed and Jackson. See the account by William H. Harbaugh, *Lawyer's Lawyer: The Life of John W. Davis* (New York: Oxford University Press, 1973), Chapter 28. See especially, Richard Kluger, *Simple Justice: The History of Brown v. Board of Education and Black America's Struggle for Equality* (New York: Alfred A. Knopf, 1976), particularly pp. 678–99. Kluger reprints a draft dissenting opinion by Reed and demonstrates conclusively that Reed intended to dissent until just two days prior to the rendering of the decision, when he yielded in the interest of "what was best for America." (At 698.) Jackson, while prepared to go along, insisted on writing a *concurring* opinion based on judicial self-restraint, warning that the Court "was declaring new law for a new day." But he was struck down by a severe coronary thrombosis—which seemed to be the catalyst in agreeing to desist from penning a separate opinion.

tentative, Conference vote was 6:3.[90] Notwithstanding the complex background and the emotional impact of the issue at hand, the Warren opinion—of which, after his retirement, he said he had written "every blessed word"[91]—was amazingly brief (just eleven pages),[92] simple, and direct—although certainly controversial! "We must look to the effect that segregation itself has on public education," he noted in nearing the heart of his Court's decision:

> In approaching this problem, we cannot turn the clock back to 1868 when the [Fourteenth] Amendment was adopted,[93] or even to 1896 when *Plessy v. Ferguson* was written. We must consider public education in the light of its full development and its present place in American life throughout the Nation. Only in this way can it be determined if segregation in public schools deprives these [Negroes] of the equal protection of the laws.
>
> Today, education is perhaps the most important function of state and local government. . . . [Education] is the very foundation of good citizenship. Today it is the principal instrument in awakening the child to cultural values, in preparing him for later professional training, and in helping him to adjust normally to his environment. . . .
>
> We come then to the question presented: *Does segregation of children in public schools solely on the basis of race, even though the physical facilities*

[90] See S. Sidney Ulmer, *Courts As Small and Not So Small Groups* (New York: General Learning Press, 1971), p. 24. Ulmer's (and Harbaugh's) claim that Frankfurter was the third holdout is vigorously rebutted by Kluger—whose account of *Brown's* dénouement is the most recent, most complete, lengthiest, and most convincing. Indeed, Frankfurter was one of the architects of unanimity, second in importance only to Warren. "F.F." did, however, have strong reservations regarding the judiciary's proper role here.

[91] As quoted by John F. Simon, *In His Own Image: The Supreme Court in Richard Nixon's America* (New York: David McKay Co., Inc., 1973), p. 55. The Chief Justice, by his own account, was determined to (a) get an unanimous vote; (b) write the opinion for the Court; and (c) "use low key unemotional language." He waited more than five months before calling for a final vote in conference; when he did he had his unanimous Court: "We took one vote, and that was it." (*The New York Times,* June 11, 1974, p. 35A.) But that did not occur until after the developments described in footnote 89, *supra.* In a letter exhibited at Harvard (October 21, 1977) commemorating Frankfurter's ninety-fifth birthday, "F.F." noted to Reed that there would have been four dissents had *Brown* been decided just one term earlier.

[92] Responding to a student's question, Warren recounted that he "purposely wrote such a short opinion so that any layman interested in the problem could read the entire opinion [instead of getting just] a little piece here and a little piece there. Hopefully this would not be the case with *Brown.* I think most of the major newspapers printed the entire decision." They did. (University of Virginia Legal Forum, April 18, 1973.)

[93] Kluger, a strong and avowed partisan of the *Brown* decision, acknowledges that painstaking research by Alexander M. Bickel, then Frankfurter's clerk, demonstrated that there was "no evidence that the framers of the Amendment had intended to prohibit school segregation." (Kluger, *op. cit.,* at 655.) In effect, Bickel had reported to his Justice that "it is impossible to conclude that the 39th Congress intended that segregation be abolished, impossible also to conclude that they foresaw it might be, under the language they were adopting." (*Ibid.,* at 654.)

*and other "tangible" factors may be equal, deprive the children of the mi-
nority group of equal educational opportunity? We believe that it does.*[94]

The Chief Justice then asserted: "Segregation of white and colored children in public schools has a detrimental effect upon the colored children. . . . *A sense of inferiority affects the motivation of a child to
learn.*"[95] And, as Earl Warren had explained a few sentences earlier, to
separate children in grade and high schools "from others of similar age
and qualifications *solely because of their race generates a feeling of inferiority as to their status in the community that may affect their hearts and
minds in a way unlikely ever to be undone.*"[96] Now followed the famous
and controversial "social science" footnote 11, which cited the writings of
those social scientists, chiefly psychologists and sociologists, on whose
findings the Court here relied. Among them were the noted black psychol-
ogist Kenneth B. Clark and Gunnar Myrdal, the Swedish sociologist whose
celebrated *An American Dilemma*[97] had caused such an uproar in the
South and the Border states when it first appeared in 1944. Wrote Warren:
"Whatever may have been the extent of psychological knowledge at the
time of *Plessy v. Ferguson,* this finding is amply supported by modern authority. Any language in *Plessy v. Ferguson* contrary to this finding is rejected."[98] Thus out went the ruling by Mr. Justice Brown for his 7:1 Court
in 1896—and up went the single dissenting vote of Mr. Justice John Marshall Harlan. All that now remained for the decision of 1954 was the dramatic conclusion that

> *in the field of public education the doctrine of "separate but equal" has no
> place. Separate educational facilities are inherently unequal. . . .* the
> plaintiffs and others similarly situated for whom the actions have been
> brought are, by reason of the segregation complained of, *deprived of the
> equal protection of the laws guaranteed by the Fourteenth Amendment.*[99]

In other words, the "equal protection of the laws" clause of the Fourteenth
Amendment now forbade the racially segregated education of public school

[94] *Brown v. Board of Education of Topeka, et al.,* 347 U.S. 483 (1954), at 492.
(Italics supplied.)

[95] *Ibid.,* at 494. (Italics supplied.)

[96] *Ibid.* (Italics supplied.)

[97] *An American Dilemma: The Negro Problem and Modern Democracy* (New
York: Harper and Bros., 1944). Republished in 1946, and, in an updated, revised
edition, by Harper & Row in 1962. For a highly critical recent evaluation of the
resort to "social science" evidence, see lawyer-anthropologist John Aron Grayzel,
"Using Social Science Concepts in the Legal Fight Against Discrimination: Servant
or Sorcerer's Apprentice," 64 *American Bar Association Journal* 1238 (August 1978).

[98] *Brown, op. cit.,* at 494. (Italics supplied.)

[99] *Ibid.,* at 495. (Italics supplied.)

children.[100] Indeed, the strong implication of the *Brown v. Board* ruling was that *any publicly* authorized or *publicly* permitted racial segregation would henceforth be unconstitutional.[101]

The Implementation Decision. Meanwhile, the 1954 decision would have to be implemented—and here the Court bowed to the counsel of Attorney-General Brownell. Refraining from an immediate desegregation order, given the revolutionary nature of the decision, the Court stayed any enforcement mandate, and ordered supportive argument in all five cases for April 1955—almost a year later. For that purpose, the Court invited all interested parties, specifically including counsel, the *amici curiae,* the Solicitor-General of the United States, and all state attorneys-general, to file briefs and, if they so chose, participate in oral argument. Most of the Southern states refused to do so, but Florida, North Carolina, Arkansas, and Texas did argue, dramatically and at length.[102] One month later, another unanimous Warren opinion (for the same Court members as its predecessor decision, except that John Marshall Harlan had replaced the deceased Mr. Justice Jackson) announced the implementation or "mandate" decision.[103] Invoking an old principle of equity law,[104] and thereby avoiding any immediate problem of overall enforcement, it mandated the *local federal courts* to direct and oversee the transition to a racially nondiscriminatory system of public school primary and secondary education "with all deliberate speed."[105] It directed these courts to order a "prompt and reasonable start," but clearly left the door ajar for consideration of the manifold local problems involved. In fact, "wide open door" may be a more appropriate description of the *initial* judicial attitude, compared to what would be a much stiffer attitude as the fifties turned into the sixties.

[100] Raoul Berger charges repeatedly and angrily that herewith Warren "revised the Fourteenth Amendment to mean exactly the opposite of what its framers designed it to mean, namely, to leave suffrage and segregation beyond federal control, to leave it with the states, where control over internal, domestic matters resided from the beginning." (*Op. cit.,* at 245.)

[101] The District of Columbia litigation had to be decided on the "due process of law" clause of Amendment Five, of course (*Bolling v. Sharpe,* 347 U.S. 497 [1954]). In effect applying a type of "reverse incorporation," the Court read the concept of "equal protection of the laws" into the "due process of law" clause of the Fifth Amendment—a policy it has embraced ever since.

[102] The Court allowed fourteen hours of argument; the usual allotment is one hour per case.

[103] *Brown v. Board of Education of Topeka, et al.,* 349 U.S. 294 (1955); and *Bolling v. Sharpe, op. cit.*

[104] For a capsule explanation of equity see my *The Judicial Process: An Introductory Analysis of the Courts of the United States, England, and France,* 4th ed. (New York: Oxford University Press, 1980), pp. 14–16.

[105] The "all deliberate speed" formula was suggested by Mr. Justice Frankfurter, who found it in a 1911 Holmes opinion dealing with monetary matters between states. (*Virginia v. West Virginia,* 222 U.S. 17, at 20.) Holmes identified it as "language of the English Chancery."

Inevitably the "child of its time," the Court had carefully separated the principle of integration—a word that appears nowhere in the decisions involved—from its actual implementation.[106] Just as the Supreme Court reflected the socio-political realities of a new day and age[107] in *Brown* I, so did it reflect the judicial-limitation realities in *Brown* II.[108] As the ensuing months and years would prove, the Court can be a leader and the conscience of the country—but in the political process of which, after all, it is a part, it has only "the power to persuade: purse and sword are in other hands," as Alexander Hamilton stated so perceptively at the Republic's dawn in his *The Federalist* # 78.

The Court would need immediate help from the executive branch. Overt or covert defiance became the rule rather than the exception in a good many areas, chiefly in the deep South. While the District of Columbia, under direct federal control, did integrate its public schools immediately—Congress had permitted segregated schools there from 1864 onward—the response in the affected states ran from bowing to the inevitable in more or less good faith, through reasonably delayed action, to absolute refusal to obey. There was occasionally even avowed, outright defiance, accompanied by flurries of violence, in Arkansas, Virginia, South Carolina, Georgia, Florida, Louisiana, Alabama and Mississippi. Many subterfuges were adopted by these states and others, such as the closing of all public schools in Prince Edward County, Virginia—where one of the five *Public School Segregation Cases of 1954* originated.[109] Public feeling ran high indeed over what the majority of the white population in the affected sectors regarded as a threat to their way of life and the right of the states to govern themselves, the latter more often than not being a camouflage for the former. Some 200 state segregation statutes would be enacted in the decade following the implementation decision.

Even Force. Still, a start, however halting and sullen, had been made; and enforcement of the decision continued to spread through a lengthy process of litigation, a host of patient efforts by many groups and individuals, courageous stances by the fifty-odd Southern federal jurists who in many ways must be recognized as the heroes of the desegregation battles

[106] See Ulmer, *op. cit.,* pp. 23–26, for an illuminating account of the various options the Court perceived in *Brown* I and II, and the Chief Justice's leadership in the cases.

[107] On this point see the interesting article by Charles L. Black, Jr., "The Lawfulness of the Segregation Decisions," 69 *Yale Law Journal* 421 (1960).

[108] Asked whether the Justices ever considered "busing" in any of the implementation decision conferences, the Chief Justice replied, "No, I don't think we ever did." (University of Virginia Legal Forum, April 18, 1973.) For a superb account of *Brown* II, see J. Harvie Wilkinson, III, *From Brown to Bakke* (New York: Oxford University Press, 1979), especially Chapters 1–9.

[109] *Davis v. County School Board of Prince Edward County, Virginia,* 347 U.S. 483.

of the decade between 1955 and 1965,[110] the repeated affirmations of the basic decisions by the United States Supreme Court,[111] and, finally, a show of federal military force when deemed necessary as a last resort. President Eisenhower, for the first three years after *Brown,* had done his best to stay out of the battle and, indeed, had done nothing either to support the Supreme Court, so heavily under fire, or to explain, let alone defend, its decisions to the country. In the judgment of many, the enormously popular and influential national hero could have achieved something here if *anyone* could. But in the fall of 1957, he found his hand forced by Governor Orville Faubus of Arkansas. Faubus, following a lengthy desegregation battle with federal and state authorities,[112] called out the National Guard to prevent duly scheduled federal court ordered public school desegregation in Little Rock, an order that involved only nine black children. When he was enjoined by the appropriate United States District Court from continued interference, he removed the Guard, thereby encouraging the lawless. Riots and disorders promptly ensued. After a confrontation with Governor Faubus at Newport, Rhode Island, failed, an angry and reluctant President Eisenhower felt compelled to federalize the Arkansas National Guard and dispatch them[113] to re-establish law and order and allow desegregation to proceed as judicially directed.[114] Five years later, in the fall of 1962, President John F. Kennedy deployed 25,000 federal troops to overcome the opposition of Mississippi, led by its governor, Ross R. Barnett, to the federal court ordered admission of black James Meredith[115] to the

[110] Jack W. Peltason, *Fifty-Eight Lonely Men: Southern Judges and School Desegregation,* rev. ed. (Urbana: University of Illinois Press, 1971), tells their story enlighteningly and engagingly.

[111] Thus, Mr. Justice Hugo Black wrote for a unanimous Supreme Court in 1964, ultimately striking down the Prince Edward County school closing and related subterfuges: "There has been entirely too much deliberation and not enough speed in enforcing the constitutional rights which we held . . . had been denied . . ." (*Griffin v. Prince Edward School Board,* 377 U.S. 218, at 229).

[112] Well told by, among others, Wilson Record and Jane Cassels Record, *Little Rock U.S.A.* (San Francisco: Chandler Publishing Co., 1960).

[113] These forces were under the command of Brigadier-General Edwin Walker who, some years later, became one of the most visible anti-integrationists and who caused considerable difficulties for the federal authorities during the Oxford, Mississippi, confrontations. (See *Associated Press v. Walker,* 388 U.S. 130, 1967.)

[114] See the Court's unanimous, seminal decision—signed and authored jointly by all nine members of the tribunal—in *Cooper v. Aaron,* 358 U.S. (1958) in which it not only sternly ordered immediate compliance with the desegregation order by lower federal courts, but reminded one and all that it is "emphatically the province and duty of the *judicial department* to say what the law is." (Italics supplied.) (For a discussion, see my *The Judicial Process, op. cit.,* p. 218.)

[115] Four years later, while on a march from Memphis to Jackson to dramatize the Negro registration drive in Mississippi, Meredith was shot and wounded in an ambush. Yet ten years later he would be the University of Mississippi's guest lecturer! (*The New York Times,* April 22, 1972, p. 32c.) And, though unsuccessfully, he ran for the Republican gubernatorial nomination in June 1972. By 1976, 475 blacks were on the Oxford campus. (*Ibid.,* October 10, p. 16m.)

University of Mississippi at Oxford. A bloody all-night battle was fought on and near the campus of "Ole Miss," with many wounded and two lives lost.[116] Eight months later President Kennedy again had to use troops, this time mobilizing the Alabama National Guard in order to overcome Governor George C. Wallace's defiance of the federal court ordered admission of blacks Vivian Malone and James Hood to the University of Alabama at Tuscaloosa.[117]

Although even token integration was often resisted in the deep South, mixed classes eventually became a reality on all levels of the public school system. "Mixed," of course, sometimes meant the presence of only one black student in an otherwise all-white classroom, but the principle was being established, and the tough financial penalties provided by Title VI of the Civil Rights Act of 1964 served to spur compliance in all but the most adamant situations. These last would be left to the judicial process; yet it was clear that in some instances, such as in Wallace-led Alabama, a course of "legal defiance," including a rejection of federal funds, would be at least temporarily pursued. In any event, on August 14, 1964, Mississippi became the *last* state to desegregate at least one school district when the Biloxi District bowed to a federal court order decreeing the desegregation of its first-grade classes. Less than six months later, the Greenville, Mississippi, School Board, facing the loss of $272,000 in federal aid-to-education funds if it failed to comply with the provisions of the Civil Rights Act of 1964 affecting such federal aid, voted unanimously to prepare a desegregation plan. Providing the first instance of non-court-ordered compliance by that state's authorities, Greenville's Mayor Pat Dunne endorsed the Board's action, pointing out that there was no alternative: "Repugnant as the law is to all of us, it's a Federal law and it's either a case of comply or close the schools."[118]

ENTER BUSING

Notwithstanding the very real and continuing desegregation progress described, the line between genuine and token *integration* has proved to be extremely difficult to draw[119]—even given such a clear mandate as that con-

[116] See University of Mississippi James W. Silver's important book *Mississippi: The Closed Society* (New York: Harcourt, Brace & World, 1966); and his colleague Russell H. Barrett's *Integration at Ole Miss* (Chicago: Quadrangle Books, 1965).

[117] Ten years later he "crowned" the first black Homecoming Queen at the same University.

[118] *The New York Times,* January 16, 1965, p. 18*l*. (At the level of higher public education, the last bastions, Alabama and South Carolina, had already fallen two years earlier.)

[119] Thus, in May 1968, obviously having reached the end of its patience, a unanimous Court ruled that the so-called "freedom of choice" desegregation plans are inadequate if they do not undo Southern school desegregation as rapidly as other available methods would. In what was its first detailed review of the adequacy of

tained in the landmark October 1969 decision in the *Holmes County* case[120] which announced the death of the "deliberate speed" concept in an 8:0 opinion, *per curiam,* highlighted by: " 'All deliberate speed' for de- segregation is no longer constitutionally permissible. . . . [T]he obliga- tion of every school district is to terminate dual school systems at once and to operate now and hereafter only unitary school systems."[121] But even assuming good faith—not always a viable assumption—how much *busing* of students does the Constitution require in order to achieve the mandated "unitary" system?[122] How much, how far, at what cost? What of housing patterns, of fatigue factors, of the relationship of ghetto and suburb, of the right of states to create administrative subdivisions?

In the face of a host of these vexatious questions, with their manifold political, economic, social, and psychological components, the Supreme Court considered the busing-to-integrate issue on its merits in an April 1971 decision of momentous significance for the entire country. Now thrust center stage, busing became—and continues to be—*the* cardinal bone of contention in the continuing and expanding efforts to implement *Brown* I and II.

The 1971 *Swann* or *Charlotte–Mecklenburg* case,[123] as it became known popularly, headed a series arising from desegregation orders to a large school district covering the Charlotte, North Carolina, metropolitan area that had a long history of maintaining two sets of segregated schools. By 1969, under court orders, half of the 30 per cent of black students in the district were in formerly all-white schools, the others remaining in virtually all-black schools. The case squarely raised the seminal question, posed by attorneys for a group of white *and* black North Carolina parents, whether the *Brown* ruling required "color-blind" assignment of students and, if so,

---

the *means* being used to implement the 1954 and 1955 *Brown* decisions, the Court— commencing a firm embrace of statistical evidence—declared that "delays are no longer tolerable"; that the "burden on a school board today is to come forward with a plan that promises realistically to work . . . *now.*" (Italics in original.) (*Green v. School Board of New Kent County,* 391 U.S. 430 [1968], at 439.) And in 1969, acting on the *first* school desegregation suit filed by the federal government in the *North,* United States District Court Judge Julius J. Hoffman (destined to be- come the much-embattled presiding judge in the "Chicago Eight" trial) ordered a suburban Chicago school district to desegregate its faculties and student bodies "forthwith." (*United States v. School District 151 of Cook County, Ill.,* 301 F. Supp. 201.)

[120] *Alexander v. Holmes County Board of Education,* 396 U.S. 19 (1969), at 20. Authorship has been attributed to Mr. Justice Black.

[121] *Ibid.* For a copy of the text of the Supreme Court's order, see *The New York Times,* October 30, 1969, p. 34. (Italics supplied.)

[122] As early as 1869, Massachusetts had authorized the expenditure of public funds to send children to and from school in horse drawn wagons and carriages. (See Wilkinson, *From Brown to Bakke, op. cit.,* Chapters 6–9, for a thorough discussion of the busing issue.)

[123] *Swann v. Charlotte–Mecklenburg Board of Education,* 402 U.S. 1.

whether busing to achieve integration was in effect unconstitutional. "We plead the same rights here that the plaintiffs pleaded in *Brown*," asserted the lawyers opposing busing—leaving to the Court another particularly complicated line-drawing problem, one charged with deep emotions.

These were not vitiated by the fact that, when the high tribunal handed down its decision that April, it was unanimous—one of the last times all nine Justices would be in agreement on racial matters.[124] Speaking for his Court, Mr. Chief Justice Burger's opinion—which reportedly went through several drafts—confounded Court watchers and the Nixon Administration alike: for it specifically upheld not only *busing* but also *racial quotas, pairing* or *grouping* of schools, and *gerrymandering* of attendance zones as well as other devices designed to remove "all vestiges of state-imposed segregation. . . . *Desegregation plans cannot be limited to the walk-in school*," he declared.[125] The Court stopped short of ordering the elimination of all-black schools or of requiring racial balance in the schools (and it made clear that its decision did *not* apply to Northern-style segregation, commonly based on *de facto* neighborhood patterns). But it said that the existence of all-black schools created a presumption of discrimination and held that federal district judges—to whom it gave extremely broad discretion—may indeed use *racial quotas*[126] as a guide in fashioning desegregation decrees. On the busing issue, the Chief Justice, in a nod to that large element among the populace favoring the neighborhood school concept, admitted that "all things being equal, with no history of discrimination, it

[124] That long standing unanimity—of almost two decades—ended on June 22, 1972, when the four Nixon appointees (Burger, Blackmun, Powell, and Rehnquist) dissented from a Supreme Court ruling that they characterized as *requiring* the imposition of "racial balance" rather than "desegregation." They protested that the majority of five (Douglas, Brennan, Stewart, White, and Marshall) had in effect equated racial balance with desegregation. (*Wright v. Council of the City of Emporia*, 407 U.S. 451.) According to one insider's account, the Court's unanimity in *Swann* was in fact deceptive: that the initial vote had actually been 6:3 *against* forced busing. (See Wilkinson, *op. cit.*, pp. 146–50.)

[125] *Swann, op. cit.*, at 15, 30. (Italics supplied.)

[126] This notwithstanding the on-its-face prohibition by §2000c of Title IV of the Civil Rights Act of 1964, which *specifically* would seem to *bar* racial quota assignments. But the Chief Justice brushed that argument aside, invoking the judiciary's "historic equitable remedial powers" in the quest of attaining of what he viewed as full compliance with the spirit as well as the letter of the equal protection of the laws clause of Amendment Fourteen. In another portent of the Court's future posture on racial quotas, in 1977 it ruled in a "multiple plurality" decision that a state (here New York), drawing up a reapportionment plan in an effort to comply with the federal Voting Rights Act of 1965, as amended, may sometimes use racial quotas that are designed to assure that blacks and other non-whites have majorities in certain legislative districts. (*United Jewish Organizations of Williamsburg v. Carey*, 430 U.S. 144.) But the Court refused (6:3) three years later to impose election by district in Mobile, Alabama, where the long-standing practice of at large election of the three-member City Commission had failed to produce a black commissioner. (*City of Mobile v. Bolden*, 446 U.S. 55.)

might well be desirable to assign pupils to schools nearest their homes. But all things are not equal," he continued, "in a system that has been deliberately constructed and maintained to enforce racial segregation."[127] The sweeping *Charlotte–Mecklenburg* ruling represented a landmark along the road to full desegregation, yet there was little doubt that the problem remained unsettled.

That it was indeed not settled would promptly be demonstrated by two landmark decisions—the first school desegregation cases to reach the Court involving a major city outside the South. One came in a Denver, Colorado, case that squarely raised the crucial issue of "Northern-style segregation," which—unlike *segregation by law* typical of the South—was the product of *economic and social patterns.* In a surprisingly decisive 7:1 holding[128] (or 6-½:1½, depending upon one's analysis) and speaking through Mr. Justice Brennan—with only Mr. Justice Rehnquist in full dissent—the Court refused to discard the *de facto-de jure* distinction, as urged upon it by concurring Justices Douglas and, especially, Powell, who also took pains to abjure forced busing. But it demonstrably expanded the *de jure* scope by making clear that even in the absence of statutorily authorized segregation policies—and none such existed in Denver or, for that matter, in Colorado, where in fact it had been statutorily *forbidden* since 1895—it was provable that the Denver school board had in fact practiced segregation by manipulating school attendance zones and school sites and favoring a "neighborhood school" policy. The Court held it was neither necessary to demonstrate total or overall segregation nor the presence of a dual school system in order to find impermissible discrimination: it was sufficient to be able to point to segregation of "a substantial portion" of the school district, with the Court thus strongly hinting that pockets of intentional segregation, be they such as a result of law, custom, or neglect, would be regarded as constituting cause for judicial proscription applicable to the entire district. This, of course, would mean busing—as an increasing number of cities in the North as well as the South was experiencing.

The Denver litigation had confined itself to a *single* school district, as had that involving Charlotte–Mecklenburg. But what of the manifold situations, particularly extant in the North, in which integration is in effect not accomplishable without *busing across district lines,* usually involving black cities and white suburbs? The *Charlotte–Mecklenburg* case had involved

---

[127] *Swann, op. cit.,* at 28. During the controversy surrounding the Charlotte-Mecklenburg school district, the North Carolina legislature enacted a law flatly forbidding any "busing assignment of any student on account of race or for the purpose of creating a racial balance or ratio in the schools." That provision, too, fell on the same day *Swann* was decided. (*North Carolina State Board of Education v. Swann,* 402 U.S. 43.)

[128] *Keyes v. School District # 1, Denver, Colorado,* 413 U.S. 189 (1973), rehearing denied, 423 U.S. 1066 (1976).

such cross-county (city-suburb) busing, but it dealt with a *single* school district! The explosive issue was joined in 1972 when U.S. District Court Judge Robert R. Merhige, Jr., sitting in Richmond, Virginia, in a momentous 325-page (!) opinion,[129] ordered a merger of that city's predominantly black public schools with those of two predominantly white suburban counties, Henrico and Chesterfield. A similarly contentious order was subsequently issued by U.S. District Court Judge Stephen J. Roth and was to involve the cross-county busing of 300,000 Detroit area children between that city and its suburbs.[130] There the similarity ended, for while the U.S. Circuit Court of Appeals for the Fourth Circuit *overruled* Judge Merhige 5:1,[131] Judge Roth's order was sustained 6:3 by the Sixth Circuit's Court of Appeals.[132] To the surprise of no one, both decisions were appealed to a somewhat less-than-eager U.S. Supreme Court.

Down came the Court, first with a "no-answer" answer in the Richmond case in a 4:4 one-sentence *per curiam* ruling, with Virginia's Mr. Justice Powell not participating: "The judgment is affirmed by an equally divided Court."[133] All eyes then turned toward Detroit, about which a decision was made in 1974. Speaking through the Chief Justice, the Court ruled (5:4) that whatever the situation in the city of Detroit itself might be or have been, the school systems in the surrounding suburbs had not been accused of unlawful segregation; that, absent proof of the latter, no constitutional power exists in the courts to decree relief balancing the racial composition of one community-wide segregated district (Detroit) with those of surrounding districts (the suburbs).[134] In bitter dissent Justices Douglas, Brennan, White, and Marshall accused the majority of taking "a giant step backward."[135]

What the Detroit landmark decision thus evidently conveyed was that the Court—recognizing the "deeply rooted" public education tradition of local control—would refuse to order cross-country or city-suburb integration, *unless* it could be proved that *intentional* segregation in one district leads to a "significant segregative effect in another district." Not surprisingly, numerous cross-country merger cases soon began to reach the Court, involving, among others, the areas around Louisville, Kentucky; Indianap-

[129] *Bradley v. School Board of the City of Richmond,* 338 F. Supp. 67.

[130] *Bradley v. Milliken,* 338 F. Supp. 582 (1972).

[131] *School Board of the City of Richmond v. Bradley,* 462 F. 2d 1058 (1972).

[132] *Bradley v. Milliken,* 484 F. 2d 215 (1973).

[133] *Bradley v. State Board of Education of the Commonwealth of Virginia,* 411 U.S. 913 (1973).

[134] *Milliken v. Bradley,* 418 U.S. 717. In the concurring Mr. Justice Stewart's words, "the multidistrict remedy contemplated by the desegregation order was an erroneous exercise of equitable authority of the federal courts." (At 756.) Joining Mr. Chief Justice Burger in the majority were Justices Stewart, Blackmun, Powell, and Rehnquist.

[135] *Ibid.,* at 782.

olis, Indiana; Wilmington, Delaware; Atlanta, Georgia; and Buffalo, New York. In its actions, the Supreme Court adhered to its announced test of whether proof of deliberate, intentional segregation had been provided. In a number of instances it so found and, for example, upheld lower-court orders mandating inter-district busing between the cities of Wilmington and Louisville and their respective suburbs, but it struck down an order directed to Atlanta and its suburbs.[136]

The busing issue[137] continued to smolder—and to create controversy of a magnitude rarely seen in the body politic. To illustrate: consistently having defied—or at least having but mildly obeyed—U.S. District Court orders to bus its children, the Boston community, led by South Boston (heavily white ethnic, very few blacks), was confronted with a series of drastic ultimata handed down by Judge W. Arthur Garrity, Jr. Rejecting or downplaying these, the Boston School Committee, an elected, popular body, subsequently found itself deprived of many of its powers in December 1975: some of its schools were placed in the hands of a court-appointed receiver. The pressures began to mount among the electorate almost everywhere: along with abortion, the busing issue became a key concern of the 1976 presidential primary races in Massachusetts; around the nation segregationist George C. Wallace was emerging victorious in the Democratic race almost entirely on the busing issue. But Boston's strife-torn public school system continued in effect to be administratively directed by Judge Garrity[138]—whose stern desegregation order was twice denied review and thus upheld, by the United States Supreme Court.[139] Even stronger measures were taken by United States District Judge Frank J. Battisti in connection with his desegregation orders affecting the Cleveland, Ohio, school system. His orders included a citation for civil contempt of court in Au-

---

[136] *Evans v. Buchanan*, 423 U.S. 963 (1975) and *Board of Education v. Newburg Area Council*, 421 U.S. 931 (1975) and *Armour v. Nix*, 446 U.S. 930 (1980), respectively. The Wilmington order was narrowly reconfirmed twice (4:3 in 1977 and 6:3 in 1980); (see *Delaware State Board of Education v. Evans*, 429 U.S. 973 and, *ibid.*, 447 U.S. 916 rehearing denied).

[137] For some post-1970 literature on busing, see the following: Robert H. Bork, *Constitutionality of the President's Busing Proposals* (Washington, D.C.: American Enterprise Institute, 1972); "The Agony of Busing Moves North," *Time Magazine*, November 15, 1971, pp. 57–64; John A. Morsell, "Busing is not the Issue," *Freedom at Issue*, May–June, 1972, pp. 12 ff.; Nicolaus Mills (ed.), *The Great School Bus Controversy* (New York: Thomas Y. Crowell, 1973); James Bolner and Robert Shanley, *Busing: The Political and Judicial Process* (New York: Praeger, 1974); Christopher Jencks, "Busing—The Supreme Court Goes North," *The New York Times Magazine*, November 19, 1972, pp. 38 ff.; and Linus A. Graglia, *Disaster by Decree* (Ithaca: Cornell University Press, 1976).

[138] Judge Garrity created a "permanent Department of Implementation (administration of racial desegregation)" with an annual payroll of $473,559 for salaries alone (as of 1977).

[139] *White v. Morgan*, 426 U.S. 935 (1975) and *McDonough v. Morgan*, 429 U.S. 1042 (1976).

gust 1980 for "incompetently administering" his program, and the appointment of an "administrator for desegregation" with power over every aspect of public education in Cleveland. The opposition to forced busing can neither simply be interpreted as merely *prima facie* evidence of racial discrimination or as racism; if it were that simple, evaluation as well as remedial action might be simpler. These labels do, of course, apply in the case of a good many opponents; but it is unquestionably also true that a good many other opponents of forced busing are neither racists nor antidesegregation obstructionists. They are opposed to busing *qua* busing for their children on understandable human grounds, and they do indeed prefer to embrace the thrust of Mr. Chief Justice Burger's *Swann* "all things being equal" hope: "assignment to schools nearest [the children's] homes"[140]—as do a sizeable segment of the black, the Hispanic, and almost all of the Chinese communities.

In what was indubitably a recognition of and response to majoritarian public sentiment on the issue, the congressional hoppers have been replete with legislation endeavoring either to amend or to strike down busing practices and orders. Most failed of passage, usually in the more liberal Senate; but a number of "riders" to annual appropriation bills prohibiting the executive departments from using federal funds "to require, directly or indirectly, the transportation of any student to a school other than the school which is nearest the student's home, except for a student requiring special education,"[141] did become law—the judiciary making quite clear, however, that it would continue to invoke its perceived powers of judicial equity in the contentious issue. A constitutional amendment to ban busing as a desegregation/integration tool failed 216:109 in the House in 1979; but late in 1980 both houses of Congress voted overwhelmingly to prohibit the Justice Department from using appropriated funds to pursue legal cases that would result in busing orders. Presidents Nixon and Ford had repeatedly called for remedial statutory or amendatory action; President Carter, however, firmly opposed such moves, and when he pointedly threatened to veto the 1980 measure Congress bowed reluctantly. Since the Republican Platform for 1980 again contained a plank against forced busing, it was a foregone conclusion that the issue had been postponed, not resolved. Indeed, a plethora of anti-busing bills were introduced early in 1981, with at least tacit backing by the Reagan Administration.

How did the Court view the volatile issue as the divided land entered the 1980s? Any response would be tentative at best; indeed, to employ a

---

[140] *Swann v. Charlotte-Mecklenburg School of Education,* 402 U.S. 1 (1971), at 28.
[141] Sec. 208 of the Health, Education and Welfare–Labor Appropriations Act for fiscal year 1978. (See *The New York Times,* March 31, 1978, p. A14.) When a lower federal court upheld the rider, the Supreme Court refused to review the decision in 1978. (*Carroll v. Department of Health, Education and Welfare,* 435 U.S. 904.)

vernacular but apposite term, the Justices' holdings have been perilously close to being "as clear as mud" on the dilemmas created by forced busing. Thus, they held (6:2) that if school authorities initially complied with a busing plan and thereby achieved a racially neutral student assignment plan, the school authorities cannot be judicially compelled to readjust busing zones each subsequent year in an effort to maintain the same initial racial mix in the face of changing population patterns.[142] Concurrently, the Court unanimously declined to review, and thus in effect upheld, a lower federal appellate court ruling that school authorities in Chattanooga, Tennessee, need not redraft a desegregation plan to reflect population shifts that had taken place *after* busing and other desegregation measures had been duly and constitutionally adopted.[143] The justices also ruled unanimously that federal tribunals may order school districts to provide costly, far-reaching, broader-than-ever *remedial* educational programs—such as remedial reading classes, teaching training, counseling, and career guidance[144]—thus seemingly embracing a compensatory approach that would avoid the busing issue *per se*. When the Court also remanded three system-wide busing order cases[145] for reconsideration because they did not meet the "purpose and intent" standard it had developed in 1976–77 as a requirement for specific findings regarding alleged violations of equal protection of the laws, the Court seemed to have embarked upon a course that required proof of *de jure* rather than *de facto* segregation for judicially ordered redress. Yet such expectations of either a predictable or consistent course were in vain—despite the fact that the same justices sat on the Court between 1975 and 1981. For 1979 and 1980 brought a series of bitterly divided compulsory busing decisions.[146] They ranged in votes from 7:2 to 5:4 in upholding lower-court busing plans and orders. Led by Justices Brennan, White, Marshall, and Blackmun, the Court had now developed a dramatic new test *cum* approach to the question of desegregation/integration, namely, that henceforth the test of compliance would not be a school board's *purpose* in acting to liquidate a dual system of education dating from pre-*Brown* days, but its *effectiveness*. In the words of Mr. Justice White, the author of the Court's sweeping decisions on school busing orders for Dayton, Ohio (5:4) and Columbus, Ohio (7:2), there is an "affirmative duty" to eliminate the *effects* of *past* discrimination, even if

---

[142] *Pasadena City Board of Education v. Spangler,* 427 U.S. 424 (1976).

[143] *Mapp v. Board of Education of Chattanooga,* 427 U.S. 911 (1976).

[144] *Milliken v. Bradley II,* 433 U.S. 267 (1977).

[145] *Dayton Board of Education v. Brinkman* (I), 433 U.S. 406 (1977).

[146] *Columbus Board of Education v. Penick,* 443 U.S. 449 (1979); *Dayton Board of Education v. Brinkman,* 443 U.S. 526 (1979); *Estes v. Metropolitan Branches of Dallas NAACP,* 444 U.S. 437 (1980); *Cleveland Board of Education v. Reed,* 445 U.S. 935 (1980); and *Austin Independent School District v. United States,* 443 U.S. 915 (1980).

there is no longer any discrimination practiced. Perhaps even more significantly, the Court adopted, albeit narrowly,[147] a new test of the burden of proof in these school desegregation cases. Traditionally, a plaintiff alleging unlawful conduct has the burden of proof; but in accordance with the 5:4 Columbus holding,[148] the burden or proof has now been shifted to the defendant school board—which in effect thus has to prove its innocence, rather than have the plaintiff prove a board's guilt. It is a fair assumption that the last word has not been heard from the Court on busing!

Much of the thrust toward school desegregation-implementation had been provided by a famed report written in 1966 by the distinguished University of Chicago sociologist, James S. Coleman, who had then demonstrated with convincing statistical evidence that while home background tended to have a greater impact than the school on children's performance, the integration of a minority of disadvantaged youngsters (chiefly nonwhite) in classrooms dominated by middle-class children (chiefly white) tended to raise the poor children's achievements without hurting those of their more affluent peers.[149] The Coleman Report, widely distributed and meeting with general approbation in the academic and governmental communities, thus became a genuine catalyst in the desegregation-integration efforts that soon began to reach a crescendo. But in mid 1975—almost a decade later—Professor Coleman issued a bombshell "second thoughts" report in which he concluded that "programs of desegregation have acted to further separate blacks and whites rather than bringing them together"; that court-ordered busing and the instability created by the assignment of great numbers of disadvantaged children to middle-class schools in the big cities "have accelerated the white flight into the suburbs and have thus led to greater racial segregation in the schools."[150] Still firmly committed to desegregation-integration, Dr. Coleman laid the blame at the doorstep of the judiciary, concluding that "it is ludicrous to attempt to *mandate* an integrated society. Integration must come through other means."[151] Primary attention, he pointed out, must focus on both education and environment; lack of special educational preparation and failure to maintain discipline

[147] *Dayton Board of Education v. Brinkman, op. cit.,* at 529.

[148] *Ibid.*

[149] *Equality of Educational Opportunity* (Washington, D.C.: U.S. Government Printing Office, 1966).

[150] *The New York Times,* June 15, 1975, Sec. 4, p. 16e. The Court's 8:0 ruling in 1976 that federal courts are empowered to order the Department of Housing and Urban Development (HUD) to provide low cost housing in a city's white suburbs to relieve racial segregation in housing within the city, may ultimately prove to be a significant counterforce. (*Hills v. Gautreaux,* 425 U.S. 284.) In writing for the Court, Mr. Justice Stewart noted: "The critical distinction between HUD and the suburban school districts in *Millikin* [pp. 341–42 *supra*] is that HUD has been found to have violated the Constitution." (At 297.)

[151] *Time Magazine,* June 23, 1975, p. 60.

would bring about, as he had warned in his 1966 report, a white backlash that had now taken the form of flight to the suburbs. As he concluded, "a large portion of that white flight has to do with the unresponsiveness of large school systems [in the inner cities], with the whole question of order and discipline in the schools, and with an undifferentiated sense of fear and disorder."[152] Readdressing the issue of "beneficial" versus "destructive" desegregation at the end of 1978, he cited "mandatory busing in large cities" as its "most destructive method" and called for its cessation forthwith.[153] In the final analysis, society must find an answer to the basic problem of the elimination of inferior schools—it is *that* goal upon which the strategies of desegregation-integration must concentrate.

SOME OTHER POST-BROWN DEVELOPMENTS

To revert to the days following *Brown* I and II, implementing the spirit of the *Public School Segregation Cases* beyond their specific educational substance became the foremost concern and task of a host of public and private groups, agencies, and individuals. It was initially in the private sector that most policy changes were effected, with the all-important and now predictable public exception of the judiciary in general and the Supreme Court in particular. Even at the national level, the legislature and executive would thus wait, for all intents and purposes, until 1957, although President Eisenhower did move on the employee-hiring front in 1955 by issuing an executive order[154] to create the Committee on Government Employment Policy. This Committee was charged with hearing individual complaints of alleged racial or religious discrimination in hiring or promotion by federal agencies. It became quite active and, on President Kennedy's assumption of office, merged with the Committee on Government Contracts (which had been created by President Truman in 1951), to become the Equal Employment Opportunities Committee (E.E.O.C.).[155] With Vice-President Johnson as its first chairman, it proved to be a far more significant body than its predecessor.

Civil Rights Act of 1957. By far the most important *legislative* action of the Eisenhower Administration in civil rights, however, was the passage of the *Civil Rights Act of 1957,* the first major legislation of its kind since Reconstruction. Enacted largely owing to the bi-partisan cooperation of Congress's Democratic leaders, House Speaker Sam Rayburn and Senate Majority Leader Lyndon B. Johnson, both from Texas—it contained three or four significant provisions. One created the United States Commission

---

152 *The* [Charlottesville, Va.] *Daily Progress,* June 1, 1975, p. 1.
153 *The Washington Post,* December 8, 1978, p. A19.
154 Exec. Order 10590, *Federal Register,* Vol. XX (1955), p. 409.
155 Exec. Order 10925, *Federal Register,* Vol. XXVI (1961), p. 1977.

"If you are thinking Sara Kate is some fly-by-night I just happened to bump into, you are dead wrong, Jim Ed."

Gaten and my uncle seemed to be heading for yet another round in their fight.

"How could I have known," Gaten said, "that posting one little note, 'Math Tutor—Affordable Rates' would have led to this. Sara Kate Colson was the first and only one who called. I must admit I was kind of taken with her. Unlike most of us at Clemson University, she didn't really seem to belong there. It was not all that unusual, though, that after a term at Parsons School of Design she would choose Clemson. She was so into textiles and design, and Clemson happened to offer one of the foremost textile programs in the country."

Jim Ed looked at Gaten. He seemed to know that Gaten wanted to talk, so he let him go on.

Gaten pulled his face into a serious frown. "I guess I was drawn to Sara Kate when in time I realized she actually didn't need help with math. I hate to admit it, but she was just as good as I was in math, if not better. Now, to beat me at that time was saying something.

"I decided she only sought help in order to free her mind to cope with an unpleasant turn of events. Her very reason for coming to Clemson turned sour. The guy she cared enough about to follow there ended up getting engaged to someone else. To this day I cannot understand how anyone could have given her up. She is so special."

A wide grin crossed Jim Ed's face. "So you decided to move in?"

My daddy shook his head. "I didn't even try it. I think we both were aware that something beyond just friendship could have developed between us, but we consciously avoided the possibility. At least I did. The time was not ripe for us. Not in South Carolina at least. So, after college, we went our separate ways."

Gaten turned his gaze towards the flower bush my mother had planted. He's thinking about my mama, I thought to myself. I was right. He was. "Besides," he added softly, "I was hopelessly in love with Berenda."

Gaten loved my mother all right. But now she was gone, and a new woman was taking over his life. He couldn't stop talking about her.

"Maybe she was drawn to me," he went on to say, "because I listened to her pour out her heart, and did her homework. Can you believe that sometimes she corrected me, her tutor?"

Gaten looked directly at Jim Ed. "You know something, she paid me anyway."

Jim Ed grunted, "And of course you took it."

Gaten's voice was sad, really sad. "I had to, Jim Ed. You know how badly I needed the money. I was living on a shoestring."

Jim Ed propped his leg upon the tongue of the spray machine, and leaned an elbow on his knee. "How well I remember," he said, looking across the land. "That's why Boot Ellis's house sits on land that used to belong to us. Papa sold him that land to help pay your tuition. Those were pretty hard times back then."

Gaten agreed. "In spite of it all, Papa still seemed to have a Midas touch. When everyone else was losing their crops and farms, he held onto his. The very fact that he could not afford to buy fertilizer one year was the reason we turned to organic farming. When that Clemson county agent checked my 4-H farming project, he couldn't believe what he saw. And Papa couldn't believe it when I got that scholarship, either. He wanted me to learn how to farm in the summer, and hold a job in the winter. Teaching school was the answer."

Jim Ed laughed. "Papa always did say there was nothing finer for farming than an old-fashioned horse-and-cow-manure mixture."

It seemed that no sooner had the two of them started getting along so good, than they quickly changed courses and started arguing again. I believe my uncle hated to see my daddy get tied up with the woman worse than I did.

It all ended up with them fussing over money. Uncle Jim Ed claimed that Gaten's education had not only cost him money, but his own education as well. I hated to hear them fuss over money.

Miss Katie said money was a bad thing, and according to the good book, it was the root of all evil. There had to be a lot of truth to that because money sure caused Gaten and Jim Ed to turn mighty evil.

Gaten seemed all tired out. His mind is all messed up, I can tell. Gaten sighed. "We all know what the real problem about Sara Kate is. Even in the eighties, we are still reluctant to address it. You know something, that is a sad, sad thing."

Jim Ed kicked the dusty ground. "I guess the thing that bothers me most is what people around here will say." He looked directly at Gaten. "And you know what they will say. We will never know how Berenda would have felt about this."

It hurt Gaten when he mentioned Berenda. It hurt me too. She was my mother. "Berenda is dead, Jim Ed," Gaten finally said in a quiet voice. A voice now drained of all its anger.

Jim Ed still had to stir the pot again. To have the last word. "If you ever allow your mind to free your thoughts to think over what you are about to get into, you will find the answer, and make the right choice, Gaten."

I never thought I would see the day Jim Ed and Gaten would turn against each other. Yet it was happening. Miss Katie said one of the signs of the end of the world would be when brother would turn against brother. Right before my very eyes, a wall had gone up between them. The end must be near. If I had a brother, or a sister for that matter, I would stick with them, through thick and thin, no matter what.

It ended up bad between them. They parted mad, two brothers set apart by anger. Separated, all because of a woman named Sara Kate.

"That old rain crow keeps on hollering," I said to Gaten after Uncle Jim Ed left. "I think I am going to look for him. Grandpa said this time of day is a good time to look for one, if you ever hope to spot one."

An old stray dog had wandered into our yard. He followed me as I started to walk away. Down the path a piece of way I stopped but didn't turn around to look back at Gaten. "Could be a big, big snake down there for all I know," I called back.

"Listen, Gaten," I continued, "there goes the rain crow again. It's a good thing Aunt Everleen took her wash off the line. We might get a gully-washer, right?" When Gaten wouldn't open his mouth, I couldn't help myself. I had to fuss at him. "If you would swallow some of that anger all swelled up inside your mad self, Gaten, you would be able to talk to somebody when they talk to you."

I started to walk away again. Every now and then I'd turn my head a little to see if, by chance, he'd decided to come with me. He didn't.

Near the edge of the woods, when I took a path through a shallow gully, overgrown with creeping kudzu vines, I heard Gaten call out, "Hey, little stranger, wait up."

"I'm looking for my little girl," he said when he caught up. He looked at the tears streaming down my face. "She wasn't crying when I saw her last. Perhaps you may have seen my little, smiling daughter?" I broke into a wide grin. I loved my daddy when he was playful. "What does she look like?" I asked.

Gaten frowned and made a serious face. "Well, now, let me see." With his hand he measured height. "She's about this tall," he said. "Her face is a little chocolate chip with big velvet brown eyes. There is a haunting beauty in the way her eyes seem to tease the lips of a perfect little mouth into an ever ready smile. She has a little button nose. Even though she is always too eager to turn it up in disgust, it's still perfect. She is a very beautiful little girl."

"What was she wearing, Mister?" I asked.

"A pair of blue jeans, torn on both knees, and a little blue tee shirt with strawberry popsicle stains all over the front."

I started to giggle. "That's me, Gaten, you've found me."

Gaten looked closely at me. He brushed dirt from my face, then with make-believe surprise said, "Oh, it is you, Clover." He grabbed my hand. His strong hand held it tightly. It was a father's hold. I was safe with him. In the evening twilight we walked hand in hand in search of the very-hard-to-find rain crow.

Everleen is whispering something I cannot hear. Not that I want to. If in the beginning it had been news to her that her husband Jim Ed didn't want his brother to get tied up with Sara Kate, I sure couldn't tell it when I told her what had happened between the brothers. All she said was, "People need to be accepted and judged by the kind of person they are inside, not on the basis of the color of their skin."

In a way, it seemed like she was kind of in favor of Gaten and Sara Kate getting together. But then you can't always guess Everleen. Lots of times she says what she doesn't mind hearing repeated in the streets. That does not mean it is necessarily what's in her heart. At least that's what my daddy always said about her.

Right now I can't stand having to sit here and listen to two people put down my daddy. It's too soon to tell if talk about Sara Kate will in time hurt me as bad. Even now, there is a little tinge of hurt or sadness when they talk so bad about her.

I get up to leave, but my leg really hurts a lot, so I limp a little and sort of drag it along. "Pick up that leg and walk right, Clover," Everleen calls out after me. "I heard once there was a little girl who dragged her leg like that. Just sliding it along like you are doing. I've asked you time and again if that leg was aching you, and every time you've said, 'No, Aunt Everleen,' then you pick it up and walk.

"Well anyway, don't you know, one day that very child turned into a snake, crawled into the bushes and vanished."

My leg still hurts, but I pick it up and walk on it anyway. I don't care how bad it hurts when I bear down on it. I can't stand having Everleen tell me that turning-into-a-snake story.

If my daddy had had any idea how much sadness his marrying Sara Kate, then up and dying, was putting me through, I don't believe he would have done it. Just living with Sara Kate is strange enough, much less having to listen to everybody talk about your daddy.

I'm not calling my daddy a fool or anything like that. All I'm saying is he up and did a fool thing when he married Sara Kate. It's true what everyone says, "Gaten just turned a fool when he met Sara Kate."

6

. . . .

An unfinished jigsaw puzzle is spread out on our dining room table. Sara Kate has arranged fresh cut flowers real pretty and placed them throughout the house. Sunlight cuts through half-closed curtains. There is the smell of food cooking, the sound of good music fills the house.

At a glance the house seems to be just a warm, ordinary household. Like the kind you see on television, a house filled with pretty things and a happy family. But after a little while what is real sweeps through, like the smell of Sara Kate's perfume sifts from room to room.

It becomes real that there is something about our house that is not all that happy. It kind of reminds me of a thick morning fog. It's there, you can see it, yet you can't put your finger on it. Like the fog, a strange, uneasy feeling has filled the house, and settled down upon us.

There is just the two of us. A stepmother and child.

Two people in a house. Together, yet apart. Aside from the music, the house is too quiet. We move about in separate ways. We are like peaches. Peaches picked from the same tree, but put in separate baskets.

I guess you would call me a scared little girl, all alone with a scared woman. I suppose there is nothing all that strange about a stepmama and a stepchild living alone. In our case, I guess it's just how we happened to end up together.

People get killed every day, get stepmothers all the time. But in this case it all happened on the same day. Only minutes after my daddy married Sara Kate he was killed.

So here we are. Two strangers in a house. I think of all the things I'd like to say to her. Think of all the things I think she'd like to say to me. I do believe if we could bring ourselves to say those things it would close the wide gap between us and draw us closer together. Yet the thoughts stay in my head—stay tied up on my tongue.

Maybe my stepmother has the same fear I have, a fear of not being accepted. In a way it reminds me of a game of Monopoly.

If Sara Kate and I ever forget who we are, and sometimes we do, then we are at ease with each other and we have a pretty good little time together. Sometimes we even laugh.

Just maybe we could learn something from each other.

Especially Sara Kate since she's the one new to the house. At least she will learn that the sound that sometimes goes boom in the night is only a shutter slamming shut. All houses have their own creaky sounds.

Right now there is hardly a sound in the house. It is so very, very dry. The drought has sucked up all the wind. Just like in the poem . . . "No wind, no rain, no motion." It's been so hot, Mr. Barnes' old rooster has stopped crowing. It seems it's even been too hot for the crickets and insects to join the nightly choir and sing.

You just wait until the fall comes. Sara Kate is going to be scared out of her wits for sure when the hoot owl cranks up. It even gives me the chills. My grandpa couldn't stand to hear the hoot owl. He used to turn a boot upside down on the fireplace hearth to quiet it down.

I guess if Sara Kate ever saw that, she'd think she had married into a completely crazy family. She probably thinks it already. I think the wake they held before Gaten's funeral all but blew her away.

On the other hand, I'm sure there are things I can learn from Sara Kate. Like what she's thinking when she purses her lips, knits her brow together and stares blankly out of the window. I just might learn that in spite of her curious ways, she might want to be my friend—that in some small way, she might even like me.

· · ·

If I had answered the telephone and hung up when I was supposed to, I would have never been trapped into listening in on Sara Kate's conversation with her mother. I still don't believe I would have eavesdropped if she hadn't laid the phone down. "Hold on a second, Mother," she said. "I must take my muffins out of the oven." Baking muffins happens to be something Sara Kate likes to do. She can make pretty ones, all right. They look like a picture in a magazine. They might would taste as good as they look, and be fit to eat, if she ever learns to put enough sugar in them.

I wanted to hang up when Sara Kate picked the phone up again, but all I needed was to have her think that I was listening on purpose. She may have thought I made it a habit to listen to her phone calls. I had sense enough to know I could not set that phone down without her knowing it. So you see I was truly trapped. I honestly had no choice but to listen.

Sara Kate seemed delighted that her mother had called. "Why don't you come down for a visit, Mother?" she asked after they'd talked for awhile.

"Why, my darling," her mother said in that same rushed, girlish voice Sara Kate has, "I've gotten things all ready for you to spend some time here. You surely have no reason to stay there now."

"There is a child, Mother."

"Oh my God," her mother gasped, "please don't tell me there is a child on the way. Don't give me a heart attack. Say you are not pregnant, Sara Kate."

"Mother, I am not pregnant. Remember, Gaten had a child. A little girl."

There was a deadly silence on the phone. A cold silence without an ounce of feeling in it.

"Come to think of it, dear, I do remember your mentioning it," said her mother.

Sara Kate's voice sounded far, far away. "Gaten's daughter is named Clover. She is a precocious ten-year-old. A darling little girl. But I must admit, it's quite a challenge for me to learn how to care for a ten-year-old."

"I'm afraid I can't help you there, dear. You see, I've never had a ten-year-old stepchild. Besides, she is really not your . . ." Her mother's voice broke off. She didn't finish the sentence, there was no need to.

"Well, if you remember, Sara Kate," her mother continued, "from the very beginning, I warned you to take a long hard look at the price you may have to pay for what you called love. Then ask yourself if it was worth it. If love happens to carry problems, then find someone without them. Problems take away love. That was and still is my advice for you."

"Good-bye, Mother," whispered Sara Kate. She then eased the receiver down so gently it hardly made a click.

Maybe she was trying to prove to herself how cool she could be.

When she passed me in the hall rushing to her room I could see silent tears creeping down her face. Sara Kate had tears, but she wasn't crying. It seemed like the same air of sadness that filled her lungs when Gaten died was vacuuming her crying into its silent self.

Maybe her mama was right. Maybe Sara Kate didn't have a reason to stay in Round Hill.

I hope Sara Kate is not sad she got tied up with Gaten and ended up with me. I hate it when she is sad like that. It's really hard on me. Because, you see, a lot of the time, actually, most of the time, I'm sad also. Really sad.

7

. . . .

*I*t sure surprised Sara Kate more than it did me when Chase Porter showed up at our house one Sunday afternoon.

I think he started liking her the first time he saw her. And to think Sara Kate wasn't even pretty then, like she is now. Purple and black bruises, fringed with white flesh, were all over her. She looked like a Band-Aid jigsaw puzzle. After all, it was only three days after the car wreck.

I watched Chase peep in his pickup mirror, run a comb through his hair and reach for his hat. He is some fine.

He told Sara Kate that he used to always come to our house when Gaten was alive. "Gaten was my friend," he said. But as far as this friend bit goes, they were not all that good of friends. Chase would come to look for a covey of doves so he could shoot his fool head off. Then he'd brag about how many he killed. Sometimes he'd talk about the peach crop. He's been inside our house one time. I know for a fact Gaten never set foot in his.

Chase Porter didn't say very much. He just looked at Sara Kate and grinned his slow grin. He's got to know he's kind of cute when he grins.

Sara Kate sure was happy he came over. He's been the only one to visit her outside of our kinfolk. Of course I'm not counting people who come to sell stuff. They've been coming ever since the day Gaten died. Yes, people do think when a man dies, he takes his wife's sense to the grave with him. They think Sara Kate hasn't got a bit of sense left over.

Chase Porter is a good catch for any woman. At least that's what Miss Katie says. "Every widow, old maid, and young girl in Round Hill has tried to get him. Even some married ones," she laughed.

I know that Chase Porter ain't hardly got all that money he makes out to have. True, he stands to get all that money his daddy's got when he dies, but old man Porter isn't dead yet.

I like Chase all right and enough. It's his daughter I can't stand. She thinks she's too much for me with her fat spoiled self. She is only ten years old and is as big as a house.

The way her daddy keeps looking at Sara Kate has gotten me to thinking. Just maybe her daddy is trying to court Sara Kate. If they get married, his daughter is dead meat if they try to hang around here.

Chase is wearing light blue jeans, a light blue dress shirt, open at the collar, and a pair of cool shades. I guess he's got on his dress-up boots on account of it being Sunday.

"You didn't happen to see my horse around here, did you, Clover?" I shake my head. Chase knows good and well he's not about to let that high-priced horse get loose. That's just an excuse to come see Sara Kate.

In a way, it's good he did come. Sure helps to spruce up Sara Kate. Having to watch him look at her with that sly grin of his makes me feel kind of funny. I don't want him to think I'm scared to stay on my own front porch just because he's there. So I say, "Care for some ice tea?" I got that from my aunt.

I pour two glasses of tea and stick a piece of lemon, all fancy-like, on the side of the glasses. I filled them so full, the tea spilled all over my hands. I had to walk real, real slow. Sara Kate looked at me, but didn't say nothing. She can't stand it when I fill something too full.

Chase is leaning against a post. His hat is kind of pulled down over his eyes. Not to keep the sun out or anything. He just thinks it's sporty, that's all. He looks down the quiet, quiet road. "Seems like everybody is in church except us," he grins. "I won't run the risk of going to church, because if I show up, the Lord might think it's time to bring the world to its end."

. . .

A whole week has passed. It's Sunday again. I'll bet you anything, sure as shooting, Chase Porter is going to bring his grinning self over here.

In a way, I guess it's good he comes. At least, all that sadness that balls up in Sara Kate's eyes sometimes will go away. I tell you, a person would have to be blind not to see she likes Chase.

"You should go out more, Sara Kate," Chase tells her. "My aunt says she'd love having you over for tea sometimes." I think to myself, your aunt ought to ask her then.

Sara Kate smiles. "Your cousin, Mary Ellen, promised to invite me to a dinner party."

Chase scratches his head and grins some more. "She is not likely to ask you, either," he says. "You see, she thinks she's pretty uppity-crusty now. Before she married my cousin, she didn't have two dimes to rub together. The high-and-mighty Mary Ellen once had to work as hard as a damn nigger woman, just to pay her rent."

Sara Kate winced when he said that right before me, and sucked in her breath. The corners of her mouth tightened.

What Chase said brought on a strange quiet. Then after it had a chance to sink in, in a rambling sort of way that made no sense at all, Chase sort of tried to apologize. To try to undo a thing he didn't at first even realize he'd done. Poor old dumb Chase. Now that it had sunk in what he'd said, he was so ashamed. He couldn't even hold his head up. Just kept his eyes fastened on his fancy boots.

For what seemed like a long time Chase kept his head down. Then he raised his eyes and looked to see if Sara Kate had been hurt by the word, nigger.

Sara Kate's face showed she'd heard him all right. Yet her face didn't show anger, just her disappointment in him. Her face just sort of closed down. She didn't choose to make something out of it. She didn't say anything and neither did Chase.

Shame had played, my daddy would have said, "its most magnificent role for Chase Porter."

Any further hurt anyone could have given wasn't necessary. I believe Sara Kate got away with him more than if she had gotten him told.

Daniel said there's a lot more ways to hurt somebody than getting them told. Like using spit for instance.

It's funny, but all this time Daniel and I thought Sara Kate would make a slip someday and say nigger. If she ever did, Daniel said, all I'd have to do is hint that folks spit in stuff people eat or drink if they say nigger. He said you don't have to even do it. If they think you did, they'll vomit the rest of their life.

Daniel couldn't fool me up to do that, though. My daddy and Grandpa would haunt me for the rest of my born days. That's way too nasty to even think of.

I don't think we'll see too much of Mr. Chase Porter with that slow easy grin for a long time.

At least after this Chase thing, I've learned a thing or two more about Sara Kate. She's not all that good and sweet all the time. She's got her mean streaks, too.

Like sometimes when she thinks Chase Porter is calling her, she will let that telephone almost ring off the hook. She will be sitting right there looking at it and she won't even pick it up.

But you know, it serves Chase right. Looks like with all the stuff you see on TV, Chase should know you can't even say something unkind about black folks today and get away with it. Much less use the word nigger.

8

. . . .

Sara Kate has stuff spread all over the kitchen table when I come in from the peach shed.

She glanced up at the wall clock. A worried frown crossed her face. "Oh, dear, I had no idea it was getting so late. I'll clear this away and start lunch. We'll shop for food as soon as we're finished."

"Some of those little pigs in a blanket you have in the freezer would go good," I say, adding, "we can throw some Tater Tots in the microwave, too."

"Oh, all right," Sara Kate said. For a change she didn't say we had to have a vegetable or salad.

I put on water to boil for ice tea. I can't drink the stuff when Sara Kate makes it. She doesn't put a drop of sugar in it. Just puts it into the fridge to get cold, then puts sugar on the table so you can sweeten it. It takes almost the whole bowl of sugar to get the cold stuff sweet.

I look at all the different things Sara Kate has been drawing. "How in the world did you learn to draw like this?" I ask her.

"I've always liked to draw since I was a child," she said, "and then when I was older, I went to school to study design and commercial art. Afterwards I apprenticed for awhile, learning textile design, fabric, wallpaper, and such. And I've been doing it ever since. I am under contract to do designs for several textile mills in the Carolinas. It's nice because I can work at home and send the designs to them."

"I wish I could draw like you," I say.

"I'll make up a box of paints for your very own, and I'll teach you. Right now we better get to the store."

Sara is reading labels in the frozen foods section at the Winn Dixie grocery store. We just left Harris-Teeter's. The music is better over here. Good dancing music is playing.

I try to stand still. I know how much Sara Kate hates it when I dance in the stores. Right now, though, I don't think I'm going to be able to keep from dancing. Everything inside of me is pulling at me, begging me to dance.

I start snapping my fingers. Sara Kate is looking at me. I look her straight in the eyes and then moon dance down the aisle. I add the new steps Daniel showed me. It's easy on the slick waxed floors.

A gray-haired woman I don't even know breaks into a

wide grin when she sees me. And then with her eyeglasses draped on a chain around her neck, a half gallon jug of Clorox in one hand, and a three-pound bag of pinto beans in the other, she dances down the aisle with me.

Sara Kate is watching us, but I don't hardly care. I just go ahead and get d.o.w.n. She has stopped frowning and I sort of believe she wishes she could dance with us.

A large sign in the store says "REGISTER TO WIN A COLOR TELEVISION." The drawing will be held in two weeks. I grab a big, big stack of entry blanks for me and Daniel to fill out. The sign says you must be over eighteen to enter, so we'll put his mama and daddy's name on them.

I see the store manager hurrying towards me. I know he wants me to put them back. I head toward Sara Kate. He is right behind me. Sara Kate is over by the tea and coffee. She picks up a box of Lipton's Blackberry Tea. I touch her on the arm. "I picked these up for you, Sara Kate."

"Thanks, honey." She doesn't even look around.

The store manager turns as red as his red hair. He scratches his head, turns to leave, stops, looks back, then walks away. There is no way he's going to take on Sara Kate Hill. She looks like she's somebody real important.

At the checkout counter Sara Kate lets me buy one bar of candy and one pack of sugar-free bubble gum. The checkout clerk looks at me, then at Sara Kate. Her long brown hair hangs in dirty ropes. Most of the clerks have their hair frizzed just like us when we get a curl. Some look like a bush, but most wear a controlled frizzy. I can't picture Sara Kate wearing any kind of frizz.

The clerk turns the Lipton tea boxes over. I can tell by her eyes she's never had peach and blackberry tea before. I haven't, either.

Sara Kate tells me to run back and get ice cream. She doesn't tell me to put any back when I bring peach, vanilla, and strawberry. I never buy chocolate. Gaten and I never liked it. We liked milk chocolate candy, though.

It's a good day to buy ice cream. It's not the third of the month when the Social Security checks come or the time for whatever check comes on the first. Best of all, the woman in front of us didn't have to write a check and turn in a thousand coupons. She did hunt in her pocketbook for a penny until Sara Kate gave her one.

The clerk blows and shrugs her shoulder when Sara Kate whispers she may not have enough money. I imagine she thinks if you can afford to buy all that high-priced stuff you ought to have plenty of money. She has enough. She takes two fifty-dollar bills that look like they've been ironed from a wallet with little tan designs on it.

Sara Kate is passing everything on the road. She is driving Gaten's truck really fast.

It's broad daylight, yet a sleepy possum wanders onto the highway. Sara Kate slams on the brakes so hard a bag of groceries slides off the seat. Her outstretched arm holds me back.

"You're going to mess around and get me killed," I fuss. "And all on account of some old possum. He ain't got no business out here in the first place. He knows he can't see this time of day with his pink eyes."

"I told you to fasten your seat belt, honey." Sara Kate is looking at the opossum. "He must be sick."

On the side of the road a dead black snake, turned belly-side up, shines like a silver belt. I'll bet anything that old sick possum was eating on it. You couldn't pay me to eat no possum.

We pass a house where an old woman is plowing through a pile of clothes at a yard sale. Her feet are stuck into a pair of worn fur-lined bedroom shoes. A bright purple garment with splashes of yellow is tucked under her arm. The main thing she seems to need is a pair of shoes.

If Sara Kate hadn't forgotten to buy bird seed, we wouldn't have had to turn right around and go back to Harris-Teeter's the very next day. And we wouldn't have run into Miss Kenyon.

Sara Kate is the only person in Round Hill that buys food for everything that flies or crawls. I can see buying seed for birds in the wintertime. But you're not supposed to feed them in the summer. We head back to the store.

I sure hope Sara Kate won't go buying the fancy dog treats and stuff she did the last time. Gideon staggered up one day all drunk up, and Sara Kate let him go in the kitchen for a glass of water. Well sir, he ate every bit of the dog food on top of the refrigerator. It didn't kill him, though.

When we drove into the parking lot and she parked right beside Miss Kenyon's car, I thought I'd die. If Sara Kate had known how much Miss Kenyon hated her guts for taking Gaten away from her, she'd never have parked there. Sara Kate wouldn't have known it was Miss Kenyon's car in the first place. She's not into cars.

Well, anyway, when we came out of the store, there was Miss Kenyon.

"Hey, Miss Kenyon," I said.

"Why, hey, Clover," she grinned, but swallowed it when she turned to Sara Kate.

"Mrs. Hill."

Sara Kate smiled, "Hi."

"I didn't know you were still in Round Hill," Miss Kenyon lied.

"Oh yes, I'm still around," Sara Kate said, "but I've been very busy."

"I suppose you're busy with your book."

"My book? I don't understand."

Miss Kenyon is almost in Sara Kate's face. "The first thing you people usually do in life is write a book. So I'm sure you've joined all the other white Southern women writers. Eager to grab at the chance to say all the things you would love to say, but afraid to say.

"You want to know how I feel about what most of your kind write? I think, if it's in your mind to write, it's in your head to say." She is stepping on Sara Kate's toes. Her face is as red as a beet.

Miss Kenyon's shopping cart was in the hot sun. Her ice cream was melting. She didn't care. Nothing could stop her. It was like a play on TV.

"If you ever write like the others, even in fiction, that our houses are dirty, our black men are shiftless, and dare use the word nigger, you'd better be prepared to leave Round Hill, South Carolina."

I don't believe Sara Kate knew how to get Miss Kenyon told off. Gaten must have figured she needed looking after. I guess that's why he married her. He would have counted on me to help her out. I couldn't let Gaten down. "Come on, Sara Kate," I said, "we got to get home."

No matter how hard I try, I cannot get this book thing out of my head. Maybe Sara Kate is writing a book about the people in Round Hill. Maybe Daniel found it, and sneaked it out when he couldn't get me to do it.

I think of the way Sara Kate was looking around Miss

Katie's house. She sure can't write that the house stinks. As soon as Miss Katie opens her door the smell of air fresheners and scented potpourri hits you. She spends days on end stuffing the strong-scented leaves, wood shavings, and dried flowers into little Ziplock plastic pouches. She gets paid two or three cents a bag. She said she made might near a hundred dollars one month.

Yep, Miss Katie's got junk. But at least you won't see roaches flying and jumping all over the place like bull frogs. I reckon not. Miss Katie's got roach powder in every crack and Ball mason jar lid she can find.

I think now of that day Sara Kate sat there flipping through all Miss Katie's *Vanity Fair* and *Forbes* magazines. Maybe Miss Kenyon was right about Sara Kate marrying my daddy to get into our lives and show us up. Miss Kenyon said we would provide the fodder she needed.

Now if Sara Kate needs a dirty house to write about, she ought to go to Skip Howe's house. Skip is one of my classmates. He is white and lives in one of the dirtiest houses I've ever seen in my whole life.

When Skip got hurt real bad cutting grass, the teacher picked me to take a fruit basket to him. Talk was that Skip's real hurt was not so much from what the lawn mower did, as what his daddy did to him for borrowing Tom Jenkins's lawn mower. Skip's daddy has been missing ever since the accident. They say his daddy liked to killed him. His mama hushed the whole thing up.

Skip had no business going over to old stingy Tom Jenkins and borrowing his lawn mower in the first place. He knew he didn't know how to use a power lawn mower. To begin with, there is not enough grass to waste your spit on in the red clay yard jammed with old wheelless cars, auto tires, rims, beer cans, and chickens. Nothing can grow. You wonder why they would even want to cut a spot of grass no bigger than a minute. Folks say, Jenkins had no business loaning people as poor as the Howes anything.

Poor Skip. He didn't know not to pull grass out of a lawn mower while it was still running.

I had to pick my steps around dog mess all over the yard, then dodge chicken mess on the front porch. On top of all the dirt inside, Skip's mama was smoking. Smoking and coughing. The fingers on her trembling hand were stained yellow as gold.

The skin on her has so many lines, it looks like chicken scratching. "Them some right pretty things you wearing honey," she said, adding, "especially them shoes." I do have on a pretty dress for a change. I said, "Thank you." I look down at my shoes. My aunt Ruby Helen sent me the dress and shoes.

I guess they do seem kind of fancy for Round Hill. One thing is for sure, Gaten would have never spent that kind of money on clothes. He claimed his money was always tied up in his peaches. "Can't ever guarantee a peach crop, baby," he always said. "Farming is a card game. You're

playing dirty pool, but you never get to hold a trump card."
Or he might have said ace, I can't remember. I do know he
did say, "The weather can call its hand anytime. And in a
second, the game is over."

Skip's mama was dressed in dirty pink cutoffs and a
sleeveless turquoise polyester blouse. A yellow plastic head-
band held her hair back. She didn't have a tooth in her
mouth. Skip was sick, yet he was dirty as he could be. Talk
about poor, they are some kind of poor.

I'm not sure Skip knows it, though. He seemed happy
enough snuggled in an old couch with springs popping out
everywhere. An old spread with foam rubber backing was
shedding all over the place. He grinned as he read all the
names signed on his get-well card.

Skip answered for me when his mama offered food. "Aw,
Ma, she don't want nothing to eat." He knew good and
well I was not about to eat a bite in that house.

Skip's mama brought him a big plate of pinto beans and
white biscuits. She brushed a few strands of bright red
hair off his forehead. Skip had a really neat baseball cap
turned sideways on his head. That's the style. Like everything they had, it was secondhand.

His mama tried to get him to take off his cap to say his
blessing and eat. But he wouldn't do it. His old hateful
daddy must have torn up his head. I will bet you anything
that even as poor as Skip is, he had some kind of new

haircut hid under that cap. I reckon, if you don't have a penny to your name, you still want to look in style. Poor Skip was some kind of ashamed when a big fat roach crawled right into his pinto beans.

Gaten always told me never to look down when someone spoke to me. But I had to look down then. I sure couldn't look at Skip. I was so sorry and ashamed for poor Skip, I could have died. I didn't care if he was white.

There was a smell in that house that was more than a smell of dirt. It wasn't Skip's hand and arm, all closed up in dirty bandages, either. After Mrs. Howe told me she was eaten up with cancer, the smell filled the room. It swallowed up the smell of everything. Even the loud-smelling pinto beans. It was the smell of death.

I told them I had to go, and split.

Gaten had our supper ready when I got out of the tub. We had skillet cornbread, hot dogs, and beans. Gaten loved him some cornbread. The beans seemed to move on my plate. I couldn't eat a bite. I told Gaten about the roaches and the cancer. He only said, "Now, now, Clover, let's not get carried away." I think of how I could fool Sara Kate into going down to their house to borrow a cup of sugar.

I think of the look that would come over Sara Kate's face if she walked into that house and Skip's mama said, "Have a seat." And I smile.

9
. . . .

Whenever I look towards Miss Katie's house now, the first thing I think of is the big prize she won. A boat.

I hope it won't be like the diamond wristwatch she got as a big prize. A black plastic thing with a diamond the size of a speck of sand staring out at you like a piece of broken glass.

The big envelope in our mailbox announcing *You May Be A 10 Million Dollar Winner* is for Miss Katie. The mailman wouldn't keep putting her mail in our box if she stopped making glue out of honey and egg whites. She uses it to glue on all those faded, rain-washed stamps she finds. Her mailbox is so loaded with ants, the mailman hates to stick his hand in it.

"I think *you* ought to take this mail to Miss Katie," I tell Sara Kate when she hands it to me to take. "It will give you a chance to visit. You always said you were going to on account of how good she's been to us since Gaten died. It

122

would be good if you get to know folks in Round Hill better, anyway."

I didn't tell Sara Kate that people were starting talk that she was a stuck-up nasty white so-and-so.

I think to myself that just maybe if Sara Kate goes with me, Miss Katie might show us the boat.

It's almost 12:30 P.M. I can tell without even looking at a clock. Through the still, hot and dry air, the theme song from "The Young and the Restless" blares out. Plunk—plunk. It seems like everybody in our section is hard of hearing.

A speeding dump truck with two wheels on the hard surfaced road, two on the dirt, rounds the curve. Sara Kate and I part. One on one side, one on the other. The sandy grit stings our faces.

Miss Katie is in her front yard. Her print dress is pulled and puffed up behind by cockleburs. Her white fluffy hair hangs in two plaits. Miss Katie looks as old as her house.

She dry spits specks of tobacco from her tongue and wipes her mouth with the back of her hand. But when she starts to talk, tiny pieces of tobacco fly out like greasy blackberry seeds. "Excuse my yard," she says. "Too hot for somebody my age to keep things up like Clover's daddy used to keep up his place. It's still kept up so good you'd think white folks lived there." She looks at Sara Kate, gives a sick grin and drops her head. Embarrassed!

Sara Kate turns her usual pinkish red. I look down at my

feet and kick the ground. I don't know what I'd do with myself sometimes if I didn't have my feet.

Miss Katie waves us in, out of the sun. "A heat stroke can slip up on a person before they know it." She moves slowly, every move studied, thought out, like an old woman. Miss Katie is old. She eases into a rocking chair and fans with a cardboard fan. It has a picture of a little black girl on it. Her hair is fixed like little girls in old TV movies. It's a funeral home fan.

Miss Katie tells us to sit down. But there are no empty chairs. She starts gathering up stuff. There is more magazines and sweepstakes mail than you can shake a stick at. Every letter shows her getting closer and closer to millions of dollars. Every stamp that ordered another magazine changed the prize to even more millions. At least that's what Miss Katie was led to believe.

Gaten once said, "If Miss Katie saved the money she spent on magazines trying to win the sweepstakes, she'd be pretty well-off for an old lady." But my daddy couldn't tell Miss Katie nothing. Nobody can.

Propped on a table crowded with whatnots, artificial flowers, and faded starched crocheted doilies that stand up is a big blue-bordered notice from American Family Publishers that reads in bold print, "THE NIGHT WHEN MRS. KATIE LEE BROWN WON THE WHOLE TEN MILLION DOLLARS!"

Sara Kate's eyes search the rooms. Rooms filled with as much stuff as a Sears & Roebuck catalog. There are store bought readymade brooms everywhere. They are neatly placed beside homemade ones, made from wild broomstraw gathered from open uncultivated farm land. The sprigs of straw are tightly tied together with strings of brightly colored print cloth.

Sara Kate tilts her head to one side like a rooster eyeing a crawling caterpillar. She studies the straw brooms. I imagine, like me, she's thinking, what on earth would Miss Katie need brooms for? There is no place to sweep. The only place you can even see the floor is in the narrow path that leads from one room to the other. A needle threader in the path shines like a brand new nickel.

Miss Katie tells her how close we are to the end of the world. Someone stole a shovel and hoe right off her front porch. She can't bring stuff like that inside, because she says it's bad luck.

Miss Katie catches me eyeing some pretty towels. "They right pretty, ain't they, Clover," she says, flashing a wide toothless grin. She brags that the teeth she ordered years and years ago from an almanac are still as good as new. They ought to be. She never wears them. They say nearly every Sunday she cries out in church, "Oh Lord, I come off and left my teeth."

I guess Miss Katie will stop giving me a couple dollars to

cut her grass. She says she's started ordering a batch of fancy hand towels from Fingerhut, in case she has to hand someone a little something. She orders more stuff. She'll send something she gets in the mail back for a free gift. Usually it's some old flower. She never reads far enough to see that if she doesn't send the plant back after so many days, then they bill her and keep sending flowers. So Miss Katie's plants keep coming and she keeps paying.

"The Young and the Restless" is still on TV. "I just have that old thing on," Miss Katie says. "I don't watch that trash. It ain't fit for no Christian." All the time, though, she is stealing quick looks. Moving her head so we don't block her view. She peeps like a crow checking out a watermelon patch. On television, an emergency broadcast signal sounds. . . . "This is an emergency test," the announcer says, "a test of the emergency broadcast system. . . . This concludes the test," he says at the end. Miss Katie shakes her head. "One day, it will be for real," she whispers.

A shaft of sunlight cuts a path across the room where Sara Kate is sitting. Miss Katie wants her to move out of the hot sun, but there is no place for her to go. The sun has zapped the wind's energy. It's as still as the painted pictures hanging on the torn wallpapered walls. A small, squeaking electric fan pushes sheets of hot air into the corners of the room.

Miss Katie's house never changes much, not even at Christmas. She just sets out little baskets of fruits, nuts, and candy on chairs or on her bed. She can't decorate. There's no place to add a single thing.

Miss Katie knocks a big bundle of S&H green stamp books to the floor and sets off a mouse trap. Kah blam! She peeps from under her hooded eyes, "There ain't a rat in this house." Sara Kate is scared to death. "I keep a trap set all the time," she explains. "Some old rat may sneak in here with his nasty self. But he sure won't live long enough to sneak around. They may crawl in, but they don't crawl out."

Miss Katie sure picked a good time to offer us something to eat. Hands that carry out bleeding rats now bring us big plates of fried pies and carrot cake loaded with thick confectioners sugar icing. She spreads a yellow napkin over my lap and plops the plate down on it.

"It's just a little something," she says. "I know how chaps are. They always want a bite of something sweet." She turned to Sara Kate. "I'll let you help yourself. I'm so glad you're here. Maybe for once Clover will eat something here. Always wants to carry it home. That's not polite, is it, Miss Sara Kate?"

Sara Kate's eyes are glued on those greasy pies. Sara Kate don't eat nobody's greasy stuff.

I pick up my pie and look at Sara Kate. She reaches for

my plate. "Oh no, young lady, you're going to have to save this for supper." She turned to Miss Katie. "Clover won't eat anything but sweets if she's allowed. Is it all right if I take it home for dessert tonight?"

Miss Katie grins, "Why sure, Miss Sara Kate. Clover is blessed to have a mama like you." Her smile faded. "Her daddy would have been so proud of you. Real proud."

"I'm clean out of new tin foil," she said, smoothing out an old wrinkled piece. I don't say nothing but I know why she is all out of tin foil. She keeps using it all up wrapping them five-dollar bills in it to send to those TV preachers.

"You must come and eat with me sometimes," Miss Katie is saying. "I had my preacher and his wife over a few months back. I made the best barbecued pig feet and tails. They said it was the best something to eat they'd had in a long time."

Sara Kate doesn't say she knows about pig feet. She'd watched Baby Joe eat plate after plate of them at the family gathering before she married Gaten. I still believe it was the sight of all that grease that made her sick.

Miss Katie shows Sara Kate a pickup notice she got for a television. She comes back to our house to use the phone. I dial the 1-800 phone number for her. She speaks really strong. "I don't have no way to get down there for my TV," she says. "You see, I don't have no car to get way down near Hilton Head, South Carolina. I have a hard time just finding somebody to carry me to the store. I don't reckon you could send it to me, could you?"

We don't know what they said to her. But she said, "Well, thank you anyhow for picking me as the winner."

Poor Miss Katie is really sad. She digs in her apron pocket for some change and tries and tries to pay Sara Kate for a toll-free call.

I think Miss Katie knows she was fooled this time. She seems tired and slowly rocks her body in a straight chair that does not move. Her arms are folded, her mouth chewing away at nothing but empty space. She swallows the empty air. Her lips quietly smack, like a box turtle eating lettuce.

Sara Kate is hurting, too. She sucks in her breath, short and quick. Her body makes little jerks like a child trying to stop crying. If she is not careful and keeps on holding all that hurt in, she's going to start working her mouth, licking her lips and making them quiet sounds like an old woman again.

We stayed around Miss Katie a long, long time. And she didn't breathe word one about her boat. What they all say is true. "Miss Katie sure won't talk about her boat."

If you think the diamond wristwatch she won was bad, you should have been there the day the UPS truck delivered the boat. It was a really big package. They say it will blow up into a big boat like a life raft. I know Miss Katie didn't expect that. The boat wouldn't have been so bad but she had to pay a big delivery charge on top of all the money she sent to them every time she sent back the easy puzzles she solved.

I might be wrong but I believe if Miss Katie had put all that money together she could have bought her a real boat to fish in.

They say when two people live together, they start to look alike. Well, Sara Kate and I have been living together for a long time and there is no way we will ever look alike.

But in strange little ways, we are starting to kind of act alike. Things like the way she helped me out with the fried pies at Miss Katie's house. And little by little, a part of me is slowly beginning to change towards Sara Kate. Even the picture of her face that shed no tears at my daddy's funeral looks different in my mind now. Maybe it's because now I know it wasn't that Sara Kate didn't cry because she didn't care. She didn't because she couldn't.

The truth is, and it's not just because Daniel says so, Sara Kate is strange. Mighty strange sometimes. Like the time I brought her some peaches. "Oh, Clover, you're so good. I love peaches." She just carried on till I said, "You know something, Sara Kate, it wouldn't hurt you one bit to come up to that peach shed for some peaches."

You won't believe this, but her eyes lit up and she thanked

me for asking her. Imagine that. Thanking somebody for something that's part theirs in the first place! On second thought, maybe she's a little scared of Everleen.

Anyway, things are shaping up pretty good between us. She doesn't get so mad anymore when I speak my mind. Everleen gets ticked off, though, if I say Sara Kate is changing towards me. She and Miss Kenyon still can't stand her.

Once when I told Everleen how Sara Kate was cleaning up everything so good, she grunted and turned her head. I could see she'd narrowed her eyes to a thin slit and was studying the fence-locust trees, lively and green in spite of the drought. Having those trees means you've got good underground water on your land. At least that's what she says.

Finally she said, "Sometimes a new broom sweeps too clean. Almost all the old family pictures except Gaten's have been swept away." Everleen is right about the pictures. It makes me a little sad that Sara Kate put them in a closet. I think I'll ask her to put them back. Other than that, the new broom can stay like it is. I'm glad Sara Kate won't make me make up my bed and clean up like Gaten used to.

Everleen is busy brushing fuzz off the peaches. "As slow as they are selling we won't need any more today," she says.

"If we do," Daniel complains, "Clover will have to carry

the baskets. I've been doing her share of work nearly all month."

Aunt Everleen turned to me, "What is that stepmama of yours doing, Clover? Sitting around drawing those flower designs and such, I guess."

I didn't say anything. I really didn't have to. My aunt nearly always answers her own questions. She moved her chair into a shady spot. "Lord knows I can't see how Sara Kate makes any money at something that piddling. But I reckon she does. Jim Ed offered her some money from what we've been taking in from the peach crop. She said, 'Thanks very much, but right now we are solvent.' One thing we can give the woman credit for, she doesn't back down from providing for you, Clover. Folks say, she stands to get a right good settlement from the accident. Thank the Lord the man had good insurance."

Everleen frowned, "Come to think of it, Sara Kate hasn't breathed a word about it to me." She fanned away bees. "I just remembered, Sara Kate sent word that she wanted to see me. She will probably tell me how much . . ."

Everleen doesn't finish. Just spreads out whatever she's thinking like peanut butter on a slice of bread leaving it there for you to select the kind of jelly needed to finish her thoughts.

Daniel is carving away on a block of wood with his daddy's sharp hunting knife. "Daniel," I warn, "you better stop fooling with that knife. If you mess around and cut your-self you're in real trouble. Sara Kate's not here to put on a tourniquet like she did when you gashed your hand before."

Aunt Everleen bristled up like a bantam rooster. "Daniel doesn't have a mama to take care of him? No mama stand-ing right here. Right before his face. Who ended up carry-ing him to the doctor for his stitches anyhow? If you chaps think I can't take care of you, maybe you both should just up and go live with Miss Sara Kate since she is such a first aid expert."

Everleen drew a long breath and sort of rolled her tongue in her mouth. She needed to spread on a little more hurt. "At least I won't have to worry about cooking for the two of you," she said. "I won't have to bake my good cakes or make my good homemade ice cream."

I can see Aunt Everleen is a little peeved with me. I guess I sort of picked the wrong time to brag on Sara Kate. Especially since Daniel and I are wearing the new shades Sara Kate bought us. I have to tell you they are the petti-est shades I've ever seen.

Through the tinted glasses the hot, bright, cloudless sky turns into a cool topaz-colored bowl. Without the shades an airplane streaking across looks like a lump of silver. With my shades on it turns into a lump of topaz floating in a topaz sky.

Aunt Everleen had not seemed too happy the day we got

the shades and I sure don't want to stir up more trouble now.

I go over to her and say, "Oh, Aunt Everleen, if you stop cooking darkness will cover the earth. Our world will look just like this . . ." I put my shades on her and step back. "Aunt Everleen," I say, "you look some kind of cool. Real cool."

I O

. . . .

Chase Porter cruises along the highway in his brand new pickup. He blows his horn and throws up a hand. We wave back.

"There goes real money," Aunt Everleen says.

"He is sure getting friendly," my uncle puts in. "Hardly a day passes that he doesn't stop by."

Everleen rolls her eyes skyward, "Believe me, it's not on account of us. Chase thinks just by chance the pretty new widow might happen to be here. I could tell by the way he was feasting his eyes on her at the wake it wasn't going to take long for him to start really looking at her. Mourning for them is short. He'll probably be going after her soon." I think to myself, you don't know it, but he already has.

A carload of tired women wearing plastic shower caps stop by the peach shed. They have finished the first shift at the textile mill. The shower caps keep the cotton out of their perms and greasy Jheri-curls. I'll bet the stores that sell the shower caps make a lot of bucks.

They buy peaches and say they have to hurry on. One of the women had had a wisdom tooth pulled when a zodiac sign was in the head. Because of the mistake she claimed she was in *some* kind of pain.

Everleen laughed, "Girl, once I would have called you backwoods backward. But now I guess you are kind of stylish high class. Maybe even getting on the level with the higher-up women since some of them look to the stars and signs for guidance. They may all do that for all we know." Everleen laughed a nose giggle. "Maybe we ought to get Miss Sara Kate a *Farmer's Almanac.*"

Now I don't believe for a minute it would make a speck of difference to Sara Kate where the sign was if she needed to plant something or have a tooth pulled. But then again it just might. It's surprising here of late to learn about the weird stuff that some of them actually believe in.

When they leave, my uncle and aunt go back to the Chase Porter business. They are riding high on their seesaw again. If Everleen says something good about Sara Kate, Jim Ed pulls her right back down to Mudville. She does the same to him when it's her turn.

"Sara Kate won't do too bad if she bags a rich cat like Chase. I still can't get the fancy lizard boots he wore to Gaten's wake out of my mind," Everleen said.

Jim Ed looked at the acres of land stretching beyond the peach orchards. "I don't know if it's the widow or this land Chase has his eye on. You know he'd stand a chance to get a portion of it if he married Sara Kate." Money is raising its ugly head for Jim Ed. You can tell when it touches his sore spot, he becomes bitter.

Everleen grunted, "I can't see that as his reason. Chase has plenty of land and will come into even more, plus money when his daddy's gone. He'll have more land and money than he'll ever need."

Jim Ed breathed a heavy sigh and shook his head. "A white man *never* gets enough land or money."

They have forgotten about some of the good stuff Chase has done. Right off hand, I really can't think of a single soul in all of Round Hill who doesn't think a lot of Chase Porter. Many times he will just up and do a good deed for someone and never let it be known that he was the person who did it. It never mattered if they were white or black.

For instance, one year a late spring freeze killed nearly everyone's peaches except his, and some peach growers down in low country. Poor Miss Annie Grace, with her old half-blind eyes, believed she had peaches in her half-acre orchard. And when she tried to bargain with Chase Porter to sell him her peaches, he didn't have the heart to tell her she didn't have peach one.

You see, there is a vine that often times grows in peach

orchards, entwined into peach trees. It's that vine that tripped up my uncle Jim Ed. It's called the trumpet vine or the trumpet honeysuckle. Well, it has these bright red-orange blossoms. It blooms around the time peaches get ripe. Anyway, Miss Annie Grace saw those blossoms in a good many trees and she thought she had peaches. Those blossoms will fool you even when you have good eyesight, much less when you can't half see to begin with.

Miss Annie Grace hopped up and sold Chase Porter her peach crop right over the telephone. Soft-hearted Chase bought her nonexistent peaches. All she wanted for the peaches, since she thought there were not that many, was for Chase to do some tractor work for her. She traded for him to disc her orchard at summer's end and send his hands in the spring to disc, prune, and spray her peaches.

What knocked everybody for a loop was seeing a small trailer full of peaches pulling out of Miss Annie Grace's orchard. What had really happened was Chase Porter's hired hands had slipped the peaches, his peaches, into her orchard. Gaten and Jim Ed couldn't even have pulled it off if they'd wanted to. The peach shed was closed. They had no peaches.

Only someone like Chase Porter would have done a thing like that anyway. He is known for doing unusual things. Anyone can see why you won't hardly find anybody in Round Hill that will speak hard of Chase.

For some school paper, my daddy once wrote, "Between farmers, there is that communality of souls. In their own special way, farmers have a unique form of religion. All are at times forced to share common experiences and hardships. Together, with usually the same reverence and respect, they bow to the weather for the outcome of their crops . . ."

I can't seem to get Sara Kate and Chase out of my mind. I guess I won't be too bent out of shape if Sara Kate takes up with Chase again. Lord knows he's trying hard enough to get her back.

I have to realize that Chase Porter is really not so bad as he seemed to be the day he messed up with the nigger word. He showed after he'd said it that he knew better. I guess he just plain forgot. Most everybody, young and old, can't remember nothing anymore. Miss Katie said she believes the microwave ovens are cooking our brain cells.

I'm beginning to see I have to speak out for Sara Kate. My aunt and uncle simply can't go on always putting the woman down. "Sara Kate is lonely," I put in for her. "Terribly lonely." The words barely leave my lips before Everleen shoots them down. "Well, look whose side our own little Clover is taking."

Yes, I am taking Sara Kate's side right now. But they can't seem to understand that just because I am, it still doesn't mean I am turning against them. Why can't they see that when you live with someone and they aren't mean or nothing they kind of grow on you?

So, I say to them, "You guys don't have to live and eat with Sara Kate every day of your life and have to watch all the sadness and loneliness that wells up inside her. And you don't have to get embarrassed and all because she does, if she happens not to be able to keep from crying in front of me."

Just thinking about it makes me start to cry. "Oh, little honey," Aunt Everleen says all sugary-like. She looks at Jim Ed and gives him one of her unspoken speeches. Not quite charades. Her body doesn't move, only her eyes. I guess you could call it eye-speak.

She pulls the words from her mouth and puts them into her eyes. They tell Jim Ed to back off Sara Kate, at least in front of me.

Since my aunt and uncle still get a little uptight about Sara Kate I decide to stop telling them some things that happen at our house. But I think I better tell Aunt Everleen how the plastic flowers got off Gaten's grave. She and Miss Katie were about to open up a full-fledged investigation.

Miss Katie had stormed up to the peach shed after she discovered the brand new plastic flowers she put on Gaten's grave were gone. She was having a living fit. "Go call the police, Everleen," she pleaded. "Go call them. Anybody low-down and dirty enough to stoop to touching something on a dead man's grave need to have the law put on them. It would be beneath me to even spit on the ground where they've stepped."

Aunt Everleen was all set to track down whoever stole the flowers.

All I could think of was someone might have seen me and Sara Kate in the graveyard that early evening.

"Sara Kate," I said, after I told her what was going on, "I think you're in trouble. I think I ought to tell Everleen." She agreed.

Come to think of it we wouldn't have even gone to the graveyard that day if the man that made Gaten's tombstone hadn't called to say he'd placed it on Gaten's grave. He insisted that Sara Kate go check it out to make sure everything was all right. He said he'd been able to get the finest marble found in the state of Georgia. Probably trying to make a big thing over it so she wouldn't be blown away by the bill.

Otherwise, I honestly don't think the woman would have gone to Gaten's grave. Sara Kate is not a graveyard visitor. I hardly think she would have bothered getting a tombstone when she did if Jim Ed hadn't kept hinting he was going to have to break down and buy one himself.

Well, anyway, there we were in the graveyard. It was after sunset but not yet dark. I stayed inside the truck. You don't catch me fooling around in a graveyard if it's broad daylight and surely not if darkness is about to sweep in.

Gaten's grave was a pathetic sight. Sun-faded plastic flowers from Family Dollar, K-Mart, or yard sales in mayonnaise jars wedged into the earth. If it had been closer to a Sunday the dried-up real flowers would still have been fresh. Sometimes people picked a fresh bouquet from their yard.

Sara Kate was snatching everything off and cramming it into a green plastic bag.

I know Sara Kate is very proper and truly smart. Real smart. If people around here could see the stuff she draws they wouldn't believe she makes up all that fancy stuff right in her head. They would declare she copied them from someone somewhere. Even so, there are things she doesn't know.

Like, for instance, among our people in Round Hill you don't go asking a widow if she likes the kind of flowers you want to put on her dead husband's grave. You just do it. The dead belong to all to remember. I can only hope and pray that no one saw us there.

I wasn't able to sort out Everleen's true feelings when I told her Sara Kate took the plastic flowers. I stopped short of telling her she threw them away.

When Sara Kate told Everleen she'd made a dreadful mistake, Everleen said, "Repent, sinner and go thy way, and sin no more." Although she smiled it didn't make her words less serious.

11

. . . . . .

*A*s soon as I hear Sara Kate thank Everleen for coming, I know I'd better stick around for awhile. Sara Kate had asked her to come. I've got to find out why. So I hide and listen. I have so many secret places in this house, it's pitiful.

Sara Kate is not one to beat around the bush. Before she even offers Everleen some ice tea, she just up and says, "I want to talk with you about Clover. I hope you have some free time."

Everleen laughs. "Today, for a change, I do have time. They poked fun at my supper last night. So that husband and son of mine won't get a bite to eat from me tonight. And they won't eat Kentucky Fried Chicken either unless they walk." She jangled a set of keys, and laughed some more.

"They sure can't go to my mama's house looking for something good to eat. Not on a Thursday night. Mama is so hooked on "The Cosby Show," she won't even cook for my daddy. He hasn't had a decent meal on Thursday night since the show started.

"Oh my goodness, gracious," she gasps. "Will you listen at me. Running off at the mouth a mile a minute. You were the one who wanted to talk."

Sara Kate sounds upset. "I'm so worried about Clover, Everleen."

"She's not down sick or nothing, is she?" The words rush out Everleen's mouth.

"Oh, no, no," Sara Kate answers hurriedly. "It's just that Clover is too troubled for a ten-year-old child. She's holding in too many thoughts about her father. Here of late, she refuses to even say his name. And if I mention him she immediately clams up."

You're right about that, Miss Sara Kate, I think to myself. I used to talk about Gaten all the time, until she started correcting every little thing I said, and kept telling me to stop talking to myself.

But, you see, when Gaten was busy working on his computer or something, he'd tell me to play his turn at tic-tac-toe. My left hand would be Gaten, my right—me. I used to beat him all the time. I still do. That's how come when I'm playing by myself sometimes, Sara Kate will hear me say, "Your turn, Gaten. . . . I beat you again, Gaten . . ."

Maybe some of the things I do make Sara Kate think I'm as crazy as Cousin California. Like the game, Killing my Shadow, for instance. It is a little crazy, I guess. You play in the hot sun. Trying to step on a shadow that moves every time you move. You can kill the shadow if you step on the head. And you can only do that at twelve o'clock sharp on most summer days. I guess I am too old to play it, but my grandpa taught me that game.

But you know, I do have sense enough to speak of how my father was, instead of how he is. I do know the past tense from the present and future. I'm not all that dumb.

But come to think of it, I'm not all that smart, either. Lots of times, I get my tenses all mixed up. To tell you the truth, this thing about my high IQ is not exactly right. Deep down I think I've fooled them all. Especially Everleen. She truly thinks I'm so smart I'm gonna make it to Washington, D.C., and out-spell everyone in that spelling bee.

Like I said before, Sara Kate is not letting up on this thing.

"There is also this leg thing, Everleen," she says. "It worries me sick to see her limp. Perhaps it's how it happens. Clover will walk normally for days on end. And then, for no apparent reason, start to limp."

There is dead silence. I know Everleen is thinking. Remember, she's been on me about that limp, too.

Sara Kate finally offers ice tea and cookies. I don't have to see them to know she will get out those fancy paper doilies and those fancy, high-priced cookies that don't taste worth a dime. That woman can spend more in a grocery store than anybody I've ever seen in my life. And we still never have anything good to eat.

Everleen has finally thought this thing out. "You know, Sara Kate, little girls grow into womanhood earlier now than they used to. And their bodies start to change. I was thirteen before my body changed over. Now that could be why Clover's leg aches her. To tell you the truth, Sara Kate, I been planning to talk to Clover, about, about, well, you know what, but I didn't. I figured with you being her stepmother and all, it was sort of your place to tell her."

Everleen knows good and well she's not telling the whole truth. She's been trying to get up enough nerve to tell me ever since we got to the M's in the dictionary. Neither one of them need to tell me. It already happened to my friend, Nairobi, when she was only nine years old. I know, because she told me. I don't care if it never starts for me.

"I can only hope, Everleen," Sara Kate is saying, "that all of this is not only in her mind. There is also this fixation that Clover has about her mother. She really thinks she can remember the things she did. Even the kind of clothes she wore."

"Sometimes the good Lord gives visions," Everleen says

quietly. My aunt can face up to anybody in this world. She never gets tongue-tied. If she is pushed into a corner, she'll survive. She will simply put the entire matter into the hands of the Lord. Grandpa always said, "It's hard to buck up against Him." It's now another round for them.

"Let's be reasonable, Everleen. Clover does not remember her mother and it's not healthy for her to believe that she does." Sara Kate's voice is firm. "I do believe that she needs medical attention. And if it's found that there is nothing wrong with her leg, then we'll know it's only in her . . ." Sara Kate stops short. She doesn't have to finish, Everleen knows what she was going to say.

Now if you know about all them half-crazy people in Everleen's family, you know good and well, the slightest hint that somebody in her family, like me, might have something wrong with their mind is going to set her off. Set her off like a match lit under a firecracker. Nobody is going to tell her she's got crazy kin.

I know my aunt is getting cross-eyed and her mouth growing out like Pinocchio's nose. That red hot temper inside her will heat up her skin like it's been microwaved. And her face will start to look all wet and greasy. She is some kind of mad then.

"What you trying to say in a nice fancy way is, the child ain't got right good sense. I don't go for some outsider coming in and trying to cook up that kind of mess." Everleen is getting loud. She starts talking loud and flat when she's mad.

I guess Sara Kate would have had me at some kind of doctor a long time ago if she knew what was really going on in my head all the time. I know for a fact what's wrong with my leg. I hurt it. Hurt it, trying to find my daddy. I was in the backyard feeding the dog when I thought for sure I heard Gaten call me. I ran to the tractor shed. Then my mind told me to check out the woods. I fell over a log and almost broke my leg, but I didn't find Gaten.

That old empty hammock in the yard bothers me a lot, too. Nobody, but nobody, ever uses it any more. It seems to still hold only the imprint of my daddy's figure.

I've never told anybody I even hurt my leg. And I sure will never tell that my leg seems to hurt more whenever I think about Gaten. I guess in a way I'm still thinking I'm just having a bad, bad dream and I'll wake up and see Gaten standing there.

Sara Kate said I keep getting those sharp pains in my eyes because I shift them so sharply and I'm always rolling my eyes. I keep cutting my eyes so sharp because sometimes it seems like I catch a glimpse of my daddy. I can understand all of that. It's what's going on in my head that worries me.

My daddy's funeral was a long time ago, but sometimes I can still hear the singing, children singing without music. Singing along with Miss Kenyon. Only Miss Kenyon wasn't singing at all. She was only opening her mouth and moving her lips. Like Aunt Ruby Helen, sadness had swallowed up her voice. The singing is sad and sounds faraway like the sound of echoes bouncing across hills.

I think of the hearse that brought my daddy's body to our house for a last good-bye. In my head, the sound of the funeral cars start and stop, but it takes a long time for the singing to stop. The funeral program called the singing accappella or something.

The singing seems so real. The wake still seems pretty real in my head, too. The soft, soft music playing so quietly you could have heard a pin drop.

The crowds of people that filed by the open casket cast silent looks, and with noiseless footsteps made silent exits.

"Mama, mama," a little girl whispered really loud. "Hush," her mama whispered back equally as loud. "Is this what they call a wake?" the little girl whispered again.

A young woman in real tight pants and spike heel shoes made a quiet entrance and stood looking down at Gaten for a long, long time. "That's Minnie Faye Baker's daughter," someone whispered. "She's right nice-looking," someone whispered back. Outside a group of happy children played handball against the brick wall. Kuh thump, kuh thump.

The whispering, a few soft coughs, and many, many soft sad sobs were the only sounds that punctured the soft strange music.

I didn't know half the people who were there. After about thirty minutes they ushered us to waiting cars. The wake was over. The next day the funeral was held, then like the wake it was over. Yet it's all still left in my head. Sadness still floating about like heavy rain clouds. I don't like death one single bit.

I wonder, when will I become too old to stop remembering all that stuff? Maybe next year.

In the kitchen, Everleen is moaning and carrying on. "Lord, Lord, if Gaten Hill had even the slightest notion somebody was thinking there was something the matter with his baby child's mind, he'd turn over in his grave. He was proud of that baby girl of his. Lord, was he some kind of proud." She sounds like she's going to cry. But she's not. She never cries unless somebody, anybody, dies.

But Sara Kate cries. "I'm sorry. So very sorry," she whispers over and over.

Except for the crying, it's quiet for a long time in the kitchen.

Everleen finally speaks. "Clover's head is all right, Sara Kate. It's in better shape than ours. If that child limps, it's because of grief and sorrow. The child can't shake her sorrow. Just a few years apart she lost her grandpa and her daddy. The poor child ain't even got no mama. Don't you understand that or do you people have no feelings for your lost loved ones?"

Sara Kate draws a sharp breath. "I don't believe I've given you any reason to say that, Everleen. Remember, I lost Gaten, too. But it's Clover we're concerned with, and I am her mama now."

Everleen must know she has gone too far. Her voice becomes soft and kind. "There is nothing wrong with our little Clover, Sara Kate. She is depressed, that's all. We can cure all that with just a little time and a whole bunch of love."

"Perhaps you're right, Everleen. But I still think we should both keep an eye on Clover."

After supper, Sara Kate and I watch television for a little while. On the coffee table is a book about girls growing up. Sara Kate has opened it to a subject on puberty. She doesn't want to be the one to have to tell me. I guess nobody wants to take on that burden. They always want to give it to someone else. I guess it's kind of good I won't have to put that burden on my daddy now. A few days later, on my bed I find a brand new little white bra and a rag doll. It seems Sara Kate knows I'm starting to grow up but yet she wants me to stay a little girl.

I do believe the leg business being in my mind is settled now. Sara Kate hasn't mentioned taking me to the doctor again. Sometimes when I'm playing, she will tell me not to hurt myself.

The only sad part is, it's only settled with Sara Kate and

my aunt. The truth is my leg really hurts a lot of the time. Right now it's hurting.

Maybe Everleen is right. The heavy load of pain and sadness is too much for my mind and soul. So my leg is helping them out.

12

. . . .

I still think back on the day I got into real serious trouble with Sara Kate. It was, after all, partially her fault to begin with. She had no business making me come all the way home every day for lunch. Even if Jim Ed or Gideon did drive me. I've always been plenty satisfied eating Everleen's cooking.

At first coming home was great. If I didn't like the fancy lunches she made, Sara Kate would let me fill up on whatever I wanted, ice cream, cookies, or snacks.

Afterwards, sometimes we would sit on the front porch for awhile. Sometimes we talked. Mostly we didn't, though. It's still kind of hard getting used to someone like Sara Kate. She just doesn't seem to fit in anyplace. For instance, for the length of time she has been here, the only company she's had outside of Gaten's people are people trying to sell something. I'll bet she has had a dozen insurance and Avon people here.

That particular day had started out bad. Sara Kate was in a terrible mood. She watched me play with my lunch. It was pretty enough, real fancy and all, but I sure didn't want to eat it. The day of the good old ice cream lunch is now history.

"Do you want to freshen up and change your clothes before you go back, Clover?" Sara Kate asked me. She kills me, always asking if I want to do something, instead of just up and telling me what she wants me to do. She knows she wants me to take off my dirty jeans and tee shirt.

"Sara Kate," I say, "looks like common sense ought to tell you not to keep on asking me if I want to do this or that. You should know good and well that I am going to say no. Strange, you didn't ask me if I wanted this nasty lunch."

She gave me a hard cold look. "Clover, I've been working really hard all morning. Yet I stopped in the middle of everything to make your lunch. It happens to be a very good one. But even if it isn't, you have got to learn to be appreciative, young lady. I happen to have feelings like anyone else."

I turned my head away, thinking to myself what she said about working so hard. It blows me away that she calls sitting down in a cool air-conditioned house, drawing and painting designs, hard work. What my aunt Everleen does is hard work, picking peaches in the hot sun, and then hanging around that hot peach shed all day trying to sell them.

Sara Kate is still eyeing me. "I suggest you eat your lunch, young lady."

Well, when I told Sara Kate she could take her lunch and shove it, she really flew off the handle. She sort of lost it. "You apologize this minute, Clover Hill," she screamed. Her face turned a bright red. Her eyes blazed.

To tell you the truth, I cannot believe I actually said what I did. I have never said anything like that before. It's truly too bad to repeat. I would have never said anything like that to Gaten. I started backing out of the door, but she stopped me.

One thing for sure, I am not afraid of the woman. Never was, never will be. There is no way anybody can be afraid of someone who is too kind-hearted to even kill a little gnat.

"Thank you very much for lunch, Miss Sara Kate," I said and ran from the house.

Sara Kate followed right behind me in the truck. When she got there, you could tell she had been crying. "Everleen," she said weakly, "we've got to talk."

I can tell you, it's not a good feeling to know that you've made a grown woman cry.

They talked all right. Sara Kate told everything that happened between us. Exactly the way it happened. She even told her exactly what I'd said.

Even as bad as it all was, I still find it kind of hard to believe that Everleen took Sara Kate's side. But I guess what's right is right. Everleen was as mad as a stinging bumblebee. "That's no way to behave, Clover Lee Hill, it's unbecoming to you," she told me. "I've been letting you get out of hand here of late. You are not a grown woman, even if you do think you are. You have no excuse for acting that way. It would be different if the woman was treating you like a dog or something.

"Now you just put in your head that you are a child. And as a child you've got to learn that many times older people know what is best for you. Whew," she blew. I guess she had fussed out. She crossed her arms in front of her. "Now you tell Sara Kate you are sorry for the way you acted."

For a long time, I just stood there. I studied Everleen's face, searching for some sign, any little thing, maybe just a slight wink, something to let me know it was just a front she was putting on to keep peace in the family. I needed a sign to let me know she was on my side. But there was no sign.

Everleen did not take her eyes from my face. She moved her hands and planted them firmly on her hips. "I am waiting on you, Clover," she said, "but I sure don't plan to stand here and wait forever."

I dropped my head. I couldn't stand to look at either one

of them. I was so glad Daniel was with his daddy, I didn't know what to do. I would have been so ashamed if he'd been there.

Finally I said, "I apologize, Sara Kate. I'm sorry for the way I acted." But then under my breath I said, ever so softly, "But you shouldn't have tried to make me eat the lunch." And dag, they both heard it.

Everleen's voice had softened, "Try to look over her little fast cutting remarks, Sara Kate. She really didn't mean any harm with that last remark. The poor little thing has just not been herself here of late.

"You see, Sara Kate, sometimes the child has to hear more around this peach shed than I'd like. I wish I didn't have to keep the kids here. Every bad word that's used sticks to their brain like a suction cup. But Lord knows, I don't know what I would do without them."

Sara Kate smiled at Everleen. "Oh, I'm beginning to learn how to handle things like that. I treat those kind of sayings, coming from a small child, like small fish. You simply toss them back into the water."

I can clearly see that Sara Kate is no longer angry with me. And it gives me a good feeling. I think just having Everleen not dump on her, plus take her side, did her all the good in the world.

Maybe Sara Kate became so happy after her talk with Everleen because she knew she was planning to clamp down tight on me. Now I imagine she believes Everleen will side with her if I get the least bit out of line.

For a few days, I have halfway been thinking that, just maybe, I will tell Sara Kate about my leg. "Sara Kate," I've made up my mind to say, "I was just thinking that, maybe, well, maybe you should take me to see that old doctor about my leg."

As usual, like with everything else, I didn't do it. I sure didn't plan for things to turn out the way they did yesterday.

Like always, I was home for lunch. It was not too bad for a change. Hamburgers on crusty seed-topped buns with pink juice running out the meat. I'm getting so I like them that way, now. Sara Kate gave me a small dish of pork-n-beans, and of course a salad. She always makes salads. She didn't eat any of the beans. She seldom does.

When we finished, she put a small plate of cookies on the table. Can you believe that just for the two of us, no company or nothing, she put a lacy paper doily under the cookies.

Well, anyway, you know that funny feeling your mouth gets when you are eating, and your mind keeps telling you, you still have half of a cookie or something left to eat. Yet you can't find it anyplace.

It's hard to explain that feeling, but the thing itself is

very, very real. That was in my mind, so I was looking everywhere, all around my plate, under my napkin.

"What are you looking for, Clover?" Sara Kate asked.

"Nothing," I said. I was looking for something and she knew it. I wouldn't say what it was, because it was too hard to put into words why I was looking so hard for half of a butter creme cookie.

I must have twisted my leg or something when I got ready to leave, because the thing started hurting me so bad, I couldn't help myself. I started crying like a newborn baby.

Sara Kate rushed behind me. Her eyes wide. "It's your leg, isn't it, Clover?"

Like I said, I wasn't ready for her to find out. Daniel and I were supposed to go fishing. Daniel was right when he said you can't hide anything from her.

"How in the world do you think my leg can keep from hurting, Sara Kate? I have to run and carry peach baskets every morning." I was still crying. "So what if it's hurting, it is my leg, you know." I had promised myself to stop being a smart aleck, but that just slipped out.

Sara Kate didn't get angry. "Let's get dressed, Clover," she said, "we are going to the doctor."

You guessed it. I wound up in the doctor's office.

The doctor was quick to see I was not about to say anything about my leg. So he started tapping, pressing, and feeling my leg. He finally said I must have injured the leg somehow. He sure didn't get it out of me first, though. I might even have kept him from finding out that I'd hurt it. The trouble was I couldn't help but say "ouch" when he pressed down too hard in one place.

I thought of the time, not too long ago, when Mr. Elijah Watson hurt his leg. They said gangrene set in. And you know what, they put him in the hospital and cut the dang leg clean off. See, Sara Kate doesn't even know stuff like that.

I decided on my own to tell the doctor I fell over a log and hurt my leg. He wanted to take X-rays of my leg. I've never had one before. They may hurt for all I know. Well, telling him what happened sure didn't help. I had to have the thing X-rayed anyway.

The doctor pointed out shadowy areas on the X-ray to Sara Kate. "There is no damage to the bones," he said. "Your daughter likely tore a ligament in the beginning and doubtless kept hurting the same leg over and over." He called me her daughter. Sara Kate had called me her daughter. She kept saying it. The only time she said Clover was when she spoke to me. Now that was really something.

I guess my leg wasn't really hurt all that bad after all. The doctor didn't put bandage one on my leg. I thought if you hurt your leg or something, they ought to bandage it up. They sure did it when Skip caught his arm in the lawn mower. Sure would have saved me from carrying peach baskets if he'd put it in a cast or up in bandages.

Since the doctor didn't make such a big deal over my leg and put me in the hospital, I figured as long as I was there it might be safe to tell him about the poison I got into my eye.

Well, that bolted Sara Kate right out of her seat. She was upset that I hadn't told her about it. She fastened her eyes on me. I do believe her eyes change color when she is angry. They didn't move. It was like they were held in place with scotch tape. "Why didn't you tell me, Clover?" she asked.

I hung my head. "I was afraid you would take me to the doctor," I whispered.

The doctor sat down in front of me, looked under both my eyelids and shined a bright light in my eyes. He said there was no damage to the eyes. But I should always let someone know if I got something in my eyes. He explained that sometimes you need to wash out the eye with special solutions.

I looked up at the doctor. He was smiling. "I won't be afraid next time," I said.

Sara Kate half-smiled. "I should certainly hope not, young lady. Now thank the good doctor and let's get on home."

I must have groaned in my sleep or something, because when I woke up Sara Kate was by my side, tucking the sheets about me. Trying to brush my hair off my forehead.

Like it could possibly fall there in the first place. She, of all people, should know that after she messed up my hair with that perm, there is no way it can fall anywhere.

My hair will fall when Aunt Everleen fixes it. She straightens it. One day at school, a little girl with her blue-eyed self had the nerve to ask me if I ironed my hair on an ironing board.

Sara Kate stayed in my room for a long time. I think she was waiting for me to fall asleep. It was a bright moonlit night. I could see her as plain as my hand before my face. She stood by the window staring into the still night.

I could also see the brown marks on the ceiling. Rain marks from a leaky roof. Poor Gaten. He fixed the roof, but didn't live long enough to paint the ceiling. I study the brown splashes and marks. If you let your eyes work on the ceiling for awhile, you can make all kinds of monsters out of them.

The next morning I was up before sunup and already bright orange-colored clouds were spread out in neat rows getting ready for the sun. Right across the doorway was the biggest spider web I'd ever seen. Smack-dab in the middle was a big spider. I was all set to cream the thing, when I thought about Sara Kate. Somehow I just couldn't bring myself to kill it. That was the first time something like that happened to me. Sara Kate's thinking is rubbing off on me for sure.

Come to think of it, Gaten may not have been so keen on killing spiders, either. I remember him telling me the story of Robert the Bruce. He said, according to legend, "Bruce, hiding from enemies in a wretched hut, watched a spider swinging by one of its threads. It was trying to swing itself from one beam to another. Bruce noticed the spider tried six times and failed. The same number of battles he had fought in vain against the English. He decided, if the spider tried a seventh time and succeeded, he also would try again. The spider did try and was successful. So Bruce tried once again and went forth to victory."

I believe I remember every single story Gaten ever told me. That man knew so much stuff, I wonder how his head held it all.

Now as far as killing goes, Sara Kate is not behind everything I don't kill. I won't kill a snail, for instance. Never have. There was one crawling on the steps right then. Its slow moving body left a nasty slimy trail. But, by dog, I didn't rub him out. I couldn't have stood the squishy mess he would have made. I watched the big spider hurry away, and went in to cook breakfast. A part of me was little by little starting to obey and care for Sara Kate without my even knowing it.

When Sara Kate came into the kitchen, I was standing on the little stool my daddy made for me, stirring a pot of cheese grits. I can solid cook grits. Gaten couldn't stand nobody's lumpy grits. I've been cooking since I was eight years old. Sara Kate made coffee while the ham and canned biscuits finished cooking. I crossed my eyes and watched her double image sip a cup of black coffee. Gaten and I always put canned Pet milk in our coffee.

Sara Kate spread somebody's homemade peach jelly on a buttered biscuit and put it on my plate. "Please don't cross your eyes, Clover."

When she is ready to eat, Sara Kate just lights in and starts eating. She doesn't ask any kind of a blessing for the food she's about to receive.

She dabbed at the corners of her mouth all dainty, like the women eating in fancy dining rooms in television movies. She raised her eyes and caught me staring at her. "Is there something wrong, Clover?" she asked.

It's funny how easy it's starting to get for me to tell Sara Kate exactly what's on my mind. "I was just wondering why you never, ever ask a blessing before you eat. Aunt Everleen says you should never stray away from the way you were raised up."

Sara Kate smiled. "In my family we never offered a blessing before meals, Clover."

I didn't say anything, but I thought to myself that was a mighty strange way to be raised up.

"Clover," she asked softly, "did Gaten offer prayer before meals?"

"Gaten wouldn't a bit more eat without saying a blessing, than he'd eat without washing his hands," I said.

"Does it make you unhappy that I don't ask a blessing?"

"No, I still say mine. Even if I do have to say it to myself."

Sara Kate laid down her fork and dabbed the corners of her mouth. I have to hand it to her, like Gaten, she eats really proper. There was a sad look in her eyes. "Clover," she said quietly, "I don't know how to say a blessing."

Someday I'm going to teach her how to ask the blessing. For sure I won't teach her one as long as Aunt Everleen's blessing. The food on the table gets cold sometimes before she finishes. She doesn't overlook a thing about the food. She gives thanks to the one who plants, weeds, gathers, cooks, and on and on.

Sara Kate hasn't asked me to teach her the blessing yet. But she will always ask me to say it before we eat. She always bows her head and closes her eyes. I know, because I always peep up at her every single time. I don't know if Sara Kate doesn't want to learn a blessing for fear she'll have to start calling on the Lord or what. One thing about her, she is not one bit religious.

I guess I'm going to have to hold all those things that happened here of late inside for awhile. Especially the spider thing. If Everleen knew that on account of what Sara Kate would have thought, I didn't kill a spider, she would declare I am natural-born crazy. Talk about having a doctor examine your head, she would hurry up and carry me to one.

It's Sunday again. The air outside is heavy with the smell of coffee and fried country ham. Inside, Sara Kate is still in her housecoat. She is drinking coffee and canned pineapple juice, and reading the Sunday *Charlotte Observer* newspaper.

Poor Gaten would have starved to death on what little cooking Sara Kate does. Sometimes I do wonder how she keeps on living. Everleen gave her a little peanut butter jar full of peach jelly and it looks like it's going to last her forever. She keeps it in the refrigerator and will stand there with the door open, eating one tiny teaspoonful. The jelly would go good on a hot butter biscuit. I have to give Daniel credit. Sara Kate is strange, strange.

I'm really hungry. I want to make me a bologna sandwich, but we don't have any white bread. There is no peanut butter. Sara Kate's spoon-eaten every bit of it. It's for sure I will have to go to my aunt's to get something good to eat.

I take the shortcut to Everleen's house. She's got to open up the peach shed at one o'clock, but she still had time to make a fresh peach cobbler for me and Sara Kate and one for her uncle Noah.

The crust on the cobbler was so juicy and good Sara Kate and I ate off the whole top. Now we have to get Everleen to put on a new crust. Gaten and I used to do it all the time.

I hate for Everleen to send me over to Noah's house on a Sunday. It was late one Sunday when he shot his sister that time. There was a boom, boom sound at his house. Then you could hear his sister screaming, and screaming like she was about to die. She was on the floor when we got there. Bright red blood was running from her hand onto the old worn wood floor.

As it turned out his sister didn't end up hurt all that bad. At the hospital they took out shotgun pellets from her hand, but missed one in her head, and gave her a tetanus shot and sent her back home. The next morning when she saw a group of her neighbors gathered in the road to talk about the shooting, she walked right down there and said all secretive-like, "Did you all hear about me getting shot last night? My fool brother shot me with his shotgun." Well, sir, all the snuff spit they'd been holding in their mouths flew right out. You could have knocked them over with a feather. She took all the gossip right out of their mouths. The woman should be on the stage.

There is not a one of Noah's old hound dogs in sight when I walk up on his porch. Maybe he's shot them, too.

They say, when the crows cry caw, caw in the spring, Noah claims they are asking, "Is the corn ready?" So he gets his shotgun and tells them, "The corn is not ready. But my shotgun is."

Part of the porch is painted bright green. The other half is just old unpainted planks, gray with age. A step is broken half in two.

His sister is long gone now. Right after the shooting she took everything she owned to Gastonia, North Carolina. But she left the bloodstains behind. She never washed them up. She told her brother they would vanish at night like daylight swallowed up by the dark. "When the daylight comes," she'd warned, "they'll come back to haunt you for your sins." Everybody says it's the Lord's truth, too. You can see them stains as plain as your hand before your face. Noah has scrubbed and scrubbed, but he can't wash them out. The house smells like a chicken scalded in hot swamp water.

Through the screen door, I can see Noah sitting near the window with his shotgun across his lap. Imagine fooling around with a gun on a Sunday.

Trouble sure can change a person. Noah used to be a right nice-looking man, his hair parted in the middle and all slicked down. And so much after-shave lotion and stuff, he smelled twice like a woman. Now he has turned into a picture of pained ugly. I think about the blood spots on the floor. A big family Bible on a table next to him is opened to a page with a picture on it. Cobwebs are everywhere. The room looks like it has been decorated for a Halloween party with spider's lace. An electric fan on the floor stirs dust balloons. They float all over the place. Maybe after all these years, Noah is trying to get saved. After the shooting he needs to do something.

I can hear his commode running. I need to go in and jiggle that handle. Gaten used to always check on stuff like that when he came over. Shucks, in the good old days I used to pick Noah's flowers in his yard, then sell them to him.

With Noah sitting there with his shotgun on his lap, I'm not about to touch that handle. I'm afraid to take the pie in and afraid to leave. I'm so scared, my hands are shaking.

Noah's mouth is stuck out like a twist clasp on a change purse. He cocks his shotgun when I drop the pie. I duck down and take off like a jack rabbit.

When I get to a patch of trees, I duck behind a bush and look back. Noah's old lazy hounds, Thunder and Lightning, are sneaking towards the pie. I think about the story of Epaminandos and how he stepped in his mother's pies. I don't turn back because I cannot bear to look.

Noah's sister's blood is still on that floor. A shotgun pellet still buried in her skull. And Everleen says Noah won't kill a dove. She claims the Lord's doing so much for Noah after they started praying for him at prayer meetings. "The Lord will help him," she said, "'cause Noah won't right in the head."

If Everleen wants to keep giving Noah stuff to eat she's going to have to take it herself. I'm not setting foot over there again.

I know what Everleen will end up saying. And it solid gets away with me when she does it. I can hear her now. "Now what would your daddy say, Clover?"

My father is dead, yet he speaks. Yes, even from the grave his hand reaches out to me. But not to comfort, only to correct.

13
· · · · · · ·

I can't figure out if Chase's daughter and niece came along to show off their new play shorts or to brag that they had been to camp. Those yellow and blue shorts are some kind of pretty. So is the girl in the yellow shorts.

"We went to camp last week," they whine through their noses at the same time. I'm not too crazy over the way Sara Kate talks, but it's way yonder better than theirs.

"I started to go to camp this summer," I say, "but I had to help sell my daddy's peaches. My daddy would have sat up in his coffin if we'd let all his peaches hit the ground. I went to Sweden, Norway, and Denmark last summer."

Sara Kate looked at me and drew quick breaths. Two, to be exact. Sucking in the same way she did when she thought I wasn't telling the truth when I said I didn't put the snake in her garden basket. I'm beginning to learn her better and better every day. There is no way she can fool me now. She

171

doesn't a bit more believe I've been to Norway and Denmark than a man in the moon. I can't see why she's getting so bent out of shape about three little towns somewhere down below Columbia. Grandpa said Norway was so little, you could spit clean across it.

The June bug I'd caught just before they drove up is digging its prickly legs into my hand. Sara Kate would die if she knew that I am planning to tie a string around the June bug's leg and make a helicopter. I guess I'd better turn it loose when she's not looking. I don't know why she got so upset over that old black snake. Looks like she'd have been glad I didn't kill him. Of course I didn't put that live snake in her basket. I won't let her know it, but I'm a little bit scared of snakes myself.

Yellow shorts whispers something to blue shorts. They giggle.

"I remember when you went, Clover," says Chase. "You told me if I lived there, I'd never stop shooting, because they have some kind of birds in Norway and Denmark."

Sara Kate's eyes are coming closer together. The green seems to darken. She's not too hot on Chase killing birds. I sure don't know how she ended up marrying Gaten. He hunted all the time, and like Grandpa would shoot anything but a dove. Maybe she didn't know that about my daddy.

Anyway, Chase's kinfolks are having a cookout on the

weekend and they are begging her to come. They don't say boo about me coming. Maybe it's because I look so bad. You see, Sara Kate fixed my hair. And that woman can't fix my kind of hair. I can't get it through her head that she can't set my hair when it's wet. My head looks like a puffed up fighting cock. They are looking at me like I'm a piece of moon rock or something. I really wish I were pretty.

My poor daddy. He always had a hard time with my hair. For years I had to ride the school bus, because my aunt messed over my hair too long to have me ready in time to ride with him. My hair would have still been a problem for Gaten. Because sure as there's a hell, Sara Kate couldn't fix it. After the peach season is over, Aunt Everleen is going to have a perm put in my hair.

Yellow shorts is telling Sara Kate about all the good stuff they are going to have at the cookout. "We are going to make two churns of homemade ice cream," she says.

"Please, please come, Sara Kate," blue shorts begs.

"I'm sorry, my dears," Sara Kate says in that smooth breathy voice of hers, "but I'm not sure yet what plans Clover may have made for us."

Chase grins his slow grin. "Clover, surely you wouldn't have anything planned that would be more fun for the two of you than the cookout?"

Sara Kate and I exchange looks. "It sounds like fun," I

say. "Well, good," Sara Kate smiles, "then it's settled. We'll be delighted to come."

Yellow shorts and blue shorts are giggling and jumping up and down like a pair of hoptoads.

So we went to the cookout. I had a good time, but it sure isn't the way I want to spend the rest of my life. I got too many curious questioning stares when I walked about between the two of them with Sara Kate holding my hand.

Chase seemed to have been having a good time. I suppose he really was. Chase Porter happens to be a man who does whatever he wants and whenever. He said he doesn't give a damn what people say or think.

Come to think of it, maybe I didn't stand out so much after all. After a few weeks of sun Sara Kate could almost pass for one of us.

I guess it's the way she wanted to look. Even after she sloshed on a hundred different kinds of creams, moisturizers, anti-wrinkle cream, and sunscreen, she still added a suntan lotion. Seems to me the sun was enough. She spends so much money on stuff to block out the sun. Looks like if she didn't want the sun to hit her she wouldn't go out of her way to tan.

It's funny how the sun works. It may darken her skin but it sure takes the color out of her brown hair. It will be blonde if she's not careful.

· · ·

It was barely getting dark when Chase drove us home from the cookout. I sat on the front steps waiting for Chase and Sara Kate to finish whatever it was that they were so seriously talking about. When they finally got out of the pickup they still stood talking at the edge of the yard.

I didn't hear Chase ask Sara Kate to marry him, nor the answer she gave him. All I know is in my presence she kissed him good-bye and said her decision not to marry him did not mean her caring for him had changed. "I think for now," she added, "loving each other is all Clover and I can handle."

Sara Kate made a pot of tea and poured a cup for each of us. She watched me dangle my legs from the kitchen stool.

"It's a good thing you were able to wear shorts to the cookout, Clover," she said. "You've outgrown practically everything. You will definitely need new school clothes. Maybe we should start shopping soon."

I think of all the money Sara Kate might spend on school stuff. "I hope you won't spend too much on new clothes," I say. "Like Grandpa always used to say, 'when push comes to shove you can always wash and wear the same clothes over and over again.'

"You see, Sara Kate," I blurt out, "if you really have the

money for school clothes I'd rather you not buy so many and save some towards a purple ten-speed bicycle for me."

My wish, practically the only wish I've ever had in my whole life, just slid right out.

Sara Kate looked surprised. She smiled, "Why, Clover, if it's a ten-speed purple bicycle you want then that's what you'll get. But we'll still have to get some new school clothes."

I smile. In my mind I can see myself racing up and down the road, cruising down every path in Round Hill. My wish has finally come true. I am going to get my purple bicycle.

14

· · · · · · ·

When I look back and think about the way I treated Sara Kate that day at lunch, I can't help thinking, what in the world would Gaten have thought? I know one thing, I really hate I acted the way I did. I ran screaming and crying to my aunt Everleen like a little wild fool.

Maybe in the way things turned out, it all happened for the good. Because, you see, after that very day, Everleen and Sara Kate became closer. All because they were both siding with each other against me. I say that about them, but secretly I'm kind of glad that they both care enough about me to make me do the right thing. Maybe, when I am older, I will tell them that.

Sometimes, Sara Kate will pop in and out at the peach shed. When she takes a break from her "art work" as Daniel calls it, she will bring Tastee Freeze ice cream. Sometimes she brings ice tea with fresh mint leaves. Aunt Everleen drinks it, but not me.

If things had not changed between the two women, Sara Kate would have never been there, that hot August day. But there she was. Standing and chatting with Everleen in one of her skimpy halter tops, and the shortest shorts I'd ever seen. It was then that we heard a weak cry for help. It was coming from over in the Elberta peaches.

"It's Jim Ed," Everleen screamed. She started to run, but stopped and started running around and around in circles. She was going to pieces. "Go find help, Everleen, we'll find Jim Ed," Sara Kate screamed, as the two of us raced in the direction of his weak cries.

Poor Uncle Jim Ed lay under a peach tree with stinging yellow jackets swarming all over him. He had gotten his foot all tangled up in a trumpet vine and fell into the army of yellow jackets feeding on a pile of peaches someone had emptied out in the grass. There was doubtless a yellow jacket nest there on the ground also.

I guess once the stinging things got hold of Jim Ed and started stinging him like crazy, he couldn't help what he did. Like he didn't have a grain of sense, instead of trying to free himself so he could try to get away, he started fighting and killing the jokers. He knew better. He'd known all his life, if you kill one yellow jacket, two or more will come in to sting you. It seemed every yellow jacket there multiplied. They were everywhere. Jim Ed is allergic to any bee sting. You could almost see him swelling up. His eyes were already swollen closed.

Sara Kate didn't seem to think twice about the stinging bees. She plunged right into them and pulled Jim Ed out. The yellow jackets were soon all over her. She was getting stung like crazy. Yet she did not cry out in pain.

Jim Ed stopped gasping for breath. You could see he wasn't breathing. Sara Kate started crying, "Oh, no, Jim Ed, we can't lose you, too." She dropped to her knees, and while I fanned away yellow jackets with peach branch leaves, she gave Jim Ed mouth-to-mouth resuscitation.

A new red Ford pickup roared right through the peach orchard. In a split second, two men that I'd never seen before leaped out, put Jim Ed in the truck, and with Sara Kate at his side, sped away. I had to try and outrun the yellow jackets.

At the hospital, the doctors said after Sara Kate had worked to revive him, they had gotten him there just in time. It was lucky she knew CPR.

Sara Kate had big welts all over her. She didn't swell up like Jim Ed, though. She is not as allergic to bee stings.

I think the people in Round Hill will talk about what she did for the rest of their lives.

· · ·

Aunt Everleen has been having migraine headaches, one right after the other, ever since Uncle Jim Ed got stung. The big problem with her headache is, she forces you to have it along with her. My aunt does not like to suffer alone. So she tells you every pain she feels, everything she sees. I not only have to feel the throbbing pain that works its way up the back of her neck, pain that moves quickly across the top of her head to the eyes; I am also forced to see the flashing lights that dance a wild fire dance on her eyeballs. I do wish she wouldn't tell me about the people and things that sway and shimmer before her eyes like heat waves. It seems to make my eyes play tricks on me.

It's a good thing Sara Kate is helping her out until Uncle Jim Ed gets back. He doesn't seem in a rush to get better. I think he enjoys going over to the Bells and watching all the baseball games on cable TV. The Bells have a satellite dish in their front yard that's bigger than their house.

"If you can drive a stick shift, you can drive a tractor, Miss Sara Kate," said Gideon. He reached her a tractor key and showed her the gears. Sara Kate made only one mistake. She took the tractor out of gear when she stopped. Gideon stopped it from rolling into a gully.

I could have shown Sara Kate how to drive the tractor. Daniel could have, too. Nobody asked us, though.

Gideon has really put a fooling on Sara Kate. He has

fooled her into paying him some money every day he's worked. "I just need a little piece of money to tide me over until tomorrow, Miss Sara Kate," he'd beg. Every day for awhile, Gideon would complain that he didn't have a lick of bread, lard, fatback, or something in his house. When Sara Kate gave him money, the next day he couldn't come to work. Or, if he did, he couldn't pick peaches.

I knew there was trouble the morning he staggered up, tipped his cap to a stack of peach baskets, and said, "Good morning. How are you feeling this fine morning?" Gideon was hitting the bottle too hard to pick peaches.

Jim Ed knew better than to let him have money every day. He would just let him push his mouth into that ugly, juicy spout he always made, and get as mad as he wanted to. Sara Kate didn't know to do that.

Poor, poor Gideon. I guess he can't help himself. I will never forget when he was in that detox place, and Daniel and I didn't see Trixie, his little dog, anywhere. We knew Gideon would die if he came home and found out his dog was gone. So we went everywhere, calling "here Trixie, here Trixie." We searched even in the dark. Trixie was nowhere to be found.

"We looked everywhere for Trixie," we told Gideon when he came home, "but we couldn't find her. She must have run away." "Dogs will run off sometimes," was all Gideon said.

Later we found out that Gideon had sold Trixie for twenty dollars. He never said a word to us about what happened to his dog. One thing is for sure, he will never fool me again.

The swelling around Jim Ed's eyes is going down. You can finally see a little of his eyes peeping out through slits, like half-opened pea pods. One good thing, he can still see. Aunt Everleen took down the "Pick Your Own" sign. She is still burning up mad that it was some customer picking in the orchard who dumped the peaches on the ground where Jim Ed got stung. It was an awful thing for a person to do just because they happened upon a tree with bigger peaches. They had no right to pour out the ones they had. It made the act even worse when they happened to pick a tree that had yellow jacket nests under it.

I believe Everleen and Sara Kate are going to become friends. Everleen has started bragging about her a little bit. My sister-in-law did such and such, she'll say. Sara Kate takes up for her. Like with the golf thing. One day, Everleen sort of over-talked herself and led a fine lawyer to think she knew golf inside and out. Trapped, she was ashamed to admit she didn't play. She doesn't even know which end of a golf club to hit the ball with. So when the handsome lawyer asked her what her handicap was, she had no idea what he was talking about. She sort of crossed her eyes and cast her what-on-earth-are-you-talking-about look. She looked down, and said real soft like, "I guess my handicap is my old arthritic left knee." Everybody except Everleen started to laugh, but when Sara Kate hurriedly said, "Everleen has a great sense of humor, and such a sharp, keen wit," then Everleen laughed, too.

After Jim Ed came back to the peach shed, Gideon straightened up and has been in the peach orchard every morning. Even things at home are going good. People are starting to drop by. People other than Jim Ed and Everleen. After the yellow jacket thing, they walk over almost every evening after we close the peach shed. They sit out under the big oaks in the front yard and talk until dark.

Gaten's hammock is still stretched between two of the trees. Sometimes Jim Ed will rest there until it's time to go home. It's almost like old times.

About the Author

Dori Sanders was born in York County, South Carolina. Her father's farm, where her family still raises Georgia Belle and Elberta peaches, is one of the oldest black-owned farms in York County. Her father was a school principal and an author. She attended York County public schools and later studied at community colleges in Prince George's and Montgomery counties in Maryland. She does most of her writing during the winter months, in Maryland, where she is associate banquet manager of a hotel near Andrews Air Force Base. In the growing season she farms the family land, cultivating peaches, watermelons, and vegetables, and helps staff Sanders' Peach Shed, her family's open-air produce stand. *Clover* is her first novel.